The Ancient Wisdom Collection (Vol. 8)

The Arthashastra & The Commentaries of Julius Caesar
— Timeless Guides to War, Governance and Leadership

A Modern Translation

Adapted for the Contemporary Reader

Kautilya (Chanakya) | Julius Caesar

Translated by Tim Zengerink

Table Of Contents

Preface - Message to the Reader

What If You Could Help Rebuild the Greatest Library in Human History?

Thousands of years ago, the Library of Alexandria stood as the crown jewel of human achievement — a sanctuary where the collected wisdom of every known civilization was gathered, preserved, and shared freely.

And then, it was lost.

Through fire, conquest, and the slow erosion of time, humanity lost not just books — but ideas, dreams, discoveries, and stories that could have changed the world forever.

Today, the Library of Alexandria lives again — and you are invited to be a part of its restoration.

Our mission is simple yet profound:

To rebuild the greatest library the world has ever known, and to translate all timeless works into every language and dialect, so that no seeker of knowledge is ever left behind again.

By joining our movement to rebuild the modern Library of Alexandria, you become part of an unprecedented mission:

- **Unlimited Access to the Greatest Audiobooks & eBooks Ever Written:**

  Instantly explore thousands of legendary works—Plato, Shakespeare, Jane Austen, Leo Tolstoy, and countless more. All instantly available to read or listen, placing a complete literary universe at your fingertips.

- **Beautiful Paperback & Deluxe Editions at Printing Cost**

  Own any title as an elegant paperback, deluxe hardcover, or stunning collectible boxset—offered to you at true printing cost, delivered straight to your door. Build your personal Library of Alexandria, crafted for beauty, built for durability, and worthy of proud display.

- **Fresh Translations for Modern Readers—in Every Language & Dialect**

  Enjoy timeless masterpieces reimagined in clear, contemporary language—no more outdated phrases or obscure references. Alongside the original versions, we're tirelessly translating these classics into every language and dialect imaginable, ensuring accessibility and understanding across cultures and generations.

- **Join a Global Renaissance of Literature & Knowledge**

  You directly support expanding our library, publishing deluxe editions at true cost, translating works into all global languages, and bringing humanity's greatest stories to people everywhere. By joining today, you're not just preserving a legacy of masterpieces; you set in motion a powerful wave of literary accessibility.

Become a Torchbearer of Knowledge.

Join us for free now at **LibraryofAlexandria.com**

Together, we will ensure that the light of human wisdom never fades again.

With gratitude and a shared love of knowledge,
The Modern Library of Alexandria Team

Visit:

www.libraryofalexandria.com

Or scan the code below:

Introduction

Empire, Intrigue, and Command:
The Statesman's Toolkit Across Civilizations

In the annals of ancient political thought and military strategy, few texts have achieved the legendary status held by the Arthashastra of Kautilya (also known as Chanakya) and the Commentaries of Julius Caesar. Though emerging from vastly different cultural and historical contexts—India during the Mauryan Empire and Rome during its late Republic—these two works converge in their focus on the mechanisms of power, governance, and warfare. They are not abstract treatises but practical manuals forged in the heat of realpolitik, authored by men who shaped the destinies of empires.

The Ancient Wisdom Collection (Vol. 8) unites these masterworks for the first time in a single volume, offering modern readers an extraordinary opportunity to examine the timeless principles of leadership, diplomacy, administration, and military conquest from two of antiquity's most cunning and capable minds. Kautilya, the chief minister and architect behind the rise of Chandragupta Maurya's dominion, penned a blueprint for building and sustaining an empire. Julius Caesar, the military general, consul, and eventual dictator of Rome, chronicled his own campaigns with a clarity and precision that made his works a model for both military education and political propaganda.

These works are neither democratic nor idealistic. They are realist documents that confront the world as it is, not as we wish it to be. And yet, their enduring relevance lies not in their cynicism but in their lucidity. They teach the reader to think strategically, to act decisively, and to govern wisely. Whether you are a leader, a student of history, or simply a seeker of practical philosophy, this volume offers a rare convergence of insight from East and West, from thought and action, from court and battlefield.

To understand what these texts offer, we must first understand the minds and contexts behind them—and how their visions of power continue to shape the modern world.

Kautilya's Arthashastra: Blueprint of the Ancient Indian State

Kautilya, also known as Chanakya or Vishnugupta, was a master strategist, political philosopher, and royal advisor credited with establishing the Mauryan Empire in the fourth century BCE. His Arthashastra, composed in Sanskrit, is one of the oldest and most comprehensive treatises on statecraft, economics, espionage, military organization, and civil administration ever written.

Unlike many classical works of political thought, the Arthashastra is unapologetically pragmatic. It does not theorize about the best form of government in the abstract; it instructs the ruler in how to obtain, hold, and expand power. It combines the roles of Machiavelli's The Prince, Sun Tzu's The Art of War, and Adam Smith's Wealth of Nations—centuries before any of these works were conceived.

The title itself is revealing: Artha means "material success" or "prosperity," and Shastra means "treatise." This is a manual on the science of success. But success, in Kautilya's view, is inseparable from order, stability, and intelligence. The king is not merely a conqueror but the protector and organizer of society. His duties include overseeing taxation, judicial proceedings, internal security, trade, agriculture, and even public morality.

Perhaps the most famous—and controversial—aspect of the Arthashastra is its advocacy of espionage and secret operations. Kautilya lays out a system of spies, informants, double agents, and political sabotage with astonishing detail. Deception, according to him, is not a moral lapse but a necessary instrument of statecraft. Truth is subordinated to the stability of the realm.

Kautilya also provides extensive guidance on war: when to wage it, when to avoid it, how to win without fighting, how to divide enemies, and how to use psychological and economic pressure to subdue rivals. He outlines six methods of foreign policy—peace, war, neutrality, alliance, double-dealing, and subjugation—all of which must be deployed with precise timing and shrewd calculation.

Despite its apparent ruthlessness, the Arthashastra is not anarchic. It values order and justice, albeit from the top down. The king is advised to avoid personal vices, surround himself with wise ministers, and ensure the welfare of his people. Dharma (moral duty), Artha (prosperity), and Kama (desire) are balanced in a triadic model of governance. But when in doubt, Artha takes precedence—because without stability, morality cannot flourish.

Reading the Arthashastra is a sobering and bracing experience. It unveils the machinery of power in all its complexity and subtlety. Yet it is also empowering: it teaches that leadership is not the domain of intuition or inheritance alone, but of disciplined thinking, calculated action, and ruthless foresight.

Caesar's Commentaries:
Narrative of Conquest, Strategy of Power

While Kautilya wrote from the perspective of an advisor and bureaucrat, Julius Caesar wrote as a commander, politician, and participant in the very events he describes. His Commentaries— primarily The Gallic War and The Civil War—are literary achievements as well as military records. They document Caesar's campaigns across Gaul and later his conflicts against Pompey and the Roman Senate during the civil war that ultimately led to the end of the Roman Republic.

Written in a third-person style that masks personal ego behind formal detachment, the Commentaries serve multiple purposes. They record logistical details of battles, troop movements, negotiations, and fortifications with remarkable clarity. But they also present Caesar as the consummate Roman leader: rational, disciplined, decisive, and just. In effect, they are works of self-justification—propaganda that reads like history.

Caesar's military genius shines through every page. He adapts swiftly to changing terrain, exploits the weaknesses of his enemies, maintains strict discipline among his men, and uses engineering as much as brute force. His writings provide insights into Roman military organization, including the use of legions, auxiliaries, sieges, and cavalry. But more than that, they reveal how warfare is also a matter of perception, diplomacy, and public opinion.

One of Caesar's most striking features is his composure under pressure. Whether surrounded by hostile tribes or facing betrayal within his own ranks, he rarely hesitates. He analyzes problems with dispassionate logic and acts with confidence. The Commentaries teach not only tactics but temperament. Leadership, for Caesar, is about commanding respect through competence.

But beneath the narrative of glory lies a deeper tension. Caesar's conquests laid the foundation for his personal dictatorship and the fall of the Roman Republic. His strategic brilliance came at the cost of civil liberties, senatorial authority, and traditional Roman institutions. He emerges from his own writings as both a hero and a harbinger of empire.

Reading Caesar alongside Kautilya reveals striking parallels: both men understood that legitimacy is not merely claimed but cultivated; that appearances matter as much as outcomes; that fear, loyalty, and advantage are tools of the ruler's trade. Yet Caesar shows us the leader as performer, warrior, and politician all in one—an embodiment of Roman virtus (strength) and gravitas (seriousness).

East and West: A Strategic Dialogue

By bringing together the Arthashastra and Caesar's Commentaries, this volume creates a strategic dialogue between East and West, between theory and practice, between the architect of empire and the general who made himself emperor. What emerges is not a unified philosophy of governance, but a toolkit of principles, tactics, and warnings relevant to any age.

Both works teach that leadership is not accidental. It requires preparation, foresight, and the ability to make hard choices. Both emphasize the importance of intelligence gathering, adaptable strategies, and understanding human nature. Both recognize that power is fragile—that it must be maintained through vigilance, persuasion, and if necessary, force.

Yet their differences are just as instructive. Kautilya sees the state as a living organism sustained by a vast network of institutions and policies. Caesar sees history through the lens of individual will and battlefield mastery. Kautilya seeks stability through system; Caesar pursues glory through action. One governs from behind the throne; the other leads from the front lines.

To study these texts together is to see leadership not as a fixed ideal but as a spectrum of skills and styles. It is to understand how empire is built—in the minds of advisors, in the speeches of generals, in the laws of ministers, and in the blood of battlefields.

In an era of global complexity and renewed interest in governance and power dynamics, these ancient voices still speak. They challenge us to rise above sentimentality, to observe the world as it is, and to act with intelligence, courage, and purpose.

Welcome to The Ancient Wisdom Collection (Vol. 8). May it sharpen your insight, deepen your judgment, and illuminate the art of leadership in all its dimensions.

Arthashastra

Kautilya

Book 1

CHAPTER I & II. THE LIFE OF A KING & THE END OF SCIENCES.

Anvikshaki, the three Vedas (Trayi), Varta (agriculture, cattle-breeding, and trade), and Danda-Niti (the science of government) are what are referred to as the four sciences.

The school of Manu (Manava) holds that there are only three sciences: the three Vedas, Varta, and the science of government, as they consider Anvikshaki to be merely a specialized branch of the Vedas.

The school of Brihaspati argues that there are only two sciences: Varta and the science of government, as they see the three Vedas as simply an abridgment or a pretext for one experienced in worldly affairs.

The school of Usanas asserts that there is only one science: the science of government, claiming that all other sciences find their beginning and end within it.

However, Kautilya contends that there are four and only four sciences, from which all knowledge concerning righteousness and wealth is derived, and therefore they are so named.

Anvikshaki encompasses the philosophies of Sankhya, Yoga, and Lokayata.

Righteous and unrighteous deeds (Dharmadharmau) are learned from the three Vedas; wealth and non-wealth from Varta; the expedient and inexpedient (Nayanayau), as well as strength and weakness (Balabale), from the science of government.

When viewed through the lens of these sciences, Anvikshaki is seen as highly beneficial to the world. It steadies the mind in times of both prosperity and adversity, and it grants clarity in foresight, speech, and action.

The Science of Anvikshaki is regarded as the light to all forms of knowledge, a simple means to accomplish all tasks, and the holder of all virtues.

[Thus ends Chapter II, "Determination of the place of Anvikshaki among Sciences" in Book I, "Concerning Discipline" of the Arthasástra of Kautilya.]

CHAPTER III. THE END OF SCIENCES.

Determination of the place of the Triple Vedas.

The three Vedas—Sama, Rik, and Yajus—are known as the triple Vedas. Together with the Atharvaveda and the Itihasaveda, they constitute the Vedas.

The Angas (limbs of the Vedas) include Siksha (Phonetics), Kalpa (Ceremonial injunctions), Vyakarana (Grammar), Nirukta (Glossarial explanation of obscure Vedic terms), Chandas (Prosody), and Astronomy.

As the triple Vedas clearly define the respective duties of the four castes and the four stages of religious life, they are considered the most useful.

The duty of a Brahman is to study, teach, perform sacrifices, officiate in others' sacrifices, and give and receive gifts.

The duty of a Kshatriya is to study, perform sacrifices, give gifts, engage in military service, and protect life.

The duty of a Vaisya is to study, perform sacrifices, give gifts, engage in agriculture, cattle-breeding, and trade.

The duty of a Sudra is to serve the twice-born (dvijati), engage in agriculture, cattle-breeding, trade (varta), and practice the professions of artisans and court-bards (karukusilavakarma).

The duty of a householder is to earn a livelihood through his profession, marry within his equal class of different ancestral Rishis, have intercourse with his wife after her monthly ablution, give gifts to gods, ancestors, guests, and servants, and consume the remaining offerings.

The duty of a student (Brahmacharin) is to learn the Vedas, perform fire-worship, practice ablution, live by begging, and devote himself to his teacher, even at the cost of his own life—or in the absence of his teacher, to the teacher's son or elder classmate.

The duty of a Vanaprastha (forest recluse) is to observe chastity, sleep on the bare ground, wear twisted locks and deer-skin, perform fire-worship, practice ablution, worship gods, ancestors, and guests, and subsist on food from the forest.

The duty of an ascetic (Parivrajaka) is to exercise complete control over the senses, abstain from all kinds of work, disown wealth, withdraw from society, beg from various places, dwell in forests, and maintain purity, both internal and external.

Harmlessness, truthfulness, purity, freedom from spite, abstinence from cruelty, and forgiveness are duties common to all.

The observance of one's own duty leads to Svarga (heaven) and eternal bliss (Anantya). If violated, the world will fall into chaos due to confusion of castes and duties.

Thus, the king must ensure that people do not stray from their duties. Whoever upholds their duty, adheres to the customs of the Aryas, and follows the rules of caste and religious life, will find happiness in this life and the next. The world, when sustained by the principles of the triple Vedas, will flourish and never perish.

[Thus ends Chapter III, "Determination of the place of the Triple Vedas" among Sciences in Book I, "Concerning Discipline" of the Arthasástra of Kautilya.]

CHAPTER IV. THE END OF SCIENCES.

Varta and Dandaniti.

Agriculture, cattle-breeding, and trade constitute Varta. It is highly valuable as it provides grains, cattle, gold, forest produce (kupya), and free labor (vishti). It is through the treasury and the army, which are solely acquired through Varta, that the king can control both his own forces and those of his enemies.

The sceptre, on which the welfare and advancement of the sciences of Anvikshaki, the triple Vedas, and Varta depend, is called Danda (punishment). The science of punishment, or the law of governance, is known as Dandaniti.

Dandaniti is the means to acquire possessions, to secure them, to improve them, and to distribute the benefits of such improvements among those who deserve them. The progress of the world relies on this science of government.

"Hence," says my teacher, "whoever desires the progress of the world must always keep the sceptre raised (udyatadanda). There is no better tool than the sceptre to bring people under control."

Kautilya, however, disagrees: whoever imposes overly harsh punishment becomes hated by the people, while one who imposes overly mild punishment becomes disrespected. But a ruler who enforces punishment fairly, according to what is deserved, earns respect. When punishment is administered with proper consideration, it encourages people to follow righteousness and pursue productive works that generate wealth and enjoyment. On the other hand, punishment given out of greed, anger, or ignorance sparks outrage, even among hermits and ascetics in the forests—let alone among householders.

When the law of punishment is neglected, disorder arises, as the proverb of the fish (matsyanyayamudbhavayati) suggests: without a magistrate (dandadharabhave), the strong will devour the weak. Under the protection of the sceptre, however, the weak can resist the strong.

The people (loka), consisting of the four castes and the four stages of religious life, will stay true to their duties and occupations when governed by the king with his sceptre, remaining devoted to their respective paths.

[Thus ends Chapter IV, "Determination of the Place of Varta and of Dandaniti" among Sciences in Book I, "Concerning Discipline" of the Arthasástra of Kautilya. "The End of Sciences" is completed.]

CHAPTER V. ASSOCIATION WITH THE AGED.

Thus, the first three sciences (of the four) depend on the science of government for their proper functioning. Danda, or punishment, which ensures safety and security of life, is itself reliant on discipline (vinaya).

Discipline is of two types: artificial and natural. Instruction (kriya) can only bring a docile being into conformity with the rules of discipline, but not an undocile being (adravyam). The study of sciences can only educate those with the mental faculties of obedience, listening, grasping, memory, discrimination, inference, and deliberation, but not those who lack such qualities.

Sciences must be studied and their teachings strictly followed under the guidance of specialized teachers.

After undergoing the ceremony of tonsure, the student must learn the alphabet (lipi) and arithmetic. Upon receiving the sacred thread, he must study the triple Vedas, the science of Anvikshaki from acknowledged teachers (sishta), the science of Varta from government superintendents, and the science of Dandaniti from both theoreticians and practical politicians (vaktriprayoktribhyah).

The prince shall observe celibacy until he reaches the age of sixteen. Then, he shall undergo the tonsure ceremony (godana) and marry.

To maintain effective discipline, the prince must always remain in the company of aged professors of the sciences, for in them alone discipline is firmly rooted.

He shall spend his mornings receiving lessons in military arts, including those related to elephants, horses, chariots, and weapons, and his afternoons listening to the Itihasa.

Itihasa includes Purana, Itivritta (history), Akhyayika (tales), Udaharana (illustrative stories), Dharmasastra, and Arthasastra.

During the rest of the day and night, the prince shall not only receive new lessons and revise old ones, but also repeatedly hear anything that has not been clearly understood.

For knowledge arises from hearing (sutra); from knowledge, steady application (yoga) becomes possible; and from application, self-possession (atmavatta) can be attained. This is what is meant by the efficiency of learning (vidhyasamarthyam).

A king who is well educated, disciplined in the sciences, dedicated to the good governance of his subjects, and committed to the welfare of all people will enjoy the earth without opposition.

[Thus ends Chapter V, "Association with the Aged" in Book I, "Concerning Discipline" of the Arthasástra of Kautilya.]

CHAPTER VI. RESTRAINT OF THE ORGANS OF SENSE.

The Shaking Off of the Aggregate of the Six Enemies.

Restraint of the organs of sense, on which success in study and discipline depends, can be achieved by abandoning lust, anger, greed, vanity (mána), haughtiness (mada), and overjoy (harsha).

The absence of confusion (avipratipatti) in the perception of sound, touch, color, taste, and scent—through the ear, skin, eyes, tongue, and nose—is what is meant by the restraint of the organs of sense. Strict adherence to the precepts of the sciences also signifies this, for the sole aim of all the sciences is the restraint of the senses.

Anyone of contrary character, who does not control their organs of sense, will perish swiftly, even if they possess the entire world.

For example: Bhoja, also known as Dándakya, perished along with his kingdom and relations after attempting to act lasciviously toward a Brahman maiden.

Similarly, Karála, the Vaideha, met the same fate. Likewise, Janamejaya was consumed by his anger against Brahmans, and Tálajangha for his vengeance against the family of the Bhrigus.

Aila, driven by greed to extract wealth from the Brahmans, and Ajabindu, the Sauvíra, faced their downfall in similar circumstances.

Ravana, driven by vanity and unwilling to return another man's wife, and Duryodhana, unwilling to part with even a portion of his kingdom, also perished.

Dambhodbhava and Arjuna of the Haihaya dynasty, in their arrogance and disdain for others, likewise fell.

Vátápi, in his overjoyed attempt to attack Agastya, and the corporation of the Vrishnis in their attempt against Dvaipáyana, also perished.

These kings, along with others, fell victim to the aggregate of the six enemies and failed to restrain their senses, leading to the downfall of their kingdoms and families.

By driving out the six enemies, kings like Ambarísha of the Jámadagnya dynasty, famous for his restraint of the senses, and Nábhága, were able to enjoy long reigns over the earth.

[Thus ends Chapter VI, "The Shaking Off of the Aggregate of the Six Enemies" in the section on "Restraint of the Organs of Sense" in Book I, "Concerning Discipline" of the Arthasástra of Kautilya.]

CHAPTER VII. RESTRAINT OF THE ORGANS OF SENSE.

The Life of a Saintly King.

By conquering the aggregate of the six enemies, the king shall restrain his organs of sense; gain wisdom through association with the aged; gain insight through his spies; ensure safety and security through constant activity; maintain his subjects in their respective duties through the exercise of authority; uphold his personal discipline through continuous study of the sciences; and win the affection of the people by connecting them with wealth and doing good deeds for them.

With his senses under control, the king shall avoid harming the women and property of others, stay free not only from lust, even in dreams, but also from falsehood, arrogance, and evil tendencies. He will steer clear of unrighteous and uneconomical activities.

By adhering to righteousness and economy, he will enjoy his desires without transgressing limits. He will never be without happiness. He may enjoy in equal measure the three pursuits of life— charity, wealth, and desire—which are all interdependent. When one of these pursuits is indulged excessively, it harms not only the other two but also itself.

Kautilya asserts that wealth, and wealth alone, is the most important, as both charity and desire rely on wealth for their fulfillment.

Those teachers and ministers who protect the king from falling prey to dangers, and who, by striking the hours of the day as determined by measuring shadows (chháyánálikápratodena), warn him of any carelessness, even in secret, shall always be respected.

Sovereignty (rájatva) is possible only with assistance. A single wheel cannot move alone. Therefore, the king must employ ministers and listen to their opinions.

[Thus ends Chapter VII, "The Life of a Saintly King," in the section of the "Restraint of the Organs of Sense," in Book I, "Concerning Discipline" of the Arthasástra of Kautilya; "Restraint of the Organs of Sense" is completed.]

CHAPTER VIII. CREATION OF MINISTERS.

"The king," says Bháradvája, "should appoint his classmates as ministers, for they can be trusted since he personally knows their honesty and ability."

"No," says Visáláksha, "because they were also his playmates and may despise him. Instead, he should appoint those whose secrets are shared with him and well-known to both. Having shared vices and habits with the king, they would not harm him for fear of betrayal."

"Such fear is common," says Parásara, "because under the threat of revealing his secrets, the king may follow their good and bad deeds. By disclosing his secrets, the king could humble himself before as many people as he confides in. Therefore, the king should appoint ministers who have demonstrated loyalty during life-threatening situations and have proven devotion."

"No," says Pisuna, "this shows devotion, but not intelligence (buddhigunah). The king should choose ministers who, when handling finances, produce as much or more than the expected revenue, demonstrating their capability."

"No," says Kaunapadanta, "such individuals may lack other essential ministerial qualities. Therefore, the king should appoint ministers whose fathers and grandfathers were also ministers. These individuals, due to their knowledge of past events and established loyalty, will never desert the king, even if offended. Faithfulness, even among animals, shows this—cows, for example, stay with their familiar herds."

"No," says Vátavyádhi, "such individuals might gain excessive influence over the king and act as though they were the king themselves. Instead, the king should appoint new individuals who are proficient in the science of politics. These new ministers will see the king as the true sceptre-bearer (dandadhara) and will not dare to offend him."

"No," says the son of Báhudantí (a woman), "a person with only theoretical knowledge and no experience in practical politics may make serious mistakes when dealing with real issues. Therefore, the king should appoint ministers from high-born families, who are wise, pure in intent, brave, and loyal, as ministerial appointments should be based solely on qualifications."

Kautilya concludes: "This is satisfactory in all respects. A person's ability is proven through their demonstrated capacity in work. Accordingly, based on differences in their abilities, their powers should be divided, and the time and place of their duties clearly determined. Such individuals should not be appointed as councillors (mantrinah) but as ministerial officers (amátyah)."

[Thus ends Chapter VIII, "Creation of Ministers" in Book I, "Concerning Discipline" of the Arthasástra of Kautilya.]

CHAPTER IX. THE CREATION OF COUNCILLORS AND PRIESTS.

A person who is native-born, from a respected family, influential, well-educated in various skills, forward-thinking, wise, has a good memory, courageous, eloquent, skilled, intelligent, enthusiastic, dignified, persistent, of pure character, approachable, firm in loyalty, and possessing good behavior, strength, health, and bravery, without procrastination or indecisiveness, affectionate, and free from qualities that cause hatred or hostility—these are the traits of a qualified minister.

Those who have only half or even a quarter of these traits belong to the middle or lower ranks.

Of these traits, native birth and influence should be verified by reliable people; education and skills by professors of the same field; practical and theoretical knowledge, foresight, memory, and approachability should be judged from successful work outcomes; eloquence, skill, and quick intelligence from how well they tell stories in conversations; endurance, enthusiasm, and bravery in times of trouble; purity of life, friendliness, and loyal devotion by regular interaction; behavior, strength, health, dignity, and freedom from laziness and indecision from close friends; and an affectionate and generous nature through personal experience.

A king's actions can be direct, indirect, or inferred.

What he directly sees is visible; what others teach him is indirect; and drawing conclusions about what hasn't been done yet from what has been accomplished is inferred.

Since actions don't all happen at the same time, come in different forms, and may occur in distant and varied places, the king must appoint his ministers to carry them out, keeping in mind the right time and place. This is the duty of the ministers.

A person whose family and character are highly praised, who is well educated in the Vedas and the six Angas, skilled in interpreting signs whether natural or accidental, knowledgeable in the science of government, obedient, and capable of preventing disasters, whether caused by nature or humans, by performing rituals from the Atharvaveda, should be appointed by the king as the high priest. The king should follow him as a student follows his teacher, as a son follows his father, and as a servant follows his master.

A Kshatriya, raised by Brahmans, guided by wise advisors, and faithfully following the teachings of the scriptures, becomes unbeatable and achieves success, even without the help of weapons.

CHAPTER X. ASCERTAINING BY TEMPTATIONS PURITY OR IMPURITY IN THE CHARACTER OF MINISTERS.

Assisted by his prime minister (mantri) and his high priest, the king shall, by offering temptations, examine the character of ministers (amátya) appointed in government departments of ordinary nature.

The king shall dismiss a priest who, when ordered, refuses to teach the Vedas to an outcaste person or to officiate in a sacrificial performance (apparently) undertaken by an outcaste person (ayájya).

Then the dismissed priest shall, through the medium of spies under the guise of classmates (satri), instigate each minister one after another, saying on oath, "This king is unrighteous; well, let us set up in his place another king who is righteous, or who is born of the same family as of this king, or who is kept imprisoned, or a neighboring king of his family and of self-sufficiency (ekapragraha), or a wild chief (atavika), or an upstart (aupapádika); this attempt is to the liking of all of us; what dost thou think?"

If any one or all of the ministers refuse to acquiesce in such a measure, he or they shall be considered pure. This is what is called religious allurement.

A commander of the army, dismissed from service for receiving condemnable things (asatpragraha), may, through the agency of spies under the guise of classmates (satri), incite each minister to murder the king in view of acquiring immense wealth, each minister being asked, "This attempt is to the liking of all of us; what dost thou think?"

If they refuse to agree, they are to be considered pure. This is what is termed monetary allurement.

A woman-spy under the guise of an ascetic and highly esteemed in the harem of the king may allure each prime minister (mahámátra) one after another, saying, "The queen is enamored of thee and has made arrangements for thy entrance into her chamber; besides this, there is also the certainty of large acquisitions of wealth."

If they discard the proposal, they are pure. This is what is styled love-allurement.

With the intention of sailing on a commercial vessel (prahavananimittam), a minister may induce all other ministers to follow him. Apprehensive of danger, the king may arrest them all. A spy under the guise of a fraudulent disciple, pretending to have suffered imprisonment, may incite each of the ministers thus deprived of wealth and rank, saying, "The king has betaken himself to an unwise course; well, having murdered him, let us put another in his stead. We all like this; what dost thou think?"

If they refuse to agree, they are pure. This is what is termed allurement under fear.

Of these tried ministers, those whose character has been tested under religious allurements shall be employed in civil and criminal courts (dharmasthaníyakantaka sodhaneshu); those whose purity has been tested under monetary allurements shall be employed in the work of a revenue collector and chamberlain; those who have been tried under love-allurements shall be appointed to superintend the pleasure-grounds (vihára) both external and internal; those who have been tested by allurements under fear shall be appointed to immediate service; and those whose character has been tested under all kinds of allurements shall be employed as prime ministers (mantrinah), while those who are proved impure under one or all of these allurements shall be appointed in mines, timber and elephant forests, and manufactories.

Teachers have decided that in accordance with ascertained purity, the king shall employ in corresponding works those ministers whose character has been tested under the three pursuits of life, religion, wealth, and love, and under fear.

Never, in the view of Kautilya, shall the king make himself or his queen an object (laksham, butt) of testing the character of his councillors, nor shall he vitiate the pure like water with poison.

Sometimes the prescribed medicine may fail to reach the person of moral disease; the mind of the valiant, though naturally kept steadfast, may not, when once vitiated and repelled under the four kinds of allurements, return to and recover its original form.

Hence, having set up an external object as the butt for all the four kinds of allurements, the king shall, through the agency of spies (satri), find out the pure or impure character of his ministers (amátya).

CHAPTER XI. THE INSTITUTION OF SPIES.

Assisted by the council of his ministers, who have been tested through espionage, the king shall proceed to create spies: spies under the guise of a fraudulent disciple (kápatika-chhátra), a recluse (udásthita), a householder (grihapaitika), a merchant (vaidehaka), an ascetic practicing austerities (tápasa), a classmate or colleague (satri), a fire-brand (tíkshna), a poisoner (rasada), and a mendicant woman (bhikshuki).

A skillful person capable of reading others' thoughts is a fraudulent disciple. After honoring such a spy with rewards of money and respect, the minister shall instruct him, "Sworn to the king and me, you shall inform us of any wickedness you discover in others."

One who is initiated into asceticism and has foresight and a pure character is called a recluse. This spy, provided with substantial funds and many disciples, shall engage in agriculture, cattle-rearing, and trade (vártakarma) on the lands assigned to him for this purpose. From the produce and profits thus earned, he shall provide all the ascetics with food, clothing, and shelter. He will also send those under his care who wish to earn a livelihood (vrittikáma) on espionage, directing each to detect a specific crime related to the king's wealth and to report it when they come to collect their wages and sustenance. Each ascetic (under the recluse) shall, in turn, send their followers on similar missions.

A farmer, fallen from his profession but possessing foresight and a pure character, is termed a householder spy. This spy shall cultivate the lands assigned to him for this purpose and maintain the farmers and others involved, as previously described.

A trader, fallen from his profession but possessing foresight and pure character, is a merchant spy. This spy shall engage in the production of merchandise on the lands allotted to him for this purpose, etc., as before.

A man with a shaved head (munda) or braided hair (jatila), desiring to earn a livelihood, is a spy disguised as an ascetic practicing austerities. Such a spy, accompanied by a group of disciples with shaved heads or braided hair, may settle in the outskirts of a city, pretending to survive on a handful of vegetables or meadow grass (yavasamushti) taken once every month or two, while secretly consuming his preferred food (gúdhamishtamáháram).

Merchant spies, pretending to be his disciples, may worship him as if he possesses supernatural powers. His other disciples may publicly declare, "This ascetic is a master of extraordinary powers."

Regarding those who, eager to learn about their future, gather around him, the ascetic may, through palmistry, predict future events based on the signals and gestures of his disciples (angavidyayá sishyasanjnábhischa) concerning the affairs of prominent people in the country—such as minor gains, destruction by fire, fear of robbers, execution of rebels, rewards for the virtuous, and forecasts of foreign matters (videsa pravrittivijnánam), saying, "This will happen today, that tomorrow, and the king will do this." His disciples shall corroborate these predictions by providing supporting facts and details.

He shall also predict not only the rewards that people with foresight, eloquence, and bravery are likely to receive from the king, but also possible changes in the appointments of ministers.

The king's minister shall conduct his duties in accordance with the predictions made by the ascetic. He shall appease, with offers of wealth and honor, those who have known reasons to be disaffected, and secretly punish those who are discontented without cause or who are conspiring against the king.

Honored by the king with rewards of money and titles, these five institutes of espionage (samstháh) shall determine the purity of character of the king's servants.

CHAPTER XII. INSTITUTION OF SPIES.

Creation of Wandering Spies.

Those orphans (asambandhinah), who must be supported by the state and are trained in the sciences, palmistry (angavidya), sorcery (máyágata), the duties of various religious orders, sleight of hand (jambhakavidya), and the reading of omens and augury (antara-chakra), are classmate spies or spies learning by social interaction (samsargavidyasatrinah).

Brave desperados from the country, who risk their lives fighting elephants or tigers primarily to earn money, are called firebrands or fiery spies (tíkshna).

Those who have no trace of filial affection, who are exceptionally cruel and lazy, are considered poisoners (rasada).

A poor widow of the Bráhman caste, who is very clever and seeks to earn her livelihood, is called a woman ascetic (parivrájiká). Honored within the king's harem, such a woman shall visit the residences of the king's prime ministers (mahámátrakuláni).

The same rule applies to women with shaved heads (munda), as well as those of the súdra caste. All of these are wandering spies (sancháráh).

Of these spies, those who are from good families, loyal, reliable, well-trained in the art of disguising themselves according to different countries and professions, and who possess knowledge of many languages and arts, shall be sent by the king to spy within his own country on the activities of his ministers, priests, army commanders, the heir-apparent, the gatekeepers, the officer in charge of the harem, the magistrate (prasástri), the collector-general (samáhartri), the chamberlain (sannidhátri), the commissioner (pradeshtri), the city constable (náyaka), the officer in charge of the city (paura), the superintendent of transactions (vyávahárika), the superintendent of manufactories (karmántika), the assembly of councillors (mantriparishad), heads of departments (adhyaksháh), the commissary-general (dandapála), and officers in charge of fortifications, borders, and wild tracts.

Fiery spies, such as those employed to hold the royal umbrella, vase, fan, and shoes, or to attend to the throne, chariot, and conveyance, shall observe the public behavior (báhyam cháram) of these officers.

Classmate spies shall report this information (i.e., that gathered by the fiery spies) to the institutes of espionage (samsthásvarpayeyuh).

Poisoners, such as a sauce-maker (súda), a cook (arálika), a water-bath attendant (snápaka), a shampooer, a bed-spreader (ástaraka), a barber (kalpaka), a toilet attendant (prasádaka), a water-servant, and servants disguised as a hunchback, a dwarf, a pigmy (kiráta), the dumb, the deaf, the simpleton, the blind; as well as artisans such as actors, dancers, singers, musicians, comedians, and a bard, along with women, shall observe the private behavior of these officers.

A mendicant woman shall report this information to the institute of espionage.

The immediate officers of the institutes of espionage (samsthánámantevásinah) shall activate their own spies using signs or written communication (samjnálipibhih) to verify the information.

Neither the institutes of espionage nor the wandering spies shall know each other.

If a mendicant woman is blocked at the entrance, the line of doorkeepers, spies disguised as parents (mátápitri vyanjanáh), women artisans, court-bards, or prostitutes shall, under the pretense of delivering musical instruments, or by using cipher-writing (gudhalekhya), or by signs, convey the information to its intended destination (cháram nirhareyuh).

Spies from the institutes of espionage may suddenly leave under the pretense of suffering from a long-standing illness, lunacy, or by causing a fire or administering poison to someone.

When the information received from these three different sources is consistent, it shall be considered reliable. If these sources frequently differ, the spies involved shall either be secretly punished or dismissed.

The spies referred to in Book IV, "Removal of Thorns," shall receive their salaries from the foreign kings (para) with whom they are employed as servants. However, if they assist both states in catching robbers, they shall receive salaries from both states (ubhayavetanáh).

Those whose sons and wives are kept as hostages shall receive salaries from two states and be regarded as under the mission of enemies. The purity of character of such individuals shall be verified through people of the same profession.

Thus, regarding kings who are enemies, allies, intermediaries, of low rank, or neutral, and concerning their eighteen government departments (ashtáldasa-tírtha), spies shall be deployed.

The hump-backed, the dwarf, the eunuch, accomplished women, the mute, and various ranks of the Mlechcha caste shall serve as spies within their households.

Merchant spies shall operate within forts; saints and ascetics shall reside in the suburbs of forts; farmers and recluses shall be positioned in the rural areas; herdsmen at the country's borders; and in forests, forest-dwellers, sramanas, and chiefs of wild tribes shall be stationed to monitor enemy movements. All these spies shall execute their duties with great speed.

Spies sent by foreign kings shall also be identified by local spies; spies will detect other spies of similar professions. It is the institutes of espionage, whether secret or open, that will activate these spies.

Those chiefs whose hostile intentions have been discovered by spies loyal to the king shall be made to live on the borders of the state, providing an opportunity to identify the spies of foreign kings.

CHAPTER XIII. PROTECTION OF PARTIES FOR OR AGAINST ONE'S OWN CAUSE IN ONE'S OWN STATE.

Having set up spies over his prime ministers (mahámátra), the king shall proceed to spy on both citizens and country people.

Classmate spies (satri) formed into opposing factions shall engage in debates in places of pilgrimage (tírtha), in assemblies, houses, corporations (púga), and among gatherings of people. One spy may begin by saying:

"This king is said to possess all the desirable qualities; he seems unfamiliar with tendencies that would cause him to oppress the citizens and country people with heavy fines and taxes."

In response to those who seem to agree with this statement, another spy may interrupt and say:

"People suffering under anarchy, as seen in the proverb of the large fish swallowing the small one (mátsyanyáyábhibhútah prajáh), first chose Manu, the Vaivasvata, as their king and allotted him one-sixth of the grains produced and one-tenth of the merchandise as sovereign dues. Supported by these payments, kings took on the responsibility of ensuring the safety and well-being (yogakshemavaháh) of their subjects and being accountable for their subjects' sins if they violated the principles of fair punishments and taxes. That is why even hermits give the king one-sixth of the grains they collect, believing it is a tax paid to the one who protects them. The king embodies both the duties of Indra (the rewarder) and Yama (the punisher), acting as a visible dispenser of punishments and rewards (heda-prasáda). Anyone who disrespects the king will also face divine punishments. Thus, kings should never be disrespected."

In this way, treacherous opponents of the sovereignty shall be silenced.

Spies shall also be aware of the rumors circulating within the state. Spies with shaved heads or braided hair shall investigate whether there is contentment or discontent among those who depend on the king's grains, cattle, and gold, among those who supply these to the king in both good and bad times, those who restrain a disaffected relative of the king or a rebellious district, and those who fend off an invading enemy or a wild tribe. The more content such people are, the more honor they shall receive; while those who are disaffected shall be won over by rewards or conciliation. Alternatively, dissension may be sown among them so that they alienate themselves from each other, from a neighboring enemy, from a wild tribe, or from a banished or imprisoned prince. If these measures fail, they may be employed in collecting fines and taxes, making them incur the displeasure of the people. Those who are overcome with enmity may be secretly punished or made to incur the anger of the entire country. Alternatively, by taking the sons and wives of such treacherous persons into state protection, they may be forced to live in mines, preventing them from offering shelter to enemies.

Those who are angry, greedy, fearful, or who despise the king serve as instruments for enemies. Spies disguised as astrologers and fortune-tellers shall ascertain the connections these individuals have with each other and with foreign kings.

Honors and rewards shall be given to those who are content, while those who are disaffected shall be brought around through conciliation, gifts, sowing dissension, or punishment.

Thus, in his own state, a wise king shall protect factions among his people, whether friendly or hostile, powerful or powerless, against the intrigues of foreign kings.

CHAPTER XIV. WINNING OVER FACTIONS FOR OR AGAINST AN ENEMY'S CAUSE IN AN ENEMY'S STATE.

The protection of parties for or against one's own cause in one's own state has been discussed. Now, similar measures concerning parties in a foreign state are to be addressed.

Those who are misled with false promises of large rewards; those whose party, although equally skillful as another in artistic work or in producing useful or profitable works, is overlooked in favor of their rival, who receives larger rewards; those who are oppressed by courtiers (Vallabhá-varuddháh); those who are invited only to be insulted; those who are harassed through banishment; those who, despite investing large sums of money, have failed in their undertakings; those who are prevented from exercising their rights or claiming their inheritance; those who have lost their rank and honors in government service; those who are marginalized by their own relatives; those whose women are violently assaulted; those who are imprisoned; those who are secretly punished; those who are warned of their wrongdoings; those whose property has been completely confiscated; those who have endured long imprisonment; and those whose relatives have been banished—these all belong to the group of provoked persons.

Those who have fallen into misfortune through their own misdeeds; those who are offended by the king; those whose sinful actions have been exposed; those who are fearful after seeing punishment given to someone guilty of the same offense; those whose lands have been confiscated; those whose rebellious nature has been suppressed by force; those who, as superintendents of government departments, have suddenly amassed great wealth; those who, as relatives of such wealthy individuals, aspire to inherit their fortune; those who are disliked by the king; and those who hate the king—all of these come under the group of alarmed persons.

He who is impoverished; he who has lost much wealth; he who is niggardly; he who is addicted to evil propensities; and he who is engaged in dangerous transactions—all these constitute the group of ambitious persons.

He who is self-sufficient; he who is fond of honors; he who is intolerant of his rival's honor; he who is esteemed low; he who is of a fiery spirit; he who is foolhardy, as well as he who is not content with what he has been enjoying—all these come under the group of haughty persons.

Of these, he who clings to a particular faction shall be so deluded by spies with shaved heads or braided hair as to believe that he is intriguing with that party. Partisans under provocation, for example, may be won over by saying, "Just as an elephant in rut, mounted by a driver under intoxication, tramples whatever it encounters, so this king, deprived of the eye of knowledge, blindly oppresses both citizens and country people with taxes and fines; it is possible to restrain him by setting up a rival elephant against him. Therefore, have the patience to wait."

Likewise, alarmed persons may be won over by telling them, "Just as a hidden snake strikes and emits venom over anything that frightens it, so this king, fearful of danger from you, will soon unleash his anger on you. So, it would be wise for you to seek safety elsewhere."

Similarly, ambitious persons may be persuaded by telling them, "Just as a cow raised by dog-keepers gives milk to the dogs but not to Bráhmans, so this king grants rewards to those without valor, foresight, eloquence, or bravery, but not to those of noble character. Therefore, another king, who is capable of distinguishing men of worth, should be sought."

In like manner, haughty persons may be swayed by telling them, "Just as a water reservoir owned by Chándálas serves only the Chándálas and not others, so this low-born king grants his favor only to people of low birth, not to Aryas like you. Therefore, another king, who is capable of recognizing the differences between men, should be sought."

All these disaffected persons, once they have agreed to these proposals, may be bound under a solemn agreement (panakarmaná) to form a coalition with the spies to achieve their aims.

Likewise, friends of a foreign king may also be won over through persuasion and rewards, while implacable enemies may be brought around by sowing discord, by threats, or by pointing out the faults of their master.

CHAPTER XV. THE BUSINESS OF COUNCIL MEETING.

Having secured the loyalty of both local and foreign parties, both within his own and the enemy's state, the king shall proceed to consider administrative measures.

All kinds of administrative actions must be preceded by careful deliberation in a well-formed council. The discussions within the council must remain entirely secret, and the deliberations must be conducted in such a way that not even birds can witness them; for it is said that the secrecy of counsels was once betrayed by parrots, minas, dogs, and other low creatures of insignificant birth. Therefore, without ensuring sufficient safeguards against any potential leaks, the king should never enter into council deliberations.

Whoever reveals the content of these counsels shall be torn to pieces. The disclosure of secrets can be detected by observing changes in the behavior and expressions of envoys, ministers, and leaders. Changes in behavior are referred to as a change in attitude (ingitamanyathávrittih), and observation of facial expressions is known as reading countenance (ákritigrahanamákárah).

Strict secrecy regarding the council's discussions must be maintained, and vigilance must be exercised over the officers involved in these deliberations until the time to act on the decisions made in the council approaches.

Carelessness, intoxication, talking during sleep, love affairs, and other vices among council members are often the causes of the betrayal of secrets.

Those who are secretive by nature or feel disregarded may reveal counsels. Therefore, it is essential to take precautions against these dangers. The disclosure of secret matters benefits people other than the king and his officials.

"Hence," says Bháradvája, "the king should deliberate on secret matters alone; for ministers have their own confidants, and those confidants, in turn, have theirs. This chain of ministers tends to the leakage of secrets.

"Thus, no outsider should be aware of the king's plans. Only those directly involved in executing the plan should know of it, either when it begins or when it is completed."

"No deliberation," says Visáláksha, "made by a single person will be successful. The nature of the work a sovereign must undertake is to be understood by considering both visible and invisible factors. The ability to perceive what is not seen, to make conclusive decisions about what is visible, to clear up doubts in matters where two opinions are possible, and to infer the whole from seeing only a part—all this is possible only through ministers. Therefore, the king should deliberate with people of wide intellect.

He should not disregard anyone but listen to the opinions of all. A wise man should even make use of the sensible utterance of a child.

"This," says Parásara, "is about gathering the opinions of others, not about keeping counsels. He should ask his ministers for their opinion on a matter similar to the one he has in mind, saying, 'This is the situation; it happened in this way; what should be done if it turns out like this?' and he should act according to their decision. In this way, both the gathering of opinions and the maintenance of secrecy can be achieved."

"Not so," says Pisuna, "because when ministers are asked for their opinions about a distant task or an accomplished or unaccomplished work, they either approach it with indifference or offer half-hearted opinions. This is a significant flaw. Therefore, the king should consult only those people who are known to provide decisive opinions about the work for which he seeks advice. By doing so, he will secure both good advice and the secrecy of counsel."

"Not so," says Kautilya, "because this kind of advice-seeking is infinite and endless. The king should consult three or four ministers. Consultation with a single minister may not lead to any definite conclusion, especially in complicated matters. A single minister may act willfully and without restraint. When deliberating with two ministers, the king may be either overpowered by their combined action or endangered by their mutual dissension. However, with three or four ministers, he will avoid serious trouble and reach satisfactory results. With more than four ministers, reaching a decision becomes burdensome, and maintaining the secrecy of counsel becomes much more difficult. Depending on the situation, time, and nature of the work in question, the king may, as he sees fit, deliberate with one or two ministers, or even by himself.

The five essential elements of every council deliberation are: means to carry out the work, command over plenty of men and wealth, allocation of time and place, remedies against dangers, and final success."

The king may ask his ministers for their opinion either individually or collectively and evaluate their competence by examining the reasons they provide for their opinions.

He should not delay when the awaited opportunity arises, nor should he engage in lengthy consultations with those whose interests he plans to harm.

The school of Manu suggests that the assembly of ministers (mantriparishad) should consist of twelve members.

The school of Brihaspati proposes that it should consist of sixteen members.

The school of Usanas recommends that it should have twenty members.

However, Kautilya asserts that the assembly should consist of as many members as the needs of the kingdom require (yathásámarthyam).

These ministers must consider all matters concerning the interests of both the king and his enemies. They should initiate work that has yet to begin, complete what has been started, improve what has already been achieved, and ensure strict compliance with orders (niyogasampadam).

The king should supervise works alongside his close officers (ásannaih), and consult with those who are distant by sending written messages (patrasampreshanena).

Indra's assembly of ministers (mantriparishad) consists of a thousand sages. They are his eyes, which is why he is called "thousand-eyed" though he possesses only two eyes.

In emergencies, the king shall summon both his ministers and the assembly of ministers (mantrino mantriparishadam cha) to inform them of the situation. He shall act according to the majority's (bhúyishtháh) suggestion or follow the course of action that leads to success (káryasiddhikaram va) they recommend.

And while performing any task, none of his enemies (pare) should know his secret, but he shall know the vulnerabilities of his enemy. Like a tortoise retracting its limbs, he should withdraw any exposed actions.

Just as offerings of food made to ancestors by someone ignorant of the Vedas are unfit for wise men to eat, so too is a person unlearned in the sciences unfit to participate in council deliberations.

CHAPTER XVI. THE MISSION OF ENVOYS.

Whoever has succeeded as a councillor is an envoy.

Whoever possesses the qualifications of a minister is a chargé-d'affaires (nisrishtárthah).

Whoever possesses the same qualifications, but with one-quarter less, is an agent entrusted with a specific mission (parimitárthah).

Whoever possesses the same qualifications, but with one-half less, is a conveyer of royal writs (sásanaharah).

Having made excellent arrangements for transportation, conveyance, servants, and sustenance, the envoy shall embark on his mission, thinking: "The enemy shall be told this; the enemy (para) will respond like this; this shall be my reply; and this is how he shall be deceived."

The envoy shall form friendships with the enemy's officers, such as those in charge of wild tracts, boundaries, cities, and rural areas. He shall also compare the military posts, war resources, and fortresses of the enemy with those of his own master. He shall assess the size and area of the forts and the state, as well as the strongholds where valuables are stored and identify the assailable and unassailable points.

Once permission has been granted, he shall enter the enemy's capital and deliver the mission exactly as entrusted to him, even if it costs him his life.

A brightness in the tone, face, and eyes of the enemy; a respectful reception of the mission; inquiries about the health of friends; participation in discussions of virtues; being given a seat close to the throne; courteous treatment of the envoy; remembrance of friends; and a conclusion of the mission with satisfaction—all these are signs of the enemy's goodwill, while their absence signifies his displeasure.

In the case of a displeased enemy, he may be told: --

"Messengers are the mouthpieces of kings, not only of you but of all; therefore, messengers, who, even in the face of weapons raised against them, must deliver their mission exactly as they were entrusted, do not deserve death, even if they are outcasts. Where, then, is the justification for putting messengers of the Bráhman caste to death? This is the speech of another. The duty of messengers is to deliver that speech exactly."

Not carried away by the respect shown to him, the envoy shall remain there until he is permitted to leave. He shall not be intimidated by the enemy's power, shall strictly avoid women and liquor, and shall sleep alone. It is well known that the intentions of envoys are often discovered while they are asleep or under the influence of alcohol.

Through the help of spies disguised as ascetics, merchants, or their disciples, or through spies posing as physicians and heretics, or through those who receive salaries from two states (ubhayavétana), the envoy shall gather information about the intrigues among those loyal to his master, the conspiracies of hostile factions, and assess the people's loyalty or disloyalty to the enemy, as well as any vulnerable points.

If there is no possibility of directly engaging in such conversations (regarding the people's loyalty), he may attempt to gather such information by listening to the talk of beggars, intoxicated and insane people, or those babbling in their sleep. He may also observe signs made at places of pilgrimage and temples or decipher paintings and secret writings (chitra-gúdha-lékhya-samjñá-bhih).

Whatever information he gathers in this way, he shall verify through further intrigues.

He shall not refute the enemy's assessment of the elements of sovereignty in his own master's kingdom but shall simply respond with, "All is known to you." Nor shall he disclose the methods employed by his master to achieve a certain goal.

If he has not succeeded in his mission but is still detained, he shall consider the situation, pondering:

Whether the enemy, recognizing the danger my master faces, seeks to avoid his own peril; whether he intends to incite an enemy or a neighboring king against my master; whether he aims to stir up internal rebellion in my master's state or provoke a wild chief (átavika) against him; whether he seeks to destroy my master by employing a friend or a king whose domain borders my master's state (ákranda); whether he aims to prevent internal troubles in his own state or avoid a foreign invasion or incursions by wild tribes; whether he intends to delay the timing of my master's military expedition; whether he seeks to gather raw materials and merchandise, repair his fortifications, or recruit a powerful army; whether he waits for the right moment to fully train his own army; or whether he seeks an alliance to remedy the current contempt caused by his carelessness—what could be the reason for detaining me like this?

Based on his assessment, the envoy may choose to stay or depart as he sees fit, or he may demand a quick resolution of his mission.

Alternatively, after delivering an unfavorable message (sásana) to the enemy and feigning fear of imprisonment or death, he may return without permission; otherwise, he may face punishment.

The duties of an envoy (dúta) include the transmission of missions, the maintenance of treaties, the issuance of ultimatums (pratápa), gaining friends, executing intrigues, sowing discord among allies, assembling secret forces, secretly removing relatives or valuable items, gathering intelligence about the movements of spies, displaying bravery, breaking peace treaties, winning the favor of the enemy's envoy and officials.

The king shall employ his own envoys to carry out such tasks and guard himself against the mischief of foreign envoys by employing counter-envoys, spies, and visible and invisible watchmen.

CHAPTER XVII. PROTECTION OF PRINCES.

Protection of Princes

Having first secured his own personal safety from his wives and sons, the king can then ensure the security of his kingdom against both immediate enemies and foreign kings.

We shall discuss "Protection of Wives" in the section on "Duties toward the Harem."

From the time of the princes' birth, the king shall take special care of them.

"For," says Bháradvája, "princes, like crabs, have a notorious tendency to devour their begetter. When they lack filial affection, it is better to punish them in secret (upámsudandah)."

"This," says Visáláksha, "is cruelty, the destruction of fortune, and the extinction of the Kshatriya race. Therefore, it is better to keep the princes under guard in a designated place."

"This," says the school of Parásara, "is like the fear of a lurking snake (ahibhayam); for a prince may suspect that his father, fearful of danger, has confined him, and may attempt to destroy his father. Therefore, it is better to keep a prince under the custody of boundary guards or inside a fort."

"This," says Pisuna, "is akin to the fear of a wolf among a flock of sheep (aurabhrakam bhayam); for after realizing the reason for his confinement, the prince may ally with the boundary guards against his father. Therefore, it is better to send him to a fort belonging to a foreign king far away from his own state."

"This," says Kaunapadanta, "is like the position of a calf (vatsasthánam); just as a man milks a cow with the help of its calf, so the foreign king may exploit the prince's father. Therefore, it is better to have the prince live with his maternal relatives."

"This," says Vátavyádhi, "is akin to the position of a flag (dhvajasthánamétat); just as in the case of Aditi and Kausika, the prince's maternal relatives may use him as a banner and continue to beg favors. Therefore, it is better to let princes dissipate their lives in sensual pleasures (grámyadharma), as indulgent sons do not oppose their permissive father."

"This," says Kautilya, "is a living death; for no sooner is a royal family with a prince or princes given to dissipation attacked than it collapses, like wood infested with worms. Therefore, when the queen reaches the age favorable for conception, priests shall offer the necessary oblations to Indra and Brihaspati. When she becomes pregnant, the king shall observe the instructions of midwifery concerning gestation and delivery. After the birth, the priests shall perform the prescribed purification ceremonies. When the prince reaches the proper age, experts shall train him under the correct discipline."

"Any one of the classmate spies," say the Ambhíyas (politicians), "may lure the prince towards hunting, gambling, liquor, and women, and provoke him to rebel against his father and seize control of the kingdom. Another spy, however, shall prevent him from committing such acts."

"There can be," says Kautilya, "no greater crime or sin than corrupting an innocent mind; just as a fresh object is stained by whatever it comes into contact with, so a young prince with a fresh mind is inclined to accept everything he is told as a legitimate teaching. Therefore, he should only be taught about righteousness and wealth (artha), not unrighteousness or non-wealth. Classmate spies should be so courteous towards him as to say, 'We are yours.' When, under the influence of youth, he turns his attention to women, impure women disguised as Aryas shall terrify him in the night and in lonely places. If he indulges in liquor, he shall be frightened by making him drink liquor adulterated with narcotics (yógapána). When fond of gambling, spies disguised as fraudulent gamblers shall terrify him. If he enjoys hunting, he shall be scared by spies posing as highway robbers. And when he desires to rebel against his father, he shall, under the pretense of compliance, be gradually dissuaded from such actions by being told: 'A king is not made by mere desire; failure in your attempt will bring your death, and success will lead you to hell, causing the people to grieve (for your father) and condemn you, the only clod (ekalóshtavadhascha).'"

When a king has an only son, who is either indifferent to worldly pleasures or is his favored child, the king may keep him under restraint. If the king has several sons, he may send some of them to places where there is no heir apparent, nor any child recently born or still in the womb.

If a prince possesses good and friendly qualities, he may be made the commander-in-chief or appointed as the heir apparent.

Sons are of three kinds: those of sharp intelligence, those of stagnant intelligence, and those of a perverted mind.

Whoever diligently practices what he has been taught regarding righteousness and wealth is of sharp intelligence. Whoever does not put into practice the good teachings he has received is of stagnant intelligence. And whoever gets entangled in dangers and despises righteousness and wealth is of a perverted mind.

If a king has an only son of the last type, efforts should be made to produce another son; or sons may be begotten through his daughters.

When a king is too old or ill to beget sons, he may appoint a maternal relative or a blood relative (kulya) of his, or a neighboring king of good and friendly qualities, to "sow the seed in his field" (kshétrebíjam, i.e., to beget a son with his wife).

But a wicked and only son shall never be placed on the royal throne.

A royal father, who serves as the only support for many people, should be favorably inclined towards his son. Except in times of danger, sovereignty falling to the eldest son is always respected. Sometimes, however, sovereignty may belong to a clan; for the corporation of clans, invincible in nature and free from the chaos of anarchy, can maintain a permanent existence on earth.

CHAPTER XVIII. THE CONDUCT OF A PRINCE KEPT UNDER RESTRAINT AND THE TREATMENT OF A RESTRAINED PRINCE.

A prince, though subjected to difficulties and assigned an unfair task, shall still loyally follow his father unless the task threatens his life, enrages the people, or causes other serious calamities. If he is given a noble or beneficial duty, he shall strive to gain the favor of the superintendent in charge of the work, complete the task with better results than expected, and present his father with both the expected profits from the work and any excess profit due to his skill. If, despite this, the king remains displeased with him and shows undue favor to another prince or other wives, the prince may request permission from the king to retire to a forest life.

If the prince fears imprisonment or death, he may seek refuge with a neighboring king known for being righteous, charitable, truthful, and not cunning, but also one who welcomes and respects guests of good character. Living under such a king's protection, he can gather men and money, establish marriage ties with influential individuals, form alliances with wild tribes, and win over factions in his father's state.

Alternatively, traveling alone, he may earn his livelihood by working in gold or ruby mines, or by crafting gold and silver ornaments or other trade goods. By forming close connections with heretics (páshanda), wealthy widows, or merchants engaged in ocean trade, he may, through the use of poison (madanarasa), rob them of their wealth and the wealth of the gods, except when such wealth is reserved for Bráhmans learned in the Vedas. He may also adopt measures used to capture villages from a foreign king. Or he may move against his father with the help of his mother's servants.

The prince, disguising himself as a painter, carpenter, court-bard, physician, buffoon, or heretic, and assisted by spies similarly disguised, may seize an opportunity to present himself armed with weapons and poison before the king, declaring: "I am the heir-apparent; it is not fitting that you alone enjoy the kingdom, which is meant for both of us, or which others rightly desire to share. I should not be excluded simply by being given double the subsistence and salary."

These are the measures that a prince under restraint might undertake.

Spies or his mother, whether natural or adoptive, may reconcile a restrained heir-apparent and bring him back to court.

Alternatively, secret emissaries armed with weapons and poison may kill a prince who has been abandoned. If the prince has not been abandoned, he may be captured at night by women prepared for the task, or by the use of liquor, or during a hunting expedition, and brought back to court.

Once brought back, the king may appease the prince with a promise of sovereignty after the king's death and keep him under guard in a designated place. If the king has many sons, a rebellious prince may be banished.

CHAPTER XIX. THE DUTIES OF A KING.

If a king is energetic, his subjects will also be energetic. If he is reckless, not only will they become reckless, but they will also undermine his efforts. Furthermore, a reckless king will easily fall into the hands of his enemies. Therefore, the king must always remain vigilant.

He shall divide both day and night into eight nálikas (1½ hours each), or according to the length of the shadow cast by a gnomon standing in the sun: a shadow of three purushás (36 angulás or inches), one purushá (12 inches), four angulás (4 inches), and no shadow, indicating midday, are the four divisions of the forenoon; the same divisions (in reverse order) are used for the afternoon.

Of these divisions, during the first one-eighth part of the day, the king shall post watchmen and attend to accounts of receipts and expenditures; during the second part, he shall look after the affairs of both the citizens and the rural population; during the third part, he shall bathe, dine, and study; during the fourth part, he shall receive revenue in gold (hiranya) and manage the appointments of superintendents; during the fifth part, he shall correspond by writs (patrasampreshanena) with his ministers and receive secret information from his spies; during the sixth part, he may engage in his favorite pastimes or personal contemplation; during the seventh part, he shall supervise elephants, horses, chariots, and infantry; and during the eighth part, he shall discuss military operations with his commander-in-chief.

At the close of the day, he shall perform the evening prayer (sandhya).

During the first one-eighth part of the night, he shall receive secret emissaries; during the second part, he shall bathe, have supper, and study; during the third part, he shall enter the bedchamber to the sound of trumpets and sleep during the fourth and fifth parts; awakened by the sound of trumpets during the sixth part, he shall recall to mind the teachings of the sciences and his duties for the day; during the seventh part, he shall consider administrative matters and dispatch spies; and during the eighth part of the night, he shall receive blessings from sacrificial priests, teachers, and the high priest. Afterward, he shall meet his physician, chief cook, and astrologer, and salute a cow with its calf and a bull by circumambulating around them before entering his court.

Or, according to his capacity, the king may modify the timetable and attend to his duties accordingly.

When in the court, he shall never keep petitioners waiting at the door, for if a king becomes inaccessible to his people and delegates his responsibilities to immediate officers, it is certain to create confusion in business, cause public dissatisfaction, and make him vulnerable to his enemies.

Therefore, he shall personally attend to the matters of the gods, heretics, Bráhmans learned in the Vedas, cattle, sacred places, minors, the elderly, the afflicted, the helpless, and women—each in the order of importance or according to the urgency of the matter.

He shall address urgent matters immediately and never delay them, for when postponed, they may become too difficult or impossible to resolve.

Seated in the room where the sacred fire is kept, the king shall attend to the concerns of physicians and ascetics practicing austerities, doing so in the presence of his high priest and teacher and after offering preliminary salutations to the petitioners.

Accompanied by those proficient in the three sciences (trividya)—but never alone, lest the petitioners be offended—he shall consider the matters of those practicing austerities, as well as those knowledgeable in witchcraft and Yóga.

For a king, his religious vow is his readiness for action; his performance of duties is his sacrifice; giving equal attention to all is his offering of fees and ablution towards consecration.

The happiness of his subjects is his happiness; their welfare is his welfare. He shall not consider what pleases him personally as good, but rather what pleases his subjects.

Therefore, the king shall always be active and diligent in his duties; the root of wealth is activity, and the root of misfortune is its opposite.

Without activity, current and future acquisitions will be lost; through activity, he can achieve both his desired goals and abundant wealth.

CHAPTER XX. DUTY TOWARDS THE HAREM.

On a site naturally best suited for the purpose, the king shall construct his harem, consisting of many compartments, one within another, surrounded by a parapet and a ditch, and secured with a door.

He shall build his own residential palace following the model of his treasury-house; or he may have his residence in the center of the delusive chamber (móhanagriha), which is equipped with secret passages built into the walls; or in an underground chamber adorned with figures of goddesses and altars (chaitya) carved into the wooden door-frame, with multiple underground exits. Another option is an upper story with a hidden staircase inside the wall and an escape passage concealed in a hollow pillar, with the entire structure designed with mechanical contrivances so it can collapse when needed.

If he fears danger from his own classmates (sahádhyáyi), such contrivances and safeguards against peril may be employed during times of danger or at other times, as he deems necessary.

No other kind of fire can burn the harem that is thrice circumambulated from right to left by a fire of human origin (manushénágnina); no other fire can be kindled there. Fire also cannot harm a harem whose walls are made of mud mixed with ashes from lightning and soaked in hail-water (karaka-vári).

Poisonous snakes will not enter buildings protected by plants like Jívanti (Fæderia Fœtida), svéta (Aconitum Ferox), mushkakapushpa (?), and vandáka (Epidendrum Tesselatum), and branches of péjáta (?) and asvattha (Ficus Religiosa).

Cats, peacocks, mongooses, and spotted deer will eat snakes. Parrots, minas (sárika), and Malabar birds (bhringarája) will shriek when they detect the smell of snake venom. The heron (crauncha) faints in the presence of poison, the pheasant (jívanjívaka) feels distress, the young cuckoo (mattakókila) dies, and the eyes of the partridge (chakóra) turn red. Thus, precautions against fire and poison shall be taken.

On one side, behind the harem, there shall be compartments for the women, equipped with all necessary medicines for midwifery and illnesses, as well as well-known pot-herbs (prakhyátasamsthávriksha) and a water reservoir. Outside these compartments shall be the residences of princes and princesses. In front of these buildings will be the toilet ground (alankára bhúmih), the council ground (mantrabhúmib), the court, and the offices of the heir-apparent and superintendents.

Between the compartments, the army under the command of the officer in charge of the harem shall be stationed for security.

When inside the harem, the king shall only see the queen after her personal purity has been assured by an old maid-servant. He shall not touch any woman unless her purity is verified, for many dangers have arisen from within the queen's chambers. For example, King Bhadrasena was slain by his own brother who hid in the queen's chamber; King Kárusa was killed by his son who hid under his mother's bed; Queen Kásirája poisoned her king by mixing poison with fried rice disguised as honey; Queen Vairantya killed her king using an anklet coated with poison; Queen Sauvíra murdered her king with a gem from her waist, smeared with poison; Queen Jálútha killed her king with a looking glass tainted with poison; and Queen Vidúratha killed her king with a weapon concealed in her hair.

Therefore, the king must always be cautious to avoid such hidden dangers. He shall prevent his wives from associating with ascetics, whether with shaved heads or braided hair, buffoons, and outside prostitutes (dási). Women of high birth should not have the opportunity to see his wives, except for the designated midwives.

Prostitutes (rúpájíva), attending the harem, must always maintain personal cleanliness by bathing frequently, and wear fresh garments and ornaments.

Eighty men and fifty women disguised as fathers, mothers, elderly persons, and eunuchs shall oversee the purity and conduct within the harem. They shall ensure that the affairs of the harem are managed in a way that brings happiness to the king.

Each person in the harem must live in the area assigned to them and shall never move into the spaces assigned to others. No one in the harem shall associate with any outsiders at any time.

The movement of all goods, whether entering or leaving the harem, shall be strictly controlled. After careful examination, these items may only reach their destination—inside or outside the harem—based on the seal-mark (mudrá) provided.

CHAPTER XXI. PERSONAL SAFETY.

On rising from bed, the king shall be greeted by groups of women armed with bows. In the second compartment, he shall be received by the Kanchuki (the one who presents the king's coat), the Ushnisi (the one who presents the king's head-dress), elderly attendants, and other members of the harem.

In the third compartment, he shall be greeted by crooked and dwarfish persons, and in the fourth compartment, by prime ministers, kinsmen, and doorkeepers holding barbed missiles in their hands.

The king shall employ as his personal attendants those whose fathers and grandfathers had served the royal family, those who are closely related to the king, those who are well-trained and loyal, and those who have provided distinguished service.

Foreigners, those who have not earned rewards or honor through good service, and even natives who are known to be engaged in inimical activities shall not be part of the king's bodyguard or the troops of the officers in charge of the harem.

In a well-guarded area, the head cook (máhánasika) shall oversee the preparation of a variety of relishing dishes. The king shall partake of these freshly prepared dishes only after first offering them as an oblation to the fire and then to birds.

The presence of poison in the dish can be inferred if the flame and smoke from the fire turn blue and crackle, or if the birds (that eat the offering) die. Other signs include: when the steam rising from cooked rice has the color of a peacock's neck and appears suddenly cool; when vegetables show an unnatural color, are watery, hardened, and seem to have dried suddenly, with blackish foam layers, lacking their natural smell, touch, and taste; when utensils reflect more or less light than usual and have a foam layer at the edges; when liquids develop surface streaks; when milk has a bluish streak in the center of its surface; when liquor or water shows reddish streaks; when curd shows black or dark streaks, and honey shows white streaks; when watery substances seem overcooked, appear blue and swollen; when dry substances shrink and change color; when hard things seem soft and soft things become hard; when tiny creatures near the dishes die; when carpets and curtains show black circular spots with loose threads and hair falling off; and when metallic vessels set with gems become tarnished as though roasted, losing their polish, color, shine, and softness to the touch— poison should be suspected in all these cases.

As for the person who has administered poison, the telltale signs include a dry and parched mouth, hesitation in speech, excessive sweating, frequent yawning, intense bodily tremors, frequent stumbling, evasion in conversation, careless work, and reluctance to remain in the place assigned to them.

Thus, physicians and experts skilled in detecting poison must always attend to the king.

After taking medicine from the storeroom, the purity of which has been confirmed through experimentation, and after both the physician, the decoctioner (páchaka), and the purveyor (póshaka) have tasted it themselves, the physician shall deliver the medicine to the king. The same procedure applies to liquor and other beverages.

Servants in charge of clothing and toiletries, after having bathed and cleaned themselves and dressed in freshly washed garments, shall provide the king with clothing and toiletries that have been sealed and received from the officer in charge of the harem.

Prostitutes shall be responsible for duties in the bathhouse, as shampooers, bedding-room attendants, washermen, and garland-makers. When presenting water, scents, fragrant powders, clothing, and garlands to the king, the servants, along with the prostitutes, must first touch these items with their eyes, arms, and breasts to ensure they are safe.

This same rule applies to anything received from someone outside the palace.

Musicians shall entertain the king only with performances that do not involve weapons, fire, or poison. Musical instruments, as well as the ornaments of horses, chariots, and elephants, must always be kept within the confines of the harem.

The king shall mount chariots or beasts of burden only after they have first been mounted by his hereditary driver or rider.

He shall board a boat only when it is piloted by a trustworthy sailor and attached to a second boat for safety. He shall never sail on a ship that has previously been weatherbeaten, and even when on a good ship, his army shall stand guard on the shore.

He shall enter water only when it is free from large fish (matsya) and crocodiles. He shall wander in forests only if they are cleared of snakes and crocodiles (gráha).

To gain proficiency in shooting arrows at moving targets, the king shall engage in sports in forests that have been cleared by hunters and hound-keepers of the dangers of highway robbers, snakes, and enemies.

He shall give audiences to saints and ascetics only when he is attended by a trustworthy bodyguard armed with weapons. When receiving envoys from foreign states, he shall be surrounded by his assembly of ministers.

When inspecting his army, he shall be attired in military dress and mount a horse, chariot, or elephant to review his troops prepared in military formation.

On occasions of entering or leaving the capital, the king's road shall be guarded on both sides by staff-bearers and cleared of armed persons, ascetics, and the crippled (vyanga).

He shall only attend festivals, fairs (yátra), processions, or sacrificial performances when these events are policed by bands of 'The Ten Communities' (dasavargikadhishthitáni).

Just as the king ensures the personal safety of others through the use of spies, a wise king shall also take care to secure his own person from external dangers.

Book 2

CHAPTER I. FORMATION OF VILLAGES.

Either by encouraging foreigners to immigrate (paradesapraváhanena) or by reducing the excessive population from the densely populated areas of his own kingdom (svadésábhishyandavámanéna vá), the king may establish new villages either on uninhabited sites or on the ruins of old settlements (bhútapúrvama vá).

Villages shall be composed of no fewer than one hundred families and no more than five hundred families of agricultural people from the súdra caste. The boundaries of these villages shall extend as far as one or two krósas (2250 yards or more) and be capable of providing mutual protection. Boundaries may be marked by natural features like rivers, mountains, forests, bulbous plants (grishti), caves, artificial constructions (sétubandha), or trees such as the sálmali (silk cotton tree), samí (Acacia Suma), and kshíravriksha (milky trees).

In the center of eight hundred villages, a stháníya (a fortress) shall be constructed; in the center of four hundred villages, a drónamukha; in the center of two hundred villages, a khárvátika; and a sangrahana in the midst of a group of ten villages.

At the borders of the kingdom, forts shall be built and manned by boundary-guards (antapála), whose duty will be to control access into the kingdom. The interior of the kingdom shall be secured by trap-keepers (vágurika), archers (sábara), hunters (pulinda), chandálas, and wild tribes (aranyachára).

Those who perform sacrifices (ritvik), spiritual guides, priests, and those learned in the Vedas shall be granted Brahmadaya lands that yield sufficient produce and are exempt from taxes and fines (adandkaráni).

Superintendents, accountants, gopas (village heads), sthánikas (regional officers), veterinary surgeons (Aníkastha), physicians, horse trainers, and messengers shall also be endowed with lands, but they shall not have the right to sell or mortgage these lands.

Prepared lands shall be given to taxpayers (karada) for their lifetime use (ekapurushikáni).

Lands that are being prepared for cultivation shall not be taken away from those who are working on them.

Lands may be confiscated from those who fail to cultivate them properly and given to others; or they may be cultivated by village laborers (grámabhritaka) and traders (vaidehaka) to prevent the original owners from paying less than they should to the government. If cultivators pay their taxes without difficulty, they may be favorably provided with grains, cattle, and money.

The king shall bestow on cultivators only such favor and tax remission (anugrahaparihárau) as will increase the treasury, avoiding any measures that might deplete it.

A king with a depleted treasury will drain the vitality of both the citizens and rural population. In the case of opening new settlements or during other emergencies, remissions of taxes may be granted.

He shall treat with fatherly kindness those who have passed the period of tax remission.

The king shall engage in mining operations and manufacturing, exploit timber and elephant forests, facilitate cattle breeding and commerce, construct roads for land and water traffic, and establish market towns (panyapattana).

He shall also build reservoirs (sétu) filled with either perennial water or water from another source. Alternatively, he may provide sites, roads, timber, and other necessary materials for those who wish to construct reservoirs on their own. The same applies to the construction of places of pilgrimage (punyasthána) and groves.

Anyone who abstains from cooperative construction (sambhúya setubhandhát) must send his servants and bullocks to carry out the work, contribute to the expenses, but will have no claim to the profits.

The king shall exercise his ownership rights (swámyam) over fishing, ferrying, and trading in vegetables (haritapanya) in reservoirs or lakes (sétushu).

Those who neglect the rightful claims of their slaves (dása), hirelings (áhitaka), and relatives shall be reminded of their duties.

The king shall provide for the maintenance of orphans (bála), the elderly, the infirm, the afflicted, and the helpless. He shall also offer support to helpless pregnant women and provide for the care of the children they give birth to.

Elders among the villagers shall be responsible for managing and improving the property of bereaved minors until they reach maturity; this applies to the property of Gods as well.

If a capable person, other than an apostate (patita) or a mother, neglects to provide for the maintenance of his or her child, spouse, mother, father, minor brothers or sisters, or widowed girls (kanyá vidhaváscha), that person shall be punished with a fine of twelve panas.

If a person adopts asceticism without making provisions for the maintenance of his wife and sons, he shall be punished with the first amercement. Similarly, anyone who converts a woman to asceticism (pravrájayatah) without providing for her will be fined.

Only those who have passed the age of reproduction may become ascetics after distributing their property among their sons. If they fail to do so, they will be punished.

No ascetic other than a vánaprastha (forest hermit), no community other than local communities (sajátádanyassanghah), and no guilds except for local cooperative guilds (sámutthávyiká-danyassamayánubandhah) shall be allowed entry into the kingdom's villages. Furthermore, villages shall not have buildings (sáláh) intended for sports and entertainment.

For the sake of maintaining peace and avoiding disturbances, actors, dancers, singers, drummers, buffoons (vágjívana), and bards (kusílava) shall not interfere with the daily work of the villagers, nor shall they attempt to exploit the villagers by seeking money, free labor, commodities, grains, or liquids in abundance. Helpless villagers are always dependent on their fields and must not be disturbed.

The king shall refrain from taking possession of any territory that is prone to invasions by enemies and wild tribes or that suffers from frequent famines and pestilence. He shall also avoid indulging in expensive and lavish sports.

The king must protect agriculture from oppressive fines, forced labor, and excessive taxes (dandavishtikarábádhaih), and he shall safeguard herds of cattle from thieves, tigers, poisonous creatures, and cattle diseases.

Furthermore, he shall ensure that roads are free from the interference of courtiers (vallabha), workmen (kármika), robbers, and boundary guards. He must also prevent roads from being damaged by herds of cattle.

In this way, the king shall not only maintain and repair the timber and elephant forests, buildings, and mines established in the past but also create new ones.

CHAPTER II. DIVISION OF LAND.

The king shall make provision for pasture grounds on uncultivable lands.

Bráhmans shall be provided with forests for the cultivation of sóma, for religious learning, and for the performance of penance. Such forests shall be made safe from dangers posed by both animate and inanimate objects, and they shall be named after the tribal lineage (gótra) of the Bráhmans residing within them.

A forest as large as the aforementioned, with only one entrance, made inaccessible by surrounding ditches, filled with plantations of delicious fruit trees, bushes, bowers, and thornless trees, with a large lake full of water and harmless animals, as well as tigers (vyála), beasts of prey (márgáyuka), male and female elephants, young elephants, and bisons—all with their claws and teeth removed—shall be established for the king's sports.

At the extreme border of the kingdom or in another suitable location, another game forest, containing game animals and open to all, shall be created. In order to obtain all types of forest produce, as mentioned elsewhere, one or several forests shall be specially designated for this purpose.

Manufactories for preparing goods from forest produce shall also be established.

Wild tracts of land shall be separated from timber forests. Elephant forests shall be created at the farthest limits of the kingdom, separated from wild areas.

The superintendent of forests, along with his team of forest guards, shall not only maintain the forests but also be aware of all the entrance and exit routes for forests that are mountainous, swampy, or contain rivers or lakes.

Anyone who kills an elephant shall be sentenced to death.

Anyone who brings in the tusks of an elephant that has died from natural causes shall be rewarded with four-and-a-half panas.

The guards of the elephant forests, along with elephant keepers, those who chain the legs of elephants, boundary guards, forest-dwellers, and those who nurse elephants, shall track herds of elephants by following the trails of urine and dung left by elephants, and by observing forest paths covered by branches of Bhallátaki (Semicarpus Anacardium). They will also look for places where elephants have slept or sat, left droppings, or destroyed the banks of rivers or lakes. They shall determine whether these signs come from herds of elephants, a single roaming elephant, a stray elephant, a leader of herds, a tusker, a rogue elephant, an elephant in rut, a young elephant, or an elephant that has escaped from captivity.

Experts in catching elephants shall follow the instructions of the elephant doctor (aníkastha) and capture elephants that possess auspicious characteristics and a good temperament.

The victory of kings in battle primarily depends on elephants, as their large size enables them to destroy the enemy's army formations, fortifications, and encampments, as well as to carry out dangerous tasks.

Elephants bred in regions such as Kálinga, Anga, Karúsa, and the East are considered the best. Those from Dasárna and western regions are of middle quality, while those from Sauráshtra and Panchajana regions are of lower quality. However, the strength and energy of all elephants can be improved through proper training.

CHAPTER III. CONSTRUCTION OF FORTS

On all four sides of the kingdom's boundaries, defensive fortifications against enemy attacks in times of war shall be constructed in areas best suited for the purpose: a water fortification (audaka), such as an island in the middle of a river or a plain surrounded by lower ground; a mountainous fortification (párvata), such as a rocky area or a cave; a desert fortification (dhánvana), such as a wild tract devoid of water and overgrown with thickets in barren soil; or a forest fortification (vanadurga) filled with wagtails (khajana), water, and dense thickets.

Of these, water and mountain fortifications are best suited for defending populous centers, while desert and forest fortifications are suited for habitation in wilderness areas (atavísthánam).

Alternatively, with preparations ready for retreat, the king may establish his fortified capital (stháníya) as the center of his sovereignty (samudayásthánam) in the middle of his kingdom. This capital should be located in a naturally strategic area, such as the bank of a river confluence, a deep pool of perennial water, or near a lake or tank. The fort may be circular, rectangular, or square in shape, surrounded by an artificial water canal and connected to both land and water routes.

Around this fort, three ditches, spaced one danda (6 ft.) apart from each other, shall be dug. These ditches shall be fourteen, twelve, and ten dandas wide, respectively, and their depth shall be one-quarter to one-half of their width. The ditches shall be square at the bottom, one-third as wide as the top, with sides constructed of stones or bricks. These ditches shall be filled with perennial flowing water or water drawn from another source, and they shall contain crocodiles and lotus plants.

At a distance of four dandas (24 ft.) from the innermost ditch, a rampart six dandas high and twice as wide shall be constructed by heaping up mud. The rampart shall be square at the bottom, oval in the center, and pressed down by the trampling of elephants and bulls. It shall be planted with thorny and poisonous bushes. Any gaps in the rampart shall be filled with fresh earth.

Above the rampart, parapets, either in odd or even numbers, with an intermediate space of 12 to 24 hastas between them, shall be built of bricks and raised to a height twice their breadth.

The passage for chariots shall be constructed from palm tree trunks or broad and thick slabs of stone, with spheres resembling the heads of monkeys carved on their surface, but never from wood, as wood is vulnerable to fire.

Square towers, uniform in shape and equipped with moveable staircases or ladders equal to their height, shall also be built.

In the 30 danda space between two towers, there shall be a broad street divided into two compartments, covered with a roof, and two and a half times as long as it is wide.

Between the towers and the broad street, an Indrakósa shall be constructed, which is made of wooden planks providing seating for three archers.

A road for the gods shall also be built, measuring two hastas wide inside (perhaps within the towers), four times as wide on the sides, and eight hastas along the parapet.

Paths (chárya) to ascend the parapet, as wide as one danda (6 feet) or two, shall also be constructed.

In an unassailable section of the rampart, a passage for escape (pradhávitikám) and an exit door (nishkuradwáram) shall be made.

Outside the rampart, movement passages shall be blocked by forming various obstacles, such as a knee-breaker (jánubhanjaní), tridents, mounds of earth, pits, wreaths of thorns, tools resembling the tail of a snake, palm leaf, triangle, dog's teeth, rods, ditches filled with thorns and covered with sand, frying pans, and water pools.

On both sides of the rampart, circular holes with a diameter of one and a half dandas shall be made, and an entrance gate, one-sixth as wide as the street, shall be fixed.

A square (chaturásra) shall be formed by successively adding one danda up to eight dandas, starting from five, or in the ratio of one-sixth the length up to one-eighth.

The rise in elevation (talotsedhah) shall be formed by adding one hasta at a time, starting from 15 hastas up to 18 hastas.

In constructing a pillar, six parts of it shall form its visible height, with twice as much (12 parts) buried in the ground, and one-fourth of the height reserved for its capital.

For the first floor, five parts shall be allocated for the formation of a hall (sálá), a well, and a boundary house; two-tenths of the floor space shall be used for two platforms opposite each other (pratimanchau). The upper storey shall be twice as high as its width, and carvings of images shall adorn it. The top-most storey shall be half or three-fourths as wide as the first floor. The side walls shall be built of bricks, and on the left side, a staircase shall circumambulate from left to right, while on the right side, a secret staircase hidden within the wall shall be constructed. A top-support with ornamental arches (toranasirah) shall extend two hastas outward. Two door panels shall each occupy three-fourths of the door space. Two sets of crossbars (parigha) shall be used to fasten the door, and an iron bolt (indrakila) the length of an aratni (24 angulas) shall secure it. A boundary gate (ánidváram) shall be five hastas wide, and four beams shall be used to secure the door against elephants. Turrets (hastinakha), raised to the height of a man's face, may be either movable or fixed, or constructed of earth in areas without water.

A turret above the gate, beginning from the top of the parapet, shall be constructed, with its front resembling an alligator for three-fourths of its height.

In the center of the parapets, a deep lotus pool shall be constructed, as well as a rectangular building with four compartments, one inside the other. A residence for the Goddess Kumiri (Kumárípuram) shall be built, with its external area one-and-a-half times the size of the innermost room. A circular building with an archway shall also be constructed. According to the space and materials available, canals (kulyá) shall be built to store weapons, and they shall be three times as long as they are broad.

These canals shall hold stones, spades (kuddála), axes (kuthári), various staffs, cudgels (musrinthi), hammers (mudgara), clubs, discus, machines (yantra), and weapons capable of killing a hundred men at once (sataghni). They shall also store spears, tridents, bamboo sticks with iron-pointed edges, camel-necked weapons, explosives (agnisamyógas), and whatever other weapons can be designed and created from the available materials.

CHAPTER IV. BUILDINGS WITHIN THE FORT.

The demarcation of the ground inside the fort shall begin by laying out three royal roads running from west to east and three from south to north.

The fort shall have twelve gates, each provided with both land and water access, kept secret.

Chariot roads, royal roads, and roads leading to drónamukha, stháníya, rural areas, and pasture grounds shall each be four dandas (24 feet) in width.

Roads leading to sayóníya (?), military stations (vyúha), burial or cremation grounds, and villages shall be eight dandas in width.

Roads to gardens, groves, and forests shall be four dandas wide.

Roads leading to elephant forests shall be two dandas wide.

Chariot roads shall measure five aratnis (7½ feet). Roads for cattle shall measure four aratnis, and roads for smaller quadrupeds and men shall measure two aratnis.

Royal buildings shall be constructed on strong, stable ground.

In the midst of the houses of people from all four castes, and to the north from the center of the ground inside the fort, the king's palace shall be built, facing either north or east, occupying one-ninth of the total area inside the fort, as described elsewhere (Chapter XX, Book I).

The royal teachers, priests, sacrificial grounds, water reservoir, and ministers shall be located to the east by north of the palace.

The royal kitchen, elephant stables, and the storehouse shall be situated to the east by south.

On the eastern side of the fort, merchants dealing in scents, garlands, grains, and liquids, along with expert artisans and people of the Kshatriya caste, shall have their residences.

The treasury, the accountant's office, and various manufacturing sites (karmanishadyáscha) shall be located south by east.

The storehouse for forest produce and the arsenal shall be situated south by west.

To the south of the city, the superintendents of the city, commerce, manufactories, and the army shall live, as well as those who trade in cooked rice, liquor, and meat, along with prostitutes, musicians, and the people of the Vaisya caste.

To the west by south, stables for asses, camels, and working horses shall be located.

To the west by north, stables for conveyances and chariots shall be situated.

To the west, artisans manufacturing worsted threads, cotton threads, bamboo mats, skins, armor, weapons, and gloves, as well as the people of the Súdra caste, shall have their dwellings.

To the north by west, shops and hospitals shall be established.

To the north by east, the treasury and stables for cows and horses shall be located.

To the north, the royal tutelary deity of the city, ironsmiths, artisans working on precious stones, and Bráhmans shall reside.

In various corners of the city, guilds and corporations of workmen shall have their residences.

At the center of the city, temples or apartments for gods such as Aparájita, Apratihata, Jayanta, Vaijayanta, Siva, Vaisravana, Asvina (divine physicians), and the honorable liquor house (Srí-madiragriham) shall be situated.

In the corners, the guardian deities of the land shall be appropriately installed.

Likewise, the principal gates—Bráhma, Aindra, Yámya, and Sainápatya—shall be constructed; and at a distance of 100 bows (dhanus = 108 angulas) from the ditch (on the counterscarp side), places of worship, pilgrimage, groves, and buildings shall be constructed.

Guardian deities for all quarters shall also be installed in their respective quarters.

Burial or cremation grounds shall be situated either to the north or east, but the burial grounds for the highest caste people shall be located to the south of the city.

Violation of this rule shall result in the first amercement as punishment.

Heretics and Chandálas shall live beyond the burial grounds.

Families of workmen shall be provided with sites suitable to their occupation and fieldwork. In addition to working in flower gardens, fruit gardens, vegetable gardens, and paddy fields assigned to them, these families shall gather grains and merchandise in abundance, as authorized.

There shall be one water well for every ten houses.

Oils, grains, sugar, salt, medicinal articles, dried or fresh vegetables, meadow grass, dried meat, haystacks, firewood, metals, skins, charcoal, tendons (snáyu), poison, horns, bamboo, fibrous garments, strong timber, weapons, armor, and stones shall also be stored in the fort in such quantities that they can last for years without causing any shortage. Old supplies shall be replaced with new ones when fresh stock is received.

Elephants, cavalry, chariots, and infantry shall each be commanded by several chiefs, as having many chiefs ensures they remain fearful of betrayal from one another and are less vulnerable to enemy plots and intrigue.

The same principle shall apply to the appointment of boundary guards and those responsible for repairing fortifications.

People dangerous to the safety of cities and countries (báhirikas) shall never be allowed to reside in forts. They may either be relocated to rural areas or forced to pay taxes.

CHAPTER V. THE DUTIES OF THE CHAMBERLAIN.

The Chamberlain (sannidhátá, meaning one who always attends upon the king) shall oversee the construction of the treasury house, trading house, grain storehouse, forest produce storehouse, armory, and jail.

He shall dig a square well, not too deep but moist with water, and pave both the bottom and sides with stone slabs. In this well, using strong timber, he shall construct a cage-like underground chamber with three stories, the topmost story at ground level. This chamber shall have multiple compartments of various designs, with floors plastered with small stones, one door, a movable staircase, and it shall be consecrated by the presence of a guardian deity.

Above this chamber, the treasury house shall be built, enclosed on both sides, with projecting roofs, and it shall open extensively into the storehouse. It shall be constructed of bricks.

The Chamberlain may employ outcast men (abhityakta-purusha) to build, at the extreme boundary of the kingdom, a grand mansion to store substantial treasure for safeguarding against dangers and calamities.

The trading house shall be a quadrangle, enclosed by four buildings with one door. It shall have pillars built of burnt bricks, many compartments, and rows of pillars on both sides, spaced apart.

The storehouse shall consist of many spacious rooms, enclosing the forest produce storehouse, which shall be separated by a wall and connected to both the underground chamber and the armory.

The court (dharmasthíya) and the office of the ministers (mahámátríya) shall be constructed in a separate location.

A jail shall also be constructed, with separate accommodations for men and women, both kept apart, and with many compartments that are well guarded.

All these buildings shall be equipped with halls (sála), pits (kháta—possibly privies), water wells, bathrooms, protections against fire and poison, as well as cats and mongooses. They shall also include the necessary provisions to worship the guardian deities appropriate to each location.

In front of the storehouse, a bowl (kunda) with a mouth as wide as an aratni (24 angulas) shall be set up as a rain-gauge (varshamána).

Assisted by experts with the necessary qualifications and equipped with tools and instruments, the Chamberlain shall attend to the reception of gems, whether old or new, as well as raw materials of superior or inferior value.

In cases of deception involving gems, both the deceiver and the accomplice shall be punished with the highest amercement. In cases involving superior commodities, they shall be punished with the middle-most amercement. For inferior commodities, the offenders shall not only be compelled to return the same but also pay a fine equal to the value of the goods.

The Chamberlain shall accept only those gold coins that have been verified as pure by the coin examiner.

Counterfeit coins shall be cut into pieces, and whoever brings in counterfeit coins shall be punished with the first amercement.

Grains that are pure and fresh shall be accepted in full measures; otherwise, a fine of twice the value of the grains shall be imposed.

The same rules shall apply to the receipt of merchandise, raw materials, and weapons.

In all departments, whether an officer (yukta), a clerk (upayukta), or a servant (tatpurusha), anyone who misappropriates amounts from one to four panas or other valuable items shall be punished with the first, middlemost, or highest amercement or even death, depending on the severity of the offense.

If the officer in charge of the treasury causes a loss of money, he shall be whipped (ghátah), while his accomplices shall receive half the punishment. If the loss is due to ignorance, he shall be censured.

If guards frighten robbers with the intent of giving them a hint, the guards shall be tortured to death.

Therefore, the Chamberlain shall, with the assistance of trustworthy individuals, handle the business of revenue collection.

He shall have such thorough knowledge of both external and internal incomes extending up to a hundred years that, when questioned, he can state without hesitation the exact amount of net balance remaining after all expenditures have been met.

CHAPTER VI. THE BUSINESS OF COLLECTION OF REVENUE BY THE COLLECTOR-GENERAL.

The Collector-General shall oversee the collection of revenue from forts (durga), rural areas (ráshtra), mines (khani), buildings and gardens (setu), forests (vana), herds of cattle (vraja), and roads of traffic (vanikpatha).

Revenue from tolls, fines, weights and measures, the town-clerk (nágaraka), the superintendent of coinage (lakshanádhyakshah), the superintendent of seals and passports, liquor sales, the slaughter of animals, threads, oils, ghee, sugar (kshára), the state goldsmith (sauvarnika), warehouses, prostitutes, gambling, building sites (vástuka), the guild of artisans and craftsmen (kárusilpiganah), the superintendent of gods, and taxes collected at the city gates or from external inhabitants (Báhirikas) all come under the category of forts.

Produce from crown lands (sita), the government's share of the produce (bhága), religious taxes (bali), taxes paid in cash (kara), taxes from merchants, the superintendent of rivers, ferries, boats, ships, towns, pasture grounds, road cess (vartani), ropes (rajjú), and ropes for binding thieves (chórarajjú) fall under the category of rural areas.

Gold, silver, diamonds, gems, pearls, corals, conch shells, metals (loha), salt, and other minerals extracted from plains and mountain slopes fall under the category of mines.

Flower gardens, fruit gardens, vegetable gardens, wet fields, and fields where crops are grown by sowing roots or seeds (múlavápáh, such as sugarcane crops) fall under the category of gardens (sétu).

Game forests, timber forests, and elephant forests come under the category of forests.

Cows, buffaloes, goats, sheep, asses, camels, horses, and mules come under the category of herds.

Land and waterways fall under the category of roads of traffic.

All of these form the body of income (áyasaríram).

Capital (múla), shares (bhága), premia (vyáji), parigha (?), fixed taxes (klripta), premia on coins (rúpika), and fixed fines (atyaya) are the various forms of revenue (áyamukha), the sources from which income flows.

The chanting of auspicious hymns during the worship of gods and ancestors, gifts, the harem, the kitchen, the messengers' establishment, the storehouse, the armory, the warehouse, the storehouse for raw materials, manufactories (karmánta), free laborers (vishti), maintenance of infantry, cavalry, chariots, elephants, herds of cows, the museum of animals, deer, birds, and snakes, as well as the storage of firewood and fodder, all constitute the body of expenditure (vyayasaríram).

The royal year, month, fortnight (paksha), day, dawn (vyushta), the third and seventh fortnights of the rainy, winter, and summer seasons (which are shorter in days), the remaining months that are complete, and the separate intercalary month are the divisions of time.

The Collector-General shall also pay attention to the work in hand (karaníya), completed work (siddham), partial work (sésha), receipts, expenditures, and the net balance.

The work of maintaining the government (samsthánam), daily routine tasks (pracháraḥ), gathering life necessities, collecting, and auditing all forms of revenue—these are considered the tasks at hand.

What has been credited to the treasury, what has been taken by the king, what has been spent in connection with the capital and not entered into the register or carried over from the previous year, and royal commands either written or orally communicated to be entered—these constitute completed work.

Preparation of plans for profitable works, recovery of unpaid fines, demands for arrears of revenue kept in abeyance, and the examination of accounts—these tasks fall under what is called partial work in hand, which may sometimes be of little or no value.

Receipts can be classified into three types: (1) current, (2) last balance, and (3) accidental (anyajátah, received from external sources).

Current receipts (vartamána) are those collected day by day.

Last balance (puryushita) refers to whatever has been carried over from the previous year, what is held by others, or what has changed hands.

Accidental receipts include what has been lost and forgotten by others, fines levied on government servants, marginal revenue (párśva), compensation collected for damage (párihínikam), gifts to the king, the property of those who have died due to epidemics (damaragatakasvam) without leaving any heirs, and treasure-troves.

The investment of capital (vikshépa), the remnants of a failed undertaking, and savings from estimated expenditures are all means to monitor and control spending (vyayapratyayah).

The rise in the price of merchandise due to the use of varying weights and measures during sales is called vyáji. Another source of profit comes from price increases driven by competitive bidding among buyers.

Expenditure is divided into two types—daily expenditure and profitable expenditure.

Daily expenditure refers to what is spent regularly every day.

Profitable expenditure refers to what is earned or spent periodically, such as once per paksha (fortnight), month, or year.

The amount spent on these two categories is termed daily expenditure and profitable expenditure, respectively.

The net balance (nívi) is what remains after deducting all incurred expenses and excluding all future revenue yet to be realized. This net balance may be newly realized or carried forward from a previous period.

Thus, a wise Collector-General shall manage the task of revenue collection, focusing on increasing income and reducing expenses.

CHAPTER VII. THE BUSINESS OF KEEPING UP ACCOUNTS IN THE OFFICE OF ACCOUNTANTS.

The superintendent of accounts shall ensure that the accountant's office is constructed with its door facing either north or east, with seats for clerks arranged separately, and with shelves for account books neatly organized.

In this office, records shall be maintained regarding the following: the number of various departments; a description of the work being carried out and the results achieved in the various manufactories (Karmánta); the amount of profit, loss, expenditure, delayed earnings, and vyáji (premia in kind or cash) realized; the status of the government agency employed; the amount of wages paid; the number of free laborers (vishti) engaged in relation to the capital invested in any work. Likewise, for gems and commodities of superior or inferior value, records shall detail their prices, the rate of barter, the counterweights (pratimána) used in weighing them, their quantity, weight, and cubical measure.

Records shall also include information about the customs, professions, and transactions of countries, villages, families, and corporations; the gains in the form of gifts given to the king's courtiers; their rights to own and enjoy lands; tax remissions granted to them; and provisions and salaries paid to them. The gains provided to the king's wives and sons in the form of gems, lands, and prerogatives, as well as provisions made to counteract evil portents, shall also be recorded. Additionally, the treaties with friendly or hostile kings, issues of ultimatum, and the payments of tribute either received from or paid to them shall be regularly entered into the prescribed registers.

From these account books, the superintendent shall provide reports on the status of work in progress, completed work, partial works, receipts, expenditures, net balances, and tasks yet to be undertaken in each of the departments.

Supervisors with corresponding qualifications shall be employed to oversee high, middling, and low-level works.

The king will ultimately suffer if he reduces the fixed expenditure for profitable works.

If a person engaged by the government for any work is absent, his sureties, who jointly received wages from the government, or his sons, brothers, wives, daughters, or servants benefiting from his work, shall bear the loss caused to the government.

The work of 354 days and nights constitutes a full year. Payment for such work shall be made in proportion to the amount completed at the end of the month of Ashádha (around mid-July). The work done during the intercalary month shall be calculated separately.

A government officer, who neglects to understand the information gathered through espionage or fails to properly supervise the work in his department as required, may cause a loss of revenue to the government. This could be due to ignorance, idleness when he is too weak to engage in active duties, inadvertence in perceiving sounds and other sensory objects, timidity when afraid of public outcry or unrighteous actions, selfish desires when he is inclined towards those pursuing their own selfish ends, cruelty resulting from anger, lack of dignity when surrounded by sycophants and needy flatterers, or by using false balances, measures, and calculations out of greed.

The school of Manu holds that the fine imposed on such an officer should equal the amount of the lost revenue multiplied by the serial number of the offense committed.

The school of Parásara maintains that the fine should be eight times the amount lost.

The school of Brihaspati suggests that it should be ten times the amount.

The school of Usanas proposes that it should be twenty times the amount.

However, Kautilya argues that the fine should be proportional to the severity of the guilt.

Accounts should be submitted during the month of Ashádha. When the accountants from different districts present themselves with sealed books, commodities, and the net revenue, they shall be kept apart in a single location to prevent any conversation among them. After hearing the totals for receipts, expenditure, and net revenue, the net amount shall be received.

If the superintendent of a department increases the net total of revenue by raising any one of the items of receipts or reducing any item of expenditure, he shall be rewarded eight times that amount. However, if the net total is decreased, the same penalty shall apply—he will be required to pay eight times the amount of the decrease.

Accountants who fail to present themselves on time or who do not submit their account books along with the net revenue shall be fined ten times the amount due from them.

If the superintendent of accounts (káranika) does not promptly proceed to receive and verify the accounts when the clerks (kármika) are ready, he shall be punished with the first amercement. If the clerks are not ready, they shall be punished with double the first amercement.

All the ministers (mahámátras) shall together report the complete and accurate accounts pertaining to each department.

Whoever among these individuals (whether ministers or clerks) offers divided counsel, remains aloof, or speaks falsehoods shall be punished with the highest amercement.

If an accountant has not prepared the table of daily accounts (akritáhorúpaharam), he may be granted one additional month for its preparation. After the lapse of that month, he shall be fined 200 panas for each additional month of delay.

If an accountant has only a small portion of the accounts concerning net revenue to prepare, he may be allowed five nights to complete it.

The table of daily accounts, along with the net revenue submitted by the accountant, shall be scrutinized by verifying it with righteous transaction norms, precedents, and through the application of arithmetical processes such as addition, subtraction, and inference, as well as through espionage. It shall be cross-checked with regard to divisions of time such as days, five nights, pakshas (fortnights), months, four-month periods, and the year.

Receipts shall be verified by considering the place and time of collection, the form of their collection (whether capital or share), the current and past production levels, the person who made the payment, the one who facilitated the payment, the officer who determined the payable amount, and the officer who received it. Expenditure shall be verified by examining the cause of profit from any source, the relevant place and time, the amount payable and paid, the officer who ordered the collection, the person who remitted the payment, the individual who delivered it, and the person who received it.

Similarly, the net revenue shall be verified in terms of place, time, and source, along with its standard of fineness, quantity, and the personnel assigned to guard the deposits and magazines (grains, etc.).

If an officer (káranika) does not facilitate, or actively prevents, the execution of the king's orders, or if he renders the receipts and expenditure in a manner other than prescribed, he shall be punished with the first amercement.

Any clerk who deviates from the prescribed format for writing accounts, enters information unknown to him, or makes double or triple entries (punaruktam), shall be fined 12 panas.

Anyone who scrapes off the net total shall face double the punishment.

If anyone consumes or conceals it, they shall be fined eight times the amount.

Anyone causing a loss of revenue shall be fined five times the amount lost (panchabandha) and be required to make good the loss. If a lie is spoken, the punishment for theft shall be imposed. If an omitted or lost entry is later entered, or is made to appear as forgotten but added after recollection, the punishment shall be double the original.

The king shall forgive minor offenses, show satisfaction even if the revenue is low, and reward (with pragraha) those superintendents who bring immense benefit to him.

CHAPTER VIII. DETECTION OF WHAT IS EMBEZZLED BY GOVERNMENT SERVANTS OUT OF STATE REVENUE.

All undertakings rely on financial resources. Therefore, primary attention shall be directed toward maintaining the treasury.

Public prosperity (prachárasamriddhih), rewarding good conduct (charitránugrahah), capturing thieves, reducing the number of unnecessary government employees, abundant harvests, prosperous commerce, freedom from troubles and calamities (upasargapramokshah), reduction in tax remissions, and income from gold (hiranyópáyanam) all contribute to financial prosperity.

On the other hand, the following are the causes of financial depletion: obstruction (pratibandha), loans (prayóga), trading (vyavahára), fabrication of accounts (avastára), causing revenue loss (parihápana), self-enjoyment (upabhóga), barter (parivartana), and defalcation (apahára).

Obstruction refers to the failure to begin an undertaking or realize its results, or to credit its profits to the treasury. In such cases, a fine of ten times the amount involved shall be imposed.

Loan refers to lending treasury money with periodic interest.

Trading refers to conducting business using government funds. Both these offenses shall be punished with a fine of twice the profit earned.

Fabrication of accounts occurs when one misrepresents the proper timing of revenue collection, either accelerating or delaying it inappropriately. Here, a fine of ten times the amount (panchabandha) shall be imposed.

Causing revenue loss refers to reducing a fixed amount of income or increasing expenditure without authorization. The punishment shall be a fine of four times the loss incurred.

Self-enjoyment occurs when one personally uses or causes others to use what belongs to the king. The penalty for this offense varies: for enjoying gems, the death sentence shall be imposed; for enjoying valuable articles, the middlemost amercement shall apply; and for articles of lesser value, they must be restored along with a fine equal to their value.

Barter refers to exchanging government-owned articles for similar articles of others, and it is covered under the same rules as self-enjoyment.

Defalcation occurs when one fails to deposit the fixed amount of revenue collected into the treasury, does not spend what has been ordered to be spent, or falsifies the net revenue collected. For defalcation, a fine of twelve times the amount shall be imposed.

There are about forty ways of embezzlement: what is realized earlier is entered later on; what is realized later is entered earlier; what ought to be realized is not realized; what is hard to realize is shown as realized; what is collected is shown as not collected; what has not been collected is shown as collected; what is collected in part is entered as collected in full; what is collected in full is entered as collected in part; what is collected is of one sort, while what is entered is of another sort;

what is realized from one source is shown as realized from another; what is payable is not paid; what is not payable is paid; not paid in time; paid untimely; small gifts made large gifts; large gifts made small gifts; what is gifted is of one sort while what is entered is of another; the real donee is one while the person entered (in the register) as donee is another; what has been taken into (the treasury) is removed while what has not been credited to it is shown as credited; raw materials that are not paid for are entered, while those that are paid for are not entered; an aggregate is scattered in pieces; scattered items are converted into an aggregate; commodities of greater value are bartered for those of small value; what is of smaller value is bartered for one of greater value; price of commodities enhanced; price of commodities lowered; number of nights increased; number of nights decreased; the year not in harmony with its months; the month not in harmony with its days; inconsistency in the transactions carried on with personal supervision (samágamavishánah); misrepresentation of the source of income; inconsistency in giving charities; incongruity in representing the work turned out; inconsistency in dealing with fixed items; misrepresentation of test marks or the standard of fineness (of gold and silver); misrepresentation of prices of commodities; making use of false weight and measures; deception in counting articles; and making use of false cubic measures such as bhájan—these are the several ways of embezzlement.

Under the above circumstances, the persons concerned, such as the treasurer (nidháyaka), the prescriber (nibandhaka), the receiver (pratigráhaka), the payer (dáyaka), the person who caused the payment (dápaka), and the ministerial servants of the officer (mantri-vaiyávritvakara), shall each be separately examined. If any one of these tells a lie, he shall receive the same punishment as the chief officer (yukta) who committed the offense. A proclamation in public (prachára) shall be made to the effect, "whoever has suffered at the hands of this offender may make their grievances known to the king."

Those who respond to the call shall receive compensation equal to the loss they have sustained.

When there are a number of offenses in which a single officer is involved, and when his guilt of parókta (embezzlement or misappropriation) in any one of those charges has been established, he shall be answerable for all those offenses. Otherwise (i.e., when it is not established), he shall be tried for each of the charges separately. When a government servant has been proven guilty of misappropriating part of a large sum in question, he shall be held accountable for the entire amount.

Any informant (súchaka) who supplies information about embezzlement just about to be perpetrated shall, if successful in proving it, receive as a reward one-sixth of the amount in question. If the informant happens to be a government servant (bhritaka), he shall receive one-twelfth of the amount for the same act. If an informant succeeds in proving only a part of a significant embezzlement, he shall still receive the prescribed share of the part of the embezzled amount proven.

An informant who fails to prove his claim shall be subject to monetary or corporal punishment and shall never be acquitted. When the charge is proven, the informant may attribute the tale-bearing to someone else or clear himself in any other way from blame. Any informant who withdraws his assertion after being influenced by the insinuations of the accused shall be condemned to death.

CHAPTER IX. EXAMINATION OF THE CONDUCT OF GOVERNMENT SERVANTS.

Those who are possessed of ministerial qualifications shall, in accordance with their individual capacity, be appointed as superintendents of government departments. While engaged in work, they shall be daily examined; for men are naturally fickle-minded and like horses at work exhibit constant change in their temper. Hence the agency and tools which they make use of, the place and time of the work they are engaged in, as well as the precise form of the work, the outlay, and the results shall always be ascertained. Without dissension and without any concert among themselves, they shall carry on their work as ordered. When in concert, they eat up (the revenue). When in disunion, they mar the work. Without bringing to the knowledge of their master (bhartri, the king), they shall undertake nothing except remedial measures against imminent dangers.

A fine of twice the amount of their daily pay and of the expenditure (incurred by them) shall be fixed for any inadvertence on their part. Whoever of the superintendents makes as much as, or more than, the amount of fixed revenue shall be honoured with promotion and rewards. My teacher holds that that officer who spends too much and brings in little revenue eats it up; while he who proves the revenue (i.e., brings in more than he spends) as well as the officer who brings in as much as he spends does not eat up the revenue. But Kautilya holds that cases of embezzlement or no embezzlement can be ascertained through spies alone. Whoever lessens the revenue eats the king's wealth. If owing to inadvertence he causes diminution in revenue, he shall be compelled to make good the loss.

Whoever doubles the revenue eats into the vitality of the country. If he brings in double the amount to the king, he shall, if the offence is small, be warned not to repeat the same; but if the offence be grave he should proportionally be punished. Whoever spends the revenue (without bringing in any profit) eats up the labour of workmen. Such an officer shall be punished in proportion to the value of the work done, the number of days taken, the amount of capital spent, and the amount of daily wages paid. Hence the chief officer of each department (adhikarana) shall thoroughly scrutinise the real amount of the work done, the receipts realised from, and the expenditure incurred in that departmental work both in detail and in the aggregate. He shall also check (pratishedhayet) prodigal, spend-thrift and niggardly persons. Whoever unjustly eats up the property left by his father and grandfather is a prodigal person (múlahara). Whoever eats all that he earns is a spendthrift (tádátvika). Whoever hoards money, entailing hardship both on himself and his servants is niggardly.

Whoever among these three types of people has the support of a strong party shall not be disturbed; but whoever does not have such support shall be captured (paryádátavyah). Whoever is stingy, despite possessing immense wealth, hoarding, depositing, or sending it out—hoarding in their own house, depositing with local citizens or country people, or sending it to foreign countries—a spy will find out the advisors, friends, servants, relatives, partisans, as well as the income and expenditure of such a stingy person. Whoever, in a foreign country, carries out the business of such a stingy person shall be persuaded to reveal the secret. When the secret is exposed, the stingy person shall be murdered, seemingly under the orders of (his) declared enemy.

Therefore, the superintendents of all departments shall carry on their respective duties together with accountants, writers, coin-examiners, treasurers, and military officers (uttarádhyaksha). Those who serve military officers and are known for their honesty and good behavior shall be spies to observe the conduct of accountants and other clerks. Each department shall be managed by several temporary heads. Just as it is impossible to avoid tasting the honey or poison that finds itself on the tip of one's tongue, it is also impossible for a government worker not to take at least a small part of the king's revenue. Just as it is impossible to see whether fish swimming under the water are drinking or not drinking, it is also impossible to detect whether government workers employed in the service are taking money for themselves.

It is possible to observe the movements of birds flying high in the sky, but it is not possible to detect the hidden motives of government workers. Government workers shall not only have their ill-gotten gains confiscated, but they shall also be transferred from one position to another, so that they cannot either misappropriate government money or keep what they have already taken. Those who increase the king's revenue rather than stealing it, and who are loyally devoted to him, shall be made permanent in their service.

CHAPTER X. THE PROCEDURE OF FORMING ROYAL WRITS.

Teachers say that the word "sásana," meaning command, is only used when referring to royal writs (sásana). Writs hold great importance for kings, as treaties and events leading to war rely on these writs.

Therefore, a person who possesses the skills of a minister, is knowledgeable about all types of customs, proficient in writing, capable of producing legible script, and quick in reading should be appointed as a writer (lékhaka).

This writer, after carefully listening to the king's orders and thoroughly considering the matter at hand, should write down the king's command.

When writing a writ addressed to a lord (ísvara), it should include a respectful mention of the lord's country, possessions, family, and name. For a writ addressed to a common man (anisvara), it should include a polite mention of the person's country and name.

The writer must take into account the addressee's caste, family, social rank, age, education (sruta), occupation, property, character (síla), blood relations (yaunánubandha), and also the place and time of writing, to create a writ that suits the position of the person being addressed.

The organization of the subject matter (arthakrama), relevance (sambandha), completeness, elegance, and clarity are the essential qualities of a writ.

The act of presenting facts in order of importance is called arrangement. When the following facts are not contradictory to the previous facts, continuing until the completion of the letter, it is called relevance.

Avoiding redundancy or a lack of words or letters, offering an impressive explanation of the subject by providing reasons, examples, and illustrations, and using appropriate, suitably strong words (asrántapada) makes for completeness.

Describing a meaningful subject in an elegant style that has a pleasing effect is sweetness.

Using words that are not colloquial (agrámya) is dignity.

The use of common and well-known words brings lucidity.

There are sixty-three alphabetical letters, starting with Akára.

The combination of letters forms a word (pada). Words are of four types—nouns, verbs, verb prefixes, and particles (nipáta).

A noun is something that represents an essence (satva).

A verb is something that does not have a fixed gender and represents an action.

'Pra' and similar words are prefixes to verbs.

'Cha' and other words that do not change are particles.

A group of words that conveys a complete meaning is called a sentence (vákya).

A combination of words (varga) consisting of no more than three words and no fewer than one word should be arranged in such a way that it harmonizes with the meaning of the words that follow.

The word "iti" is used to indicate the completion of a writ and also to mark an oral message, as in the phrase "váchikamasyeti," meaning an oral message along with this (writ).

There are thirteen purposes for which writs are issued: calumniation (nindá), commendation, inquiry, narration, request, refusal, censure, prohibition, command, conciliation, promise of help, threat, and persuasion.

Calumniation (nindá) involves speaking badly about someone's family, appearance, and actions.

Commendation (prasamsá) involves praising someone's family, person, and actions.

Asking, "How is this?" is inquiry.

Explaining something as "this way" is narration (ákhyána).

Requesting by saying "give" is a request.

Saying, "I do not give" is refusal.

Saying, "This is not worthy of you" is censure (upálambhah).

Telling someone "do not do this" is prohibition (pratishedha).

Saying "this must be done" is a command (chódaná).

Saying "what I am, you are too; whatever I own, you own as well" is conciliation (sántvam).

Offering help in a difficult situation is a promise of help (abhyavapattih).

Pointing out potential future harm is a threat (abhibartsanam).

Persuasion comes in three forms: persuasion for the purpose of gaining money, persuasion when someone fails to fulfill a promise, and persuasion during times of trouble.

There are also different types of writs: writs of information, writs of command, and writs of gift. Additionally, there are writs of remission, writs of license, writs of guidance, writs of reply, and writs of general proclamation.

"This is what the messenger says," and "this is what the king says." If there is truth in what the messenger has said, then the agreed-upon item should be handed over immediately. The messenger has informed the king about all the enemy's actions (Parakára). This is the writ of information, which is said to take many forms.

Whenever, and especially when it concerns government officials, the king issues an order either for punishment or reward, it is called a writ of command (ájnálékha).

When the intention is to bestow honor upon someone who has earned it, either to help ease their suffering (ádhi) or as a gift (paridána), writs of gift (upagrahalekha) are issued.

Whenever a favor (anugraha) is announced in accordance with the king's orders for specific castes, cities, villages, or countries, it is known as a writ of remission (paríháralékha) by those familiar with it.

Similarly, permission (nisrishti) is either given verbally or in writing, and it is called a verbal order or a writ of license.

When various natural disasters or confirmed human-made troubles are believed to be the reason for taking action, writs of guidance (pravrittilékha) are issued to attempt remedies.

After reading a letter and discussing how to respond to it, a reply made according to the king's orders is called a writ of reply (pratilékha).

When the king commands his viceroys (isvara) and other officers to protect and provide material assistance to travelers, whether on roads or within the country, it is called a writ of general proclamation (sarvatraga lekha).

Negotiation, bribery, causing dissension, and open attack are methods of strategy (upáya).

Negotiation comes in five types: praising the qualities of the enemy, discussing shared relationships, pointing out mutual benefits, highlighting future opportunities, and emphasizing shared interests.

When the family, person, occupation, behavior, education, property, and other qualities of the enemy are acknowledged with careful attention to their merit, it is called praising the qualities (gunasankírthana).

When it is shown that both parties share relatives, blood relations, teachers (maukha), a priestly hierarchy (srauva), family, and friends, it is known as narrating mutual relationships (sambandhópakhyána).

When both sides—the king's party and the enemy's party—are shown to be helpful to each other, it is called pointing out mutual benefit (parasparópakárasamdarsanam).

Inducement such as saying, "If this is done in this way, such results will benefit both of us," is called showing vast future prospects (Ayátipradarsanam).

Saying, "What I am, you are as well; you may use whatever is mine in your works," is called identity of interests (átmópanidhánam).

Offering money is known as bribery (upapradána).

Creating fear, suspicion, and making threats is called sowing dissension.

Killing, harassing, and looting is considered attack (danda).

The faults in a writ include clumsiness, contradictions, repetition, poor grammar, and misarrangement.

Writing on a black and ugly leaf (kálapatrakamacháru) or with uneven and uncolored (virága) writing causes clumsiness (akánti).

If one part of a letter contradicts an earlier part, it causes contradiction (vyágháta).

Repeating something that has already been stated before is considered repetition.

Using words incorrectly in terms of gender, number, tense, or case is poor grammar (apasabda).

Improper paragraph divisions (varga), omitting necessary divisions, and violating any other essential qualities of a writ are considered misarrangement (samplava).

Having studied all sciences and having carefully observed the forms of writing in use, these rules for writing royal writs have been laid down by Kautilya for the benefit of kings.

[Thus ends Chapter X, "The Procedure of Forming Royal Writs," in Book II, "The Duties of Government Superintendents," of the Arthasástra of Kautilya. End of the thirty-first chapter from the beginning.]

CHAPTER XI. EXAMINATION OF GEMS THAT ARE TO BE ENTERED INTO THE TREASURY.

The Superintendent of the treasury, in the presence of qualified individuals, shall accept into the treasury whatever should be admitted, including gems (ratna) and items of both high and low value.

Támraparnika refers to pearls produced in the Támraparni; Pándyakavátaka refers to pearls obtained in Pándyakavata; Pásikya refers to those produced in the Pása; Kauleya refers to those produced in the Kúla; Chaurneya refers to those produced in the Chúrna; Mahéndra refers to pearls obtained near the Mahéndra mountain; Kárdamika refers to those produced in the Kárdama; Srautasíya refers to those produced in the Srótasi; Hrádíya refers to those found in the deep pool of water known as Hrada; and Haimavata refers to pearls obtained near the Himalayas. These are the various types of pearls.

Pearls are found in oyster shells, conch shells, and other miscellaneous sources.

Pearls that resemble the lentil (masúra), those made of three segments (triputaka), those resembling a tortoise (kúrmaka), semi-circular pearls, multi-layered pearls, double pearls (yámaka), scratched pearls, rough-surfaced pearls, spotted pearls (siktakam), those resembling the water-pot of an ascetic, those that are dark brown or blue in color, and those poorly drilled are considered inauspicious.

The best pearls are those that are large, round, without a flat bottom (nistalam), bright, white, heavy, smooth to the touch, and well-drilled.

There are several types of pearl necklaces: Sirshaka, Upasirshaka, Prakándaka, Avaghátaka, and Taralapratibandha.

A necklace made of 1,008 strings of pearls is called Indrachchhanda.

Half of that, or 504 strings, is called Vijayachchhanda.

Sixty-four strings form an Ardhahára.

Fifty-four strings form a Rasmikalápa.

Thirty-two strings form a Guchchha.

Twenty-seven strings form a Nakshatramála.

Twenty-four strings form an Ardhaguchchha.

Twenty strings form a Mánavaka, and half of that, or ten strings, is called Ardhamánavaka.

The same necklaces, when containing a gem at the center, retain their names with "Mánavaka" added to their respective titles.

When all the strings in a necklace are of the sirshaka pattern, it is called a pure necklace (suddhahára), and the same applies to strings of other patterns. A necklace with a gem in the center is also called Ardhamánavaka.

A necklace with three slab-like gems (triphalaka) or five slab-like gems (panchaphalaka) in the center is called Phalakahára.

A single string of pearls is called a pure Ekávali, and with a gem in the center, it is called Yashti. When the string is adorned with gold globules, it is called Ratnávali.

A string made of alternating pearls and gold globules is called Apavartaka.

Strings of pearls with a gold wire between two strings are called Sopánaka.

When this type of string has a gem in the center, it is called Manisópánaka.

The above descriptions also apply to the formation of head-strings, bracelets, anklets, waist-bands, and other similar varieties of jewelry.

Kauta, which is obtained from Kúta; Mauleyaka, which is found in Múleya; and Párasamudraka, which is found beyond the ocean, are several varieties of gems.

A gem that has a pleasant color like that of the red lotus flower, the Párijáta flower (Erithrina Indica), or the rising sun is called the Saugandhika gem.

A gem that is the color of the blue lotus flower, sirísha (Acacia Sirisa), water, fresh bamboo, or the feathers of a parrot is known as the Vaidúrya gem. Pushyarága, Gómútraka, and Gómédika are other varieties of this type.

A gem characterized by blue lines, one that is the color of the Kaláya flower (a type of phraseolus), or one that is intensely blue, as blue as the Jambu fruit (rose apple), or as blue as the clouds is called the Indraníla gem. Other types of gems include Nandaka (pleasing gem), Sravanmadhya (which appears to pour water from its center), Sítavrishti (which appears to pour a cold shower), and Súryakánta (sunstone).

Gems may be hexagonal, quadrangular, or circular. They are dazzling, pure, smooth, heavy, brilliant, transparent (antargataprabha), and illuminating. These are the qualities of fine gems.

However, gems with a faint color, sandy layers, spots, holes, poor perforation, or scratches are considered defective.

Inferior gems include Vimalaka (pure), Sasyaka (plant-like), Anjanamúlaka (deep-dark), Pittaka (like the bile of a cow), Sulabhaka (easily obtainable), Lohitaka (red), Amritámsuka (with white rays), Jyótírasaka (glowing), Maileyaka, Ahichchhatraka (found in the country of Ahichchhatra), Kúrpa, Pútikúrpa, Sugandhikúrpa, Kshírapaka, Suktichúrnaka (like the powder of an oyster shell), Silápraválaka (coral-like), Pulaka, and Súkrapulaka.

The remaining ones are metallic beads (káchamani).

Sabháráshtraka, which is found in the country of Sabháráshtra; Madhyamaráshtraka, found in the Central Province; Kásmaka, from the country of Kásmaka; Srikatanaka, found near the mountain Vedótkata; Manimantaka, from the vicinity of the mountain Maniman or Manimanta; and Indravánaká are varieties of diamonds.

Diamonds are sourced from mines, streams, and other miscellaneous locations.

The color of a diamond may resemble that of a cat's eye, the Sirísha flower (Acacia Sirísa), cow urine, cow bile, alum (sphatika), the Málati flower, or any of the previously mentioned gems.

The best diamonds are those that are large, heavy, hard (prahárasaham, capable of withstanding blows), regular in shape (samakóna), able to scratch the surface of vessels (bhájanalékhi), refractive of light (kubrámi), and brilliant.

Inauspicious diamonds are those that lack angles, are uneven (nirasríkam), or are bent to one side (párasvápavrittam).

Alakandaka and Vaivarnaka are the two types of coral that have a ruby-like color, are very hard, and are free from internal contamination by other substances.

Sátana coral is red and smells like earth; Gósirshaka is dark red and has a fishy smell; Harichandana is the color of parrot feathers and smells like tamarind or mango fruit, as does Tárnasa; Grámeruka coral is red or dark red and smells like goat urine; Daivasabheya is red and smells like a lotus flower, as does Aupaka (Jápaka); Jongaka and Taurupa corals are red or dark red and soft; Maleyaka coral is reddish-white; Kuchandana coral is as black as Agaru (resin of the aloe), or red, or dark red, and is very rough; Kála-parvataka coral has a pleasant appearance; Kosákaraparvataka, which comes from a mountain shaped like a bud, is black or variegated black; Sítódakíya coral is black and soft, with a lotus-flower scent; Nágaparvataka, from the Naga mountain, is rough and has the color of Saivala (Vallisneria); and Sákala coral is brown.

Light, soft, moist (asyána, not dry), as greasy as ghee, pleasantly fragrant, adhesive to the skin, mildly scented, long-retaining both its color and scent, tolerant of heat, absorptive of heat, and comfortable on the skin—these are the characteristics of sandalwood (chandana).

As for Agaru (Agallochum, resin of aloe): Jongaka is black or variegated black with spots; Dongaka is black; and Párasamudraka is variegated in color and smells like cascus or Navamálika (jasmine).

Agaru is heavy, soft, greasy, has a long-lasting fragrance that can be detected from afar, burns slowly with continuous smoke, has a uniform scent, absorbs heat, and adheres so firmly to the skin that it cannot be easily removed by rubbing. These are the qualities of Agaru.

Regarding Tailaparnika: Asókagrámika, from Asókagráma, is meat-colored and smells like a lotus flower. Jongaka is reddish-yellow and smells like a blue lotus flower or cow's urine. Grameruka is greasy and smells like cow's urine. Sauvarnakudyaka, from the land of Suvarnakudya, is reddish-yellow and smells like Mátulunga (citron fruit or sweet lime). Púrnadvipaka, from the island of Púrnadviipa, smells like a lotus flower or butter. Bhadrasríya and Páralauhityaka are nutmeg-colored, and both smell like Kushtha (Costus Speciosus). Antarvatya is the color of cascus and also smells like Kushtha. Kaleyaka, from the land of Svarna-bhúmi, is yellow and greasy. Auttaraparvataka, from the northern mountain, is reddish-yellow.

These fragrant substances are considered commodities of superior value (Sára).

The fragrance of Tailaparnika substances lasts regardless of whether they are made into a paste, boiled, or burned. Their scent remains unchanged and unaffected even when mixed with other substances. These substances share similar qualities with sandalwood and Agaru.

Kántanávaka, Praiyaka, and Auttaraparvataka are varieties of skins.

Kántanávaka is peacock-neck-colored, and Praiyaka is variegated with blue, yellow, and white spots. Both are eight angulas (inches) long.

Bisí and Mahábisí are products of Dvádasagráma (twelve villages).

Bisí is of indistinct color, hairy, and variegated with spots. Mahábisí (great Bisí) is rough and almost white. Both are twelve angulas long.

Syámika, Kálika, Kadali, Chandrottara, and Sákulá are other types of skins obtained from Aroha (Arohaja).

Syámika is brown with variegated spots, and Kálika is brown or the color of a pigeon. Both of these are eight angulas long. Kadali is rough and two feet long; when Kadali has variegated, moonlike spots, it is called Chandrottarakadali and is one-third of its length. Sákulá is variegated with large, round spots similar to those seen in a type of leprosy (kushtha) or has tendrils and is spotted like a deer's skin.

Sámúra, Chínasi, and Sámúli are skins procured from Báhlava (Bahlaveya).

Sámúra is thirty-six angulas long and black; Chínasi is reddish-black or blackish-white; and Sámúli is wheat-colored.

Sátina, Nalatúla, and Vrittapuchchha are skins from aquatic animals (Audra).

Sátina is black; Nalatúla is the color of Nala grass fibers; and Vrittapuchchha, which has a round tail, is brown.

These are the varieties of skins.

Among skins, the best are those that are soft, smooth, and hairy.

Blankets made of sheep's wool may be white, purely red, or as red as a lotus flower. They may be made by sewing worsted threads (khachita), woven with woolen threads of various colors (vánachitra), made from different pieces (khandasanghátya), or woven with uniform woolen threads (tantuvichchhinna).

There are ten types of woolen blankets: Kambala, Kauchapaka, Kulamitika, Saumitika, Turagastarana, Varnaka, Talichchhaka, Váravána, Paristoma, and Samantabhadraka.

Among these, the best blanket is the one that is as slippery (pichchhila) as a wet surface, has fine hair, and is soft.

That blanket which is made up of eight pieces and is black in color is called Bhingisi, used as rainproof; similarly, Apasáraka serves the same purpose. Both of these blankets are products of Nepal.

Samputika, Chaturasrika, Lambara, Katavánaka, Praváraka, and Sattalika are blankets made from the wool of wild animals.

The fabric produced in the country of Vanga (Vangaka) is a white and soft fabric (dukúla). That produced in the Pándya region (Paundraka) is black and as soft as the surface of a gem. The fabric from Suvarnakudya is red like the sun, as soft as a gem's surface, woven while the threads are very wet, and of either uniform (chaturasra) or mixed texture (vyámisravána).

There are single, half, double, treble, and quadruple garments, which are various forms of the same fabric.

The above explanation applies to other types of fabrics, such as Kásika, Benarese products, and Kshauma, which is manufactured in Pándya (Paundraka).

Mágadhika (a product of the Magadha country), Paundraka, and Sauvarnakudyaka are fibrous fabrics.

Nágavriksha (a species of tree), Likucha (Artocarpus Lakucha), Vakula (Mimusops Elengi), and Vata (Ficus Indica) are the sources of their fibers.

The fiber from Nágavriksha is yellow (pita); that from Likucha is wheat-colored; that from Vakula is white, and the rest is butter-colored.

Of these, the fiber produced in Suvarnakudya is considered the best.

This also explains fabrics such as kauseya (silk cloth) and chinapatta (fabrics of Chinese manufacture).

Regarding cotton fabrics, those from Madhura, Aparánta (the western parts), Kálinga, Kási, Vanga, Vatsa, and Mahisha are considered the best.

For other kinds of gems (not previously mentioned), the superintendent shall determine their size, value, species, form, utility, treatment, and repair of old gems, as well as any undetectable adulteration. The superintendent shall also assess their wear and tear over time and location, as well as remedies for those that are inauspicious (himsra).

[Thus ends Chapter XI, "Examination of Gems that are to be entered into the Treasury," in Book II, "The Duties of Government Superintendents," of the Arthasástra of Kautilya. End of the thirty-second chapter from the beginning.]

CHAPTER XII. CONDUCTING MINING OPERATIONS AND MANUFACTURE.

Possessed of knowledge in the science of copper and other minerals (Sulbádhátusástra), experienced in the processes of distillation and condensation of mercury (rasapáka), and skilled in testing gems, the superintendent of mines, aided by experts in mineralogy and equipped with mining laborers and the necessary tools, shall examine mines. These mines may show signs of having been exploited before, indicated by mineral waste (kitta), crucibles, charcoal, and ashes, or they may be newly discovered in plains or mountain slopes containing mineral ores. The richness of these ores can be determined by their weight, deep color, strong smell, and taste.

Liquids that seep from pits, caves, slopes, or deep excavations of known mountains, which have the color of the fruit of rose-apple (jambu), mango, or fan palm, which are yellow like ripe turmeric, sulphur of arsenic (haritála), honeycomb, or vermilion, which shine like the petals of a lotus or the feathers of a parrot or peacock, and which are near bodies of water or shrubs of similar color, and are greasy (chikkana), clear (visada), and heavy, are ores of gold (kánchanika). Similarly, liquids that spread like oil when dropped in water, to which dirt and filth adhere, and which amalgamate with copper or silver more than one hundred percent (satádupari veddhárah) are also gold ores.

Substances that have a similar appearance to the above but with a piercing smell and taste are Bitumen.

Ores that are found in plains or on mountain slopes, which are yellow, copper-red, or reddish-yellow in color, marked with blue lines, and resemble black beans (masha, Phraseolus Radiatus), green beans (mudga, Phraseolus Mungo), or sesame seeds; those that are marked with spots like curd drops and shine like turmeric, yellow myrobalan, lotus petals, aquatic plants, liver, or spleen; those containing sandy layers within and marked with circular or svastika-shaped figures; and those containing globular masses (sagulika), which, when roasted, do not crack but emit much foam and smoke, are gold ores (suvarnadhátavah) used to form amalgams with copper or silver (prativápárthasté stámrarúpyavedharáh).

Those ores that have the color of a conch-shell, camphor, alum, butter, pigeon, turtle-dove, Vimalaka (a kind of precious stone), or the neck of a peacock; which shine like opal (sasyaka), agate (gomédaka), cane sugar (guda), and granulated sugar (matsyandika); those with the color of the kovidára flower (Bauhinia Variegata), lotus, patali flower (Bignonia Suaveolens), kalaya (a kind of phraseolus), kshauma (flax), and atasi (Linum Usitatissimum); those found combined with lead or iron (anjana); those that smell like raw meat, are disjointed gray or blackish-white, and are marked with lines or spots; and those which, when roasted, do not crack but emit foam and smoke—these are silver ores.

The heavier the ores, the greater the quantity of metal they contain (satvavriddhih).

Impurities in ores, whether superficial or deeply embedded, can be removed, and the metal extracted when the ores are chemically treated with Tikshna urine (mútra) and alkalies (kshára). The ores are also smeared with a mixture of the powder of Rajavriksha (Clitoria Ternatea), Vata (Ficus Indica), and Pelu (Carnea Arborea), along with cow's bile, and the urine and dung of a buffalo, an ass, and an elephant.

Metals become soft when treated with the powder of kandali (mushroom) and vajrakanda (Antiquorum), together with the ashes of barley, black beans, palása (Butea Frondosa), and pelu (Carnea Arborea), or with the milk of both cows and sheep. Any metal split into a hundred thousand parts can be softened when it is soaked three times in a mixture made from honey (madhu), madhuka (Bassia Latifolia), sheep's milk, sesame oil, clarified butter, jaggery, kinva (ferment), and mushroom.

Permanent softness (mridustambhana) can also be achieved when the metal is treated with the powder of cow's teeth and horn.

Ores found in plains or on mountain slopes, which are heavy, greasy, soft, tawny, green, dark, bluish-yellow (harita), pale-red, or red, are copper ores.

Ores that are the color of kákamechaka (Solanum Indica), pigeon, or cow's bile, and are marked with white lines and smell like raw meat, are the ores of lead.

Those ores that are variegated in color like saline soil or have the color of a burnt lump of earth are the ores of tin.

Those ores that are orange (kurumba), pale-red (pándurohita), or the color of the flower of sinduvára (Vitex Trifolia) are the ores of tíkshna (steel or iron).

Those ores that are the color of the leaf of kánda (Artemisia Indica) or the leaf of birch are the ores of vaikrintaka.

Precious stones are those that are pure, smooth, effulgent, resonant (when struck), very hard (satatívrah), and of light color (tanurága).

The yield of mines may be used for purposes that are commonly practiced.

The commerce in commodities made from mineral products shall be centralized, and there should be established punishments for the manufacturing, selling, or purchasing of such commodities outside the prescribed areas.

A mine laborer who steals mineral products, except for precious stones, shall be punished with a fine of eight times their value.

Any person who steals mineral products or carries on mining operations without a license shall be bound in chains and forced to work as a prisoner.

Mines that yield minerals used for making vessels (bhánda) or that require a large investment to extract may be leased out for a fixed share of the output or a fixed rent (bhágena prakrayena va). Mines that can be worked without much outlay shall be exploited directly by government agencies.

The superintendent of metals (lóhádhyakshah) shall oversee the production of copper, lead, tin, vaikrintaka (possibly mercury), árakúta (brass), vritta (?), kamsa (bronze or bell-metal), tála (sulphur of arsenic), and lodhra (?), as well as the manufacturing of commodities (bhánda) from these metals.

The superintendent of mint (lakshnádhyakshah) shall manage the production of silver coins (rúpyarúpa) composed of four parts copper and one-sixteenth part (másha) of one of the metals: tíkshna (steel or iron), trapu (tin), sisa (lead), or anjana (antimony). The coins shall be in denominations of a pana, half a pana, a quarter, and one-eighth.

Copper coins (támrarúpa), made of four parts of an alloy (pádajívam), shall be issued in denominations of a máshaka, half a máshaka, a kákani, and half a kákani.

The examiner of coins (rúpadarsaka) shall regulate currency both as a medium of exchange (vyávahárikim) and as legal tender admissible into the treasury (kosapravesyám). The premia levied on coins paid into the treasury shall be: 8 percent, known as rúpika; 5 percent, known as vyáji; one-eighth pana per cent, as párikshika (testing charge); along with a fine of 25 panas to be imposed on offenders, excluding the manufacturer, seller, purchaser, and examiner. The superintendent of ocean-mines (khanyadhyakshah) shall oversee the collection of conch-shells, diamonds, precious stones, pearls, corals, and salt (kshára) and regulate commerce in these commodities. Once the crystallization of salt is complete, the superintendent of salt shall promptly collect both the money-rent (prakraya) and the government's share of salt. By selling the government's share of salt, he shall realize not only its value (múlyam) but also a 5 percent premium (vyájím), both in cash (rúpa). Imported salt (ágantulavanam) shall pay one-sixth of its value (shadbhága) to the king. The sale of this share (bhágavibhága) shall fetch a 5 percent premium (vyáji) and an 8 percent premium (rúpika), both in cash (rúpa). Purchasers of this salt shall also pay a toll (sulka) and compensation (vaidharana) equivalent to the loss caused to the king's commerce. If they fail to pay, they shall be fined 600 panas. Adulteration of salt shall be punished with the highest amercement, as will the unauthorized manufacture of salt by individuals other than hermits (vánaprastha). Men learned in the Vedas, those engaged in penance, and laborers may carry salt for their own food, but salt and alkalies for any other purposes shall be subject to toll payment. Thus, in addition to collecting from mines the ten kinds of revenue, such as: value of the output (múlya), the share of the output (vibhága), a 5 percent premium (vyáji), the testing charge on coins (parigha), fines previously announced (atyaya), toll (sulka), compensation for losses entailed on the king's commerce (vaidharana), fines determined based on the severity of crimes (danda), coinage (rúpa), an 8 percent premium (rúpika), the government shall maintain a state monopoly over both mining and commerce in minerals. Thus, taxes (mukhasangraha) on all commodities intended for sale shall be prescribed once and for all.

[Thus ends Chapter XII, "Conducting Mining Operations and Manufacture," in Book II, "The Duties of Government Superintendents," of the Arthasástra of Kautilya. End of the thirty-third chapter from the beginning.]

CHAPTER XIII. SUPERINTENDENT OF GOLD IN THE GOLDSMITH'S OFFICE.

In order to manufacture gold and silver jewelry, keeping each material separate, the superintendent of gold shall establish a goldsmith's office (akshasála) consisting of four rooms and one door. In the center of the high road, a trained, skilled goldsmith of high birth and reliable character shall be appointed to run the shop.

Jámbúnada, which is the product of the Jambu river; Sátakumbha, extracted from the mountain of Satakumba; Hátaka, from the mines known as Hátaka; Vainava, from the mountain Vénu; and Sringasúktija, extracted from sringasúkti (?) are the varieties of gold.

Gold may be found either pure, amalgamated with mercury or silver, or alloyed with other impurities as mine gold (ákaródgata). The best gold is that which is the color of lotus petals, ductile, glossy, produces no continuous sound (anádi), and glittering. Gold that is reddish-yellow (raktapíta) is of middle quality, while red-colored gold is of low quality. Impure gold is of a whitish color.

Impure gold shall be fused with lead in a quantity four times that of the impurity. When gold becomes brittle due to contamination with lead, it shall be heated with dry cow dung (sushkapatala). If the gold splits into pieces due to hardness, it should be heated and then drenched in oil mixed with cow dung (taila-gomaye).

Mine gold that becomes brittle due to contamination with lead shall be heated while wrapped in cloth (pákapatráni kritvá) and hammered on a wooden anvil. Alternatively, it can be drenched in a mixture made of mushroom and vajrakhanda (Antiquorum).

Tutthodgata, extracted from the mountain Tuttha; Gaudika, a product of the country known as Gauda; Kámbuka, extracted from the mountain Kambu; and Chákraválika, from the mountain Chakravála, are the varieties of silver.

The best silver is white, glossy, and ductile, while silver of the reverse quality is considered bad.

Impure silver shall be heated with lead, using one-fourth the quantity of the impurity. When the silver becomes full of globules, white, glowing, and the color of curd, it is considered pure.

When the streak of pure gold made on a touchstone is the color of turmeric, it is termed suvarna. If one to sixteen kákanis of gold in a suvarna (of sixteen máshakas) are replaced with one to sixteen kákanis of copper, and the copper becomes inseparably alloyed with the rest of the gold, the sixteen varieties (carats) representing the standard of the purity of gold (shodasavarnakáh) will be achieved.

First, a streak with suvarna should be made on a touchstone, and then, next to it, a streak with a piece of the gold to be compared. If a uniform streak made on the smooth surface of the touchstone can be wiped off, swept away, or appears due to the sprinkling of glittering powder (gairika) using the nail, an attempt at deception can be inferred.

If the edge of the palm dipped in a solution of vermilion (játihinguláka) or sulphate of iron (pushpakásísa) in cow's urine touches gold (suvarna), it turns white.

A touchstone with a soft, shining luster is considered the best. The touchstone from the Kálinga country, which is the color of green beans, is also the best. A touchstone of even or uniform color is ideal for the sale or purchase of gold. The one that has the color of an elephant, tinged with green and capable of reflecting light (pratirági), is good for selling gold. The touchstone that is hard, durable, uneven in color, and does not reflect light is good for purchasers (krayahitah). The best touchstone is grey, greasy, uniformly colored, soft, and glossy.

Gold that maintains the same color when heated (tápo bahirantascha samah), is as glittering as tender sprouts, or is the color of the flower of kárandaka (?), is considered the best.

Black or blue discoloration in gold is considered an impurity (apráptaka).

We will discuss the balance and weights under the "Superintendent of Weights and Measures" (Chapter XIX, Book II). In accordance with the instructions provided there, silver and gold (rúpyasuvarnam) may be exchanged.

No person who is not an employee shall enter the goldsmiths' office. Any person who enters without permission shall be executed (uchchhedyah). Any workman who enters the office carrying gold or silver shall forfeit the same.

Goldsmiths engaged in preparing various types of ornaments, such as kánchana (pure gold), prishita (hollow ornaments), tvashtri (gem-setting in gold), and tapaníya, as well as blowers and sweepers, shall only enter or exit the office after a thorough examination of their person and dress. All their instruments, along with their unfinished work, shall remain where they were working. The amount of gold they received and the ornamental work they were crafting shall be placed in the center of the office. Finished items shall be examined in both the morning and evening, and then locked up with the seals of both the manufacturer and the superintendent (kárayatri, the person commissioning the work).

Kshepana, guna, and kshudra are three kinds of ornamental work.

Setting jewels (kácha, glass beads) in gold is called kshepana.

Thread-making or string-making is called guna.

Solid work (ghana), hollow work (sushira), and the manufacture of globules with rounded orifices are considered kshudra, which refers to basic or ordinary work.

For setting jewels in gold, five parts of káñchana (pure gold) and ten parts of gold alloyed with four parts of copper or silver shall be used. Here, the pure gold shall be kept separate from impure gold.

For setting jewels in hollow ornaments (prishitakácha karmanah), three parts of gold will hold the jewel, and four parts will be used for the base.

For tvashtri work, copper and gold shall be mixed in equal quantities.

For solid or hollow silver articles, silver may be mixed with half the amount of gold; alternatively, using a powder or solution of vermilion, gold equal to one-fourth the amount of the silver ornament may be applied (vásayet) as a coating.

Pure and glittering gold is called tapaníya. When tapaníya is combined with an equal quantity of lead and heated with rock salt (saindhav'ika) until it reaches its melting point under dry cow dung, it becomes the basis for gold alloys of various colors such as blue, red, white, yellow (harita), parrot green, and pigeon gray.

The coloring ingredient for gold is one kákaní of tíkshna, which has the color of a peacock's neck, tinged with white, and is dazzling, being full of copper (pitapúrnitam).

Pure or impure silver (tára) may be heated four times with asthituttha (copper sulfate mixed with powdered bone), then four more times with an equal quantity of lead, again four times with dry copper sulfate (sushkatuttha), followed by three times in a skull (kapála), and lastly twice in cow dung. Silver that has undergone these seventeen stages of treatment with tuttha (shodasatutthátikrántam), and is finally heated to a white light with rock salt, can be alloyed with suvarna in proportions ranging from one kákani to two máshas. The resulting suvarna takes on a white color and is called sveta-tára.

When three parts of tapaníya (pure gold) are melted with thirty-two parts of sveta-tára, the alloy becomes reddish-white (svetalohitakam). When three parts of tapaníya are combined with thirty-two parts of copper, the alloy becomes yellow (píta, red!). When three parts of the coloring ingredient (rágatribhága, i.e., tíkshna mentioned earlier) are heated with tapaníya, the compound turns yellowish-red (píta). When two parts of sveta-tára and one part of tapaníya are heated together, the alloy turns as green as mudga (Phraseolus Mungo). When tapaníya is soaked in a solution containing half the quantity of black iron (káláyasa), it turns black.

If tapaníya is twice soaked in this solution mixed with mercury (rasa), it takes on the color of a parrot's feathers.

Before these varieties of gold are put to use, their test streaks shall be taken on a touchstone. The process of assaying tíkshna and copper shall be thoroughly understood. Consequently, the various counterweights (avaneyimána) used in weighing diamonds, rubies, pearls, corals, and coins (rúpa), as well as the proportional amounts of gold and silver needed for various types of ornaments, can be properly understood.

Uniform in color, equal in the color of its test streak to standard gold, free from hollow bulbs, ductile (sthira), very smooth, free from alloys, pleasing to wear as an ornament, not overly dazzling yet glittering, appealing in its consistency of mass, and pleasing to the mind and eyes—these are the qualities of tapaníya, pure gold.

[Thus ends Chapter XIII, "The Superintendent of Gold in the Goldsmiths' Office," in Book II, "The Duties of Government Superintendents," of the Arthasástra of Kautilya. End of the thirty-fourth chapter from the beginning.]

CHAPTER XIV. THE DUTIES OF THE STATE GOLDSMITH IN THE HIGH ROAD.

The State Goldsmith shall employ artisans to manufacture gold and silver coins (rúpyasuvarna) from the bullion of citizens and country people. The artisans employed in the office shall perform their tasks as ordered and within the prescribed time. If, using the excuse that no specific time or nature of the work was given, they spoil the work, they shall forfeit their wages and pay a fine equal to twice the amount of their wages. If they delay the work, they shall forfeit one-fourth of their wages and pay a fine equal to twice the forfeited amount.

The goldsmith of the mint shall return coins or ornaments of the same weight and quality (varna) as the bullion (nikshepa) received at the mint. Except for coins that have been worn out or have diminished in value (kshínaparisírna), the same coins may be returned to the mint even after many years.

The state goldsmith shall gather from the artisans employed in the mint information regarding pure gold, metallic mass (pudgala), coins (lakshana), and the rate of exchange (prayóga).

When a suvarna coin (weighing 16 máshas) is manufactured from gold or silver, an additional one kákani (one-fourth másha) of the metal shall be given to the mint to account for the loss during the manufacturing process. The coloring ingredient (rágaprakshépa) shall be two kákanis of tíkshna (copper sulfate?), with one-sixth being lost during the manufacturing process.

If the quality (varna) of a coin weighing less than the standard másha is lowered, the artisans responsible shall be punished with the first amercement. If the weight of the coin is less than the standard weight, they shall be punished with the middlemost amercement. Deception involving balances or weights shall result in the highest amercement. Deception in the exchange of manufactured coins (kritabhándopadhau) shall also be punished with the highest amercement.

Anyone who causes gold or silver items to be manufactured anywhere other than the mint, or without being observed by the state goldsmith, shall be fined 12 panás. The artisan who performs such work shall, if caught, be fined twice that amount. If not caught, measures described in Book IV shall be taken to detect the offense. Once detected, the artisan shall either be fined 200 panás or have his fingers cut off.

Weighing balances and counterweights must be purchased from the superintendent responsible for them; otherwise, a fine of 12 panás shall be imposed.

The types of artisan work (kárukasma) include compact work (ghana), compact and hollow work (ghanasushira), soldering (samyúhya), amalgamation (avalepya), enclosing (samghátya), and gilding (vásitakam).

False balances (tulávishama), removal (apasárana), dropping (visrávana), folding (petaka), and confounding (pinka) are various means employed by goldsmiths to deceive the public.

False balances include those with bending arms (sannámini), those with a high helm or pivot (utkarnika), those with a broken head (bhinnamastaka), those with a hollow neck (upakanthi), those with faulty strings (kusikya), those with defective cups or pans (sakatukakshya), those that are crooked or shaky (párivellya), and those combined with a magnet (ayaskánta).

When pure alluvial gold is replaced with an equal portion of Triputaka (a mixture of two parts silver and one part copper), this deceitful practice is termed copper-removal (triputakávasáritam). When an equal portion of gold is replaced with copper, it is also termed copper-removal (sulbávasáritam). If vellaka is used to replace an equal portion of gold, it is called vellaka-removal. When pure alluvial gold is replaced with gold half mixed with copper, it is called gold removal (hemávasáritam).

Goldsmiths use various tools and methods for stealing gold, including a crucible with a hidden base metal, metallic excrement, pincers, tongs, metallic pieces (jongani), and borax (sauvarchikálavanam).

When, by intentionally causing the crucible containing bullion to burst, a few sand-like particles of gold are mixed with other particles of a base metal and formed into a mass, this deceitful act is called dropping (visrávana). Likewise, when examining the folded or inlaid leaves of an ornament (áchitakapatrapariksháyám), if silver is substituted for gold or if base metal particles are substituted for gold, it is also termed dropping (visrávana).

Folding (petaka), whether firm (gádha) or loose (abhyuddhárya), is employed in soldering, preparing amalgams, and enclosing a piece of base metal between two pieces of superior metal.

When a lead piece (sísarúpa—lead coin) is firmly covered with gold leaf using wax (ashtaka), this act is called gádhapetaka, or firm folding. When it is loosely covered, it is called loose folding.

In amalgams, a single or double layer of superior metal is used to cover a piece of base metal. Copper or silver may be placed between two leaves of superior metal. A copper piece (sulbarúpya) may be covered with gold leaf, with the surface and edges smoothened. Similarly, a piece of any base metal may be covered with a double layer of copper or silver, with the surface and edges smoothened.

The two forms of folding may be detected by heating, by testing on a touchstone (nikasha), or by noticing the absence of sound when it is rubbed (nissabdollekhana). Loose folding can be identified using the acid juice of badarámla (Flacourtia Cataphracta or jujube fruit) or in saltwater. This covers folding (petaka).

In a compact and hollow piece (ghana-sushire rúpe), small particles of gold-like mud (suvarnamrinválukáh) or bits of vermilion (hingulakalkah) are heated to adhere firmly inside the piece. Even in a solid piece (dridhavástuke rúpe), wax-like mud from Gándhára mixed with particles of gold-like sand is heated to make it stick. These impurities can be removed by hammering the pieces while they are red hot.

In an ornament or coin (sapari-bhánde vá rúpe), salt mixed with hard sand (katusarkará) is heated in flame to make it firmly adhere to the item. This salt and sand can be removed by boiling (kváthana).

In some pieces, mica may be firmly fixed inside using wax and covered with a double leaf of gold or silver. When such a piece with mica or glass inside is suspended in water (udake), one side dips more than the other. Alternatively, if pierced by a pin, the pin moves easily through the layers of mica inside (patalántareshu).

Spurious stones and counterfeit gold and silver may be substituted for real ones in compact and hollow pieces (ghanasushira). They can be detected by hammering the pieces while red hot. This is the process of confounding (pinka).

Therefore, the state goldsmith must have a thorough knowledge of the species, characteristics, color, weight, and composition (pudgala-lakshana) of diamonds, precious stones (mani), pearls, corals, and coins (rúpa).

There are four ways deception can occur when examining new pieces or repairing old ones: hammering, cutting, scratching, and rubbing.

When, under the excuse of detecting the deception known as folding (petaka) in hollow pieces or in threads or cups made of gold or silver, the articles in question are hammered, this act is termed hammering.

When a lead piece (covered over with gold or silver leaf) is substituted for a real one and its interior is cut out, this is termed cutting (avachchhedanam).

When compact pieces are scratched using tíkshna (copper sulfate?), the act is called scratching (ullekhana).

When gold or silver articles are rubbed with a piece of cloth that has been painted with the powder of sulphuret of arsenic (haritála), red arsenic (manassila), vermilion, or with the powder of kuruvinda (black salt?), this is termed rubbing.

Through these acts, gold and silver articles (bhándáni) undergo diminution, but no other kind of damage is inflicted on them.

In all articles that are hammered, cut, scratched, or rubbed, the loss can be determined by comparing them with intact pieces of the same type. In amalgamated pieces (avalepya) that are cut off, the loss can be identified by cutting off an equal portion of a similar piece. For pieces whose appearance has changed, they should be frequently heated and drenched in water.

The state goldsmith shall infer deception (kácham vidyát) when the artisan preparing the articles exhibits undue attention to throwing away materials, counterweights, fire, anvils (gandika), working instruments (bhandika), the seat (adhikarani), the assaying balance, folds of their dress (chellachollakam), their head, thigh, or if they appear preoccupied with flies, are eager to examine their own body, or closely monitor the water-pot or firepot.

Regarding silver, a bad smell like that of rotten meat, hardness due to any alloy (mala), projection (prastína), and discoloration may be signs of adulteration.

Thus, articles of gold and silver, whether new, old, or of bad or unusual color, must be examined, and appropriate fines as described above shall be imposed.

[Thus ends Chapter XIV, "The Duties of the State Goldsmith in the High Road" in Book II, "The Duties of Government Superintendents" of the Arthasástra of Kautilya. End of the thirty-fifth chapter from the beginning.]

CHAPTER XV. THE SUPERINTENDENT OF STOREHOUSE.

The superintendent of the storehouse (Koshthágára) shall supervise the accounts related to agricultural produce (síta); taxes under Ráshtra (country parts); commerce (krayima); barter (parivartna); grains obtained through begging (prámityaka); grains borrowed with a promise to repay (ápamityaka); production of rice, oils, and similar products (simhanika); accidental revenue (anyajáta); reports to verify expenditures (vyayapratyaya); and recovery of past arrears (upasthánam). Whatever agricultural produce is brought in by the superintendent of agriculture (from crown lands) is referred to as sítá.

Taxes such as fixed taxes (pindakara); taxes paid as one-sixth of the produce (shadbhága); provisions provided by the people for the army (senábhakta); taxes levied for religious purposes (bali); taxes or subsidies paid by vassal kings and others (kara); taxes collected on the occasion of the birth of a prince (utsanga); taxes collected when there is a margin for such collection (párśva); compensation in the form of grain for damage done by cattle to crops (párihínaka); gifts presented to the king (aupáyanika); and taxes levied on lands below tanks, lakes, etc., constructed by the king (kaushtheyaka)—all fall under the category of 'Ráshtra.'

The sale proceeds of grains, purchased grains, and the collection of interest on grain debts (prayogapratyádána) are considered commerce. The profitable exchange of grains for other grains is termed barter (parivarthana). Grains obtained through begging are termed prámityaka. Grains borrowed with a promise to repay them are referred to as ápamityaka.

The pounding of rice, the splitting of pulses, the frying of grains and beans, the production of beverages (suktakarma), the preparation of flour by those who depend on such work, the extraction of oil by employing shepherds and oil-makers, and the manufacture of sugar from sugarcane juice are known as simhanika.

Anything lost, forgotten, or found forms accidental revenue (anyajáta). Investment, remnants of a failed venture, and savings from an estimated outlay serve as ways to verify and check expenditures (vyayapratyaya). The amount or quantity of compensation claimed for using a different balance or for any error in taking a handful is called vyáji. The collection of past dues is termed 'upasthána' or 'recovery of past arrears.'

Regarding grains, oils, sugar, and salt, the section on grains will be covered under the duties of the 'Superintendent of Agriculture.'

[Thus ends Chapter XV, "The Duties of the Superintendent of Storehouse" in Book II, "The Duties of Government Superintendents" of the Arthasástra of Kautilya.]

Clarified butter, oil, serum of flesh, and pith or sap (of plants, etc.) are termed oils (sneha). Decoction (phánita), jaggery, granulated sugar, and sugar-candy are termed kshára.

Saindhava, which is the product of the Sindhu region; Sámudra, produced from seawater; Bida; Yavakshara, nitre; Sauvarchala, the product of the country of Suvarchala; and udbhedaja, extracted from saline soil, are termed lavana, or salt.

The honey of bees, as well as the juice extracted from grapes, is called madhu.

A mixture made by combining one of the following substances—sugarcane juice, jaggery, honey, grape juice, the essence of the fruits of jambu (Eugenia Jambolana) and the jaka tree—with the essence of meshasringa (a type of plant) and long pepper, with or without the addition of the essence of chirbhita (a kind of gourd), cucumber, sugarcane, mango fruit, and the fruit of myrobalam, the mixture being prepared to last for a month, six months, or a year, constitutes the group of astringents (sukta-varga).

The fruits of trees bearing acid fruits, such as karamarda (Carissa Carandas), vidalámalka (myrobalam), matulanga (citron tree), kola (small jujube), badara (Flacourtia Cataphracta), sauvíra (large jujube), and parushaka (Grewia Asiatica), come under the group of acid fruits.

Curds, acids prepared from grains, and similar items are classified as acids in liquid form.

Long pepper, black pepper, ginger, cumin seed, kiratatikta (Agathotes Chirayta), white mustard, coriander, choraka (a plant), damanaka (Artemisia Indica), maruvaka (Vangueria Spinosa), sigru (Hyperanthera Moringa), and similar substances, including their roots (kánda), are classified under the group of pungent substances (tiktavarga).

Dried fish, bulbous roots (kándamúla), fruits, and vegetables form the group of edibles (sakavarga).

Of the store thus collected, half shall be kept in reserve to ward off the calamities of the people, and only the other half shall be used. Old collections shall be replaced by new supplies.

The superintendent shall also personally supervise the increase or decrease sustained in grains when they are pounded (kshunna), frayed (ghrishta), reduced to flour (pishta), fried (bhrashta), or dried after being soaked in water.

The essential part (sára, i.e., the portion fit for food) of kodrava (Paspalam Scrobiculatum) and vrihi (rice) is one-half; for sáli (a kind of rice), it is less by one-eighth part; for varaka (Phraseolus Trilobus), it is less by one-third part; for priyangu (panic seed or millet), it is one-half; for chamasi (barley), mudga (Phraseolus Mungo), and masha (Phraseolus Radiatus), it is less by one-eighth part; for saibya (simbi), it is one-half; for masúra (Ervum Hirsutum), it is less by one-third part compared to the raw material or grains from which it is prepared.

Raw flour and kulmasha (boiled and forced rice) will amount to one and a half times the original quantity of the grains. Barley gruel and its flour, when baked, will yield twice the original quantity.

Kodrava (Paspalam Scrobiculatum), varaka (Phraseolus Trilobus), udáraka (Panicum), and priyangu (millet) will increase three times the original quantity when cooked. Vríhi (rice) will increase four times when cooked. Sáli (a type of rice) will increase five times when cooked.

Grains will increase twice the original quantity when moistened, and two and a half times when soaked to the point of sprouting.

Grains, when fried, will increase by one-fifth of the original quantity, and leguminous seeds (kaláya) will double in quantity when fried, as will rice.

Oil extracted from atasi (linseed) will be one-sixth of the seed quantity; oil from seeds such as nimba (Azadirachta Indica), kusámra (?), and kapittha (Feronia Elephantum) will yield one-fifth; and oil from tila (sesame), kusumba (a type of kidney bean), madhúka (Bassia Latifolia), and ingudi (Terminalia Catappa) will yield one-fourth.

Five palas of kárpása (cotton) or kshauma (flax) will yield one pala of threads.

Rice prepared in such a way that five drónas of sáli yield ten ádhakas of rice is suitable for feeding young elephants; eleven ádhakas from five drónas are fit for elephants with a bad temper (vyála); ten ádhakas from the same amount are for elephants trained for riding; nine ádhakas for war elephants; eight ádhakas for infantry; eleven ádhakas for army chiefs; six ádhakas for queens and princes; and five ádhakas from the same quantity are for kings.

One prastha of pure, unsplit rice, one-fourth prastha of súpa (soup or broth), and clarified butter or oil equal to one-fourth part of the súpa will suffice to form one meal for an Arya.

For low castes (avara), one-sixth prastha of súpa and half the quantity of oil will be sufficient for one meal.

For women, the same rations, reduced by one-fourth, will form a meal. For children, half the above rations will suffice.

For cooking twenty palas of meat, half a kutumba of oil, one pala of salt, one pala of sugar (kshára), two dharanas of pungent substances (katuka, spices), and half a prastha of curd will be necessary. For larger quantities of meat, the same ingredients should be proportionally increased.

For cooking sákas (dried fish and vegetables), the above ingredients should be added in one and a half times the quantity. For dried fish, the ingredients are to be doubled.

Rations for elephants and horses will be described in connection with the "Duties of Their Respective Superintendents."

For bullocks, one drona of masha (Phraseolus Radiatus) or one drona of barley, cooked with other ingredients prescribed for horses, is the requisite quantity of food, in addition to one tula of oilcakes (ghánapinyaka) or ten ádhakas of bran (kanakuttana-kundaka). For buffaloes and camels, the quantity is doubled.

For asses, red spotted deer, and deer with white stripes, half a drona.

For antelopes and large red deer, one ádhaka.

For goats, rams, and boars, half an ádhaka or one ádhaka of grain, along with bran.

For dogs, one prastha of cooked rice. For hamsa (geese), krauncha (herons), and peacocks, half a prastha.

From the above measures, the quantity of rations sufficient for one meal for other beasts, cattle, birds, and rogue elephants (vyála) can be inferred.

Charcoal and chaff may be provided for iron smelting and lime-kilns (bhittilepya).

Bran and flour (kánika) may be given to slaves, laborers, and cooks. Surplus bran and flour may also be given to those who prepare cooked rice and rice cakes.

The necessary instruments include weighing balances, weights, measures, millstones (rochani), pestles, mortars, wooden contrivances for pounding rice (kuttakayantra), contrivances for splitting seeds (rochakayantra), winnowing fans, sieves (chálani), grain baskets (kandoli), boxes, and brooms.

Sweepers, preservers, those who weigh (dharaka), those who measure grains (mápaka), supervisors of grain measuring, those in charge of the supply of commodities to the storehouse (dápaka), suppliers (dáyaka), workers who receive compensation for errors in grain measuring (sáláкáipratigráhaka), slaves, and laborers are collectively referred to as vishti.

Grains are heaped on the floor; jaggery (kshára) is bound with grass-rope (múta); oils are stored in earthenware or wooden vessels; and salt is heaped on the ground.

[Thus ends Chapter XV, "The Superintendent of Storehouse," in Book II, "The Duties of Government Superintendents," of the

Arthasástra of Kautilya. End of the thirty-sixth chapter from the beginning.]

CHAPTER XVI. THE SUPERINTENDENT OF COMMERCE.

The Superintendent of Commerce shall ascertain the demand or absence of demand, and the rise or fall in the price of various kinds of merchandise, whether produced on land or in water, and whether transported by land or water routes. He shall also determine the appropriate time for the distribution, centralization, purchase, and sale of these goods.

Merchandise that is widely distributed shall be centralized, and its price increased. Once the increased price becomes widely accepted, a new rate shall be declared. Merchandise produced locally by the king shall be centralized, while imported goods shall be distributed to various markets for sale. Both types of goods shall be sold at favorable prices to the public.

The Superintendent shall avoid setting profits so high as to cause harm to the people.

Commodities for which there is frequent demand shall not be restricted by time limits for sale, nor shall they suffer from the disadvantages of centralization (sankuladosha). Alternatively, peddlers may sell the king's merchandise at a fixed price in multiple markets, paying necessary compensation (vaidharana) proportional to any losses incurred (chhedánurúpam).

The amount of vyáji (profit margin) due on commodities sold by cubical measure is one-sixteenth of the total quantity (shodasabhágo mánavyáji); for commodities sold by weight, it is one-twentieth; and for those sold by number, it is one-eleventh of the total.

The Superintendent shall show favor to those who import foreign merchandise. Mariners (návika) and merchants who import foreign goods shall be granted a remission of trade taxes so that they may derive some profit (áyatikshamam pariháram dadyát).

Foreigners importing merchandise shall not be sued for debts unless they are part of local associations or partners (anabhiyogaschárthesshvágantúnámanyatassabhyopakári bhyah).

Those selling the king's merchandise must always deposit their sale proceeds in a wooden box placed in a designated location, with a single aperture at the top. During the eighth part of the day, they shall submit a sales report to the superintendent, stating, "This much has been sold, and this much remains." They must also hand over the weights and measures. These are the rules for local commerce.

Regarding the sale of the king's merchandise in foreign countries:—

The superintendent must first compare the value of local produce with that of foreign produce that can be obtained in barter. He will then calculate whether there is any profit left after covering the necessary payments to the foreign king, such as tolls (sulka), road-cess (vartaní), conveyance-cess (átiváhika), tax payable at military stations (gulmadeya), ferry charges (taradeya), subsistence for the merchant and his followers (bhakta), and the portion of merchandise owed to the foreign king (bhága).

If no profit can be made by selling local produce in foreign countries, the superintendent must consider whether any local produce can be profitably bartered for foreign goods. He may then send one-quarter of his valuable merchandise via safe routes to different markets on land. To maximize profits, the deputed merchant may build friendships with forest guards, boundary guards, and the officers in charge of cities and country parts under the foreign king. The merchant must take precautions to protect both his treasure (sára) and his life from danger. If he cannot reach the intended market, he may sell the merchandise at any market free from all dues (sarvadeyavisuddham).

Alternatively, the merchant may take his merchandise to other countries by river routes (nadípatha).

The merchant must also gather information about conveyance charges (yánabhágaka), subsistence during the journey (pathyadana), the value of foreign goods that can be obtained in exchange for local merchandise, occasions of pilgrimages (yátrakála), methods to ward off journey dangers, and the history of commercial towns (panyapattanacháritra).

Having gathered information about transactions in commercial towns along riverbanks, the merchant should transport his goods to profitable markets and avoid unprofitable ones.

[Thus ends Chapter XVI, "The Superintendent of Commerce," in Book II, "The Duties of Government Superintendents," of the Arthasástra of Kautilya. End of the thirty-seventh chapter from the beginning.]

CHAPTER XVII. THE SUPERINTENDENT OF FOREST PRODUCE.

The Superintendent of Forest Produce shall collect timber and other products from the forests by employing those who guard the productive forests. He shall initiate productive works in the forests and impose appropriate fines and compensations for any damage caused to productive forests, except in cases of natural calamities.

The following are classified as forest products:

Sáka (teak), tinisa (Dalbergia Ougeinensis), dhanvana (?), arjuna (Terminalia Arjuna), madhúka (Bassia Latifolia), tilaka (Barleria Cristata), tála (palmyra), simsúpa (Dalbergia Sissu), arimeda (Fetid Mimosa), rájádana (Mimosops Kauki), sirisha (Mimosa Sirísha), khadira (Mimosa Catechu), sarala (Pinus Longifolia), tálasarja (sal tree or Shorea Robesta), asvakarna (Vatica Robesta), somavalka (a kind of white khadíra), kasámra (?), priyaka (yellow sal tree), dhava (Mimosa Hexandra), and others are considered strong timber (sáradáruvarga).

The bamboo group includes utaja, chimiya, chava, vénu, vamsa, sátina, kantaka, and bhállúka.

The creeper group includes vetra (cane), sokavalli, vási (Justicia Ganderussa?), syámalatá (Ichnocarpus), and nágalata (betel).

The fibrous plant group (valkavarga) includes málati (Jasminum Grandiflorum), dúrvá (panic grass), arka (Calotropis Gigantea), sana (hemp), gavedhuka (Coix Barbata), and atasí (Linum Usitatissimum).

Plants used for making ropes (rajjubhánda) include munja (Saccharum Munja) and balbaja (Eleusine Indica).

Táli (Corypha Taliera), tála (palmyra or Borassus Flabelliformis), and bhúrja (birch) yield leaves (patram).

Flowers are yielded by kimsuka (Butea Frondosa), kusumbha (Carthamus Tinctorius), and kumkuma (Crocus Sativus).

Bulbous roots and fruits form the group of medicinal plants.

Poisons include kálakúta, vatsanábha, háláhala, meshasringa, mustá (Cyperus Rotundus), kushtha, mahávisha, vellitaka, gaurárdra, bálaka, márkata, haimavata, kálingaka, daradaka, kolasáraka, ushtraka, and others. Snakes and worms kept in pots also constitute the group of poisons.

Skins include those from animals such as godha (alligator), seraka (?), dvípi (leopard), simsumára (porpoise), simha (lion), vyághra (tiger), hasti (elephant), mahisha (buffalo), chamara (bos grunniens), gomriga (bos gavaeus), and gavaya (the gayal).

Other animal products include bones, bile (pittha), snáyu (?), teeth, horn, hooves, and tails of the above animals, as well as other beasts, cattle, birds, and snakes (vyála).

Metals include kálayasa (iron), támra (copper), vritta (?), kámsya (bronze), sísa (lead), trapu (tin), vaikrintaka (mercury?), and árakuata (brass).

Utensils (bhanda) are made from cane, bark (vidala), and clay (mrittiká).

Other forest products include charcoal, bran, and ashes.

The forest produce also includes menageries of beasts, cattle, and birds, as well as the collection of firewood and fodder.

The Superintendent of Forest Produce shall carry out the manufacture of all kinds of articles, either within or outside the capital city, that are essential for daily life or for the defense of forts.

[Thus ends Chapter XVII, "The Superintendent of Forest Produce," in Book II, "The Duties of Government Superintendents," of the Arthasástra of Kautilya. End of the thirty-eighth chapter from the beginning.]

CHAPTER XVIII. THE SUPERINTENDENT OF THE ARMOURY.

The Superintendent of the Armoury shall employ skilled and experienced workmen to manufacture wheels, weapons, mail armor, and other related instruments within a specified time and for fixed wages. These items are to be used in battles, for the construction or defense of forts, or for destroying the cities or strongholds of enemies.

All weapons and instruments shall be stored in places properly designated for them. They shall be regularly dusted, moved from one location to another, and exposed to the sun. Weapons susceptible to heat and moisture (úshmopasneha) or prone to being eaten by worms shall be stored in secure locations. They shall also be inspected periodically in terms of their category, shape, characteristics, size, source, value, and total quantity.

The following are immovable machines (sthirayantrám): Sarvatobhadra, Jamadagnya, Bahumukha, Visvásagháti, Samgháti, Yánaka, Parjanyaka, Ardhabáhu, and Úrdhvabáhu.

The following are movable machines: Pánchálika, Devadanda, Súkarika, Musala, Yashti, Hastiváraka, Tálavrinta, Mudgara, Gada, Spriktala, Kuddála, Ásphátima, Audhghátima, Sataghni, Trisúla, and Chakra.

Weapons with ploughshare-like edges (halamukháni) include Sakti, Prása, Kunta, Hátaka, Bhindivála, Súla, Tomara, Varáhakarna, Kanaya, Karpana, and Trásika.

Bows are made from different materials: tála (palmyra), chápa (a kind of bamboo), dáru (a type of wood), and sringa (bone or horn), and are known as kármuka, kodanda, druna, and dhanus, respectively.

Bow-strings are made from múrva (Sansviera Roxburghiana), arka (Catotropis Gigantea), sána (hemp), gavedhu (Coix Barbata), venu (bamboo bark), and snáyu (sinew).

Different kinds of arrows include Venu, Sara, Saláka, Dandásana, and Nárácha. The arrowheads are made of iron, bone, or wood and are designed to cut, rend, or pierce.

Swords include Nistrimsa, Mandalágra, and Asiyashti, with handles made of rhinoceros or buffalo horn, elephant tusk, wood, or bamboo root.

Razor-like weapons include Parasu, Kuthára, Pattasa, Khanitra, Kuddála, Chakra, and Kándachchhedana.

Other weapons include Yantrapáshána, Goshpanapáshána, Mushtipáshána, Rochaní (mill-stone), and stones.

Armor varieties include Lohajáliká, Patta, Kavacha, and Sútraka, made from iron or skins combined with the hoofs and horns of porpoise, rhinoceros, bison, elephant, or cow.

Likewise, sirastrána (cover for the head), kanthatrána (cover for the neck), kúrpása (cover for the trunk), kanchuka (a coat extending as far as the knee joints), váravána (a coat extending as far as the heels), patta (a coat without cover for the arms), and nágodariká (gloves) are varieties of armor.

Veti, charma, hastikarna, tálamúla, dharmanika, kaváta, kitika, apratihata, and valáhakánta are instruments used in self-defense (ávaranáni).

Ornaments for elephants, chariots, and horses, as well as goads and hooks to guide them in battlefields, are considered accessory items (upakaranáni).

In addition to these, other delusive and destructive contrivances (as discussed in Book XIV) and any new inventions by expert workmen shall also be kept in stock.

The Superintendent of Armoury shall carefully assess the demand and supply of weapons, their application, their wear and tear, as well as their decay and loss.

[Thus ends Chapter XVIII, "The Superintendent of the Armoury," in Book II, "The Duties of Government Superintendents," of the Arthasástra of Kautilya. End of the thirty-ninth chapter from the beginning.]

CHAPTER XIX. THE SUPERINTENDENT OF WEIGHTS AND MEASURES.

The Superintendent of Weights and Measures shall oversee the manufacturing of standardized weights. Ten seeds of másha (Phraseolus Radiatus) or five gunja (Cabrus Precatorius) equal one suvarna-másha. Sixteen máshas equal one suvarna or karsha. Four karshas equal one pala. Eighty-eight white mustard seeds equal one silver-másha. Sixteen silver máshas or twenty saibya seeds equal one dharana. Twenty grains of rice equal one dharana of a diamond.

The various units of weight include: Ardha-másha (half a másha), one másha, two máshas, four máshas, eight máshas, one suvarna, two suvarnas, four suvarnas, eight suvarnas, ten suvarnas, twenty suvarnas, thirty suvarnas, forty suvarnas, and one hundred suvarnas.

A similar series of weights shall also be created in dharanas.

Weights (pratimánáni) shall be made from iron or stones found in the regions of Magadha and Mekala, or from materials that neither contract when wetted nor expand under heat.

Starting with a lever that is six angulas long and weighs one pala, ten balances shall be made, with each successive balance increasing by one pala in weight and eight angulas in length. Each balance will have a scale-pan attached on one or both sides.

A balance known as samavrittá, with a lever 72 angulas long and weighing 53 palas in its metallic mass, shall also be made. A scale-pan weighing five palas will be attached to its edge. The horizontal position of the lever (samakarana) when weighing a karsha shall be marked at the point where, when held by a thread, it balances horizontally. To the left of this mark, symbols for 1 pala, 12, 15, and 20 palas shall be indicated. After this, each place of tens up to 100 shall be marked. In the place of Akshas, the sign of Nándi shall be inscribed.

Likewise, a balance called parimáni, with twice the metallic mass of samavrittá and measuring 96 angulas in length, shall be made. On its lever, markings for 20, 50, and 100, in addition to the initial weight of 100, shall be engraved. Twenty tulas equal one bhára, and ten dharanas equal one pala. One hundred such palas equal one áyamáni, which is a measure of royal income.

The public balance (vyávaháriká), servants' balance (bhájiní), and harem balance (antahpurabhájiní) shall decrease successively by five palas when compared to áyamáni. Each pala in these balances will fall short of the áyamáni by half a dharana. The metallic mass of the levers in each balance will successively decrease in weight by two ordinary palas and in length by six angulas.

With the exception of flesh, metals, salt, and precious stones, all other commodities weighed in the two first-named balances shall have an excess of five palas (prayáma) given to the king.

A wooden balance with an 8-hand-long lever, equipped with measuring marks and counterpoise weights, shall be erected on a pedestal resembling that of a peacock.

Twenty-five palas of firewood will be required to cook one prastha of rice. This is the unit for calculating any greater or lesser quantity of firewood.

Thus, the weighing balance and weights are discussed. Then, with 200 palas of másha grains, one drona becomes an áyamána (a measure of royal income). A public drona will contain 187½ palas; a servants' drona (bhájaníya) will contain 175 palas; and a harem drona (antahpurabhájaníya) will contain 162½ palas.

Adhaka, prastha, and kudumba are each one-quarter of the unit before them. Sixteen dronas equal one vári, twenty dronas equal one kumbha, and ten kumbhas equal one vaha.

Cubic measures shall be made of dry and strong wood, so that when filled with grains, the conically heaped-up portion standing above the mouth of the measure equals one-fourth of the measured grains. Alternatively, measures may be made so that the heaped-up portion can fit inside the measure. Liquids, however, shall always be measured level to the mouth of the measure.

For wine, flowers, fruits, bran, charcoal, and slaked lime, twice the quantity of the heaped-up portion (i.e., one-fourth of the measure) shall be given as excess. The price of a drona is 1¼ panas, an ádhaka is ¾ pana, a prastha is 6 máshas, and a kudumba is 1 másha.

The price of liquid measures will be double the price of dry measures. The price of a set of counter-weights is 20 panas, and the price of a tulá (balance) is 6⅔ panas.

The Superintendent shall charge 4 máshas for stamping weights or measures. A fine of 27¼ panas shall be imposed for using unstamped weights or measures.

Traders shall pay one kákaní per day to the Superintendent as a charge for stamping weights and measures.

Those who trade in clarified butter shall give to purchasers 1/32 part more as taptavyáji (i.e., compensation for the decrease in the quantity of ghee due to its liquid condition). Those who trade in oil shall give 1/64 part more as taptavyáji.

While selling liquids, traders shall give 1/50 part more as mánasráva (i.e., compensation for the decrease in quantity due to overflow or adhesion to the measuring can).

Half, one-fourth, and one-eighth portions of the kumbha measure shall also be manufactured. Eighty-four kudumbas of clarified butter are considered equal to one wáraka of ghee, while sixty-four kudumbas of clarified butter are equal to one wáraka of oil (taila). One-quarter of a wáraka is referred to as ghatika, either of ghee or oil.

[Thus ends Chapter XIX, "Balance, Weights and Measures," in Book II, "The Duties of Government Superintendents," of the Arthasástra of Kautilya. End of the fortieth chapter from the beginning.]

CHAPTER XX. MEASUREMENT OF SPACE AND TIME.

The Superintendent of Lineal Measure shall possess knowledge of measuring both space and time. Eight atoms (paramánavah) are equal to one particle thrown off by the wheel of a chariot. Eight such particles are equal to one likshá. Eight likshás are equal to the middle of a yúka (louse) of medium size. Eight yúkas are equal to one yava (barley) of medium size. Eight yavas are equal to one angula (¾ of an English inch), or the middle joint of the middle finger of a man of medium size may be taken as equal to one angula. Four angulas are equal to one dhanurgraha. Eight angulas are equal to one dhanurmushti. Twelve angulas are equal to one vitasti, or one chháyápaurusha. Fourteen angulas are equal to one sama, sala, pariraya, or pada.

Two vitastis are equal to one aratni or one prájápatya hasta. Two vitastis plus one dhanurgraha are equal to one hasta, used in measuring balances, cubic measures, and pasture lands. Two vitastis plus one dhanurmushti equal one kishku or one kamsa. Forty-two angulas are equal to one kishku, as used by sawyers and blacksmiths for measuring the grounds for army encampments, forts, and palaces. Fifty-four angulas equal one hasta, used in measuring timber forests. Eighty-four angulas are equal to one vyáma, used in measuring ropes and digging depth in terms of a man's height. Four aratnis are equal to one danda, dhanus, nálika, or paurusha. One hundred and eight angulas are equal to one garhapatya dhanus (a measure used by carpenters called grihapati), used for measuring roads and fort walls. The same 108 angulas are equal to one paurusha, a measure used in building sacrificial altars. Six kamsas or 192 angulas are equal to one danda, used in measuring lands gifted to Bráhmans. Ten dandas are equal to one rajju. Two rajjus are equal to one paridesa (square measure). Three rajjus are equal to one nivartana (square measure). The same three rajjus, plus two dandas on one side, equal one báhu (arm). One thousand dhanus are equal to one goruta (the sound of a cow). Four gorutas are equal to one yojana.

Thus, lineal and square measures are dealt with.

Then, with regard to measures of time:

The divisions of time are: truti, lava, nimesha, káshthá, kalá, náliká, muhúrta, forenoon, afternoon, day, night, paksha (fortnight), month, ritu (season), ayana (solstice), samvatsara (year), and yuga (age). Two trutis are equal to one lava. Two lavas are equal to one nimesha. Five nimeshas are equal to one káshthá. Thirty káshthás are equal to one kalá. Forty kalás are equal to one náliká, which is the time taken for one ádhaka of water to flow out of a pot through an aperture the same diameter as a 4-angula-long wire made of 4 máshas of gold. Two nálikas are equal to one muhúrta. Fifteen muhúrtas are equal to one day or one night.

Such a day and night occur in the months of Chaitra and Asvayuja. After six months, the duration of day and night increases or decreases by three muhúrtas.

When the shadow is eight paurushas (96 angulas), it is 1/18th of the day. When it is six paurushas (72 angulas), it is 1/14th of the day. When four paurushas, it is 1/8th. When two paurushas, it is 1/6th. When one paurusha, it is ¼th. When the shadow is eight angulas, it is 3/10th of the day (trayodasabhágah); when four angulas, it is 3/8th. When no shadow is cast, it is considered midday.

Likewise, when the day declines, the same process in reverse order shall be observed. It is in the month of Ashádha that no shadow is cast at midday. After Ashádha, during the six months from Srávana onward, the length of the shadow successively increases by two angulas. During the next six months from Mágha onward, it successively decreases by two angulas.

Fifteen days and nights together make up one paksha. The paksha during which the moon waxes is called sukla (white), and the paksha during which the moon wanes is called bahula.

Two pakshas make one month (mása). Thirty days and nights together make one prakarmamása (work-a-month). The same 30 days and nights, with an additional half day, make one solar month (saura). The same 30 days and nights, less by half a day, make one lunar month (chandramása). Twenty-seven days and nights make a sidereal month (nakshatramása).

Once in thirty-two months, there comes one malamása, a "profane month" (an extra month added to the lunar year to harmonize it with the solar). Once in thirty-five months, there is a malamása for Asvaváhas. Once in forty months, there is a malamása for hastiváhas.

Two months make one ritu (season). Srávana and Proshthapada make the rainy season (varshá). Asvayuja and Kárthíka make the autumn (sarad). Márgasírsha and Phausha make the winter (hemanta). Mágha and Phalguna make the dewy season (sisira). Chaitra and Vaisákha make the spring (vasanta). Jyeshthámúlíya and Ashádha make the summer (grishma).

The seasons from sisira and upward are the summer solstice (uttaráyana), and those from varshá and upward are the winter solstice (dakshináyana). Two solstices (ayanas) make one year (samvatsara). Five years make one yuga.

The sun "carries off" (harati) 1/60th of a whole day every day, thus completing one full day every two months (ritau). Likewise, the moon falls behind by 1/60th of a whole day every day, falling behind by one day every two months. Thus, in the middle of every third year, they (the sun and the moon) make one adhimása (additional month), the first in the summer season and the second at the end of five years.

[Thus ends Chapter XX, "Measurement of Space and Time," in Book II, "The Duties of Government Superintendents," of the Arthasástra of Kautilya. End of the forty-first chapter from the beginning.]

CHAPTER XXI. THE SUPERINTENDENT OF TOLLS.

The Superintendent of Tolls shall establish both the toll-house and its flag near the large gate of the city, with the flag facing either the north or the south. When merchants arrive at the toll gate with their merchandise, four or five collectors shall record who the merchants are, where they come from, the amount of merchandise they are bringing, and where the sealmark (abhijnánamudrá) was first placed on the merchandise.

Merchants whose merchandise has not been stamped with the sealmark shall pay double the toll. For using counterfeit seals, they shall pay eight times the toll. If the sealmark is effaced or torn, the merchants in question shall be compelled to stand in the ghatikásthána (a place for public punishment). When a seal meant for one type of merchandise is used for another or when the merchandise is falsely named (námakrite), the merchants shall pay a fine of 1¼ panás for each load (sapádapanikam vahanam dápayet).

The merchandise shall be placed near the flag of the toll-house, and the merchants shall declare its quantity and price, then cry out three times, "Who will purchase this quantity of merchandise for this price?" They shall hand over the merchandise to anyone who demands it for that price. If buyers offer a higher price, the enhanced amount, along with the toll on the merchandise, shall be paid into the king's treasury. If the merchants reduce the quantity or price of the merchandise to avoid a high toll, the excess shall be taken by the king, or the merchants shall be made to pay eight times the toll. The same punishment shall apply if the price of merchandise packed in bags is lowered by showing an inferior sample or when valuable goods are covered with a layer of inferior ones.

If the price of merchandise is increased beyond its proper value due to fear of bidders raising the price, the king shall receive the enhanced amount or twice the toll on it. The same punishment or eight times the toll shall be imposed on the Superintendent of Tolls if he conceals merchandise.

Therefore, commodities shall be sold only after they are accurately weighed, measured, or numbered.

In the case of inferior goods or those exempt from tolls, the toll amount due shall be determined after careful consideration.

Merchants who pass beyond the flag of the toll-house without paying the toll shall be fined eight times the amount of the toll due from them. Those traveling to and from the city shall ascertain whether the toll has been paid on any merchandise going along the road.

Commodities intended for marriages, or taken by a bride from her parents' house to her husband's (anváyanam), or intended for presentation, or taken for the purpose of performing sacrifices, confinement of women, worship of gods, the ceremony of tonsure, investiture with the sacred thread, gift of cows (godána, made before marriage), any religious rite, consecration ceremony (dikshá), and other special ceremonies, shall be exempt from tolls.

Those who lie about such goods shall be punished as thieves.

Anyone smuggling part of their goods without paying toll, mixing it with goods on which toll has already been paid, or breaking open a bag to hide goods in order to use the same toll pass for a second portion of merchandise, shall lose the smuggled goods and be fined the value of the smuggled amount.

Someone who, after falsely swearing by cow dung, smuggles goods shall face the highest penalty.

If a person imports banned items like weapons, armor, metals, chariots, precious stones, grains, or cattle, they will not only be punished according to other laws but will also have to forfeit the goods. If these items were brought in to be sold, they must be sold outside the city walls, toll-free.

The officer in charge of boundaries (antapála) shall collect a pana-and-a-quarter as road tax (vartani) for each load of goods.

They shall charge one pana for each single-hoofed animal, half a pana for each head of cattle, and a quarter of a pana for smaller four-legged animals.

They will also collect a másha for each head-load of merchandise.

The officer is responsible for compensating merchants for any losses suffered within their region.

After thoroughly inspecting foreign goods for quality, the officer shall stamp them with a seal and send them to the toll superintendent.

Alternatively, they may send a spy disguised as a merchant to inform the king about the amount and quality of the goods. The king will then pass this information to the toll superintendent to show the king's all-knowing power. The superintendent will tell the merchants that a certain merchant has brought in a certain amount of high or low-quality merchandise, which cannot be hidden, emphasizing that this knowledge is due to the king's wisdom.

For hiding inferior goods, eight times the toll shall be charged; for hiding or covering up superior goods, they shall be confiscated.

Anything harmful or useless to the country will be blocked, while goods of great benefit, including rare seeds, will be allowed in without paying tolls.

CHAPTER XXII. REGULATION OF TOLL-DUES.

Merchandise, whether it comes from outside the city (báhyam, i.e., from country parts), is produced inside the city (ábhyantaram, i.e., manufactured inside forts), or is imported from foreign countries (átithyani), shall all be subject to tolls, both when exported (nishkrámya) and imported (pravésyam).

Imported goods shall pay 1/5th of their value as a toll.

For flowers, fruits, vegetables (sáka), roots (múla), bulbous roots (kanda), pallikya (?), seeds, dried fish, and dried meat, the superintendent shall collect 1/6th of their value as toll.

For conch-shells, diamonds, precious stones, pearls, corals, and necklaces, experts familiar with the production cost, timing, and quality of the items shall determine the toll amount.

For fibrous garments (kshauma), cotton cloths (dukúla), silk (krimitána), mail armor (kankata), sulphuret of arsenic (haritála), red arsenic (manassilá), vermilion (hingulaka), metals (lóha), and coloring materials (varnadhátu); as well as sandalwood, agarwood (agaru), spices (katuka), ferments (kinva), clothing (ávarana), and similar items; wine, ivory, skins, raw materials for making fiber or cotton garments, carpets, curtains (právarana), and products derived from worms (krimijáta); and wool and other products from goats and sheep, he shall collect 1/10th or 1/15th as toll.

For cloths (vastra), quadrupeds, bipeds, threads, cotton, scents, medicines, wood, bamboo, fibers (valkala), skins, and clay pots; as well as grains, oils, sugar (kshára), salt, liquor (madya), cooked rice, and similar items, he shall collect 1/20th or 1/25th as toll.

Gate dues (dvárádeya) shall be 1/5th of toll dues, though this tax may be waived if circumstances call for such a favor. Goods shall not be sold where they are grown or produced.

When minerals and other goods are purchased from mines, a fine of 600 panás shall be imposed.

When flowers or fruits are purchased from flower or fruit gardens, a fine of 54 panas shall be imposed.

When vegetables, roots, or bulbous roots are purchased from vegetable gardens, a fine of 51¾ panas shall be imposed.

When any type of grass or grain is purchased from a field, a fine of 53 panas shall be imposed.

Permanent fines of 1 pana and 1½ panas shall be collected on agricultural produce (sítátyayah).

Therefore, based on the customs of the country or community, the rate of tolls shall be set for both new and old commodities, and fines shall be proportionate to the seriousness of the offenses.

CHAPTER XXIII. SUPERINTENDENT OF WEAVING.

The Superintendent of Weaving shall employ qualified persons to manufacture threads, coats, cloths, and ropes.

Widows, crippled women, young girls, mendicant or ascetic women, women forced to work due to failure to pay fines, mothers of prostitutes, elderly female servants of the king, and temple dancers who have ceased to attend temple service shall be employed to cut wool, fiber, cotton, fluff, hemp, and flax.

Wages shall be determined according to whether the threads spun are fine, coarse, or of medium quality, in proportion to the amount of work done, and the quantity of thread produced. Those who produce a greater quantity shall be rewarded with oil and dried myrobalan fruit cakes. They may also be employed to work on holidays with the promise of additional rewards.

If the amount of thread spun falls short, considering the quality of the raw material, wages shall be reduced accordingly.

Weaving can also be done by artisans who are capable of producing a set quantity of work within a specified time and for a fixed wage.

The superintendent shall closely associate with the workmen.

Those who manufacture fibrous cloths, garments, silk-cloths, woolen cloths, and cotton fabrics shall be rewarded with presentations such as scents, garlands of flowers, or any other prizes of encouragement.

Various kinds of garments, blankets, and curtains shall be produced.

Those skilled in the craft shall manufacture mail armor.

Women who do not leave their homes, whose husbands are away, or those who are disabled or young girls may, when compelled to work for their livelihood, be given work through the courtesy of maid-servants of the weaving establishment.

Women who can present themselves at the weaving house shall, at dawn, be allowed to exchange their spun threads for wages. Only enough light as is necessary to examine the threads shall be used. If the superintendent looks at the face of these women or discusses any other work, he shall be punished with the first amercement. Delay in paying wages shall result in the middle amercement, and the same punishment shall apply when wages are paid for incomplete work.

A woman who, after receiving wages, does not turn out the required work shall have her thumb cut off.

Those who misappropriate, steal, or run away with the raw materials shall be punished in the same way.

Weavers, when guilty of offenses, shall be fined from their wages in proportion to their offenses.

The superintendent shall closely associate with those who manufacture ropes and mail armor, and he shall also oversee the manufacture of straps and other necessary items.

He shall oversee the production of ropes from threads and fibers and the production of straps from cane and bamboo bark, which are used for training or tethering draft animals.

[Thus ends the section on "The Superintendent of Weaving."]

CHAPTER XXIV. THE SUPERINTENDENT OF AGRICULTURE.

Being knowledgeable in the science of agriculture, which deals with the planting of bushes and trees (krishitantragulmavrikshsháyurvedajñah), or with the help of those trained in these sciences, the Superintendent of Agriculture shall collect seeds at the proper time from all kinds of grains, flowers, fruits, vegetables, bulbous roots, roots, pállikya (?), fibre-producing plants, and cotton.

He shall employ slaves, laborers, and prisoners (dandapratikartri) to sow these seeds on crown-lands that have been regularly and thoroughly ploughed.

The work of these individuals shall not be disrupted by any shortage of plows (karshanayantra) or other essential tools, nor by the lack of bullocks. Nor shall there be any delay in securing for them the services of blacksmiths, carpenters, drillers (medaka), ropemakers, and those skilled in catching snakes or similar tasks.

Any loss caused by negligence on the part of these workers shall result in a fine equal to the value of the loss.

The average rainfall in the Jangala region is 16 dronas; it is one and a half times greater in moist regions (anúpánám). For countries that are agriculturally suited (désavápánam), the rainfall is 13½ dronas in the Asmaka region, 23 dronas in Avanti, and immense amounts in the western regions (aparántánám), the borders of the Himalayas, and regions where water channels are used for agriculture (kulyávápánám).

When one-third of the necessary rainfall occurs both in the early and late months of the rainy season and two-thirds falls in the middle, the rainfall is considered evenly distributed (sushumárúpam).

A forecast of such rainfall can be made by observing the position, movement, and "pregnancy" (garbhádána) of Jupiter (Brihaspati), as well as the rise, set, and movement of Venus, and the natural or unnatural appearance of the sun.

From the sun, the sprouting of seeds can be predicted; from the position of Jupiter, the formation of grains (stambakarita) can be foretold; and from the movement of Venus, the likelihood of rainfall can be inferred.

Three are the clouds that continuously rain for seven days; eighty are they that pour minute drops; and sixty are they that appear with the sunshine—this is termed rainfall. Where rain, free from wind and unmingled with sunshine, falls so as to render three turns of ploughing possible, there the reaping of a good harvest is certain.

Hence, according as the rainfall is more or less, the superintendent shall sow the seeds which require either more or less water.

Sáli (a kind of rice), vríhi (rice), kodrava (Paspalum Scrobiculatum), tila (sesamum), priyangu (panic seeds), dáraka (?), and varaka (Phraseolus Trilobus) are to be sown at the commencement (púrvávápah) of the rainy season.

Mudga (Phraseolus Mungo), másha (Phraseolus Radiatus), and saibya (?) are to be sown in the middle of the season.

Kusumbha (safflower), masúra (Ervum Hirsutum), kuluttha (Dolichos Uniflorus), yava (barley), godhúma (wheat), kaláya (leguminous seeds), atasi (linseed), and sarshapa (mustard) are to be sown last.

Or seeds may be sown according to the changes of the season.

Fields that are left unsown (vápátiriktam, i.e., owing to the inadequacy of hands) may be brought under cultivation by employing those who cultivate for half the share in the produce (ardhasítiká); or those who live by their own physical exertion (svavíryopajívinah) may cultivate such fields for ¼th or 1/5th of the produce grown; or they may pay (to the king) as much as they can without entailing any hardship upon themselves (anavasitam bhágam), with the exception of their own private lands that are difficult to cultivate.

Those who cultivate irrigating by manual labour (hastaprávartimam) shall pay 1/5th of the produce as water-rate (udakabhágam); by carrying water on shoulders (skandhaprávartimam) ¼th of the produce; by water-lifts (srotoyantraprávartimam), ⅓rd of the produce; and by raising water from rivers, lakes, tanks, and wells (nadisarastatákakúpodghátam), ⅓rd or ¼th of the produce.

The superintendent shall cultivate wet crops (kedára), winter crops (haimana), or summer crops (graishmika) based on the availability of laborers and water. Rice and similar crops are considered the best to grow (jyáshtha), vegetables (shanda) are of medium difficulty, and sugarcane (ikshu) is the most challenging (pratyavarah) because it is prone to various issues and requires significant care and cost to harvest.

Lands that are beaten by river foam (phenághátah), such as riverbanks, are ideal for growing plants like pumpkins, gourds, and other vines (valliphala). Areas frequently flooded (paríváhánta) are good for growing long pepper, grapes (mridvíká), and sugarcane. The areas near wells are best suited for growing vegetables and roots, while low-lying grounds (hariníparyantáh) are suitable for growing green crops. The spaces between rows of crops are suitable for planting fragrant plants, medicinal herbs, cascus roots (usínara), híra (?), beraka (?), pindáluka (lac), and similar plants.

Medicinal herbs that typically grow in marshy areas should be planted not only in suitable grounds but also in pots (sthályam). Grain seeds need to be exposed to mist and heat (tushárapáyanamushnam cha) for seven nights, while kosi seeds should be treated the same way for three nights. The cut ends of sugarcane and similar seeds (kándabíjánam) should be coated with a mixture of honey, clarified butter, hog fat, and cow dung. Bulbous root seeds (kanda) should be coated with honey and clarified butter, while cotton seeds (asthibíja) should be treated with cow dung. Water pits at the roots of trees should be burned and manured with cow bones and dung at the appropriate times.

Once the seeds sprout, they should be fertilized with a fresh haul of small fish and watered with the milk of the snuhi plant (Euphorbia Antiquorum).

Where there is the smoke caused by burning tWhere there is smoke created by burning the essence of cotton seeds and the shed skin of a snake, snakes will not stay in that area.

When sowing seeds, always begin by planting a handful of seeds soaked in water along with a piece of gold. While doing this, recite the following mantra:

"Prajápatye Kasyapáya dévája namah. Sadá Sítá medhyatám déví bíjéshu cha dhanéshu cha. Chandaváta hé."

This means: "Salutations to the god Prajápati Kasyapa. May agriculture always thrive, and may the Goddess reside in both seeds and wealth. Channdavata he."

Provisions should be provided to watchmen, slaves, and laborers according to the amount of work they complete. They shall receive a monthly wage of one and a quarter pana. Artisans shall also be compensated with wages and provisions based on the amount of work they do.

People who are well-versed in the Vedas and those practicing penance may take ripe flowers and fruits from the fields to worship their gods, as well as rice and barley for performing the ágrayana, a sacrificial ceremony marking the beginning of the harvest season. Similarly, those who make a living by gleaning grains from fields may collect leftover grains after the main harvest has been removed.

Grains and other crops should be gathered immediately after each harvest. A wise person leaves nothing behind in the fields, not even chaff. Once harvested, crops should be stacked in tall piles or shaped into turrets. The piles should not be packed too tightly, and their tops should not be small or low. Threshing floors from different fields should be located near each other. Workers in the fields should always have access to water but not to fire.

[Thus ends Chapter XXIV, "The Superintendent of Agriculture" in Book II, "The Duties of Government Superintendents" of the Arthasástra of Kautilya. End of the forty-fifth chapter from the beginning.]

CHAPTER XXV. THE SUPERINTENDENT OF LIQUOR.

By employing men skilled in the production of liquor and ferments (kinva), the Superintendent of Liquor will manage the liquor trade not only in forts and rural areas but also in military camps. Based on the supply and demand (krayavikrayavasena), the sale of liquor can either be centralized or spread out.

A fine of 600 panas will be imposed on all violators involved in the liquor trade, except for those who are manufacturers, buyers, or sellers. Liquor must not be taken out of villages, and liquor shops should not be located too close to each other.

To prevent workers from neglecting their tasks, and Aryas (noble people) from compromising their dignity and virtuous conduct, and to avoid irresponsible behavior by troublemakers, liquor should only be sold to trustworthy individuals in small quantities—one-fourth or half-a-kudumba, one kudumba, half-a-prastha, or one prastha. People of known good character may be permitted to take liquor out of the shop.

Alternatively, everyone may be required to consume liquor inside the shops to detect any stolen goods or items of value like sealed deposits, unsealed deposits, items given for repair, or stolen goods that customers may have obtained unlawfully. If customers are found with gold or other possessions that do not belong to them, the superintendent will arrange for their arrest outside the shop. Similarly, those who spend excessively or beyond their means will also be arrested.

Fresh liquor should not be sold below its proper price, except for low-quality liquor, which may be sold elsewhere or given to slaves or workers as payment. It can also be used as a drink for draft animals or as food for pigs.

Liquor shops should have several rooms, each with separate beds and seats. The drinking room should have fragrances, flower garlands, water, and other amenities suitable to the season to ensure customers' comfort.

Spies positioned in the shops will observe whether the customers' spending is normal or unusual and whether there are any unfamiliar faces. They will also assess the value of the clothing, jewelry, and gold left by customers who may be intoxicated.

When customers under intoxication lose any of their belongings, the merchants of the shop shall not only make good the loss but also pay an equivalent fine. Merchants seated in half-closed rooms shall observe the appearance of local and foreign customers who, in real or false guise of Aryas, lie down in intoxication along with their beautiful mistresses.

Of various kinds of liquor such as medaka, prasanna, ásava, arista, maireya, and madhu:

Medaka is manufactured with one drona of water, half an ádaka of rice, and three prastha of kinva (ferment).

Twelve ádhakas of flour (pishta), five prastha of kinva (ferment), with the addition of spices (játisambhára) together with the bark and fruits of putraká (a species of tree), constitute prasanná.

One hundred palas of kapittha (Feronia Elephantum), 500 palas of phánita (sugar), and one prastha of honey (madhu) form ásava.

With an increase of one-quarter of the above ingredients, a superior kind of ásava is manufactured; and when the same ingredients are lessened to the extent of one-quarter each, it becomes of an inferior quality.

The preparation of various kinds of arista for various diseases is to be learned from physicians.

A sour gruel or decoction of the bark of meshasringi (a kind of poison) mixed with jaggery (guda) and with the powder of long pepper and black pepper or with the powder of triphala (a mixture of 1 Terminalia Chebula, 2 Terminalia Bellerica, and 3 Phyllanthus Emblica) forms Maireya.

To all kinds of liquor mixed with jaggery, the powder of triphala is always added.

The juice of grapes is termed madhu. Its own native place (svadesa) is the commentary on such of its various forms as kápisáyana and hárahúraka.

One drona of either boiled or unboiled paste of másha (Phraseolus Radiatus), three parts more of rice, and one karsha of morata (Alangium Hexapetalum) and similar ingredients form kinva (ferment).

In the making of medaka and prasanna, five karshas of the powder of each of páthá (Clypea Hermandifolia), lodhra (Symplocos Racemosa), tejovati (Piper Chaba), eláváluka (Solanum Melongena), honey, the juice of grapes (madhurasa), priyangu (panic seeds), dáruharidra (a species of turmeric), black pepper, and long pepper are added as sambhára, the necessary spices.

The decoction of madhúka (Bassia Latifolia) mixed with granulated sugar (katasarkará), when added to prasanna, gives it a pleasing color.

For ásava, the required amount of spices includes one karsha of the powder of each of chocha (bark of cinnamon), chitraka (Plumbago Zeylanica), vilanga, and gajapippalí (Scindapsus Officinalis), and two karshas of the powder of each of kramuka (betel nut), madhúka (Bassia Latifolia), mustá (Cyprus Rotundus), and lodhra (Symplocos Racemosa).

The addition of one-tenth of the above ingredients (such as chocha, kramuka, etc.) is referred to as bíjabandha.

The same spices that are added to prasanná are also added to white liquor (svetasurá).

The liquor that is produced from mango fruits (sahakárasurá) may have a higher concentration of mango essence (rasottara) or spices (bíjottara). It is called mahásura when it contains sambhára (the spices described above).

When a handful (antarnakho mushtih, meaning as much as can be held in the hand while bending the fingers so the nails are hidden) of the powder of granulated sugar dissolved in the decoction of moratá (Alangium Hexapetalum), palása (Butea Frondosa), dattúra (Datura Fastuosa), karanja (Robinia Mitis), meshasringa (a kind of poison), and the bark of milky trees (kshiravriksha), mixed with half of the paste made from the powders of lodhra (Symplocos Racemosa), chitraka (Plumbago Zeylanica), vilanga, páthá (Clypea Hermandifolia), mustá (Cyprus Rotundus), kaláya (leguminous seeds), dáruharidra (Amomum Xanthorrhizon), indívara (blue lotus), satapushpa (Anethum Sowa), apámárga (Achyranthes Aspera), saptaparna (Echites Scholaris), and nimba (Nimba Melia) is added to a kumbha of liquor payable by the king, it makes the liquor very pleasant. Five palas of phánita (sugar) are added to the above mixture to enhance its flavor.

On special occasions (krityeshu), families (kutumbinah) shall be permitted to make white liquor (svetasura), arishta for medicinal use, and other types of liquor.

During festivals, fairs (samája), and pilgrimages, the right to manufacture liquor for four days (chaturahassaurikah) shall be granted.

The Superintendent shall collect daily fines (daivasikamatyayam), or license fees, from those who are allowed to produce liquor on these occasions.

Women and children shall be assigned the task of collecting 'sura' and 'kinva' (ferment).

Those who deal in liquor other than that made by the king shall pay a five percent toll.

Regarding sura, medaka, arishta, wine, phalámla (acid drinks made from fruits), and ámlasídhu (spirit distilled from molasses):

After determining the day's sale of these types of liquor, the difference between royal and public measures (mánavyáji), and the surplus profit made from such sales, the Superintendent shall set the amount of compensation (vaidharana) owed to the king. This compensation applies to local or foreign merchants who cause loss to the king's liquor trade. The Superintendent shall always choose the most beneficial course of action.

[Thus ends Chapter XXV, "The Superintendent of Liquor" in Book II, "The Duties of Government Superintendents," of the Arthasástra of Kautilya. End of the forty-sixth chapter from the beginning.]

CHAPTER XXVI. THE SUPERINTENDENT OF SLAUGHTER-HOUSE.

When a person traps, kills, or harms deer, bison, birds, and fish that are protected by the state or live in state-protected forests (abhayáranya), they shall be punished with the highest fine.

Householders who trespass in protected forests will be punished with the middlemost fine.

If someone traps, kills, or harms either fish or birds that do not prey on other animals, they shall be fined 26¾ panas. If the same is done to deer or other animals, the fine will be twice as much.

For captured wild animals, the superintendent shall take one-sixth; for fish and birds of prey, they will take one-tenth or more, and for deer and other animals (mrigapasu), one-tenth or more as toll.

One-sixth of live animals, such as birds and beasts, shall be released in state-protected forests.

Elephants, horses, or animals resembling a human, bull, or donkey living in oceans, as well as fish in tanks, lakes, channels, and rivers, and game-birds such as krauncha (a kind of heron), utkrosaka (osprey), dátyúha (a type of cuckoo), hamsa (flamingo), chakraváka (brahmany duck), jivanjívaka (a type of pheasant), bhringarája (Lanius Malabaricus), chakora (partridge), mattakokila (cuckoo), peacocks, parrots, and maina (madanasárika), along with other auspicious animals, both birds and beasts, shall be protected from any harm.

Those who break this rule shall be punished with the first level of amercement.

Butchers must sell only fresh and boneless meat of animals (mrigapasu) that were just killed.

If they sell bony meat, they shall provide an equal compensation (pratipákam). If any weight is lost due to using a false balance, they shall pay eight times the weight difference.

Calves, bulls, and milch cows are not to be slaughtered. Those who slaughter or torture them to death shall be fined 50 panas.

The meat of animals killed outside the slaughterhouse (parisúnam), headless, legless, or boneless meat, rotten meat, and the meat of animals that have suddenly died shall not be sold. Otherwise, a fine of 12 panas will be imposed.

Vicious animals such as cattle, wild beasts, elephants (vyala), and fish living in state-protected forests shall, if they become dangerous, be trapped and killed outside the forest preserve.

[Thus ends Chapter XXVI, "The Superintendent of Slaughterhouse" in Book II, "The Duties of Government Superintendents" of the Arthasástra of Kautilya. End of the forty-seventh chapter from the beginning.]

CHAPTER XXVII. THE SUPERINTENDENT OF PROSTITUTES.

The Superintendent of Prostitutes shall appoint a prostitute (ganiká), whether born into a prostitute's family or not, and known for her beauty, youth, and accomplishments, to the king's court with an annual salary of 1,000 panas.

A rival prostitute (pratiganiká) shall also be appointed with half that salary (kutumbárdhéna).

If the appointed prostitute goes abroad or dies, her daughter or sister shall take her place and receive her property and salary. Alternatively, her mother may substitute another prostitute. If none of these are available, the king shall take possession of her property.

To enhance the prestige of the prostitutes serving the king, who hold the royal umbrella, golden pitcher, and fan while attending him on his litter, throne, or chariot, they shall be ranked according to their beauty and splendid jewelry, into first, middle, and highest ranks. Their salaries shall be fixed accordingly, in thousands of panas.

A prostitute who has lost her beauty shall be appointed as a nurse (mátriká).

To regain her freedom, a prostitute shall pay 24,000 panas as ransom, and the son of a prostitute shall pay 12,000 panas.

From the age of eight, a prostitute shall perform music before the king.

Those prostitutes, female slaves, and elderly women who are no longer able to serve in terms of enjoyment (bhagnabhogáh) shall work in the king's storehouse or kitchen.

A prostitute who chooses to place herself under the protection of a private individual and stops attending the king's court must pay a monthly fee of one pana-and-a-quarter to the government.

The superintendent shall oversee the earnings, inheritance, income (áya), expenditure, and future income (áyati) of every prostitute and also curb their extravagant spending.

If a prostitute entrusts her jewelry to anyone other than her mother, she shall be fined 4¼ panas.

If she sells or mortgages her property (svapateyam), she shall be fined 50¼ panas.

A prostitute shall be fined 24 panas for defamation, twice that amount for causing injury, and 50¼ panas, along with 1½ panas, for cutting off someone's ear.

When a man forces a prostitute against her will or has relations with a prostitute girl (kumári), he shall be punished with the highest amercement. However, if he has relations with a willing underage prostitute, he shall be punished with the first amercement.

If a man confines or abducts a prostitute against her will, or disfigures her by causing injury, he shall be fined 1,000 panas or more, up to twice the amount of her ransom (nishkraya), depending on the severity of the crime and the social position of the prostitute (sthánaviseshena).

If a man harms a prostitute appointed at the court (praptádhikáram), he shall be fined three times the amount of her ransom.

If a man harms the mother, young daughter, or rúpadási (a female attendant) of a prostitute, he shall be punished with the highest amercement.

In all cases, for a first-time offense, the punishment shall be the first amercement; for a second-time offense, twice that amount; for a third-time offense, three times that amount. For a fourth offense, the king may impose any punishment he deems appropriate.

If a prostitute refuses to yield her person under the king's orders, she shall receive 1,000 lashes with a whip or pay a fine of 5,000 panas.

If a prostitute refuses to provide her services after receiving payment, she shall be fined twice the amount of the fees.

If, in her own house, a prostitute denies her paramour enjoyment, she shall be fined eight times the amount of the fees unless the paramour is unassociable due to disease or personal defects.

If a prostitute murders her paramour, she shall be burned alive or thrown into water.

If a paramour steals the jewelry or money of a prostitute, or deceives her by not paying the agreed fees, he shall be fined eight times that amount.

Every prostitute shall report her daily earnings (bhoga), future income (áyati), and the identity of her paramour (under her influence) to the superintendent.

These same rules shall apply to actors, dancers, singers, musicians, buffoons (vágjivana), mimics (kusílava), rope-dancers (plavaka), jugglers (saubhika), wandering bards or heralds (chárana), pimps, and unchaste women.

When performers of these types come from foreign lands to hold shows, they shall pay 5 panas as a license fee (prekshávetana).

Every prostitute (rúpájivá) shall pay twice the amount of one day's earnings (bhogadvigunam) to the government each month.

Those who teach prostitutes, female slaves, and actresses in arts such as singing, playing musical instruments, reading, dancing, acting, writing, painting, playing instruments like the vina, pipe, and drum, reading the thoughts of others, making scents and garlands, massage techniques, and the art of attracting and captivating others, shall be provided maintenance by the state.

They (the teachers) shall train the sons of prostitutes to become chief performers (rangopajívi) on the stage.

The wives of actors and others of similar professions, who have been taught various languages and the use of signals (sanja), shall, along with their relatives, be employed to detect wrongdoers and to eliminate or mislead foreign spies.

[Thus ends Chapter XXVII, "The Superintendent of Prostitutes" in Book II, "The Duties of Government Superintendents," of the

Arthasástra of Kautilya. End of the forty-eighth chapter from the beginning.]

CHAPTER XXVIII. THE SUPERINTENDENT OF SHIPS.

THE Superintendent of Ships shall oversee the records related to navigation, not only on oceans and river mouths but also on natural or artificial lakes and rivers near fortified cities such as stháníya and others.

Villages located on seashores or riverbanks and lakes shall pay a fixed amount of tax (kliptam). Fishermen must give one-sixth of their catch as a fee for their fishing license (naukáhátakam). Merchants shall pay the customary toll levied in port towns, and passengers arriving on the king's ship shall pay the appropriate sailing fees (yátrávetanam). Those who use the king's boats for gathering conch shells and pearls shall pay the appropriate hire (naukáhátakam), or they may use their own boats.

The duties of the superintendent of mines will also apply to the superintendent of conch shells and pearls. The superintendent of ships must closely follow the customs of commercial towns and the orders of the superintendent of towns (pattana, or port town). When a ship battered by weather arrives at a port, he shall show it fatherly care and concern.

Ships carrying merchandise that has been damaged by water may either be exempted from tolls or have their tolls reduced by half, allowing them to depart when it is time to sail. Ships that dock at harbors along their journey may be asked to pay tolls. Pirate ships (himsríká), vessels bound for enemy territories, and those violating the rules and customs of port towns shall be destroyed.

Large boats (mahánávah) equipped with a captain (sásaka), a steersman (niyámaka), and crew members to handle the ropes, hold the sickle, and pour out water, shall be launched on large rivers that cannot be forded even during winter and summer. Small boats shall be used in rivers that overflow during the rainy season.

Fording or crossing rivers without permission shall be prohibited to prevent traitors from escaping. If someone crosses a river at an improper place or during unusual times, they shall be punished with the first amercement. If a person crosses a river at the regular place and time without permission, they shall be fined 26¾ panas.

Exemptions to cross rivers at any time and place shall be granted to fishermen, carriers of firewood, grass, flowers, and fruits, gardeners, vegetable dealers, herdsmen, people pursuing suspected criminals, messengers following other messengers, servants delivering supplies, provisions, and orders to the army, those using their own ferries, and those supplying villages in marshy districts with seeds, essentials, commodities, and other necessary items.

Bráhmans, ascetics (pravrajita), children, the elderly, the afflicted, royal messengers, and pregnant women shall be provided with free passes by the superintendent to cross rivers.

Foreign merchants who frequently visit the country and are known to local merchants shall be permitted to land in port towns.

The following individuals shall be arrested: anyone abducting another's wife or daughter, someone carrying off another's wealth, a suspicious person, someone with a disturbed appearance, anyone without baggage, a person attempting to conceal or evade notice of a valuable load, someone who has just changed their attire, anyone who has renounced or removed their usual garb, someone pretending to be an ascetic, someone feigning illness, anyone who appears alarmed, someone secretly carrying valuable items or on a secret mission, anyone carrying weapons or explosives (agniyoga), someone holding poison, and anyone who has traveled a long distance without a pass.

A minor quadruped, as well as a man carrying some load, shall pay one másha. A head-load, a load carried on shoulders (káyabhárah), a cow, and a horse shall each pay 2 máshas. A camel and a buffalo shall each pay 4 máshas. A small cart (laghuyána) shall pay 5 máshas, and a cart of medium size drawn by bulls (golingam) shall pay 6 máshas, while a big cart (sakata) shall pay 7 máshas. A head-load of merchandise shall pay ¼ másha, which explains the toll for other types of loads. In big rivers, ferry-fees are double the amounts listed above.

Villages near marshy areas shall provide the ferry-men with the prescribed amount of food and wages. At boundaries, ferry-men shall collect tolls, carriage-cess, and road-cess. They shall also confiscate the property of anyone traveling without a pass. The Superintendent of Boats shall compensate for losses caused by a boat's failure due to overloading, sailing at the wrong time or place, lack of ferry-men, or inadequate repairs. Boats should be launched between the months of Ashádha (excluding the first seven days) and Kártika, with the ferryman's evidence recorded and the daily income remitted.

[Thus ends Chapter XXVIII, "The Superintendent of Ships" in Book II, "The Duties of Government Superintendents" of the Arthasástra of Kautilya. End of the forty-ninth chapter from the beginning.]

CHAPTER XXIX. THE SUPERINTENDENT OF COWS.

The Superintendent of Cows shall supervise the following:

(1) Herds maintained for wages (vétanópagráhikam), (2) Herds surrendered for a fixed amount of dairy produce (karapratikara), (3) Useless and abandoned herds (bhagnotsrishtakam), (4) Herds maintained for a share in dairy produce (bhágánupravishtam), (5) Classes of herds (vrajaparyagram), (6) Cattle that strayed (nashtam), (7) Cattle that are irrecoverably lost (vinashtam), and (8) The amassed quantity of milk and clarified butter.

(1) When a cowherd, buffalo-herdsman, milker, churner, and hunter (lubdhaka), all fed by wages, graze milch cows (dhenu) in

groups of hundreds (satam satam)—since if they graze the herds for the profit of milk and ghee, they might starve the calves to death—this system of rearing cattle is termed "herds maintained for wages."

(2) When a single person rears a hundred heads of cattle (rúpasatam), comprising equal numbers of aged cows, milch cows, pregnant cows, heifers, and calves (vatsatari), and gives the owner 8 várakas of clarified butter annually along with the branded skin of any dead cows, this system is called "herds surrendered for a fixed amount of dairy produce."

(3) When those who rear a hundred heads of cattle, made up of equal numbers of afflicted cattle, crippled cattle, cattle that can only be milked by a familiar person, cattle that are difficult to milk, and cattle that kill their own calves, give a share of the dairy produce in return to the owner, it is termed "useless and abandoned herd."

(4) When, out of fear of cattle-lifting enemies (parachakrátavibhayát), cattle are placed under the protection of the superintendent, who receives 1/10th of the dairy produce for this service, it is termed "herds maintained for a share in dairy produce."

(5) When the superintendent classifies cattle into categories such as calves, steers, tameable ones, draught oxen, bulls to be trained for yoking, bulls kept for breeding, cattle fit only for meat supply, buffaloes, and draught buffaloes; and female calves, female steers, heifers, pregnant cows, milch cows, barren cows—whether cows or buffaloes—calves that are one or two months old, as well as those that are even younger; and when he brands all of them, including the calves that are one or two months old, along with any stray cattle that have remained unclaimed for a month or two in the herds; and when he registers their branded marks, natural marks, color, and the distance between their horns, that system is known as "class of herds."

(6) When an animal is carried off by thieves, ends up in another herd, or strays without being recognized, it is considered "lost."

(7) When an animal gets stuck in a quagmire or falls off a precipice, dies from disease or old age, drowns in water, is killed by the fall of a tree or riverbank, is beaten to death with a staff or stone, struck by lightning, devoured by a tiger, bitten by a cobra, carried off by a crocodile, or caught in a forest fire, it is deemed "irrecoverably lost."

Cowherds shall make every effort to keep their cattle safe from such dangers.

Anyone who injures or causes harm to a cow, or who steals or helps another steal a cow, shall be sentenced to death.

If a person substitutes an animal bearing the royal brand with a privately owned one, they shall be punished with the first amercement.

When someone retrieves local cattle from thieves, they shall receive the promised reward (panitam rúpam), and if someone rescues foreign cattle from thieves, they shall receive half its value.

Cowherds must provide care and remedies to calves, elderly cows, or cows suffering from diseases.

They shall graze the herds in forests that are specifically assigned as pasture grounds for various seasons, where thieves, tigers, and other dangerous animals are driven away by hunters with the help of their hounds. To keep away snakes and tigers and as a way to track the location of the herds, bells shall be tied around the necks of timid cattle. Cowherds shall allow their cattle to enter rivers or lakes that are uniformly deep, wide, and free from mud and crocodiles, and they must protect them from any dangers in these circumstances.

Whenever an animal is captured by a thief, a tiger, a snake, or a crocodile, or if the animal becomes weak due to old age or illness, cowherds must report it; otherwise, they will be required to compensate for the loss.

If an animal dies naturally, the cowherds shall surrender the skin with the brand mark if it is a cow or buffalo; the skin with the ear (karnalakshanam) if it is a goat or sheep; the tail with the branded skin if it is a donkey or camel; and simply the skin if it is a young animal. In addition to the above, they must also return the fat (vasti), bile, marrow (snáyu), teeth, hooves, horns, and bones.

Cowherds may sell either fresh or dried meat. They shall give buttermilk to the dogs and hogs as drink, and keep a small amount of buttermilk in a bronze vessel for preparing their own meal. They may also use curdled milk or cheese (kíláta) to make their oilcakes more appetizing (ghánapinyáka-kledartha).

Anyone who sells a cow from the herds shall pay the king one-fourth of the cow's value (rúpa). During the rainy season, autumn, and the first part of winter (hemanta), the cows shall be milked twice a day (morning and evening). During the latter part of winter, as well as spring and summer, they shall be milked only once in the morning. Any cowherd who milks a cow a second time during these seasons shall have their thumb cut off.

If a cowherd misses the proper time for milking, he will lose the profit from that milk. The same rule applies if a cowherd neglects the opportune time to pierce a bull's nose for a ring, or to tame or train it for the yoke.

When one drona of cow's milk is churned, it will yield one prastha of butter. The same quantity of buffalo's milk will yield one-seventh prastha more, and milk from goats or sheep will yield half a prastha more. The exact amount of butter in all types of milk should be determined by churning, since the supply of milk and butter depends on factors such as the nature of the soil and the quality and quantity of the fodder and water.

If someone causes a bull from a herd to fight with another bull, he shall be punished with the first amercement. If the bull is injured in such a fight, the person will be punished with the highest amercement.

When grazing, cattle should be grouped into herds of ten, organized by color. Depending on the protective strength of the cowherds and the capacity of the cattle to travel, cowherds should decide whether to graze the cattle near or far.

Sheep and other animals should be shorn of their wool every six months. The same rules apply to herds of horses, donkeys, camels, and pigs.

For bulls fitted with nose-rings and capable of carrying heavy loads or traveling as fast as horses, the daily diet should consist of half a bhára of meadow grass (yavasa), twice that amount of ordinary grass (trina), one tulá (100 palas) of oilcakes, ten ádhakas of bran, five palas of salt (mukhalavanam), one kudumba of oil for rubbing on the nose (nasya), one prastha of drink (pána), one tulá of meat, one ádhaka of curis, one drona of barley or cooked másha (Phaseolus radiatus), and one drona of milk. In place of milk, half an ádhaka of surá (liquor), one prastha of oil or ghee (sneha), ten palas of sugar or jaggery, and one pala of ginger root (sringibera) may be given.

The same provisions, reduced by one-quarter, will serve for mules, cows, and donkeys, while buffaloes and camels should be provided with double the quantity of these rations. Draught oxen and milk cows should receive food based on how long the oxen are worked and how much milk the cows produce. All cattle should be given plenty of fodder and water.

This is how herds of cattle should be raised and maintained.

A herd of 100 donkeys or mules should contain five male animals, a herd of goats or sheep should have ten, and a herd of ten cows or buffaloes should have four male animals.

[Thus ends Chapter XXIX, "The Superintendent of Cows" in Book II, "The Duties of Government Superintendents" of the Arthasástra of Kautilya. End of the fiftieth chapter from the beginning.]

CHAPTER XXX. THE SUPERINTENDENT OF HORSES.

The Superintendent of Horses shall record the breed, age, color, identifying marks, group or class, and the native place of each horse. He shall categorize the horses as follows: (1) those kept in sale-houses for sale (panyágárikam), (2) those recently purchased (krayopágatam), (3) those captured in wars (áhavalabdham), (4) those of local breed (ájátam), (5) those sent there for assistance (sáháyyakágatam), (6) those mortgaged (panasthitam), and (7) those temporarily housed in stables (yávatkálikam).

He shall report to the king about horses that are considered inauspicious, crippled, or diseased.

Every horseman shall know how to properly manage and make economic use of whatever provisions he has received from the king's treasury and storehouse.

The superintendent shall have stables constructed that are spacious enough to accommodate the number of horses to be kept. The stables should be twice as wide as the length of a horse, with four doors facing the four cardinal directions. The central floor should be designed for horses to roll on, and the front of the stable should have wooden seats at the entrance. The stable should house animals like monkeys, peacocks, red spotted deer (prishata), mongoose, partridges (chakora), parrots, and maina birds (sárika).

Each horse's room should be four times as wide or long as the length of the horse, with a central floor paved with smooth wooden planks, and separate compartments for fodder (khádanakoshthakam). There should also be passages for the removal of urine and dung, and the door should face either north or east. The orientation of the quarters (digvibhága) may be based on practical considerations or in relation to the position of the building.

Steeds, stallions, and colts shall be housed separately.

A horse that has just given birth to a colt shall be given a drink of 1 prastha of clarified butter for the first three days. Afterward, it shall be fed 1 prastha of flour (saktu) and made to drink oil mixed with medicine for ten nights. Following this period, it shall be given cooked grains, meadow grass, and other food appropriate for the season.

A colt that is ten days old shall be given a kudumba of flour mixed with ¼ kudumba of clarified butter and 1 prastha of milk until it is six months old. Afterward, the rations shall be increased by half as much each month, with the addition of 1 prastha of barley until it turns three years old. From three to four years old, it shall be fed one drona of barley. By the age of four or five, the colt reaches full development and becomes fit for work.

The face (mukha) of the best horse measures 32 angulas; its body length is five times the length of its face, its shank measures 20 angulas, and its height is four times the length of its shank. Horses of medium and lower sizes are shorter by two and three angulas respectively in these measurements.

The circumference (parínáha) of the best horse is 100 angulas, while medium and smaller horses are five parts (panchabhágávaram) smaller in measurement.

The diet for the best horse consists of 2 dronas of any grain, such as rice (sáli or vríhi), barley, or panic seeds (priyangu), which may be soaked or cooked, as well as cooked mudga (Phraseolus Mungo) or másha (Phraseolus Radiatus). Additionally, the horse should receive 1 prastha of oil, 5 palas of salt, 50 palas of flesh, 1 ádhaka of broth (rasa) or 2 ádhakas of curd, and 5 palas of sugar (kshára) to make its diet more palatable, along with 1 prastha of liquor (súrá) or 2 prasthas of milk.

This same quantity of food and drink shall be provided to horses that are fatigued from long journeys or from carrying loads.

For care, 1 prastha of oil should be given for enema (anuvásana), 1 kudumba of oil for rubbing over the nose, and 1,000 palas of meadow grass. Twice as much ordinary grass (trina) shall also be provided, and hay or grass shall be spread over an area of 6 aratnis.

The same quantity of rations, less by one-quarter, is given to horses of medium and smaller sizes. A draught horse or stallion of medium size should receive the same amount as the best horse, while those of smaller size will receive the same quantity as a horse of medium size. Steeds and párasamas are provided with one-quarter less rations. Colts are given half the rations provided to steeds. This outlines how rations are distributed.

Those who prepare the food for horses, grooms, and veterinary surgeons are also entitled to a share of the rations (pratisvádabhajah). Stallions that have become incapacitated due to old age, illness, or the hardships of war, and are thus no longer fit for battle but only consume food, should be allowed to mate with mares for breeding purposes in the interest of the citizens and the country.

The best horse breeds come from the regions of Kámbhoja, Sindhu, Aratta, and Vanáyu. Those from Báhlíka, Pápeya, Sauvira, and Taitala are of middle quality, and all others are considered ordinary (avaráh). These three types of horses—best, middle, and ordinary—can be trained for war or riding, depending on whether they are fierce (tíkshna), gentle (bhadra), or slow (manda).

The regular training of a horse is meant to prepare it for war (sánnáhyam karma). The different types of riding are circular movement (valgana), slow movement (níchairgata), jumping (langhana), gallop (dhorana), and responding to signals (nároshtra).

There are different styles of circular movement (valgana): Aupavenuka, vardhmánaka, yamaka, álídhapluta, vrithatta, and trivacháli. The same types of movements, but with the head and ears kept upright, are called slow movements. These are performed in sixteen ways: Prakírnaka, prakírnottara, nishanna, pársvánuvritta, úrmimárga, sarabhakrídita, sarabhapluta, tritála, báhyánuvritta, panchapáni, simháyata, svádhúta, klishta, slághita, brimhita, and pushpábhikírna.

Different forms of jumping include jumping like a monkey (kapipluta), jumping like a frog (bhekapluta), sudden jumping (ekapluta), jumping with one leg (ekapádapluta), leaping like a cuckoo (kokila-samchári), dashing with the chest almost touching the ground (urasya), and leaping like a crane (bakasamchari).

Galloping is classified as flying like a vulture (kánka), dashing like a water-duck (várikánaka), running like a peacock (máyúra), half the speed of a peacock (ardhmáyúra), dashing like a mangoose (nákula), half the speed of a mangoose (ardha-nákula), running like a hog (váráha), and half the speed of a hog (ardha-váráha).

Movement that follows a signal is called nároshtra. Carriage horses can travel distances of six, nine, or twelve yojanas in a day.

Five, eight, and ten yojanas are the distances that should be covered by riding horses. Trotting according to its strength, trotting with good breathing, and trotting while carrying a load on its back are the three kinds of trot. Trotting according to strength, trotting combined with circular movement, ordinary trotting, medium-speed trotting, and regular speed are also different types of trotting.

Qualified instructors shall give directions for making proper ropes that will be used to tether the horses. Charioteers shall take care of the manufacturing of all necessary war equipment for horses. Veterinary surgeons shall administer the required treatments to prevent the horse's body from growing too much or shrinking and adjust the horse's diet according to seasonal changes.

Those who move the horses, those who tie them in the stables, those responsible for supplying meadow grass, those who cook grains for the horses, stable guards, grooms, and those responsible for treating poisons should perform their assigned duties properly, or they will forfeit their daily wages.

Anyone who rides a horse that is kept inside the stables either for rituals like waving lights or for medical treatment will be fined 12 panas. If, due to defects in medicine or carelessness in treatment, a disease worsens, a fine of twice the cost of the treatment shall be imposed. If the wrong medicine is administered, or if the treatment is neglected, resulting in an adverse outcome, the fine will be equivalent to the value of the horse. The same rule applies to cows, buffaloes, goats, and sheep.

Horses must be washed, covered with sandalwood powder, and adorned with garlands twice a day. On new moon days, sacrifices should be made to Bhútas, and on full moon days, auspicious hymns should be chanted. Not only on the ninth day of the Asvayuja month, but also at the start and end of journeys, and during times of illness, priests should wave lights to invoke blessings on the horses.

CHAPTER XXXI. THE SUPERINTENDENT OF ELEPHANTS.

The Superintendent of Elephants shall take proper steps to protect elephant forests and supervise the operations regarding the standing or lying in stables of elephants, whether male, female, or young, when they are tired after training. He shall also examine the proportional quantity of rations and grass, the extent of training given to them, their accoutrements and ornaments, as well as the work of elephant doctors, trainers of elephants in warlike feats, and grooms such as drivers, binders, and others.

An elephant stable shall be constructed to be twice as broad and twice as high as the length of the elephant, with separate apartments for female elephants, a projected entrance, and posts called kumári, with the door facing either east or north.

The space in front of the smooth posts, where elephants are tied, shall form a square with one side equal to the length of the elephant and shall be paved with smooth wooden planks and provided with holes for the removal of urine and dung.

The space where an elephant lies down shall be as broad as the length of the elephant and be equipped with a flat form raised to half the height of the elephant for leaning on.

Elephants used in war or for riding shall be kept inside the fort, while those still being tamed or of bad temper shall be kept outside.

The first and the seventh of the eight divisions of the day are the two times for bathing the elephants. The time following these two periods is for their food. Forenoon is designated for exercise, while the afternoon is the time for drinking. Two parts of the night are reserved for sleep, and one-third of the night is spent in staying alert.

Summer is the season for capturing elephants.

Only elephants that are 20 years old should be captured.

Young elephants (bikka), infatuated elephants (mugdha), elephants without tusks, diseased elephants, those suckling their young (dhenuká), and female elephants (hastiní) shall not be captured.

An elephant that is seven aratnis tall, nine aratnis long, and ten aratnis in circumference, and is therefore inferred to be 40 years old, is considered the best.

An elephant that is 30 years old is of middle quality, while one that is 25 years old is of the lowest class.

The diet for the last two classes of elephants shall be reduced by one-quarter based on their classification.

For an elephant measuring seven aratnis in height, the rations shall include 1 drona of rice, ½ ádhaka of oil, 3 prasthas of ghee, 10 palas of salt, 50 palas of meat, 1 ádhaka of broth (rasa), or twice that quantity (2 ádhakas) of curd. To make the food flavorful, 10 palas of sugar (kshára), 1 ádhaka of liquor, or twice the quantity of milk (payah), shall be added. For external use, 1 prastha of oil shall be used to smear over the body, and 1/8 prastha of oil for the head and for lighting the stables. Additionally, 2 bháras of meadow grass, 2¼ bháras of ordinary grass (sashpa), 2½ bháras of dry grass, and any amount of stalks of various pulses (kadankara) shall be given.

An elephant in rut (atyarála) and 8 aratnis tall shall receive the same rations as an elephant of 7 aratnis.

The rest of the elephants, measuring 6 or 5 aratnis in height, shall receive rations proportionate to their size.

A young elephant (bikka) captured for the mere purpose of playing with it shall be fed milk and meadow grass.

The physical attributes of an elephant's splendor are classified as follows: one that is blood-red (samjátalóhita), one that is fleshy, one whose sides are evenly grown (samaliptapakshá), one whose girths are full or equal (samakakshyá), one whose flesh is evenly distributed, one with a smooth back (samatalpatala), and one with a rough surface (játadrónika).

Depending on the seasons and their physical splendor, elephants, whether sharp or slow of sense (bhadra and mandra), as well as elephants possessing characteristics of other beasts, shall be trained and taught to perform suitable tasks.

CHAPTER XXXII. TRAINING OF ELEPHANTS.

Elephants are classified into four categories based on their training: tameable (damya), those trained for war (sánnáhya), those trained for riding (aupaváhya), and rogue elephants (vyála).

Tameable elephants are divided into five groups: those that allow a person to sit on their withers (skandhagata), those that permit being tethered to a post (stambhagata), those that can be taken to water (várigata), those that lie down in pits (apapátagata), and those attached to their herd (yúthagata). All of these elephants should be cared for as attentively as a young elephant (bikka).

Military training consists of seven types: drill (upasthána), turning (samvartana), advancing (samyána), trampling down and killing (vadhávadha), fighting other elephants (hastiyuddha), attacking forts and cities (nágaráyanam), and general warfare.

The first steps in this training include binding the elephants with girths (kakshyákarma), putting on collars (graiveyakakarma), and making them work with their herd (yúthakarma).

Elephants trained for riding are categorized into seven types: those that allow a person to mount while in the company of another elephant (kunjaropaváhya), those that allow riding when led by a war elephant (sánnáhyopaváhya), those taught to trot (dhorana), those trained in various movements (ádhánagatika), those that move with the use of a staff (yashtyupaváhya), those that move with an iron hook (totropaváhya), those that move without the use of whips (suddhopaváhya), and those helpful in hunting.

The initial training steps for these include autumnal work (sáradakarma), rough or mean work (hínakarma), and learning to respond to signals.

Rogue elephants can only be controlled in one way—through punishment. These elephants exhibit a deep distrust of work, are stubborn, unruly, unstable, willful, or behave erratically due to the influence of rut.

Rogue elephants whose training is unsuccessful may be classified as purely roguish (suddha), clever in roguery (suvrata), perverse (vishama), or exhibiting all kinds of vices.

Rogue elephants whose training fails may be classified as purely roguish (suddha), clever in roguery (suvrata), perverse (vishama), or possessing all kinds of vices.

The appropriate types of fetters and other necessary means to control them shall be determined by the elephant doctor. Tether posts (álána), collars, girths, bridles, leg chains, and frontal fetters are some of the different binding instruments used for control.

Hooks, bamboo staffs, and machines (yantra) are also instruments used for handling elephants. Necklaces such as vaijavantí and kshurapramála, along with litters and housings, are the ornaments for elephants.

War accoutrements include mail armor (varma), clubs (totra), arrow bags, and machines. Elephant doctors, trainers, expert riders, and others involved in taking care of elephants, including those who groom them, prepare their food, provide grass, tether them, clean the stables, and watch the stables at night, all have responsibilities in maintaining elephants' well-being.

Elephant doctors, watchmen, sweepers, cooks, and others involved in elephant care shall receive 1 prastha of cooked rice, a handful of oil, and 2 palas of sugar and salt from the storehouse. Additionally, except for the doctors, others shall also receive 10 palas of meat.

Elephant doctors shall provide necessary medical care to elephants that, during journeys, suffer from disease, exhaustion, rut, or old age.

Offenses such as allowing stables to accumulate dirt, failing to provide grass, making an elephant lie on hard, unprepared ground, striking its vital parts, allowing a stranger to ride it, riding it at improper times, leading it through impassable water routes, or letting it enter thick forests are punishable with fines. These fines shall be deducted from the rations and wages owed to the offenders.

During the Cháturmásya period (July, August, September, and October) and at the junction of two seasons, a ritual of waving lights shall be performed three times. Sacrifices to Bhútas for the safety of elephants shall also be carried out on new-moon and full-moon days by commanders.

When it comes to tusks, leaving a portion of the tusk near its root, equal to twice its circumference, the remaining part of the tusk shall be cut off once every 2½ years for elephants born in river-irrigated regions (nadija), and once every 5 years for mountain elephants.

[Thus ends Chapter XXXII, "The Training of Elephants" in Book II, "The Duties of Government Superintendents" of the Arthasástra of Kautilya. End of the fifty-third chapter from the beginning.]

CHAPTER XXXIII. THE SUPERINTENDENT OF CHARIOTS; THE SUPERINTENDENT OF INFANTRY AND THE DUTY OF THE COMMANDER-IN-CHIEF.

The duties of the Superintendent of Horses will also explain those of the Superintendent of Chariots. The Superintendent of Chariots shall oversee the construction of chariots.

The best chariot shall be 10 purushas in height (which is 120 angulas) and 12 purushas in width. Following this model, seven more chariots with the width decreasing by one purusha each time, down to a chariot of 6 purushas in width, shall be made. He shall also construct chariots for gods (devaratha), festal chariots (pushyaratha), battle chariots (sángrámika), travelling chariots (páriyánika), chariots for attacking enemy strongholds (parapurabhiyánika), and training chariots.

He shall assess the skills of troops in shooting arrows, hurling clubs and cudgels, wearing armor, using equipment, driving chariots, fighting while seated in a chariot, and controlling the chariot horses.

He shall also handle the accounts for provisions and wages paid to those either permanently or temporarily employed to make chariots and other necessary items. He must ensure that the workers are content and well-rewarded (yogyarakshanushthánam) and measure the distance of roads.

The same rules apply to the Superintendent of Infantry. This superintendent must understand the exact strength or weakness of hereditary troops (maula), hired troops (bhrita), corporate troops (sreni), as well as the armies of friendly or hostile kings and wild tribes.

He must also be familiar with fighting in lowlands, open battle, fraudulent attacks, fighting under cover of trenches (khanakayuddha), or from heights (ákásayuddha), and fighting during the day and night. Additionally, he must be trained in the necessary drills for such warfare.

He shall be able to assess whether troops are fit or unfit for emergency situations.

With attention to the position of the entire army (chaturangabala), trained in handling all kinds of weapons and leading elephants, horses, and chariots, the Commander-in-Chief must be capable of ordering advance or retreat (áyogamayógam cha).

He must know what type of terrain is more advantageous for his army, the most favorable time for battle, the enemy's strength, how to cause dissension in a united enemy force, how to rally his own scattered troops, how to scatter an enemy's forces, how to lay siege to a fortress, and when to launch a full-scale attack.

Always mindful of the discipline his army must maintain, not just in camping and marching, but in the heat of battle, he shall name the regiments (vyúha) after trumpets, boards, banners, or flags.

[Thus ends Chapter XXXIII, "The Superintendent of Chariots, the Superintendent of Infantry, and the Duties of the Commander-in-Chief" in Book II, "The Duties of Government Superintendents" of the Arthasástra of Kautilya. End of the fifty-fourth chapter from the beginning.]

CHAPTER XXXIV. THE SUPERINTENDENT OF PASSPORTS.

The Superintendent of Passports shall issue passes at the rate of one masha per pass. Whoever holds a pass shall have the freedom to either enter or leave the country. Whoever, being a native of the country, enters or leaves without a pass shall be fined twelve panas. If someone presents a false pass, they shall be punished with the first amercement. A foreigner who commits the same offense shall be punished with the highest amercement.

The Superintendent of Pasture Lands shall check the passes. Pasture grounds will be established between any two dangerous areas. Valleys will be cleared of the threat of thieves, elephants, and other wild animals.

In barren areas of the country, tanks, shelter buildings, and wells shall be constructed, along with flower gardens and fruit gardens. Hunters with their hounds shall scout the forests. When thieves or enemies are approaching, they must hide by climbing trees or mountains to avoid capture, and blow conch-shells or beat drums to give warning. Regarding the movements of enemies or wild tribes, hunters may send messages by releasing the pigeons of the royal household with passes (mudrá), or by setting fires and creating smoke signals at different intervals.

The superintendent shall also be responsible for the protection of timber and elephant forests, keeping roads in good condition, arresting thieves, ensuring the safety of merchant travel, protecting cows, and overseeing the transactions of the people.

[Thus ends Chapter XXXIV, "The Superintendent of Passports, and the Superintendent of Pasture Lands," in Book II, "The Duties of Government Superintendents," of the Arthasástra of Kautilya. End of the fifty-fifth chapter from the beginning.]

CHAPTER XXXV. THE DUTY OF REVENUE-COLLECTORS; SPIES IN THE GUISE OF HOUSEHOLDERS, MERCHANTS AND ASCETICS.

After dividing the kingdom (janapada) into four districts and further classifying the villages (gráma) into three ranks—first, middle, and lowest—he shall assign them to one of the following categories: villages exempt from taxation (paribáraka); those that supply soldiers (áyudhíya); those that pay their taxes in the form of grains, cattle, gold (hiranya), or raw materials (kupya); and those that provide free labor (vishti) or dairy products in place of taxes (karapratikara).

It is the duty of the Gopa, the village accountant, to manage the accounts of five or ten villages as instructed by the Collector-General. The Gopa shall establish village boundaries, mark plots of land as cultivated, uncultivated, plains, wet lands, gardens, vegetable gardens, fences (váta), forests, altars, temples, irrigation works, cremation grounds, feeding houses (sattra), places where water is provided to travelers (prapá), pilgrimage sites, pasture grounds, and roads. By doing so, he will define the boundaries of various villages, fields, forests, and roads, and he will record the details of gifts, sales, charities, and any remission of taxes related to fields.

Additionally, after numbering the houses as either taxpaying or non-taxpaying, the Gopa shall record the total number of inhabitants in all four castes in each village, and he shall also account for the number of cultivators, cowherds, merchants, artisans, laborers, slaves, and both biped and quadruped animals. At the same time, he shall calculate the amount of gold, free labor, tolls, and fines that can be collected from each house.

He shall also keep records of the number of young and old men living in each house, along with their personal history (charitra), occupation (ájíva), income (áya), and expenditures (vyaya).

Similarly, the Sthánika, the district officer, shall oversee the accounts of one-quarter of the kingdom. In the areas under the supervision of the Gopa and Sthánika, commissioners (prodeshtárah) specially appointed by the Collector-General will not only inspect the work and methods used by the village and district officers but will also collect the special religious tax known as bali (balipragraham kuryuh).

Spies disguised as householders (grihapatika), acting under the orders of the collector-general for espionage, shall verify the accuracy of the accounts kept by village and district officers regarding the fields, houses, and families in each village. This includes the area and yield of crops in the fields, ownership rights and any tax remissions related to houses, and the caste and profession of each family.

They shall also assess the total number of people and animals (janghágra) as well as the income and expenditures of each household. They will investigate the reasons behind the migration of people, whether leaving or arriving, especially those who are habitual wanderers, and monitor the movement of men and women of questionable character (anarthya), as well as foreign spies.

Similarly, spies disguised as merchants will assess the quantity and price of royal merchandise such as minerals, products from gardens, forests, and fields, or manufactured goods. Regarding foreign merchandise of superior or inferior quality arriving by land or water, they will investigate the tolls, road taxes, transportation fees, military taxes, ferry charges, and the one-sixth portion merchants are required to pay. They will also check the expenses merchants incur for their own sustenance and for storing their goods in warehouses (panyágára).

Spies disguised as ascetics, under the collector-general's orders, will gather information on the actions, whether honest or dishonest, of farmers, cowherds, merchants, and heads of government departments.

In locations such as places of worship, crossroads, ancient ruins, near tanks, rivers, bathing areas, pilgrimage sites, hermitages, desert regions, mountains, and dense forests, spies disguised as old and notorious thieves, along with their band of students, shall investigate the reasons for the arrival, departure, and resting of thieves, enemies, and overly brave individuals.

The collector-general shall diligently attend to the kingdom's affairs. Likewise, his subordinates, as part of the espionage network, shall work with their colleagues and followers to carry out their duties.

[Thus ends Chapter XXXV, "The Duty of Revenue Collectors; Spies under the Guise of Householders, Merchants, and Ascetics," in Book II, "The Duties of Government Superintendents" of the Arthasástra of Kautilya. End of the fifty-sixth chapter from the beginning.]

CHAPTER XXXVI. THE DUTY OF A CITY SUPERINTENDENT.

Like the Collector-general, the Officer in charge of the Capital City (*Nágaraka*) shall look to the affairs of the capital.

A *Gopa* shall keep the accounts of ten households, twenty households, or forty households.

He shall not only know the caste, *gotra*, the name, and occupation of both men and women in those households, but also ascertain their income and expenditure.

Likewise, the officer known as *Sthánika* shall attend to the accounts of the four quarters of the capital.

Managers of charitable institutions shall send information (to *Gopa* or *Sthánika*) as to any heretics (*Páshanda*) and travellers arriving to reside therein.

They shall allow ascetics and men learned in the Vedas to reside in such places only when those persons are known to be of reliable character.

Artisans and other handicraftsmen may, on their own responsibility, allow others of their own profession to reside where they carry on their own work (i.e., in their own houses).

Similarly, merchants may on their own responsibility allow other merchants to reside where they themselves carry on their mercantile work (i.e., their own houses or shops).

They (the merchants) shall make a report of those who sell any merchandise in forbidden places or at forbidden times, as well as of those who are in possession of any merchandise other than their own.

Vintners, sellers of cooked flesh, and sellers of cooked rice, as well as prostitutes, may allow any other person to reside with them only when that person is well-known to them.

They (vintners, etc.) shall make a report of spendthrifts and fool-hardy persons who engage themselves in risky undertakings.

Any physician who treats in secret a patient suffering from ulcers or the effects of unwholesome food or drink, as well as the master of the house where such treatment occurs, will only be considered innocent if they report the situation to either the *Gopa* or *Sthánika*. Otherwise, both the physician and the master of the house will be held equally guilty along with the patient.

Householders must report any strangers arriving at or departing from their homes; failing to do so will make them guilty of any crime committed during that night. Even when no crime seems to have been committed, they will still be fined 3 panas for failing to report such movements.

Travelers on highways or footpaths must apprehend any person they come across who is injured, carrying weapons, struggling with a heavy load, avoiding others timidly, indulging in excessive sleep, appearing fatigued from a long journey, or seeming unfamiliar with the place, particularly within or outside the capital, in temples, places of pilgrimage, or burial grounds.

Spies shall also search for suspicious individuals in deserted houses, the workshops or homes of vintners, sellers of cooked rice and flesh, gambling houses, and in the abodes of heretics.

The lighting of fires is prohibited during the middle two parts of the day, divided into four equal parts during the summer. A fine of 1/8th of a pana shall be imposed for starting a fire during this time.

Householders may carry out cooking operations outside their homes.

If a house-owner does not have ready at hand five water pots, a *kumbha* (large pot), a *dróna* (large vessel), a ladder, an axe, a winnowing basket, an elephant-driving hook, pincers, and a leather bag, he shall be fined ¼th of a pana.

They must also remove thatched roofs. Blacksmiths and others who work with fire must live together in a single designated area.

Every houseowner must remain by the door of their house at night. Water vessels must be kept in rows, in the thousands, without causing disorder. These vessels should be placed not only along big streets and at intersections but also in front of royal buildings.

Any houseowner who does not run to help extinguish a fire, regardless of what is burning, shall be fined 12 panas. A renter (one who occupies a rented house) shall be fined 6 panas for not helping to put out the fire.

Whoever carelessly sets a fire shall be fined 54 panas. Whoever intentionally sets a fire shall be thrown into the fire as punishment.

Whoever throws dirt in the street shall be fined 1/8th of a pana. Whoever causes mud or water to accumulate in the street shall be fined ¼th of a pana. Whoever commits the above offenses on the king's road shall be fined double the amount.

Whoever excretes feces in places of pilgrimage, water reservoirs, temples, and royal buildings shall be fined beginning with one pana, with the fines increasing according to the severity of the offense. But when such excretions are due to the use of medicine or disease, no punishment shall be imposed.

Whoever throws inside the city the carcass of animals such as a cat, dog, mongoose, or snake shall be fined 3 panas. Whoever throws in the carcass of an ass, camel, mule, or cattle shall be fined 6 panas. Whoever throws in a human corpse shall be fined 50 panas.

When a dead body is taken out of the city through a gate other than the prescribed one or through a path other than the usual path, the first amercement shall be imposed; and those who guard the gates through which the dead body is taken out shall be fined 200 panas.

When a dead body is buried or cremated outside the designated burial or cremation grounds, a fine of 12 panas shall be imposed.

The time interval between six *nálikas* (2 2/5 hours) after nightfall and six *nálikas* before dawn shall be marked by the sound of a trumpet, signaling a prohibition on public movement.

Once the trumpet has been sounded, anyone moving near the royal buildings during the first or last *yáma* (3 hours) of the restricted period shall be fined one pana and a quarter. During the middle *yámas*, the fine shall be double that amount. Anyone found moving outside the royal buildings or the fort shall be fined four times that amount.

Anyone arrested in suspicious places or caught committing a criminal act shall be examined.

Anyone found moving near royal buildings or climbing the fortifications of the capital shall be punished with the middlemost amercement.

However, those who go out at night for the purpose of midwifery or medical treatment, to carry a dead body to the burial or cremation grounds, to walk with a lamp in hand, to visit the city officer, to investigate the cause of a trumpet sound, to extinguish a fire, or with the authority of a pass shall not be arrested.

On nights when movement is allowed (chárarátrishu), those who go out in disguise, those who venture out despite being forbidden, and those who carry clubs or weapons shall be punished in accordance with the seriousness of their crime.

Those watchmen who stop someone they should not stop, or who fail to stop someone they should stop, shall be punished with twice the amount of the fine levied for untimely movement.

When a watchman has carnal connection with a slave woman, he shall be punished with the first amercement; when he has such connection with a free woman, he shall be punished with the middlemost amercement; when he has carnal connection with a woman arrested for untimely movement, he shall be punished with the highest amercement; and when he has such connection with a woman of high birth (kulastrí), he shall be put to death.

When the officer in charge of the city (nágaraka) fails to report to the king whatever nocturnal disturbance of animate or inanimate nature (chetanâchetana) has occurred, or when he is careless in performing his duties, he shall be punished according to the gravity of his offense.

He shall conduct daily inspections of reservoirs of water, roads, secret passages for going out of the city, forts, fort walls, and other defensive structures. He shall also keep in his custody any objects he finds that have been lost, forgotten, or left behind by others.

On days corresponding to the king's birth star, as well as on full moon days, young, old, sick, or helpless prisoners (anátha) shall be released from the jail (bandhanâgâra); or those who are of charitable disposition or who have made agreements with the prisoners may release them by paying an appropriate ransom.

Once a day or once every five nights, prisoners may be released from jail, taking into account the work they have completed, the whipping they have undergone, or an adequate ransom paid in gold.

Whenever a new country is conquered, when an heir apparent is installed on the throne, or when a prince is born to the king, prisoners are generally set free.

Book 3

CHAPTER I. DETERMINATION OF FORMS OF AGREEMENT; DETERMINATION OF LEGAL DISPUTES.

In the cities of Sangrahana, Dronamukha, and Sthániya, and at places where districts meet, three individuals who are well-versed in Sacred Law (dharmasthas) and three ministers of the king (amátyas) shall oversee the administration of justice.

(Valid and Invalid Transactions)

They shall consider as invalid any agreements (vyavahára) made in secret, inside homes, during the night, in forests, in secluded areas, or through fraudulent means.

The proposer of such an agreement and any accomplices shall be punished with the first amercement. [A fine ranging from 48 to 96 panas is called the first amercement; from 200 to 500 panas, the middlemost amercement; and from 500 to 1,000 panas, the highest amercement. See Chap. XVII, Book III.]

The witnesses (srotri = voluntary hearers) shall each be fined half of the above amount, and the persons who accepted the agreement shall bear any loss they have incurred.

However, agreements made in the presence of others, or those that do not have any other grounds for invalidation, shall be considered valid.

Agreements concerning matters like inheritance division, sealed or unsealed deposits, or marriage, or those involving women who are either suffering from illness or do not leave their homes, and agreements made by individuals who are not known to be of unsound mind, shall be valid, even if they were entered into inside homes.

Transactions involving robbery, duels, marriages, or the execution of the king's orders, as well as agreements made by individuals who typically conduct their business during the early part of the night, shall be valid even if they take place at night.

For those who spend most of their lives in forests, whether they are merchants, cowherds, hermits, hunters, or spies, their agreements, even if made in the forests, will be considered valid. If fraudulent agreements are involved, only those entered into by spies will be valid.

Agreements made by members of any association among themselves will also be valid, even if made in private. However, any other agreements made in seclusion or under similar conditions, unless specified otherwise, will be considered void.

Similarly, agreements made by dependent or unauthorized individuals, such as a father's mother, a son, a father who has a son, an outcast brother, the youngest brother in a family with shared interests, a wife who has a husband or son, a slave, a hired laborer, anyone too young or too old to manage business, a convict (abhisasta), a cripple, or an afflicted person, will not be considered valid unless the individual is specifically authorized to do so.

Even if an authorized person enters into an agreement, it will be void if at the time of making the agreement they were provoked, anxious, intoxicated, or if they were a lunatic or haunted. In all of these cases, the person who proposed the agreement, their accessory, and the witnesses will each be punished according to the rules specified above.

However, agreements entered into personally by someone within their community at the right place and time will be valid, as long as the circumstances, the nature of the agreement, its description, and the qualities of the case are believable.

Such agreements, with the exception of orders (Adesa, likely referring to a bill of exchange) and hypothecations, can still be binding even if made by a third person. This concludes the determination of the forms of agreement.

(The Trial.)

The year, season, month, fortnight (paksha), date, nature, and location of the event, the amount of the debt, as well as the country, residence, caste, gotra, name, and occupation of both the plaintiff and the defendant—both of whom must be capable of suing or defending (kritasamarthávasthayoh)—must first be recorded. After that, the statements of both parties will be taken in the order appropriate to the case. These statements will then undergo a thorough examination.

(The offence of Parokta.)

If either party, instead of addressing the main issue, brings up unrelated matters; if their previous statements contradict their later ones; if they insist on considering the opinion of a third person, even when it's not relevant; if, after starting to answer the main question, they abruptly stop despite being ordered to continue; if they introduce topics other than those they initially raised; if they retract their own statements; if they reject the testimony given by their own witnesses; or if they secretly converse with their witnesses when they shouldn't— these actions constitute the offence of "Parokta."

(Punishment for Parokta.)

The fine for *Parokta* (bringing up unrelated matters or changing the subject during a trial) is five times the amount in question. The fine for *Svayambadi* (making claims without evidence) is ten times the amount.

(Payments for Witnesses.)

Fees for witnesses (*purushabhritih*) shall amount to 1/8th of the total sum in dispute (*astánga*). Additionally, provisions may be made to cover the travel expenses of the witnesses, based on the amount of the lawsuit. These two types of costs shall be borne by the losing party.

(Countersuits.)

In cases other than duels, robbery, or disputes among merchants or trade-guilds, the defendant is not allowed to file a counterclaim against the plaintiff. Similarly, no counterclaim can be made on behalf of the defendant.

(Adjournments.)

The plaintiff must respond quickly after the defendant has answered the questions at issue. If not, the plaintiff will be guilty of parokta, as they are expected to know the key details of the case, while the defendant may not. The defendant is allowed three or seven nights to prepare their defense. If the defendant is not ready within that time, they will be fined between 3 and 12 panas. If they still fail to respond after three fortnights, they will be fined for parokta, and the plaintiff will be able to recover the amount in question from the defendant's property. However, if the plaintiff is suing only for the return of a favor (pratyupakarana), no decree will be passed.

The same punishment will apply to defendants who fail to defend their case.

If the plaintiff is unable to prove their case, they will also be guilty of parokta. If the plaintiff cannot substantiate the case against a defendant who has passed away or is ill, they will need to pay a fine and perform the defendant's funeral rites as determined by the witnesses. However, if the plaintiff successfully proves the case, they may be allowed to take possession of the property pledged to them. If the plaintiff is not a Bráhman and fails to prove their case, they may be required to perform ceremonies to drive out demons (rakshoghna rakshitakam).

- In virtue of the king's power to ensure that the duties of the four castes and the four stages of religious life are observed, and to prevent the violation of these duties, the king is seen as the fountain of justice (dharmapravartaka).

- Sacred law (Dharma), evidence (Vyavahára), history (Charitra), and royal edicts (Rájasásana) are the four pillars of Law. In order of importance, each is superior to the one preceding it.
- Dharma represents eternal truth governing the world; Vyavahára is based on the testimony of witnesses; Charitra refers to historical tradition (sangraha) upheld by the people; and Rájasásana is the order or edict of the king.
- The duty of a king is to protect his subjects with justice, and by doing so, he secures his place in heaven. A king who neglects this duty or disturbs social order wields his power (danda) in vain.
- It is power, and power alone, exercised impartially and in proportion to guilt—whether against his own son or his enemy—that sustains both this world and the next.
- A king who administers justice in accordance with sacred law (Dharma), evidence (Vyavahára), history (Samsthá), and royal edicts (Nyáya) will be able to conquer the world within the four quarters (Chaturantám mahím).
- If there is a disagreement between history and sacred law, or between evidence and sacred law, the matter should be resolved according to sacred law.
- However, if sacred law (sástra) conflicts with rational law (Dharmanyáya, or the king's law), reason should take precedence, as the original text of sacred law may not always be available.
- Self-assertion (svayamváda) by either party has often proven faulty. Only through examination (anuyoga), honesty (árjava), evidence (hetu), and oath-taking (sapatha) can a person win their case.
- If witness testimony reveals contradictions in the statements of either party, or if spies discover that one party's cause is false, the judgment shall go against that party.

CHAPTER II. CONCERNING MARRIAGE. THE DUTY OF MARRIAGE, THE PROPERTY OF A WOMAN, AND COMPENSATIONS FOR REMARRIAGE.

Marriage comes before all other transactions in life (vyavahára). The giving of a well-adorned maiden in marriage is called Bráhma marriage. The union of a man and a woman to jointly perform sacred duties is known as Prájápatya marriage.

When a maiden is given in marriage in exchange for a couple of cows, it is called Arsha. When a maiden is given to a priest who officiates in a sacrifice, it is called Daiva. The voluntary union of a maiden with her lover is referred to as Gándharva marriage. When a maiden is given after receiving a significant amount of wealth (súlka), it is known as Asura. The abduction of a maiden is called Rákshasa, and if the abduction happens while she is asleep or intoxicated, it is called Paisácha marriage.

Of these, the first four types are ancient ancestral customs and are considered valid when approved by the father. The remaining types require approval from both the father and the mother, as they receive the súlka, or bride price, given by the bridegroom for their daughter. If one parent has passed away, the surviving parent will receive the súlka. If both parents have died, the maiden herself shall receive it. Any form of marriage is acceptable as long as it pleases all parties involved.

(Property of Women.)

A woman's property includes her means of living (vritti) or jewelry (ábadhya). If her means of living are worth more than two thousand, they should be officially given to her. There is no limit to the amount of jewelry she can own. A wife is not wrong to use this property to support her son, daughter-in-law, or herself when her husband is away and has not left anything for her care. In times of trouble, like illness, famine, or danger, or for charitable acts, her husband can also use this property. No one can complain if this property is used with the mutual agreement of a couple who have twins. Likewise, no complaint will be made if this property is used for three years by couples married under the first four types of marriage. However, in Gándharva and Asura marriages, the use of this property must be paid back with interest. In Rákshasa and Paisacha marriages, using this property will be treated as theft. This is how the responsibility of marriage is handled.

When her husband dies, a woman who wishes to live a religious life should immediately receive both her endowment and jewelry (sthápyábharanam) and any remaining súlka owed to her. If she does not already have these in her possession, even though they were supposed to be given to her, she will get both of them along with any interest that has accumulated. If she wants to remarry (kutumbakáma), she will be given whatever her father-in-law, her husband, or both gave her at the time of her remarriage (nivesakále). The right time for a woman to remarry will be explained when talking about the long absence of husbands.

If a widow marries a man who was not chosen by her father-in-law, she will lose whatever her father-in-law or husband gave her. The relatives (gnátis) of a woman must return to her any property she left with them. Whoever fairly takes a woman under his care must also take care of her property. No woman will succeed in claiming her husband's property. If she lives a religious life, she may enjoy it (dharmakámá bhunjíta). A woman with sons cannot freely use her own property (strídhana), as it will be passed on to her sons. If a woman tries to take her own property for the purpose of supporting her sons, she must set it aside in their name. If a woman has several sons, she must keep her property in the same condition as it was when her husband gave it to her. Even if the property was given to her with the freedom to enjoy and manage it, she must still put it in her sons' names.

A widow who has no children but stays loyal to her deceased husband may, under the care of her teacher, enjoy her property for as long as she lives, as property is given to women to protect them from misfortune. After her death, her property will go to her relatives (dáyáda). If the husband is still alive and the wife dies, her sons and daughters will split her property. If there are no sons, the daughters will inherit it. If there are no daughters either, the husband will take back the súlka, which he gave to her, and her relatives will take back any gifts or dowry they had given her. This is how a woman's property is handled.

(Re-marriage of Males.)

If a woman has no children, no male children, or is barren, her husband must wait for eight years before marrying another. If she only gives birth to a dead child, he has to wait for ten years. If she only has daughters, he must wait for twelve years. After this time, if he wants to have sons, he may marry another woman. If he breaks this rule, he must pay her not only the sulka (the dowry), her property (strídhana), and an appropriate monetary compensation (ádhivedanikamartham), but also a fine of 24 panas to the government. He must give the sulka and property (strídhana) even to women who didn't receive these things when they married him, as well as giving his wives their proper compensation and enough to live on (vritti). Then he can marry as many women as he wants because women are meant to bear sons. If many or all of his wives are having their period at the same time, he must lie with the wife he married first or with the one who has given birth to a living son. If he hides the fact that a wife is menstruating or neglects to lie with any of them after their menstruation, he will be fined 96 panas.

None of his wives who either have sons, are pious, barren, give birth to a dead child, or are beyond the age of menstruation should be forced to sleep with him if she doesn't want to. If the man doesn't want to, he doesn't have to lie with his wife if she has leprosy or is mentally ill. However, if a woman wishes to have sons, she may lie with men who have such diseases.

- If a husband has a bad character, is away for a long time, becomes a traitor to his king, endangers his wife's life, falls from his caste, or loses his virility, his wife can leave him.

[Thus ends Chapter II, "The Duty of Marriage, the Property of a Woman, and Compensation for Remarriage," in Book III, "Concerning Law," of the Arthasástra of Kautilya. End of the fifty-ninth chapter from the beginning.]

CHAPTER III. THE DUTY OF A WIFE; MAINTENANCE OF A WOMAN; CRUELTY TO WOMEN; ENMITY BETWEEN HUSBAND AND WIFE; A WIFE's TRANSGRESSION; HER KINDNESS TO ANOTHER; AND FORBIDDEN TRANSACTIONS.

Women reach their legal majority at the age of twelve, and men at the age of sixteen. If, after reaching adulthood, they disobey lawful authority (asusrúsháyám), women shall be fined 15 panas, while men shall be fined twice that amount.

(Maintenance of a woman.)

A woman who is entitled to claim maintenance for an unlimited period shall be provided with as much food and clothing (grásaccHádana) as necessary or even more, based on the income of the person responsible for maintaining her (yatha-purushaparivápam vá). If the period for which she is entitled to support is limited, then a fixed amount of money, determined in proportion to the maintainer's income, shall be given to her. This also applies if she has not received her sulka, property, or compensation (due to her if her husband remarries). If, after separating from her husband, she places herself under the protection of someone from her father-in-law's family (svasrakula) or chooses to live independently, then her husband shall not be liable for her maintenance. Thus, the determination of maintenance is addressed.

(Cruelty to women.)

Women of disobedient nature shall be taught proper behavior through general expressions such as "You, half naked; you, fully naked; you, cripple; you, fatherless; you, motherless" (nagne vinagne nyange pitrke matrke vinagne ityanirdesena vinayagrahanam). Alternatively, three light blows, either with bamboo bark, a rope, or the palm of the hand, may be given on her hips. Any violation of these guidelines will be punished with half the penalty for defamation or physical harm. The same punishment applies to a woman who, driven by jealousy or hatred, acts cruelly toward her husband. Penalties for engaging in inappropriate behavior, either at the door or outside her husband's house, are addressed elsewhere. Thus, cruelty to women is addressed.

(Enmity between husband and wife.)

A woman who despises her husband, has gone through seven cycles of her menses, and loves another man must immediately return to her husband both the endowment and jewelry she received from him and allow him to lie with another woman. A man who dislikes his wife must let her seek refuge either in the house of a mendicant woman, with her legal guardians, or with her relatives. If a man falsely accuses his wife of adultery with one of her or his relatives, or with a spy—an accusation that can only be proven by eyewitnesses (drishtilinge)—or accuses her of trying to leave him unjustly, he shall be fined 12 panas. A woman who despises her husband cannot end their marriage without his consent, nor can a man divorce his wife against her will. However, if there is mutual hatred, divorce may be agreed upon (parasparam dveshánmokshah). If a man fears harm from his wife and desires a divorce, he must return to her everything he gave her at the time of marriage. If a woman, fearing danger from her husband, seeks a divorce, she will forfeit her claim to her property. Marriages performed in accordance with the customs of the first four types of marriages cannot be dissolved.

(Transgression.)

If a woman engages herself in amorous sports, For drinking against an order, a woman shall be fined 3 panas. She shall pay a fine of 6 panas for going out during the day to attend sports or visit a woman or watch a spectacle. If she goes out to see another man or for sports, the fine shall be 12 panas. For the same offenses committed at night, the fines shall be doubled. If a woman abducts another woman while she is asleep or intoxicated (suptamatta-pravrajane), or if she drags her husband to the door of the house, she shall be fined 12 panas. If she leaves her house at night, the fine shall be double the previous amount. If a man and a woman exchange signals for the purpose of sensual enjoyment or carry on secret conversations for the same reason, the woman shall be fined 24 panas, and the man shall pay double that amount. A woman showing off her hair, the tie of her dress around her waist, her teeth, or her nails shall pay the first amercement, and a man doing the same shall pay twice the first amercement.

For having conversations in suspicious places, whips may be used as punishment instead of fines. In the center of the village, an outcaste (chandála) may whip such women five times on each side of their bodies. A woman can avoid being whipped by paying a pana for each whip (panikam vá praharam mokshayet). Thus, transgression is dealt with.

(Forbidden transactions.)

For a man and a woman who, though forbidden, engage in any mutual transaction, the woman shall be fined 12, 24, and 54 panas, depending on whether the help consists of (i) small items, (ii) heavy items, or (iii) gold or gold coins (hiranyasuvarnayoh); the man shall be fined double the above amounts. For a similar transaction between a man and a woman who are forbidden to associate (agamvayoh), half of the above punishment shall be imposed. The same punishment applies for any other forbidden transaction between men and women. Thus, forbidden transactions are addressed.

- Treason, transgression, and wandering at will shall cause a woman to lose her rights not only to (i) strídhana, her personal property of over 2,000 panas and her jewelry, (ii) áhita, compensation she received for allowing her husband to marry another woman, but also (iii) sulka, the money her parents received from her husband.

Thus concludes the section on "The Duty of a Wife; Maintenance of a Woman; Enmity between Husband and Wife; a Wife's Transgression; and Forbidden Transactions" in the portion "Concerning Marriage" from the book "Concerning Law" of the Arthasástra of Kautilya.

CHAPTER IV. VAGRANCY, ELOPEMENT AND SHORT AND LONG SOJOURNMENTS.

If a woman leaves her husband's house for any reason other than danger, she shall be fined 6 panas. If she leaves against her husband's direct order, she shall be fined 12 panas. If she goes beyond her neighbor's house (prativesagrihatigatáyah), she shall be fined 6 panas. If she allows her neighbor into her house, accepts alms from a mendicant, or brings in the goods of a merchant, she shall be fined 12 panas. If she continues to do so even after being explicitly forbidden, she shall be punished with the first amercement. If she goes beyond the surrounding houses (parigrihátigatáyam), she shall be fined 24 panas. If she takes another man's wife into her house without any legitimate reason, she shall be fined 100 panas. However, if this happens without her knowledge or against her orders, she will not be held accountable.

My teacher says: For the sake of avoiding danger, it is not wrong for a woman to seek the help of a man who is a kinsman of her husband, a wealthy and respectable man (sukhávastha), the head of the village, one of her legal guardians (anvádhikula), or someone from the family of a mendicant woman, or any of her own male relatives.

But Kautilya raises the question: How can good women (sádhvíjana) even know if the family of her own male relatives is virtuous? It is not an offense for a woman to go to her relatives' houses under situations like death, illness, calamities, or childbirth. Whoever stops her from going in such situations shall be fined 12 panas. If a woman hides herself during such events, she will forfeit her endowment. If her relatives hide her to exempt her from aiding in such situations, they shall lose the remaining balance of sulka, the money due to them from her husband for her marriage. Thus, issues of vagrancy are addressed.

(Elopement or Criminal Rendezvous.)

If a woman leaves her husband's house and goes to another village, she shall not only pay a fine of 12 panas but also forfeit her endowment and jewelry (sthápyábharanalopascha). If she goes to any other place under any pretense other than for subsistence or pilgrimage (bharmádánatirthagamanábhyámanyatra), even if she is in the company of a suitable man, she shall pay a fine of 24 panas and lose all social privileges (sarvadharmalopascha). The man who permits such a woman to accompany him on his journey shall be punished with the first amercement. If both the man and woman share similar sinful ideals in life (tulyasreyasoh) and live a corrupt life (pápiyasoh), each of them shall be punished with the middle-most amercement. However, if the man she accompanies is a near relative, he shall not be punished. If a relative takes a woman with him despite being forbidden, he shall be fined half of the middlemost amercement.

If, on the road, in a forest, or in any hidden place, a woman falls into the company of another man or, for the purpose of pleasure, joins a suspicious or forbidden man, she shall be guilty of elopement (sangrahanam vidyát). It is no offense for women to be in the company of actors, performers, singers, fishermen, hunters, herdsmen, vintners, or other men who usually travel with their women. If a man takes a woman with him on his journey despite being forbidden to do so, or if a woman accompanies a man despite being forbidden, half of the fines previously mentioned shall apply to both of them. Thus, the issue of elopement is dealt with.

(Re-marriage of women.)

Wives belonging to the Súdra, Vaisya, Kshatriya, or Bráhman caste, who have not borne children, should wait for their husbands who have gone abroad for a short time for at least a year. However, if they have given birth to children, they should wait for their absent husbands for more than a year. If they have been provided with maintenance, they should wait twice the length of time mentioned. If they are not provided for, their well-to-do relatives (gnátis) should maintain them for either four or eight years. After this period, the relatives should allow them to remarry, after taking what was given to them at the time of their marriage.

If the husband is a Bráhman who is studying abroad, his wife, if childless, should wait for him for ten years; if she has borne children, she should wait for twelve years. If the husband is of the Kshatriya caste, his wife should wait for him until her death. Even if she has children with a second husband of the same caste (savarna) to prevent the extinction of her family line, she will not face disgrace for this (savarnatascha prajátá ná pavádam labheta).

If the wife of an absent husband lacks maintenance and is neglected by her wealthy relatives, she may remarry someone of her choice who can support her and alleviate her suffering.

A young wife (kumárí) married according to the customs of the first four kinds of marriage (dharmaviváhát), whose husband has gone abroad and is heard from, should wait for him for seven menstrual cycles (saptatirthányákánksheta), provided she has not publicly mentioned his name. If she has announced his name, she should wait for him for a year. If the husband has gone abroad and is not heard from, the wife should wait for him for five menstrual cycles. However, if the husband has not been heard from, the wife should wait for ten menstrual cycles.

If the wife has only received a part of the marriage payment (sulka) from her absent husband who is not heard from, she should wait for him for three menstrual cycles. If he is heard from, she should wait for seven cycles. If she has received the full marriage payment, she should wait for five cycles if the husband is not heard from, and ten cycles if he is heard from. Afterward, with the permission of judges (dharma-sthairvisrishtá), she may marry a man of her choice, as neglecting his wife after her monthly purification is, according to Kautilya, a failure in duty (tirthoparodho hi dharmavadha iti Kautilyah).

For husbands who have been away for a long time (dirgrhapravásinah), who have become ascetics, or who have passed away, their childless wives should wait for seven menstrual cycles. If they have children, they should wait for a year. Afterward, the wife may marry her husband's brother. If her husband had multiple brothers, she should marry the next in age to her late husband, someone virtuous who can protect her, or the youngest unmarried brother. If no brothers are available, she may marry someone from her husband's gotra or a close relative. If there are several suitable candidates, she should choose the closest relation to her deceased husband.

- If a woman remarries someone who is not a relative (dáyáda) of her late husband, she and the man she marries, along with those who arranged and consented to the marriage, will be punished as if they had eloped.

[Thus ends Chapter IV, "Vagrancy; Elopement; and Short and Long Sojournments," in the section "Concerning Marriage" in Book III, "Concerning Law" of the Arthasástra of Kautilya. End of the Section "Concerning Marriage". End of the sixty-first chapter from the beginning.]

CHAPTER V. DIVISION OF INHERITANCE.

Sons whose fathers, mothers, or ancestors are still alive cannot act independently (anísvarah). After the time of the parents or ancestors, the division of ancestral property among the descendants from the same ancestor will occur, calculating the shares based on lineage (per stirpes, meaning according to fathers).

Any self-acquired property of the sons, except that which was gained using the parental property, is not subject to division. Sons or grandsons up to the fourth generation from the first ancestor also have designated shares (amsabhájah) in the property acquired through their undivided ancestral property, as the line of descent (pindah) remains unbroken up to the fourth generation (avichchhinnah). However, those whose lineage from the first ancestor has been broken (vichchhinnapindáh, i.e., beyond the fourth generation) shall divide the property equally. Those who have been living together shall redistribute their property, regardless of whether they had previously divided their ancestral property or had never received such property at all. Among the sons, the one who has brought prosperity to the ancestral property will also receive a share of the profit.

If a man dies without male children, his brothers or those who have been living with him (saha jívino vá) shall inherit his movable property (dravyam), while his daughters (born of marriages other than the first four types) will inherit his immovable property (riktham). If he has sons, they will inherit the property. If he has only daughters born from marriages following the customs of the first four types of marriage, these daughters will inherit the property. If there are neither sons nor daughters of such marriages, the deceased man's father will inherit the property if he is alive. If the father is also deceased, the deceased's brothers and their sons will inherit it. If there are many fatherless brothers, they will divide the property among themselves, and each of the sons of these brothers will receive the share due to his father (piturekamamsam). If the brothers (sodarya) are the sons of different fathers, they will divide the property according to their paternal lines.

Among a deceased man's father, brother, and brother's sons, the latter shall depend on the former for their shares if the former are still living. This also applies to the youngest or eldest claiming their own share of the inheritance.

When a father distributes his property while still alive, he shall not make any distinction when dividing it among his sons. He must not deprive any of his sons of their rightful share without sufficient reason. After the father's death, the elder sons shall show kindness and consideration to the younger ones, as long as the younger ones are not of bad character.

(Time of dividing inheritance.)

The division of inheritance shall take place when all inheritors have reached their legal age. If the division occurs before this, the minors shall receive their shares free from any debts. The shares belonging to the minors shall be kept in the safe custody of their maternal relatives or trustworthy elders from the village until the minors reach maturity. The same rule applies to those who have gone abroad. Unmarried brothers shall also receive the same amount for marriage expenses as was spent on their married brothers. Likewise, unmarried daughters shall receive an appropriate dowry, payable at the time of their marriage.

Both assets and liabilities must be divided equally.

My teacher suggests that even the smallest items, such as mud vessels, should be equally divided among the poor. However, Kautilya holds that this is unnecessary, as the rule is that all existing property is to be divided, but nothing that does not exist. After declaring before witnesses the total amount of shared property, as well as the property that constitutes additional shares for the brothers (based on birth order), the division of inheritance shall proceed. Any property that was divided unfairly, deceptively, or concealed shall be redivided.

Property that has no rightful heir shall be given to the king, except for the property of a woman, a deceased person for whom no funeral rites have been performed, or a miserly man—excluding property belonging to a Bráhman learned in the Vedas. The property of the learned shall be given to those well-versed in the three Vedas.

Persons who have fallen from their caste, those born of outcastes, and eunuchs shall have no share in the inheritance. This also applies to idiots, lunatics, the blind, and lepers. However, if such individuals have wives with property, their children who are not afflicted by the same conditions shall inherit. All these individuals, except for those who have fallen from caste, shall be entitled only to food and clothing.

- If any of these individuals were married before falling from caste or suffering from these afflictions, and if their family line risks becoming extinct, their relatives may beget sons for them and allot these sons a proportionate share of the inheritance.

[Thus ends Chapter V, "Procedure of Portioning Inheritance" in the section of "Division of Inheritance" in Book III, "Concerning law" of the Arthasástra of Kautilya. End of the sixty-second chapter from the beginning.]

CHAPTER VI. SPECIAL SHARES IN INHERITANCE.

Goats shall be the special shares of the eldest sons born of the same mother among Bráhmans; horses among Kshatriyas; cows among Vaisyas; and sheep among Súdras. Blind animals of the same type shall be the special shares of the middle sons; animals with a variegated color shall be the special shares of the youngest sons. In the absence of quadrupeds, the eldest shall receive an additional share of the whole property, excluding precious stones, as this act alone will bind him to his duty to his ancestors.

This method follows the rules observed among the followers of Usanas.

When the father passes away, his carriage and jewelry shall be the special share of the eldest son; his bed, seat, and the bronze plate from which he took his meals shall go to the middle son, while black grains, iron, household utensils, cows, and a cart shall go to the youngest. The remaining property, or even the aforementioned items, may be divided equally among the sons. Sisters shall not have a claim to inheritance but will receive their mother's bronze plate and jewelry after her death.

If the eldest son is impotent, he shall receive only one-third of the special share usually given to the eldest. If he follows a condemnable occupation or has abandoned religious duties, he shall receive only one-quarter of the special share. If he is reckless in his actions, he shall receive nothing.

This rule also applies to the middle and youngest sons. Of these two, the one who demonstrates manliness shall receive half of the special share usually given to the eldest.

Regarding sons born of different wives:

Of sons born to two wives, if only one wife has gone through all the necessary religious ceremonies, or if neither wife observed the necessary rites as maidens, or if one of the wives gave birth to twins, primogeniture is decided by birth.

Shares in inheritance for sons such as Súta, Mágadha, Vrátya, and Rathakára depend on the abundance of paternal property. Other sons of inferior birth, not among the aforementioned categories, shall depend on the eldest for their subsistence. Dependent sons shall receive equal divisions.

For sons born to a Bráhman father from the four castes, the son of a Bráhman woman shall take four shares; the son of a Kshatriya woman shall take three shares; the son of a Vaisya woman shall take two shares; and the son of a Súdra woman shall take one share.

The same rule applies to Kshatriya and Vaisya fathers who have begotten sons in three or two castes, respectively.

An Anantara son of a Bráhman, meaning a son begotten by a Bráhman with a woman of the next lower caste, shall, if endowed with manly or superior qualities (mánushopetah), take an equal share with other sons of lesser qualities. Similarly, Anantara sons of Kshatriya or Vaisya fathers, if they possess manly or superior qualities, shall take either half or equal shares with others.

An only son born to two mothers from different castes shall inherit the entire property and be responsible for maintaining the relatives of his father.

A Palrasava son, begotten by a Bráhman on a Súdra woman, shall receive one-third of the share. A sapinda (agnate) or a kulya (nearest cognate) of the Bráhman shall take the remaining two-thirds, being obliged to perform funeral rites. In the absence of agnates or cognates, the deceased father's teacher or student shall take the remaining shares.

- Alternatively, on the wife of such a Bráhman, a sagotra (relative from the same family name) or a mátribandha (relative from the mother's side) may beget a natural son (kshetraja), and this son may inherit the wealth.

[Thus ends Chapter VI, "Special Shares of Inheritance" in the section of "Division of inheritance" in Book III, "Concerning law" of the Arthasástra of Kautilya. End of the sixty-third chapter from the beginning.]

CHAPTER VII. DISTINCTION BETWEEN SONS.

My teacher says that the seed sown in another's field shall belong to the owner of that field. Others argue that, since the mother is merely the receptacle for the seed (mátá bhastrá), the child must belong to the one whose seed it is. Kautilya, however, says that the child belongs to both living parents.

The son born to a man from his wife who has gone through all the necessary ceremonies is called aurasa, a natural son. Equal to him is the son of an appointed daughter (putrikáputra). The son begotten on a wife by another man, appointed for the purpose, who is of the same gotra as the husband or of a different gotra, is called kshetraja. Upon the begetter's death, the kshetraja son will be the son to both fathers, follow the gotras of both, offer funeral libations to both, and inherit the immovable property (ríktha) of both. Of the same status as the kshetraja is he who is secretly begotten in the house of relatives and is called gúdhaja, the secretly born.

The son cast off by his natural parents is called apaviddha and belongs to the man who performs the necessary religious ceremonies for him. The son born of a maiden before wedlock is called kánína. The son born to a woman married while carrying is called sahodha. The son of a remarried woman (punarbhátáyáh) is called paunarbhava. A natural son can claim relationships with both his father and his father's relatives, but a son born to another man can have relationships only with his adopter.

Of the same status as the latter is he who is given in adoption with water by both the father and mother, known as datta. The son who, either by his own will or following his relatives' intent, offers himself as the son of another is called upagata. He who is appointed as a son is called kritaka, and the one who is purchased is called kríta.

Upon the birth of a natural son, savarna sons will inherit only one-third of the property, while the asavarna sons will receive only food and clothing.

Sons begotten by Bráhmans or Kshatriyas on women of the next lower caste (anantaráputráh) are called savarnas, but sons born of women two castes lower are called asavarnas. The son begotten by a Bráhman on a Vaisya woman is called Ambashtha, and the son of a Bráhman on a Súdra woman is called Nisháda or Párasava. The son begotten by a Kshatriya on a Súdra woman is known as Ugra, while the son of a Vaisya on a Súdra woman is considered a Súdra. Sons begotten by men of impure life, from any of the four castes, on women of lower castes next to their own are called Vrátyas. The above types of sons are called anuloma, sons begotten by men of higher castes on women of lower castes.

Sons begotten by a Súdra on women of higher castes are called Ayogava, Kshatta, and Chandála. When begotten by a Vaisya, they are Mágadha and Vaidehaka, and by a Kshatriya, they are called Súta. However, the individuals known as Súta and Mágadha in the Puránas are distinct and hold greater merit than either Bráhmans or Kshatriyas. The above types of sons are pratiloma, meaning sons born from men of lower castes and women of higher castes, originating from kings who violate all dharmas.

The son begotten by an Ugra on a Nisháda woman is called Kukkuta, and in reverse, when begotten by a Nisháda on an Ugra woman, the son is called Pulkasa. The son begotten by an Ambhashtha on a Vaidehaka woman is named Vaina, and the reverse order of that combination produces a son called Kusílava. An Ugra fathering a child with a Kshatta woman creates a son named Vapáka. These and other such sons are known as Antarálas, or mixed castes.

A Vainya becomes a Rathakára or chariot-maker by profession. Members of this caste shall marry within their own group. They should continue to follow the customs and occupations of their ancestors. They may either become Súdras or join other lower castes, except for Chandálas.

A king who guides his subjects according to these rules will ascend to heaven; otherwise, he will fall into hell.

- The offspring of mixed castes (Antarálas) shall receive equal shares of inheritance. Partition of inheritance shall follow the customs of the country, caste, guild (sangha), or village of the inheritors.

[Thus ends Chapter VII "Distinction between Sons" in the section of "Division of Inheritance" in Book III, "Concerning law" of the Arthasástra of Kautilya. End of "Division of Inheritance". End of the sixty-fourth chapter from the beginning.]

CHAPTER VIII. BUILDINGS.

Disputes concerning property (Vástu) are to be settled based on evidence provided by people living in the neighborhood. Houses, fields, gardens, buildings of any kind (setubandhah), lakes, and tanks are all considered Vástu.

The attachment of a house's roof to the transverse beam using iron bolts is called setu (karna-kílaya-sabandho'anugriham setuh). Houses must be constructed according to the stability of the setu, and new houses should be built without encroaching on the property of others.

The foundation (pade bandhah) should measure 2 aratnis by 3 padas. All permanent houses, except for temporary structures built for the confinement of women for ten days, must be equipped with a dunghill (avaskara), a water course (bhrama), and a well (udapánum). Failure to comply with this rule will result in the first amercement.

This rule also applies to the construction of closets, pits, and water courses for festive occasions.

Each house should have a water course with sufficient slope and a length of 3 padas or 11 aratnis, ensuring that water either flows continuously or falls directly into the drain. Violating this rule will incur a fine of 54 panas.

An apartment, starting with a pada or an aratni, should be built measuring 3 padas by 4 padas for placing a fire for worship (agnishtham), a waterbutt (udanjaram), a corn mill (rochaním), or a mortar (kuttinín). Non-compliance with this rule will result in a fine of 24 panas.

The space between any two houses or between the extended portions of any two houses shall be 4 padas, or 3 padas. The roofs of neighboring houses may either be 4 angulas apart, or one of them may overlap the other. The front door (anidváram) should measure a kishku, and there should be no obstacle inside the house that blocks the opening of either leaf of the door. The upper story must have a small but high window. If the window obstructs a nearby house, it must be closed. The owners of houses can build their homes in whatever way they mutually agree upon, as long as they avoid anything harmful. To prevent rain from causing damage, the roof should be covered with a broad mat that cannot be blown away by the wind. The roof should also not be of a type that easily bends or breaks. If this rule is violated, it shall be punished with the first amercement. The same punishment applies for causing inconvenience by constructing doors or windows that face those of neighboring houses, except when these houses are separated by the king's road or a public road.

If any pit, steps, water-course, ladder, dung-hill, or any other part of a house causes inconvenience to outsiders, blocks their enjoyment, or results in water collecting and damaging the wall of a neighboring house, the owner shall be fined 12 panas. If the inconvenience is caused by feces or urine, the fine shall be doubled. Watercourses or gutters must allow free passage for water; otherwise, the fine will be 12 panas.

The same fine of 12 panas shall apply not only to a tenant who refuses to leave after being asked but also to a homeowner who evicts a renter who has paid their rent, unless the renter is involved in defamation, theft, robbery, abduction, or falsely claiming ownership. Anyone who voluntarily leaves a house must pay the remaining balance of the annual rent.

If any member of a group does not participate in building a structure meant for the common use of all members, or if anyone obstructs another member from using any part of that structure, they shall be fined 12 panas. Similarly, if someone interferes with another's enjoyment of such a structure, they shall be fined double that amount.

- With the exception of private rooms and parlors (angana), all other open areas of houses, as well as any rooms where a fire is kept burning for worship or where a mortar is located, should be made available for common use.

[Thus ends Chapter VIII, "House-building" in the section of "Buildings" in Book III, "Concerning Law" of the Arthasástra of Kautilya. End of the sixty-fifth chapter from the beginning.]

CHAPTER IX. SALE OF BUILDINGS, BOUNDARY DISPUTES, DETERMINATION OF BOUNDARIES, AND MISCELLANEOUS HINDRANCES.

Wealthy individuals among relatives or neighbors shall, one after another, take the opportunity to purchase land or other holdings. Neighbors of good standing, numbering forty and different from the buyers mentioned earlier, shall gather in front of the property up for sale and announce its availability. An accurate description of the exact boundaries of fields, gardens, buildings, lakes, or tanks must be declared in front of the village elders or elders of the neighborhood. If, after shouting three times, "Who will purchase this at such and such a price?" no objections are raised, the buyer may proceed with the purchase of the property in question. If, at this point, the value of the property increases due to bidding even among members of the same community, the increased amount, along with the toll on the value, shall be handed over to the king's treasury. The person bidding (vikrayapratikroshtá) shall pay the toll. Bidding for a property in the absence of its owner shall be punished with a fine of 24 panas. If the owner does not come forward even after seven nights, the bidder may take possession of the property. Selling the property or buildings (vástu) to anyone other than the bidder shall be punished with a fine of 200 panas; if the property in question is other than buildings (vástu), the fine for the offense shall be 24 panas. Thus, the rules for the sale of buildings are outlined.

(Boundary disputes.)

In all disputes over boundaries between two villages, the neighboring elders from five or ten nearby villages (panchagrámí or dasagrámí) shall investigate the case, using evidence drawn from natural or man-made boundary markers. Senior cultivators and herdsmen, or others with prior knowledge of the area, as well as any individuals familiar or unfamiliar with the disputed boundary markers, shall first describe the markers in question. Then, dressed in unusual attire (viparítaveshah), they shall lead the group to the location. If the boundary markers they described are not located, a fine of 1,000 panas shall be imposed on the person providing false or misleading information. However, if they reach the correct location, the party that has encroached on the boundary or destroyed the markers shall be fined similarly. The king shall then distribute for beneficial use any landholdings without boundary markers or those that have ceased to be maintained by any individual.

(Disputes about fields.)

Disputes over fields shall be resolved by the elders of the neighborhood or village. If their opinions differ, a decision shall be sought from a group of honest and respected individuals, or the disputants may choose to divide the disputed holding equally. If neither of these methods succeeds, the king shall take possession of the holding (vástu) in question. The same rule applies to holdings for which no claimant comes forward; such holdings may also be beneficially distributed among the people. Any forcible occupation of a holding shall be punished as theft.

If someone occupies a holding on justifiable grounds, they shall pay the rightful owner a rent, with the amount set based on what is reasonably needed for the subsistence of the cultivator working the holding. Encroachment upon boundaries shall be punished with the first amercement. Destroying boundary markers shall be fined 24 panas. These rules also apply to disputes concerning forest hermitages, pasture lands, main roads, cremation grounds, temples, sacrificial sites, and places of pilgrimage. Thus, the determination of boundaries is addressed.

(Miscellaneous hindrances.)

All kinds of disputes will be settled based on the evidence provided by neighbors. Regarding pasture lands, fields, flower gardens, threshing floors, houses, and stables for horses, priority will be given to resolving issues for the first person in line before addressing those of anyone who comes afterward. Exceptions are made for forests belonging to Brahmins, places with Soma plants, temples, and sites of sacrifice and pilgrimage. Anyone who causes damage to seeds sown in someone else's fields by using a shortcut to reach tanks, rivers, or fields must pay the affected party compensation equal to the amount of the damage.

If the owner of any wet fields, parks, or buildings causes harm to similar property owned by others, the fine will be double the amount of the damage caused.

The water from a lower tank should not be allowed to flood any field that is irrigated by a higher tank.

The natural flow of water from a higher tank to a lower one must not be stopped unless the lower tank has remained unused for three continuous years. Anyone breaking this rule will be punished with the first level of penalty. The same punishment applies to draining a tank of its water. Any type of structure, including bridges or dams, that has been neglected for five consecutive years will be forfeited, except in cases of natural disaster.

(Remission of taxes.)

When constructing new works, such as tanks or lakes, taxes on the lands below these tanks will be waived for five years. For repairs on neglected or ruined works of this kind, a four-year tax exemption is given. Improvements or expansions of waterworks will have a three-year tax exemption. For new works acquired by mortgage or purchase, a two-year tax exemption will apply on lands below these works. If uncultivated land is acquired for farming, whether by mortgage, purchase, or any other means, the tax exemption will last for two years.

Out of the crops grown by irrigation using wind power, bullocks, or from tanks, fields, parks, flower gardens, or any other method, a portion of the produce, not so large as to burden the cultivators, should be provided to the Government.

Individuals who cultivate lands below tanks or similar works owned by others, either by paying a fixed price, an annual rent, or a share of the crops grown, or who are permitted to cultivate the land rent-free, must maintain these tanks and structures in good condition; otherwise, they will be fined double the amount of the damage caused.

- Those who divert the water of tanks or similar works at any place other than the designated sluice gate will be fined 6 panas; those who block the water flow from the sluice gate of a tank carelessly will be fined the same amount.

[Thus ends Chapter IX, "Sale of buildings, boundary disputes, determination of boundaries, and miscellaneous hindrances" in the section of "Buildings" in Book III, "Concerning Law" of the Arthasástra of Kautilya. End of the sixty-sixth chapter from the beginning.]

CHAPTER X. DESTRUCTION OF PASTURE-LANDS, FIELDS AND ROADS, AND NON-PERFORMANCE OF AGREEMENTS.

People who block or interfere with the flow of water intended for farming will face the first level of punishment. Anyone constructing buildings on someone else's property to attract pilgrims, including places of worship or temples, or who sells, mortgages, or causes the sale or mortgage of long-established charitable structures, will be subject to the middle level of punishment. Witnesses to such actions will face the highest level of punishment, except in cases involving neglected or ruined buildings. If there are no claimants for rundown religious buildings, villagers or charitable individuals are allowed to repair them.

(Blocking the roads.)

The rules regarding types of roads and paths were covered in the section on fort construction.

Blocking roads meant for common animals or people will incur a fine of 12 panas; blocking roads for superior animals, 24 panas; for roads used by elephants or leading to fields, 54 panas; for roads leading to buildings or forests, 600 panas; for roads to burial grounds or villages, 200 panas; for roads to a fortress, 500 panas; and for roads leading to regions, pasture grounds, or district centers, 1,000 panas. These fines also apply to excessively deep plowing on any of these roads, and a quarter of these fines apply if the plowing only affects the surface.

If a cultivator or neighbor encroaches on a field during the sowing season, they will be fined 12 panas, except when the encroachment results from unavoidable disasters, other disturbances, or extreme hardship coming from the field itself.

(Settling in villages.)

Taxpayers may sell or mortgage their fields only to other taxpayers; Brahmins may sell or mortgage their Brahmadaya, or gifted lands, only to those who also possess such lands. Otherwise, they will face the first level of punishment. The same penalty applies to any taxpayer who settles in a village where taxpayers do not reside. If one taxpayer takes over the place of another, they shall have rights to all holdings except the house of the previous owner, although the house itself may also be granted to the new resident.

If someone cultivates another person's inalienable land when the owner is not farming it, that person must return the land after enjoying its use for five years, receiving fair compensation for any improvements made on the land. Individuals who are not taxpayers and live abroad will retain ownership rights to their lands.

(The Head-man of the village.)

When the headman of a village needs to travel for business concerning the entire village, the villagers shall take turns accompanying him. Those unable to accompany him must pay a fee of 1½ panas for every yojana.

If the headman expels anyone from the village, except in cases involving a thief or an adulterer, he will be fined 24 panas, and the villagers will face the first level of punishment if they do the same.

The re-entry of a person previously expelled from the village is clarified in the section on the "settlement of people in villages."

Around each village, an enclosure of timber posts must be constructed, extending 800 angulas in distance from the village boundary.

(Trespassing cattle.)

Pasture lands, plains, and forests may be used for grazing cattle.

For camels or buffaloes that are allowed to stray after grazing in pasture grounds, the fine will be ¼ of a pana; for cows, horses, or asses, it will be 1/8 of a pana; for smaller animals, 1/16 of a pana. If cattle are found lying on these lands after grazing, the fines will be double the above amounts. For cattle that continually stay near the pasture grounds, the fines will be four times the above rates.

Bulls released in the name of the village deity, cows within ten days of calving that remain in the enclosure, or bulls kept specifically for breeding purposes will not be fined. If animals are proven guilty of eating crops, their owner or owners will pay double the amount of the crop loss. People driving their cattle through a field without informing the owner will be fined 12 panas. If someone allows their cattle to stray, they will be fined 24 panas, and cowherds allowing cattle under their care to stray will be fined half of that. The same penalty applies to letting cattle graze in flower gardens.

Breaking the fence of a field will incur twice the previous fine. If cattle stray and consume grains stored in a house, on a threshing floor, or in a courtyard, the owners of the cattle will have to provide adequate compensation.

If animals kept in reserve forests are found grazing in a field, it should be reported to the forest officers, and the animals will be driven out without harm. Stray cattle should be driven away with ropes or whips, and anyone who harms them will face punishment for assault or violence. Those who encourage cattle to graze in others' fields or are caught in the act must be thoroughly prevented. This concludes the guidelines for preventing damage to pasture lands, fields, and roads.

(Non-performance of agreement.)

The fine imposed on a cultivator who comes to a village for work but does not fulfill his duties will go to the village. He must return double the wages he accepted with the promise to work, along with double the value of any food and drink he was provided. If the work involves a sacrificial ceremony, he must also pay double the wages for not participating.

Anyone who does not contribute to the preparations for a public show will lose, along with their family, the right to attend the event. If someone who did not help prepare for a public performance is caught secretly listening or watching, or if anyone refuses to contribute to a project beneficial to all, they will be required to pay double the value of their expected contribution. The orders of any person acting for the common good must be respected. Disobedience in such a case will result in a fine of 12 panas. If others unite to harm or beat the person giving orders for the public benefit, each participant will pay twice the standard fine for such an offense.

If one of the offenders is a Brahmin or someone of higher status, they will face punishment first. A Brahmin who chooses not to join a village sacrificial ceremony will not be forced but may be persuaded to contribute his share.

These rules also apply to any failure to fulfill agreements among regions, castes, families, and assemblies.

- Those who work together to construct public buildings along roads, which benefit the entire country, and those who not only beautify their villages but also guard them will receive favorable recognition from the king.

[Thus ends Chapter X "Destruction of pasture lands, fields, and roads," in the section of "Buildings" in Book III, "Concerning Law" of the Arthasástra of Kautilya; end of "Buildings"; and of non-performance of agreements.' End of the sixty-seventh chapter from the beginning.]

CHAPTER XI. RECOVERY OF DEBTS.

An interest rate of one and a quarter panas per month per cent is considered fair. A rate of five panas per month per cent constitutes commercial interest. An interest rate of ten panas per month per cent is common among forest regions, while twenty panas per month per cent is usual among sea traders. Any person who exceeds, or causes another to exceed, the above rates of interest shall be punished with the first level of punishment; and those who are witnesses to such transactions shall each pay half the amount of the fine imposed.

The nature of the transactions between creditors and debtors, upon which the welfare of the kingdom depends, shall be thoroughly scrutinized at all times. In times of a good harvest, interest on grains shall not exceed half of its value in money. Interest on investments in stocks (prakshepa) shall be set at one-half of the profit and should be paid as each year expires. If it is allowed to accumulate due to either intention or the absence of the receiver or payer abroad, the amount to be paid shall be twice the share or the original principal.

A person who demands interest before it is due, or who attempts to represent the total amount of both the principal and its interest as the principal alone, shall be fined four times the amount under dispute. A creditor who sues for four times the amount they initially lent shall also pay a fine of four times the unjust amount. Of this fine, the creditor shall pay three-fourths, while the debtor shall pay the remaining one-fourth.

Interest on debts owed by persons engaged in prolonged sacrifices (dírghasatra), suffering from illness, detained in the houses of their teachers for learning, or who are minors or too impoverished, shall not accumulate.

A creditor who refuses to receive payment of his debt shall pay a fine of 12 panas. If this refusal is due to some justifiable reason, then the amount, free from any further interest, shall be held in safe custody by others. Debts neglected for ten years, except in the cases of minors, elderly persons, sick individuals, those involved in calamities, those traveling abroad or fleeing the country, and in cases of national disturbances (rájyavibhrama), shall not be reclaimed.

Sons of a deceased debtor are responsible for repaying the principal with interest. In the absence of sons, the deceased's kinsmen who claim a share of his estate, or any sureties such as joint partners in the debt, shall repay the debt. No other kind of surety shall be considered valid; the surety of a minor is weak and ineffective.

A debt for which there is no specified time or place for repayment shall be paid by the sons, grandsons, or any other heirs of the deceased debtor. Any debt with no specified time or place for repayment, and for which life, marriage, or land has been pledged, shall be borne by the debtor's sons or grandsons.

(Regarding many debts against one.)

Except when a debtor is going abroad, no debtor shall be sued simultaneously for more than one debt by one or two creditors. Even if the debtor is going abroad, he shall repay his debts in the order in which they were borrowed or shall first settle debts owed to the king or a learned Brahmin.

Debts contracted mutually by a husband and wife, a son and father, or between brothers with undivided interests shall be deemed irrecoverable.

Cultivators or government servants shall not be detained for debts while engaged in their official duties or work.

A wife, even if unaware of the debt (pratisrávaní), shall not be detained for a debt contracted by her husband, except in cases involving herdsmen or joint cultivators. However, a husband may be detained for a debt contracted by his wife. If it is confirmed that a man fled the country without addressing the debt contracted by his wife, he shall be subject to the highest level of punishment; if this is disputed, reliance shall be placed on witnesses.

(Witnesses.)

It is required to present three witnesses who are reliable, honest, and respected. A minimum of two witnesses acceptable to both parties is necessary in debt cases; never shall one witness alone be considered sufficient.

The following individuals are not eligible to serve as witnesses: brothers of the wife, co-partners, prisoners, creditors, debtors, enemies, dependents, or those previously punished by the Government. Also ineligible are persons legally barred from transactions, the king, those learned in the Vedas, those dependent on village provisions, lepers, individuals with bodily eruptions, outcasts, individuals of low occupation, the blind, the deaf, the mute, egotistical individuals, females, or government servants, except in cases involving dealings within their own community.

In disputes involving assault, theft, or abduction, individuals other than a wife's brothers, enemies, or co-partners can act as witnesses. In cases of secret dealings, a single woman or man who has privately seen or heard them may testify, except if they are the king or an ascetic. In cases of prosecution, masters can testify against servants, priests or teachers against disciples, and parents against sons. Other individuals may also act as witnesses in criminal cases.

If masters, servants, or other similarly related persons sue each other, they will be punished with the highest level of penalty. Creditors found guilty of making false claims (parokta) shall be fined ten times the amount involved, but if unable to pay such a fine, they shall pay at least five times the amount claimed. Thus concludes the section on witnesses.

(Taking oaths.)

Witnesses shall be presented before Brahmins, along with vessels of water and fire. A Brahmin witness shall be instructed, "Tell the truth." A Kshatriya or a Vaisya witness shall be told, "If you speak falsehood, may you fail to receive the rewards of your sacrificial and charitable deeds; but, after defeating your enemies in battle, may you become a beggar, carrying a skull in your hand."

A Sudra witness shall be warned as follows: "If you speak falsely, may all your good deeds, whether from a previous life or after your death, go to the king, and may any sins the king has committed fall upon you. Fines will also be levied on you, for facts as they were heard or seen will certainly be revealed in time."

If witnesses are found to have made a unanimous false agreement within seven nights, a fine of 12 panas shall be imposed. If they are found to have done so within three fortnights, they shall pay the full amount being claimed in the dispute.

If witnesses disagree in their testimonies, judgment shall be based on the statements of a majority of pure and respectable witnesses; or the average of their statements may be followed; or the amount in dispute may be claimed by the king. If witnesses testify to a lesser amount than claimed, the plaintiff shall be fined in proportion to the extra amount claimed; if they testify to a greater amount, the excess shall go to the king. In cases where the plaintiff proves himself ignorant or foolish, or when difficulty arises due to the witnesses' poor hearing at the time of the transaction or due to unclear writing, or where the debtor is deceased, only the evidence of witnesses shall be relied upon.

The followers of Usanas state: "Only in cases where witnesses prove themselves senseless or foolish, and when investigating the place, time, or nature of the transaction proves futile, shall the three levels of fines be imposed."

The followers of Manu assert: "False witnesses shall pay a fine ten times the amount, whether the sum lost is true or false."

The followers of Brihaspati declare: "When witnesses have muddied a case due to their ignorance, they shall be tortured to death."

"No," says Kautilya. "Witnesses must pay attention to the truth of what they hear when they are called to testify in any matter; if they did not pay attention, they shall be fined 24 panas; if they testified to a false case without thorough scrutiny, they shall be fined half of this amount."

- Each party shall produce witnesses who are not far removed either by time or place from the event in question; witnesses who are greatly removed either by time or place, or who are unwilling to appear, shall be compelled to present themselves by order of the judges.

[Thus ends Chapter XI, "Recovery of debts" in Book III, "Concerning Law" of the Arthasástra of Kautilya. End of the sixty-eighth chapter from the beginning.]

CHAPTER XII. CONCERNING DEPOSITS.

The rules concerning debts shall also apply to deposits. In cases where forts or regions of the kingdom are destroyed by enemies or wild tribes, where villages, merchants, or herds of cattle suffer attacks from invaders, where the kingdom itself is devastated, where widespread fires or floods result in the complete destruction of villages or partially damage immovable properties, with movable properties having been saved beforehand, or where sudden fires or floods prevent even movable properties from being salvaged, or when a ship loaded with goods is either sunk or looted by pirates, deposits lost in any of these situations shall not be reclaimed.

If the depositary has used the deposit for personal comfort, they shall not only pay compensation (bhogavetanam) determined according to the circumstances of place and time but shall also pay a fine of 12 panas. Any loss in the value of the deposit due to its use shall also be restored, along with an additional fine of 24 panas. Deposits that are damaged or lost through any cause must also be compensated in full.

When the depositary is either deceased or suffering from calamities, the deposit shall not be claimed. If the deposit has been mortgaged, sold, or lost, the depositary shall not only restore four times its value but shall also pay a fine equal to five times the value stipulated (pancbabandho dandah). If the deposit has been exchanged for a similar one by the depositary or lost in any other manner, its value shall be compensated.

(Pledges.)

The same rules shall apply in cases involving pledges whenever they are lost, consumed, sold, mortgaged, or misappropriated. A pledge that is productive, known as a usufructuary mortgage, shall never be lost to the debtor, nor shall any interest on the debt be charged. However, if the pledge is unproductive, as in the case of hypothecation, it may be lost, and interest on the debt shall continue to accumulate. A pledgee who does not return the pledge when the debtor is ready to redeem it shall be fined 12 panas.

In the absence of the creditor or mediator, the debt amount may be placed in the safekeeping of the village elders, allowing the debtor to reclaim the pledged property; alternatively, with its current value established and no future interest accruing, the pledge may be left where it is. If there is an increase in the value of the pledge or if there is reason to believe it may depreciate or be lost soon, the pledgee may, with permission from the judges or based on evidence from the officer responsible for pledges, sell the pledge either in the presence of the debtor or under the oversight of experts who can assess the validity of such concerns.

An immovable property pledged for enjoyment, whether through labor or without labor, shall not be allowed to lose its value while generating interest on the loaned amount and covering the maintenance expenses.

A pledgee who enjoys the pledged property without permission shall forfeit both the debt and shall pay the net profit they derived from it. The rules concerning deposits shall also be applicable to other matters related to pledges.

(Property entrusted to another for delivery to a third party)

The same rules shall apply to orders (ádesa) and property entrusted for delivery to a third party (anvádhi).

If a merchant entrusts a messenger with property for delivery to a third person and the messenger does not reach the intended destination or is robbed by thieves, the merchant shall bear no responsibility for the property; similarly, the family of a messenger who dies while en route shall not be held liable for the entrusted property.

For all other matters, the rules regarding deposits shall also apply here.

(Borrowed or hired properties.)

Properties either borrowed (yáchitakam) or hired (avakrítakam) must be returned in the same intact condition as when they were received. If, due to a long passage of time or distance, or because of inherent defects in the properties themselves, or due to unforeseen accidents, borrowed or hired properties are lost or destroyed, they need not be compensated for. The rules concerning deposits shall also apply here.

(Retail sale.)

Retail dealers who sell merchandise belonging to others, at prices specific to particular localities and times, shall hand over to the wholesale dealers the full amount of the sale proceeds and profit they have realized. The rules regarding pledges shall apply in this context as well. If, due to time or distance, there is a decrease in the value of the merchandise, retail dealers shall pay the value and profit at the rate that was in effect when they originally received the merchandise.

Servants who sell commodities at prices set by their masters shall not make any profit. They shall only return the actual sale proceeds. If prices decline, they shall only return as much of the sale proceeds as they receive at the lower rate.

However, merchants who are members of trade guilds (samvyavaharikeshu), or who are known to be trustworthy and are not condemned by the king, need not repay the value of merchandise that is lost or destroyed due to its inherent defects or unforeseen accidents. But for merchandise affected by time or distance, they shall return as much of its value and profit as remains after accounting for the wear and tear of the goods.

For all other matters, the rules regarding deposits shall also apply here. This explains retail sales.

(Sealed deposits.)

The rules established concerning unsealed deposits (upanidhis) shall also apply to sealed deposits. A person who hands over a sealed deposit to anyone other than the rightful depositor shall be punished. In the event that a depositary denies having received a deposit, the previous circumstances (púrvápadánam) surrounding the deposit, as well as the character and social standing of the depositor, shall serve as the only evidence. Artisans (káravah) are considered to naturally possess an impure character, and it is not customary for them to make deposits for valid reasons.

When a depositary denies having received a sealed deposit that was not deposited for a credible reason, the depositor may be granted secret permission from the judges to present witnesses whom he might have discreetly stationed behind a wall (gúdhabhitti) during the deposit.

In the midst of a forest or on a voyage, an elderly or ailing merchant might entrust a valuable article with a specific secret mark to a depositary and proceed on his way. Upon sending details of this deposit to his son or brother, the latter may request the sealed deposit. If the depositary does not return it without issue, he shall not only lose his credibility but shall also face punishment for theft in addition to being required to return the deposit.

A trustworthy individual, intending to renounce worldly life and become an ascetic, may leave a sealed deposit marked with a secret sign in the custody of another and, after several years, return to claim it. If the depositary denies it dishonestly, he shall be made to restore the deposit and shall also face punishment for theft.

If a person with a sealed deposit marked with a secret sign becomes fearful while passing through a street at night and, fearing capture by the police for walking at an odd hour, entrusts the deposit to someone before continuing on his way, and is subsequently jailed, he may later request the deposit back. Should the depositary deny this claim dishonestly, he shall be forced to restore it and will face punishment for theft.

A member of the depositor's family may recognize the sealed deposit in another person's possession and may request not only the deposit but also information about the depositor's whereabouts. If the custodian denies either request, he shall be treated in the same way as in the previous cases.

In all these situations, it is essential to inquire how the disputed property came into the depositary's possession, the circumstances connected to the transactions surrounding the property, and the plaintiff's social standing and wealth (arthasámarthyam).

The above rules shall apply to all types of transactions between any two people (mithassamaváyah).

- Therefore, all agreements should be entered into openly and in the presence of witnesses, without secrecy. Whether dealing with one's own people or others, the circumstances of the time and place should first be carefully considered.

[Thus ends Chapter XII "Concerning Deposits" in Book III, "Concernig Law" of the Arthasástra of Kautilya. End of the sixty-ninth chapter from the beginning.]

CHAPTER XIII. RULES REGARDING SLAVES AND LABOURERS.

The selling or mortgaging of the life of a Sudra who is not a born slave, has not reached adulthood, and is Arya by birth shall be punished by a fine of 12 panas; for a Vaisya, the fine is 24 panas; for a Kshatriya, 36 panas; and for a Brahmin, 48 panas. If persons who are not kin engage in the sale or mortgage of such individuals, they shall face the three levels of amercement, and in severe cases, capital punishment. Purchasers and those who abet these actions shall also be punished. It is not considered a crime for Mlechchhas to sell or mortgage the life of their own children. However, an Arya shall never be subjected to slavery.

If the life of an Arya is mortgaged to alleviate family difficulties, to obtain money for fines or legal decrees, or to reclaim confiscated household goods, the family members must redeem him as soon as possible, especially if he is a youth or an adult capable of providing assistance.

A person who has willingly enslaved himself once shall, if guilty of an offense (nishpatitah), remain a slave for life. Likewise, any person whose life has been twice mortgaged by others shall, if found guilty of an offense, be enslaved for life. Both types of individuals shall be bound to lifelong servitude if they are found attempting to flee to foreign lands.

Deceiving a slave of his earnings or denying him the rights he has as an Arya shall be punished by half the fine normally levied for enslaving the life of an Arya.

A person who unknowingly mortgages the life of a convict, deceased person, or an afflicted individual shall be entitled to recover the value paid for the slave from the original mortgager.

Employing a slave to handle the dead, clean waste, or clear away food remnants; forcing a slave to remain unclothed; harming or insulting them; or violating the chastity of a female slave shall result in the forfeiture of the amount paid for that slave. Violating the chastity of nurses, female cooks, or female servants who are joint cultivators or of similar class shall immediately grant them freedom. Any act of violence toward an attendant of high birth entitles him to escape servitude. If a master has relations with a nurse or pledged female slave against her will, he shall face the first level of amercement, while a stranger doing the same shall face the middle level of amercement.

If a man commits or assists in committing rape with a girl or female slave pledged to him, he shall forfeit the purchase value and pay a monetary sum (sulka) to her, in addition to a fine double that amount to the Government.

The offspring of a man who has sold himself into slavery shall be considered Arya. A slave shall have the right to retain not only his earnings, provided they do not interfere with his master's work, but also any inheritance received from his father.

By paying the amount for which one was enslaved, a slave shall regain Arya status. This rule applies equally to those who were born into slavery or pledged as slaves.

The amount required for a slave to secure freedom shall be equivalent to the price for which he was originally sold.

Any person enslaved for fines or court decrees (dandapranítah) shall earn the amount through labor. An Arya captured in war shall pay for his freedom a sum proportional to the risk endured during his capture, or half of that amount.

If a slave under eight years old, who has no relatives—whether born in the master's household, inherited, purchased, or acquired by any other means—is employed in menial tasks against his will, or is sold or mortgaged in a foreign land; or if a pregnant female slave is sold or pledged without arrangements made for her confinement, the master shall face the first level of amercement. The buyer and any abettors shall also be punished similarly.

Failing to release a slave upon receipt of the required ransom shall be penalized with a fine of 12 panas; confining a slave without valid reason (samrodhaschákaranát) shall also carry the same punishment.

A slave's property shall pass to his kinsmen; if no relatives are present, the master shall inherit it.

If a master begets a child by a female slave, both the child and the mother shall immediately be recognized as free. If, for subsistence, the mother must remain in servitude, her brother and sister shall be freed.

Selling or mortgaging the life of a male or female slave once freed shall result in a fine of 12 panas, except in cases of voluntary enslavement. Thus concludes the rules regarding slaves.

(Power of Masters over their hired servants.)

Neighbors shall be aware of the terms of agreement between a master and his servant. The servant shall receive the wages that were promised. If wages were not agreed upon in advance, the amount shall be determined based on the work completed and the time spent on it (karmakálánurúpam—according to the prevailing rate). When wages have not been previously set, a cultivator shall receive one-tenth of the crops grown, a herdsman one-tenth of the clarified butter produced, and a trader one-tenth of the sale proceeds. Wages that were agreed upon beforehand shall be paid and received as promised.

Artisans, musicians, physicians, entertainers, cooks, and other workers who voluntarily offer their services shall be paid the same wages as others in similar positions, or as determined by skilled persons (kusaláh) in that profession.

Disputes concerning wages shall be resolved based on evidence provided by witnesses. If no witnesses are available, the master who assigned work to the servant shall be questioned. Failure to pay agreed wages shall incur a fine of ten times the amount due (dasabandhah), or 6 panas; misappropriation of wages shall be punished with a fine of 12 panas or five times the amount of wages (panchabandho vá).

If a person, while being swept away by floods, trapped in a fire, or in peril from elephants or tigers, is rescued on the condition that he would give his rescuer all his property and even offer his sons, wife, and himself as slaves, he shall instead pay only an amount as determined by experts. This rule shall apply to all situations in which assistance is provided to a person in distress.

* A public woman shall honor her agreements, as promised; however, insistence on fulfilling an agreement that is ill-considered or inappropriate shall not be enforced.

[Thus ends Chapter XIII, "Rules regarding slaves" in the section of "Rules regarding slaves" and the "Right of Masters" in the section of "Rules regarding Labourers" in Book III, "Concerning Law" of the Arthasástra of Kautilya. End of the seventieth chapter from the beginning.]

CHAPTER XIV. RULES REGARDING LABOURERS; AND CO-OPERATIVE UNDERTAKING.

A servant who neglects or unreasonably delays work after receiving wages shall be fined 12 panas and detained until the work is completed. However, if a worker is incapable of performing the task, is engaged in a low-level job, is suffering from illness, or is affected by calamities, they shall be given some leniency or allowed to have the work done by a substitute. Any loss caused to the employer due to this delay shall be compensated by additional work from the servant.

An employer may freely engage another person to complete the work, provided there are no restrictive conditions preventing the original employee from taking on other work, nor shall the employee seek work elsewhere.

An employer who does not assign work to his laborer, or an employee who does not complete the employer's task, shall be fined 12 panas. An employee who has received wages for specific work that remains incomplete shall not leave to take up other work on his own accord.

My preceptor asserts that an employer not assigning work when the employee is prepared should be considered as if the work has been performed by the employee.

However, Kautilya disagrees, arguing that wages should only be paid for work actually completed, not for work left undone. If an employer assigns only a portion of the work to the laborer and does not assign the rest, though the laborer is ready to finish it, then the incomplete portion of work shall still be considered finished. Yet, if circumstances, such as changes in time or place, or if the work quality by the laborer is unsatisfactory, the employer may reasonably withhold satisfaction with the work performed. Moreover, if the laborer is left unchecked, he may exceed the agreed amount of work, resulting in a loss for the employer.

The same rules shall apply to guilds of workmen (sanghabhritáh).

Workmen guilds shall have a grace period of seven nights beyond the agreed deadline to fulfill their contracts. Beyond this time, they shall find substitutes to ensure the work is completed. Without their employer's permission, guild members shall neither leave any work unfinished nor take anything from the worksite. A fine of 24 panas shall be imposed for taking anything, and 12 panas for leaving work incomplete. Thus conclude the rules regarding laborers.

Guilds of workmen (sanghabhritáh, those employed by companies) as well as those engaged in cooperative work (sambhúya samutthátarah) shall divide their earnings (vetanam, or wages) either equally or as agreed among themselves.

Cultivators or merchants shall, either at the end or midway through their cultivation or manufacturing process, pay their laborers a share proportional to the work completed. If the laborers, upon leaving work midway, provide suitable replacements, they shall receive their wages in full.

In the case of commodities being manufactured, wages shall be paid according to the amount of work completed, as such payment is unaffected by any potential gains or losses in the subsequent sale of merchandise (by peddlers or otherwise).

A healthy person who abandons his company after work has begun shall be fined 12 panas, as no one shall leave the company of his own accord. Any individual found secretly neglecting his share of work shall be pardoned (abhayam) for the first offense and be assigned a proportionate amount of new work, with the promise of a corresponding share of earnings. In cases of repeated negligence or if the person seeks employment elsewhere, they shall be expelled from the company (pravásanam). If the offense is severe (maháparádhe), the person shall be treated as condemned.

(Co-operation in sacrificial acts.)

Priests cooperating in a sacrifice shall divide their earnings either equally or according to a prior agreement, except for specific portions that are due to any individual priest. If a priest participating in sacrifices such as Agnishtoma, etc., passes away after the consecration ceremony, his claimant shall receive 1/5th of the promised or prescribed gift (dakshiná); after the ceremony consecrating the purchase of Soma, 1/4th; after the Madhyamopasad or Pravargyodvásana ceremony, 1/3rd; and after the Maya ceremony, 1/2 of the share. In the Sutya sacrifice, if the priest passes after the Prátassavana ceremony, 3/4ths of the share shall be paid; after the Madhyandina ceremony, the full present shall be given, as the payment of presents shall be completed by that stage. In every sacrifice, except Brihaspatisavana, it is customary to provide presents. The same rule shall apply to the presents due in Aharganas, sacrifices by this name.

The remaining priests, retaining the remainder of the present, or any other relatives of a deceased priest, shall perform the funeral rites for the deceased for a period of ten days and nights.

If the sacrificer (the one who initiated the sacrifice) dies, the remaining priests shall complete the sacrifice and retain the presents. If a sacrificer dismisses a priest before completing the sacrifice, he shall be punished with the first amercement. If the sacrificer who dismisses a priest has not kept the sacrificial fire, or is a preceptor, or one who has already performed sacrifices, the fines shall be 100, 1000, and 1000 panas respectively.

Since sacrificial merits diminish when performed in the company of certain individuals—such as a drunkard, a man married to a Sudra woman, a Brahmin murderer, one who has violated the chastity of his preceptor's wife, a recipient of condemnable gifts, a thief, or one whose sacrificial acts are reproachable—it is permissible to dismiss such a priest without penalty.

[Thus ends Chapter XIV, "Rules regarding labourers, and Co-operative undertaking" in the section of "Rules regarding slaves and labourers," in Book III, "Concerning Law" of the Arthasástra of Kautilya. End of the seventy-first chapter from the beginning.]

CHAPTER XV. RESCISSION OF PURCHASE AND SALE.

A merchant who refuses to deliver merchandise that he has sold shall be fined 12 panas unless the merchandise is inherently defective, hazardous, or unsuitable.

Merchandise with inherent flaws is termed naturally bad; items liable to confiscation by the king, or susceptible to loss from thieves, fire, or floods, are deemed dangerous; and goods lacking all good qualities or made by deceased persons are considered intolerable.

The time allowed for rescinding a sale is one night for merchants, three nights for cultivators, five nights for herdsmen, and seven nights for transactions involving precious items or goods of mixed qualities (vivrittivikraye).

Merchandise likely to perish soon may, if it does not result in a loss to others, be granted early disposal privileges by restricting the sale of similar merchandise elsewhere that is not as perishable. Violation of this rule shall result in a fine of 24 panas or one-tenth of the value of merchandise sold in contravention of this rule.

If a buyer attempts to return a purchased item and it is neither naturally bad, dangerous, nor intolerable, he shall be fined 12 panas. The rescission rules applying to a seller shall likewise apply to the purchaser.

(Marriage Contracts)

As regards marriages among the three higher castes, the rejection of a bride before the rite of pánigrahana (the clasping of hands) is considered valid; similarly, among the Sudras, when observing religious rites. Even in cases where the rite of pánigrahana has taken place, the rejection of a bride is valid if it is later discovered that she has previously lain with another man. However, this rule does not apply to brides and bridegrooms of pure character and high family. Any person who has given a girl in marriage without disclosing her guilt of having been with another man shall be fined 96 panas and shall also be required to return the sulka and strídhana. Similarly, any person who accepts a girl in marriage without revealing the faults of the bridegroom shall pay double the aforementioned fine and forfeit the sulka and strídhana paid for the bride.

(Sale of bipeds and quadrupeds)

If bipeds or quadrupeds are sold as strong, healthy, and clean when they are actually unclean or suffering from leprosy or other diseases, the seller shall be fined 12 panas. The period allowed for rescinding the sale is three fortnights for quadrupeds and one year for humans, as it is possible to ascertain their true condition within this time.

- An assembly convened for this purpose shall, in cases of rescinding sales or gifts, make a decision that ensures neither the giver nor the receiver is harmed by the outcome.

[Thus ends Chapter XV, "Rescission of purchase and sale" in Book III, "Concerning Law" of the Arthasástra of Kautilya. End of the seventy-second chapter from the beginning.]

CHAPTER XVI. RESUMPTION OF GIFTS, SALE WITHOUT OWNERSHIP AND OWNERSHIP.

Rules concerning the recovery of debts shall also apply to the resumption of gifts. Invalid gifts shall be kept in the safe custody of designated individuals. Anyone who has given away not only his entire property but also his sons, wife, and even his own life as a gift shall bring this for consideration by those authorized to annul such gifts. Gifts or charitable donations made to wicked individuals or for unworthy purposes, financial support to malevolent or cruel persons, and promises of sexual enjoyment to the unworthy shall be settled by these authorized individuals so that neither the giver nor the receiver is harmed by the outcome.

Those who extort any kind of assistance from timid individuals by threatening them with legal punishment, defamation, or financial loss shall be punished as if guilty of theft, and the individuals who yield such assistance shall likewise be penalized.

Cooperating in harming a person and showing insolence towards the king shall be punished with the highest amercement. No son or heir claiming the property of a deceased person shall be obliged, against his will, to pay the value of any bail borne by the deceased (prátibhávyadanda), any remaining balance of a dowry (sulkasesha), or gambling stakes, nor shall he be bound to fulfill promises of gifts made by the deceased under the influence of alcohol or love. Thus concludes the section on resumption of gifts.

(Sale without ownership.)

As regards the sale of property by someone without ownership: Upon discovering a lost item in another person's possession, the rightful owner shall arrange for the offender's arrest through the court's judges. If time or location does not allow for this, the owner shall personally apprehend the offender and bring him before the judges. The judge shall inquire as to how the offender acquired the property. If the offender explains how he obtained it but cannot produce the person who sold it to him, he shall be released and forfeit the property. However, if the seller is produced, he shall not only repay the value of the property but also face the punishment for theft.

If someone in possession of stolen property flees or hides until the property is entirely consumed, he shall pay its full value and also receive the punishment for theft.

After proving his claim to the lost property (svakaranam kritva), the rightful owner shall be permitted to reclaim it. If he cannot substantiate his title, he shall be fined five times the value of the property (panchabandhadandah), and the property shall be seized by the king.

If the owner reclaims a lost item without obtaining court permission, he shall be subject to the first level of amercement.

Stolen or lost items, when discovered, shall be held at the toll-gate. If no claimant appears within three fortnights, the items shall be taken by the king.

The rightful owner of a lost or stolen biped shall pay a ransom of 5 panas before reclaiming it. Likewise, the ransom for a single-hoofed animal shall be 4 panas; for a cow or buffalo, 2 panas; for minor animals, 1/4 of a pana; and for items such as precious stones or raw materials, five percent of their value.

Any property of his subjects that the king recovers from enemy forests or territories shall be returned to its rightful owner. Any property stolen by thieves that the king cannot retrieve shall be compensated from the king's treasury. If the king is unable to compensate for these losses, he shall either authorize a self-appointed agent (svayamgráha) to retrieve them or provide an equivalent ransom to the affected party. An adventurer may keep whatever the king generously grants him from the spoils taken from an enemy's land, excluding the life of an Arya and the property of gods, Brahmins, or ascetics.

Thus concludes the rules regarding the sale of property by someone without ownership.

(Ownership.)

As to the title of an owner to his property: Owners who have left their country where their property lies shall continue to retain their title to it. When owners—excluding minors, the elderly, those afflicted with disease or calamities, those sojourning abroad, or those who have abandoned their country during national disturbances—neglect their property, allowing it to remain under the enjoyment of others for ten years, they shall forfeit their title to it.

Buildings left in the enjoyment of others for a period of 20 years shall not be reclaimed. However, the mere occupation of buildings belonging to others by kinsmen, priests, or heretics during the absence of the king shall not entitle them to a right of possession. The same rule applies with regard to open deposits, pledges, treasure troves (nidhi), boundary markers, or any property belonging to kings or priests (srotriyas).

Ascetics and heretics shall reside in a large area without disturbing each other. However, a new resident shall be provided with space occupied by an old resident. If the old resident is unwilling to yield the space, he shall be removed.

The property of hermits (vánaprastha), ascetics (yati), or bachelors learning the Vedas (Brahmachári) shall, upon their death, be inherited in succession by their preceptors, disciples, spiritual brothers (dharmabhrátri), or classmates.

Whenever hermits, ascetics, or similar individuals are required to pay any fines, they may perform penance, offer oblations to the gods, conduct fire worship, or perform the ritual known as Mahákachchhavardhana in the name of the king, observing the ritual for as many nights as the number of panas required to satisfy the fine. Heretics (páshandáh) who lack either gold or gold-coins shall observe fasting in the same manner, except in cases involving defamation, theft, assault, and the abduction of women. In these instances, they shall be compelled to undergo conventional punishment.

- The king shall, under the penalty of fines, prohibit any willful or improper actions by ascetics, as vice overwhelming righteousness will, in the long run, bring ruin upon the ruler himself.

[Thus ends Chapter XVI, "Resumption of gifts, sale without ownership, and ownership" in Book III, "Concerning Law" of the Arthasástra of Kautilya. End of the seventy-third chapter from the beginning.]

CHAPTER XVII. ROBBERY.

Sudden and direct seizure (of person or property) is termed sáhasa, while fraudulent or indirect seizure (niranvaye'pavyayanecha) is regarded as theft.

The school of Manu holds that the fine for the direct seizure of precious stones and superior or inferior raw materials shall equal their value. According to the followers of Usanas, it should be twice the value of the items. However, Kautilya asserts that the fine should correspond to the severity of the crime.

For articles of small value, such as flowers, fruits, vegetables, roots, turnips, cooked rice, skins, bamboo, and earthenware pots, the fine shall range from 12 to 24 panas. For items of moderate value, like iron (káláyasa), wood, roping materials, and herds of smaller animals, the fine shall range from 24 to 48 panas. For items of higher value, such as copper, brass, bronze, glass, ivory, and vessels, the fine shall range from 48 to 96 panas. This is termed the first amercement.

In cases of seizure involving large animals, people, fields, houses, gold, gold coins, or fine fabrics, the fine shall range from 200 to 500 panas, known as the middlemost amercement.

My preceptor holds that forcibly detaining or causing others to detain men or women in prison or forcibly releasing them from imprisonment shall be punished with fines ranging from 500 to 1,000 panas. This is termed the highest amercement.

A person who induces another to commit sáhasa according to a plan devised by themselves shall be fined double the value of the person or property seized. An instigator who hires someone to commit sáhasa with the promise, "I shall pay you as much gold as you require," shall be fined four times the value.

The school of Brihaspati believes that if an abettor, with the promise, "I will pay you this amount of gold," induces someone else to commit sáhasa, the abettor shall be required to pay the promised amount of gold along with an additional fine. However, Kautilya holds that if an abettor justifies their actions by claiming anger, intoxication, or loss of sense (moham), they shall be punished as previously described.

- In all fines below one hundred panas, the king shall collect an additional eight percent as rúpa, and in fines exceeding one hundred panas, an additional five percent. These two forms of exaction are deemed just, given that people are prone to sin on one hand, and kings are naturally subject to misguidance on the other.

[Thus ends Chapter XVII, "Robbery" in Book III, "Concerning Law" of the Arthasástra of Kautilya. End of the seventy-fourth chapter from the beginning.]

CHAPTER XVIII. DEFAMATION.

Calumny, contemptuous speech, or intimidation constitutes defamation.

Among insulting expressions directed at one's physical attributes, habits, education, occupation, or nationality, calling a person with a deformity by their true name, such as "the blind" or "the lame," shall be punished with a fine of 3 panas; calling them by a false name incurs a fine of 6 panas. If the blind, the lame, etc., are mocked with ironic terms, such as "a man of beautiful eyes" or "a man of beautiful teeth," the fine shall be 12 panas. The same applies when a person is insulted with terms referring to conditions such as leprosy, lunacy, or impotency. Insulting expressions in general, whether true, false, or sarcastic toward the insulted person, shall be punished with fines exceeding 12 panas when directed at individuals of equal rank.

If the insulted persons are of superior rank, the fines shall be doubled; if of lower rank, they shall be halved. For defaming the wives of others, the fines shall be doubled.

If the abuse arises from carelessness, intoxication, or loss of sense, the fines shall be halved.

Regarding the verification of leprosy or lunacy, physicians or neighbors shall serve as authorities.

For evidence of impotency, testimony may come from women, the examination of urine scum, or the low specific gravity of feces in water (i.e., the sinking of feces in water).

(Speaking ill of habits.)

If, among Brahmins, Kshatriyas, Vaisyas, Sudras, and outcastes (antávasáyins), any person of a lower caste abuses the habits of someone of a higher caste, the fines imposed shall increase, beginning from 3 panas and upward, with the progression starting from the lowest caste. If any person of a higher caste abuses someone of a lower caste, the fines imposed shall decrease, beginning from 2 panas.

Contemptuous expressions such as "a bad Brahmin" shall also be punished according to the above rule.

The same rules shall apply to defamatory remarks regarding learning (sruta), the professions of buffoons (vágjívana), artisans, or musicians, as well as relating to specific nationalities such as Prájjunaka or Gándhára.

(Intimidation)

If a person intimidates another by using expressions like "I shall render thee thus," the bravado shall be punished with a fine that is half of what would be imposed on a person who actually carries out such an act.

If a person, being unable to fulfill his threat, claims provocation, intoxication, or loss of sense as his excuse, he shall be fined 12 panas.

If a person who is capable of causing harm and acts under the influence of enmity intimidates another, he shall be compelled to provide lifelong security for the well-being of the intimidated person.

- Defamation of one's own nation or village shall be punished with the first amercement; defamation of one's own caste or assembly shall incur the middlemost amercement; and defamation of gods or temples (chaitya) shall be penalized with the highest amercement.

[Thus ends Chapter XVIII, "Defamtion" in Book III, "Concerning Law" of the Arthasástra of Kautilya. End of the seventy-fifth chapter from the beginning.]

CHAPTER XIX. ASSAULT.

Touching, hitting, or injuring someone is considered assault.

When a person touches another person's body below the navel with a hand, mud, ashes, or dust, he will be fined 3 panas. If the touch involves something unclean, like the foot or spit, the fine is 6 panas. If touched with saliva, urine, feces, or similar substances, the fine is 12 panas. If this action happens above the navel, the fines are doubled, and if on the head, the fines are quadrupled.

If the same offense is committed against a person of higher rank, the fine will be twice as much; if against a person of lower rank, the fine will be half the amount stated. If the offense is directed toward another person's wife, the fine is doubled.

If the offense happens because of carelessness, intoxication, or loss of reason, the fines are reduced by half.

For grabbing someone by the legs, clothes, hands, or hair, the fines will be more than 6 panas. Actions like squeezing, wrapping arms around, pushing, dragging, or sitting on another person will be punished with the first level of amercement.

Running away after making someone fall will result in a fine equal to half of those listed above.

The limb of a Sudra used to strike a Brahmin will be cut off.

(Striking.)

For striking, compensation must be paid, and the fine imposed will be half of what is levied for touching. This rule also applies to Chandalas and other persons considered profane when committing the same offense. Striking with the hand shall incur a fine of less than 3 panas; striking with the leg will result in a fine twice that amount; and striking with an instrument that causes swelling shall be punished with the first level of amercement. Striking in a way that endangers life shall be punished with the middle level of amercement.

(Hurting.)

Causing a bloodless wound with a stick, mud, a stone, an iron bar, or a rope shall be punished with a fine of 24 panas. Causing the blood to gush out, excepting cases where it is diseased or bad blood, shall be punished with double the fine.

Beating a person nearly to the point of death, though without causing blood, or breaking a person's hands, legs, or teeth, tearing off the ear or the nose, or breaking open the flesh of a person except in cases of ulcers or boils, shall be punished with the first amercement. Causing injury to the thigh or the neck, wounding the eye, or harming in such a way as to impede eating, speaking, or any other bodily movement shall not only be punished with the middlemost amercement but shall also require the payment of compensation (to the sufferer) sufficient to cover his treatment and cure. If circumstances of time or place do not permit the immediate arrest of an offender, he shall be handled as described in Book IV, which treats the measures to suppress the wicked.

Each individual in a confederacy of persons who have inflicted harm on another person shall be punished with double the usual fine.

My preceptor holds that quarrels or assaults of a remote date shall not be grounds for a complaint.

However, Kautilya holds that there shall be no acquittal for an offender. My preceptor believes that he who is the first to bring a complaint of a quarrel should win, as it is the pain that drives one to seek justice.

However, Kautilya disagrees; whether a complaint is lodged first or last, it is the testimony of witnesses that must be relied upon. In the absence of witnesses, the nature of the injury and other circumstances connected with the quarrel in question shall serve as evidence. A sentence of punishment shall be passed on the very day that a defendant accused of assault fails to answer the charge made against him.

(Robbery in quarrels.)

A person stealing anything amidst the commotion of a quarrel shall be fined 10 panas. The destruction of articles of small value shall be punished with a fine equal to the value of the articles, in addition to an adequate compensation paid to the sufferer. Destruction of large items shall require compensation equal to their value and a fine twice the value of the items. In cases involving the destruction of items such as clothes, gold, gold coins, vessels, or merchandise, the first amercement along with the value of the articles shall be imposed.

Causing damage to the wall of another man's house by striking it shall be fined 3 panas; breaking open or demolishing it shall result in a fine of 6 panas, in addition to the cost of restoring the wall.

Throwing harmful substances into someone's house shall incur a fine of 12 panas; throwing objects that endanger the lives of the inhabitants shall be punished with the first amercement.

For causing pain with sticks or similar objects to minor animals, a fine of one or two panas shall be imposed; if blood is drawn, the fine shall be doubled. For larger animals, double the fines stated above shall be imposed, along with adequate compensation to cover the animals' treatment and recovery.

Cutting off the tender sprouts of fruit-bearing, flowering, or shade-providing trees in city parks shall result in a fine of 6 panas; cutting minor branches of such trees shall result in a fine of 12 panas; and cutting large branches shall result in a fine of 24 panas. Cutting the trunks of these trees shall be punished with the first amercement, and felling them shall incur the middlemost amercement.

For plants that bear flowers, fruits, or provide shade, half of the above fines shall be levied.

The same fines shall apply in cases involving trees grown in places of pilgrimage, forests dedicated to hermits, or in cremation or burial grounds.

- For similar offenses related to trees marking boundaries, those which are worshipped or marked for observation (chaityeshválakshiteshucha), or trees grown in royal forests, double the aforementioned fines shall be imposed.

[Thus ends Chapter XIX, "Assault" in Book III, "Concerning law" of the Arthasástra of Kautilya. End of the seventy-sixth chapter from the beginning.]

CHAPTER XX. GAMBLING AND BETTING AND MISCELLANEOUS OFFENCES.

With the purpose of identifying spies or thieves, the Superintendent of Gambling shall centralize all gambling activities and impose a fine of 12 panas if gambling takes place elsewhere.

My preceptor believes that in disputes concerning gambling, the winner should be punished with the first amercement and the loser with the middlemost amercement, as the loser, though not skillful enough to achieve his desire to win, cannot tolerate his defeat.

However, Kautilya disagrees: if the penalty for the loser were doubled, no one would dare to bring complaints to the king. Nevertheless, gamblers are naturally inclined to play deceitfully.

Therefore, the Superintendents of Gambling shall be upright and provide dice at a rental rate of one kákani per pair. If any player substitutes dice through sleight of hand instead of using the provided ones, he shall be fined 12 panas. A deceitful player shall be punished with the first amercement, pay fines applicable for theft and deception, and forfeit the stakes he has won.

The Superintendent shall collect not only 5 percent of the stakes won by each winner, along with the rental for supplying dice and other necessary items, but also fees for providing water, accommodation, and the license fee.

Additionally, the Superintendent may manage transactions involving the sale or mortgage of items. If he neglects to prevent sleight-of-hand tricks and other deceptive practices, he shall be fined twice the amount levied on the deceitful gamblers.

These rules shall also apply to betting and challenges, except in cases related to learning and art.

(Miscellaneous offences.)

As regards miscellaneous offenses:

When a person fails to return borrowed, hired, or deposited property at the required place or time; sits in the shade for more than one and a quarter hours (ayáma) beyond the prescribed time; evades payment at military stations or river crossings by claiming to be a Brahmin; or loudly invites others to engage in disputes with his neighbors, he shall be fined 12 panas.

When a person fails to deliver property entrusted to him for another, drags the wife of his brother by the hand, has relations with a public woman kept by another, sells merchandise known for its bad reputation, breaks open the sealed door of a house, or harms any of the forty householders or neighbors, a fine of 48 panas shall be imposed.

When a person misappropriates funds collected as a household agent, forcibly violates the chastity of an independently living widow, when an outcast (Chandála) touches an Arya woman, when a person fails to assist another in danger without cause, or invites to a religious feast Buddhists (Sákya), Ajívakas, Sudras, or exiled persons (pravrajita), a fine of 100 panas shall be imposed.

When an unauthorized person administers an oath to an offender, undertakes government work without authorization, renders minor animals impotent, or induces a female slave to miscarry through medicine, he shall be punished with the first amercement.

If between father and son, husband and wife, brother and sister, maternal uncle and nephew, or teacher and student, one abandons the other when neither has renounced their duties, or if a person leaves behind another in the center of a village after bringing them there for help, the first amercement shall be levied.

If a person abandons a companion in the middle of a forest, he shall be punished with the middlemost amercement.

If a person threatens and abandons a companion in the forest, he shall be fined with the highest amercement.

When individuals who started a journey together abandon each other as described above, half the corresponding fine shall be imposed.

When a person illegally confines another, releases someone from prison, or detains a minor unlawfully, a fine of 1,000 panas shall be imposed.

Fines shall vary according to the ranks of the people involved and the severity of the crimes.

Mercy shall be shown to pilgrims, ascetics engaged in penance, the diseased, those suffering from hunger, thirst, or travel fatigue, villagers from rural areas, those who have endured much punishment, and those without means.

Transactions involving gods, Brahmins, ascetics, women, minors, the elderly, the sick, and the helpless shall, even if not complained of, be settled by the judges themselves, and excuses of time, place, or possession shall not be considered in such cases.

Individuals known for learning, intelligence, bravery, noble birth, or great works shall be shown honor.

• Judges shall settle disputes impartially, without circumvention, with minds unaffected by moods or circumstances, remaining pleasant and accessible to all.

Book 4

CHAPTER I. PROTECTION OF ARTISANS.

Three Commissioners (pradeshtárah) or three ministers shall be responsible for implementing measures to suppress disturbances to peace (kantakasodhanam kuryuh).

Those individuals who are expected to relieve hardship, who can instruct artisans, who are trustworthy with deposits, who can design and plan artistic work, and who are relied upon by artisan guilds, may receive deposits from the guilds. The guilds (sreni) shall have their deposits returned to them in times of distress.

Artisans shall fulfill their engagements according to the agreed-upon time, place, and form of work. Those who delay their commitments, claiming no agreement on time, place, and form of work, shall, except in cases of trouble or calamity, forfeit one-fourth of their wages and be fined an amount equal to twice their wages. They shall also compensate for any resulting losses or damages. Artisans who work against given instructions shall not only forfeit their wages but also be fined an amount equal to twice their wages.

(Weavers.)

Weavers shall increase the threads supplied to them for weaving cloths in the proportion of 10 to 11 (dasaikádasikam). If they fail to do so, they shall not only pay a fine equal to twice the loss in threads or the value of the entire yarn but also forfeit their wages. In weaving linen or silk cloths (kshaumakauseyánam), the increase shall be in the ratio of 1 to 1½. In weaving fibrous or woolen garments or blankets (patronakambáladukúlánám), the increase shall be 1 to 2.

If there is any loss in length, the value of the loss shall be deducted from the wages, and a fine equal to twice the loss shall be imposed. Any loss in weight (tuláhíne) shall be punished with a fine equal to four times the amount of the loss. If different types of yarn are substituted, the fine shall be twice the value of the original yarn.

The same rules shall apply to the weaving of broad cloths (dvipatavánam).

The acceptable loss in weight of woolen threads due to threshing or shedding of hair is 5 palas.

(Washermen.)

Washermen shall wash clothes either on wooden planks or on stones with a smooth surface. Washing on any other surface shall result in a fine of 6 panas, along with the payment of compensation equal to the damage caused.

If washermen wear clothes other than those marked with the symbol of a cudgel, they shall be fined 3 panas. A fine of 12 panas shall be imposed for selling, mortgaging, or renting out the clothes of others.

In cases of substituting clothes with others, they shall be fined an amount equal to twice the value of the clothes and be required to return the original ones.

For keeping clothes overnight that are to be made as white as a jasmine flower, or are meant to attain their natural color after washing on smooth stones, or are to be made simply whiter by dirt removal, proportional fines shall be levied. For keeping clothes intended for a light tinting more than five nights, clothes meant to be made blue more than six nights, or clothes to be made as white as flowers or as glossy as lac, saffron, or blood and requiring significant skill for brilliance more than seven nights, the wages shall be forfeited.

Trustworthy individuals shall act as judges in disputes regarding color, and experts shall assess the appropriate wages.

For washing high-quality garments, the wage shall be one pana; for garments of medium quality, half a pana; and for lower-quality garments, one-fourth of a pana.

For rough washing on large stones, the wage shall be one-eighth of a pana.

In the first wash of red-colored clothes, a loss of one-fourth of the color is expected; in the second wash, one-fifth of the color is lost, explaining the color losses in subsequent washes. The rules concerning washermen also apply to weavers.

Goldsmiths who, without informing the government, purchase silver or golden articles from unclean sources without altering the form of the articles shall be fined 12 panas; if they purchase such articles and alter their form (e.g., by melting), they shall be fined 24 panas. If they purchase these items from a thief, they shall be fined 48 panas. If they secretly melt an item and purchase it below its value, they shall face the penalty for theft, as they would for deception involving manufactured articles. When a goldsmith steals gold equal to the weight of a másha (1/16th of a suvarna) from a suvarna, he shall be fined 200 panas; if he steals silver equal to the value of a másha from a silver dharana, the fine shall be 12 panas. This illustrates the proportional increase of penalties. When a goldsmith removes the entire weight of gold (karsha) from a suvarna by the apasárana method or any other deceptive combination (yoga), he shall be fined 500 panas. Contaminating gold or silver in any way shall be regarded as a loss of their intrinsic color.

One másha shall be the fee for crafting a silver dharana; for a suvarna, it shall be one-eighth of that amount, with fees doubling based on the skill of the craftsman. This indicates the proportional rise in fees.

The fee for crafting articles from copper, brass, vaikrinataka, and árakúta shall be five percent. In crafting items from copper, a loss of one-tenth of the material is expected. If the weight loss amounts to a pala, a fine equal to twice the value of the loss shall be imposed. This shows the increase in penalties based on loss. In crafting items from lead or tin, a loss of one-twentieth of the mass is expected. For each pala of these materials, a fee of one kákani shall be charged. In crafting iron articles, one-fifth of the mass will be lost, with a fee of two kákanis for each pala. This further explains the proportional increase in fees.

When a coin examiner declares an unacceptable current coin as suitable for entry into the treasury or rejects an acceptable coin, he shall be fined 12 panas. If the examiner misappropriates a másha from a current coin of a pana, after the tax (Vyájí) of five percent on the coin has been paid, he shall be fined 12 panas. This demonstrates the proportional rise in fines. When someone manufactures, accepts, or exchanges a counterfeit coin, he shall be fined 1,000 panas; if a counterfeit coin is placed into the treasury, the offender shall be sentenced to death.

(Scavengers.)

Of any precious items that sweepers come across while sweeping, one-third shall be kept by them, and two-thirds shall go to the king. However, any precious stones found shall be fully surrendered to the king. Seizing precious stones shall incur the highest amercement.

A discoverer of mines, precious stones, or treasure troves shall, upon reporting the find to the king, receive one-sixth of it as their share. However, if the discoverer is a peon (bhritaka), his share shall be only one-twelfth of it.

Treasure troves valued beyond 100,000 shall be taken entirely by the king. If of lesser value, the discoverer shall receive one-sixth as his share.

Treasure troves that a person of pure and honest life can prove to be their ancestral property shall be taken in full by that person. Claiming a treasure trove without such proof shall incur a fine of 500 panas. Secretly taking possession of a treasure trove shall be punished with a fine of 1,000 panas.

(Medical Practice).

Physicians who undertake medical treatment without informing the government of the disease's dangerous nature shall, if the patient dies, be punished with the first amercement. If a patient under treatment dies due to the physician's carelessness, the physician shall face the middlemost amercement. If a disease worsens due to a physician's negligence or indifference (karmavadha), it shall be regarded as assault or violence.

(Musicians)

Bands of musicians (kúsílavah) shall reside in a fixed place during the rainy season. They shall be careful not to give excessive indulgence or cause excessive loss (atipátam) to anyone. Violation of this rule shall be punished with a fine of 12 panas. They may hold performances as they wish, following the customs of their region, caste, family, profession, or association.

The same rules shall apply to dancers, mime artists, and other mendicants.

For offenses, mendicants shall receive as many lashes with an iron rod as the number of panas imposed on them.

Wages for the works of other types of artisans shall be similarly determined.

Thus, traders, artisans, musicians, beggars, buffoons, and other idlers—who are thieves in effect, though not in name—shall be restrained from oppressing the country.

[Thus ends Chapter I, "Protection of artisans" in Book IV, "The Removal of Thorns" of the Arthasástra of Kautilya. End of the seventy-eighth chapter from the beginning.]

CHAPTER II. PROTECTION OF MERCHANTS.

The Superintendent of Commerce shall allow the sale or mortgage of any old commodities (purána bhándanám) only when the seller or mortgagor of such articles proves his ownership of the same. With a view to prevent deception, he shall also supervise weights and measures.

A difference of half a pala in such measures as are called parimání and drona is not considered an offense. However, a difference of a full pala in these measures shall be punished with a fine of 12 panas. Fines for greater differences shall be increased proportionally.

A difference of one karsha in the balance called tulá is not an offense. However, a difference of two karshas shall incur a fine of 6 panas, with fines for greater differences increased proportionally.

A difference of half a karsha in the measure called ádhaka is not an offense; however, a difference of one karsha shall incur a fine of 3 panas. For greater differences, fines shall be increased proportionally. Fines for differences in weight in other types of balances shall be inferred based on this rule.

If a merchant, using a false balance, buys a greater quantity of a commodity and sells a lesser quantity under the same nominal weight by using the same or another false balance, he shall be punished with double the fines stated above.

Any deception by a seller to the extent of one-eighth part of articles valued at a pana and sold by number shall incur a fine of 96 panas.

The sale or mortgage of articles such as timber, iron, gemstones, ropes, skins, earthenware, threads, fibrous garments, and woolen clothes as superior when they are actually inferior shall be punished with a fine of eight times the value of the articles thus sold.

If a trader sells or mortgages inferior items as superior, goods from one region as if they were from another, adulterated products, or deceitful mixtures, or if he subtly substitutes other items for those just sold (samutparivartimam), he shall be fined 54 panas and shall also be required to compensate for the loss.

To determine fines for any such fraudulent sales, the rate shall be two panas for a loss valued at one pana, and 200 panas for a loss valued at 100 panas.

Those who conspire to lower the quality of artisans' work, obstruct their income, or interfere with their sale or purchase shall be fined 1,000 panas.

Merchants who conspire either to prevent the sale of goods or to manipulate the buying or selling prices of commodities shall be fined 1,000 panas.

Middlemen who cause a merchant or a purchaser to lose one-eighth of a pana by substituting, through tricks of hand, false weights or measures or other inferior items shall be punished with a fine of 200 panas. Fines for greater losses shall be proportionally increased, beginning from 200 panas.

The adulteration of grains, oils, alkalis, salts, scents, and medicinal articles with similar items of no quality shall be punished with a fine of 12 panas.

It is the responsibility of the trader to calculate the daily earnings of middlemen and to fix that amount on which they are authorized to live, as the income which falls between sellers and purchasers (i.e., brokerage) differs from profit.

Only authorized persons shall collect grains and other merchandise; any collection of such items without permission shall be confiscated by the Superintendent of Commerce.

Therefore, merchants shall display a favorable attitude toward the people in the sale of grains and other commodities.

The Superintendent of Commerce shall fix a profit margin of five percent above the set price for local commodities and ten percent on foreign produce. Merchants who raise the price or realize profit even to the extent of half a pana above this on the sale or purchase of commodities shall be punished with a fine starting from five panas for realizing 100 panas up to 200 panas.

Fines for greater price enhancements shall be increased proportionally.

If there is a failure to sell collected merchandise wholesale at the established rate, the rate shall be adjusted.

In cases of obstruction to traffic, the Superintendent shall grant necessary concessions.

When there is an oversupply of merchandise, the Superintendent shall centralize its sale and prohibit the sale of similar merchandise elsewhere until the centralized stock is cleared.

Showing goodwill towards the public, merchants shall sell this centralized stock for daily wages.

The Superintendent shall, considering the cost of outlay, quantity manufactured, amount of toll, interest on the outlay, hire, and other kinds of accessory expenses, determine the price of such merchandise, taking into account whether it was manufactured long ago or imported from a distant country (desakálántaritánám panyánám).

[Thus ends Chapter II, "Protection of merchants" in Book IV "The Removal of Thorns" of the Arthasástra of Kautilya. End of the seventy-ninth chapter from the beginning.]

CHAPTER III. REMEDIES AGAINST NATIONAL CALAMITIES.

There are eight kinds of providential visitations: they are fire, floods, pestilential diseases, famine, rats, tigers (vyáláh), serpents, and demons. From these calamities shall the king protect his kingdom.

(Fire.)

During the summer, villages shall conduct cooking activities outdoors. Alternatively, they shall equip themselves with the ten remedial instruments (dasamúlí).

Precautionary measures against fire have been discussed in the context of the duties assigned to the superintendents of villages as well as those related to the king's harem and retinue.

On regular days, and especially on full-moon days, offerings, oblations, and prayers shall be made to honor fire.

(Floods.)

Villagers residing along riverbanks shall, during the rainy season, relocate to higher grounds. They shall prepare wooden planks, bamboos, and boats. Through bottle gourds, canoes, tree trunks, or boats, they shall rescue individuals being swept away by floods. Persons neglecting rescue efforts, except those lacking boats or other means, shall be fined 12 panas. On new and full-moon days, rivers shall be worshipped. Those skilled in sacred magic and mysticism (máyáyogavidah), as well as individuals learned in the Vedas, shall perform incantations to guard against excessive rain.

During drought shall Indra (sachínátha), the Ganges, mountains, and Mahákachchha be worshipped.

(Pestilences.)

Such remedial measures as will be treated of in the 14th book shall be taken against pestilences. Physicians with their medicines, and ascetics and prophets with their auspicious and purificatory ceremonials shall also overcome pestilences. The same remedial measures shall be taken against epidemics (maraka = killer). Besides the above measures, oblations to gods, the ceremonial called, Mahá-kachchhavardhana, milking the cows on cremation or burial grounds, burning the trunk of a corpse, and spending nights in devotion to gods shall also be observed.

With regard to cattle diseases (pasuvyádhimarake), not only the ceremony of waving lights in cowsheds (nirájanam) shall be half done, but also the worship of family-gods be carried out.

(Famines.)

During famine, the king shall show favour to his people by providing them with seeds and provision (bíjabhaktopagráham).

He may either do such works as are usually resorted to in calamities; he may show favour by distributing either his own collection of provisions or the hoarded income of the rich among the people; or seek for help from his friends among kings.

Or the policy of thinning the rich by exacting excessive revenue (karsanam), or causing them to vomit their accumulated wealth (vamanam) may be resorted to.

Or the king with his subjects may emigrate to another kingdom with abundant harvest.

Or he may remove himself with his subjects to seashores or to the banks of rivers or lakes. He may cause his subjects to grow grains, vegetables, roots, and fruits wherever water is available. He may, by hunting and fishing on a large scale, provide the people with wild beasts, birds, elephants, tigers or fish.

(Rats.)

To ward off the danger from rats, cats and mongooses may be let loose. Destruction of rats that have been caught shall be punished with a fine of 12 panas. The same punishment shall be meted out to those who, with the exception of wild tribes, do not hold their dogs in check.

To destroy rats, grains mixed with the milk of the milk-hedge plant (snuhi: Euphorbia Antiquorum), or grains combined with ingredients discussed in the 14th book may be left on the ground. Ascetics and prophets may perform auspicious ceremonies, and on new and full-moon days, rats may be worshipped.

Similar measures may also be taken to counter threats from locusts, birds, and insects.

(Snakes.)

When facing a threat from snakes, experts skilled in remedies for snake poison shall use incantations and medicines. Alternatively, snakes may be destroyed collectively, or those learned in the Atharvaveda may perform auspicious rites. On new and full-moon days, snakes may be worshipped. This outlines the measures to be taken against threats from water-dwelling animals.

(Tigers.)

To eliminate tigers, the carcasses of cattle mixed with the juice of the madana plant, or calves' carcasses filled with the juices of madana and kodrava plants, may be placed in appropriate locations. Hunters or keepers of hounds may capture tigers by entrapping them in nets. Armed individuals in protective armor may also kill tigers using weapons.

Failure to aid a person seized by a tiger shall be punished with a fine of 12 panas, and an equal reward shall be given to anyone who kills a tiger. On new and full-moon days, mountains may be worshipped.

Similar methods may be employed against attacks from wild animals, birds, or crocodiles.

(Demons.)

Individuals acquainted with Atharvaveda rituals and experts in sacred magic and mysticism shall perform ceremonies to ward off dangers from demons. On full-moon days, the worship of Chaityas shall be conducted by placing offerings on a verandah, including an umbrella, a picture of an arm, a flag, and some goat's flesh.

In all situations of demonic threat, the incantation "we offer thee cooked rice" shall be used.

The king shall always protect the afflicted among his people as a father would protect his sons.

Ascetics skilled in magical arts, who possess supernatural powers to ward off natural visitations, shall therefore be honored by the king and encouraged to reside within his kingdom.

[Thus ends Chapter III, "Remedies against national Calamities" in Book IV, "The Removal of Thorns," of the Arthasástra of Kautilya. End of the eightieth chapter from the beginning.]

CHAPTER IV. SUPPRESSION OF THE WICKED LIVING BY FOUL MEANS.

Measures necessary for the protection of countries were briefly addressed in the description of the duties of the Collector-general. Now, we shall discuss in detail such measures as are effective in removing disturbances to peace.

The Collector-general shall employ spies disguised as people endowed with supernatural abilities, those engaged in penance, ascetics, travelers of the world (chakra-chara), bards, buffoons, mystics (prachchhandaka), astrologers, prophets foretelling the future, individuals skilled in reading auspicious or inauspicious times, physicians, lunatics, the dumb, the deaf, the intellectually disabled, the blind, traders, painters, carpenters, musicians, dancers, vintners, and manufacturers of cakes, meat dishes, and cooked rice, and send them throughout the country to gather intelligence.

These spies shall determine the integrity or corruption of villagers or the Superintendents of villages and report accordingly.

If any person is discovered to live a concealed life of corruption (gúdhajívi), a spy familiar with such conduct shall be deployed to engage with him.

By forming a connection with the suspect, who may be either a judge or a commissioner, the spy may ask that a misfortune involving a friend of the spy be averted in exchange for a certain amount of money. If the judge agrees to the arrangement, he shall be proclaimed a receiver of bribes and banished. The same rule shall apply to commissioners.

A spy may inform the village assembly (grámakútam) or its superintendent that a wealthy but wicked man is facing difficulties and suggest that they take advantage of the situation to extract money from him. If either the assembly or the superintendent complies with the spy's suggestion, banishment shall be imposed with a proclamation of "extortion."

By pretending to be accused of a crime, a spy may approach false witnesses, offering them substantial sums of money. If they agree, they shall be declared as false witnesses and banished.

Manufacturers of counterfeit coins shall be dealt with in the same manner.

If any person is believed to use magical charms, drugs, or rituals performed on cremation grounds to obtain the love of women for others, a spy may approach him and ask for assistance in winning back the affections of a wife, daughter, or daughter-in-law, whom the spy claims to love, in exchange for a sum of money. If the individual consents, he shall be proclaimed as one practicing witchcraft (samvadanakáraka) and banished.

Similar actions may be taken against those engaged in harmful witchcraft practices that are detrimental to others.

Anyone suspected of using poison (rasa = mercury) on others, due to their talk of it, selling or purchasing mercury, or using it to prepare medicines, may be approached by a spy with a request to poison a particular enemy in exchange for a sum of money. If he agrees, he shall be proclaimed a poisoner (rasada) and banished.

Similar measures may be applied to those who handle medicines prepared from the madana plant.

Anyone suspected of manufacturing counterfeit coins, evidenced by frequent purchases of various metals, alkalis, charcoal, bellows, pincers, crucibles, stoves, and hammers, having hands and clothing stained with ashes and smoke, or possessing other necessary tools for illegal minting, may be approached by a spy posing as an apprentice. Gradually betraying him, the spy shall expose his guilt, and the accused, upon being proclaimed a manufacturer of false coins, shall be banished.

Similar actions may be taken against those who dilute gold by mixing it with alloys or deal with counterfeit gold (suvarna = coin?).

There are thirteen types of criminals who, secretly attempting to live by dishonest means, disrupt the peace of the country. Depending on whether their offenses are minor or severe, they shall either be banished or made to pay an adequate compensation.

[Thus ends Chapter IV, "Suppression of the wicked living by foul means" in Book IV "The Removal Thorns" of the Arthasástra of Kautilya. End of the eighty-first chapter from the beginning.]

CHAPTER V. DETECTION OF YOUTHS OF CRIMINAL TENDENCY BY ASCETIC SPIES.

On using the opportunities provided by ordinary spies sent in advance, special spies pretending to be endowed with supernatural powers may, under the pretense of knowing incantations that allow rapid escape, invisibility, or the unsealing of tightly fastened doors, entice highway robbers into committing robberies. Similarly, under the guise of knowing incantations that attract the love of women, they may lure adulterers into engaging in criminal activities intended to expose their criminal intentions.

These enthusiastic recruits, thus persuaded, may then be taken to a village where persons disguised as men and women have been pre-positioned, and which is a different village than the one intended to be reached. The youths may be told that reaching the desired village on time is difficult and that the power of incantation must be demonstrated here and now.

Pretending to open doors with the power of incantation, the youths may be invited to enter. In the midst of alert watchmen, who are actually acting in concert, the youths may be rendered "invisible" by incantation and directed to proceed further inside. Making the watchmen appear sleepy, the youths may be instructed to move the beds of the watchmen confidently, believing in the spell's protection. Individuals disguised as wives of others may then, under the apparent influence of incantation, interact favorably with the youths.

Once the youths have seemingly experienced these magical powers, they may be taught recitations and other procedures as part of this art. They may then be asked to test the effectiveness of their new knowledge by looting houses containing marked valuables or money, and subsequently apprehended in the act. They may also be captured while attempting to sell, buy, or mortgage items marked with identifying symbols, or while under intoxication induced by medicinal drinks (yogasurámatta).

From these apprehended youths, details of their past activities and the identities of their accomplices may be gathered.

Spies disguised as old and notorious thieves may similarly infiltrate robber gangs and, through similar strategies, lead to the robbers' arrests.

The Collector-general shall present these arrested robbers to the public and announce that their capture is due to the king's instructions, as the king has mastered the divine art of catching robbers. He shall proclaim, "I will continue to apprehend other robbers repeatedly, and it is your duty, citizens, to prevent any of your kin from engaging in wicked deeds."

Any person identified through spy reports as having been a robber of yoking ropes, whips, or other agricultural implements may be detained and informed that their capture is the result of the king's omniscient power. Spies, disguised as old and notorious robbers, herdsmen, hunters, or hound keepers, may infiltrate criminal groups living in forests and conspire with them to raid villages or caravanserais that, according to a prior arrangement, are stocked with counterfeit gold and other items. During the ensuing chaos, these criminals may be killed by armed men positioned there for this purpose. Or, when these robbers have secured a haul of stolen treasure, they may be given food laced with the intoxicating juice of the madana plant or apprehended either while sleeping, exhausted from constant movement, or while under the influence of intoxicating medicinal beverages consumed during religious festivals.

The Collector-general shall publicly display these and other apprehended criminals, proclaiming the omniscient power of the king to the people at large.

[Thus ends Chapter V, "Detection of youths of criminal tendency by ascetic spies," in Book IV, "The Removal Thorns" of the Arthasástra of Kautilya. End of the eighty-second chapter from the beginning.]

CHAPTER VI. SEIZURE OF CRIMINALS ON SUSPICION OR IN THE VERY ACT.

In addition to the measures taken by spies posing as prophets, further actions based on suspicious behavior or possession of stolen items may also be undertaken.

(Suspicion.)

Persons to be suspected include those whose families subsist on limited inheritance; who have little comfort; who frequently change their residence, caste, or names, including those of their family (gotra); who conceal their occupations; who have adopted a lavish lifestyle involving meat, condiments, alcohol, perfumes, garlands, fine clothing, and jewelry; who spend money extravagantly; who often associate with promiscuous women, gamblers, or vintners; who frequently leave their place of residence; whose business dealings, journeys, or destinations are hard to decipher; who travel alone in secluded areas like forests and mountainous regions; who hold private meetings in isolated locations close to or far from their homes; who rush to treat fresh wounds or boils; who constantly hide in the inner rooms of their homes; who are overly devoted to women; who are keen to gather information about the women and property of others; who associate with people of questionable knowledge and work; who loiter in the dark behind walls or under cover; who buy rare or suspicious items at odd times or places; who are known for hostile behavior; whose caste and occupation are disreputable; who maintain false appearances or wear different caste symbols; who abandon their ancestral customs with false justifications; whose notoriety is well-known; who, though overseeing villages, are fearful of appearing before the prime minister and either hide or go elsewhere; who breathe heavily from fear while sitting alone; who display unusual anxiety or heart palpitations; whose faces are pale and dry, with indistinct and stammering voices; who frequently travel with armed companions; or who present a threatening demeanor.

These and other individuals may be suspected of being murderers, robbers, or offenders guilty of misappropriating treasure troves or deposits, or of being any other kind of deceivers secretly engaged in foul means for survival.

Thus, the capture of criminals based on suspicion is addressed.

(Seizure of Stolen Articles.)

Concerning the capture of criminals caught in the very act: Information regarding items that are either lost or stolen shall, if these items are not located, be shared with those who deal in similar goods. Traders who conceal items about which they have previously received such information shall be condemned as accomplices. If they are found to have been unaware of the item's loss, they may be acquitted upon returning the item.

No one shall, without informing the Superintendent of Commerce, mortgage or purchase any old or second-hand item for personal use.

Upon receiving information about the sale or mortgage of old items, the Superintendent shall question the seller about the item's origin. The seller may state: it is an inheritance; it was received from a third party; it was purchased by him; it was made to order; or it is a secret pledge. He may then specify the time and place where it was obtained. Alternatively, he may provide evidence concerning the price and commission (kshanamúlyam) for which it was acquired. If his account of the item's background is verified, he shall be acquitted.

If, however, the item is identified as one lost by another person whose description of the item's background matches the prior account, the item shall be deemed to belong to that individual who is proven to have owned it for an extended period and whose life is known to be pure. For, while even animals are found to bear identifying features such as color, gait, and form, there should be no difficulty in identifying items like raw materials, jewels, or vessels, which are products of a unique source, specific materials, a particular manufacturer, and intended for a definite purpose.

The possessor of the disputed item may argue that the item is either borrowed or hired, a pledge or sealed deposit, or an article obtained from a certain person for resale. If he substantiates his claim by presenting a reference person, he shall be released; otherwise, the reference person may deny any involvement in the matter.

In cases where a person is found in possession of an article lost by another and claims to have received it as a gift from a third person, he must support this by presenting as witnesses not only those who gave or facilitated the transfer of the article to him but also those who, as mediators, custodians, bearers, or witnesses, arranged for the transfer.

If a person claims that the item in his possession was thrown away, lost, or forgotten by a third party, he must establish his innocence by providing evidence regarding the time, location, and circumstances of finding the item. Failing to do so, he must return the item and pay a fine equal to its value, or he may be punished as a thief.

Thus, the seizure of criminals caught in the act is addressed.

(Circumstantial Evidence.)

Concerning the apprehension of criminals based on circumstantial evidence:

In instances of housebreaking and theft, circumstances such as entry and exit through means other than doors, breaking a door with specialized tools, breaking windows with or without latticework, removing the roof in multi-story houses, ascending and descending stairs, breaking walls, tunneling, or utilizing techniques needed to access secret hoards of treasure (known only from internal sources) shall indicate the involvement of insiders in the crime. Conversely, when these clues do not suggest insider involvement, they indicate external agents. When both types of clues are present, they imply the participation of both internal and external individuals.

Regarding crimes suspected to be committed by internal agents:

Any individual of a miserable appearance, present at the scene, associated with known rogues or thieves, and found with tools used in theft; a woman from a poor family or one who has placed her affections elsewhere; servants of similarly questionable character; any person overly prone to sleep or suffering from lack of sleep; any individual showing signs of exhaustion, with a pale, dry face, a stammering and unclear voice, watching others or excessively grieving; any person bearing signs of climbing heights; anyone with a scratched or wounded body or torn clothing; anyone whose legs and hands show evidence of scraping or scratching; anyone with hair and nails dirty or freshly broken; anyone who has just bathed and applied sandalwood paste; anyone who has oiled their body and recently washed hands and feet; anyone with identifiable footprints matching those left near the house; anyone whose broken garlands, sandalwood marks, or pieces of clothing match fragments found in or near the house; anyone whose sweat or scent of drink matches fragments of dress left in or near the house—these individuals and others fitting this description shall be thoroughly examined.

A citizen or someone known for adulterous habits may also be under suspicion.

- A commissioner (pradeshtá), along with his team of gopas and sthánikas, shall work to uncover external thieves; meanwhile, the city officer (nágaraka) shall investigate internal suspects within fortified towns under these outlined circumstances.

[Thus ends Chapter VI, "Seizure of criminals on suspicion or in the very act," in Book IV, "'The Removal of Thorns" of the Arthasástra of Kautilya. End of the eighty-third chapter from the beginning.]

CHAPTER VII. EXAMINATION OF SUDDEN DEATH.

In cases of sudden death, the corpse shall be smeared with oil and examined.

A body showing traces of mucus and urine, with bloated organs, swollen hands and legs, open eyes, and ligature marks around the neck, may indicate death by suffocation and suppression of breathing.

A body with contracted arms and thighs may suggest death by hanging.

A corpse with swollen hands, legs, and belly, sunken eyes, and an inflated navel may also point to death by hanging.

A body with a stiff rectum and eyes, tongue bitten between the teeth, and a swollen belly may indicate drowning.

A corpse covered in blood, with injured or broken limbs, may be evidence of death caused by beatings with sticks or ropes.

A body with fractures and broken limbs may suggest it was thrown down from a height.

A corpse with darkened hands, legs, teeth, and nails, loose skin, fallen hair, reduced flesh, and a face marked with foam and saliva may indicate poisoning.

A body with similar symptoms but with bleeding bite marks may suggest death from bites by serpents or other venomous creatures.

A corpse found sprawled, with disheveled clothing, showing signs of severe vomiting and purging, may indicate death due to the administration of the juice of the madana plant.

Death from any of the above causes is sometimes disguised as voluntary hanging, with ligature marks placed around the neck to create the appearance of self-inflicted death.

In suspected cases of poisoning, the undigested portion of meat may be tested in milk. If extracted from the stomach and thrown into a fire, the sample may be declared poisoned if it produces a "chitchita" sound and shows rainbow-colored flames. Additionally, if the stomach (hridayam) remains unburnt while the rest of the body has turned to ashes, the dead man's servants may be questioned about any violent or cruel treatment they may have received from the deceased. Similarly, relatives of the dead, such as a person living in misery, a woman who may have placed her affections elsewhere, or any relative defending a woman who was deprived of her inheritance by the deceased, may also be examined.

The same examination shall apply to cases where an already deceased body has been staged to look as if it were hanged.

Any investigation into death from alleged voluntary hanging shall consider past harm or wrongdoings committed by the deceased.

All instances of sudden death typically involve one or more of the following motives: offense to women or kin, inheritance disputes, professional competition, rivalry, commerce, guilds, or any legal disputes—each a source of anger, and anger, in turn, is a cause of death.

When, due to mistaken identity, one is murdered by hired hands, thieves for money, or the enemies of another, the relatives of the deceased shall be questioned as follows:

Who summoned the deceased? Who was with him? Who accompanied him on his journey? And who took him to the place where he was found dead?

Those present in the area of the murder shall also be individually questioned as follows:

By whom was the deceased brought there? Did they (the witnesses) notice any armed person hiding nearby and showing signs of distress?

Any lead provided by these witnesses shall be pursued in the subsequent investigation.

- After examining the personal belongings of the deceased, such as travel items, clothing, jewelry, or other possessions found on the body, those who supplied or were involved with these items shall be questioned regarding the deceased's companions, place of residence, reasons for the journey, profession, and other activities.
- If a man or woman, driven by passions like love, anger, or other sinful impulses, commits or incites suicide by ropes, weapons, or poison, their body shall be dragged by a Chandala along the public road with a rope.
- Such individuals shall not receive cremation rites, nor any traditional funeral ceremonies normally performed by relatives.
- Any relative who conducts funeral rites for such persons shall either forfeit the right to their own funeral rites or be abandoned by their family and kin.
- Anyone associating with persons who perform forbidden rites shall, along with any other associates, lose within a year the right to conduct or oversee sacrifices, to teach, and to give or receive gifts.

[Thus ends Chapter VII, "Examination of sudden death," in Book IV, "The Removal of Thorns" of the Arthasásatra of Kautilya. End of the eighty-fourth chapter from the beginning.]

CHAPTER VIII. TRIAL AND TORTURE TO ELICIT CONFESSION.

Whether the accused is a stranger or a relative of the complainant, the defendant's defense witness shall be questioned thoroughly in the presence of the complainant. These questions will cover detailed aspects of the defendant's life, including his country of origin, caste, family background, full name, occupation, assets or property, close friends, and usual place of residence. The responses provided by the defense witness will then be carefully cross-checked against the defendant's own statements on these same points to ensure consistency. Any discrepancies between the witness's account and the defendant's statements may affect the credibility of the defense.

Next, the defendant will be asked for a detailed account of his actions during the day leading up to the alleged crime, covering both the specific tasks he engaged in and the people he interacted with. Furthermore, he will need to specify where he spent the night prior to his apprehension, including any individuals he may have been with or places he visited. If the defendant's answers to these questions are substantiated by credible and reliable referees or witnesses, he shall be exonerated of the charges. However, if his statements lack reliable corroboration, he may be subjected to more rigorous interrogation, which may include torture if there is substantial reason to suspect guilt (anyatha karmapráptah).

If more than three days have passed since the commission of a crime, any person suspected of the crime shall not be detained solely on the basis of suspicion, as, after this time, there may be too few details to justify a full questioning unless there exists strong evidence that establishes a link between the suspect and the alleged crime.

Further, individuals who wrongfully accuse an innocent person of theft, or those who knowingly conceal a thief and prevent their apprehension, shall be held accountable and subject to the same penalties as if they had committed the theft themselves. This rule is in place to discourage false accusations and to ensure that no innocent individual is subjected to undue punishment based on deceit or malice.

Moreover, if a person accused of theft can demonstrate that the complainant has personal enmity, rivalry, or longstanding hatred towards him, then this established motive of animosity shall be enough to acquit the accused, as it casts reasonable doubt on the legitimacy of the Any person who unlawfully confines an innocent individual (parivásayatah suddham) shall be penalized with the first amercement.

Establishing guilt against a suspected individual shall require the presentation of concrete evidence. This may include instruments or tools linked to the accused, involvement of any accomplices or abettors, the stolen items themselves, and any middlemen involved in the selling or purchase of the stolen goods. The credibility of these evidences shall be carefully assessed in relation to the location of the theft, the circumstances surrounding the possession of the stolen article, and the means by which it was circulated or disposed of.

If none of these evidences are present and the accused expresses significant distress, he shall be considered innocent. Often, innocent individuals are wrongly accused due to unfortunate circumstances, such as merely being near the scene of the crime, having a similar appearance, attire, or weapons as the true thief, or possessing items resembling those that were stolen. Cases like that of Mándavya, who under the threat of torture admitted to theft despite his innocence, illustrate that accidental coincidences often lead to wrongful detainment. Therefore, only definitive and conclusive evidence shall be required to confirm guilt (tasmátsamáptakaranam niyamayet).

Certain individuals are exempt from torture, including the uneducated, minors, the elderly, the infirm, intoxicated individuals, the mentally unwell, those suffering from hunger or thirst, travelers fatigued from long journeys, those who have overeaten, those who have confessed willingly (átmakásitam), and those who are physically very weak. None of these groups shall be subjected to physical coercion.

Among the group of spies, including courtesans, those providing water and other refreshments to travelers, storytellers, innkeepers offering accommodations, any spy who shares a similar skill or background to the suspect may be released to discreetly observe the suspect's activities, as discussed in the context of misappropriation involving sealed deposits.

Those individuals whose guilt is strongly suspected shall be subjected to physical examination through torture (áptadosham karma kárayet), provided that evidence or behavior has raised substantial suspicion of their involvement in the alleged crime. However, certain groups are exempt from these harsher measures. Women who are currently pregnant or who have recently given birth—specifically within one month postpartum—shall be entirely spared from any form of physical torture due to their condition. In cases where women are involved, the extent of physical examination or punishment shall be set to half of the standard severity prescribed for men. Alternatively, women, with no exceptions, may be subjected to a thorough process of cross-examination (vákyanuyogo vá) in order to verify their statements or gather information, thus avoiding any physical punishment.

Furthermore, individuals of the Brahman caste, especially those esteemed for their knowledge of the Vedas, along with ascetics who have renounced worldly affairs, shall be exempt from physical punishment altogether. Instead, they shall only be subject to surveillance and espionage to gather evidence of any alleged wrongdoing, given the high respect accorded to their roles in society.

Anyone who disregards or violates these protective regulations shall face the first amercement as punishment, demonstrating the state's commitment to enforcing these exemptions responsibly. The same level of penalty shall be applied if any person, regardless of status, suffers fatal consequences from the use of torture, underscoring the gravity of inflicting excessive harm.

There are four main categories of torture (karma) utilized for punitive purposes: these include six different types of fines or penalties (shatdandáh), seven specific forms of whipping or flogging (kasa), two methods of suspension from above (upari nibandhau), and one particular method involving water known as the water-tube (udakanáliká cha).

In cases where individuals are deemed to have committed particularly serious or grave offenses, a series of nine types of blows using a cane shall be administered as part of the physical penalty: these include 12 hard strikes to each thigh, which is intended to induce pain without permanent harm; 28 targeted blows with a specially designated stick from the naktamála tree, whose wood is traditionally used for its punitive impact; 32 strikes to each palm and each sole of the feet, to inflict controlled pain without disabling injury; and two strikes specifically aimed at the knuckles, with the hands clasped together in such a way that the position resembles a scorpion.

Further methods of disciplinary suspension include two types where the individual is suspended face-down (ullambane chale), a method designed to disorient and discomfort. Additionally, the punishment may involve burning one joint of a finger after making the accused drink rice gruel as a way to increase sensitivity to the burning sensation. In other cases, the accused may be subjected to heating of the body for an entire day after being made to drink oil, which heightens the body's sensitivity to the heat. Another form of torture involves forcing the individual to lie on coarse green grass overnight during the cold winter season, exposing them to the discomfort of the rough surface and low temperatures.

Together, these methods constitute the full range of 18 types of physical punishment, carefully outlined to address different levels of perceived offenses, while aiming to balance the punitive and deterrent effects of these forms of punishment.

The instruments used by the accused in the commission of their crime, such as ropes, clubs, arrows, spades, knives, and similar items, shall be publicly displayed on the back of an ass as a mark of disgrace and a warning to others. Each day, a different form of torture may be employed as a means of progressively intensifying the punishment.

For those criminals who have acted with prior threats, robbing after having announced their intentions, or those who have partially used the stolen goods, been apprehended in the very act, or caught with the stolen items in their possession, stricter punishments apply. Criminals who have attempted to seize the king's treasury or committed a severe crime against the state or society may, by the king's order, be subjected repeatedly to any or all of the forms of torture previously described, depending on the gravity and impact of their offenses.

Regardless of the crime, a Bráhman offender shall not be subjected to physical torture. Instead, their punishment involves marking their crime in a manner that makes their transgressions known to society. The face of a convicted Bráhman shall be branded with a symbol that signifies the nature of their offense. For theft, a symbol of a dog shall be used; for murder, a mark of a headless body shall indicate the crime; for committing sexual misconduct with the wife of a teacher, the image of the female part (bhaga) shall be branded; and for drinking liquor, the emblem of a vintner's flag shall be imprinted.

After the branding has created a lasting wound and the offense has been publicly proclaimed, the king shall determine the Bráhman's ultimate fate. He may be banished from the kingdom, casting him out of society, or sentenced to a life of forced labor in the mines, where he shall remain permanently as a punishment befitting his crime. This approach ensures that justice is served while observing the societal norms and respecting the unique position of Bráhmans within the law.

[Thus ends Chapter VIII, "Trial and Torture to Elicit Confession" in Book IV, "The Removal of Thorns" of the Arthasástra of Kautilya. End of the eighty-fifth chapter from the beginning.]

CHAPTER IX. PROTECTION OF ALL KINDS OF GOVERNMENT DEPARTMENTS.

COMMISSIONERS appointed by the Collector-general shall first check (the proceedings of) Superintendents and their subordinates.

Those who unlawfully seize valuable articles or precious stones from either mines or large-scale manufactories shall face the punishment of beheading, as their crime is deemed a significant offense. For individuals who take ordinary items or essential goods from manufactories producing items of lesser value, the penalty shall be the first amercement, aligning the severity of punishment with the relative value of the seized items.

If anyone takes items valued between 1/16 and 1/4 of a pana from manufactories or from the king's granary, the fine imposed shall be 12 panas. For items valued from 1/4 to 1/2 a pana, the fine shall be 24 panas. Seizing items valued from 1/2 to 3/4 of a pana shall result in a fine of 36 panas, and for items valued between 3/4 and 1 pana, the penalty shall be 48 panas.

Those who seize items valued between 1 and 2 panas shall face the first amercement. For items valued between 2 and 4 panas, the penalty shall be the middle amercement, and for items valued between 4 and 8 panas, the highest amercement shall apply. Should anyone seize items worth between 8 and 10 panas, they shall be sentenced to death due to the gravity of the offense.

When a person unlawfully takes raw materials, finished goods, or similar commodities valued at half the above amount from courtyards, shops, or arsenals, the penalties outlined above shall apply similarly.

Should an individual seize items of only 1/4 of the listed values from the government treasury, granaries, or the offices of superintendents, they shall be fined at double the amount indicated in the original penalties.

It has already been established within the laws of the king's harem that anyone who attempts to intimidate or signal thieves to escape shall be punished with torture leading to death, as this act facilitates crime.

If anyone other than a government official commits theft during daylight hours, stealing from fields, threshing yards, houses, or shops, and takes items such as raw materials, finished goods, or everyday necessities valued between 1/16 and 1/4 of a pana, they shall either be fined 3 panas or be paraded through the streets. During this procession, their body shall be smeared with cow dung, and an earthenware pan containing a burning light shall be tied around their waist (sarávamekhalayá), serving as a public mark of disgrace for their offense.

When any person steals articles valued between 1/4 and 1/2 of a pana, they shall face a fine of 6 panas. Alternatively, they may be punished by having their head shaved or by being exiled (mundanam pravrajanam vá). If someone steals articles valued between 1/2 and 1/3 of a pana, the fine imposed shall be 9 panas, or the offender may be publicly paraded through the streets, with their body covered in cow dung or ashes, or an earthenware pan with a blazing light tied around their waist as a mark of disgrace. For theft of items worth between 1/3 and 1 pana, the penalty shall be a fine of 12 panas, or the offender may have their head shaved or face banishment.

When a person is caught stealing goods valued between 1 and 2 panas, they shall be fined 24 panas, or alternatively, their head may be shaved with a piece of brick, or they may be exiled. For theft of items valued between 2 and 4 panas, the fine shall be 36 panas; for items between 4 and 5 panas, the fine shall be 48 panas. If the value of the stolen articles ranges between 5 and 10 panas, the offender shall face the first amercement. If the stolen items are worth between 10 and 20 panas, the penalty shall be a fine of 200 panas; for goods worth 20 to 30 panas, the fine shall rise to 500 panas; for articles worth 30 to 40 panas, the fine shall reach 1,000 panas. Any person stealing articles valued between 40 and 50 panas shall be condemned to death, as this is considered an extreme offense.

If a person forcibly seizes items, whether during the early part of the day or night, valued at half the amounts specified above, they shall face double the fines previously outlined. If an armed individual seizes goods by force, regardless of the time of day, valued at 1/4 of the amounts listed, they shall be subject to the same fines.

A master of a household (kutumbádhyaksha), a superintendent, or an independent officer (mukhyaswámi) who issues or utilizes unauthorized orders or seals shall be punished based on the severity of their transgression, either with the first, middlemost, or highest amercement, or they may face the death penalty or another appropriate punishment reflecting the gravity of the offense.

A judge who threatens, intimidates, ejects, or unjustly silences one of the disputants in their court shall first be punished with the first amercement. Should the judge defame or abuse either disputant, the punishment shall be doubled. A judge who fails to inquire about essential matters, asks irrelevant questions, omits previously asked questions, or improperly aids a party by suggesting answers shall face the middlemost amercement as punishment.

If a judge neglects to investigate necessary details, delves into irrelevant matters, causes delays out of spite, unnecessarily prolongs a case to exhaust the involved parties, avoids or sidesteps statements leading to a case's resolution, assists witnesses by providing hints, or reopens cases that have already been settled, they shall be subject to the highest amercement. A judge who repeats any of these offenses shall be both fined double the previous amount and dismissed from their position to prevent further judicial misconduct.

If a clerk fails to record exactly what the parties have stated, instead entering details that were not actually said, or disregards statements that were poorly worded (duruktam), or changes statements that were clearly expressed to make them seem contradictory or ambiguous, he shall be penalized with either the first amercement or a fine proportionate to the seriousness of his error.

When a judge or commissioner levies an unjust fine in gold, they shall be required to pay a fine either double the amount unjustly levied or, if they have imposed a sum either exceeding or falling short of the legal limits, they shall be fined eight times the amount of the improper imposition.

If a judge or commissioner enforces an unjust corporal punishment, they shall either face the same punishment or be fined twice the ransom amount that would typically be applied for such an offense. Should a judge intentionally misstate the correct sum or endorse as true an amount that is actually false, the penalty shall be eight times that amount.

If an officer releases or causes the release of detainees from confinement (cháraka), or interferes with prisoners' access to basic activities such as sleeping, sitting, eating, or other necessary actions, they shall be subject to fines starting from 3 panas and increasing with the severity of the infraction.

If anyone releases or facilitates the release of debtors from confinement, they shall not only be fined with the middlemost amercement but shall also be held responsible for covering the full debt owed by the released debtor.

Anyone who releases or arranges the release of prisoners from formal jails (bandhanágára) shall face the death penalty, and all of their property shall be confiscated as part of the punishment.

If the superintendent of jails detains anyone without clearly stating the cause or justification for the detention (samkrudhakamanákhyáya), he shall be fined 24 panas. If he imposes any form of unjust torture, the fine shall be 48 panas. For transferring a prisoner to another location or depriving a detainee of necessary food and water, the penalty shall be 96 panas. If the superintendent harasses or extorts bribes from a prisoner, he shall face the middlemost amercement. Should he beat a prisoner to the point of death, the fine shall be a substantial 1,000 panas.

In cases where a person commits sexual assault with a female prisoner, slave, or a woman hired for work within the jail, the first amercement shall apply. If he commits this offense against the widow of a thief or any man who has died in an epidemic (dámara), the penalty shall be the middlemost amercement. However, if an Arya woman in detention is assaulted, the offender shall receive the highest amercement.

If an inmate in lock-up commits assault upon an Arya woman in the same facility, he shall face the death penalty on the very grounds of the offense. Similarly, any officer who assaults an Arya woman detained for improper movement at night (akshanagrihitáyám) shall also be hanged at the scene. When such an offense is committed with a woman who is enslaved, the punishment shall be the first amercement.

An officer who facilitates a prisoner's escape from lock-up without breaking it open shall be subjected to the middlemost amercement. If the officer breaks open the lock-up to allow a prisoner to escape, he shall be condemned to death. Should he permit a prisoner to escape from a more secure jail facility, the sentence is death, with complete confiscation of his property.

Through enforcing such suitable punishments, the king shall rigorously test the conduct of government officials. Once officials of proven integrity are established, they shall, in turn, oversee the conduct of the people in both urban and rural settings.

[Thus ends Chapter IX, "Protection of all kinds of Government Departments" in Book IV, "The Removal of Thorns" of the Arthasástra of Kautilya. End of the eighty-sixth chapter from the beginning.]

CHAPTER X. FINES IN LIEU OF MUTILATION OF LIMBS.

When government servants (arthachara) commit certain offenses, such as violating a sacred institution (tírthághata) or engaging in pickpocketing (granthibheda), the penalties they face increase in severity with repeated infractions. On the first offense, they may either have their index finger amputated or pay a fine of 54 panas, depending on the discretion of the ruling authority or the legal severity attributed to the crime. Should these individuals repeat the offense a second time, they shall either lose another finger or pay a heightened fine of 100 panas. With a third offense, the consequences escalate even further: they shall forfeit their right hand or be subject to a substantial fine of 400 panas. Upon a fourth offense, no leniency is offered, and they shall be subject to execution, the means of which may vary according to the king's directive or the established customs governing capital punishment.

If a person steals or harms animals, such as roosters, mongooses, cats, dogs, or pigs, valued at less than 54 panas, they face a penalty reflecting both the offense and the value of the animals. For the initial infraction, they shall have the tip of their nose cut off, or alternatively, pay a fine of 54 panas. Should these animals belong to individuals of the Chandala caste or wild tribes, the fine shall be reduced by half, reflecting a lesser severity.

Further provisions address those who steal or capture animals of greater value or specific rarity. Anyone found guilty of taking wild animals, livestock, birds, elephants, tigers, fish, or other animals confined in traps, enclosures, or pits must return the stolen animals and pay a fine equal to their value to compensate for the loss and any potential distress caused by their absence.

In cases where forest resources are stolen—be it valuable raw materials, wild animals, or plants—a fine of 100 panas shall be imposed as a penalty. Should anyone be guilty of theft or destruction involving animals kept in infirmaries or other welfare institutions, the imposed fine will be twice that amount, signaling the elevated consequence due to the intended purpose of the animals' care.

When individuals steal minor tools, personal belongings, or other valuable items from artisans, musicians, or ascetics, they will face a fine of 100 panas. For larger items, or agricultural implements crucial to a trade or livelihood, the imposed fine shall be twice this amount.

If a person enters a fort without authorization, especially with an intent to remove valuables through a concealed passage or an opening in the walls, this intrusion shall be punished by beheading. Alternatively, the offender may pay a substantial fine of 200 panas, the choice of which may depend on the surrounding circumstances or the individual's intent.

For the theft of carts, boats, or smaller animals such as minor livestock, the penalty involves the amputation of one leg or payment of a fine totaling 300 panas.

In cases involving fraudulent gambling activities, such as where a gambler substitutes or manipulates dice rented for a kákaní or employs sleight of hand to deceive the opponent, they shall have their hand amputated or pay a penalty amounting to 400 panas.

Those who serve as accomplices, either to a thief or to an adulterer, will face significant penalties. The accomplice, along with any woman who voluntarily engages in adultery with the knowledge of its nature, shall have both their ears and noses removed or, alternatively, pay a fine of 500 panas each. Meanwhile, the primary offender—the thief or adulterer—will face double this penalty, further establishing accountability.

If an individual is caught stealing larger animals, kidnapping a male or female slave, or seizing items belonging to a deceased person, also known as pretabhándam, they shall face severe repercussions. Both of the offender's legs will be amputated, or they may choose to pay a hefty fine of 600 panas as retribution for the gravity of the offense.

Should a person brazenly attack or cause injury to the limbs of someone from a higher caste, or a teacher, or if they display disrespect by climbing onto the horse, elephant, or coach of the king, this individual shall lose one leg and one hand or be fined 700 panas.

When a Súdra falsely claims the identity of a Bráhman, it is considered a serious offense. Additionally, those who commit acts of theft involving property consecrated to deities, who conspire against the king, or who intentionally blind another person shall face the ultimate form of retribution: either the blinding of their own eyes through a poisonous ointment, or the imposition of an exorbitant fine of 800 panas to fully account for their crime.

When a person enables the release of a thief or an adulterer, falsifies or omits portions when transcribing the king's orders, abducts a girl or a slave who is carrying gold, engages in deceitful transactions, or sells spoiled meat, they shall face severe penalties. The offender may have two legs and one hand amputated or pay a substantial fine of 900 panas, reflecting the gravity of these transgressions.

Should anyone be found selling human flesh, the punishment shall be death, as this crime is seen as utterly reprehensible and deserving the highest level of punitive response.

If an individual steals images of deities or animals, abducts people, or unlawfully seizes another person's fields, houses, gold, coins, precious stones, or crops, they too shall face severe consequences.

They may either be sentenced to beheading or required to pay the highest level of amercement, depending on the specific context of the offense.

- In determining the suitable penalties, several factors must be carefully considered: the social standing of the individuals involved, the specific nature and seriousness of the offense, whether the motivation behind the crime was substantial or minor, and the context of past and present circumstances. The timing and location of the offense are also important, as they can influence the assessment of intent and impact.
- Furthermore, the commissioner is tasked with making a fair and balanced judgment, taking into account the distinctions among offenders, whether they are members of the royal family or commoners. This deliberate approach ensures that the severity of punishment is properly aligned with the first, middlemost, or highest amercements, reflecting a just response to the nature of each crime and the individuals involved.

[Thus ends Chapter X, "Fines in lieu of mutilation of limbs" in Book IV, "The Removal of Thorns" of the Arthasástra of Kautilya. End of the eighty-seventh chapter from the. beginning.]

CHAPTER XI. DEATH WITH OR WITHOUT TORTURE.

If a man kills another during a quarrel, he shall be subjected to death by torture. If someone is wounded in a fight and dies within seven nights, the person responsible for the wound shall face immediate execution. Should the wounded individual die within a fortnight, the offender shall be required to pay the highest level of amercement. If the wounded person succumbs to the injury within a month, the responsible party shall pay a fine of 500 panas along with an appropriate compensation to the bereaved family.

When someone injures another using a weapon, the highest amercement shall apply. If the act was committed under intoxication, the offender's hand shall be amputated; if the injury results in immediate death, the perpetrator shall be executed.

In cases where a person causes a woman to miscarry by physical harm, medication, or repeated harassment, the punishments are staggered: the highest amercement for physical harm, the middlemost for causing abortion through medication, and the first amercement for harassment that leads to miscarriage.

Individuals who bring violent death to others, frequent prostitutes, inflict unjust penalties, spread false or defamatory rumors, assault or obstruct travelers, engage in housebreaking, or harm royal animals such as elephants, horses, or carriages shall face hanging.

Anyone who attempts to destroy or steal the remains of those executed for these offenses shall face the same punishment or be subject to the highest amercement.

If a person provides support to murderers or thieves—be it food, clothing, materials, shelter, guidance, or any other form of assistance—they shall be fined with the highest amercement. If such support was given without knowledge of the criminal activities, the individual shall receive a public reprimand.

If the sons or wives of murderers or thieves are found innocent of involvement, they shall be acquitted. However, if any evidence shows their cooperation in the crime, they will be taken into custody.

Anyone who conspires against the kingdom, forces entry into the king's private quarters, incites wild tribes or enemies to rebel, or spreads discontent in forts, villages, or the army shall be burned alive from head to toe. If a Bráhman is guilty of such actions, he shall instead be drowned.

Anyone who kills their father, mother, son, brother, teacher, or an ascetic shall face execution by burning of both head and skin. If they insult any of these individuals, their tongue shall be cut out; if they bite or injure any body part of these persons, the corresponding limb shall be removed.

When a man kills another without cause or steals a group of cattle, he shall be beheaded. For these purposes, a group or herd of cattle is defined as ten or fewer animals.

If someone intentionally breaches the dam of a full tank, they shall be drowned in that same tank. If the tank was empty, they shall pay the highest amercement, and if it was already in disrepair due to neglect, they shall pay the middlemost amercement.

Anyone who administers poison to another or a woman who murders someone shall be sentenced to drowning.

A woman who kills her husband, teacher, or child; sets fire to property; administers poison; or mutilates another's body shall be torn apart by bulls. This punishment shall apply regardless of whether she is pregnant or within a month of childbirth.

Anyone who sets fire to pasture lands, grain fields, threshing yards, houses, or forests (whether for timber or shelter for elephants) shall be cast into flames.

Any person who insults the king, reveals confidential information from the royal council, attempts to harm the king, or desecrates the kitchens of Bráhmans shall have their tongue cut out.

If a civilian steals weapons or armor, they shall be executed by archers. A soldier committing the same act shall face the highest amercement.

Anyone who castrates another shall face the removal of their own generative organ.

Anyone who mutilates another's tongue or nose shall have their fingers cut off.

- Such severe punishments as these are recorded in the texts of wise sages, but it is advised that if the crime is not especially cruel, the offender may be given a simple execution instead.

[Thus ends Chapter XI, "Death with or without torture" in Book IV, "The Removal of Thorns" of the Arthasástra of Kautilya. End of the eighty-eighth chapter from the beginning.]

CHAPTER XII. SEXUAL INTERCOURSE WITH IMMATURE GIRLS.

Anyone who defiles a young maiden of equal caste before she reaches maturity shall either lose his hand or be fined 400 panas; should the maiden lose her life as a result, the offender shall face the death penalty.

Anyone who defiles a maiden who has reached maturity shall either lose his middle finger or pay a fine of 200 panas, in addition to providing adequate compensation to her father.

No one is permitted to engage in sexual relations with a woman without her consent.

If a man defiles a consenting maiden, he shall be fined 54 panas, while the maiden shall pay half that amount.

When a man impersonates someone who has already paid the marriage fee to a woman (to deceive her into intercourse), he shall either lose his hand or pay a fine of 400 panas, in addition to reimbursing the marriage fee.

If a man has relations with a maiden who has reached maturity but remains unwed after seven cycles of menses, and she was betrothed to him but not yet married, he shall neither be considered guilty nor owe her father compensation, for her father has forfeited authority over her by delaying the marriage.

It is not an offense for a man of equal caste and rank to engage with a maiden who has remained unmarried three years after her first menses. Nor is it an offense for a man of another caste to engage with a maiden who has been without marriage and jewelry for more than three years after her first menses, as this lack of paternal provision constitutes neglect of her rightful dowry, akin to theft.

Anyone who, under the guise of securing a bride for someone else, instead obtains her for a third party shall pay a fine of 200 panas.

No man shall engage in sexual intercourse with a woman against her will.

If a man replaces the bride initially promised with another woman, he shall be fined 100 panas if the substituted bride is of the same rank, and 200 panas if she is of a lower rank. The substituted bride shall also be fined 54 panas, and the man shall be required to return the marriage fee along with any additional expenses the bridegroom incurred in preparation for the marriage.

If a man, after agreeing to marry a particular maiden, later refuses to do so, he shall be fined double the amount previously specified for such substitutions.

In cases where a man marries a woman of a different bloodline than he originally agreed to or makes false claims about her qualities, he shall pay a fine of 200 panas, return the marriage fee, and cover any expenses related to the marriage preparations.

It is strictly prohibited for a man to force a woman into a relationship or sexual act against her will, regardless of circumstances.

If a woman willingly consents to be with a man of her own caste and social rank, she shall be fined 12 panas, while any other woman who encourages or assists in this situation shall be fined double, paying 24 panas. A woman who aids a man in coercing a maiden into a relationship against her will shall be fined 100 panas, and she must also compensate the maiden with an appropriate marriage fee as a form of restitution.

A woman who voluntarily offers herself to a man without any prior marriage arrangement shall become a slave to the king, forfeiting her freedom as a consequence.

When a man engages in relations with a woman outside of the village boundaries or spreads false stories regarding such matters, the fines imposed shall be doubled.

In the case of a man forcibly abducting a maiden, he shall be fined 200 panas. However, if the maiden was adorned with valuable golden jewelry, the offender shall face the maximum possible fine. If several men are involved in the abduction of a maiden, each individual shall be subject to the same penalty.

When a man engages in relations with the daughter of a harlot, he shall pay a fine of 54 panas and additionally provide the girl's mother with a sum equivalent to sixteen times her daily income, acknowledging the impact of his actions.

If a man violates the daughter of his male or female slave, he shall pay a fine of 24 panas and also provide the maiden with an adequate marriage fee and suitable jewelry, ensuring she has the means for her future well-being and social standing.

When a man engages in a relationship with a woman held in servitude due to an unpaid ransom, he shall not only pay a fine of 12 panas, but also provide her with appropriate clothing and necessary support for her well-being.

In all such cases, anyone who aids or encourages the principal offender shall receive the same punishment as the offender himself.

If a relative or servant of a man who is absent takes under his protection a woman of questionable character who is the absentee's wife, he may do so legally (in effect, marrying her). However, while under such protection, the woman must wait for her husband's return. If the husband returns and has no objections, both the protector and the woman shall be acquitted of any wrongdoing. If the husband objects, the woman shall have her ears and nose cut off as punishment, while her protector shall be put to death as an adulterer.

If a man falsely accuses someone of theft while the true issue is adultery, the false accuser shall be fined 500 panas.

A person who lets an adulterer go free by accepting a bribe shall pay a fine amounting to eight times the value of the gold or payment received.

The occurrence of adultery may be proven by evidence such as physical confrontation, abduction, visible marks on the bodies of those involved, expert evaluations based on the situation, or testimonies from the women implicated.

When a man rescues a woman from enemies, dense forests, or floodwaters, or when he saves the life of a woman abandoned in a forest, left helpless in times of famine, or discarded as if she were deceased, he may have her companionship if both parties consented during the rescue.

However, if the woman is of high caste, has children, and shows no inclination for a romantic relationship, she may be freed from any obligations to him upon payment of an adequate ransom.

- Women who have been saved from thieves, floodwaters, famine, national disasters, or from abandonment or being lost in forests, or those cast out as though dead and later brought to safety, may become the companion of their rescuer if both have mutually agreed upon it.
- However, women who have been cast out by royal decree or by their own families, as well as those of high caste, those unwilling to be rescued, or women with children, shall not be taken either for ransom or for companionship.

[Thus ends Chapter XII, "Sexual Intercourse with Immature Girls," in Book IV, "The Removal of Thorns" of the Arthasástra of Kautilya. End of the eighty-ninth chapter from the beginning.]

CHAPTER XIII. PUNISHMENT FOR VIOLATING JUSTICE.

Anyone who forces a Bráhman to consume forbidden food or drink shall be subject to the highest penalty. For compelling a Kshatriya to do so, the penalty shall be the middle amercement; for a Vaisya, the first amercement; and for a Súdra, a fine of 54 panas.

Those who willingly consume any food or drink that is condemned shall be declared outcasts.

If anyone forces entry into another's home during the day, they shall be fined with the first amercement; if it happens at night, the fine shall be the middlemost amercement. If someone enters another's home with a weapon, whether day or night, they shall face the highest amercement.

If beggars, peddlers, lunatics, or disturbed individuals try to enter a house by force, or if neighbors force entry into a home during an emergency, they will not be penalized provided there was no explicit prohibition against such entry.

Those who go onto their own roof after midnight shall be fined with the first amercement; those who climb onto another's roof will face the middlemost amercement.

Breaking the fences of villages, gardens, or fields shall also incur the middlemost amercement.

Traders are to inform the headman of the village regarding the value and nature of their merchandise before halting in any area of a village. If any portion of their goods, not securely transported out of the village during the night, is stolen or lost, the headman shall compensate for the loss.

Merchandise stolen or lost on routes between villages shall be the responsibility of the superintendent of pasture lands. If there is no such pasture officer, the Chorarajjuka officer shall cover the loss. If merchandise is lost in an area without even this level of protection, the people on the boundary of that area shall compensate. If there are no boundary people, residents from the five or ten nearest villages shall make up for the loss.

Harm caused by building weak houses, using carts with no support, or carts with broken beams, sharp objects hanging above, damaged support, or missing coverings, as well as harm caused by a cart falling into a pit, a tank, or off a dam, shall be considered assault.

Cutting down trees, stealing the rope used to tie a tameable animal, using untrained animals, and throwing sticks, mud, stones, rods, or arrows at chariots or elephants, as well as raising or waving an arm against chariots or elephants, will also be treated as assault.

If the driver of a chariot shouts "get out" to a passerby, he will not be held responsible for any collision.

If a person is killed by an elephant because they provoked it, the person who died is considered responsible. The family of the deceased should offer nearly a full kumbha of liquor, along with garlands, scents, and enough cloth to wash the tusks of the elephant. This is because death caused by an elephant is seen as having the same honor as taking a sacred bath after a horse-sacrifice. This offering is known as "washing the legs."

However, if an innocent passerby is killed by an elephant, the driver shall be fined the highest penalty.

If the owner of a horned or tusked animal fails to prevent their animal from harming someone, they shall be fined the first amercement. If the owner refuses to help after being asked to, the fine will be doubled.

If a person causes or permits animals with horns or tusks to harm or kill each other, he is responsible for paying a fine equal to the value of the animals that were harmed or lost, and he must also compensate the owner or any other person who suffered a loss. When someone rides over an animal that has been released in the name of the gods, or over a bull, ox, or young female calf, they will face a fine of 500 panas. Anyone who drives away these animals will be penalized with the highest amercement.

When a person takes away lesser animals that are valuable for their wool or milk, or for carrying or riding purposes, they must pay a fine equal to the animal's worth and also return it. The same fine and restitution apply if someone drives these animals away for reasons unrelated to religious ceremonies for gods or ancestors.

In cases where an animal with a broken or removed nose-ring, or one not properly trained for yoking, injures someone, or when an animal charges at a person or causes harm by pulling backward with its cart, or if it becomes confused due to crowding of people or other animals, the owner is not held responsible. However, when injuries are caused in any other circumstance, fines are applied according to prior rules, and any loss of animal life due to such incidents must be compensated. If the driver of the cart or carriage that caused harm is underage, the responsible adult in the cart will be fined. If there is no adult present, any passenger of age will be fined, or the driver himself if he is an adult. Carts driven by minors or unaccompanied by any person of age will be seized by the king.

Any actions involving witchcraft that are intended to harm others will have the same harm inflicted back on the person responsible. If witchcraft is done only to inspire love between a wife and her husband or to help a lover gain affection from a maiden, it is not considered an offense. However, when such acts cause harm to others, the perpetrator will face a fine set at the middlemost amercement.

If someone uses witchcraft to try to win the affections of his father's or mother's sister, his maternal uncle's wife, his teacher's wife, or his own daughter-in-law, daughter, or sister, he will have a limb cut off and be put to death. Any woman who willingly consents to such a relationship with the offender will face the same punishment. A woman who chooses to engage with a slave, servant, or hired worker will receive the same penalty.

If a Kshatriya is found guilty of adultery with a Bráhman woman who is unprotected, he will be punished with the highest amercement. If a Vaisya commits the same act, he will lose all his property. If a Súdra is guilty of this offense, he will be wrapped in mats and burned alive.

Anyone found guilty of adultery with the queen of the kingdom will be punished by being burned alive in a vessel (kumbhílpákah). If a man engages in adultery with a woman of a lower caste, he will be branded on his forehead with a mark indicating his punishment and banished, or he will be reduced to the same caste as the woman. Should a Súdra or svapáka commit adultery with a woman of a low caste, that man shall be sentenced to death, and the woman will have her ears and nose cut off as punishment.

Adultery involving a nun (pravrajitá) is punishable with a fine of 24 panas, which the nun herself must also pay if she consents to the act. If a man forces himself upon a harlot, he will face a fine of 12 panas. In cases where several people attempt to use witchcraft to influence a single woman, each person involved will be fined 24 panas.

Any man who engages in intimate acts with a woman in a way that goes against the natural order (a-yonau) will be subject to the first amercement. Likewise, a man found having relations with another man will also face the first amercement.

- A person who, in a senseless state, engages in intimate acts with animals will face a fine of 12 panas. If the same act is committed with idols representing goddesses (daivatapratimá), the fine will be doubled.
- If the king imposes punishment on an innocent person, he must dedicate a fine equal to thirty times the amount of the wrongful penalty to the god Varuna by casting it into water. This amount will subsequently be distributed among the

Bráhmans.

- Through this act of atonement, the king will be absolved of the sin of unjust punishment, as King Varuna is considered the ruler over the sins of men.

Book 5

CHAPTER I. CONCERNING THE AWARDS OF PUNISHMENTS.

Actions necessary to remove disturbances to public order, both in fortified cities and rural areas, have been discussed. Now, we will proceed to address measures to suppress acts of treason against the king and his kingdom.

For those officials who serve the king but hold hostile feelings or who have aligned with his enemies, a spy on a secret mission or one disguised as an ascetic, loyal to the king's cause, shall act as previously described. Alternatively, a spy skilled in creating discord may be deployed, as will be explained in the section on "Invasion of an Enemy's Villages."

The king, in the name of righteousness, may discreetly punish those courtiers or groups of influential officials who pose a threat to the kingdom and who cannot be dealt with openly in daylight.

A spy may instigate the brother of a disloyal minister and, with suitable incentives, bring him to the king for a meeting. The king, after bestowing upon him the right to control and enjoy the wealth of his treacherous brother, may arrange for him to confront his brother; and if he murders his brother with a weapon or poison, he shall also be executed on the same spot, under the charge of committing parricide.

This measure illustrates the approach for dealing with a disloyal Pârasava (offspring of a Bráhman and a Sûdra wife) and a seditious son of a servant.

Alternatively, under the influence of a spy, the brother of a disloyal minister may claim inheritance rights. If the claimant, while resting at night near his brother's residence or elsewhere, is killed by an aggressive spy (tîshna), it may then be declared, "Alas! the claimant to inheritance has been murdered (by his own brother)." The king, aligning himself with the aggrieved party, may proceed to punish the disloyal minister.

Spies, in the presence of a seditious minister, may openly threaten to strike his inheritance-claiming brother. Then, as "the claimant lies by the door, etc.," the procedure continues as outlined.

This tactic also applies to causing a fraudulent conflict between two disloyal ministers within a family where a father or son has had improper relations with a daughter-in-law, or a brother with the wife of another brother.

A spy may appeal to the ego of a seditious minister's son, who is known for his gentle demeanor and respectable conduct, by telling him, "Although you are like a prince, you are held here in fear of enemies." The king may privately honor this misguided individual, saying, "Fearing harm from the minister, I have delayed your official appointment, even though you have reached the age to be recognized as my heir." The spy may then encourage him to kill the minister. Once the task is completed, the son, too, will be executed in the same place on the charge of parricide.

A wandering woman, skilled in deception, may enchant the wife of a rebellious minister by using particular herbs or potions that stir feelings of love. Through this influence, the woman might persuade the minister's wife to act against him, potentially leading to his poisoning.

If this method proves ineffective, the king has other ways to address the disloyalty of the minister. He might assign him to lead a regiment of poorly trained soldiers along with fiery spies on a high-risk mission. Such tasks could include suppressing a rebellious wild tribe or an unruly village, setting up a new local governor in a region close to the wilderness, controlling a highly rebellious city, or securing a caravan carrying tributes to the king from a neighboring territory. During the disorder that might arise in any of these missions, whether during the day or at night, the fiery spies or those disguised as robbers may kill the minister and declare to all that he perished in the line of duty.

In another strategy, while preparing for a military expedition or engaging in a royal game, the king may summon his disloyal ministers for a meeting. Fiery spies with concealed weapons may accompany the ministers and, upon reaching the royal pavilion, will offer themselves for a search to enter the inner chamber. When the guards find weapons on these spies, they will declare them as accomplices of the seditious ministers. This incident will be made public, and the ministers will be executed, with replacements hanged in place of the fiery spies, protecting the king's plan from any exposure.

During recreational outings outside the city, the king may house disloyal ministers in accommodations adjacent to his own. Here, a woman of disrepute, posing as the queen, could be planted in their quarters to tarnish their reputations. Once discovered, the ministers could be publicly disgraced and punished according to the prior instructions, linking them to a scandal.

Another plan involves a sauce maker or sweetmeat maker gaining the trust of a disloyal minister by saying, "Only someone of your status deserves such special delicacies." Once the minister approves, the cook may lace a small amount of sauce, sweetmeat, or water with poison, secretly switching these with items in the king's lunch when he is outside the city. Upon public revelation of this incident, the king may order the execution of both the minister and the cook, branding them as poisoners and traitors to the crown.

If a disloyal minister shows a fascination with witchcraft, a spy pretending to be a skilled sorcerer may deceive him into believing that certain ritualistic objects, like a pot containing an alligator, a tortoise, or a crab, could help him achieve his ambitions. The spy could convince him that by performing rituals using these items, he could obtain supernatural assistance. While the minister becomes absorbed in this supposed ritual, the spy could seize the opportunity to end his life, either by poisoning him or striking him with a concealed iron rod. Publicly, it would be announced that the minister's own fixation on dangerous witchcraft led to his untimely end.

A spy disguised as a physician might deceive a disloyal minister into thinking he has a terminal or incurable illness. This way, the spy can secretly administer poison while pretending to prescribe medicine or dietary advice. Likewise, spies posing as sauce-makers or sweetmeat vendors may seek any opportunity to poison him when they find a chance.

These are covert techniques for dealing with traitorous individuals who pose a threat to peace and stability. When dealing with individuals conspiring against both the king and his realm:

If a dangerous conspirator needs to be eliminated, another similarly disloyal figure can be enlisted, accompanied by a group of untrained soldiers and fiery spies. They might be given a complex assignment such as, "Travel to this fort or district, assemble an army or gather taxes; confiscate wealth from a courtier; bring the daughter of a noble by force; build a new fortress; lay out a garden; construct a trade route; establish a settlement; set up a mine; establish timber or elephant reserves; demarcate a new district or frontier; and restrain or punish anyone who defies or hinders your tasks." A second conspirator or group may then be sent to counter the first group's activities under similar instructions. If a conflict arises between the two parties, spies in the guise of fiery or undercover operatives may throw weapons, causing death and chaos. They can then arrest others and use the scene as grounds for their punishment.

When disputes erupt in rebellious towns, villages, or families—perhaps over boundaries, land yields, property damages, livestock injuries, or even during public celebrations or festivals—whether the disputes are genuine or ignited by spies, the spies may throw weapons and declare, "This is what happens to those who defy this leader." The conspirators can then be arrested and penalized.

Similarly, when conflicts arise between disloyal factions, fiery spies may set their fields, granaries, or homes ablaze, assault their family members or livestock, and claim that their actions were done on orders from the rebels themselves. As a result, others will face arrest and punishment. Spies can also arrange for meetings between conspirators in strongholds or rural areas under the guise of shared feasts, during which poisoners could act, resulting in poisonings that lead to further arrests and penalties.

A mendicant woman could skillfully deceive a disloyal district chief by convincing him that the wife, daughter, or daughter-in-law of a rival seditious chief is enamored with him. She could accept any jewelry the misled chief gives her for this supposed love interest and then present it to the rival chief, alleging that the first chief, in youthful arrogance, is pursuing his wife or daughter. This deception may spark a bitter feud between the two chiefs, potentially leading to a deadly night duel and retribution against both sides.

In cases where loyalty needs to be tested, the prince or a commander might show favor to a group of enemies subdued by one faction, only to later show disapproval. Meanwhile, others subdued by a separate faction could be dispatched to confront the first group, accompanied by a mix of untrained soldiers and undercover operatives, helping to turn the disloyal groups against each other in the process.

In this way, any surviving sons of these conspirators who remain calm and unaffected by these events will inherit their father's wealth and property, proving their loyalty. By managing disloyal factions with these consistent methods, the kingdom will establish loyalty among the people. This process will ensure the enduring loyalty of the population to the king's descendants and prevent any unrest or troubles caused by seditious elements.

With patience and foresight, the king, assured of stability both now and in the future, may choose to enforce punishments discreetly. These punishments may apply not only to his own subjects who pose a threat but also to those who support or act on behalf of the enemy's cause. By doing so, the king maintains a secure realm, ensuring peace while dealing with threats quietly and effectively.

[Thus ends Chapter I, "Concerning the Awards of Punishments" in Book V. "The Conduct of Courtiers" of the Arthasástra of Kautilya. End of the ninety-first chapter from the beginning.]

CHAPTER II. REPLENISHMENT OF THE TREASURY.

If the king finds himself in urgent need of funds and faces significant financial strain, he may resort to additional revenue collection from his subjects. In areas where the primary livelihood depends on rainfall and grain is abundant, he may request either one-third or one-fourth of the grain harvest based on the resources and capacity of the people there. However, he must refrain from placing demands on subjects residing in regions of moderate or lower productivity. This exemption also extends to people who contribute substantially to the kingdom, such as those aiding in the construction of fortifications, public gardens, buildings, trade routes, the development of unused lands, the mining sector, and forest preservation efforts for timber and elephant habitats. Similarly, he must not impose extra demands on border residents or individuals struggling to maintain basic sustenance. Instead, he should offer grain and livestock to support those involved in reclaiming and cultivating barren lands.

The king may consider purchasing a quarter of the remaining grain stock from his subjects, ensuring sufficient reserves for seeds and personal sustenance are set aside. The property and resources of forest-dwelling tribes and Bráhmans skilled in Vedic knowledge should be avoided entirely for revenue collection; however, if their goods are needed, they should be bought at a fair market price. Should these methods prove insufficient, the collector-general's officials might encourage the farming communities to cultivate crops during the summer. To ensure compliance, they may issue a notice that doubled fines will be imposed for violations among the peasantry and facilitate the sowing of seeds during planting seasons. Upon the ripening of crops, officials may respectfully request a share of ripened produce, while refraining from gleaning or disturbing grains and vegetables that have naturally fallen to the ground. These scattered grains serve an important role in offerings to gods and ancestors, feeding livestock, and supporting mendicants and village staff.

For those who attempt to hide their harvested grain, a penalty of eight times the concealed amount in each variety is due. Anyone caught stealing crops from another's field must pay a fine of fifty times the value if the thief belongs to the same community; however, a foreign thief shall face a death sentence. Officials may levy one-fourth of the grain yield from cultivators and one-sixth of forest produce and resources such as cotton, wax, woven materials, tree bark, hemp, wool, silk, medicinal herbs, sandalwood, flowers, fruits, vegetables, firewood, bamboo, meat, and dried meat. Half of all ivory and animal hides may also be claimed. Those trading any goods without the king's permission shall face the first level of amercement. This encompasses the guidelines for revenue collection among cultivators.

Merchants who trade in valuable goods like gold, silver, diamonds, precious stones, pearls, coral, horses, and elephants must contribute 50 karas. Those dealing in cotton threads, cloth, copper, brass, bronze, sandalwood, medicinal products, and alcohol are required to pay 40 karas. Traders in grains, liquids, metals, and those dealing in carts must pay 30 karas. For those trading in glass or engaging in fine craftsmanship, the fee is 20 karas. Artisans of lesser-quality goods, along with those who manage brothels, are to pay 10 karas. Those trading in firewood, bamboo, stones, pottery, cooked foods, and vegetables are expected to pay 5 karas. Performers and prostitutes shall contribute half of their earnings. Goldsmiths, however, will have their entire stock confiscated, with no leniency shown for their offenses, as their trade is known for dishonesty under the guise of respectability. Thus are the levies upon merchants established.

People raising poultry and pigs must hand over half of their livestock to the government. Those raising smaller animals are expected to give up one-sixth of their animals. Herdsmen keeping cows, buffaloes, mules, donkeys, and camels are to offer one-tenth of their herds. Those who manage brothels are to collect revenue with the help of women renowned for beauty and youth serving under the king's command. These are the obligations for livestock keepers.

These demands are intended to be imposed only once and not to be repeated. In the absence of such demands, the collector-general may seek contributions from both citizens and rural inhabitants by using pretexts related to various governmental projects. Leading citizens, brought in through agreement, should publicly provide notable donations, thereby encouraging others to contribute similarly. Undercover agents posing as common citizens may publicly criticize those who give less, stirring competition among contributors. Affluent individuals may be encouraged to offer as much gold as they can spare. Those who willingly or charitably offer their wealth to the king should be honored with positions in court or tokens of prestige like an umbrella, turban, or valuable ornaments as thanks for their generosity.

Spies, disguised as mystics or sorcerers, may collect funds for the supposed safety of the state. They are permitted to collect money not only from societies of heretics or temples but also from estates of deceased persons or households affected by fires, provided that these funds are not designated for the enjoyment or use of Bráhmans.

The Superintendent of Religious Institutions may consolidate various properties belonging to the deities of both cities and rural areas and transfer this wealth to the king's treasury. Alternatively, under the cover of religious events, such as establishing a deity's shrine, setting up an altar, opening an ascetic's sacred space, or interpreting omens, the king may collect resources through ceremonies or gatherings. Another means might include proclaiming the miraculous presence of a god, highlighted by a sacred tree in the royal gardens that has produced untimely blooms or fruit.

Or, by sparking a false panic over an "evil spirit" residing in a prominent city tree, where a person is hidden and making eerie, unsettling sounds, the king's spies, disguised as holy ascetics, could initiate a campaign to collect offerings. Claiming that the offerings are necessary to appease this spirit and send it away, they could draw funds from the people. Similarly, spies might invite the public to witness a supposedly mythical serpent with multiple heads in a well connected to an underground tunnel system, charging a fee for those who wish to catch a glimpse of this "rare" creature. To add authenticity, they could plant a drugged cobra in a borehole within an idol of a serpent, a temple corner, or even in the hollow of an anthill, using the sedated snake to heighten the sense of mystique and power. Believers would be enticed to pay to view this serpent. For those who are skeptical by nature, spies could prepare a special "sacred water," subtly mixed with anesthetic ingredients. When these nonbelievers drink it, their sudden lethargy and drowsiness would be blamed on a divine presence, supposedly cursing those who doubt.

If the people remain unconvinced, an outcast could be secretly bitten by a cobra, an incident spies would later use as an example of the dangers of ignoring or defying these sacred events. With this, more revenue could be gathered to "appease the gods."

Meanwhile, a royal spy disguised as a wealthy merchant could pose as the business partner of a real, affluent merchant. Together, they would gather a large sum from sales, deposits, and loans. Once the fund grew to a significant amount, the spy could arrange to be "robbed" of all their collective assets. This strategy would also apply to officials like the royal coin examiner or the state goldsmith, who could stage similar thefts by pretending they'd lost significant assets in the course of their duties.

Alternatively, a spy, posing as a trader, or even an established merchant widely known for his dealings, could take loans or valuables from other traders, requesting gold and goods in pledges for foreign trade. After obtaining a sizable amount of resources, this supposed merchant would also arrange for a sudden nighttime robbery, claiming to be a victim of thieves.

In another tactic, prostitute-spies posing as virtuous women could captivate seditious individuals, luring them with their charms. As soon as these rebellious individuals are seen within the residences of these women, they could be arrested, and all their wealth confiscated. Or, in cases where rival seditious groups within a family argue or clash, spies trained as poisoners could target one faction, using the altercation to accuse the other group, confiscating their property as punishment.

A planted outcast might act as though he were a high-born man demanding repayment of a "large debt" supposedly left with the seditious person, or he could lay claim to an inheritance. He could also claim to be a servant or slave of the person and assert ownership over his wife, daughter, or daughter-in-law. Stationing himself outside the target's residence or nearby at night, he could await his moment, at which point a spy would arrange his death, declaring loudly, "This is the fate of one claiming what is rightfully his." In turn, this accusation could be used to strip the seditious person and his associates of their possessions, effectively neutralizing both the immediate threat and future unrest from similar groups.

Or a spy disguised as an ascetic may approach a seditious individual, tempting him with promises of great wealth or influence through the use of witchcraft, saying, "I am skilled in witchcraft that can bring endless wealth, gain entry into the king's court, win the love of any woman, eliminate one's enemies, prolong life, or grant a son if desired." If the seditious person agrees to pursue this forbidden magic, the spy could set up an elaborate scene involving ritual offerings. This might take place near an altar in a burial ground, where a small amount of money and the body of a man or child had already been hidden. The spy would offer up rich sacrifices of meat, wine, and perfume, claiming these offerings are essential for success. Once the ritual is over, the buried treasure is uncovered, but it is made to appear minimal. The spy would then explain that the wealth gained was small because the offerings weren't grand enough, suggesting that the seditious person should buy more valuable offerings to increase his gains. The spy would then catch him in the act of buying these extravagant items, providing ample evidence of his activities.

In a further twist, a female spy, disguised as a grieving mother, might raise an alarm, crying out that her child has been sacrificed for witchcraft, drawing public condemnation on the seditious person involved.

If a seditious person secretly practices sorcery at night, performs rituals in the forest, or indulges in amusements in a secluded park, fiery spies could eliminate him under cover of night and dispose of the body as though it were that of a social outcast.

Alternatively, a spy disguised as the servant of a seditious person could mix counterfeit coins with his own wages, planting them to be found, leading to the seditious person's arrest. Another spy, posing as a goldsmith, might work within the household of a rebellious individual and accumulate various tools needed to make counterfeit coins, setting up the seditious person for arrest on charges of fraud.

In another strategy, a spy disguised as a physician might declare a healthy yet seditious person to be ill and administer poison under the guise of medicine. Or a spy acting as the servant of a suspected person could ask another spy—disguised as a trustworthy friend—for an explanation of how letters from the king's enemies or items essential to a royal ceremony ended up in his master's possession. The spy himself could even pretend to offer explanations, further sowing doubt about the seditious person's loyalty.

These measures, as intricate as they may seem, are reserved strictly for dealing with the seditious and the wicked, ensuring that innocent individuals are never subjected to these severe tactics.

Just as fruits are picked from a garden only when they have fully ripened, so too should revenue be collected only when it becomes due or "ripe." Gathering taxes or revenue prematurely, just like harvesting unripe fruit, can harm the source, potentially leading to significant losses and creating a great deal of unnecessary hardship. Therefore, it is essential that revenue collection is timed carefully, ensuring that the source remains undisturbed and productive, so it may continue to yield resources without interruption.

[Thus ends Chapter II, "Replenishment of the Treasury" in Book V, "The Conduct of Courtiers" of the Arthasástra of Kautilya. End of the ninety-second chapter from the beginning.]

CHAPTER III. CONCERNING SUBSISTENCE TO GOVERNMENT SERVANTS.

In line with the needs of his forts and provinces, the king should allocate a portion, ideally less than one-fourth of the total revenue, to support his officials and retainers. Their well-being should be secured through suitable compensation to keep them motivated and dedicated to their duties. Importantly, this allocation should not compromise principles of righteousness or sound financial practices.

The sacrificial priest, the royal teacher, the minister, the court priest, the commander of the army, the crown prince, the queen, and the king's mother are each to receive an annual allowance of 48,000 panas. This generous provision helps ensure they remain steadfast, avoiding temptations that could lead to disloyalty or dissatisfaction.

Door-keepers, the superintendent of the royal harem, chief officials overseeing governance, the chief chamberlain, and the head of financial collection should each receive 24,000 panas. This amount supports their role, making them reliable and effective in their duties.

For the prince, his nurse, the chief constable, the town overseer, the superintendent of judicial or trade matters, heads of manufacturing, council ministers, as well as superintendents of territories and borders, an annual allocation of 12,000 panas is advised. This amount aims to strengthen their loyalty and make them formidable allies of the king.

Leaders of various military divisions, including those heading elephant, cavalry, chariot, and infantry units, along with commissioners, are each to be allotted 8,000 panas, enabling them to command respect within their respective ranks.

Lastly, superintendents responsible for managing infantry, cavalry, chariots, elephants, and the guards overseeing forests for timber and elephants should each receive 4,000 panas.

The chariot driver, the army physician, the horse trainer, the carpenter, and those responsible for rearing animals are each to receive 2,000 panas annually, recognizing their essential contributions to military operations and animal care.

Individuals who offer counsel, including the foreteller, omen reader, astrologer, storyteller, bard, and members of the priest's retinue, along with various departmental heads, are to be allocated 1,000 panas each. This ensures these roles are honored for their cultural and administrative importance.

For trained soldiers and the accounting and writing staff, an annual wage of 500 panas is appropriate to support their diligent and accurate service. Musicians are granted 250 panas, though trumpeters are awarded double this amount in acknowledgment of their skill in ceremonial music. Artisans and carpenters, who are crucial for both construction and maintenance, are to be given 120 panas each.

Lower-ranked support staff, including caretakers for animals and attendants tasked with miscellaneous duties, those serving the king directly, bodyguards, and coordinators of free labor, are designated an annual wage of 60 panas to reflect their support roles.

The king's chosen companion, the elephant driver, sorcerers, mountain miners, attendants of various types, teachers, and scholars are given a special honorarium that ranges from 500 to 1,000 panas based on their skill and merit.

Messengers are compensated by the distance they travel, with a rate of 10 panas per yojana. If their journey spans from 10 to 100 yojanas, their rate doubles to ensure the strenuous travel is rewarded adequately.

Any representative of the king participating in royal sacrifices like the Rájasúya ceremony will receive three times the amount that others of similar learning would be given, highlighting their elevated role. Meanwhile, the charioteer of the king in these sacrifices is awarded 1,000 panas for his role.

Spies, whether they are disguised as tricksters, impartial observers, householders, merchants, or ascetics, are granted 1,000 panas each, recognizing the value of their intelligence gathering. Lower-ranked spies, including village servants, fiery spies, poisoners, and wandering mendicant women, are compensated with 500 panas, acknowledging their work in gathering and reporting information essential for the king's security and strategy.

Servants who lead spies are to be compensated with 250 panas, or adjusted according to the level of work they complete. Superintendents responsible for overseeing one hundred or one thousand community units (vargas) will regulate the subsistence, wages, profits, appointments, and transfers of the people under their command.

However, officers appointed to guard the royal palaces, forts, and rural areas are exempt from reassignment. Chief officers, tasked with overseeing these secure locations, should be numerous and maintain long-term, stable appointments in these roles.

When a servant dies while on duty, provisions will be made for their surviving family members, including their children, spouses, and dependent relatives. Furthermore, during times of mourning, illness, or childbirth, the king shall show favor and generosity to these affected families. In times of financial constraint, the king may distribute forest goods, livestock, or even portions of land along with a small monetary gift. If he wishes to encourage settlement on undeveloped lands, payments will be made solely in currency; however, to ensure fairness across all villages, no single village shall be exclusively allocated to any servant.

Through these measures, the king not only ensures the livelihood of his servants but also rewards them according to their skills, knowledge, and dedication. For payments, the king may substitute one adhaka in place of the standard 60 panas, allowing for compensation in kind.

Foot soldiers, horses, chariots, and elephants will undergo thorough military training at sunrise on all days except those marked by planetary conjunctions. The king will be present to observe and assess the readiness of his forces during each training session. Weapons and armor must bear the royal seal before being entered into the armory, ensuring that they are accounted for and securely maintained. Armed individuals are restricted in movement unless they possess a valid passport permitting them to carry weapons.

If any weapons are lost or damaged, the superintendent responsible will bear the cost, reimbursing double the value of each lost or spoiled item, with records kept of all damaged or disposed weapons. Boundary guards are instructed to confiscate weapons and armor from caravans lacking the required travel passport.

When preparing for a military campaign, the king will activate his army. On these missions, spies disguised as merchants will deliver essential supplies to military outposts, doubling the supplies with a promise of repayment later. This strategy allows the king's merchandise to reach a wider market, simultaneously ensuring profitable returns on wages paid out.

By maintaining careful oversight of income and expenses, the king will prevent financial and military challenges. These arrangements ensure both subsistence and fair wages for all in service.

- Spies, prostitutes, craftsmen, singers, and senior military officers are tasked with closely observing the behavior of military personnel, assessing whether their actions are honorable or dishonorable.

[Thus ends Chapter III, "Concerning Subsistence to Government Servants" in Book V, "The Conduct of Courtiers" of the Arthasástra of Kautilya. End of the ninety-third chapter from the beginning.]

CHAPTER IV. THE CONDUCT OF A COURTIER.

Anyone with worldly experience and understanding of its affairs might, through the help of a trusted ally, seek the patronage of a king who is known for his pleasant nature and possesses all the qualities of a true ruler. He may consider aligning himself with any king whom he perceives as appreciative of wise counsel and good-hearted in character, even if that king lacks great wealth or the full strength of sovereignty. However, he should avoid associating with a king of a corrupt nature, for no matter how vast his power, a ruler devoid of good temperament and driven by a dislike for the science of governance and an inclination towards wrongful deeds cannot sustain his rule.

Upon gaining an audience with a virtuous king, he should provide the king with instruction in the sciences, and the king's silent acceptance of his teachings will strengthen his standing. When consulted on important matters, present or future, that require insight and deliberation, he may confidently and wisely offer his advice without fear of opposition from the council, ensuring that his guidance aligns with principles of righteousness and prudence. He may further advise the king, saying, "According to the principle that delays in quelling strong alliances of wrongdoers should be avoided, you should act firmly against the wicked, especially if they are well-supported. Also, refrain from disregarding my counsel, character, or secrets, and allow me to signal you with subtle gestures if you are about to deliver a punishment under impulse or anger."

With these understandings, the courtier may begin his duties. He should sit close to the king, distinguished from the seats of other courtiers. He must refrain from subtle criticisms of any assembly member's opinions, making unbelievable statements, laughing loudly without reason, or causing excessive noise. He should avoid speaking in whispers, private exchanges within the council, appearing publicly in royal attire, showing arrogance, jesting inappropriately, openly seeking gifts or promotions, looking sidelong or biting his lips, frowning at others, interrupting the king, making enemies of powerful factions, or associating with women, go-betweens, messengers of foreign rulers, foes, dismissed officers, or those of questionable character. He must avoid excessive adherence to a single course of action and contact with any union or alliance of men.

- Without missing timely moments, he should advocate for the king's interests; in the presence of trusted friends, he may speak of his own interests, and discuss the concerns of others when the time and place are fitting, all while upholding the principles of righteousness and economy.
- When consulted, he should advise the king on matters that are both beneficial and pleasing, avoiding the suggestion of

anything harmful even if it might appeal to the king. If the king is open to it, he may, in private, offer guidance that, though unwelcome, is in the king's best interest.

- He may choose silence over sharing anything offensive and should refrain from mentioning topics the king dislikes, as many, even those who are otherwise unfavored, have gained influence simply by avoiding such subjects. When a king seeks only pleasing news, indifferent to its negative effects, a wise advisor will observe this and act accordingly.
- In moments of jest, he should restrain his laughter, avoiding hurtful remarks or blaming others unfairly. He should demonstrate patience towards personal slights and cultivate a resilience as steadfast as the earth itself.
- A wise person will keep self-preservation at the forefront of his mind, understanding that service to a king is akin to living within fire—where fire may harm parts of the body, the king has the ability to shape or even destroy the lives of his servants, impacting not only the individual but also his family, including his children and wife.

[Thus ends Chapter IV, "The Conduct of a Courtier" in Book V, "The Conduct of Courtiers" of the Arthasástra of Kautilya. End of the ninety-fourth chapter from the beginning.]

CHAPTER V. TIME-SERVING.

When serving as a minister, the courtier must present the king with an accurate account of the net revenue after all forms of expenditure are covered. He should give detailed information, clarifying specifics like the nature of work that is either external or internal, secretive or open, costly or trivial. In all the king's pursuits, be it hunting, gambling, drinking, or pleasures, he should be close at hand, striving through careful persuasion to prevent the king from succumbing to negative habits or falling victim to the plots, schemes, or deceit of enemies. At all times, he must attempt to interpret the king's thoughts and expressions.

In guiding the king's scattered thoughts toward resolution, the courtier should pay close attention to the cues the king displays—indications of his inclinations, anger, joy, sadness, resolve, fear, or his shifts between opposing emotions.

When the king is favorably disposed towards the courtier, he displays it through particular gestures and actions: he shows enjoyment in recognizing the courtier's insights; listens attentively; offers him a seat and welcomes him in private; shows trust even in uncertain situations; engages in pleasant conversation; takes initiative in noticing details without needing reminders; tolerates reasonable suggestions; gives orders with a gentle demeanor; extends his hand in friendly gestures; refrains from ridicule when commendable things are said; praises the courtier's qualities when he is not present; recalls the courtier at mealtime; seeks his company in leisure; consults him when faced with concerns; respects those who follow him; confides in him; honors him increasingly; provides him with wealth; and alleviates his burdens. Each of these actions serves as a sign of the king's satisfaction with the courtier.

When the opposite occurs, the courtier should recognize the king's displeasure. Here are further indications, expressed clearly:

Signs of dissatisfaction include the king's angry demeanor when the courtier is near; avoidance or refusal to hear him; reluctance to offer him a seat or grant him audience; a noticeable change in tone or expression while conversing with him; seeing him with one eye or brow furrowed; biting the lips; visible perspiration; heavy breathing or unexplained smiles; talking to himself; sudden shifts in body posture; reaching for another's hand or chair; unsettling another person present; mocking the courtier's knowledge, background, or heritage; criticizing his colleague with similar flaws; condemning a person of opposite character flaws; censuring his adversary; ignoring his accomplishments; fixating on his shortcomings; paying undue attention to others entering the room; excessive gifting; dishonesty; and noting changes in how visitors to the court behave.

In observing signs of change, the courtier should even consider the behavior of animals around the king, as these too may reveal the underlying disposition of his sovereign.

- Kátyáyana asserts that this king dispenses his favors generously, extending them to all.
- Kaninka Bháradvája observes that the Krauncha bird has moved from the right to the left, implying a subtle change in fortune or direction.
- Dírgha Chárayana remarks that this king is like grass, likely suggesting pliability or being easily influenced.
- Ghotamukha compares him to a damp cloth, indicating softness or perhaps yielding nature.
- Kinjalka likens him to an elephant pouring out water, a symbol of power and grandeur, yet potentially wasteful in the process.
- Pisuna advises to consider him as a chariot-horse, suggesting he serves as a vehicle for others' ambitions. Pisuna's son adds that seeking favor with the king's opponent may lead to personal hardship or disapproval.

When the flow of wealth and honor ceases, such a king may indeed be left behind; alternatively, one might gain insight into both the king's character and his own shortcomings and adjust his behavior accordingly. Another option is to align with one of the king's most trusted allies for protection and favor.

- Living with the king's trusted friend, the courtier must strive to eliminate his master's flaws by leveraging his own network of friends to influence matters indirectly. Once this is achieved, he should return to his original position, regardless of whether the king remains in power or has passed away.

[Thus ends Chapter V "Time-serving" in Book V, "The Conduct of Courtiers" of the Arthasástra of Kautilya. End of the ninety-fifth chapter from the beginning.]

CHAPTER VI. CONSOLIDATION OF THE KINGDOM AND ABSOLUTE SOVEREIGNTY.

The minister shall skillfully deflect any dangers threatening the king. Long before any risk to the king's life appears imminent, the minister should, in collaboration with his own allies and followers, allow visitors to see the king only once a month or every two months. On other occasions, he may excuse the king's absence by claiming the king is involved in rituals meant to prevent national calamities, eliminate enemies, extend life, or ensure an heir.

When appropriate, the minister may even show a false king to the public or to messengers from allies or adversaries. This false king would direct all communication through the minister, making him the spokesperson in every interaction. Orders from the king would appear to come through the minister, channeled via the gatekeeper and the officer of the harem, and any decisions of mercy or punishment towards wrongdoers would be delivered indirectly.

Both the treasury and the military forces shall be overseen by two reliable and confidential officials, centralized in a single, secure location within the fort or on the kingdom's boundary. Members of the royal family, including princes and other close kin, may be deployed for challenging assignments, such as seizing a commander who has become a threat along with his followers, leading expeditions, or carrying out visits to the families of the king's allies.

Any neighboring king who appears likely to invade can be invited under the pretense of a festival, wedding, elephant capture, horse trade, or other land dealings, and captured. Alternatively, an ally might be enlisted to keep this potential invader occupied until a suitable agreement can be negotiated. Or the neighboring ruler could be encouraged to quarrel with hostile tribes or rivals. Should any member of his family be held in captivity, an offer of territorial gains could turn him against his own.

By garnering support from the nobility and princes of the royal family, the minister may install and publicly present the heir-apparent. Or, having eliminated all threats to the kingdom as outlined in the instructions on punishment, he might take charge of administration himself.

If, however, one of the neighboring kings continues to cause trouble, the minister might invite him with the promise, "Come here, and I shall make you king," and then dispose of him; or he might restrain this king through strategic means to keep him from posing any threat.

Finally, having gradually shifted the responsibilities of governance to the heir-apparent, the minister may formally announce the king's passing to the people.

If the king passes away while in enemy territory, the minister may form an alliance between the enemy and a trusted ally posing as the deceased king's adversary and then withdraw. Alternatively, he might install one of the neighboring kings in the fort of the deceased ruler and then withdraw. He could also set up the rightful heir on the throne and direct the army to face the enemy, using all available defensive strategies if the enemy advances, as laid out in other teachings on averting danger.

Kautilya states, "In such situations, the minister should assume full powers of sovereignty."

Bháradvája disagrees, arguing, "If the king is on his deathbed, the minister might instead provoke discord between the royal family's princes and influential nobles, allowing them to weaken each other. Any who then threaten the kingdom could be executed under the justification of preserving public order. By secretly disciplining the key members of the royal family and securing control, the minister may rightfully claim the throne. After all, in matters of power, even fathers and sons are known to turn against each other for the sake of the kingdom. Why should the minister, the chief guardian of the realm, be an exception?

"Moreover," Bháradvája continues, "one should not reject what has fallen into their hands through circumstance, for people say that a woman who pursues a man out of her own volition, if later dismissed, may turn to curse him."

- "An opportunity will present itself only once to a man who is vigilant and prepared, and it will not come again if he later wishes to complete his endeavor."

"But it is unrighteous," says Kautilya, "to undertake actions that provoke the anger of the people, nor is it a recognized standard. Therefore, he should appoint as ruler a son of the king who possesses virtuous qualities. If there is no prince of good character, he may put forward a less favorable prince, a princess, or the pregnant queen and say to the other ministers: 'This is your lineage (kshepa); consider both the heritage of this (child) and your own bravery and descent; this (child) is merely a symbol, and you are the leaders; now, how should I proceed?'"

While he speaks, those already taken into confidence should reply: "Who else, other than someone under your guidance, is fit to safeguard the multitude of the kingdom's four castes?" The remaining ministers will undoubtedly agree. Thus, he should install a prince, princess, or the pregnant queen and present them to the royal kin as well as to emissaries from allies or adversaries. He should grant the ministers and military officers enhanced stipends and wages, assuring them, "This (child) will further elevate your standing upon reaching adulthood." He should also make similar promises to the chief officers governing the forts and provincial areas, as well as to parties aligned with both allies and foes. Afterward, he should make all necessary arrangements for the prince's education and training.

Alternatively, he may install as the successor a child born of the princess by a man of her own caste. He should appoint as the prince's representative someone from the same family who is of modest valor and attractive appearance, to prevent the mother from being distressed with undue anxieties. He should ensure she is protected justly and refrain from indulging himself in luxuries. For the king, he may provide new chariots, horses, jewels, clothing, attendants, and residences.

- When the prince reaches maturity, the minister may suggest to the prince that he take over the responsibilities of governance, thus relieving the minister of the intellectual burden. He may choose to step away from his position if the king shows dissatisfaction but remain in his role if the king is pleased with his service.
- If he finds himself disillusioned with the life of a minister, he may choose to withdraw to a secluded forest or embark on a prolonged sacrificial ritual, ensuring that he informs the queen of all the measures and persons assigned to guide and protect the prince's upbringing.
- Even if the king is heavily influenced by powerful chiefs, the minister can, through the king's trusted advisors, guide him in the principles of governance, using stories and examples from the ancient texts, such as the Itihása and Purána, to reinforce his teachings.
- Should circumstances require, the minister may assume the guise of a skilled ascetic to endear himself to the king further. Once he has secured the king's trust, he can take effective steps to curb any seditious influences that might threaten the stability of the kingdom.

Book 6

CHAPTER I. THE ELEMENTS OF SOVEREIGNTY.

The elements of sovereignty consist of the king, the minister, the country, the fort, the treasury, the army, and the friend.

The foremost qualities of an ideal king include the following: He should come from a noble lineage, possess a godly disposition, and be endowed with valor. He seeks wisdom from the experience of elders, is virtuous, honest, and consistent in nature, showing gratitude and commitment to large and noble ambitions. His zeal is strong, he avoids procrastination, and he commands power to influence neighboring rulers. The king's mind is resolute, supported by a council of skilled ministers, and he values discipline—qualities that make his character both inviting and admirable.

In regard to intellectual qualities, a king should demonstrate inquiry, attentive listening, perceptiveness, a strong memory, thoughtful reflection, careful deliberation, insightful inference, and unwavering adherence to decisions.

Enthusiasm manifests in valor, a firm purpose, swift action, and moral integrity.

A ruler of self-possession exhibits a keen intellect, an impressive memory, and an alert mind. He is energetic, powerful, skilled in various arts, virtuous, and discerning in matters of rewards and punishment. Such a king maintains dignity, identifies dangers and solutions, exercises foresight, and seizes opportunities wisely based on place, time, and effort. He understands when treaties or warfare are necessary and maneuvers deftly with treaties and obligations to exploit his enemy's weaknesses. This king makes lighthearted jokes without compromising his dignity or confidentiality, remains calm, avoids anger, greed, and stubbornness, and is not prone to rashness or gossip. He addresses others with a pleasant demeanor, respects customs and traditions, and upholds the wisdom imparted by the elderly.

The qualifications of a minister have been previously discussed at various stages in this work.

A good country is defined by strategic capital cities, centrally and at the kingdom's borders, capable of providing sustenance not only to residents but also to outsiders in times of crisis. It deters enemies and possesses the strength to withstand neighboring threats. Such a region is free from muddy, rocky, uneven, or desert terrains, and avoids issues with conspirators, wild beasts, or vast wilderness. A prosperous country is visually appealing, blessed with fertile lands, rich mines, abundant timber and elephants, and vast grazing lands. It is artfully structured, with concealed passageways, plentiful livestock, reliable water sources independent of rain, an integrated network of land and waterways, and is enriched with varied commercial goods. It bears the capacity for a large army and supports significant taxation, while being populated by diligent and ethical farmers, intelligent landowners, skilled laborers, and a citizenry renowned for loyalty and high character.

The qualities of ideal forts have already been discussed in detail.

An exemplary treasury is one that is acquired justly, whether through inheritance or self-earned, and is rich in gold, silver, and an array of large, colorful gems and gold coins. Such a treasury is capable of supporting the kingdom through long periods of hardship or calamity.

The best kind of army is one that has been consistently maintained over generations, directly from the king's father and grandfather. It is strong and devoted, with soldiers who are well-respected and content with their families. This army is loyal and willing to stay in distant locations as required, standing invincible in all circumstances. Its soldiers are skilled in various combat techniques, proficient with multiple forms of weaponry, and are ready to share in the king's fortunes, whether for better or worse. Due to their loyalty, they are never prone to internal disputes with the king. Furthermore, an ideal army is comprised entirely of warriors from the Kshatriya caste, emphasizing its strength and commitment.

The best kind of ally or friend, also handed down from father and grandfather, is one who has stood the test of time. This friend is rational, steadfast, always open to reasonable persuasion, and unshakable in their loyalty. Such an ally is capable of swiftly organizing and preparing for warfare on a large scale, adding resilience and reliability to the kingdom's support network.

On the other hand, the most dangerous enemy is one who lacks royal heritage, who is driven by greed, possesses a weak council of ministers, and leads a populace that is disloyal and discontented. This enemy is frequently engaged in unjust actions, shows poor character, indulges in unworthy pleasures, and lacks zeal and strategic insight. Their actions are marked by indiscretion, helplessness, and ultimately cause harm to themselves and those they lead. Such an enemy is feeble and thus easily overthrown, for they are already weakened from within.

- Apart from the enemy, these seven elements—each possessing the ideal qualities described—are regarded as the essential limbs of sovereignty.
- A wise king has the capability to uplift and transform even the weakest, poorest, and most troubled parts of his sovereignty into ones that are thriving and content. Conversely, a ruler with wicked intentions and poor judgment will undoubtedly ruin even the most prosperous, loyal, and stable elements of his kingdom.
- Therefore, a king who lacks integrity and engages in corrupt habits, regardless of his power or status as an emperor, will inevitably face downfall, either through the uprising of his own people or at the hands of his enemies.
- On the other hand, a wise and politically astute king, even one ruling over a modest territory, can harness the strength of these essential elements to extend his influence across the entire earth, securing victories without experiencing defeat.

- [Thus, ends Chapter I "The Elements of Sovereignty" in Book VI, "The Source of Sovereign States" of the Arthasástra of Kautilya. End of the ninety-seventh chapter from the beginning.]

CHAPTER II. CONCERNING PEACE AND EXERTION.

The acquisition and safeguarding of property rely on the stability of peace and the vigor of industry.

Industry, or vyayama, is the effort put forth to accomplish the goals of any undertaking. Peace, on the other hand, is the condition where the results of these efforts are enjoyed without disruption. Together, peace and industry are secured through the wise application of six-fold royal policy.

Positions in sovereignty can experience three possible states: deterioration, stagnation, or progress. These states are influenced by both human and providential causes. Human-driven influences are represented by policy (naya) and impolicy (apanaya), while fortune (aya) and misfortune (anaya) reflect the providential.

Providential events are those that are unforeseen; fortune here is described as the attainment of a sought-after outcome that once seemed unreachable. Human causes are those anticipated or driven by foresight; when goals are reached as anticipated, they are the result of good policy. Impolicy, on the other hand, brings harmful outcomes, which can sometimes be foreseen, while providential misfortunes are entirely beyond foresight.

The conqueror is the king whose good character and well-composed sovereignty make him the source of wise policy. The king situated immediately on the boundary of the conqueror's land is termed the enemy, while the king lying just beyond the enemy, separated from the conqueror only by the enemy, is called the friend of the conqueror.

An adversary of nearby and substantial strength is an enemy, and he becomes vulnerable when facing hardship or when he has strayed into corrupt actions. Such an enemy becomes susceptible to attack when he lacks support, but if equipped with some assistance, he is only subject to harassment or weakening. These various states represent different approaches to an enemy.

In front of the conqueror and in proximity to the enemy, other kings are aligned: first, the conqueror's friend; next, the enemy's ally; followed by the conqueror's friend's friend, and finally, the ally of the enemy's friend.

Behind the conqueror's position are situated a rearward enemy (parshnigraha), a rearward friend (akranda), the ally of the rearward enemy (parshnigrahasara), and the ally of the rearward friend (akrandasara).

A rival of equal noble lineage, positioned directly beside the conqueror, is regarded as a natural enemy, while one who opposes the conqueror indirectly by stirring up antagonism and creating adversaries is considered an artificial, or factitious, enemy.

A king who has inherited a long-standing alliance, established by his forefathers and situated next to the territory of the conqueror's immediate adversary, is a natural ally. On the other hand, an ally whose friendship is based primarily on self-preservation and security is regarded as an acquired friend.

The king whose territory lies between both the conqueror and his primary enemy, and who is strong enough to assist either side in unity or in separation, or to resist either one independently, is called the Madhyama or mediatory king.

Beyond the reach of these local powers lies a more distant, highly powerful king capable of extending support or opposition to the conqueror, his enemy, or the Madhyama king, either individually or collectively. This figure, wielding considerable influence, is known as the neutral king (udasina). Together, these roles comprise the twelve primary kings within the geopolitical framework.

A "Circle of States" includes the conqueror, his friend, and the friend of that friend, forming a triplet of primary kings. Each of these kings has five foundational elements of sovereignty—namely, a trusted minister, a secure country, a fortified stronghold, a wealthy treasury, and a capable army. In this arrangement, a single Circle of States contains eighteen primary elements. Similarly, other circles are structured with different central figures, such as the conqueror's enemy, the Madhyama king, or the neutral king, thereby forming three additional Circles of States, each with its distinct configuration.

Altogether, these formations create four essential Circles of States, composed of twelve primary kings, sixty sovereign elements, and a combined seventy-two elements of statecraft and governance.

Each of the twelve kings in these Circles must be considered with regard to their sovereignty, strength, and ultimate objectives. Here, strength represents power, and happiness is seen as the end goal of sovereignty.

Strength is classified into three types: first, intellectual strength, which is rooted in wisdom and careful planning; second, the strength of sovereignty, represented by a well-funded treasury and a robust army; and third, physical strength, which is manifest through martial prowess and combat capability.

The end of statecraft is similarly divided into three kinds: the end of deliberation, achieved through wise counsel and planning; the end of sovereignty, attained by leveraging the power of governance; and the end of martial power, secured through steadfast perseverance and military force.

A king's standing is determined by the extent of his power and his capacity for ensuring happiness: if he possesses both in greater measure than another, he is deemed superior; if in lesser measure, he is inferior; and if equal, he stands on par. Thus, a wise king must always strive to enhance his power and elevate his state's happiness to gain advantage over rivals.

A king whose elements of sovereignty are on par with those of his enemy should utilize his righteous conduct and the influence of allies or those hostile to his enemy to eclipse his opponent's power. Alternatively, he may assess the potential for his enemy's self-undoing, contemplating: "Though my enemy may have great power now, his own actions—such as using harsh language, imposing severe penalties, and mismanaging wealth—will likely damage his rule. Even if he achieves some short-term victories, he may succumb to his own vices, such as indulging in excessive hunting, gambling, drinking, or women. If his subjects are already discontented, he may become weak and arrogant, making him vulnerable to my advance."

The conqueror may also consider the likelihood of his enemy retreating, thinking, "Should he be attacked, my enemy might flee with his resources to a fort or remote area. Though his army is strong, his lack of loyal friends or a secure fortification may still render him vulnerable to my strategies."

Furthermore, if a distant king is eager to subdue his own rival and would also support my cause in defeating this enemy when my resources are stretched, then it may be strategic for me to momentarily permit my enemy to consolidate his strength and enjoy temporary success, anticipating future opportunities. In situations where I am called upon to act as a Madhyama king or mediating force, I can better position myself to take advantage of my opponent's vulnerabilities as they unfold.

- By extending the boundaries of his Circle of States to encompass his friend's lands, the conqueror can align the neighboring kings as the spokes of this circle, positioning himself firmly as its central axis. This arrangement places the conqueror at the heart of a network, directing influence outward with the support of allies.

- An enemy who can be weakened or subdued will, when situated between the conqueror and his allied friend, seem to gather power, yet this apparent growth in strength is merely a fleeting illusion, as his position is strategically vulnerable within the conqueror's expanding circle.

Book 7

CHAPTER I. THE SIX-FOLD POLICY, AND DETERMINATION OF DETERIORATION, STAGNATION AND PROGRESS.

The Circle of States serves as the foundation for six principal forms of strategy in statecraft, shaping how rulers interact with allies, enemies, and those they govern. My teacher identifies these six forms as peace (sandhi), war (vigraha), neutrality (ásana), preparations for conflict (yána), alliance (samsraya), and a combined approach involving peace with one side and war with another, often referred to as a double policy (dvaidhíbháva). However, Vátavyádhi posits that all six ultimately derive from two fundamental strategies—peace and war—as each of the six approaches originates from these two primary forms of statecraft. In contrast, Kautilya holds that these six approaches, given their unique functions and respective applications, merit individual recognition as distinct strategies.

Each of these six forms of policy has a particular purpose. Peace involves agreements and assurances to avoid conflict, while war comprises offensive measures and direct confrontation. Neutrality is a stance of non-engagement, whereby the ruler refrains from favoring any side in a conflict. Marching or making preparations involves mobilizing resources and readiness to engage in conflict should circumstances require it. Alliance signifies reliance on a stronger power for protection and support. Lastly, a double policy allows a ruler to maintain peace with one faction while pursuing conflict with another. Together, these six forms offer a range of choices for navigating complex relationships with other states.

Each form of policy is best suited to a specific situation. A ruler who finds himself weaker than an adversary should seek peace to avoid unnecessary losses. Conversely, a ruler confident in his superior strength may consider war as a means to expand his influence. When a king believes he is neither vulnerable to threats nor capable of overcoming his enemy, neutrality provides a safe course. A ruler with abundant resources and an advantageous position may decide to march forward and assert dominance over a foe. A ruler lacking sufficient power to protect himself may best secure his survival by aligning with a stronger ally, while a king who sees strategic merit in supporting one side and opposing another may choose the double policy, balancing peace with one ally while confronting a shared adversary. Each of these forms serves a distinct role, allowing a ruler to respond with flexibility to a variety of circumstances.

A wise king will select whichever policy aligns best with his goals, enabling him to construct fortifications, improve infrastructure, establish roads, expand agriculture, found new settlements, exploit mineral and forest resources, and hinder similar developments by his enemies. When a king observes his strength increasing in both quality and quantity faster than that of his adversary, he may temporarily ignore his rival's attempts to advance, knowing that his own growth will soon outpace the competition.

If two rival kings find themselves progressing toward their respective goals at an equal rate, they may see mutual benefit in negotiating peace. In contrast, no ruler should engage in any strategy that brings about a reduction in his own gains without producing an equivalent disadvantage for his enemy. Such a situation leads to deterioration and risks weakening his own kingdom over time. However, if the king foresees that his temporary losses will be offset by future gains that ultimately surpass his rival's, he may accept minor setbacks to secure a longer-term advantage.

When two rulers, though facing difficulties, anticipate an equal benefit in the future, they, too, may find peace preferable to prolonged conflict. The state in which neither growth nor decline is evident, where the kingdom neither advances nor recedes, is termed stagnation, a condition that a wise ruler will seek to avoid, ensuring that his policies and efforts always serve to strengthen and expand his power and influence over time.

Whoever thinks his stagnancy to be of a shorter duration and his prosperity in the long run to be greater than his enemy's may neglect his temporary stagnation.

My teacher says that if any two kings, who are hostile to each other and are in a stationary condition expect to acquire equal amount of wealth and power in equal time, they shall make peace with each other.

"Of course," says Kautilya, "there is no other alternative."

Or if a king thinks:--

"That keeping the agreement of peace, I can undertake productive works of considerable importance and destroy at the same time those of my enemy; or apart from enjoying the results of my own works, I shall also enjoy those of my enemy in virtue of the agreement of peace; or I can destroy the works of my enemy by employing spies and other secret means; or by holding out such inducements as a happy dwelling, rewards, remission of taxes, little work and large profits and wages, I can empty my enemy's country of its population, with which he has been able to carry his own works; or being allied with a king of considerable power, my enemy will have his own works destroyed; or I can prolong my enemy's hostility with another king whose threats have driven my enemy to seek my protection; or being allied with me, my enemy can harass the country of another king who hates me; or oppressed by another king, the subjects of my enemy will immigrate into my country, and I can, therefore, achieve the results of my own works very easily; or being in a precarious condition due to the destruction of his works, my enemy will not be so powerful as to attack me; or by exploiting my own resources in alliance with any two (friendly) kings, I can augment my resources; or if a Circle of States is formed by my enemy as one of its members, I can divide them and combine with the others; or by threats or favour, I can catch hold of my enemy, and when he desires to be a member of my own Circle of States, I can make him incur the displeasure of the other members, and fall a victim to their own fury,"--if a king thinks thus, then he may increase his resources by keeping peace.

Or if a king considers:

"My land is naturally well-defended with mountains, forests, rivers, and strategically placed forts with only one secure entrance, and it is populated with experienced soldiers and established groups of fighters. Therefore, it can easily repel any assault from my enemy. Or, by positioning myself within my stronghold at the border, I can effectively hinder my enemy's efforts. Additionally, internal conflicts and diminished morale may soon weaken my enemy, causing his projects to fail on their own. Or, should he face an attack from another ruler, I could encourage his people to migrate to my land." With such thoughts, he might decide to maintain open hostilities to expand his resources at the enemy's expense.

Alternatively, a king might reason:

"My enemy lacks the strength to disrupt my undertakings, just as I am not strong enough to damage his. Even if he attempts an attack, he will suffer greatly, like a dog fighting a boar, while my resources remain intact." In this case, the king could maintain neutrality, confident that his resources would grow as his enemy weakens himself.

Or, a king might think:

"By mobilizing my army, I could successfully damage my enemy's enterprises, and I have solid arrangements to protect my own." This would allow him to increase his resources by moving forward with a campaign.

Yet, if a king concludes:

"I am not strong enough either to weaken my enemy's efforts or to shield my own resources against his attacks," he would be wise to seek protection from a more powerful ruler, aiming to improve his condition gradually, moving from deterioration to stability, and from stability to advancement.

Finally, a king might assess:

"By forming an alliance with one ruler, I can continue strengthening my own resources, while engaging in warfare with another enables me to hinder my enemy's progress." This would allow him to follow a dual policy of selective peace and war, thereby enhancing his resources and strategic influence.

- Therefore, a king within the circle of sovereign states should utilize the six-fold policy with strategic wisdom, aiming to transition his kingdom from a state of decline to stability and, from there, towards a state of flourishing progress.

[Thus ends Chapter I, "The Six-fold Policy and Determination of Deterioration, Stagnation and Progress" in Book VII, "The end of the Six-fold Policy" of the Arthasástra of Kautilya. End of the ninety-ninth chapter from the beginning.]

CHAPTER II. THE NATURE OF ALLIANCE.

When the benefits of peace and war are evenly matched, peace should be chosen, as the disadvantages—such as loss of strength, wealth depletion, prolonged absence from home, and moral repercussions—are always linked to war.

This principle also applies when comparing neutrality with war. Between dual policy (pursuing peace with one while engaging in war with another) and alliance, dual policy is preferable; for by adopting dual policy, a king can strengthen his position while remaining focused on his own objectives, whereas a king in an alliance is bound to support his ally at his own expense.

An alliance should be formed with a king stronger than the neighboring adversary; if such a king is unavailable, then it is wise to foster goodwill with the neighboring enemy. This can be achieved through strategic support, either financially, militarily, or by ceding a portion of territory while maintaining a cautious distance. For kings, there is no greater danger than forming an alliance with a considerably powerful king, except in situations where an enemy is actively attacking.

A king without strength should adopt the stance of a defeated ruler towards his closest enemy. However, when signs of his own rising influence become evident—such as his enemy's vulnerability due to severe illness, internal strife, the growth of other enemies, or misfortune affecting a friend of the enemy—then he can find a reason to free himself from subordination. For example, he could feign a need for ritual purification to protect his enemy from impending calamity, using it as an opportunity to escape the enemy's court. If in his own lands, he should avoid contact with his ailing foe, and if in close proximity, he may seize the chance to eliminate the enemy whenever circumstances allow.

A king positioned between two powerful neighboring rulers should seek protection from the stronger of the two or align with the one he finds most trustworthy. Alternatively, he may establish peace with both on equal terms and then work to create rivalry between them, telling each that the other is a threat whose tyranny could lead to their downfall, thus sowing discord. Once divided, he may try to subdue each of them separately using secretive or indirect methods.

If necessary, he may seek refuge with two nearby kings of significant power, allowing them to help him counter an immediate enemy. He could also forge an alliance with a leader fortified in a stronghold, adopting a dual strategy—making peace with one king while waging war with the other. Alternatively, he may adapt his actions based on the changing dynamics of peace and war, acting as circumstances dictate. Aligning himself with traitors, adversaries, and tribal chiefs plotting against both neighboring kings could also prove advantageous.

Pretending to be closely allied with one of the kings, he might exploit the other's vulnerabilities by employing the help of enemies and tribal forces. Forming a Circle of States by befriending both kings is another option. Alternatively, he could ally with a mediating king or a neutral ruler, using their support to overpower one or even both of the neighboring kings. Should both kings cause him harm, he may seek the protection of a just and righteous king, whether from the mediating, neutral, or allied circles. This protector should be one whose subjects are loyal and support the ruler's happiness and peace, someone who can help him regain his lost standing, who shares a historical or familial bond with his ancestors, and in whose realm he can rely on numerous powerful allies.

- When faced with two powerful kings who are friendly with one another, a ruler should establish an alliance with the one he both favors and who favors him in return. This mutual preference and goodwill form the most reliable basis for forging a strong and beneficial alliance.

[Thus ends Chapter II, "The Nature of Alliance" in Book VII, "The end of the Six-fold Policy" of the Arthasástra of Kautilya. End of the hundredth chapter from the beginning.]

CHAPTER III. THE CHARACTER OF EQUAL, INFERIOR AND SUPERIOR KINGS; AND FORMS OF AGREEMENT MADE BY AN INFERIOR KING.

A king who seeks to expand his own power should apply the six-fold policy carefully.

Agreements of peace should be made with those kings of equal or superior strength, while a weaker king may be engaged in battle. A king who wages war against one much stronger will be as vulnerable as a foot-soldier challenging an elephant, risking inevitable defeat. Similarly, when two kings of equal power clash, the outcome is likely to damage both, just as two clay pots striking each other would break. In contrast, when a stronger king confronts a weaker one, the outcome resembles a stone shattering an earthen pot, ensuring the stronger king's victory.

If a stronger king dismisses a weaker one's proposal for peace, the lesser king should adopt the stance of a vassal, showing humility as a subordinate before a superior. But when two kings of equal might resist peace, then one should return to the other the same level of opposition he has received, since peace between two equals only emerges when they possess comparable strength. As iron can only meld with iron when heated, so too does equal force forge harmony between kings.

When a weaker king shows complete submission, peace should be granted; for an overly troubled or angered lesser king, much like an uncontrolled fire, may retaliate fiercely and find support from nearby allies. If a king perceives that his ally's subjects, despite being overtaxed and impoverished, have not yet fled to his own domain due to fear of being called back, he may choose, even with limited strength, to challenge his ally openly. Likewise, if a king locked in battle with another observes that the suffering populace of his enemy does not rally to him due to the hardships of war, he should, though stronger, consider peace or lessen the burdens of conflict.

When two kings are equally matched in battle and one sees his difficulties as more severe than his opponent's, realizing that resolving his enemy's issues might lead to an increased threat, he should seek peace despite his resources. If a king experiences neither harm to his rival nor benefit to himself, he should adopt a stance of neutrality, even if he holds an advantage.

Lastly, if a king assesses his enemy's problems as impossible to fix, he may advance against that foe, confident of victory, regardless of his own inferior power.

When a king perceives himself beset by impending dangers or significant troubles, he should, despite his superior strength, seek the protection of another for stability. If he recognizes that his goals can be best met by forming peace with one ruler while engaging in conflict with another, he should—even with greater power—adopt a dual strategy, balancing both alliance and opposition.

In this way, the six forms of state policy come into play, each used in combination as circumstances demand.

Now, as for their specific application:

- When a king of lesser power finds himself under attack by a stronger ruler leading a Circle of States, he should humbly seek peace by offering resources such as treasure, troops, himself, or even his land.
- If the agreement includes the condition that a set number of troops or the elite of his army must be presented upon request, this type of peace is called átmámisha, or "offering himself as flesh."
- An agreement where the commander of the army, along with the heir-apparent, is required to present themselves upon request is termed purushántarasandhi, or "peace with hostages other than the king himself." This type is beneficial for self-preservation since it does not necessitate the king's direct attendance.
- If the terms require that the king himself or another delegate should march with the army to a designated place when needed, it is called adrishtapurusha, or "peace without a specific individual as a representative." This arrangement contributes to the safety of both the king and the principal commanders of his army.

- In the first two forms of peace, a woman of status may be given as a pledge, while in the last form, there should be a covert plan to seize the enemy. These describe the various peace arrangements that hinge upon the provision of the king's forces.
- When wealth is offered to free the other elements of sovereignty, such peace is known as parikraya, or "price."
- Likewise, when peace is reached by giving an amount of money that can be carried on a person's shoulders, it's termed upagraha, or "subsidy," and this form comes in various arrangements. Due to distance or prolonged storage, sometimes the promised tribute may accrue arrears. Nevertheless, since this type of payment can be reasonably postponed, it's considered preferable to agreements where a woman is given as a pledge.
- When both parties reach peace through amicable union, it's called suvarnasandhi, or "golden peace." The opposite of this is kapála, meaning "half of a pot," a type of peace involving the payment of a vast sum of money.
- In the first two forms, one should provide materials, elephants, horses, and troops; in the third, gold; and in the fourth, one should avoid payment by citing losses incurred from previous efforts. These illustrate types of peace agreements reached through monetary terms.
- When a part of the territory is ceded to keep the rest of the kingdom and its people secure, this is known as ádishta, or "ceded," and benefits a ruler who seeks to rid the ceded area of thieves and other malefactors.
- When the entire territory, excluding the capital and weakened by resource exploitation, is ceded, it's called uchchhinnasandhi, or "peace cut off from profit," which serves a king wishing to bring hardship upon his adversary.
- When freedom for the kingdom is secured by agreeing to pay the produce of the land, this agreement is called avakraya, or

"rent." An agreement involving the promise to pay even more than the land produces is known as paribhúshana, or "ornament."

- Among these options, the first is preferable; however, the last two, which are based on yielding the land's produce, should only be agreed upon when circumstances force one to submit to a stronger power. These illustrate types of peace achieved by ceding territory.

- These three kinds of peace are to be concluded by a lesser king who must yield to the strength of a more powerful ruler due to the specific conditions of his resources, prevailing circumstances, and the timing involved.

[Thus ends Chapter III, "The Character of Equal, Inferior, and Superior Kings; and Forms of Agreement made by an Inferior King" in Book VII, "The end of the Six-fold Policy" of the Arthasástra of Kautilya. End of the hundred and first chapter from the beginning.]

CHAPTER IV. NEUTRALITY AFTER PROCLAIMING WAR OR AFTER CONCLUDING A TREATY OF PEACE; MARCHING AFTER PROCLAIMING WAR OR AFTER MAKING PEACE; AND THE MARCH OF COMBINED POWERS.

Remaining neutral, or deciding to proceed with action only after declaring either peace or war, has been outlined. Sthána (remaining quiet), ásana (withdrawing from hostility), and upekshana (neglect) all align with the concept of ásana, or neutrality. As for the distinctions between these three aspects: Sthána involves remaining steady with a specific policy; ásana is the act of holding back from hostilities to serve one's own interests; and upekshana means taking no steps at all against an opponent.

When two rulers are both interested in extending their power but also desire peace, and neither can advance successfully against the other, they may each decide to maintain a stance of quiet after either declaring war or reaching a peaceful understanding.

When a ruler sees he has the means to defeat an enemy of equal or greater power—either through his own forces, with support from allies, or using wild tribes—then, having fortified his defenses against both internal and external threats, he may decide to remain quiet after declaring a state of war.

When a king is confident that his people are brave, united, and prosperous enough to sustain their own work without interruption, while also able to interfere with the enemy's efforts, he may then choose to stay neutral after declaring war.

Should a ruler recognize that his enemy's subjects are mistreated, impoverished, greedy, and often harassed by hostile armies, thieves, or wild tribes, and might thus be won over through intrigue; or that his own agricultural and commercial sectors are thriving while those of his enemy are dwindling; or that the enemy's people, suffering from famine, might relocate to his own lands; or that, despite any declines in his own agricultural or trade returns and any growth in his enemy's, his people will remain loyal and not defect to the enemy; or that by declaring war he could seize the enemy's grain, cattle, and gold by force; or that he could halt the enemy's damaging trade imports to protect his own economy; or that valuable trade could flow toward his lands instead of the enemy's; or that war would prevent the enemy from dealing with traitors, enemies, wild tribes, and rebels and would lead to conflict among them; or that his own ally would swiftly accumulate wealth without significant losses and would stand by him on his march, since no ally would miss the chance to acquire fertile land and a prosperous ally like himself—then, with a view to weakening his enemy and showcasing his strength, he may choose to stay neutral after proclaiming a state of war.

However, my teacher contends that if a king takes such a passive approach, his enemy might use this opportunity to overpower him.

Kautilya disagrees, saying, "The aim in maintaining quiet after proclaiming war is to weaken the enemy's resources rather than allowing him to grow stronger." He believes that once a king gains enough strength, he will be ready to confront and defeat his enemy. Additionally, any adversary of this enemy will likely support the quiet king to protect their own interests. For this reason, any king with adequate resources may consider staying quiet after proclaiming war.

If this strategy of remaining neutral after declaring war brings about negative results, then switching to neutrality after making peace might be more favorable.

When a king finds his strength bolstered by keeping quiet post-declaration of war, he should consider launching an attack on his enemy.

If a king notices that his enemy has become entangled in difficulties, that these troubles are beyond the enemy's control to fix, and that the enemy's subjects are suffering, mistreated, unhappy, impoverished, or disunited, thus making them prone to deserting their ruler; or that his enemy's land has succumbed to devastating calamities like fire, floods, diseases, epidemics, or famine, weakening its defenses and draining its resources—then it may be time to move forward with an attack after proclaiming war.

If a king is fortunate enough to have a strong ally ahead and a dependable supporter behind him, both with loyal and courageous citizens, while his foes lack these strengths, then he can feel secure in advancing with his powerful ally holding back the enemy in the front and the supporter containing any threats from behind. With these favorable conditions, he can march forward after proclaiming war against the primary enemy ahead.

Should a king see the chance to achieve victory swiftly on his own, he may press on against the main enemy while proclaiming war on those behind him; otherwise, he should secure peace with those rearward enemies before advancing.

If a king feels he cannot confront his enemy alone but finds it necessary to proceed, he should arrange to march with the support of kings of comparable, greater, or lesser power, depending on the needs of his campaign.

For objectives with clearly defined goals, the distribution of spoils should be set in advance; however, if the objective involves numerous or varied targets, the spoils should be divided as circumstances demand. When it's not possible to forge such an alliance, he might request assistance in the form of an army for a fixed portion of the spoils or ask an ally to accompany him, agreeing to an equal share.

If the prospect of gain is highly probable, the shares should be fixed; if uncertain, they should remain flexible.

- A share of profit based on the strength of the army provided is the first approach; assigning shares according to the effort each participant contributes is the most effective. Profits may also be divided in proportion to the success achieved or the resources initially invested.
- [Thus ends Chapter IV, "Neutrality after Proclaiming War or after Concluding a Treaty of Peace; Marching after Proclaiming War or after Making Peace; and the March of Combined Powers," in Book VII, "The end of the Six-fold Policy" of the Arthasástra of Kautilya. End of the hundred and second chapter from the beginning.]

CHAPTER V. CONSIDERATIONS ABOUT MARCHING AGAINST AN ASSAILABLE ENEMY AND A STRONG ENEMY; CAUSES LEADING TO THE DWINDLING, GREED, AND DISLOYALTY OF THE ARMY; AND CONSIDERATIONS ABOUT THE COMBINATION OF POWERS.

If a king has two enemies—one weaker but vulnerable and one stronger, and both are struggling—which one should he attack first?

The stronger enemy should be attacked first. Once this enemy is defeated, the weaker enemy can then be targeted, as this one will likely surrender willingly to the conqueror after seeing the powerful opponent fall. The stronger enemy, however, would never surrender so easily.

Now, if faced with a choice between a weaker enemy in serious trouble or a stronger enemy facing only minor difficulties, which one should the conqueror go after first? My teacher suggests that, for an easier conquest, the vulnerable enemy facing worse troubles should be attacked first.

Kautilya, however, disagrees. He argues that the conqueror should aim for the stronger enemy with minor troubles. Even if the troubles of this stronger enemy are less severe, they will increase under attack. While attacking the weaker enemy may worsen that enemy's troubles, leaving the stronger one alone might allow him to overcome his issues and unite with the weaker enemy or another rival positioned behind the conqueror.

When there are two vulnerable enemies, one known for integrity but facing serious troubles, and another of vicious character facing lighter troubles, but with unfaithful subjects, which one should be attacked first?

If the conqueror attacks the virtuous enemy with serious troubles, that enemy's loyal subjects will likely come to his aid. In contrast, the vicious enemy's subjects—disloyal and unmotivated—will probably not support their ruler. These disloyal subjects could even weaken a strong ruler. For this reason, the conqueror should go after the enemy whose subjects cannot be trusted.

Now, given a choice between an enemy whose subjects are poor and greedy and another whose subjects feel oppressed, which one should he attack first?

My teacher suggests that the conqueror should march against the enemy whose subjects are poor and greedy, as they are more easily won over by schemes and can be quickly stirred up. However, the subjects who feel oppressed are less likely to be swayed and can be calmed by punishing their leaders.

Kautilya disagrees. He argues that, although these subjects may be poor and greedy, they remain loyal to their ruler and will stand firmly by his side, ready to counter any intrigue against him. Loyalty, he notes, is the foundation of all other virtues. Therefore, the conqueror should focus his attack on the enemy whose subjects feel oppressed.

Next, which enemy should be targeted: a powerful but corrupt enemy or a weaker but righteous one? The answer is the powerful enemy with a corrupt nature. When this enemy is attacked, his subjects are unlikely to support him; instead, they may even work against him or join forces with the conqueror. In contrast, if the virtuous enemy is attacked, his subjects will stand by him, or even die with him.

- By disrespecting the virtuous and praising the corrupt; by allowing unjust and unnatural killings to occur;
- by disregarding the observance of moral and just traditions; by engaging in unjust deeds and ignoring just actions;
- by doing things that should be avoided and failing to do what should be done; by withholding rightful payments and demanding what should not be taken;
- by failing to punish the guilty and harshly punishing the less guilty; by arresting the innocent and letting those who should be caught go free;
- by taking on dangerous tasks while neglecting profitable ones; by failing to protect people from thieves and by seizing their wealth;
- by abandoning courageous efforts and discouraging noble deeds; by offending the leaders of the people and looking down upon those who are honorable;
- by disrespecting the elderly, by acting deceitfully and lying; by

failing to address issues and neglecting ongoing tasks;

- and by being careless in ensuring the security and welfare of his people and their property, the king fosters poverty, greed, and resentment among his subjects;

- when people are impoverished, they become greedy; when they become greedy, they grow discontented; when discontented, they willingly side with the enemy or turn against their own ruler.

Therefore, no king should allow situations to arise that lead to poverty, greed, or disaffection among his people. If such issues do arise, he must act swiftly to address them.

Of the three—impoverished people, greedy people, or disaffected people—which is the most dangerous?

An impoverished population constantly fears oppression and ruin, whether through excessive taxation or other means, and will naturally seek relief from poverty, support rebellion, or even consider fleeing elsewhere.

A greedy population remains perpetually unsatisfied and is susceptible to enemy manipulation.

A disaffected population will rise against its ruler, especially in collaboration with the enemy.

If the decline in population arises from a lack of resources, such as gold or grain, it signals a kingdom-wide threat and is difficult to resolve. However, a shortage of capable people can be offset by acquiring wealth and supplies. Greed, though limited to a few high-ranking officials, can be resolved or appeased by allowing them to acquire spoils from an enemy. Disaffection or disloyalty can be quelled by eliminating key leaders, as without leadership, the people are more manageable and less likely to be swayed by external enemies. When a population is too fearful to withstand hardships, it may scatter if its leaders are subdued, but when controlled, it can endure difficulties.

After thoroughly assessing the reasons for making peace or engaging in war, a king should form alliances with rulers who are both powerful and of good moral character to act against an enemy.

A "king of considerable power" refers to one who has the strength either to defeat or capture an enemy behind his ally or to offer sufficient support to his ally during a campaign.

A "king of righteous character" is one who remains committed to fulfilling promises, regardless of whether the outcome is favorable or not.

Should the conqueror march with a single, stronger ally or with two allies of equal strength?

It is generally more advantageous to march with two allies of equal strength. If aligned with a superior king, an ally might seem under the influence of that stronger power. Marching with two equally powerful allies allows for flexibility, and should those allies be skilled in tactics, they can be split if necessary. Moreover, if one of these allies proves untrustworthy, the other two can work together to counter any betrayal or discord caused by the third.

Should a king march with a single ally of equal power or two allies of lesser strength?

Marching with two allies of lesser power is preferable; the conqueror can assign different tasks to each, maintaining command over both. Once the primary objective is achieved, the lesser allies are more likely to withdraw respectfully, satisfied by their support for a more dominant partner.

- To ensure the reliable behavior of an ally known for inconsistent character, the conqueror should carefully monitor the ally's conduct until the mission is complete. This can be done by making surprise inspections at critical moments or by securing the ally's loyalty with his family, such as by holding his wife as a pledge.

- Even when genuinely motivated by friendship, a conqueror should exercise caution with an ally of equal power, especially if that ally achieves notable success. Success can often shift an ally's approach, and an ally who feels empowered may alter his stance, even towards a stronger conqueror.

- An ally of greater strength should be trusted with caution since prosperity has the potential to change intentions. Such an ally, even if content with a modest share of the gains, may later take advantage, perhaps even claiming twice what was initially agreed.

- The primary conqueror, pleased with victory, should ensure the fair dismissal of his allies by providing their rightful shares. Rather than competing with them for the rewards, he should be willing to yield when necessary. By doing so, the king can cultivate respect and loyalty from the entire Circle of States.

[Thus ends Chapter V, "Considerations about Marching against an Assailable Enemy and a Strong Enemy; Causes Leading to the Dwindling, Greed, and Disloyalty of the Army; and Considerations about the Combination of Powers" in Book VII, "The end of the Six-fold Policy" of the Arthasástra of Kautilya. End of the hundred and third chapter from the beginning.]

CHAPTER VI. THE MARCH OF COMBINED POWERS; AGREEMENT OF PEACE WITH OR WITHOUT DEFINITE TERMS; AND PEACE WITH RENEGADES.

In this way, the conqueror can effectively manage the second key factor in his strategy: the neighboring enemy. He should prompt his nearby rival to join him in a joint campaign, proposing, "You advance in that direction, and I will move in this direction. We will share the spoils equally."

If the loot is to be shared equally, it represents a peace agreement; if divided otherwise, it signals dominance over the enemy. A peace agreement can either include a clear commitment to achieve a specific goal (paripanita) or have no concrete objectives (aparipanita).

When the agreement specifies, "You proceed to that region, and I shall proceed here," it is a peace agreement aimed at achieving a set objective in a particular location.

If the terms involve, "You remain engaged for this duration, while I remain engaged similarly," it constitutes an agreement with a fixed timeframe.

Where the terms are, "You aim to complete that task, and I will focus on this one," it becomes an agreement to achieve distinct goals.

When the conqueror reasons, "My ally (formerly my rival) must cross unfamiliar terrain filled with mountains, forests, rivers, forts, and deserts, lacking food supplies, inhabitants, grazing areas, firewood, and water, and distant and unlike other lands, making it challenging for his army to operate; while I will travel through a territory offering the complete opposite advantages," he should form an agreement centered on a specific location.

Similarly, if the conqueror considers, "My ally must engage in action without sufficient supplies and endure harsh weather—rainy, hot, or cold seasons—that hinder his forces over an ill-suited period, whereas I can work in ideal conditions," then he should base the agreement on timing.

If the conqueror sees that "my ally's task is temporary and insignificant, irritating his people, consuming excessive time and resources, and potentially causing harm, going against righteousness, alienating the Madhyama and neutral kings, and risking friendships, whereas my task yields opposite results," he should structure the agreement around achieving specific goals.

Additionally, agreements may combine location and time, time and objective, location and objective, or all three elements—location, time, and objective. This approach produces a total of seven possible forms of peace agreements.

Long before making such an agreement, the conqueror has to fix his own work and then attempt to overreach his enemy.

When a peace agreement is made with a hasty, careless, and short-sighted enemy who has fallen into hardship, without specifying exact terms regarding time, location, or objectives—solely for the purpose of mutual peace—the conqueror can exploit the situation to catch the enemy off guard at their weak points. This approach is referred to as peace with no definite terms (aparipanita). An old saying illustrates this strategy:

"By keeping one neighboring enemy entangled with another, a wise king can then turn his attention to a third king. After defeating this third adversary of equal power, he can claim his territory."

There are several additional forms of peace: peace with no specific objective (akritachikírshá), peace with binding conditions (kritasleshana), breaking of peace (kritavidúshana), and the restoration of broken peace (apasírnakriyá).

Battles also come in three varieties: open battle, deceptive battle, and silent battle, in which the enemy is covertly eliminated, without any formal declaration or mention of war.

When a new peace agreement is established using tactics like negotiation, and when the rights of the parties—whether they are equal, inferior, or superior in power—are clearly defined, it is called peace with no specific end, meaning it aims solely for security and stability.

Peace with binding terms occurs when allies secure the agreement by ensuring its conditions are strictly followed, maintaining unity and avoiding any risk of discord.

Breaking of peace arises when, through spies or traitors, proof of the other king's breach of trust or treachery is established, justifying the annulment of the agreement.

Restoration of broken peace refers to the act of reconciling and reinstating cooperation with a servant, ally, or other former member who had defected.

There are four types of those who leave their master and later return: the first has a reason both for leaving and returning; the second has no reason for either; the third has a reason for leaving but none for returning; and the fourth has no reason for leaving, but a reason to come back.

Anyone who left due to the master's own shortcomings and returns upon recognizing the master's good character or realizing flaws in the enemy's kindness is to be accepted back. Such a person, after weighing his circumstances, has legitimate reasons both for leaving and returning. Recognizing the value of this judgment, he should be reconciled and welcomed, as his return signals respect for the master's virtues or a desire to amend past misjudgments.

If a person deserted because of his own failings and returns without regard for the kindness or merits of either his old or new master, he shows a lack of loyalty and stability. This type of fickle behavior, coupled with the absence of a compelling reason for his actions, indicates he does not merit the trust or forgiveness of reconciliation, as his unpredictable nature could disrupt the harmony within the court.

A person who abandoned his master due to the master's faults but returned out of his own inadequacies or difficulties should be considered a deserter. Since he had a reason to leave but not a genuine reason to return, his motives must be thoroughly scrutinized. Welcoming back someone in this category should be approached cautiously, ensuring the interests of the court are not compromised by one who left only to return in unfavorable circumstances.

In the case of one who returns under the influence of the enemy or with intentions of undermining his former master, the situation requires a meticulous examination. This person may harbor ill will toward his former master, either through natural inclination or by fear of retribution, should the former master regain power over his current master. Additionally, he may return after realizing that his new master's aims might be harmful or ruthless, reflecting his apprehension for his own safety. Such individuals need careful scrutiny. If their motives are honest, they should be welcomed respectfully; if not, it is best to keep them at a distance to protect the court from potential harm.

Individuals who left of their own fault but returned due to the cruelty or ill nature of their new master should be considered deserters who had no valid reason to leave initially but developed a legitimate reason to return. Their actions suggest they are more likely to follow a leader of good character, and such individuals require careful assessment to determine their loyalty before any decision is made regarding their return.

If a king determines, "This deserter brings me valuable information about my enemy's weaknesses, is aligned with my allies, and can be easily rallied against cruel and corrupt figures or groups," he may deem this individual worthy of trust and retain him as an asset within his service. Such a person's awareness of enemy flaws and potential usefulness could outweigh concerns about his past desertion.

My teacher advises that any person who has failed to achieve results in his duties, weakened in strength, sought personal gain from his skills instead of devotion, was driven by greed, overly inquisitive about foreign lands, indifferent to the bonds of friendship, or entangled with strong enemies, should be disregarded. Such individuals are considered unfit for service as they lack the virtues required for steadfast loyalty and allegiance to the court.

However, Kautilya counters this view, suggesting that abandoning individuals for these reasons shows timidity, poor management, and lack of patience in discerning true potential. He proposes that only those who pose harm to the king's interests should be removed, while those who threaten the enemy's interests could be useful allies. If an individual's actions seem harmful to both parties, then a thorough investigation should precede any decision.

- In situations where peace with an otherwise unworthy king becomes necessary, the conqueror must establish defenses at points where his power might pose a risk. By fortifying vulnerable positions, the conqueror can ensure that his interests are protected while still maintaining an alliance of convenience.

- To restore broken peace, a renegade or anyone showing sympathy toward the enemy should be kept at a strategic distance, where they remain valuable to the state but are not a direct threat. This positioning allows the state to utilize the renegade's skills or influence while minimizing risks, ensuring he contributes to the state until the end of his life.

- Alternatively, such an individual could be directed to oppose the enemy directly, perhaps as a captain of the army responsible for guarding remote or wild areas vulnerable to enemy incursions. Placing him in a boundary role serves both as an act of control and as a practical use of his skills, keeping him from the heart of state affairs.

- Another option might involve sending him on missions to engage in discreet trade dealings involving either new or old goods in foreign territories. This covert operation, intended to keep him preoccupied with complex overseas dealings, could later be used as a means to accuse him of conspiracy with the enemy, should the need arise.

- In cases where the future peace of the state absolutely requires it, a renegade deemed dangerous may be removed without delay. Swift, decisive action can neutralize any further threats that he might pose, preventing long-term repercussions.

- A deeply ingrained, wicked nature that has developed from ongoing association with enemies is as hazardous as the untrustworthy presence of a snake close by. Just as a pigeon feeding on the seeds of the plaksha (holy fig-tree) endangers the salmali (silk-cotton) tree by threatening its habitat, so too does a person of a corrupt nature continuously menace the peace and safety of the state.

- When battle is waged openly in broad daylight and within a specific location, it is classified as open battle. However, strategies that involve pretending to attack from one direction while planning an assault from another, or capturing and eliminating an enemy when he is least prepared or when he is already troubled, fall under the category of treacherous combat.

- Treachery also includes bribing a section of the enemy's army while methodically destroying another section. Meanwhile, silent warfare is characterized by cunning efforts to sway the principal officers of the enemy's forces through subtle intrigue, rather than direct confrontation. This tactic undermines the enemy's structure from within, silently destabilizing their power.

[Thus ends Chapter VI, "The March of Combined Powers; Agreement of Peace with or without Definite Terms; and Peace with Renegades," in Book VII, "The end of the Six-fold Policy" of the Arthasástra of Kautilya. End of the hundred and fourth chapter from the beginning.]

CHAPTER VII. PEACE AND WAR BY ADOPTING THE DOUBLE POLICY.

The conqueror can outmaneuver his closest enemy as follows:

By forming an alliance with a neighboring king, the conqueror can initiate a campaign against another nearby ruler. If the conqueror anticipates that the enemy will not target his rear nor join forces with any vulnerable foe he intends to attack, he considers himself safe from facing unfavorable odds. In this arrangement, the ally not only aids in gathering revenue and resources but also suppresses any internal dissidents troubling the conqueror, deals with wild tribes and their strongholds, and destabilizes the targeted enemy, either pushing them toward a vulnerable state or forcing them into a peace agreement. Moreover, the ally, once satisfied with his share of benefits, may even assist in converting other potential foes of the conqueror into friendly entities. In this way, the conqueror can declare war on one adversary while making peace with another, securing either military support through funds or financial backing to support his army from neighboring kings.

When kings of varying strength—superior, equal, or inferior—agree to an alliance with the conqueror and provide him with armies or wealth in amounts directly proportional to the strength they lend, this arrangement is known as an "even peace." Conversely, if the contributions differ from what the situation demands, this is called "uneven peace," and if the contributions are particularly advantageous to one side, it is termed "deceptive peace" or "atisandhi."

When a powerful king finds himself beset by challenges or unfortunate events, a weaker king may propose an arrangement where the powerful king lends military support in exchange for a portion of the profits, proportional to the strength he contributes. Should the more powerful king find such terms insulting or opportunistic, he may respond with an act of war; otherwise, he might agree to the arrangement if it serves his interests.

In another instance, a weaker king, intending to strengthen his own resources and revenue, may approach a stronger ruler for military assistance to secure his rear and protect his home territories during his campaign, offering a larger share of the profits than the strength of the army lent would usually warrant. If the superior king considers the weaker ruler sincere, he may accept the proposal; however, if suspicions arise, he might instead initiate a counterattack.

A weaker king, who is fortified with defensive strongholds and alliances, may need to make a brief advance to capture an enemy or secure a valuable prize without an all-out battle. In this situation, he may seek assistance from a more powerful but troubled ally, proposing a smaller profit share than the worth of the army provided would usually justify. If the stronger ruler feels disrespected or sees an opportunity, he may retaliate, but if he sees the benefit, he may instead accept the offer and provide his support.

When a powerful king, who is unburdened by any troubles, wishes to bring about losses in men and resources to his enemy through that enemy's unwise actions, or intends to send his own army abroad under the guise of assistance, or aims to entangle his enemy in a conflict with a hostile force, or to stir up troubles for a vulnerable and weakened enemy by setting an inferior king against him, or if he genuinely desires peace for its own sake with sincere intentions, he may agree to accept a smaller portion of the profit (in exchange for providing an army to another). This way, he gains financially through his alliance, assuming his ally shares his good intentions; otherwise, he may simply declare war on the ally.

A king may also deceive or support an equal in the following ways:

When a king offers peace to an equal in strength, with a condition that he receives that ally's army—one strong enough to counter a rival force, or to secure his territory's front, center, and rear, or to protect his friend, or to defend any other vulnerable region of his land—in exchange for a profit share proportional to the army's strength, the latter king may accept if he believes the offer is sincere. Otherwise, he may resort to war.

When an equal in power, who has access to an alternate military force, seeks an ally's army due to weakened sovereignty and multiple threats, and requests this in return for a smaller share of profit than the contribution deserves, the stronger ally may reject the request or accept it if necessary.

When a king, currently under duress, with his plans vulnerable to the ambitions of nearby rulers, and who is still gathering his forces, seeks assistance from an equal in strength, offering a larger share of profit than the army's worth warrants, his ally may choose to assist him if the proposal appears genuine. If not, a declaration of war remains a possibility.

Moreover, if a king wishes to weaken a rival king who is already struggling due to diminished resources, or to ruin his otherwise highly profitable ventures, or if he plans to strike when the rival is within reach or during a campaign, he may increase demands on an assailable rival (whether that rival is equal, inferior, or even superior in power) by repeatedly requesting aid. The targeted king may agree to these demands if he believes doing so will help him preserve his power by using the ally's army to destroy an enemy's stronghold or pillage an ally of the enemy, or to devastate that enemy's outlying territories. Alternatively, he may use his ally's forces to strengthen his own through their exposure to battles in favorable conditions, thereby positioning himself to either subdue his ally or persuade the ally's army to his side.

When a king wishes to control another king, whether stronger or weaker, by holding him as an assailable enemy to be overpowered later, especially after utilizing his help to defeat a third opponent, or if he wants to reclaim funds previously paid out (like subsidies), he may propose a peace agreement to that king with terms offering to pay more than the cost of his army. If the king receiving this proposal is strong enough to retaliate, he may respond with a declaration of war; if he is not as powerful, he may either accept the terms or choose to remain allied with the assailable enemy instead. Alternatively, he could offer troops filled with traitors, hostile elements, and unpredictable forces.

When a king of greater power finds himself in trouble due to weakened resources or allies and seeks assistance from a lesser king's army, offering a profit share equal to the value of the troops provided, the lesser king, if he has the strength to resist, might declare war; otherwise, he might agree to the proposal.

Similarly, a stronger king might ask a weaker king for troops in return for a profit share less than the cost of the army provided. The weaker king, if powerful enough to oppose this, may opt to declare war; if not, he may simply accept the terms as they are.

- Both the king being approached for peace and the king proposing peace should carefully evaluate the intentions behind the peace proposal. After considering the potential benefits and outcomes, each should decide on the course of action that promises the most favorable results.

[Thus ends Chapter VII "Peace and War by Adopting the Double Policy" in Book VII, "The end of the Six-fold Policy" of the Arthasástra of Kautilya. End of the hundred and fifth chapter from the beginning.]

CHAPTER VIII. THE ATTITUDE OF AN ASSAILABLE ENEMY; AND FRIENDS THAT DESERVE HELP.

If an assailable enemy at risk of being attacked wishes to assume the conditions that led two kings to ally against him or to drive a wedge between them, he may propose peace to one of these kings by offering twice the profit expected from their current alliance. Once an agreement is reached, the enemy can then emphasize the toll of war, such as the loss of men and wealth, the difficulty of fighting abroad, the moral consequences, and the personal hardships that the king would otherwise endure. If the king accepts this reasoning, the promised amount may be paid, or the agreement may be dissolved by sowing distrust between that king and other rulers.

If a king's objective is to see his ally suffer loss in a poorly planned venture, to disrupt a rival's successful enterprises, or to strike his enemy while he's off-guard or on the march, he may agree to take only a small gain for now and plan to ask for additional support later, potentially in alliance with the vulnerable enemy's foe.

When a king's primary aim is to support a friend, to weaken an adversary, or to secure substantial returns down the line by ensuring his ally's success now, he may be wise to set aside the offer of immediate profit in favor of smaller, future gains from his ally.

In cases where a king wishes to defend his ally from internal conspirators, other enemies, or a stronger ruler who threatens his ally's survival, and he hopes to set a precedent for reciprocal aid in the future, he may take no present or future compensation.

However, if a king intends to undermine an enemy's subjects, disrupt an ally's peace, or break an alliance due to suspicion of betrayal or pending attacks, he may preemptively demand a larger payment than usual. Under these circumstances, his ally may request a delay or installment plan, either now or later, which can also apply to prior situations discussed.

The conqueror and his rival each support their allies based on how steadfast and loyal those allies are, how feasible and beneficial their projects seem, and the dedication of their subjects to these causes.

Whoever undertakes a feasible task begins a manageable endeavor; whoever starts a task that is unblemished by poor reputation begins a commendable project; whoever initiates a task promising substantial returns begins a profitable effort; and whoever remains dedicated without rest until the task is completed shows true resolve. The one who enjoys loyal, devoted subjects has the advantage of securing assistance and seeing any project through to success without risking his favor or influence. Friends with these qualities, when won over by the conqueror or his enemy, provide immense support. Friends who lack these qualities, however, should not be aided.

Between two kings—the conqueror and his rival—who share the same ally, the king who supports a truly loyal friend has the upper hand. By supporting a genuine ally, he not only strengthens his position but avoids the losses of men, resources, and the strains of campaigning abroad. Meanwhile, the other king, who may inadvertently aid an ungrateful rival, risks wasting resources and even emboldening an enemy who resents any perceived favoritism.

If the conqueror and his rival both find an ally in the same mediatory (Madhyama) king, the one who assists a loyal and genuine friend gains an advantage. Helping a trustworthy ally brings mutual benefit and security, while the other king risks losing resources, enduring the burdens of distant ventures, and inadvertently empowering a resentful enemy. However, when the Madhyama king is unreliable and misuses assistance, investing his energies in futile endeavors and providing little in return, the rival gains an edge over the conqueror.

This principle equally applies to a neutral king under the same conditions.

In situations where a king considers aiding either a Madhyama or a neutral king with part of his army, it's wise to discern the ally's qualities carefully. If the king chooses to support an ally who is courageous, adept with weapons, resilient, and genuinely loyal, he may unintentionally put himself at risk, especially if his enemy, by contrast, supports someone with opposing, less dependable qualities—allowing the enemy to gain a strategic advantage.

When a king successfully accomplishes an objective with the aid of a friend who expects future military assistance in return, he may select among his different types of armies—be it his own hereditary army, hired forces, a collective army of regional groups, his ally's troops, or an army of wild tribes. He should consider sending those troops that are well-prepared for diverse terrains and seasons or, alternatively, select forces such as those from an enemy or wild tribes located far enough to avoid immediate repercussions.

If the king suspects his ally might misuse his forces by deploying them into hazardous or hostile regions, unfavorable wilderness, or during challenging seasons that would weaken his own military, he could defer sending his troops, citing other pressing uses for them, and instead offer assistance by other means. However, if he must lend his army, he should send only units accustomed to the prevailing conditions, ensuring they'll remain stationed until the ally's objective is fulfilled and that they'll be protected from undue risk. When his ally's task is completed, the king should seek a valid reason to recall his troops. Alternatively, he might send forces filled with those harboring animosity, traitors, or wild tribes—forces potentially unreliable to the ally—or, by establishing a truce with the ally's vulnerable enemy, subtly undermine the alliance.

- When all kings involved in an agreement, regardless of whether they hold equal, lesser, or greater power, gain an equal benefit from the alliance, this arrangement is known as peace (sandhi). However, if the benefit gained is uneven, with one party profiting less than others, it is regarded as defeat (vikrama). This principle defines the nature of peace and war.
- [Thus ends Chapter VIII, "The Attitude of an Assailable Enemy; and Friends that Deserve Help," in Book VII, "The end of the Six-fold Policy" of the Arthasástra of Kautilya. End of the hundred and sixth chapter from the beginning.]

CHAPTER IX. AGREEMENT FOR THE ACQUISITION OF A FRIEND OR GOLD.

Among the three gains—gaining a friend, acquiring gold, and securing territory—which result from the march of allied forces, the gain mentioned last is more valuable than the previous ones. Territory is prioritized since it can enable the acquisition of both friends and wealth. Between the acquisition of a friend and that of gold, each can be used to obtain the other, and both hold their distinct advantages.

An agreement made on the terms "let us gain a friend," for instance, is known as even peace. If one party acquires a friend while the other is left with an adversary, this is seen as uneven peace, and if one side benefits more significantly than the other, it is viewed as deception. In the case of even peace, the one who gains a friend of strong character or assists an old friend out of difficulties is ultimately the greater beneficiary, for support given in challenging times strengthens the friendship.

Now, of the two—an enduring but somewhat unyielding friend or a more recent, submissive ally, each secured by helping them in difficult times—which is preferable? My teacher believes a long-standing friend of independent nature is better, as they may not be as supportive but will also not cause harm. However, Kautilya argues that a recent friend who shows submissive qualities is better, as such a friend is more likely to provide meaningful help when needed; for, after all, the essence of friendship lies in assistance.

When comparing two equally loyal friends—one a new ally with substantial resources and potential for mutual gain, and the other a long-standing ally with limited resources—my teacher asserts that a new friend with ample resources is preferable because such a friend can offer significant support swiftly and help sustain larger ventures. Kautilya, however, disagrees, favoring the long-standing friend of more limited means. He argues that a new, wealthy friend might waver in their loyalty if they encounter significant material loss from their help or might seek a reciprocal arrangement. Meanwhile, a loyal, enduring friend, even if less resourceful, will provide sustained support over the long term due to the strength of the long-established relationship.

Which is preferable: a powerful but slow-to-respond ally, or a smaller, more responsive ally? My teacher suggests that a powerful ally, though slow to act, brings an impressive strength that can achieve large goals when finally moved to action. However, Kautilya argues that a smaller, more easily mobilized ally is preferable, as such a friend is ready at the right moment to act and, due to limited power, can be directed by the conqueror as needed. A powerful ally, in contrast, cannot be so easily maneuvered.

Next, which is better: scattered forces, or a standing army that is not entirely loyal? My teacher maintains that scattered forces are preferable because, though spread out, they are more likely to obey when summoned. Kautilya disagrees, favoring a standing army that, even if not immediately loyal, can be won over through diplomatic and strategic measures. Gathering scattered forces in time is more challenging, as their individual lives and duties often delay their collective mobilization.

Is it better to have a friend with a large population or a friend with abundant gold? My teacher believes that a friend with a vast population is better because such a friend wields considerable power and can undertake any mission when needed. Kautilya, however, values a friend rich in gold, as wealth is always useful, whereas an army is not always essential. Gold can procure troops and other desired resources as necessary.

Between an ally with gold and one with extensive territory, which is preferable? My teacher asserts that a friend with gold is advantageous, as they can support heavy expenses wisely. But Kautilya argues that territory is superior, as it can yield both friends and wealth. Therefore, an ally with vast land is ultimately more valuable.

Even when the allies of both the conqueror and his enemy have similarly sized populations, they may still differ in traits like bravery, resilience, willingness to cooperate, and readiness for military formation. Similarly, when both allies are equally wealthy, they may differ in qualities such as willingness to grant requests, generosity, and consistent availability.

Regarding this topic, the following sayings are well known:

- A truly good friend possesses six qualities: being long-standing, submissive, easily motivated, connected through family ties, powerful, and of a harmonious nature.
- A long-standing friend is one who values the relationship out of genuine, disinterested motives, upholding the friendship simply for the sake of friendship itself and preserving its legacy over generations.
- A submissive friend is one whose generosity can be enjoyed in various ways and is of three types: one who offers benefits exclusively to a single ally, one who benefits both the conqueror and the enemy, and a third type who offers benefits that extend to everyone.
- A steadfast friend, though less yielding, is one who stands firm, whether in offering or receiving help, maintaining a forceful stance toward adversaries, possessing numerous strongholds, and commanding a large army that includes wild tribes, demonstrating a lasting but resolute and independent nature.
- A friend who seeks alliance primarily for self-preservation during times of threat or trouble is a temporary and submissive friend.
- A true friend remains aligned with a single purpose, providing support reliably, staying unchanged, and maintaining a friendly nature even in hardship.
- An amicable friend is one who is inherently loyal. A friend who also sides with the enemy is changeable, while one who is neutral toward both the conqueror and his enemy is considered a friend to both.
- A friend who holds hostility toward the conqueror or is equally loyal to the conqueror's enemy is harmful, regardless of whether he actively helps or simply possesses the capacity to assist.
- A friend who aids the enemy's allies, dependents, vulnerable

persons, or relatives is a mutual friend, valued by both the enemy and the conqueror.

- A friend with expansive and fertile lands, who is self-sufficient, strong but somewhat idle, tends to withdraw support if his ally falls into disrepute or hardship.
- A weaker ally, cautious and adaptive to both the conqueror's and enemy's influence without forming enmities, is known as a common friend.
- Lastly, one who ignores a friend's request for help, whether the need is clear or not, disregards his own potential danger by neglecting loyalty.

The question arises: which is preferable—a quick, smaller gain or a distant, larger gain?

My teacher argues that a quick, smaller gain is better since it enables the fulfillment of immediate objectives.

Kautilya, however, disagrees: a distant, larger gain that continually yields benefits, like a productive seed, is preferable; otherwise, only then should an immediate smaller gain be considered.

- Thus, when deciding, a king who wishes to fortify his power should carefully evaluate the lasting benefits of a continuous gain or a share in such a lasting gain before marching in alliance with others.

[Thus ends Chapter IX, "Agreement for the Acquisition of a Friend or Gold" in the section of "Agreement for the Acquisition of a Friend, Gold, or Land and Agreement for Undertaking a Work," in Book VII, "The end of the Six-fold Policy" of the Arthasástra of Kautilya. End of the hundred and seventh chapter from the beginning.]

CHAPTER X. AGREEMENT OF PEACE FOR THE ACQUISITION OF LAND.

The agreement to acquire land is termed a peace agreement for the acquisition of territory.

Of the two kings entering this agreement, the one who acquires a fertile, productive land rich with crops gains the upper hand.

If both kings acquire similarly fertile lands, the one who takes such land by defeating a powerful enemy gains the advantage; not only does he acquire land, but he also weakens an adversary and thereby strengthens his own position. True, conquering a weaker enemy offers its own merit, but the land gained is often poor, and former allies in the vicinity may now become adversaries.

When enemies are equally powerful, the one who secures land after conquering a fortified opponent gains the edge; capturing a fortress not only secures the territory but also helps contain wild tribes.

Acquiring land from a wandering foe has a further distinction— whether the acquired land borders a powerful or powerless enemy. Land near a powerless enemy is more manageable, while that bordering a powerful adversary requires constant defense, draining men and resources.

Which is preferable: gaining fertile land near a persistent enemy or sterile land near a temporary one?

My teacher suggests fertile land near a persistent enemy is preferable since it yields resources to maintain a strong army capable of subduing the enemy.

Kautilya, however, disagrees: rich land attracts many adversaries, and a constant enemy will remain hostile, whether or not conciliated with men and money. A temporary enemy, on the other hand, may remain calm due to either fear or favor. Land bordered by multiple forts sheltering bandits, foreigners, and wild tribes is land with a persistent enemy; land of the opposite character has only a temporary enemy.

Which is better, a small, nearby piece of land or an extensive, distant one?

A small, nearby territory is better, as it can be more easily acquired, secured, and defended, unlike the other, which is challenging on all fronts.

Of these two types of land, which is preferable—one self-sustaining or one that requires external defense?

Self-sustaining land is preferable, as it supports its own military and financial needs, unlike the latter, which serves merely as a remote military outpost.

Finally, is it better to acquire land from a foolish king or a wise one?

Acquiring land from a foolish king is better, as it can be easily gained and held without fear of it being reclaimed, whereas land obtained from a wise and beloved king presents a far greater challenge.

Of two enemies—one that can only be harassed and another that is fully reducible—acquiring land from the reducible one is the better choice. When this enemy is attacked, having little to no external aid, he tends to flee, taking his army and wealth along, often abandoned by his subjects. In contrast, the other enemy, who can only be harassed, remains steady with the support of his forts and allies.

Among two fortified kings, the one with forts on flat land is easier to subdue than one whose fort lies within a river's embrace; a fort on a plain is accessible, vulnerable to assault, and may be taken with the enemy inside. However, a fort surrounded by a river demands double the effort to overcome and offers a natural supply of water and other essentials to sustain its defenders.

When choosing between capturing land from a king with a river fort and another with mountainous fortifications, taking land from the former is preferable. A river fort can be attacked using elephants aligned to form a bridge across the river, wooden bridges, or boats. Additionally, the river may not always have a deep flow and can potentially be drained. In contrast, a mountain fort is inherently defensive and challenging to besiege or climb; even if one part of its defense falls, the remaining forces can retreat safely. Such a fort provides strategic advantages, allowing defenders to hurl rocks or trees down onto attackers.

Which is easier: taking land from those fighting on plains or from those defending from low grounds? Land is easier to seize from the latter, as they battle under challenging conditions of both timing and terrain, whereas those on the plains can readily fight at any moment and location.

Between two enemies, one who defends from ditches and another from elevated ground, seizing land from the former is advantageous. Defenders in ditches can be valuable as they are accustomed to fighting both from within trenches and with weapons in hand, whereas those fighting from higher ground depend solely on their weapons.

- Whoever, well-versed in political strategy, captures land from these and other types of enemies will stand out in strength, overshadowing both allied partners and any rivals outside the alliance.

[Thus ends Chapter X, "Agreement of Peace for the Acquisition of Land" in the section of "Agreement for the Acquisition of a Friend, Gold, or Land and Agreement for Undertaking a Work," in Book VII, "The End of the Six-fold Policy" of the Arthasástra of Kautilya. End of the hundred and eighth chapter from the beginning.]

CHAPTER XI. INTERMINABLE AGREEMENT.

The agreement that is established under the mutual understanding, "Let us cultivate and settle on this unused or waste land," is known as an interminable agreement. This type of agreement involves both parties contributing to develop a previously uncultivated or deserted tract of land, with each party aiming to gain advantages, whether in terms of crop production, revenue, or strategic control.

When one of the parties takes the lead in colonizing a fertile portion of this land, managing to sow and gather a harvest earlier than the other, that party gains a marked advantage, as it can reap immediate benefits, secure resources, and assert a stronger presence on the land. This initial success in securing crops is likely to make the cultivating party less dependent on external resources, enhancing their standing in the partnership and strengthening their claim over the cultivated area.

Now, if a choice has to be made between colonizing an extensive plain or a smaller area rich in water sources, the latter option is generally preferable. A limited but well-watered area is advantageous as it allows for continual crop and fruit cultivation year-round, without the reliance on seasonal rains. This sustained productivity supports a dependable source of income and food, which in turn sustains population growth and stability. The smaller, well-watered land also requires fewer resources to manage, whereas vast plains, although expansive, may demand substantial investment for irrigation and infrastructure.

Of the various plains available for colonization, one that supports the cultivation of both early and late-season crops, requires minimal labor, and has low irrigation needs is ideal. Such land provides a continuous yield, increasing food security and economic stability for the settlers. In contrast, a plain with higher water needs and limited crop cycles is less favorable, as it might demand greater investment in both labor and water resources for a sustainable return.

When considering watery lands, one that enables the cultivation of grains is more valuable than one that primarily yields other types of crops. Grains serve as a staple food and can be stored over long periods, providing sustenance in times of scarcity. Additionally, a steady grain supply reduces dependency on external sources, strengthening the colony's independence. However, if two watery areas are compared—one small and grain-rich, and the other extensive but producing a range of crops other than grains—the larger area may offer greater benefits. With its vast expanse, the larger area not only supports specialized agricultural practices, such as the cultivation of spices or medicinal plants, but also provides ample room for constructing forts and defensive structures, which enhance security and stability. Moreover, this diversity in agricultural output and available space supports the growth of trade, which can generate additional revenue and help sustain the population.

If a choice is presented between land rich in grains and land abundant in mineral resources, the latter contributes significantly to the treasury, while the former can support both the treasury and essential stockpiles of food. A supply of grains is critical for maintaining storehouses that feed both civilians and soldiers, especially during extended military campaigns or in times of crisis. However, territory with rich mineral deposits, especially those yielding precious metals, holds considerable value as it allows for wealth accumulation, which can be used to fund further territorial expansion or other strategic investments.

My teacher argues that when choosing between two types of forests, one that produces timber and another home to elephants, the timber forest should be prioritized, as it provides resources for constructing essential infrastructure, stockpiling for emergencies, and supporting general livelihood needs. Timber forests are invaluable for building, and with timber supplies readily available, a kingdom can ensure its infrastructural needs are met.

Kautilya, however, counters this view by emphasizing that while timber forests are indeed valuable, they can be cultivated and grown in various locations. An elephant forest, however, is unique and cannot simply be replicated. Elephants are crucial for military purposes, and they contribute significantly to a kingdom's ability to conquer and defend against powerful enemies. The strength of an army is amplified by having trained elephants, which can overpower cavalry and infantry alike, playing a decisive role in warfare. Hence, an elephant forest is strategically indispensable, especially for a kingdom intending to expand its influence.

Among different types of routes, land routes are preferable as they are long-standing, reliable, and can be maintained more effectively over time, whereas water routes, though sometimes useful, may be less dependable due to changing conditions, navigability, and seasonal restrictions.

Another important consideration is whether to settle a land with a dispersed population or one with an organized community. The former, with scattered inhabitants, is easier to control and manage. Such populations are generally less prone to internal discord and are more resilient against the influence of external enemies. In contrast, a community of closely-knit people may be more vulnerable to collective anger, influenced easily by charismatic figures or external pressures, making them more susceptible to manipulation by enemies. In the event of calamities, these populations may also struggle with coping as a group, while a dispersed population is more resilient and adaptable.

Lastly, when colonizing a land with people of varying social classes, it is advantageous to begin with the lowest caste, as these individuals are versatile, highly serviceable, and numerous. The lowest caste can perform a wide array of essential functions that support the colony's development and provide a stable workforce for various tasks, ensuring the colony's productivity and longevity. This foundation provides a secure base for further settlement, allowing for a gradual expansion that sustains economic and social stability.

Between cultivated and uncultivated areas, the uncultivated land is often more valuable, especially if it has rich soil suitable for various types of farming activities. When it's fertile, able to support pasturelands, manufacturing, mercantile activities like lending and borrowing, and attracts wealthy merchants, it holds even more potential than already cultivated land.

When comparing a tract of land that has forts with one that is densely populated, the latter is more beneficial. A well-populated area embodies a complete kingdom, full of life and productivity. In contrast, an unpopulated region, like a barren cow, offers little in terms of prosperity or productivity.

If a king seeks to reclaim land previously sold to another for colonization, particularly after the purchaser has depleted his resources in the attempt, he should strategically make an agreement with a buyer who is weak, of low birth, lacking in vigor, isolated, unprincipled, inclined toward wrongful behavior, resigned to fate, and careless in actions. Such a buyer, if unfit for colonization, will struggle and likely fail, losing both his men and money. A man born to a low position may initially attract a following due to wealth or power, but his subjects may abandon him to avoid being adversely affected by his weakness. A leader who lacks vitality won't be able to command his forces effectively, resulting in an army that dwindles due to his inability to support it. Similarly, a person with wealth who is unwilling to spend or show generosity will struggle to rally support or find assistance. A colonizer with a poor moral character or one addicted to harmful habits is easily removable from a settlement and may even endanger its security. Furthermore, one who resigns himself to fate without taking bold, deliberate action will achieve nothing, and an indiscreet individual will lack the strategic judgment to colonize successfully. This type of colonizer, lacking discretion, is considered the least effective.

My teacher asserts that an imprudent colonizer might reveal vulnerabilities in his sponsor, the conqueror. However, Kautilya argues that while such a colonizer might expose these weaknesses, he also paves the way for his own downfall at the hands of the conqueror.

In situations where there is a shortage of suitable individuals for colonizing waste land, the conqueror may arrange for the settlement of such areas as will be discussed in greater detail later under the topic "Capture of an Enemy in the Rear."

The arrangement described above is what is known as a verbal agreement (abhihitasandhi), where the terms are openly communicated. If a powerful king pressures another to sell a portion of land that is fertile and desirable to him, the weaker king might agree to sell under a transparent arrangement. This is referred to as "unconcealed peace" (anibhritasandhi), where the terms are explicitly understood.

If a king of comparable power requests land from another under similar circumstances, the seller should carefully weigh whether he can potentially reclaim the land, maintain control over it, bring his enemy under submission through the transfer, or gain enough wealth or alliances from the sale to strengthen his future endeavors.

This evaluation equally applies when a less powerful king considers buying land, ensuring he gains a strategic advantage.

- In these matters, a king who is skilled in the principles of political science and who manages to secure friends, resources, and land with or without a settled population will strategically position himself to surpass the other rulers aligned with him.

[Thus ends Chapter XI, "Interminable Agreement" in the section of "Agreement for the Acquisition of a Friend, Gold, or Land and Agreement for Undertaking a Work", Book VII, "The End of the Six-fold Policy" of the Arthasástra of Kautilya. End of the hundred and ninth chapter from the beginning.]

CHAPTER XII. AGREEMENT FOR UNDERTAKING A WORK.

When an agreement is made with the terms "Let us have a fort built," it is called an agreement to undertake a specific work. Among two kings, the one who constructs a strong, nearly impenetrable fort on land naturally suited for fortification with minimal labor and expense gains an advantage over the other.

When considering different types of forts—such as those on plains, those surrounded by rivers, and those on mountains—the last type listed is generally superior to the previous. As for irrigation projects, a system that provides a perennial water supply is better than one reliant on diverted sources, and of these perennial sources, the one that can irrigate the most extensive area is most advantageous.

In planting timber forests, the king who establishes a forest producing valuable resources, expanding into wild regions and with a river at its edge, gains an upper hand. A forest with a river is self-sustaining and can serve as a refuge during difficult times. For game forests, the king who cultivates a dense forest of fierce animals near the enemy's animal-filled forests, causing disturbances to the enemy and extending into elephant reserves near the border, is at an advantage.

My teacher argues that between two lands—one densely populated with non-warriors and the other with a small number of brave fighters—the latter is more advantageous since even a few brave soldiers can easily overpower a larger group of timid individuals, leading to the collapse of the enemy's army.

Kautilya disagrees, stating that a larger number of less capable people is preferable. Such a population can perform support tasks in the military camp, assist soldiers actively in the battlefield, and create an intimidating impression simply through sheer numbers. Further, discipline and training can instill courage and motivation in even the timid.

When it comes to mines, the king who can exploit a valuable, easily accessible mine with minimal labor and expense holds an advantage. When comparing a smaller mine yielding high-value materials and a larger mine producing items of lesser value, my teacher argues that the former is preferable. Precious materials such as diamonds, gemstones, pearls, corals, gold, and silver can collectively far outweigh the quantity of common commodities.

Kautilya, however, contends that a large, long-lasting mine yielding lesser-value commodities is more advantageous. The wealth generated from accumulating vast quantities of these items can be used to purchase rare, high-value items as needed, making a large mine with continuous yield a significant asset.

This brings us to the important topic of selecting trade routes. My teacher suggests that between two options—one trade route by water and another by land—the water route is preferable. This is because it tends to be less expensive while also providing the potential for greater profits.

However, Kautilya offers a different perspective, arguing that water routes often face various obstacles, can be unreliable, pose immediate dangers, and lack adequate defenses. In contrast, land routes do not suffer from these disadvantages and are generally more reliable.

When considering water routes, Kautilya points out that a path along the shore is superior to one that runs through the open ocean. The shore route connects numerous trading port towns, making it more accessible. Similarly, river navigation is favorable since it is usually continuous and allows for dangers that can be avoided or managed.

Regarding land routes, my teacher asserts that a route leading toward the Himalayas is better than one heading south. Kautilya, however, disagrees. He explains that aside from items like blankets, animal skins, and horses, many valuable trade goods—such as conch shells, diamonds, precious stones, pearls, and gold—are readily available in the southern regions.

For routes going south, Kautilya emphasizes the importance of selecting a trade route that passes through numerous mines, is well-frequented by people, and is less costly or burdensome. Alternatively, a route that allows for the acquisition of a wide variety of merchandise is also a strong choice.

This leads to considerations for trade routes headed east or west. Between a cart track and a footpath, the cart track is preferred as it allows for larger-scale preparations and transport. Similarly, routes that can accommodate pack animals like donkeys or camels, regardless of the terrain or time of year, are considered beneficial for trade.

Kautilya's analysis also addresses routes intended solely for foot traffic, known as amsa-patha or shoulder-paths, where individuals carry merchandise on their backs. While these paths may have limitations, they can still serve important roles in trade networks, particularly in regions where other forms of transport are impractical.

- It is considered a significant loss for the conqueror to engage in any work that ultimately benefits the enemy, as such endeavors only serve to strengthen his opponent. Conversely, engaging in tasks that hinder the enemy's progress is viewed as a gain for the conqueror. In situations where the benefits from both sides are equal, the conqueror must recognize that his own situation is stagnant, showing no real advancement or improvement.
- Similarly, it is unwise for the conqueror to commit to a project that requires a substantial outlay of resources yet yields minimal returns. On the other hand, a project that reduces costs while enhancing output is deemed beneficial. If the output of a project matches its costs, the conqueror must once again acknowledge that he is in a stagnant condition, neither gaining nor losing ground.
- Therefore, it is crucial for the conqueror to seek out opportunities for fortification and other initiatives that are not only cost-effective but also promise greater profits and enhanced power. This approach ensures that the agreements made for undertaking various works lead to meaningful progress and improvement rather than stagnation.

[Thus ends Chapter XII, "Agreement for Undertaking a Work," in the section of "Agreement for the Acquisition of a Friend, Gold, or

Land and Agreement for Undertaking a Work"' in Book VIII, "The End of the Six-fold Policy" of the Arthasástra of Kautilya. End of the hundred and tenth chapter from the beginning.]

CHAPTER XIII. CONSIDERATIONS ABOUT AN ENEMY IN THE REAR.

When the conqueror and his enemy both attempt to capture the rear of their respective foes, who are preoccupied with attacking others, the one who successfully takes the rear of an opponent with abundant resources gains significant advantages. This is because a king with vast resources must first eliminate his frontal enemy, who is currently under attack, before he can address the threat posed by the rear. In contrast, an enemy lacking resources may not have realized their desired profits and, therefore, poses a lesser threat.

If both enemies are equally resourced, the conqueror who manages to capture the rear of an opponent who has made extensive preparations will also find greater advantages. This is due to the fact that a king who has prepared extensively must deal with his rear enemy only after neutralizing the threat posed by his frontal adversary. Conversely, a king with minimal preparations may find his movements hindered by the broader Circle of States, making him less formidable.

In scenarios where both sides have equal troop strength, capturing the rear of an enemy who has engaged a wandering foe will yield more benefits. A king who has marched against a wandering enemy will likely need to deal with the rear enemy only after securing an easy victory against his initial target. This is unlike a king who confronts a fortified enemy; he may find himself repelled during the assault on the enemy's defenses and, upon retreating, caught between the rear enemy and the frontal adversary, who is protected by strong fortifications.

These principles apply equally to various enemy scenarios discussed previously. When enemies are of similar caliber, the conqueror who targets the rear of a king confronting a virtuous adversary stands to gain more, as the attacking king may lose the support of his own subjects due to the moral implications of his actions. On the other hand, an attack against a wicked king can bolster the attacker's standing with the populace, earning him their goodwill.

Similar reasoning applies when considering those who have marched against an extravagant king or one who lives hand-to-mouth, as well as against a miserly ruler. The dynamics remain consistent when examining confrontations involving allies, where the principles of strategic advantage and resource management continue to hold true.

When two enemies are in play—one focused on attacking a friend and the other targeting an enemy—the one who strikes at the rear of the latter gains significant advantages. This is because a king who has initiated hostilities against a friend can more easily negotiate peace with that friend and subsequently turn his attention toward the rear enemy. It's generally simpler to make amends with a friend than to engage in conflict with an enemy.

In another scenario involving two kings, where one is intent on destroying a friend and the other is focused on an enemy, the king who targets the rear of the first king stands to gain more. A ruler attacking an enemy typically has the backing of his allies, which helps him subdue the rear enemy. In contrast, a king destroying his own allies may find himself isolated and at a disadvantage.

When both the conqueror and his adversary are attacking the rear of an enemy while attempting to enforce the collection of what is not rightfully owed to them, the one whose foe has already suffered significant losses—in terms of both resources and personnel—will benefit more. Conversely, when they aim to collect what is legitimately due to them, the one whose enemy has already lost both profits and troops will reap greater advantages.

If the enemy being targeted is capable of retaliating, and the assailant's rear enemy has fortified himself on one of the assailant's flanks, then the rear enemy has the upper hand. This is because a rear enemy positioned on one of the assailant's sides can not only align with the assailable enemy but also pose a direct threat to the assailant's base. In contrast, a rear enemy situated directly behind the assailant can merely harass the rear without being able to mount a more strategic assault.

- Kings who have the ability to disrupt an enemy's rear and block his movements fall into three categories: those positioned directly behind the enemy and those on either side, each forming a group capable of hampering the enemy's plans.
- A king positioned between a conqueror and his foe is known as an "antardhi," or one who stands between two rulers. If this intermediary king possesses strongholds, alliances with wild tribes, and other types of support, he becomes a formidable barrier, effectively obstructing even the mightiest of forces.

When both the conqueror and his rival are set on capturing a Madhyama king by attacking his rear, the one who manages to sever the Madhyama king's ties with his allies and, in doing so, transforms an enemy into a friend, gains a more favorable position; for a former enemy forced into peace will provide stronger support than an ally coerced to uphold a compromised alliance. This same strategy applies when attempting to win over a neutral king.

Between attacks from the rear and those from the front, the former is often preferable when it enables treacherous warfare (mantrayuddha), where subterfuge and strategy can be more effectively employed.

My teacher believes that in open warfare, both sides ultimately suffer due to heavy losses in men and resources, and even the victor appears weakened because of these costs.

However, Kautilya disagrees, asserting that the enemy's total destruction is worth significant losses of men and money.

When losses of men and resources are equal, the conqueror who first fully annihilates his front-line enemy and then turns to his rear adversary gains a distinct advantage. If both the conqueror and his enemy are each tackling their respective frontal foes, the one who first destroys a deeply antagonistic front-line enemy with abundant resources reaps the greatest benefits.

This approach illustrates the strategy for neutralizing various enemies and wild tribes:

- When an enemy exists both in the rear and front, along with an assailable target ready to be marched against, the conqueror should consider the following plan:
- The rear enemy typically encourages the frontal enemy to strike at the conqueror's ally. To counter this, the conqueror should set the ákranda (the enemy of the rear enemy) against the rear enemy's ally, provoking conflict between them to weaken the rear enemy's plans. Similarly, he should instigate hostilities between the allies of both the ákranda and the rear enemy.
- In parallel, the conqueror should ensure his own ally engages the frontal enemy's friend in conflict, thereby distracting them. To further protect himself, he should enlist the assistance of his ally's ally to counter any threat posed by the friend of his enemy's friend.
- With the support of his ally, the conqueror should keep his rear enemy contained and, using his ally's ally, prevent any attack from his rear enemy against the ákranda (his rear ally).
- By enlisting the help of his allies, the conqueror should bring the Circle of States, both in his rear and front, under his influence. He should place messengers and spies in each state within this Circle, and continually weaken his enemies' strength, all the while maintaining secrecy over his strategies and alliances.
- For the ruler who fails to conceal his strategies, his

accomplishments, even if momentarily successful, will ultimately collapse—just as surely as a damaged raft lost on the sea.

[Thus ends Chapter XIII, "Considerations about an Enemy in the Rear," in Book VII, "The End of the Six-fold Policy" of the Arthasástra of Kautilya. End of the hundred and eleventh chapter from the beginning.]

CHAPTER XIV. RECRUITMENT OF LOST POWER.

When the conqueror faces an attack from a united front of enemies, he can approach their leader with a peace proposal: "Let us make peace. I offer you gold, and I am your ally. Your advantage will double, and it's unwise to bolster the power of your allies who now show a friendly face, for as they grow stronger, they will turn on you in time."

Alternatively, he might appeal to the leader's sense of caution to dismantle the coalition: "Just as you now unite to attack someone as harmless as I am, these same allies will target you in your times of prosperity or hardship. The lure of power can change loyalties; it's best to dissolve this alliance."

Once the alliance weakens, the conqueror could direct the leader to focus on the weakest of the enemies or persuade the leader to turn the alliance's weaker members against him. He may use any approach beneficial to his own cause to provoke dissatisfaction among the allied ranks. Offering the leader a more profitable prospect could tempt him into a separate agreement, creating division. Those who serve both states may praise the leader's benefits and subtly mock the unity of the coalition, saying, "It appears you have banded together nicely."

If some of the allies are already unstable, they could be encouraged to break the agreement, and those drawing income from both alliances can remind them of their previous warnings, ensuring further discord. Once disunited, the conqueror can ally himself with any isolated leader.

If there's no primary leader, the conqueror can reach out to the one who initiated the alliance, the most resolute, the people's favorite, the most fearful, the one whose friendship aligns through royal ties, a trusted ally, or even a wandering adversary — in this particular order.

For each type, he must employ suitable tactics: gain favor with the alliance's initiator by showing deference; win over the resolute one through greetings and respect; secure an alliance with the people's favorite by offering twice the expected gains; satisfy the greedy by promising men and money; calm the fearful by presenting a hostage; solidify royal ties by forming closer bonds; please an old friend by extending goodwill and dropping hostilities; and aid and align with the wandering enemy. Using appropriate approaches—conciliation, gifts, sowing discord, or even threats, as detailed under "Troubles"—the conqueror should aim to win over any of these individuals.

He who is facing difficulties and fears an attack from his enemy should, by offering military and financial support, establish a peace agreement with the enemy that includes clear terms on location, timing, and tasks. He should also amend any offenses he may have caused by breaching previous treaties. If lacking in support, he should seek allies among his relatives and friends. Additionally, constructing a well-fortified stronghold can provide him with much-needed defense, as having protection from forts and friends commands respect from both his people and his enemies.

One who lacks the wisdom to deliberate effectively should surround himself with knowledgeable advisors and consult experienced elders with extensive learning. This will help him achieve his objectives.

For someone without a robust treasury and military, his focus should be on fortifying the fundamental elements of his sovereignty. A stronghold is essential, as the land provides the resources to build wealth and support an army, and a secure fort offers refuge for both the king and his forces.

Waterworks, such as irrigation systems, are vital for ensuring a steady supply of crops, as they help provide consistent crop yields regardless of rainfall. Well-maintained trade routes are crucial for strategic advantage over enemies; through these routes, armies and spies move, essential equipment like weapons, armor, chariots, and draft animals are procured, and travel becomes more accessible for both exit and entry.

Mines are a foundational source for resources used in warfare. Similarly, forests rich in timber supply the materials necessary for constructing forts, vehicles, and chariots, all of which are indispensable in sustaining a fortified and well-prepared kingdom.

Elephant forests provide elephants essential for warfare and transportation. Pasturelands support cows, horses, and camels, which are vital for pulling chariots. If he lacks these resources in his own territory, he should seek to acquire them from his relatives or allies. In the absence of a proper army, he should strive to attract brave individuals from guilds, thieves' networks, wild tribes, non-local groups, and spies skilled in causing harm to enemies.

In times of vulnerability, he may need to adopt the approach of a weaker king when dealing with a more powerful one, focusing on diplomacy to avoid threats from both enemies and allies.

- Thus, by leveraging his loyal supporters, wise counsel, treasury, and military, he can escape the grip of his adversaries.

[Thus ends Chapter XIV, "Recruitment of Lost Power," in Book VII, "The End of the Six-fold Policy" of the Arthasástra of Kautilya. End of the hundred and twelfth chapter from the beginning.]

CHAPTER XV. MEASURES CONDUCIVE TO PEACE WITH A STRONG AND PROVOKED ENEMY; AND THE ATTITUDE OF A CONQUERED ENEMY.

When a weaker king is under attack from a stronger foe, he should look for protection from an ally who is more powerful than the enemy and beyond the reach of the enemy's skill in planning intrigues. Among kings equal in strategic abilities, the distinction should be made by assessing stable prosperity and the support of experienced advisors.

If a superior ally isn't available, the weaker king should seek out allies of equal power who, combined, match the strength of the enemy but remain beyond the enemy's influence over wealth, military force, or intrigue. Among kings who are equally equipped with resources, army, and clever tactics, preference should be given to those capable of making substantial preparations.

If allies of equal power are not an option, he should turn to lesser kings who are loyal, enthusiastic, capable of resistance, and also beyond the enemy's sway. In choosing among kings equally enthusiastic and action-oriented, preference should be given to those who can secure strategic battlefields. Among those with equal battlefield advantages, priority should go to those who are consistently prepared for war. Among kings who possess both favorable terrain and readiness, distinction should be based on their weaponry and armor supply.

If no allies can be found, the weaker king should take refuge in a fortified location where the enemy's large army cannot disrupt the steady supply of food, fodder, firewood, and water, thus causing the enemy substantial losses in both men and resources. If multiple forts are available, preference should be given to those well-suited for storing and securing provisions. Kautilya advises that refuge should be taken in a fort populated with loyal inhabitants and stocked with ample supplies. Additionally, the choice of such a fort is supported by the following reasons:

"I shall confront the enemy by aligning with his adversary's ally, or by seeking support from a mediating king or a neutral ruler. With the assistance of a neighboring king, wild tribes, a relative of the enemy, or an imprisoned prince, I will either seize or devastate his kingdom. I will stir up chaos within his fort, land, or camp using my loyal followers already embedded there. When he draws near, I will eliminate him through secret means, whether by weapons, fire, poison, or other hidden strategies as I see fit. I shall exhaust his resources by pushing him into costly undertakings, either initiated by himself or manipulated by my spies. By inflicting significant losses, I will create discord among his allies or sow discontent within his army.

I will cut off his camp's supply lines to weaken him, or I might feign surrender to introduce vulnerabilities within his ranks and eventually overpower him using all my resources. If his spirit wanes, I will impose my terms for peace. If I block his movements, he will encounter hardships from all quarters; and when he is defenseless, I will crush him using my hereditary army, or perhaps with the aid of his own enemies or wild tribes. I will safeguard my extensive domain by fortifying my stronghold, where the united forces of myself and my allies will be unbeatable. My troops, trained to fight from valleys, pits, or under cover of darkness, will create traps for him on his path, particularly if he is engaged in pressing matters.

As he faces continual losses, he will weaken on arrival, reaching this hostile territory in an unfavorable place and at an unfavorable time. With fortifications and wild tribes in his way, he will find access to my lands costly in terms of men and resources. Unable to secure advantageous positions for his or his allies' armies, and afflicted by disease, he will be in a state of distress when he reaches my stronghold—and, once here, he will have no chance of retreat."

In the absence of such favorable conditions, or if the enemy's army proves overwhelmingly strong, one might have to abandon the fort and flee. My teacher argues that, in such a scenario, one could charge toward the enemy like a moth to a flame, as a brave confrontation would lead to one outcome or another—either honorable death or possible victory for one who disregards the risks to life.

Kautilya, however, advises a different approach. If conditions exist that favor a peace agreement, he suggests making peace with the enemy. If no such conditions arise, one may try to achieve peace through strategic threats or secure an ally. Alternatively, a messenger could be sent to the enemy with an invitation for peace. Another method might be to honor and reward the enemy's envoy, conveying to him, "Here is the king's armory, the queen's residence, and the princes; I and this kingdom are yours, with the approval of the royal family."

Once under the protection of the enemy, the king should serve his protector as a loyal subordinate, catering to his protector's occasional needs. Any fortifications, acquisition efforts, marriage alliances, installation ceremonies for an heir, commercial ventures, capturing elephants, setting up secret battle spots, marching campaigns, and festivities must be undertaken only with his protector's approval. Additionally, he should request permission for any treaties with the settlers in his territory and for punishing anyone fleeing his lands. If citizens or villagers turn hostile or unfaithful, he may petition his protector for a new territory or eliminate disloyal individuals through covert means as would befit dealing with traitors. He must refrain from accepting even a favorable offer of territory from a friend without the protector's knowledge, although he may still consult with the protector's ministers, priest, army chief, or heir.

The king should support his protector in every feasible way. During public worship or prayers, he should lead his people in praying for the protector's long life and continuously proclaim his loyalty and dedication to the protector.

- A conquered king, faithfully serving his strong protector, should always avoid associating with people of doubtful loyalty and show full allegiance, serving loyally and diligently within the protector's circle.

[Thus ends Chapter XV, "Measures Conducive to Peace with a Strong and Provoked Enemy and the Attitude of a Conquered Enemy," in Book VII, "The End of the Six-fold Policy" of the Arthasástra of Kautilya. End of the hundred and thirteenth chapter from the beginning.]

CHAPTER XVI. THE ATTITUDE OF A CONQUERED KING.

To create financial strain on his protector, a powerful vassal king who aims to expand his territory may, with the protector's consent, launch a campaign in regions where the land and climate are advantageous for his army's maneuvers. Ideally, this would be against an enemy lacking strongholds or defensive structures, with the vassal having no immediate threats in his rear. However, if there are rear threats, he should take steps to secure his defenses before marching forward.

For weaker kings, he should use conciliation and gifts to bring them under control, while for stronger kings, he should employ tactics like sowing discord and making strategic threats. Depending on the circumstances, he may use one, some, or all of these approaches to subdue both his immediate and distant rivals.

In practicing conciliation, he should offer promises to safeguard villages, protect forest dwellers, secure herds of cattle, and ensure the safety of trade routes. He can also grant pardons to those who have been exiled, fled, or committed transgressions.

The policy of gifting may involve granting land, valuable items, and even daughters in marriage, along with assurances of safety. To instill division among enemies, he could incite a neighboring king, a wild tribal leader, a relative of the enemy, or an imprisoned prince to stir up internal conflicts.

He should confront his enemy directly in an open battle, through a well-coordinated ambush, via conspiracy, or during the upheaval of a strategic capture of the enemy's fortress. Each method provides an opportunity to bring the enemy to submission.

The vassal may reinstate deposed kings who show spirit and can strengthen his forces. Similarly, he may reinstate those who possess strong financial or military resources, as they could bolster his own with funds and forces, or those who are knowledgeable in land management and could provide access to territories.

Among his allies, different types of friends offer various benefits:

- A friend offering diverse resources (chitrabhoga) aids with gems, valuable commodities, raw materials from commercial hubs, resources from villages and mines, or animals for transportation from timber and elephant forests.
- A friend offering abundant support (mahábhoga) provides wealth and military assistance.
- A friend offering comprehensive support (sarvabhoga) contributes army forces, funds, and land.
- A friend offering limited support (ekatobhogi) provides defense against an enemy on one front.
- A friend offering dual support (ubhayatobhogi) aids both the vassal and the vassal's adversary, as well as their allies.
- Finally, a friend offering complete support on all fronts (sarvatobogi) aids in dealing with the enemy, the enemy's allies, any neighboring threats, and wild tribes, ensuring a stable advantage across all borders.

If he has an enemy in his rear, a wild chief, or a particularly strong enemy who can be appeased by offering land, he should provide each with a strategically chosen piece of territory. To an enemy with fortifications, he should grant land that is disconnected from his own territory; to a wild chief, he should offer land with little means of subsistence; to a relative of the enemy, a piece of land that can easily be reclaimed; to a former enemy held as a prisoner, land that has not been captured from the enemy's territory; to an armed corporation, land constantly troubled by external threats; and to a coalition of such groups, land adjacent to a more powerful ruler. For a military corporation skilled in warfare, he should assign land troubled by both internal strife and external threats. If dealing with a belligerent king who desires conflict, he should give land unsuitable for military maneuvers. To a supporter of his enemy, he should offer barren land; to an exiled prince, land stripped of resources; to a ruler who has recommitted to peace after breaking it, a land that requires considerable resources for settlement; to a deserted prince, land with minimal defenses; and finally, to his own protector, an inhospitable piece of territory.

In continuing relations with these figures, he should maintain his approach toward those most helpful and steady in their support. For those opposed to him, he should work behind the scenes to sway them. To loyal allies, he should provide assistance to enable even more help, rewarding and honoring them generously. If an ally is in difficulty, he should offer support. When receiving visitors, he should accommodate their preferences and make efforts to ensure their satisfaction. He should avoid any dismissive, threatening, slanderous, or harsh language, and he must protect those he has promised safety, as a father would. For the guilty, he should announce their crimes publicly before punishing them, and for minor offenders, he should deliver discreet, secret punishments to avoid any suspicion from his protector.

He must refrain from seizing the lands, possessions, families, or any inheritance of defeated kings. Instead, he should restore these to the slain king's relatives. For a king who has passed away while allied with him, he should place the rightful heir on the throne. By showing such respect, the conqueror will ensure that defeated kings, seeing the protection of their lands and families, will remain loyal and encourage their descendants to support the conqueror's family for generations.

Should he disregard these policies and covet the lands, treasures, or families of those he has conquered or imprisoned, he will incite hostility within the surrounding kingdoms, driving the Circle of States to turn against him. Even his own ministers may grow resentful and seek safety within this circle, harboring plans against his life and rule.

- Therefore, conquered kings who are allowed to remain in their lands under a policy of conciliation will remain faithful to the conqueror, extending their loyalty to his descendants for generations.

[Thus ends Chapter XVI, "The Attitude of a Conquered King," in Book VII, "The End of the Six-fold Policy," of the Arthasástra of Kautilya. End of the hundred and fourteenth chapter from the beginning.]

CHAPTER XVII. MAKING PEACE AND BREAKING IT.

The terms sama (quiet), sandhi (peace agreement), and samádhi (reconciliation) are interchangeable, each referring to an arrangement that nurtures mutual trust and harmony between rulers. The essence of these agreements is to create stability and peace that all parties can rely upon.

One of my teachers holds the view that peace based solely on an honesty pledge or oath is somewhat unreliable and susceptible to change, while peace founded upon a secured pledge, like a hostage or a tangible guarantee, offers stronger stability and is less likely to be broken. However, Kautilya disagrees with this, stating that peace rooted in an honesty pledge or oath is enduring and steadfast, not only in this world but in the spiritual realm as well. The tangible guarantee or hostage is useful only for reinforcing the physical aspects of the agreement in this world and for establishing confidence on both sides.

In the past, kings known for their integrity would often form peace alliances with a simple declaration, "We are joined in peace," signifying a bond that they expected to endure without question. However, if there was any fear of an integrity breach, leaders might enhance the pact's strength with a solemn oath, swearing upon revered items or symbols of significance and strength, such as fire, water, the front of a chariot, the shoulder of an elephant, the sturdy brick of a fort wall, or even materials like precious gold. By invoking these items in their oaths, they bound themselves to a greater degree, pledging that breaking the promise would bring ruin upon the violator, forsaken by these powerful symbols of prosperity and stability.

In cases where the risk of violating an oath remained, peace could be further stabilized with the involvement of prominent figures, such as revered ascetics or high-ranking nobles, acting as guarantors. These guarantors added a layer of trustworthiness and weight to the agreement. Among such guarantors, the one who holds the greatest sway or influence over the enemy's actions provides the most substantial assurance, whereas selecting a figure without much control is ineffective and can even invite deception.

When the treaty requires hostages, especially children, strategic choices come into play. For instance, offering a princess as a hostage can be advantageous, as a princess often brings challenges to her captors due to her potential influence, while a prince may be seen as a more straightforward hostage with fewer implications. If there are multiple sons, choosing which to send is also significant: sending a high-born, brave, wise son who is well-trained in military arts, or an only son, generally benefits the captor more than the family surrendering him. Therefore, sending a lower-born son with limited inheritance rights or a son who lacks intellect and has no training in military arts can reduce the disadvantage to the family giving him. In such cases, a timid or unskilled son, or one of many, is less valuable in political terms, as he is not integral to the continuity of the kingdom.

Among sons, loyalty and wisdom may weigh differently: people are usually loyal to a high-born son, even if he isn't particularly wise, whereas a wise son, though low-born, will generally excel at the practical aspects of governance. However, when it comes to effective statecraft, a high-born prince who collaborates with experienced advisors often outshines a low-born but wise son.

When choosing between a wise prince and a brave prince, the wise prince, despite possibly being less bold, has intellectual strengths that favor him in many situations, while the brave prince, even if not particularly wise, embodies courage and can be invaluable in battle. Yet, in the long run, a wise prince's strategic foresight and planning capabilities enable him to surpass even the most courageous warriors, just as a skilled hunter can ultimately overcome even a formidable elephant through craftiness and cunning.

- This careful approach to alliances and hostages illustrates that true strength and stability in peace agreements come not only from power but from strategic choices about who is pledged, the nature of the pledge, and the intent behind these alliances.

Regarding the comparison between a brave prince and a trained prince, a brave prince, even if untrained, possesses the natural ability and inclination for battle, while a trained prince, though possibly less courageous, can aim accurately and hit his targets. Despite the trained prince's accuracy, a brave prince's strong will and commitment to his principles make him stand out, as bravery often leads to a more determined approach to governance and warfare.

When it comes to a king with multiple sons versus a king with only one son, the former has the advantage of being able to offer one son as a hostage while keeping the others safe, which allows him to break the peace if necessary without endangering his lineage. On the other hand, a king with only one son lacks this flexibility and may need to approach peace agreements with more caution.

In cases where the king hands over all his sons as hostages, it becomes crucial to consider the king's ability to father more sons in the future. If both kings have this potential, the advantage lies with the king who can beget capable sons, as this promises strong heirs to continue his line. If both kings can produce able sons, the advantage then goes to the king likely to have a son sooner, as this reduces the risk posed by having all sons held as hostages.

If a king has only one son who is also brave and lacks the capacity to have more sons, he should consider surrendering himself instead of his only son as an assurance of peace. However, if a king is in a position of rising power, he may consider breaking the peace agreement altogether.

Should the prince be held as a hostage, clever strategies can be employed for his potential escape. Carpenters, artisans, and covert agents stationed with the prince might assist him, creating a secret escape route through an underground tunnel. Additionally, dancers, actors, singers, musicians, entertainers, royal poets, swimmers, and certain individuals skilled in covert operations may be placed within the enemy's service to covertly support the prince. These individuals should have unrestricted access to the palace, allowing them to blend in and move freely, providing the prince with potential opportunities to disguise himself and escape at night.

Similarly, female agents and spies posing as entertainers or other service workers within the enemy's palace might also serve as valuable assets. The prince could slip away, disguised as one of these workers, carrying their tools, dishes, or other belongings as cover. Moreover, cooks, confectioners, attendants, and others assigned to serve the enemy king could assist the prince's escape by concealing him under various items, such as food trays, blankets, or ceremonial objects. Servants responsible for maintaining the palace, handling the king's chariots, preparing his bed, assisting with personal grooming, or drawing bath water may also provide cover for the prince. Using the cover of darkness, he could escape disguised as one of these attendants, blending into the palace's usual routines to slip away unnoticed.

These tactics exemplify the clever methods that can be employed to facilitate the prince's escape and ensure his safety, even when he is held as a hostage.

Or the prince might appear to be in spiritual communion with the god Varuna, secluded in a reservoir connected to the palace by an underground tunnel, or he could be escorted there under cover of night. Spies disguised as traders might then distribute poisoned cooked rice and fruit to the sentinels, incapacitating them. Alternatively, on religious occasions, such as offerings to the gods or ceremonies honoring ancestors, the prince could serve the guards rice and beverages mixed with the juice of the madana plant, inducing them to fall asleep, thus giving him an opening to escape.

He might also secure his freedom by bribing the guards directly. Spies, posing as city officials, court bards, or physicians, could further assist by setting fire to a building filled with valuable items to cause a distraction, or merchants with spy affiliations could set ablaze stores filled with commercial goods, diverting attention. In order to throw off any pursuers, the prince could leave a dummy body in his quarters and set the room on fire, giving the impression he perished in the flames. He might then escape through a loosened house joint, an open window, or a tunnel.

Alternatively, disguised as a carrier of goods like glass beads or pots, the prince could slip away under the cover of night. If he seeks further concealment, he might enter the quarters of ascetics and emerge disguised as one of them, whether shaven-headed or with twisted hair. Another tactic might involve posing as a person with a peculiar illness, a forest-dweller, or even being carried out disguised as a corpse. He could also escape by impersonating a widowed woman following a funeral procession, blending in among mourners.

Spies disguised as forest people could misdirect any pursuers by sending them on the wrong path, while the prince himself would take an alternate route. Hiding among carts and drivers, he might merge into a caravan to avoid detection. If closely trailed, he could lead his followers into an ambush or, in its absence, lay a trail of gold coins or poisoned morsels along the road, prompting his pursuers to pause and investigate while he takes a different path.

Should he be captured, the prince could attempt to win over his captors with offers of conciliation or by serving them poisoned food. Meanwhile, his father, staging a sacrifice for Varuna or exploiting an accidental fire, might place a decoy body as a false martyr, using it to publicly accuse the enemy of murdering his son, thereby creating an opportunity to launch a counter-attack.

- Or, in a final act of defiance, the prince might draw a concealed sword, striking at his guards with swift force and escaping with the help of his previously hidden spies.

[Thus ends Chapter XVII, "Making Peace and Breaking It," in Book VII, "The End of the Six-fold Policy" of the Arthasástra of Kautilya. End of the hundred and fifteenth chapter from the beginning.]

CHAPTER XVIII. THE CONDUCT OF A MADHYAMA KING, A NEUTRAL KING, AND OF A CIRCLE OF STATES.

The third and fifth states from a madhyama king (a king who is a mediator or positioned between other powers) are generally friendly to him, while the second, fourth, and sixth states are usually unfriendly. If this madhyama king shows favor to both the friendly and unfriendly states, the conqueror should align himself amicably with the madhyama. But if the madhyama king does not favor these states, then the conqueror should instead seek friendship directly with those states.

When the madhyama king aims to secure an alliance with a potential ally of the conqueror, the conqueror should act decisively. By mobilizing his own allies and the allies of his friend against the madhyama, and by distancing the madhyama king from his allies, the conqueror can maintain and secure his own alliance. Alternatively, the conqueror might rouse the surrounding Circle of States against the madhyama king by declaring, "This madhyama king has grown overly ambitious and is plotting our ruin; let us unite and thwart his advances."

If this Circle of States is supportive, the conqueror can proceed to enhance his own power by suppressing the ambitions of the madhyama king. But if the Circle of States does not fully support him, the conqueror should instead bolster his friend with men and resources. Then, through conciliation and gifts, he should sway either the leader of the madhyama king's opposition or a nearby ruler who is hostile toward the madhyama, or a ruler who has been in a state of mutual reliance with the other kings, or those who are hesitant to act due to distrust of one another. By winning over a single ally, he doubles his strength; by securing a second, he triples it. With these accumulated allies, the conqueror can then proceed against the madhyama king.

However, if conditions—either of location or timing—are unfavorable for this approach, the conqueror should instead secure peace by allying with an enemy of the madhyama king or by instigating traitorous elements to unify against the madhyama. If the madhyama king threatens the conqueror's allies, the conqueror should step in to prevent this aggression, reassuring his friend with, "I will protect you as long as you remain vulnerable." He must extend tangible support, particularly when his ally's resources are weak or depleted. Should the madhyama king attempt to displace one of the conqueror's friends, the conqueror should immediately offer assistance and either provide new lands to this ally or ensure that they remain under his own protection, thus preventing them from seeking protection elsewhere.

In cases where some of the conqueror's allies, particularly those who are either reducible or vulnerable to the madhyama king, start to side with the madhyama, the conqueror should consider forming a strategic peace with a third king. Likewise, if certain allies of the madhyama king, especially those who are similarly vulnerable to the conqueror, demonstrate a capacity for both offense and defense and turn friendly towards the conqueror, then he should make peace with them as well. By doing so, the conqueror not only achieves his own objectives but also manages to appease and influence the madhyama king.

If the madhyama king is eager to secure the conqueror's potential ally as his own, the conqueror can either make peace with another ruler or try to deter his friend from switching allegiance, advising him with words like, "It is unworthy of you to abandon a friend who values your companionship." Alternatively, the conqueror may choose to remain passive if he believes that the Circle of States might resent the friend's disloyalty. In situations where the madhyama king seeks to ally with the conqueror's enemy, the conqueror should covertly support this enemy with resources and troops, ensuring his assistance is unnoticed by the madhyama.

If the madhyama king aims to befriend the neutral king, the conqueror should attempt to sow discord between them. He should seek the protection of whichever—madhyama or neutral king—is respected by the Circle of States. The behavior of the madhyama king often mirrors that of the neutral king. If the neutral king intends to form an alliance with the madhyama, the conqueror should work to obstruct the neutral king's plans to overpower a foe, support an ally, or secure the services of another neutral king's army. In this way, the conqueror can strengthen his position, suppress his enemies, and extend aid to his allies, even if these allies have acted unfavorably toward him.

The conqueror's potential adversaries include a king of malicious disposition who is generally harmful, a rear-enemy allied with a frontal enemy, a weakened foe facing difficulties, and one who waits for the conqueror to encounter trouble before launching an attack.

Conversely, kings likely to align with the conqueror include those who march alongside him toward a shared goal, those who march with him but for different reasons, those who wish to join forces to attack a mutual enemy, those who march together after forming a peace agreement, those with personal objectives, those rising together with others, those willing to trade armies or treasuries, and those adopting the dual strategy of allying with one while fighting another.

Neighboring kings who may serve the conqueror's interests include a neighboring ruler fearing an attack from a powerful adversary, one positioned between the conqueror and his enemy, the rear-enemy of a dominant ruler, one who has voluntarily submitted to the conqueror, one who surrenders out of fear, and one already subdued. The same holds true for those kings who are positioned next to the immediate foes of the conqueror.

- Among these kings, the conqueror should prioritize supporting the friend who shares the conqueror's objectives in opposing their common enemy, using this alliance to hold the enemy at bay.
- Once the enemy has been subdued and if the friend, having gained in strength, begins to resist the conqueror's influence, the conqueror should take measures to turn neighboring rulers, including those adjacent to the neighbor, against this now unsubmissive friend.
- Alternatively, the conqueror might support a relative of the friend or an imprisoned prince in claiming his lands, or act in a way that keeps the friend dependent on the conqueror's assistance to maintain his loyalty.
- The conqueror should refrain from assisting a friend who is in continuous decline, ensuring instead that the friend remains neither so weak as to require constant help nor so strong as to become a threat. A skilled ruler maintains balance, positioning allies to neither deteriorate nor exceed their assigned influence. When, with the desire of getting wealth, a wandering friend (i.e., a nomadic king) makes an agreement with the conqueror, the latter should so remove the cause of the

friend's flight that he never flies again.

- When a friend is equally accessible to both the conqueror and the enemy, the conqueror should first work to sever that stubborn friend's alliance with the enemy. Once the friend is isolated, he can be subdued, and the conqueror may then turn to defeating the enemy.

- If a friend maintains a neutral stance, the conqueror should subtly arrange for the friend to incur the animosity of his closest adversaries. When the friend is embroiled in conflicts with them, the conqueror can step in and offer assistance, securing loyalty through this aid.

- When a friend, due to his weakness, seeks protection from both the conqueror and the enemy, the conqueror should support him with military forces, ensuring that the friend remains reliant on this aid and refrains from shifting loyalties.

- Alternatively, the conqueror might remove the friend from his current territory, relocating him to a different region. In this way, the conqueror retains control, with the option to administer punishment or reward, depending on the friend's loyalty.

- Alternatively, the conqueror might weaken a friend who has become too powerful, or eliminate him if he fails to support the conqueror in times of danger yet enjoys the conqueror's protection during peaceful times.

- If an enemy aggressively turns against his own adversary (who is the conqueror's ally) when the adversary is already burdened by troubles, the ally should, without exposing his vulnerabilities, take action to suppress this enemy.

- However, if a friend takes no further action after initially opposing a troubled enemy, the enemy will overcome his difficulties and ultimately subdue the inactive friend.

- A strategist well-versed in political science should carefully assess the stages of advancement, decline, stagnation, attrition, and collapse, as well as the application of every form of strategic maneuver.

- One who understands the intricate interdependencies within the sixfold policy can skillfully manipulate and command rulers as if they were bound in a web of alliances and rivalries crafted by his own design.

Book 8

CHAPTER I. THE AGGREGATE OF THE CALAMITIES OF THE ELEMENTS OF SOVEREIGNTY.

When several calamities strike at once, the first consideration should be to assess whether a proactive offense or a strategic defense is more manageable. National calamities, whether they arise from natural events, mismanagement, or external factors, often reflect a blend of bad fortune and poor decision-making. The term vyasana (translated as vices or calamities) encompasses the opposite of virtue, signifying not only a lack of positive qualities but also the escalation of adverse conditions and hardships. Vyasana, in essence, signifies a force that diminishes one's prosperity and stability, undermining well-being at the personal or national level.

My teacher asserts that among various calamities—including distress afflicting the king, his ministers, the general population, fortifications, finances, the army, or allies—the distress of the king is the most consequential, with each subsequent calamity listed in descending order of seriousness.

Bháradvája, however, contends that between the distress of the king and that of his ministers, ministerial distress is more severe. Ministers bear the weight of council deliberations, securing the realization of strategies, overseeing projects, managing finances and expenditures, mobilizing and maintaining the army, defending the kingdom from both internal and external threats, preserving order, protecting the kingdom's heir, ensuring the smooth installation of successors, and enacting solutions to ongoing or anticipated crises. In the absence of capable ministers, these critical duties suffer, and the king—like a bird stripped of its wings—is deprived of effective action, giving rise to unchecked enemy schemes. Ministerial distress poses an immediate threat to the king's life and stability, for ministers are the bedrock of his security and protection.

Kautilya argues differently, prioritizing the king's welfare above all. According to Kautilya, the king is the linchpin of the kingdom's structure. His role encompasses appointing ministers, priests, and administrators; addressing the challenges facing his people; tackling kingdom-wide issues; and driving forward-looking policies to benefit the realm. Should ministers face challenges, the king has the authority to replace them. A just and vigilant king ensures order through merit-based rewards and just punishments, which foster loyalty and balance among his people. The king's character, ultimately, sets a standard that permeates throughout society, shaping whether the people thrive or falter. Hence, the king is the aggregate force that embodies and directs the people's collective strength and progress.

Visáláksha holds a distinct view, asserting that between the distress of ministers and that of the people, the troubles facing the people are more serious. National wealth, military strength, resources, skilled labor, transport networks, and other essentials rely on the vitality of the general populace. Without the people, a kingdom's resources dwindle, second in importance only to the presence of a competent king and ministers.

Kautilya counters this argument by emphasizing that the effective functioning of the kingdom depends heavily on the role of the minister. Ministers coordinate and execute the king's vision, ensuring the public's safety, advancing land development, protecting property from enemies, expanding the army, maintaining financial health, managing resources, and deploying solutions to ongoing crises. Ministers play a foundational role in securing the kingdom's stability and its people's prosperity, ensuring that these functions are consistently and effectively executed.

The school of Parásara argues that, between distress of the people and issues arising from poor fortifications, the latter is far more troubling. Fortified towns serve as repositories for both treasury and military resources, offering a safe haven for the population. These fortifications provide strength beyond what mere citizens or rural people can offer, becoming powerful instruments of defense in times of threat. They afford the king a secure stronghold, while the people themselves are a shared asset, accessible to both the king and his enemy.

Kautilya disagrees, asserting that forts, financial resources, and the military ultimately rely on the populace for support. It is the people who uphold the construction of buildings, facilitate trade, sustain agriculture, manage livestock, and contribute bravery, stability, and other resources. Natural barriers like mountains and islands often serve as defensive structures in inhabited lands, whereas standalone forts become essential only in countries with limited open lands. In regions dominated by agriculture, lack of fortifications can be a source of distress, while in areas with largely martial populations, scarcity of cultivated lands or resources can pose serious challenges.

Pisuna claims that the absence of financial resources outweighs the troubles arising from lack of fortifications. Fort repairs, structural upkeep, and strategic maneuvers—such as funding espionage efforts to capture an enemy's stronghold—are made possible through wealth. Financial resources provide control over people, influence over allies and adversaries, encouragement for outsiders, and means for sustaining and mobilizing an army. Treasure can be relocated in times of crisis, but a fort cannot be so easily moved.

Kautilya counters, emphasizing that the fort itself safeguards both the treasury and the army, while supporting covert operations, controlling loyalists, maintaining the armed forces, receiving allies, and repelling threats, whether from enemies or wild tribes. Without fortifications, treasury resources are at risk of falling into enemy hands. For those who possess a well-fortified base, Kautilya notes, there is a shield against total ruin.

Kaunapadanta argues that of the two—lack of financial resources or the absence of an effective military—lacking a capable army is the greater detriment. A proficient army is vital for maintaining control over friends and enemies alike, for the possibility of swaying enemy forces, and for managing the overall administration of the kingdom. Without a military force, the treasury itself becomes vulnerable to seizure. While financial shortages may be mitigated by harvesting resources from lands, acquiring raw materials, or capturing an adversary's territory, the military's loyalty is paramount, as soldiers might even defect to the enemy or cause instability, endangering the king's life and bringing calamity.

Yet, Kautilya asserts that financial resources remain the key to observing virtuous acts and fulfilling material needs. Depending on shifts in location, timing, and strategic priorities, either finance or the army may momentarily hold more influence. The military can safeguard existing wealth, but wealth is the enduring foundation that secures both the treasury and the military. Given the dependency of all national activities on financial health, Kautilya concludes that financial distress is ultimately the most significant threat.

Vátavyádhi claims that between the distress of the army and that of an ally, it is more serious when an ally faces difficulties. An ally, even if not directly supported with resources or if stationed far away, can still play a crucial role. He fends off both rear and frontal enemies, subdues the allies of enemies, and keeps wild tribes at bay. Moreover, in times of crisis, an ally provides support in the form of funds, troops, and additional lands.

Kautilya, however, disagrees, arguing that a well-maintained and powerful army ensures the loyalty of allies, and can even encourage an enemy to adopt a friendly posture. When a task can be accomplished equally well by the army or by an ally, the choice between the two should depend on the strategic benefits of timing, location, and anticipated gains. During sudden campaigns, or when threats arise from external enemies, wild tribes, or internal rebellions, relying solely on allies can be risky. Friends are generally dependable only when financial support is available; when resources are scarce, alliances may falter, especially if an enemy has grown stronger. Therefore, Kautilya asserts, assessing the severity of various calamities across the elements of sovereignty should involve carefully weighing the current strength of both army and allies.

- When a portion of one element within sovereignty is affected by troubles, the potential to accomplish a task can be assessed based on the extent, loyalty, and strength of the unaffected and serviceable part.
- When two elements of sovereignty experience troubles simultaneously, they should be evaluated according to their trends—whether they are advancing or in decline—assuming that the remaining elements are in stable and positive condition and do not require further assessment.
- However, if the calamities affecting a single element threaten to destabilize or destroy the remaining elements, then these calamities, regardless of whether they impact the foundational or another specific element, are indeed of the utmost severity and urgency.

[Thus ends Chapter I, "The Aggregate of the Calamities of the Elements of Sovereignty," in Book VIII, "Concerning Vices and Calamities" of the Arthasástra of Kautilya. End of the hundred and seventeenth chapter from the beginning.]

CHAPTER II. CONSIDERATIONS ABOUT THE TROUBLES OF THE KING AND OF HIS KINGDOM.

The king and his domain serve as the core elements of any state's foundation, and their stability is essential for the overall strength and prosperity of the realm.

The challenges that a king faces may stem from either internal or external sources. Internal threats, though often less visible, are frequently more dangerous than external ones; they can be likened to the lurking threat of a hidden serpent that quietly waits to strike. Within internal threats, those arising specifically from ministers or close advisors are considered the most hazardous, as they have intimate access to the ruler's trust and influence. For this reason, it is vital that the king personally maintains control over the state's key functions—namely, the treasury and the military forces—to prevent manipulation from within his own court.

When comparing the vulnerabilities of divided rule versus foreign rule, both scenarios pose serious risks to stability. Divided rule—where governance is shared between two kings—often leads to conflict due to rivalry, jealousy, and conflicting loyalties, resulting in inefficiencies and eventual collapse. In contrast, foreign rule, which arises when a foreign power seizes control of a kingdom while the rightful ruler still lives, can be even more damaging. Foreign rulers typically view the conquered territory as an alien possession, exploiting it for its resources while treating it as disposable. Such rulers may strip the country of its wealth, treat it as a commercial asset, and leave it impoverished. When the citizens inevitably lose their loyalty to these foreign rulers, the latter are often quick to abandon the territory, leaving it weakened and destabilized.

In evaluating a blind king—one lacking knowledge in governance—and a king who deviates from wise policies, my teacher argues that a blind king is inherently more dangerous. A blind king, being untrained in the sciences of administration and strategy, acts impulsively, stubbornly, and often at the behest of others. His inability to make informed decisions leads to the downfall of the kingdom. On the other hand, a king who occasionally errs against wisdom can be brought back on course when his actions clearly diverge from sound governance. Kautilya, however, has a different view, asserting that a blind king, despite his limitations, can still be guided by competent advisors who help steer him toward correct policies. An erring king, however, particularly one who chooses to act against established wisdom, poses a graver risk, as his deliberate misjudgments are likely to lead to long-term damage to the state and its people.

When considering a sick king versus a new ruler, my teacher believes that a king suffering from illness may lose his throne due to ministerial conspiracies or may even lose his life due to the physical toll of managing state affairs, especially if he lacks the strength to keep control. A new ruler, on the other hand, often garners immediate support from the populace by performing popular actions such as adhering to his duties, lowering taxes, and bestowing gifts and favors upon the people. Kautilya counters this perspective by emphasizing that a sick king, even amid his illness, continues to uphold his duties out of necessity, knowing that the welfare of the kingdom depends on his role. A new ruler, however, can be unpredictable; assuming that his newly acquired lands are entirely his by right, he may act impulsively without considering the consequences. Such a king is prone to tolerating the aggressions of neighboring kings who seek to exploit his lack of control, or he may find himself overpowered by internal conflicts, as he lacks the same level of authority and established relationships with state elements as an experienced ruler. Furthermore, Kautilya differentiates between various types of kings in this context: there is a distinction between a king who is morally diseased and one who suffers from physical ailments, just as there is a difference between a high-born ruler and one of humble birth.

In comparing a high-born but weak king with a strong but low-born king, my teacher argues that people may be inclined to accept a weak but noble-born ruler out of respect for lineage, but they would ultimately resist an ineffective or unfit ruler, regardless of his birth. Conversely, if they prioritize strength and power, they may more easily accept a strong, low-born leader, allowing him to wield influence and control due to his personal capabilities rather than his heritage.

No, Kautilya says, people will naturally follow a high-born king, even if he is weak, because a thriving people tend to respect a king with noble roots. They also make sure the schemes of a strong but low-born person fail, as there is an old saying that having virtues strengthens friendships.

The loss of crops is more damaging than losing a few handfuls of grain since the hard work that went into it is destroyed. A lack of rain is worse than too much rain.

- The relative seriousness or insignificance of any two types of troubles affecting the key parts of sovereignty, following the order of the different types of distress, determines whether to take an offensive or defensive approach.

[Thus ends Chapter II, "Considerations about the Troubles of the King and of his Kingdom," in Book VIII, "Concerning Vices and Calamities," of the Arthasástra of Kautilya. End of the hundred and eighteenth chapter from the beginning.]

CHAPTER III. THE AGGREGATE OF THE TROUBLE OF MEN.

Understood! I'll ensure every sentence is translated exactly without any shortening, maintaining a line-by-line structure to preserve the original meaning and length. Here is the expanded version:

Ignorance and lack of discipline are the root causes of a person's troubles. A person without proper training fails to recognize the harm that can come from indulging in vices. Now, we will discuss these vices in detail:

There are three types of vices that stem from anger, while those arising from desire fall into four categories. Between these two types, anger is considered worse, as it drives one to act against all in its path. In most cases, kings who gave in to anger have been reported to fall prey to the rage of the people. On the other hand, kings who were addicted to pleasure have often succumbed to severe illnesses brought about by excess and the depletion of their resources.

No, says Bháradvája, anger is the trait of a righteous person. It is the very foundation of courage; it acts as a force to eliminate despicable individuals, and it instills fear among the people, keeping them under control. Anger is always an essential trait for the prevention of wrongdoing. On the other hand, desire is linked to the pursuit of pleasurable outcomes, the willingness to forgive, acts of generosity, and efforts to endear oneself to others. Desire is necessary for anyone who wishes to enjoy the benefits of their achievements.

No, says Kautilya, anger leads to enmity and stirs up conflict with adversaries, and it is consistently associated with pain. Addiction to pleasure (káma) results in loss of respect, financial ruin, and throws the one addicted into the company of thieves, gamblers, hunters, musicians, and other undesirable characters. Among these issues, enmity is more dangerous than disrespect, as a disrespected person becomes vulnerable to betrayal by both their people and their enemies, while a hated person is actively destroyed. Conflict with enemies is more severe than financial loss, as financial loss causes distress in one's resources, while enmity poses a risk to life itself. Suffering from vices is more significant than keeping poor company, for undesirable company can be abandoned immediately, but suffering from vices brings enduring harm. Therefore, anger is the more serious of the two evils.

Which is worse: the abuse of words, misuse of wealth, or the imposition of oppressive punishment?

Visáláksha argues that, when comparing the abuse of language to the misuse of money, the harm done through harsh words is more severe. For, when harshly spoken to, a brave person is moved to retaliate; harsh words, like a nail that pierces the heart, provoke anger and bring pain to all the senses.

No, says Kautilya, money as a gift can ease the anger caused by harsh words, while the misuse of money itself can lead to the loss of one's means of livelihood. Misuse of money involves giving, taking, losing, or neglecting wealth altogether.

The School of Parásara argues that misuse of money is more harmful than excessive punishment because good deeds and pleasures in life rely on wealth; even the fabric of society is tied to it. Thus, its misuse is a far greater danger.

No, says Kautilya, people would rather risk large sums than their own lives. Excessive punishment not only risks one's well-being but also exposes one to similar punishment from one's enemies.

This completes the set of evils arising from anger.

Next are the four vices rooted in desire: hunting, gambling, women, and drinking.

Pisuna asserts that hunting is the worse of the two vices, compared to gambling. Hunting leads to dangers such as encounters with robbers, enemies, wild animals, and fire, disorientation, fear, hunger, thirst, and even death. In gambling, however, a skilled gambler can achieve success, like Jayatsena and Duryodhana did.

No, says Kautilya, in gambling, one party is always bound to suffer defeat, as seen in the tale of Nala and Yudhishthira. Wealth won in gambling, much like a mere piece of meat, often brings enmity. The harms of gambling include failing to appreciate hard-earned wealth, gaining wealth unethically, losing wealth without enjoying it, ignoring basic needs, and falling ill from irregular meals. In hunting, however, benefits include physical exercise, reduced phlegm, bile, fat, and sweat, the development of skills in aiming at both moving and still targets, learning how animals behave when provoked, and engaging in an occasional journey.

Kaunapadanta argues that addiction to gambling is a worse vice than addiction to women. Gamblers are known to play all hours, even by lamplight at night, disregarding events as grave as the death of a family member. A gambler easily shows anger when spoken to during tough times. In the case of attachment to women, however, conversations about virtue and prosperity are still possible during daily routines like bathing, dressing, or eating. Moreover, it's feasible to manage a woman's behavior in a way that could support the king's welfare or even end the relationship discreetly under the guise of illness if necessary.

No, says Kautilya, it is possible to distract someone from gambling, but much harder from women. The consequences of addiction to women include failing to observe duties, neglecting immediate tasks, inability to focus on political matters, and slipping into the vice of drinking.

Vátavyádhi contends that addiction to women is more harmful than drinking, pointing to various forms of childishness often seen among women, which is elaborated in the section on "The Harem." By contrast, drinking offers sensory enjoyment, pleases others, garners followers' favor, and provides a means of relaxing after hard work.

No, says Kautilya, being involved with women can lead to children, the need for self-defense, changes in relationships within the harem, and can avoid consequences if outside women are deemed unsuitable. Drinking brings both positive and negative results, but its ill effects are striking: loss of wealth, madness in otherwise reasonable men, a lifeless appearance while living, indecency, neglect of sacred knowledge, and the loss of life, assets, and friendships. It severs ties with respectable people, brings suffering, and often leads to wasting wealth on music and singing.

Of the two vices, gambling and drinking, gambling causes gain or loss of stakes for one side or the other. Even animals display divisive tendencies and aggression under its influence. Particularly in assemblies or alliances with unified interests, gambling has been known to divide and ruin them. Worst of all evils is engaging in unworthy activities, as this completely diminishes one's capacity for wise governance and political insight.

- The pursuit of what is generally condemned stems from desire, while anger manifests in acts that oppress those who are good. Since both of these tendencies lead to numerous harms, they are regarded as the most destructive of all vices.
- Therefore, a person with good judgment should seek the company of the wise and, by mastering their own passions, rid themselves of both anger and desire, as these impulses give rise to further evils and undermine the very foundation of a stable life.

[Thus ends Chapter III, "The Aggregate of the Troubles of Men," in Book VIII. "Concerning Vices and Calamities" of the Arthasástra of Kautilya. End of the hundred and nineteenth chapter from the beginning.]

CHAPTER IV. THE GROUP OF MOLESTATIONS, THE GROUP OF OBSTRUCTIONS, AND THE GROUP OF FINANCIAL TROUBLES.

Natural calamities include fires, floods, disease outbreaks, famine, and epidemics like maraka.

My teacher believes that between fires and floods, fire's destruction is worse because it's beyond remedy. In contrast, most troubles, aside from fire, can be alleviated, and flood-related troubles eventually subside.

Kautilya disagrees, arguing that fires typically affect a single village or part of one, while floods can sweep away entire regions, affecting many villages at once.

According to my teacher, of pestilence and famine, pestilence is worse as it disrupts all kinds of work, causes illness and death, and prompts people to flee, leading to a halt in activities, while famine doesn't stop work entirely and still allows for some trade, livestock use, and tax collection.

Kautilya, however, notes that pestilence generally devastates a limited area and can be remedied, while famine affects the whole region, depriving everyone of their means to live.

This view also explains the impact of maraka.

My teacher believes that the loss of common people obstructs everyday work more than the loss of leaders.

Kautilya disagrees, explaining that it is possible to replace common people due to their sheer numbers. For common people's benefit, leaders must be preserved, as they're often one in a thousand— uniquely brave and wise, serving as a foundation for the community.

On troubles within one's own Circle of States versus those of an enemy's, my teacher asserts that internal troubles are more harmful and unmanageable since an external threat can either be fought off or kept away with allies or by negotiating peace.

Kautilya counters, saying that internal problems can be resolved by containing or eliminating problematic leaders, and such issues may impact only parts of a kingdom, whereas an enemy's Circle of States can cause destruction, burning, and devastation across many areas.

My teacher claims that discord among citizens is more damaging, as it can create disunity and invite enemy invasion, whereas disputes between kings bring benefits like better wages and tax relief for the people.

Kautilya has a different view, noting that internal disputes can be quelled by detaining the leaders or removing the causes, and infighting among citizens can actually encourage productivity as they compete, ultimately benefiting the country. However, conflicts between kings lead to widespread suffering, requiring twice as much effort to manage and causing more significant harm to the people.

My teacher believes that of a king who enjoys leisure activities and a people who are also sportive, a populace given to amusements is more damaging to productivity since their playfulness affects the kingdom's work, while a king inclined to enjoyment benefits artisans, entertainers, and merchants.

But Kautilya disagrees, arguing that when a country takes to recreation, it is generally a minor interruption, and after some leisure, the people return to work. In contrast, a king given to indulgence disrupts governance by favoring courtiers, seizing resources, and causing delays in production and industry.

My teacher suggests that between a favored wife and a prince, the prince causes more harm by indulging his followers, extracting resources, and obstructing work, whereas a wife devoted to personal enjoyment only involves herself in such pursuits.

Kautilya sees it differently. He notes that any misbehavior of a prince can be managed through the minister and priest, while the favored wife's influence, often coupled with her willfulness and poor associations, is harder to control.

According to my teacher, trouble from a corporation of people versus that from a leader is harder to manage when dealing with the people's group. Being large in number, they can disrupt through theft and disorder, while a single leader may only interfere with certain tasks.

Kautilya holds a different view, pointing out that a corporation can be controlled or subdued, as it follows the king's fortunes and can be kept in check by detaining a few members or the leader. On the other hand, a leader with strong backing poses greater risks by threatening the well-being and assets of others.

In considering the chamberlain versus the revenue collector, my teacher suggests the chamberlain, with his tendency to meddle in operations and impose fines, is more burdensome, while the collector focuses on the income of his own department.

Kautilya disagrees, arguing that the chamberlain may intercept offerings meant for the treasury, but the collector may prioritize his revenue over the king's or even divert it altogether, interfering with the kingdom's finances.

Regarding the boundary superintendent and a trader, my teacher believes that the superintendent hampers commerce by tolerating theft and overtaxing, whereas a trader benefits the kingdom by creating wealth through fair exchanges.

Kautilya argues the opposite, noting that the boundary superintendent can promote trade by welcoming goods and fostering exchanges, whereas traders often collude to manipulate prices for profit, increasing or decreasing values to their advantage.

Finally, when weighing land held by a noble against land reserved for cattle grazing, which is more beneficial?

My teacher argues that land occupied by a high-born individual is highly productive, supplying manpower to the army. For this reason, it should not be taken over, as the owner might retaliate and cause disturbances. Meanwhile, land used for cattle grazing, which can be cultivated, should be freed up for crops since agricultural land is more valuable than grazing land.

However, Kautilya holds a different view. Though land used by a noble is indeed useful, it should still be reclaimed to prevent potential issues from arising if the noble becomes rebellious. On the other hand, land reserved for cattle grazing generates revenue from livestock and does not need to be confiscated unless it directly interferes with farming activities.

My teacher also says that between robbers and wild tribes, robbers are more troublesome. They are constantly on the lookout for opportunities to abduct people at night, ambush others, and steal substantial amounts of wealth. Wild tribes, on the other hand, are more organized under a leader, generally sticking to nearby forests and only causing limited damage.

Kautilya disagrees, suggesting that robbers typically target only those who are careless, making them easier to identify and catch. In contrast, wild tribes often have fortified bases and are numerous and courageous, willing to launch attacks even in broad daylight. They can seize and devastate large areas, similar to small kingdoms.

Between animal forests and elephant forests, ordinary animals are numerous and provide ample resources, such as meat and hides. They naturally limit the growth of grass and are relatively easy to manage. Elephants, however, are quite the opposite and have been known to cause substantial damage to territories, even after they have been captured and tamed.

Benefits from one's own country, like grains, cattle, gold, and raw materials, are essential for sustaining the population in times of crisis, whereas foreign resources lack the same reliability and accessibility during hardships.

This comprises the group of molestations.

When movement is restricted by a local leader, it's called an internal obstruction; however, restrictions due to an enemy or a wild tribe are external obstructions.

This makes up the group of obstructions.

Financial troubles stemming from these two kinds of obstructions and the molestations listed above include revenue stagnation, loss of wealth through tax exemptions given to leaders, dispersed revenue, inaccurate revenue records, and funds held by neighboring kings or wild tribes.

Thus concludes the group of financial troubles.

- To ensure the country's prosperity, one should strive to prevent the causes of such troubles, address them effectively when they arise, and actively remove both obstructions and financial difficulties.

[Thus ends Chapter IV, "The Group of Molestations, the Group of Obstructions, and the Group of Financial Troubles" in BookVIII, "Concerning Vices and Calamities," of the Arthasástra of Kautilya. End of the hundred and twentieth chapter from the beginning.]

CHAPTER V. THE GROUP OF TROUBLES OF THE ARMY, AND THE GROUP OF TROUBLES OF A FRIEND.

The troubles that weaken an army encompass a wide range of situations, each of which affects the army's ability to fight effectively. These troubles include, but are not limited to: an army that feels disrespected by its leadership, one that suffers from deep humiliation, another that has not been paid, one plagued by illness, one that has just arrived without proper preparation, one exhausted from a prolonged journey, and one physically worn out. Additionally, an army that has suffered recent losses, faced outright defeat, had its front lines broken, or one that is suffering from severe weather or stationed in an unsuited terrain can be seriously impaired. Furthermore, an army can be troubled by frustration over unmet expectations, or can be affected by soldiers who have fled from previous battles, troops preoccupied with family concerns, individuals with divided loyalties, segments angered due to conflicts with the leadership, troops who have previously served in other states, and those that specialize in specific maneuvers or terrains that do not align with the current battlefield.

Among these, there are specific remedies that can improve the condition of an army in some situations but not all. For instance, an army that feels disrespected may recover and become battle-ready if leadership takes steps to restore honor and morale. However, an army that is deeply humiliated and has lost faith in its cause will be harder to rally. In cases where an army is either unpaid or plagued by illness, payment can renew loyalty and readiness, while sick troops are simply unfit for combat, regardless of external efforts. Similarly, when dealing with a freshly arrived army and one that is tired from travel, the newly arrived soldiers can be positioned and integrated, while long-traveled forces require rest before they are battle-ready. An exhausted army can be rejuvenated through adequate sleep, nourishment, and rest, while an army that has suffered significant loss, particularly of its leaders, is greatly weakened and must regroup to restore strength.

When comparing an army repelled in combat with one that has had its front lines broken, the repelled forces may reengage if reinforced with fresh troops, while an army suffering heavy casualties in its front lines will find it difficult to recover morale and strength. Troops weakened by harsh weather conditions may be readied for battle if given proper clothing and gear, whereas those stationed in unsuitable terrain cannot move freely and are likely to suffer in their combat effectiveness. Armies disappointed by unmet expectations can be brought back to readiness if they are satisfied, but soldiers who have previously fled from battle are unreliable.

Furthermore, some soldiers may be deeply attached to their families, causing distractions, and they may be made ready by temporarily separating them from familial ties, while troops who have defected to the enemy or have divided loyalties are inherently unreliable, posing risks similar to those of internal enemies. This array of potential challenges demonstrates the various ways in which an army's strength can be impacted, as well as the necessary measures that might either remedy or fail to address these unique trouble

Among armies facing issues of internal conflict, those with only a faction that is provoked or agitated can still be mobilized if that faction is pacified through careful negotiation, conciliation, or other strategic methods. However, a disunited army, whose members have developed estrangement or hostility toward each other, should not be relied upon in combat due to lack of cohesion. For forces that have resigned from service in one or multiple states, an army that departed from a foreign state without signs of conspiracy can still be led into battle under trusted commanders or spies. In contrast, an army that has resigned from several states carries greater risk and should not be deployed due to its potential for disloyalty or danger.

When considering armies trained in specialized maneuvers, one accustomed to specific strategies in both encampment and battle tactics can be effective. Yet, troops trained only to operate within specific territories or environments are limited and may not be suitable for unfamiliar or varied conditions. Armies facing obstructions are also to be handled with care. Troops blocked in one direction may still be redirected against an enemy from another direction, but an army encircled on all sides lacks the necessary mobility and should be spared from combat until freed.

For armies whose supplies have been disrupted, the specific nature of the shortage determines their readiness. Troops deprived of grain can be supported by acquiring food from alternative sources, either bringing in foodstuffs or supplying the army with movable and immovable provisions like livestock or preserved goods. However, an army cut off entirely from reinforcements and provisions is unsustainable and should not be sent to battle without reestablishing these essential resources.

Armies based domestically, as opposed to those stationed with allies, offer different strategic advantages. Those stationed within one's own country can be more easily disbanded or called back if dangers arise, whereas forces placed under an ally's protection, removed in both time and distance, present challenges in mobilization and may not be effective in immediate threats.

With armies containing traitorous elements or those fearing attack from the rear, troops infiltrated by traitors may still be of use if they are carefully isolated and placed under the command of a trusted leader. However, an army fearing a rear assault is compromised in morale and should not be exposed to the front lines until that threat is addressed. Armies that have lost communications with their central command can regain effectiveness once communication is restored, ideally with the support of civilians and local populations. Yet, a force entirely without leadership, whether that be the king or another figure of authority, lacks direction and should be restructured before deployment.

Finally, for troops that have lost a key leader or lack training, those with missing leaders may recover strength if a new, capable commander is appointed. However, untrained troops lack the necessary discipline and experience to function effectively in battle and should be drilled or properly instructed before any engagement.

- To protect his army from troubles, a king should focus on eliminating vices and challenges within the ranks, recruit capable new men, avoid areas where an enemy could stage an ambush, and ensure harmony among the army's officers.
- A wise king constantly watches for any threats posed by his enemy and remains ready to strike when the opposing army faces difficulties.
- When the king identifies any source of trouble for his people, he must quickly and carefully implement countermeasures to neutralize it.
- A friend who either independently, in alliance with others, or under another ruler's influence has turned against his own ally; a friend who has been left out due to a lack of ability to sustain loyalty, or due to greed or apathy; and
- A friend who has been swayed by another and withdrawn from

battle should all be managed with caution.

- A friend who, in adopting a strategy of making peace with one ally and planning an attack against another, has aligned with someone preparing to advance—either alone or in alliance—against his own ally;

- A friend who is unable to overcome his own difficulties due to fear, contempt, or indifference; a friend cornered in his own territory or forced to flee in fear;

- A friend who is discontented because he has paid too much, because he has not received his rightful due, or because he remains dissatisfied even after receiving what was owed to him;

- A friend who has willingly paid excessively or has been compelled by another to pay more than his fair share;

- A friend who is held under undue pressure or who, after breaking ties of loyalty, has sought to establish friendship elsewhere—each of these scenarios requires careful handling.

- A friend neglected because of a lack of capability to retain his loyalty, or a friend who turns hostile despite an ally's attempts to prevent it—such friends are rarely retained, and even if they are, they often drift away.

- A friend who understands the obligations of friendship, who is honorable, or who may feel disappointed due to lack of communication, or who, despite his enthusiasm, is not equipped for the task, or who retreats in fear from another source of threat;

- Or a friend who becomes fearful at witnessing another ally's downfall, or who fears a coalition of enemies, or who is influenced by traitors to abandon his friendship—this type of friend is likely to be won over, and once gained, is steadfast in loyalty.

- Therefore, one must be careful to avoid causes that could undermine a friendship, and if such causes do arise, they should be resolved by showing a warm and genuine approach to restore and strengthen the bond.

Book 9

CHAPTER I. THE KNOWLEDGE OF POWER, PLACE, TIME, STRENGTH, AND WEAKNESS; THE TIME OF INVASION.

The conqueror should thoroughly assess his own strength and that of his enemy. After carefully considering factors like resources, terrain, timing, march readiness, army recruitment, potential outcomes, as well as expected losses, profits, and risks, he should proceed only if he can mobilize his full force. Otherwise, it's best to remain at rest.

My teacher asserts that enthusiasm surpasses sheer power. A king who is energetic, brave, healthy, skilled in arms, and who drives his army with fervor can overcome even a powerful rival. A smaller force, led by a determined king, is capable of achieving its goals. Conversely, a king lacking in enthusiasm will fail, no matter how strong his army may be.

However, Kautilya disagrees, claiming that strength holds greater importance than enthusiasm alone. Through sheer power, a king can outmaneuver another who relies solely on zeal. By acquiring or allying with an enthusiastic king and brave soldiers, he can leverage the enthusiasm of his armies—be they cavalry, elephants, chariots, or other forces—moving them swiftly and decisively. Throughout history, powerful rulers, regardless of gender, age, or physical limitations, have achieved dominion by enlisting or purchasing the support of passionate allies.

My teacher also holds that power—meaning wealth and army—outweighs skill in intrigue because, while a king may be skilled in strategy, he is powerless without resources. Without power, he is like seeds withering in a drought, vulnerable to losing his kingdom.

Kautilya, however, contends that skill in intrigue is superior. A leader with insight and knowledge of statecraft can achieve success with minimal effort by applying strategies like conciliation, subterfuge, spies, and even chemical methods. This adept use of intrigue enables him to outwit those rulers who rely solely on enthusiasm and brute force. Hence, among enthusiasm, power, and skill for intrigue, the one who possesses the quality ranked later in this sequence has the advantage over those holding the earlier ones.

In terms of territory, or space, it signifies the land itself. A vast stretch of earth—such as the thousand yojanas (a unit of measure) from the Himalayas to the ocean—is the dominion of a true emperor, encompassing varied landscapes like forests, villages, waterfalls, plains, and rugged areas. In this diversity, a king should initiate ventures that reinforce his power and wealth. The best land is one where his army finds strategic maneuverability and that challenges his enemy; the worst is land that offers no advantage, and somewhere in between is a land of mixed characteristics.

Time, as another vital factor, includes the cold, hot, and rainy seasons and periods such as day, night, fortnight, month, season, solstice, year, and five-year cycles (Yuga). In these cycles, a ruler should embark on initiatives that promote his power and success. The most advantageous time is one that benefits his army's movements and disadvantages his enemy; the least favorable is time that reverses this balance, while a time of both advantages and drawbacks is moderate in quality.

My teacher argues that among the three factors—strength, location, and timing—strength is ultimately the most crucial. When a person is endowed with sufficient strength, they are more likely to overcome any hindrance, whether caused by rough terrain or difficult seasonal conditions, such as intense heat, biting cold, or continuous rain. A powerful king can still prevail over obstacles if he possesses adequate strength, as his resources and resilience can carry him through. Some, however, assert that location may be even more critical; they offer the analogy of a dog that, if positioned well on solid ground, can drag even a crocodile, but if that same crocodile pulls the dog into lower ground, it gains the advantage. In this sense, the right setting or advantageous ground can be as valuable as raw strength.

Another school of thought holds that timing is the most vital of the three. Those who prioritize timing often point out that by day, a crow can easily kill an owl, yet as night falls, the owl becomes dominant and can kill the crow. Thus, even the strengths of the most able creature can be influenced or thwarted by timing.

Kautilya, however, disagrees with these singular views, arguing that strength, location, and timing each play vital roles that enhance and complement each other. He contends that whoever can effectively harness all three factors will have a considerable advantage. A ruler should, therefore, take care to secure each element of strength, location, and timing in preparation for an advance. Once these are in place, the conqueror should allocate part of his forces, roughly one-third to one-fourth, to protect his base of operations from potential rear threats posed by enemies or wild tribes in the vicinity. Then, equipped with the remainder of his force and ample resources, he should aim to attack during the month of Mārgaśīrṣa (December). At this time, he can capitalize on the enemy's outdated, stale food supplies, as the opponent is unlikely to have stocked fresh provisions or repaired his fortifications. This timing enables the conqueror to devastate his enemy's most recently harvested crops, which are generally set aside for the rainy season, as well as autumnal reserves.

If his objective is to spoil both autumn harvests and spring stockpiles, the king should initiate his advance during the month of Chaitra (March). This allows him to strike his enemy's autumn crops before they can be fully secured and also attack early preparations for the next season. For further advantage, he might choose to march in Jyestha (May-June), particularly if the enemy's stores of fodder, firewood, and water have already been partially depleted. Since many rulers overlook maintaining adequate supplies during these months, it would also be an ideal time to compromise the enemy's fortifications.

By doing so, the conqueror can disrupt both the spring harvests and summer provisions, inflicting a dual loss on his foe.

Alternatively, he could consider a dewy-season campaign, particularly if his opponent's territory is naturally dry, with limited access to fodder and water, making it difficult for the enemy to sustain his forces. A summer march might also be effective if his opponent's territory is prone to mist that could obstruct visibility, and if the terrain is marked by deep valleys, dense thickets, and natural foliage that would serve the conqueror's purposes. Moreover, if his enemy's country has ample water resources that are also suitable for maneuvering his own army while impeding the enemy's, he might choose to strike during the rainy season to use the weather to his advantage.

Planning the length of the march is equally critical. Longer marches are best conducted between Mārgaśīrṣa (December) and Taisha (January), as these are the months when food and weather conditions permit sustained campaigns. Campaigns of medium length may be scheduled between March and April when the climate is moderate, allowing troops to endure without becoming overexposed to extreme weather. Short campaigns are most effectively carried out between May and June, where swift action is essential to capitalize on short bursts of readiness. However, if a ruler finds himself hampered by his own difficulties, it is usually advisable to remain stationary and avoid overextending his resources.

The concept of advancing against an enemy under duress has already been outlined in the context of "Marching After Declaring War," providing additional guidance on timing and readiness.

My teacher suggests that nearly all campaigns should capitalize on any visible struggles faced by an enemy. Yet Kautilya offers a more cautious view, advising that a ruler should advance only when his own resources are sufficiently robust to manage any unexpected turns of events, as it is often difficult to fully ascertain the extent of an enemy's distress. However, if an opportune situation arises, where the conqueror is reasonably certain of reducing or subduing the enemy, a campaign could proceed confidently.

In seasons with mild temperatures, the conqueror should rely predominantly on an elephant-heavy army. Elephants, although invaluable in strength, are highly susceptible to health issues like leprosy if made to work in hot weather without sufficient water for bathing and drinking. Under such circumstances, they tend to become sluggish and resistant to orders. On the other hand, if the opponent's land is abundant in water, the rainy season provides a fitting time for deploying an elephant-centric army. Against an enemy stationed in an area with minimal rainfall or muddy water supplies, an army composed primarily of donkeys, camels, and horses would be most effective. These animals are better suited to such conditions, making them ideal for campaigns where the terrain and climate challenge the enemy's defenses.

When marching against a desert, the rainy season is the ideal time to deploy the full composition of the army—elephants, horses, chariots, and infantry—ensuring each unit is suited to the harsh, arid environment with added rainfall. For the march itself, the conqueror should carefully organize a plan that outlines both short and long stretches of travel, adjusted to match the landscape's various types. Whether moving across level ground, rough terrain, valleys, or wide plains, each route should account for the challenges unique to each setting, allowing for adaptable progress based on the land's conditions.

When the intended task or objective is minimal, the campaign against any enemy should be brief to avoid unnecessary resource drain. Conversely, if the task is more substantial, requiring considerable effort or larger-scale conquest, the campaign should be proportionately extended, allowing time to accomplish more complex goals effectively. In times of rain, it's wise to establish camps in regions farther afield, where they can safely continue operations without facing setbacks due to weather, enabling the conqueror to maintain readiness and avoid stagnation even amid challenging conditions.

[Thus ends Chapter I, "The Knowledge of Power, Place, Time, Strength and Weakness, the Time of Invasion," in Book IX, "The Work of an Invader," of the Arthasástra of Kautilya. End of the hundred and twenty-second chapter from the beginning.]

CHAPTER II. THE TIME OF RECRUITING THE ARMY; THE FORM OF EQUIPMENT; AND THE WORK OF ARRAYING A RIVAL FORCE.

The best times to recruit different types of troops—such as hereditary soldiers, hired soldiers, corporations of soldiers, allied forces, and wild tribes—are based on the king's careful evaluation of his own resources, the enemy's capabilities, the nature of the mission, and the anticipated conditions. Each type of troop has distinct strengths, and the decision to deploy one over the other should be based on strategic priorities.

For the king, hereditary troops are a valuable asset, especially when he recognizes their reliability and attachment to his rule. If the king finds that his hereditary forces exceed his defensive needs and that having a large group idle could lead to dissatisfaction or even unrest among the ranks, he should opt to use them in action. Their loyalty is a significant advantage, especially if he fears that his enemy's own hereditary forces are large and skilled, requiring a more adept and connected army to counter them. Additionally, if the landscape and weather conditions are generally favorable for the march, hereditary troops are a dependable choice due to their endurance and unity, both crucial in extended or challenging campaigns. Hereditary forces are unlikely to be swayed by the enemy's intrigues, making them preferable when loyalty and unity are essential.

However, if the king's hired army is significantly larger than his hereditary force, and the enemy's army is known to be weaker or smaller in numbers, hired soldiers become an appropriate choice. This option is particularly useful if the campaign relies more on clever tactics than sheer force, as the hired army can bring a distinct flexibility to the strategy. If the journey's path and conditions are manageable, and the king can trust that his hired soldiers won't be swayed by enemy influences, this option allows him to utilize their skills without compromising loyalty. Hired forces work well when the enemy is not especially powerful and when they can perform with minimal risk of subversion by enemy schemes.

In situations where the king relies on corporations of soldiers, these forces serve him well if they are trustworthy and if their primary purpose is to defend his state during his absence. When a campaign is expected to be short, or if the enemy's forces also consist largely of soldier corporations, this force becomes particularly useful. Soldier corporations are cohesive units and thus are not easily divided by the enemy's tactics, making them well-suited for situations requiring solid frontlines and quick adaptability against a similar corporate army.

In certain cases, if the king has a strong alliance with another ruler, an allied army can be particularly effective. This allied force can not only aid in his own country's defense but can also support his campaign when he marches out. If he plans to move against the enemy for a limited period and anticipates more open warfare than tactical skirmishes, then allied forces are advantageous, as they bring additional resources and fresh troops to the effort. The king could place allied forces in territories that need monitoring—wild regions, cities, or open plains—while he advances his own troops to engage the enemy directly. This distribution of forces allows for strategic positioning where his ally's forces engage the enemy's supporters, keeping the main field free for his own army's maneuvers. If the king's success strongly depends on this ally, or if the ally is well-positioned nearby and deserving of the king's favor, the allied forces are a valuable addition, particularly when his friend's army is large and readily available.

In each case, the king should weigh the potential impact of his choice on both the short-term and long-term security of his kingdom. By understanding the strengths, weaknesses, and specific functions of each type of force, he can ensure that his approach is tailored to achieve the greatest advantage in his march against the enemy.

When a king believes that he can skillfully manipulate his strong enemy into fighting another rival over a city, plain, or stretch of wild land, he knows that this conflict will help him achieve one or another of his goals—much like an outcast benefits from a fight between a dog and a pig. Through this confrontation, he might see the disruptive power of his enemy's allies or wild tribes diminished, thus weakening them in the long run. If he assesses that he can redirect his immediate and powerful adversary's focus to another area, this diversion could help him relieve internal unrest, particularly if it's incited by his enemy. If he senses that the right time has come, perhaps with other rivalries heating up or minor kings becoming restless, he can leverage the enemy's forces to serve his ends by stoking such conflicts.

This strategy also sheds light on the best timing to use wild tribes in warfare. When the king sees that the enemy's path leads through areas inhabited by wild tribes, and that the road will be particularly challenging for the enemy's army to traverse, he might decide it's an ideal moment to deploy these native forces. Such wild tribes often prove invaluable in such terrains, and like using one wood-apple to split another, the tribes can be set against a smaller enemy force to weaken or even destroy it.

A well-trained and prepared army—one that is large, composed of various groups, and so devoted that it rises for battle whether paid or unpaid, even seeking plunder when the opportunity arises—is truly a formidable force. This type of force can withstand adverse weather, disband without major consequence, and be nearly impossible for an enemy to overcome. The ideal compact army is one in which all its members share the same homeland, caste, and training background, creating a cohesive and powerful military unit that can function as a united front against enemies.

These are the optimal times for gathering forces to prepare for a campaign. Among these different kinds of armies, payment to wild tribes is best provided through either raw goods or the allowance to claim spoils from conquered areas.

When the enemy's army is nearing, it's essential to obstruct their advance, push them back, delay their progress, or lead them astray with deceptive promises so that their timing becomes misaligned. This way, after the ideal marching period has passed, the enemy may find themselves at a disadvantage. Throughout these maneuvers, one must remain ever-watchful, strengthening one's own resources while ensuring that any efforts the enemy makes to bolster their forces are thwarted.

Among the different types of armies, the first mentioned generally holds the advantage over the next in the sequence. A hereditary army, bound to its master by tradition and consistently trained, offers distinct advantages over a hired force. This loyalty-driven force depends on the welfare of its leader, giving it a unity of purpose and resilience.

Of hired forces, those that remain close, rise quickly, and display unwavering loyalty are more valuable than loosely organized corporations of soldiers.

A company of soldiers, especially one that is native to the land, shares the same goals as the king, and is driven by similar sentiments of rivalry, anger, and hope for victory and reward, is more effective than the forces of an allied king. Even if such a company of soldiers is located further away and needs more time to mobilize, its unity of purpose makes it superior to the allied army.

An enemy's army led by an Arya, a noble or respected leader, is a better force than a wild tribe's army, as both types of forces are motivated by the prospect of plunder. However, in the absence of loot and when faced with difficulties, these armies can become a liability, as unpredictable as a snake in hiding.

My teacher asserts that, among armies composed of different castes—Brahmins, Kshatriyas, Vaishyas, or Shudras—the army led by Brahmins is preferable for its bravery. Each of these castes contributes something unique, yet each subsequent group is less desirable than the previous in this order.

Kautilya, however, disagrees, arguing that an army of Brahmins might be easily swayed by the enemy's flattery and acts of respect, possibly defecting to the enemy's side. Therefore, he suggests that an army of Kshatriyas, trained in the skills of weaponry and combat, is more reliable. Alternatively, an army composed of the numerically strong Vaishyas or Shudras could also be advantageous due to its sheer size.

In preparing his army, the king should assess his forces in relation to his enemy's, thinking strategically: "This is the strength of my enemy's forces; and this is how my army will counter it."

To counter an army that includes elephants, it's essential to have a force equipped with specialized items like large machines, the sakatagarbha (a siege device), wooden rods (kuntas), short dual-handled weapons (prasas), kharvatakas (presumably tactical implements), sturdy bamboo sticks, and heavy iron clubs. Each of these tools and weapons is effective against the massive power of elephants.

To confront an enemy army that relies on chariots, soldiers should be well-supplied with stones, clubs, armor, hooks, and plenty of spears. These can disrupt the momentum of chariot forces and pose serious obstacles to their movement.

For countering cavalry, a similar force equipped with the same weapons is also recommended.

To combat elephants directly, foot soldiers armored with protective gear are effective, as they can withstand the impact and pressure of these formidable animals.

For fighting heavily armored infantry, cavalry is advantageous as it provides speed and agility to outmaneuver the slower, well-protected soldiers.

When preparing to oppose an army composed of all four traditional components—elephants, chariots, cavalry, and infantry—the best approach is to deploy a mix of armored men, chariots, soldiers equipped with defensive weapons, and a well-prepared infantry. This blend of forces can counter each element of a diverse enemy army.

- Therefore, by carefully evaluating the strengths and capabilities within the various branches of one's own four-part army (composed of elephants, chariots, cavalry, and infantry), one should enlist the appropriate men and equip them accordingly. This will ensure that the army is adequately prepared to counter the unique threats and strengths posed by the enemy's forces, positioning the king's forces for successful engagement and defense.
- [Thus ends Chapter II, "The Time of Recruiting the Army, the Form of Equipment, and the Work of Arraying a Rival Force," in Book IX, "The Work of an Invader," of the Arthasástra of Kautilya. End of the hundred and twenty-third chapter from the beginning.]

CHAPTER III. CONSIDERATION OF ANNOYANCE IN THE REAR; AND REMEDIES AGAINST INTERNAL AND EXTERNAL TROUBLES.

Of the two issues—having a minor disturbance in the rear and achieving a significant gain at the front—a minor disturbance in the rear is actually more concerning. This is because any small annoyance at the back can quickly be magnified by traitors, enemies, and hostile tribes, who may exploit it. Meanwhile, members within one's own state may become unsettled by the pursuit of large-scale profit at the front.

If a ruler finds himself in this situation while under the protection of another, he should aim to weaken the influence and resources of the enemy in the rear. To secure the gains at the front, it may be prudent to send either the commander of the army or the heir-apparent to lead the forces. Alternatively, if the ruler himself is confident in his ability to keep the rear secure, he may choose to personally go forward to receive the gain.

Should the ruler fear internal unrest while advancing, it may be wise to bring along any leaders whose loyalty is in question. If the threat lies externally, he should prepare by keeping the families—sons and wives—of suspected traitors within the capital as a precaution. Further, he could split the forces under the officer managing the border territories into smaller units, each led by separate chiefs. If the risk of rebellion is high, it may even be necessary to cancel the march altogether, as internal turmoil is often more perilous than external threats.

The emergence of disloyalty from critical figures like a minister, priest, commander-in-chief, or heir-apparent is regarded as a serious internal issue. Such enemies within should be dealt with—either by resolving the ruler's own faults that may have provoked them or by exposing the risk posed by an external threat. If the priest is gravely treacherous, solutions may include confinement or banishment. If the heir-apparent is guilty, confinement or, if necessary, capital punishment could be considered—particularly if there is another son who can succeed him. Similar measures would apply to cases involving a minister or commander-in-chief.

In situations where a son, brother, or other royal family member attempts to seize control, they may be placated by offering them incentives. If this approach fails, alternative conciliatory measures include allowing them to retain their current holdings, brokering a formal agreement, or creating intrigue through an enemy. Providing them with land acquired from an enemy or involving other hostile figures may also help resolve the issue. Another option is to send them on a mission that aligns them with unfriendly forces, which may result in a fitting outcome. Additionally, enlisting the help of a frontier king or hostile tribe to manage the situation can be effective, as can employing strategies typically used in liberating an imprisoned prince or capturing enemy villages.

Finally, discontent among lower-ranking ministers represents internal ministerial unrest. Even in such cases, appropriate strategic measures should be adopted to prevent or address these challenges effectively.

Provoking unrest among external officials, such as a district chief, the officer in charge of borders, the head of wild tribes, or a recently conquered king, is referred to as external trouble. To manage this, it is strategic to set these figures against one another. If one of them is particularly fortified, he may be neutralized through the intervention of a neighboring king, a tribal chief, a relative, or an imprisoned prince. Alternatively, a friendly ally can be enlisted to prevent this individual from aligning with an enemy. A spy might also discourage the figure from such alliances by presenting a warning: "This enemy manipulates you, merely using you to turn against your own lord. When you've served his purpose, he'll send you to fight others or place you in an inhospitable location, far from your loved ones. Weakened, you'll be cast aside, perhaps even sold back to your lord, or perhaps he'll abandon you entirely after making peace with your own ruler. The wisest course is to join forces with your own lord's most reliable ally."

If he consents to this reasoning, he should be welcomed and rewarded. Should he decline, the spy might then say, "I am here specifically to ensure you don't become an enemy agent." Failing that, covert action may be necessary: the spy could arrange for his assassination through hidden agents or by embedding supposed loyalists around him, who are quietly tasked with eliminating him. This brings external troubles to an end, while encouraging similar disruptions within the enemy's own ranks.

In situations where an individual possesses the influence to either cause or alleviate disturbances, intrigue may be employed to sway them. However, with those who demonstrate reliability, are capable of effective action, and show a proven loyalty to their allies in times of success or adversity, counter-intrigue (pratijápa) may be used to ensure their allegiance. In assessing loyalty, it's crucial to consider whether someone has a cooperative or stubborn temperament.

When a stubborn-minded foreigner begins to sow intrigue among local figures, it often takes the following form: "If he kills his own master and joins me, I gain twice: my enemy's defeat and his land's acquisition. Or, should my enemy kill him, I stand to benefit as well. Those associated with the deceased and others implicated might then, fearing the same fate, disrupt my enemy's peace, especially as he finds himself isolated. Or, if my enemy's suspicions shift to any other compromised individual, I can leverage this to incite internal strife, ultimately targeting and weakening those under his command."

When a local person with a stubborn nature engages in intrigue with a foreign ally, it generally follows this pattern: "I will either loot this king's treasury or dismantle his army. I'll arrange for my master's assassination by using this foreigner's resources. If my master agrees, I'll encourage him to march against an external enemy or a nearby wild tribe, bringing confusion to his Circle of States and stirring up animosity among his neighboring rulers. This will make it easier to dominate and manipulate him—or perhaps I'll even take control of the kingdom myself. Once I have him in chains, I'll claim both his land and any nearby territories. Alternatively, I'll provoke his enemy to march, then arrange for the enemy's assassination under the guise of goodwill, or take over the enemy's capital while it's left unguarded."

When someone with a cooperative nature initiates a plot with the intent of mutual gain, it's wise to form an agreement with him. However, if a person with a stubborn disposition devises such a plan, he should be allowed to proceed on his course and then deceived when the opportunity arises. Thus, each approach should be carefully weighed and chosen accordingly.

- Enemies within one's own enemy's ranks, subjects from among subjects, subjects who may be influenced by enemies, and enemies who have access to subjects—all should be vigilantly monitored. A wise ruler or advisor should always guard against threats, securing both his own person and his interests from dangers posed by both his subjects and his adversaries.

[Thus ends Chapter III, "Consideration of Annoyance in the Rear, and Remedies Against Internal and External Troubles," in Book IX, "The Work of an Invader," of the Arthasástra of Kautilya. End of the hundred and twenty-fourth chapter from the beginning.]

CHAPTER IV. CONSIDERATION ABOUT LOSS OF MEN, WEALTH, AND PROFIT.

A reduction in skilled and loyal soldiers is what is referred to as kshaya, or loss of men, a state that can weaken the operational strength of a kingdom. Similarly, when there is a significant decrease in both gold and grain supplies, it is known as a loss of wealth, which undermines the economic stability and resources available for governance and defense. When the anticipated gain from an undertaking is expected to outweigh these potential losses, only then should a ruler consider advancing against an enemy.

Certain qualities define an anticipated gain. Ideally, it should be both attainable and secure, possibly requiring repayment but with minimal risk, widely acceptable or even favorable to the people, able to withstand the criticisms of opponents, obtainable within a manageable time frame, achievable with minimal loss of life, requiring only modest financial expenditures, large in scale, productive over time, harmless to the people and realm, just and fair in nature, and accessible without excessive delay.

A gain that can be achieved easily and kept securely without the necessity of returning it to others is known as "receivable." On the other hand, a gain that must later be repaid or relinquished to another is termed "repayable," a situation that can be precarious and often leads to misfortune. However, if the ruler considers that by taking on a repayable profit he will diminish his enemy's treasury, drain their army, or weaken their critical resources; or if he sees that the acquisition will exploit his enemy's mines, forests, irrigation systems, and trade routes; or if he anticipates the enemy's people will suffer or begin to migrate, possibly leading to internal rebellion, he may feel justified in moving forward. The condition becomes even more favorable if he can set one of his enemy's allies or other rivals against them, or cause the enemy to flee to a distant ally for protection. Additionally, the ruler may reason that by temporarily managing the enemy's lands and returning them improved, he may ultimately gain a devoted ally. With such reasoning, even a repayable gain may be wisely pursued. In this way, both receivable and repayable profits are considered, each carrying its respective benefits and risks.

A profit acquired from a corrupt ruler by a virtuous king tends to please the king's own people and is often seen favorably by others; but a gain obtained through opposite circumstances, particularly by betraying allies or abandoning virtues, tends to provoke resentment or anger. Profits taken on the advice of ministers who are self-serving or treacherous may also create dissatisfaction among loyal subjects, who may say, "This ruler has damaged our interests and drained our resources." Similarly, a gain acquired without regard for the counsel of honest ministers may lead them to complain, "The king grows wealthy while harming his own supporters." Conversely, a profit acquired through judicious actions that consider both allies and ministers will tend to be pleasing to all, reflecting wise governance and good judgment. In this manner, it is essential to discern between favorable and provoking gains.

A gain obtained by simply mobilizing and marching the army directly to the objective is considered a quick gain, as it does not require lengthy planning or delay. A gain achieved through strategic negotiation and careful planning incurs minimal loss of life and maintains the strength of the army. Likewise, a gain that primarily requires only the expenditure for essential provisions, without depleting the treasury, involves minimal financial risk. A gain that is immediately substantial and clearly beneficial to the kingdom is known as vast.

In making these evaluations, a ruler must carefully assess each type of gain's merits, considering that each advantage should ideally That which provides a stable source of income or assets is considered productive, as it generates wealth and resources continuously. When an undertaking can be achieved without any accompanying issues or risks, it is viewed as harmless, as it does not disrupt the lives or well-being of the people. Any gain acquired through fair and rightful means, without unjust actions or deception, is just. A gain obtained smoothly, without causing friction or obstruction from allies, is regarded as a primary or first profit, as it paves the way for future cooperation and mutual benefit.

When profits from two opportunities seem comparable, a wise ruler should evaluate various factors before deciding. He should weigh the suitability of the location, the season or timing of the action, the required strength, and available means. He must also consider the impact on relations—whether it will strengthen loyalty or provoke discontent—and the level of intrigue or stability involved. Furthermore, he should assess the proximity or remoteness of the profit, its immediate and long-term effects, whether it is of consistent value or likely to fluctuate, its abundance, and its practical utility. After thoroughly examining these elements, he should proceed only with the profit that embodies the most advantageous qualities.

Certain obstructions, however, can hinder the path to profit and must be managed. These include impulsive passion, rash anger, excessive timidity, unwarranted mercy, self-consciousness, or disregard for the traditional values of nobility. Arrogance, misplaced pity, excessive spiritual pursuits, rigid commitment to virtuous behavior, deception, poverty, jealousy, and disregard for immediate gains can also obstruct profit. Additional obstacles include unnecessary generosity, lack of confidence, fear, low tolerance for hardship, and over-reliance on auspicious signs, such as lunar phases and astrological predictions.

- One must realize that wealth eludes those who rely too heavily on omens and stars. In reality, wealth itself is the star that guides other wealth. What power do stars hold over one's prosperity? Those who are skilled and persistent in their efforts will surely amass wealth, even if it requires countless attempts.
- Wealth attracts wealth, just as elephants are subdued and controlled by counter-elephants. In this way, steadfastness and practical action are the true guides to prosperity.

[Thus ends Chapter IV, "Consideration about Loss of Men, Wealth and Profit,' in Book IX, "The Work of an Invader," of the Arthasástra of Kautilya. End of the hundred and twenty-fifth chapter from the beginning.]

CHAPTER V. EXTERNAL AND INTERNAL DANGERS.

When a treaty or settlement is formed improperly, outside the best interest of the state, it leads to weak policies that open doors to various dangers. The types of dangers include: those that originate externally but are supported internally; those that start internally and find external support; those with both origins and backing from external sources; and those that are wholly internal.

When foreign agents conspire with local men, or locals plot with foreigners, the outcome of such combined scheming becomes particularly dangerous. Generally, those who support a scheme have greater leverage than its originators. If the primary instigators are quashed, others will be discouraged from undertaking new plots. Foreigners usually struggle to gain the allegiance of locals through intrigue, just as locals find it difficult to sway foreigners. Foreign efforts typically fail and often end up inadvertently bolstering the king's position.

To handle internal abettors supporting foreign schemes, the king should use conciliation and gifts. Conciliation involves satisfying a person of influence through respect and honor. Gifts might include lowering taxes or offering key roles in the administration.

When foreign entities support internal conspiracies, the king should counter with strategies of division and force. For instance, spies disguised as friends can warn foreign agents that, "This person intends to deceive you through his own spies, who appear as insiders." Spies masquerading as traitors can also join conspiracies to drive a wedge between foreign agents and local traitors. Specialized spies, known as fiery spies, could gain the trust of traitors and then eliminate them using weapons or poison, or even lure foreign agents to gatherings where they can be eliminated.

When foreigners plot with other foreigners or locals with other locals, the unified intent behind such plans poses a grave threat. If wrongdoing is fully eliminated, there will be no guilty parties left to spread discontent; however, if only one guilty individual is removed, their guilt may spread to others. Therefore, if foreign agents carry out a conspiracy, the king should deploy both division and force. Spies posing as friends may tell the foreign conspirators, "Your leader, eager to enrich himself, is bound to turn against you all." Fiery spies might infiltrate the ranks of the foreign conspirators' supporters, striking them down with weapons or poison. Other spies can then reveal or betray the plot's abettor, ensuring the conspiracy collapses.

This strategic approach helps protect the king's state against both foreign and internal dangers that arise from poorly considered alliances and treaties.

When local individuals conspire with others within their own ranks, the king should apply the appropriate strategic methods to suppress the plot. Conciliation should be employed toward those who outwardly appear content or who are either naturally discontented or have shown signs of dissent. Gifts may be extended under the guise of expressing satisfaction with a loyal individual's consistent character or concern for their well-being. A spy, posing as a close ally, could advise the locals, "The king is seeking to understand your true feelings, so be honest with him." Alternatively, conspirators can be turned against one another by insinuating, "This person has been reporting your actions to the king." For conspiracies that persist, more forceful methods may be deployed, following guidelines established in the chapter on "Punishments."

Of the four identified types of dangers, internal threats should be addressed first. It has already been noted that internal dangers, like the stealthy menace of a hidden snake, are generally more severe than external ones.

- One should recognize that within these four types of dangers, those named first tend to be less serious than those mentioned later, especially when influential figures are involved in the threat. If, however, the danger stems from minor players, simpler methods of resolution may be sufficient to eliminate it.

[Thus ends Chapter V, "External and Internal Dangers" in Book IX, "The Work of an Invader," of the Arthaśāstra of Kautilya. End of the hundred and twenty-sixth chapter from the beginning.]

CHAPTER VI. PERSONS ASSOCIATED WITH TRAITORS AND ENEMIES

There are two categories of individuals who can be considered innocent in relation to conspiracies or conflicts: those who have actively chosen to distance themselves from traitors within the kingdom and those who have intentionally stayed away from any affiliation with external enemies. Recognizing the value of maintaining unity among his people, the king should carefully employ a variety of strategic methods to separate loyal citizens and country folk from traitors. In doing so, he should avoid using force whenever possible, as it is extremely difficult to impose harsh punishments on a group of influential individuals without potentially stirring greater discontent or undesirable consequences. However, when a leader or prominent figure of a rebellious group poses a risk to the unity and safety of the kingdom, the king can take measures against them, as indicated in the guidelines on "Punishments."

To ensure that his people remain uninfluenced by external enemies, the king should rely on strategic methods such as conciliation, persuasion, or careful countermeasures to undermine any attempts by the enemy's principal agents, who may be working to create alliances or gain support within the kingdom. The king's ability to secure and effectively utilize competent agents for such delicate operations largely depends on his skills, but it is equally reliant on the wisdom and support of his ministers, who play a vital role in ensuring these efforts reach the desired outcome. Thus, the success achieved through trusted and capable agents is a collaborative effort between the king and his ministers, and this combined approach provides the stability needed to counter the effects of any conspiracy or faction.

When a victory is achieved despite the presence of both traitors and loyal subjects within the ranks, this is known as "mixed success." In situations where loyalty and disloyalty are blended, success is best pursued by relying on those who are confirmed to be loyal, as it is impossible to accomplish lasting victory with unreliable support.

Success, when entangled with the involvement of both allies and enemies, is described as "success contaminated by an enemy." When this occurs, it should be managed with the assistance of trusted allies, as it is far easier to secure a positive outcome with a dependable ally than with an enemy who might have ulterior motives or hidden agendas.

When a friend or ally appears hesitant or uncooperative, intrigue should be deployed to win them over, preferably through repeated strategic influence. Spies can play a crucial role here, as they can subtly work to draw the reluctant ally away from the enemy's influence, gradually encouraging alignment with the king. If the king's allies form a combined alliance, it can also be advantageous to approach the least influential ally first, as this may lead to a fracturing of the group, causing allies in middle or leading positions to reconsider their alignment. Another approach is to focus on winning over a key middle-ranked ally within the alliance; securing a central position ally often weakens the unity of those on either extreme, making it challenging for them to maintain cohesion. In essence, the king should employ any methods that can foster division within the allied ranks of his opponents.

To win the favor of a virtuous king, he may be swayed by appeals to noble qualities, such as acknowledging his high birth, family legacy, learning, and reputation for integrity. Emphasizing the history of relationships his ancestors held with those now seeking his alliance, or reminding him of previous benefits received and the absence of hostility shown toward him, can further secure his cooperation.

Or a king who harbors good intentions, one whose enthusiasm and spirit have waned, or who has exhausted his strategic resources after numerous conflicts, or who has suffered significant losses in men and wealth, or has endured the hardships of traveling far from his kingdom, or who sincerely seeks a dependable friend, or is concerned about potential threats from another, or values friendship above all else—such a king may be brought to form an alliance through conciliation.

In the case of a king driven by greed or weakened by losses in his army, he may be persuaded with carefully chosen gifts delivered through trusted intermediaries, such as ascetics or chiefs, who have been positioned with him for this purpose. Gifts used in this context fall into five categories: the remission of obligations due for payment, continuation of an existing provision, repayment of previously received items, offerings from one's own treasury, and support in carrying out a voluntary raid on another's assets.

If two kings both fear potential hostilities and territorial encroachment from each other, seeds of discord can be effectively planted between them. The more fearful of the two might be threatened with destruction and convinced by statements like, "This other king, while feigning peace with you, is plotting against you; and he has even granted his ally permission to openly pursue peace with your enemies."

Should merchandise or key goods be on their way from either the conqueror's own land or another allied land into an enemy's territory, spies may spread rumors that these supplies are sourced from a person whom the enemy had intended to attack. When such commodities have accumulated in large quantities, a message might be sent to the enemy, saying: "These goods and trade items are being offered by me to you; if you declare war against the coalition of kings or withdraw from their alliance, you will receive the remaining tribute." Spies can then relay to other members of the coalition, "These goods have been offered by your enemy as support for this other king."

To create further discord, the conqueror might obtain unique merchandise specific to his enemy's land, items that are rarely seen or unknown outside of that region. Spies, posing as merchants, could then sell these unique goods to other significant enemies, hinting that this merchandise was a direct gift to the conqueror from the enemy whose land originally produced it.

Or, by providing wealth and honors to those known to be particularly treacherous among the enemy's people, the conqueror can arrange for these individuals to remain close to the enemy, armed with weapons, poison, or fire. One of the enemy's ministers could be eliminated, and the minister's family—his sons and wife—might be influenced to claim that he was murdered at night by a specific person. The enemy's own ministers could then interrogate each family member of the deceased minister to determine the cause of death. If they provide the agreed-upon response, they may be released; otherwise, they would be detained for further questioning. A trusted advisor to the enemy might then privately suggest to the enemy king that he should be wary of another minister who may be plotting against him. An agent, receiving payment from both the conqueror and enemy states, could then secretly encourage the suspicious minister to eliminate the king himself.

Alternatively, enthusiastic and powerful rulers may be subtly encouraged by the conqueror to seize territory from a rival king while keeping their peace treaty intact. Spies could then alert the targeted king to the impending attacks, causing him to retaliate and weaken the invading force's provisions and followers. Meanwhile, additional spies, pretending to be allies, could convince these attacking kings that it's essential to destroy the targeted king entirely.

If an enemy's courageous soldier, prized elephant, or renowned horse dies or is secretly killed or stolen by spies, others could then spread the rumor within the enemy's ranks that this loss resulted from infighting among the enemy's own followers. The person responsible for these covert eliminations might be encouraged to repeat the task, promised payment of any remaining compensation. The payment would come from a dual-state agent, further sowing division within the enemy's ranks and even convincing some members to defect to the conqueror's side.

This tactic also applies to the enemy's commander-in-chief, prince, or military officers, using similar methods to incite internal divisions and mistrust. Furthermore, the conqueror can use this approach to foster distrust among allied states, strategically planting seeds of discord that weaken their cooperation.

Undercover spies might also take direct action against a fortified enemy of low character or one already beset by challenges, executing the target without needing additional support. If any of the concealed spies find an opportune moment, they could act alone, using weapons, poison, or fire to eliminate the target. A fiery spy, who excels in direct action, can often accomplish independently what would otherwise require a full team and resources.

These actions reflect the four strategic forms of diplomacy: conciliation, gift, dissension, and conciliatory coercion. Conciliation, the most straightforward, is a singular strategy. Gifts, which usually follow conciliation, involve two elements. Dissension adds a third layer, as it follows both conciliation and gifts. Conciliatory coercion is the most complex, involving all four elements in a sequence.

These strategies also apply to dealing with internal or local adversaries, with a slight variation. Chief messengers familiar with regional operations could be dispatched to one of these local enemies, either to negotiate a treaty or to instigate the elimination of a specific figure. Upon receiving a positive response, the messengers could inform their master of the progress, and dual-state agents might secretly inform the target's people or other adversaries, saying, "This individual is, in truth, a dangerous ruler."

When one individual fears or dislikes another, spies can heighten this tension by telling one of them, "This person is secretly negotiating with your enemy and may soon betray you; you should secure peace with the king immediately and focus on removing this threat." Spies might also arrange alliances or marriages with individuals who have previously had no affiliation, thus creating new loyalties and separating them from former allies. Through the influence of a neighboring king, a wild tribe leader, a member of an enemy's family, or an imprisoned prince, spies may work to eliminate enemies situated just outside the kingdom.

Spies may also utilize caravans or wild tribes to ambush and kill a local enemy along with his forces. Alternatively, those pretending to support a local adversary and belonging to the same caste can wait for an opportune moment to assassinate him. Hidden spies might also eliminate local threats through fire, poison, or weapons.

- When a country is overrun with local enemies, they can be subdued by having them consume poisoned drinks. A particularly shrewd and stubborn enemy may be dealt with through the use of spies or by offering him food, such as meat, that has been covertly poisoned and given under the guise of goodwill.

[Thus ends Chapter VI, "Persons Associated with Traitors and Enemies," in Book IX, "The Work of an Invader," of the Arthasástra of Kautilya. End of the hundred and twenty-seventh chapter from the beginning,]

CHAPTER VII. DOUBTS ABOUT WEALTH AND HARM; AND SUCCESS TO BE OBTAINED BY THE EMPLOYMENT OF ALTERNATIVE STRATEGIC MEANS.

The intense desires and unchecked passions of a ruler or leader can provoke discontent and disloyalty among their own people, while poor strategies and unwise decisions can ignite hostility from external enemies. These tendencies are seen as the hallmarks of a life driven by reckless or demoniac influences. Anger, in particular, creates discord within the ranks and stirs up frustration, which can lead to a chain of internal issues. Certain types of wealth and resources can also inadvertently empower adversaries if managed poorly. These forms of wealth—dangerous wealth, provocative wealth, and wealth of uncertain outcomes—pose a risk not only to stability but also to overall strength and security.

Dangerous wealth refers to resources or gains that may ultimately fortify an enemy's position or create dependencies that weaken one's own standing. This type of wealth might include assets shared with neighboring kings that could later serve their purposes more than one's own, wealth obtained but repayable to an enemy, or resources that might lead to financial or personnel losses. Examples of dangerous wealth are resources seized like personal property, or profits made at the expense of prior alliances, which might cause the wider Circle of States to view such actions unfavorably. Furthermore, if wealth in the front lines creates vulnerabilities in the rear or if it comes from betraying allies, such acquisitions are dangerous because they invite resentment, potentially from both enemies and former allies alike.

Provocative wealth refers to assets that, when acquired, lead to fear or resentment, either from one's own people or from external forces. Provocative wealth may trigger anger, jealousy, or fear, even within the heart of one's own state, or it may stoke the envy or ambitions of other kings. When contemplating whether a particular form of wealth is provocative or benign, it's crucial to weigh the possibility of it being misinterpreted or feared by others. Questions may arise, such as, "Will acquiring this wealth provoke an adversary or threaten peace? Will this wealth be first provocative, but later harmless? Will providing this wealth as support to an enemy's troops foster ill will among allies?" Such uncertainties reveal that it's often better to question whether acquiring the wealth is wise rather than to accept it and risk potential conflicts or harm.

There are also six varieties of wealth that may ultimately prove harmful: wealth that generates more wealth, wealth that yields no returns, wealth that results in harm, harm that leads to wealth, harm that has no productive outcome, and harm that only worsens over time.

"Wealth that generates more wealth" can refer to situations where neutralizing an enemy in the front eventually allows for a decisive advantage over an adversary at one's rear. This type of wealth builds upon itself by ensuring further stability and security. "Wealth that yields no returns," however, may arise when offering military assistance to a neutral king without any strategic gain in return. In this case, the investment is unreciprocated and produces no tangible benefit, leaving resources and effort expended without reward.

"Wealth that results in harm" may include tactics that undermine an enemy's internal unity, leading to immediate gains but sowing seeds for potential backlash or retaliation. "Harm that leads to wealth" involves offering support, like men or money, to a neighboring adversary of one's primary enemy, as this kind of harm may reduce the enemy's influence and provide indirect gains.

Withdrawing after encouraging a weaker king with limited resources to act against another is termed as "harm that yields no benefit." This type of harm doesn't result in any favorable outcome or profit, as the efforts exerted don't contribute towards one's own advantage. Similarly, if a weaker party provokes a stronger king and then remains inactive, this can lead to further detrimental effects, a scenario known as "harm that yields only more harm." Among these situations, it is better to pursue the first option listed—indirect harm without benefit—than to face the risk of further detrimental consequences. This approach exemplifies a strategic procedure to follow when setting plans in motion.

If the conditions surrounding one's efforts are highly favorable for gaining wealth, it is known as a situation where "wealth flows from all directions." However, if an enemy in the rear obstructs the acquisition of wealth from various directions, the situation shifts, becoming dangerous wealth that is fraught with uncertainties. In either of these cases, success can still be achieved by leveraging support from a friend or an enemy of the rear adversary, thus securing a means to proceed forward.

In cases where fear of surrounding enemies looms from all directions, it can be considered a critical threat, or "dangerous trouble." If, however, a friend steps in to assist in managing this looming threat, the situation may still hold uncertainties, but the danger becomes more manageable. Success in these cases can be pursued by rallying support from a nomadic force or from an enemy who stands opposed to the rear-enemy, thereby diffusing some of the immediate tension from all sides.

When profitable wealth becomes impossible to secure due to formidable blockages posed by enemies, it is termed "dangerous wealth." Whether in such a case of obstruction or when there are favorable conditions for wealth from all directions, one should consider advancing to gain wealth with potential. If there are equal prospects from two sources, the leader should target the wealth source that is both vital, conveniently close, reliable, and obtainable with the least resistance or cost.

When the threat of harm exists from two separate quarters, it is known as wealth endangered by dual opposition. Similar to situations where wealth is endangered from all sides, success is most likely if a network of allies can be engaged. In the absence of friendly support, the leader should attempt to reduce the threat from one side by securing an alliance with a power that can be easily swayed. For dangers coming from two quarters, an alliance with a power of greater strength is advised; and if danger arises on all fronts, all available resources should be deployed to counteract it.

In circumstances where warding off these threats proves impossible, retreat may be the wisest course, abandoning possessions to preserve life. Survival enables a potential return to power at a later stage, as exemplified in the historic cases of Suyátra and Udayana, who regained strength and reestablished power through resilience and timing.

When there's a chance of gaining wealth from one direction and the risk of an attack from another, this is known as a scenario filled with both opportunity and threat. In this case, the leader should advance towards the potential wealth if it will empower him to counter the attack. If this is not feasible, his focus should be on preventing the anticipated attack. This also applies when wealth and threat loom from multiple sides.

If there's a looming threat from one side, while potential wealth from another side is uncertain, this is a situation of doubt involving both wealth and danger from two fronts. Here, it is wise to address the threat first; once this is managed, efforts can shift towards acquiring the uncertain wealth. This approach also applies when similar doubts arise about wealth and harm from multiple directions.

When there is wealth expected from one quarter, but potential harm is uncertain from another, it's known as a scenario involving both wealth and ambiguous harm from two sides. In this case, he should carefully try to neutralize any possible threats against each part of his kingdom in order of importance. It is often better to risk a friend under uncertain threats rather than jeopardize the army; similarly, the army can be sacrificed under uncertain conditions rather than risking the treasury. If all elements of sovereignty cannot be fully protected from harm, he should at least prioritize securing some.

Among these elements, first safeguard those human elements that are most loyal and free from dissenters or opportunistic individuals. For non-human resources, focus on preserving those assets that are highly valuable and essential. Any elements that can be easily secured should be protected through simpler means such as peace agreements, maintaining neutrality, or forming strategic alliances with one side while keeping other adversaries at bay. Resources or elements requiring more effort may call for additional strategies.

Of the three stages—deterioration, stagnation, and progress—focus should be on securing progress first. If, however, the current environment indicates that a stage of deterioration or stagnation may lead to greater long-term gains, reverse this order. This approach can also apply to potential harm and gains, both midway or towards the end of a campaign.

Given that doubts around profit and risk are always present in any campaign, it is wiser to secure wealth that aids in weakening an enemy from the rear, discourages the enemy's allies, replenishes losses of men and resources, funds extended operations abroad, manages obligations, and safeguards the kingdom. Further, any doubts about security or economic prospects within one's own territory should never be tolerated, as they undermine stability directly within the homeland.

This explains the situation of potential harm during the midst of an expedition. However, towards the end of a campaign, it's preferable to gain wealth by either subduing or completely overcoming a weaker or vulnerable enemy rather than finding oneself in a situation of uncertain risk. This is because unresolved threats might allow enemies to create significant disruptions. However, for someone who is not leading a coalition of states, it may be more acceptable to endure uncertain wealth or risk at either the midpoint or the conclusion of an expedition, as they are not bound to carry on with the campaign to the same extent.

In strategic terms, wealth, virtue, and pleasure form a grouping of three kinds of benefits. Among these, the focus should always be on securing the first in the list, as each subsequent element in the order relies on the stability of the former.

In contrast, harm, sin, and sorrow represent the triad of harmful consequences. When addressing these, priority should be given to tackling the first type listed before considering the others, as this sequence best preserves order and minimizes disruption.

Thus, decisions on wealth or harm, virtue or sin, and pleasure or sorrow involve considering three types of uncertainties. When choosing among these, it's wise to prioritize the first option in the list, ensuring that, where feasible, these initial choices support successful outcomes. In this way, the assessment of strategic opportunities comes to completion, marking the end of the discourse on dangers.

As for addressing risks in dangerous situations and times, specific approaches are suggested depending on the source of troubles. In cases where issues arise from sons, brothers, or other family members, the best approach is through conciliation and offering gifts. When dealing with unrest from citizens, local populace, or military chiefs, the most effective methods are distributing gifts and fostering internal divisions. And in situations involving conflicts with neighboring kings or hostile tribes, planting seeds of discord and exerting coercion tend to yield the best results. This hierarchy of methods follows a set order of actions. In other situations, these methods might be used in the opposite sequence.

The complexity of overcoming adversaries and friends alike often demands multiple strategic approaches, as each method complements the others. For suspected ministers within an enemy's ranks, conciliation may suffice without additional measures. Treacherous ministers require gifts; alliances among states call for sowing dissension; and powerful figures must be countered through direct coercion.

When faced with a mix of severe and mild threats, the strategic approach can involve a specific single measure, an alternative among measures, or a combination of methods.

- "By this alone and no other" refers to applying a single, targeted method.
- "By this or that" implies selecting an alternative approach.
- "By this as well as by that" indicates employing multiple strategies together.

In total, these options form 15 distinct types of strategic combinations: four single methods, six pairwise combinations, four combinations of any three methods, and one involving all four methods. Reversing these combinations offers the same number of strategic approaches.

A king achieving success through only one of these methods is known as one of "single success"; using two, he is known as one of "double success"; with three, he attains "treble success"; and with four, he is one of "fourfold success."

Virtue serves as the foundation for wealth, while enjoyment stands as wealth's ultimate purpose. Achieving wealth that fulfills virtue, prosperity, and enjoyment is known as "universal success" (sarvárthasiddhi). These are the various forms of success.

Providential afflictions such as fire, floods, illness, widespread disease (pramara), fever (vidrava), famine, and supernatural disturbances are considered significant threats. Success in preventing these disasters involves performing worship to the gods and honoring Bráhmans.

• Whether supernatural disturbances are nonexistent, abundant, or in normal quantities, the prescribed rites from the Atharvaveda, along with those conducted by skilled ascetics, should be observed for securing success.

Book 10

CHAPTER I. ENCAMPMENT.

On a site deemed most suitable according to architectural science, the leader (náyaka), carpenter (vardhaki), and astrologer (mauhúrtika) should outline a circular, rectangular, or square area for the camp. This camp should ideally have four gates, six roads, and nine sections, aligned according to the available space. For added security, the camp should include ditches, parapets, walls, doors, and watchtowers, all aimed at guarding against potential threats.

The king's quarters should occupy one of the nine divisions, ideally positioned toward the north from the camp's center and spanning a length of 1,000 bows and a width of half that. To the west of this lies the harem, with the harem's own security forces stationed at its edge. Directly before the king's quarters is a space dedicated to worshipping the gods; to the right is where the finance and accounting offices should be placed; and to the left, stables for the elephants and horses used by the king. A perimeter, set 100 bows away from the center, should feature four prominent pillars (sakatamedhi) along with walls.

In the first of the four divisions within this perimeter, accommodations should be arranged for the prime minister and the chief priest. To the right of this, provisions for storage and kitchens are required, while to the left, supplies for raw materials and weaponry should be stored. The second division is designated for the king's hereditary forces, as well as cavalry and chariots. Outside this perimeter, hunters and dog keepers should be stationed with trumpets and controlled fire, alongside spies and sentinels. Additionally, wells, raised mounds, and thorn barriers should be strategically placed to safeguard against enemy attacks.

Eighteen teams of rotating sentinels are responsible for the king's safety, each taking shifts in turn. To monitor the movements of spies, a daily schedule of activities should be maintained. Further regulations include prohibitions on disputes, drinking, social gatherings, and gambling within the camp, with a passport system in place for identification. The boundary officer (in charge of camp borders) should oversee the behavior of the commander-in-chief and ensure that all military protocols are closely followed.

The instructor (prasástá), with his own attendants as well as carpenters and laborers, should travel ahead along the chosen route, preparing the road by digging wells for water to ensure readiness.

Chapter II: The March of the Camp and Protection of the Army During Hardships and Attacks

With a detailed list of villages and forests along the march route, noting each location's capacity to supply grass, firewood, and water, the pace of the army's march should be adjusted according to scheduled short and extended halts. Provisions for food and other necessities must be carried in amounts double that which might be required in an emergency. Should there be no separate means to transport provisions, the army itself should carry these supplies, or they may be stockpiled at a central depot.

The army's formation during the march should follow a specific order: the leader (náyaka) at the forefront, the harem and the king positioned centrally, bodyguards (báhútsára) stationed on the flanks, and at the outer edges, elephants and additional troops. The troops accustomed to forest terrain should flank all sides, ensuring protective coverage. Other sections of the force, including the camp followers, the commissariat, and any allied armies, should independently choose their routes to guarantee tactical advantage. Armies positioned effectively for terrain will have an upper hand over those in poorly suited locations.

The quality of the army determines its daily progress: armies of the lowest quality can advance a single yojana (approximately 5.5 miles), armies of middle quality cover one and a half yojanas, and armies of the highest quality can march up to two yojanas per day. Therefore, the army's pace can be easily determined. The commander should march at the rear and establish his encampment at the forefront of the advancing force.

When encountering an obstacle on the march, the army should adjust its formation according to the terrain and threat level. In situations where the path is clear, the army should arrange itself in a crocodile formation at the front, a cart-like formation at the rear, and a diamond formation along the sides, providing protective layers from all angles. When confined to a narrow path that allows passage for only a single file, the army should adopt a pin-like formation to proceed with minimal risk. When peace has been established with one ally but conflict is expected with another, it is crucial to arrange defenses for allied forces bringing support, especially against potential attacks from a rear enemy, his allies, or other nearby kings who could intervene. Any obstructed paths should be cleared after a thorough inspection to secure a safe route forward. Likewise, a detailed review of financial resources, the army's strength, the power of allied and enemy forces, and wild tribes, along with an assessment of upcoming weather and seasonal conditions, is essential for a well-informed march.

If intelligence suggests that enemy fortifications and supplies are weakening or that unrest is brewing within the enemy's hired troops or allied forces, a cautious, slower approach is warranted. This slower advance may also be appropriate if intrigue and espionage measures require additional time or if there are signs that the enemy might seek negotiations. Conversely, if a swift assault is advantageous, the march should proceed at maximum speed.

Rivers and other bodies of water can be crossed using various methods: elephants, bridges, boats, or makeshift platforms constructed from logs, bamboo clusters, rafts, or even large baskets coated with hides. For a more discreet crossing, the army may also use lightweight items like dried gourds or specialized rafts designed to support the load. Should the enemy obstruct a crossing, the army could consider crossing further upstream or downstream, thus flanking the enemy and setting up an ambush.

The leader should ensure the safety and morale of his forces when they face challenging terrains, such as extended deserts without water or areas lacking sufficient grass, firewood, and water. Provisions should also be made to protect the army when traversing harsh or unfamiliar roads, particularly in mountainous regions marked by muddy ground, waterlogged patches, rivers, and steep hills. The army must also be shielded against enemy harassment when fatigued or weakened by hunger and thirst after a long journey, especially in precarious situations like crowded narrow paths or difficult passages. Protection protocols are equally necessary during halts for rest, meals, or sleep; in times of widespread illness or pestilence; and when soldiers or animals (such as horses and elephants) are weakened or afflicted by disease. Any sign of diminishing strength or morale, whether due to physical hardship or low supplies, requires heightened security and vigilance to keep the army intact and prepared. Furthermore, if the enemy's forces find themselves in any of these distressing situations, they should be swiftly attacked to exploit their vulnerability.

When the enemy's forces are constrained to travel along a single-file route, the invading commander should assess the enemy's true strength by carefully observing the volume of food supplies, grass, bedding, and other essentials they transport, along with tools like fire pots, banners, and weaponry. To maintain strategic advantage, the commander should take steps to conceal his own army's supplies and strength from enemy eyes.

- With a stronghold positioned in a mountainous region or along a river in his own territory, complete with all essential resources, the commander should strategically station his forces or establish his camp. This secure position not only offers natural defenses but also ensures access to necessary provisions and reinforces his ability to defend or advance against the enemy effectively.

[Thus ends Chapter II, "March of the Camp; and Protection of the Army in Times of Distress and Attack" in Book X, "Relating to

War" of the Arthasástra of Kautilya. End of the hundred and thirtieth chapter from the beginning.]

CHAPTER III. FORMS OF TREACHEROUS FIGHTS; ENCOURAGEMENT TO ONE'S OWN ARMY AND FIGHT BETWEEN ONE'S OWN AND ENEMY'S ARMIES.

He who commands a strong, well-prepared army, who has succeeded in strategic planning, and who has effectively addressed potential threats can initiate an open confrontation if he holds a position advantageous to his forces; otherwise, he should consider engaging in a more deceptive, tactical assault.

An opportune moment to strike is when the enemy's forces are weakened by internal troubles or are under heavy attack, or if the commander holds a strong position and can strike the enemy while they are trapped in a less favorable setting. A leader who maintains firm control over his state and resources may exploit the enemy's own internal dissidents, foreign enemies, or hostile groups, creating the illusion of his own defeat to lure the enemy out of their secure position and into vulnerability. When the enemy has regrouped tightly, elephants can be employed to scatter their forces; once the enemy pursues, believing the false retreat, the commander can turn back and strike. After a frontal attack, elephants and cavalry can again target the fleeing enemy as they turn their backs. If an attack at the front is not favorable, a strike from behind is wise, and likewise, if a rear attack is unwise, a frontal or side approach should be considered.

By pitting the enemy against their own traitors, hostile factions, or warring tribes, the commander can then advance with his fresh forces and strike when the enemy is exhausted. Or, the enemy can be tricked into thinking victory is within reach through a feigned defeat involving a traitor's forces, leading to an ambush where the confident enemy can be overpowered by the commander's full-strength army. The vigilant commander may surprise the enemy when they are complacent, misled into thinking that their rival's resources—merchants, camps, and carriers—have been devastated. Or, by disguising his formidable forces to appear weak, he can provoke the enemy's bravest fighters into attacking, setting them up for defeat. Capturing enemy livestock or destroying valued assets may lure these brave forces into an ambush.

If an enemy's men are harassed continuously through the night to deprive them of sleep, they can be struck in the daytime when fatigue and sun exposure sap their strength, while the commander's troops rest in shaded areas. For a night assault, he may equip his elephant troops with flame-retardant cloth and leather armor, ensuring protection while engaging the enemy under cover of darkness. Striking in the late afternoon can exploit the enemy's fatigue from morning preparations, while a direct advance against the whole army as they face the sun capitalizes on their visual disadvantage.

A desert, dangerous terrain, marshes, mountains, valleys, unstable boats, cattle obstacles, formations like a cart, mist, and night all serve as strategic lures (sattras) to draw the enemy into a disadvantageous position against the invader. These natural features and formations act as enticing traps that can mislead or hinder the enemy's movement.

The most opportune moment for launching a treacherous assault is at the very beginning of the enemy's advance. As for an open and honorable engagement, a just king should first assemble his troops, specifying the planned location and time for battle, and address them with words of unity and purpose: "I, like you, serve this land and am bound to its defense; together, we are stewards of this country, its protection our shared duty. The enemy before us is yours to confront under my command."

The king's minister and priest should further inspire the soldiers with words of valor and dedication: "The Vedas declare that those who perform sacrifices, giving their best, and those who serve in bravery reach the same sacred destination. Just as the sacrificers achieve a high state after their final ritual ablutions, so too do the courageous find their reward in valor."

Two verses on this matter go as follows:

- Beyond the realms that Bráhmans, in their pursuit of heaven, reach through dedicated sacrifices and penances lie the places reserved for brave warriors who lose their lives in noble battles. These warriors are destined to attain this honored state without delay, their courage earning them an immediate place beyond the earthly.
- Let the fate of a new vessel filled with consecrated water, covered in darbha grass, be denied to the man who does not stand and fight in return for the sustenance given by his master. Such a person, neglecting his duty, faces not honor but the punishment of descent into the depths of suffering.

Astrologers and other close advisors of the king should inspire confidence in the army by emphasizing the unbreakable formation of their array, the king's alignment with divine powers, and his profound wisdom. At the same time, they should work to instill fear in the enemy. The day before the battle, the king should observe a fast, resting on his chariot with his weapons nearby. He should also make offerings into the sacred fire, reciting Atharvaveda mantras, and arrange for prayers both for the victory of his forces and for those who, by their brave death on the battlefield, will ascend to heaven. The king should submit himself humbly to the blessings of Bráhmans and position the core of his forces with warriors distinguished by bravery, skill, noble birth, and loyalty, and who remain content with the honors and rewards they've received.

The king should be positioned among trusted warriors—his father, sons, brothers, and others skilled with weapons, without distinctive flags or headgear for protection. He may ride an elephant or chariot if the army is primarily mounted, or choose to ride the animal most familiar or expertly trained within his forces. An individual disguised as the king should be assigned the task of overseeing the alignment of the troops.

Soothsayers and court poets should praise heaven as the ultimate destination for the courageous and damnation for the cowardly, extolling the caste, clan, lineage, achievements, and virtues of the soldiers. The priest's attendants should announce the favorable outcomes of any protective spells cast. Spies, builders, and astrologers should report on the positive results of their own strategies while declaring the shortcomings of the enemy's efforts.

After ensuring that the troops are well-motivated with rewards and honors, the commander-in-chief should address the soldiers, proclaiming rewards for valor in battle as follows: one hundred thousand panas for killing the enemy king, fifty thousand for killing the enemy's commander-in-chief or heir-apparent, ten thousand for slaying the chief of the brave, five thousand for taking down an elephant or a chariot, one thousand for killing a horse, a hundred panas for slaying the chief of the infantry, twenty panas for presenting an enemy's head, and double pay plus any loot acquired. This incentive structure should be communicated to each group of ten soldiers to inspire their commitment to victory.

The army's support should be close at hand: physicians equipped with surgical tools, ointments, healing oils, and cloth for treating the wounded, along with women prepared with food and drink to nourish the fighters, all encouraging them with words of support from behind the lines.

The army should be arranged in a strategic formation on favorable terrain, ideally facing away from the south and with the sun at their back, ready to advance. If the terrain is unfavorable, horses should be run to test the ground's stability. An army forced into an unsuitable position and pushed into retreat will be vulnerable, either as it stands or as it retreats. On the other hand, if the army stands firm or advances from a favorable position, it is poised to defeat the enemy, whether standing or moving.

The terrain should be carefully assessed: whether it is flat, uneven, or a mix, and whether this applies to the front, sides, or rear of the formation. On level ground, a staff-like or circular formation is ideal, while uneven terrain calls for formations designed for dense movement or maneuverable, separated units.

If the enemy's army is thoroughly broken, the invader should consider negotiating peace. If the armies are equally matched, peace should be made if requested. However, if the enemy's forces are inferior, they should be decisively defeated—except if they hold a strong position and are willing to fight to the last.

- When an enemy's defeated and scattered army regroups with renewed vigor, showing disregard for their own lives, their rage becomes nearly unstoppable; therefore, it's unwise to provoke or further pressure a broken army that is regaining its momentum.

[Thus ends Chapter III, "Forms of Treacherous Fights; Encouragement to One's Own Army, and Fight Between One's Own and Enemy's Armies," in Book X, "Relating to War," of the Arthasástra of Kautilya. End of the hundred and thirty-first chapter from the beginning.]

CHAPTER IV. BATTLEFIELDS; THE WORK OF INFANTRY, CAVALRY, CHARIOTS, AND ELEPHANTS.

Ideal positions for infantry, cavalry, chariots, and elephants are essential in both battle and camp.

The army's different divisions benefit from terrain suited to their training: soldiers practiced in desert terrains, forests, valleys, or open plains; those trained for fighting from ditches or elevated positions, whether in daytime or at night; elephants accustomed to riverine, mountainous, marshy, or lake regions; and horses familiar with specific terrains should each have a battlefield that aligns with their particular strengths.

The best ground for chariots is one that is even and stable, lacking mounds or pits from previous movement of wheels or animals, free from natural obstructions like trees, shrubs, and roots, and clear of any boggy patches, sandy areas, or thorny clusters.

For elephants, horses, and infantry, either even or slightly uneven grounds are suitable, whether for camp or combat.

For horses, an ideal terrain contains minor stones, trees, and small pits that can be leaped over, with minimal thorns.

For infantry, the terrain is best when it has larger stones, a mix of dry and green trees, and natural features like ant-hills.

Elephants perform best on uneven terrain with hills and valleys that can be assaulted, trees that can be uprooted, and soft, muddy soil free from sharp thorny growths.

For infantry, the ideal terrain is slightly uneven yet spacious and free from thorns.

For horses, the terrain should be doubly expansive, dry, and free of tree roots, mud, or gravel that could harm hooves.

Elephants fare well on terrain with soft mud, water, dust, grass, and low-lying weeds, clear of thorny barriers or overhanging branches from large trees.

Chariots need terrain that includes lakes, open spaces, and areas free from mounds and wetlands, providing room to maneuver and turn.

These conditions outline the ideal grounds for each type of military unit in camp or battle, helping each division perform optimally in its element.

Securing occupied positions in camps and forests; holding onto ropes for safe passage while crossing rivers or enduring strong winds; managing or safeguarding supplies and new troops as they arrive; overseeing military discipline; extending the line of troops; protecting flanks; launching the initial assault; dispersing enemy forces; trampling down any remaining threats; setting up defenses; capturing and releasing positions strategically; guiding the army in new directions; transporting treasury assets and royal family members; striking the rear of the enemy's forces; chasing down fleeing opponents; maintaining pursuit; and regrouping when needed—these tasks define the role of horses in battle.

Elephants, meanwhile, have specific responsibilities, such as leading the front line; preparing roads, camps, and water access points; securing flanks; standing firmly or crossing through water obstacles; performing forced entries into fortified positions; managing fire either to start or extinguish it; overpowering one of the enemy's four military divisions; rallying dispersed soldiers; breaking apart tightly formed enemy ranks; providing protection from threats; trampling over opposing forces; intimidating and scattering them; displaying grandeur and might; seizing or abandoning specific points; breaking down walls, gates, and towers; and carrying the treasury—these are all within the domain of elephants.

For chariots, their tasks include shielding the army; defending against assaults from all four divisions of the enemy; capturing and releasing positions during combat; reassembling scattered troops; disrupting and scattering enemy formations; instilling fear with their presence; showcasing majesty and grandeur; and generating a thunderous, intimidating noise—all essential roles of the chariots in battle.

Infantry tasks include the consistent transport of weapons to all locations on the battlefield and engaging in direct combat.

Lastly, free laborers play a vital role in checking camps, clearing roads, constructing and reinforcing bridges, and ensuring safe passage along wells and rivers. They are also tasked with transporting machinery, weaponry, armor, essential tools, and provisions, as well as retrieving fallen soldiers along with their equipment and armor.

This division of labor across each military component ensures that each unit contributes to the army's success in a coordinated and effective manner.

- A king with limited cavalry can bolster his forces by mixing bulls alongside his horses; similarly, if he lacks sufficient elephants, he can strengthen the center of his army by placing mules, camels, and carts strategically to supplement his forces.

[Thus ends Chapter IV, "Battlefields; the Work of Infantry, Cavalry, Chariots and Elephants," in Book X, "Relating to War," of the Arthasástra of Kautilya. End of the hundred and thirty-second chapter from the beginning.]

CHAPTER V. THE DISTINCTIVE ARRAY OF TROOPS IN RFSPECT OF WINGS, FLANKS, AND FRONT; DISTINCTION BETWEEN STRONG AND WEAK TROOPS; AND BATTLE WITH INFANTRY, CAVALRY, CHARIOTS AND ELEPHANTS.

Once the camp is securely fortified at a distance of five hundred bows from the enemy's reach, the preparations for engaging in battle can begin. This distance provides a defensive buffer, and fortifications are strategically chosen to ensure that both the position and resources are advantageous for the army. The commander-in-chief, alongside the primary leader of the army, should allocate the elite troops to a favorable and discreet location where they remain hidden from the enemy's view, ready to be deployed at a critical moment. Meanwhile, the main bulk of the army should be arranged in a carefully structured formation to ensure both effective offense and defense.

To maintain the flow and organization of troops, there is a specific spatial arrangement for each unit: infantrymen are spaced at intervals of one sama (14 angulas) to allow for coordinated movement without overcrowding; cavalry units are spaced three samas apart to maneuver freely and effectively in support or attack; chariots are spaced four samas apart to allow for greater mobility; and elephants are given the largest space, at two to three times the distance between chariots, due to their size and need for maneuverability. This systematic spacing ensures that each type of unit can perform optimally without interference from others, allowing a unified and dynamic response during battle.

Each bow, the unit of distance used for positioning, measures five aratnis, which total 120 angulas. To organize forces, archers should be stationed five bows apart to maintain range capabilities without crowding; cavalry should be positioned three bows apart, optimizing for swift and versatile responses to enemy advances or retreats; chariots and elephants should each be placed five bows apart, maximizing the stability and impact of these larger units.

The layout of the army includes spacing known as aníkasandhi between the different sections—wings, flanks, and the central front—measuring five bows between each section to create clear pathways. For effective combat ratios, three infantrymen are assigned to counter one enemy cavalry unit. Fifteen soldiers, or alternatively five horses, are allocated to counter each enemy chariot or elephant, allowing for a targeted opposition that optimizes both resources and tactical effectiveness. In addition, each cavalry unit, chariot, or elephant has fifteen attendants (pádagopa) responsible for maintaining them, which includes handling equipment and preparing them for battle.

The standard chariot array includes a carefully organized formation of three groups (aníka), each consisting of three chariots positioned at the front, with identical group formations positioned along the two flanks and two wings of the army. In total, this creates a unified array comprising forty-five chariots, 225 horses, and 675 soldiers, with an equal number of attendants providing necessary support for these units. This formation, known as an even array, offers balanced strength and allows coordinated movements across all fronts. When circumstances permit, additional chariots may be added in groups of two until the number reaches twenty-one, resulting in a diverse set of ten possible arrangements of odd-numbered arrays.

Any surplus forces, which might be referred to as ávápa, are allocated to areas where their strengths can best be utilized. Two-thirds of these additional chariots should be stationed along the flanks and wings to reinforce vulnerable areas, while the remaining third is placed at the front to support offensive maneuvers. The surplus chariots thus strategically balance both offensive and defensive capabilities, enhancing the overall flexibility of the formation.

Specific terms categorize different configurations of force levels within the army. Ávápa, or surplus, refers to the presence of additional forces beyond the basic requirements; pratyávápa denotes a shortfall in infantry that requires immediate reinforcement; anvávápa describes the situation when there is an excess in one type of military constituent, such as an abundance of chariots or horses; and atyávápa is a term used when there is an undesirable surplus, particularly of traitorous or unreliable troops, which could undermine the army's integrity. Based on the available resources and intelligence on the enemy's numbers, a well-prepared leader should aim to increase their forces from four up to even eight times the enemy's surplus forces or any detected shortfall in the enemy's infantry strength. This careful calculation allows the army to maximize its own potential and secure an advantageous position before engaging in battle, ensuring readiness to meet or even exceed the necessary measures for a successful confrontation.

The arrangement of elephants in battle mirrors the setup used for chariots, yet offers its own distinct configurations. An array combining elephants, chariots, and cavalry can be structured with elephants placed at the circular array's endpoints, horses and primary chariots stationed along the flanks for added force and maneuverability. In an arrangement where elephants hold the front, chariots guard the flanks, and cavalry fills the wings, this configuration is particularly effective for breaching the enemy's central forces; conversely, positioning elephants on the flanks, chariots in front, and horses on the wings will prove advantageous for harassing the enemy's extremities. When organizing a formation solely with elephants, the battle-trained elephants should take the lead, riding-trained elephants are set on the flanks, while rogue elephants occupy the wings to create additional unpredictability.

For a cavalry array, armored horses are positioned upfront to face direct confrontation, with unarmored horses securing the flanks and wings, providing both offense and defense. Infantry formations consist of armored soldiers at the front for durability, archers positioned in the rear for ranged support, and unarmored troops on the wings, or alternatively, cavalry on the wings, elephants on the flanks, and chariots in front to bolster attack versatility. Many other strategic adjustments may be made, adapting to effectively counter the specific strengths and weaknesses of the opposing force.

The strongest army combines robust infantry with elephants and horses distinguished for their lineage, strength, youthfulness, vigor, endurance in older age, combat readiness, skill, resilience, noble spirit, obedience, and disciplined behaviors. To optimize the force's arrangement, one-third of the finest infantry, cavalry, and elephants should be placed at the forefront, while two-thirds of the best troops are distributed across both the flanks and wings. A formation ordered by strength—from strongest to weakest—is arranged in direct order; if interspersing strong and weak units in a mix, the order is then reversed. An understanding of all variations of these configurations is crucial for effective battlefield adaptation.

Positioning weaker troops at the army's ends risks exposing them to the enemy's strongest attacks. Instead, stationing elite forces at the forefront, with equally reinforced wings, offers better protection. By arranging one-third of the best units at the rear and the weaker forces within the center, the formation becomes adept at resisting an enemy's assault. When engaged, this setup allows the commander to strike with one or two units stationed at the wings, flanks, and front, while the rest can converge on and capture the enemy from multiple angles.

If the enemy's force is notably weaker, with limited horses and elephants, and if internal intrigues are disrupting their command, the conqueror should capitalize on this vulnerability by attacking with his strongest divisions. Reinforcing any section of the army that appears weak in numbers will ensure an advantage. Troops should be concentrated along the enemy's weakest side or along areas where danger is anticipated.

There are varied tactical approaches to war when fighting with cavalry, such as direct charges, circling around the enemy, bypassing to attack from behind, and retreating to regroup and disrupt the enemy's halt. Additional methods include amassing forces, using curved and circular maneuvers, diversions, removing the rear guard, attacking from the front, flanks, and rear, rescuing broken ranks, and taking down a disrupted enemy formation.

For elephants, warfare strategies include all but miscellaneous maneuvers, with options like breaking up the enemy's four main divisions either in isolation or collectively, dispersing their flanks, wings, and front, trampling their ranks, and catching them off guard while asleep.

Chariots operate similarly but lack certain tactics, such as disturbing halts, direct charges, tactical retreats, and fighting while stationary. The infantry, in contrast, is adaptable to almost any environment and capable of engaging effectively at all times and locations, excelling particularly in surprise assaults.

In summation, the structured diversity in formations and tactical maneuvers across the different types of troops—whether elephants, cavalry, chariots, or infantry—empowers a well-prepared army to adapt dynamically to any battlefield conditions. The appropriate configuration and use of tactics depend on the type of enemy, terrain, and available resources, ensuring that the army is equipped to handle and adapt to every possible scenario.

- He should arrange formations in both odd and even arrays, ensuring that the strength of the four key components— infantry, cavalry, chariots, and elephants—remains balanced across the setup. The king, once he has reached a distance of approximately 200 bows from the enemy line, should secure his position with the reserve forces of his army.
- He must avoid entering battle without a reserve, as this backup force is crucial for rallying and regrouping any scattered troops and maintaining the coherence and strength of the army during the fight.

[Thus ends Chapter V, "The Distinctive Array of Troops in Respect of Wings, Flanks and Front; Distinction between Strong and Weak Troops; and Battle with Infantry, Cavalry, Chariots and Elephants," in Book X, "Relating to War," of the Arthasástra of Kautilya. End of the hundred and thirty-third chapter from the beginning.]

CHAPTER VI. THE ARRAY OF THE ARMY LIKE A STAFF, A SNAKE, A CIRCLE, OR IN DETACHED ORDER; THE ARRAY OF THE ARMY AGAINST THAT OF AN ENEMY.

Wings and front positioned to enable swift turns against the enemy form what is called a snake-like array, or bhoga. According to the teachings of Brihaspati, an array constructed with two wings, two flanks, a front, and a reserve serves as a foundational setup. The main formations—staff-like, snake-like, circle-like, and detached—are varied applications of this basic structure involving wings, flanks, and front.

When the army is aligned to face forward in a single broad line, this setup is called a staff-like array, or danda. If the arrangement follows a sequential line, where one unit follows directly behind another, it forms a snake-like array, or bhoga. When positioned in a circular arrangement that faces all directions, it is known as a circle-like array, or mandala. And when arranged in smaller, separated units that can act independently, it's called a detached order array, or asamhata.

The staff-like array with equal strength across wings, flanks, and front holds the name danda. If its flanks project forward, it becomes known as pradara, signifying its intent to break through enemy formations. When the wings and flanks are pulled back, making it particularly stable, it's known as dridhaka, or firm. If the wings are extended, creating a resilient formation, the array is called asahya, or irresistible. When the wings are structured and the front bulges outward, this is known as an eagle-like array.

These configurations have additional names when arranged in reverse: "a bow," "the center of a bow," "a hold," and "a strong hold." An array with bow-like wings is termed sanjaya (victory); if the front also projects forward, it is called vijaya (conqueror). When its flanks and wings take on the appearance of a staff, it is referred to as sthúlakarna (big ear); if its front is doubled in strength, it becomes visálavijaya (vast victory). With wings stretched forward, it forms chamúmukha (face of the army), while in a reversed formation, it is named ghashásya (face of the fish).

When the staff-like array positions units one behind the other, it is described as a pin-like array. If two such lines are created, it forms an aggregate, or valaya, and with four lines, it becomes known as an invincible array. These are the variations of the staff-like formation.

The snake-like array, when wings, flanks, and front differ in depth, is identified as sarpasári (serpentine movement) or gomútrika (resembling the winding trail of a cow's path).

When the formation has two lines in front with wings positioned like in the staff-like setup, it's called a cart-like formation; the reverse of this is known as a crocodile-like formation. A cart-like array that includes elephants, horses, and chariots is called váripatantaka. These are the types of the snake-like formations.

In the circle-like formation, where the difference between wings, flanks, and front fades away, it is known as sarvatomukha (facing all directions), or sarvatobhadra (all-auspicious), ashtáníka (eight divisions), or vijaya (victory). These represent the variations of the circle-like formation.

When the wings, flanks, and front are each placed separately, it is called a detached-order formation. If five divisions of the army are arranged in this detached way, it is known as vajra (diamond) or godha (alligator). When four divisions are separated, it is called udyánaka (park) or kákapadi (crow's foot). When three divisions are arranged in this style, it is called ardhachandrika (half-moon) or karkátakasringi. These are the variations of the detached-order formation.

The formation where chariots are placed at the front, elephants on the wings, and horses at the rear is known as arishta (auspicious). A formation where infantry, cavalry, chariots, and elephants stand one behind the other is called achala (immovable). The formation where elephants, horses, chariots, and infantry line up in order, one behind the other, is known as apratihata (invincible).

The conqueror should counter the pradara formation with the dridhaka; dridhaka with the asahya; the syena (eagle-like formation) with chápa (bow-like formation); a hold formation with a strong-hold formation; the sanjaya with the vijaya; the sthúlakarna with the visálavijaya; and the váripatantaka with sarvatobhadra. The conqueror may use the durjaya formation to strike at any other types of formations.

Of infantry, cavalry, chariots, and elephants, each is best opposed by the next type listed in order; and a small part of the army should be met by a larger one. For every group of ten members within each part of the army, there should be one commander, called a padika; ten padikas report to a senápati; and ten senápatis report to a náyaka, or leader.

The different sections of the army formations should be named according to trumpet sounds, flags, and signs. Success in organizing the army's formations, gathering forces, setting up camp, marching, retreating, launching attacks, and keeping formations balanced relies on choosing the right time and place for action.

By showing the full strength of his army, using secret tactics, deploying fiery spies to attack the enemy when distracted, employing witchcraft, spreading word of the conqueror's divine favor, using carts, and decorating elephants with impressive ornaments;

By inciting traitors, driving herds of cattle into the enemy's midst, setting the enemy's camp ablaze, targeting the wings and rear of their forces, or sowing seeds of discord through agents posing as servants;

Or by spreading rumors that the enemy's fortress was burned or captured, or that a member of his family, an ally, or a wild chief had rebelled—through these and similar strategies, the conqueror should create panic and confusion within the enemy's ranks.

An arrow shot by an archer may or may not strike down a single man, but a cunning scheme crafted by wise minds can eliminate even those yet unborn.

Book 11

CHAPTER I. CAUSES OF DISSENSION; AND SECRET PUNISHMENT.

Obtaining support from corporate groups is more beneficial than acquiring an army, an ally, or immediate profits. Through conciliation and rewards, the conqueror should secure the loyalty and support of corporations that are either powerful enough to withstand the enemy or are already favorably inclined toward him. As for groups opposing him, he should weaken them by sowing division among them and, if needed, discreetly punishing them.

The warrior corporations, or kshattriyasrení, from regions like Kámbhoja, Suráshtra, and others, sustain themselves through agriculture, trade, and skill with weapons. Other groups, like those from Lichchhivika, Vrijika, Mallaka, Mudraka, Kukura, Kuru, and Pánchála, operate under royal titles.

Spies should be deployed within these groups to observe any existing jealousy, rivalry, or grudges. They should then exploit these tensions, inciting well-crafted dissensions by subtly informing one member, "This person criticizes you." Spies posing as teachers or advisors can encourage conflicts during discussions on subjects like science, arts, or sports. Fiery spies could stir up tension by publicly praising lesser-known leaders in public spaces, such as taverns or theaters, or by discreetly stoking the ambitions of low-born princes with remarks on their lineage. They could interfere with social customs by urging senior members to dine or marry among lower ranks, or they could amplify frustrations by contrasting traditional roles in birth, bravery, and social status.

Additionally, fiery spies might instigate disputes at night by tampering with properties, animals, or individuals entangled in legal issues. In all such disturbances, the conqueror should support the lesser factions with funds and reinforcements, using them to undermine the dominant group. Once these groups are fractured, he could arrange to relocate them, or he might unite and resettle them in fertile areas within their territory under structured "five-household" and "ten-household" units, training them in military tactics as they build up. Established fines should deter any rebellious alliances among these groups.

He may choose to appoint a prince of noble lineage, who is perhaps dethroned or imprisoned, as the heir-apparent to rally loyalty. Spies, acting as astrologers or other trusted figures, should subtly highlight this prince's royal qualities and encourage respected leaders of the corporations to show loyalty to him, framing the prince as the heir ready to hear their concerns. The conqueror should also send funds and supporters to these loyalists to help win over additional backers.

During moments of unrest, spies disguised as tavern-keepers should distribute hundreds of cups of liquor mixed with madana plant juice, under the pretense of celebrating events like a birth, marriage, or death. Around the entrances to temples, altars, and other guarded locations, spies should create the impression that they are discussing deals with the corporations' enemies, including promises of payment, bags of money stamped with the enemy's golden seal, and rewards. When approached by members of the corporations, the spies might confess, "We've sided with your enemy," challenging them to fight.

Another tactic is to seize livestock and valuable items belonging to the corporations, giving the best of these items to their chief, thereby stirring resentment within the group. When the corporations question the missing goods, the spies could reply that the items were gifted to the chief, inciting internal conflict. This strategy outlines how to spark discord in camps and among wild tribes.

Alternatively, a spy might approach a self-assured son of a corporation chief, saying, "You're the son of a noble king, kept here out of fear of enemy threats." Once the young man is convinced, the conqueror can secretly aid him with troops and resources, encouraging him to challenge the corporations. Once his purpose is fulfilled, the conqueror might then exile him.

Spies managing entertainers or dancers, actors, and musicians could also work to sway the corporation chiefs, using alluring women to captivate them. By sending this woman to someone else or spreading rumors that another man has forcefully taken her, spies could provoke conflict between those competing for her attention. During the resulting altercation, fiery spies can incite further strife, declaring, "This man has met his fate because of his infatuation."

A woman who has rejected a suitor but was later forgiven might approach another chief, saying, "That man has been harassing me when my heart belongs to you; I can't stay here while he's around." This can lead the latter to kill the former.

Additionally, if a woman is forcefully taken at night, she might work with fiery spies or use poison herself to bring about her attacker's death in a park or pleasure house, later claiming, "My beloved was murdered by this person."

An undercover spy disguised as an ascetic might apply a special ointment, supposedly a charm to win the affection of a beloved woman, but mixed with poison, to a man eager to impress his lover. Afterward, the spy would disappear, and other spies would attribute the event to the actions of an enemy.

Women spies, such as widows with covert instructions, might engage in a dispute over a deposit allegedly held by the king. During this quarrel, their beauty would catch the attention of the corporation chiefs as they appeal to the king to resolve their issue.

A harlot, dancer, or singer might arrange to meet a man in a secluded house. When he arrives, hopeful to see her, fiery spies would either kill him or abduct him.

A spy might approach a chief known for his interest in women, saying, "In a nearby village, a poor man has passed away, leaving a beautiful widow who would be a fitting wife for a king. Claim her as your own." After the woman is seized, an ascetic spy could appear before the corporation half a month later, accusing the chief: "This man has wrongfully taken my main wife, sister-in-law, sister, or daughter." If the corporation then punishes the chief, the conqueror should ally with the corporation, encouraging them against corrupt members. Fiery spies should frequently send an ascetic spy to walk at night. Select spies should accuse the chief, saying, "This man has committed the heinous act of killing a Bráhman and has also engaged in adultery with a Bráhman woman."

Another spy disguised as an astrologer might describe a maiden's fortune to a chief, saying, "This young woman is meant to be the wife of a king and will bear a royal son. You should either offer all your wealth for her or take her by force." If she cannot be secured, the spies should provoke a conflict. If she is seized, a quarrel will naturally follow.

A female beggar spy might approach a chief who is devoted to his wife and say, "Another chief, proud of his youth, has sent me to entice your wife and sent this letter and jewelry as a gift for her. Your wife is innocent, but this man must be stopped. I'm deeply concerned for your success in this."

Whether the quarrels arise on their own or are fueled by spies, the conqueror should support the weaker party with men and funds, setting them against the corrupt individuals or prompting them to relocate elsewhere.

By these methods, he should establish himself as the singular ruler of all corporations. Under his singular protection, the corporations should remain vigilant against all forms of betrayal.

- The leader of corporations should gain the trust and affection of all the people by living a life of integrity, mastering his desires, and choosing actions that are respected and valued by everyone under his leadership.

Book 12

CHAPTER I. THE DUTIES OF A MESSENGER.

When a king with limited resources faces an attack from a stronger enemy, he should submit to the enemy along with his sons and yield as a reed bends in flowing water.

Bháradvája argues that surrendering to a more powerful force is like bowing before Indra, the rain god, gaining favor through humility. However, Visáláksha believes a weak king should instead fight with all his resources, for courage can overcome hardships; fighting is the duty of a Kshatriya, even if it leads to either victory or defeat.

Kautilya disagrees, stating that one who constantly bows to the powerful lives without hope, like a crab on a riverbank, and one who fights with a small force against a mighty enemy perishes, much like a man trying to cross the sea without a boat. Therefore, a weak king should either seek protection from a powerful ruler or sustain himself in an unbreakable fortress.

Invaders can be of three types: a just conqueror, a demon-like conqueror, and a greedy conqueror. The just conqueror accepts respect and loyalty as sufficient, so a weak king should seek refuge under such a leader. A greedy conqueror, fearing threats from his own enemies, is content with what he can safely claim in land or wealth; hence, a weak king should satisfy such a conqueror with offerings of wealth. The demon-like conqueror, however, will only be appeased by seizing all—territory, treasure, family, and even the life of the conquered. Therefore, a weak king should keep such a conqueror at bay with both land and wealth.

When any of these types threatens a weak king, he should try to prevent the invasion by negotiating a peace treaty, strategizing through intrigue, or employing covert warfare on the battlefield. The king could sway the enemy's men with diplomacy or gifts and prevent betrayal within his ranks by creating discord among them or punishing dissenters. Spies, working secretly, may be deployed to capture the enemy's fort, territory, or camps using weapons, poison, or fire. Additionally, he may harass the enemy's rear forces or damage their lands with the help of allied wild tribes. An imprisoned prince or a branch of the enemy's family might even be encouraged to seize the enemy's territory.

After causing this damage, the king might then send an envoy to the enemy to negotiate peace. Alternatively, he may seek a peaceful resolution without risking offense. However, if the enemy continues his advance, the weak king could offer peace by pledging a quarter of his wealth and forces, with payment arranged within a day and night.

If the enemy proposes peace on the condition that the weaker king surrenders a portion of his army, the king may send over his wildest elephants and least controllable horses, or those with poison-treated equipment. If the enemy demands the surrender of his chief officers, he could assign his forces that include traitors, rival factions, and hostile wild tribes under a trusted officer's command, ensuring that both his enemy and these disruptive forces are mutually harmed. Alternatively, he might send troops composed of fiery spies, provided he first pacifies his own discontented followers. The king could also strategically transfer his loyal, hereditary forces who can inflict damage on the enemy during vulnerable moments.

If the enemy seeks wealth as a term of peace, the king might offer valuable items that are difficult to sell or raw materials that are ineffective for warfare. If peace hinges on ceding a portion of land, he may yield lands that are recoverable, already exposed to attacks from other enemies, lack natural defenses, or would require substantial investment to settle and maintain. If the demand is for a larger surrender, he could concede all lands except his capital, securing his position in the heart of his domain.

- He should craftily maneuver to make the enemy accept something that is vulnerable to another force's interference.

Above all, the king should prioritize his own safety over the preservation of wealth, for wealth that leads to ruin is of little value.

[Thus ends Chapter I, "The Duties of a Messenger, and Request for Peace," in Book XII, "Concerning a Powerful Enemy," of the Arthasástra of Kautilya. End of the hundred and thirty-sixth chapter from the beginning.]

CHAPTER II. BATTLE OF INTRIGUE.

If the enemy insists on disregarding peace, he should be warned:

"Kings have fallen by succumbing to the set of six hostile forces; it is not in your interest to follow the example of these misguided rulers. Take heed of virtue and safeguard your wealth. Those advising you to confront danger, risk sin, and compromise your assets are enemies disguised as friends. Engaging with those who disregard their own lives is hazardous; it's sinful to cause widespread bloodshed, and it's wasteful to abandon reliable wealth and a trustworthy ally in me. That king you face has many allies he could align against you, leveraging resources that he gains through your efforts against me, attacking from all sides. He has not yet lost the favor of the Circle of the madhyama and neutral States, unlike you, who have weakened your influence over them. These states, thus, await the chance to turn against you. Endure temporary losses of men and resources to break ties with this risky ally. We will then be able to undermine his influence in that stronghold over which he has lost authority. So, do not listen to those posing as friends but are actually enemies, nor should you risk your loyal friends' wellbeing, empower your true enemies to succeed, or entangle yourself in dangers that threaten life and property."

If, despite this warning, the enemy disregards the advice, the weaker king should secretly incite disloyalty among the enemy's ranks, using tactics outlined in the sections on "The Conduct of Corporations" and "Enticement of the Enemy through Secret Means."

Fiery spies and poison should be employed to destabilize the enemy, especially in matters crucial to the enemy's personal safety as discussed in "Safety of His Own Person." Keepers of courtesans may tempt and captivate key leaders in the enemy's army with youthful and alluring women. Fiery spies could then provoke discord among these leaders if one or more falls in love, sparking conflicts that might lead the defeated to either leave or even support the weak king in his efforts.

Additionally, spies disguised as ascetics could provide a love-struck enemy leader with poison, suggesting it's a medicinal potion to fulfill their romantic desires.

A spy, disguised as a merchant, might lavish gifts upon a close maid-servant of the beautiful queen (of the enemy) under the pretense of courting her, only to abandon her later. Another spy, posed as a servant to this maid-servant, may hand her a medicinal potion, saying it's meant to rekindle the merchant's affection if applied by her to his person. Once the maid-servant finds this effective, she could be persuaded to tell the queen that the same potion would secure the king's affections. The potion could then be substituted with poison for use on the king.

A spy posing as an astrologer may subtly convince the enemy's prime minister that he possesses all the attributes of a king. Meanwhile, a mendicant woman could hint to the minister's wife that she has the traits of a queen and will bear a prince. Or another woman, acting as if she were the minister's wife, might relay to him: "The king has been harassing me, and an ascetic woman has delivered this letter and jewelry to me."

Spies disguised as royal cooks could, under the pretense of following the king's orders, deliver coveted wealth to the minister, purportedly intended for use in an imminent campaign. A spy posing as a merchant could then, by various means, acquire this wealth and notify the minister of the readiness of all preparations for the mission. In this way, by employing one, two, or even three strategic maneuvers, the ministers from each faction among the allied enemies could be lured away from their respective kings on a false expedition, leaving those kings unsupported.

Spies serving under the enemy's officer in charge of waste lands could alert the townsfolk and rural people within the enemy's fortified cities to the officer's perceived alliance with the populace. They might say, "The officer in charge of waste lands warns the warriors and officials, saying, 'The king has barely survived a recent danger and has only just returned alive. Don't hoard wealth or create rivals, or you'll face execution.'" Once a crowd gathers, fiery spies could lure the citizens outside the town and assassinate their leaders, declaring, "This fate awaits anyone who ignores the warnings of the officer overseeing the waste lands." On the waste lands, these spies might scatter weapons, coins, and bloodstained ropes as if a violent struggle occurred. Other spies would then circulate the story that the officer in charge is brutalizing and robbing the people.

Similarly, spies could sow discord between the enemy's collector-general and the local population. By publicly addressing the collector-general's servants in the village square at night, fiery spies could announce, "Anyone who unjustly oppresses the people will be dealt with in this manner." When news of the collector-general's or the waste lands officer's wrongdoings spreads widely, the spies might incite the people to overthrow one of them, installing in his place a family member or an imprisoned figure under the spies' influence.

- Spreading false rumors of impending danger to the enemy, spies could incite panic by setting fire to the royal harem, the town gates, and the storehouses holding grain and other provisions, as well as assassinating the sentinels assigned to guard these places.

[Thus ends Chapter II, "The Duties of a Messenger and Battle of Intrigue," in Book XII, "Concerning a Powerful Enemy," of the

Arthasástra of Kautilya. End of "Battle of Intrigue." End of the hundred and thirty-seventh chapter from the beginning.]

CHAPTER III. SLAYING THE COMMANDER-IN-CHIEF AND INCITING A CIRCLE OF STATES.

Spies working for the enemy king or his close allies might, under the guise of friendship, suggest in front of other allies that the king is angry with leaders of the infantry, cavalry, chariots, and elephants. Once these leaders gather with their forces, fiery spies, having avoided the night guards, could pretend to act under the enemy king's orders by summoning these leaders to a particular place, then assassinating them as they depart. Other nearby spies would then declare that this action was indeed an order from the enemy king. Spies could also approach exiles from the kingdom, warning, "This outcome is exactly as we warned; for your safety, you might consider leaving for another place."

Similarly, spies could tell those whose requests have been denied by the king that the officer overseeing the waste lands was instructed by the king to handle them: "This individual has requested something inappropriate from me, which I denied. He is conspiring with my enemy. Find a way to subdue him." After planting this idea, the spies would follow their typical procedures.

In cases where requests were granted, spies could inform such individuals that the king has given secret orders to the officer in charge of the waste lands, stating, "Those people demanded what was owed, so I granted it to win their trust. But they are plotting with my enemy. Make arrangements to suppress them." The spies would then continue with their standard actions.

Spies might also approach those who refrain from asking for what they are due from the king, telling them that the officer in charge of waste lands has been instructed: "These individuals don't make their rightful requests of me. What reason could they have other than a fear that I'm aware of their guilt? Take measures to subdue them." The spies would then proceed with their usual methods.

This illustrates how to handle those aligned with the enemy.

A spy who serves as the enemy king's personal attendant might inform him that certain ministers are meeting secretly with agents of a rival king. Once convinced of this, the king could be shown certain deceptive people as supposed "envoys of the enemy," with spies pointing them out directly.

To weaken the enemy, chief army officers might be persuaded with promises of land and gold to turn against their own forces and defect from their leader. If a son of the commander-in-chief lives in or near the fortress, a spy might tell him, "You are the most capable of your father's sons, yet you're ignored. Why remain passive? Claim your rightful position by force, or risk being eliminated by the heir-apparent."

Alternatively, a family member of the commander or the king, or someone held in captivity, could be bribed with gold and instructed, "Undermine the inner strength of the enemy, or weaken his forces stationed on the border."

Or, wild tribes might be enticed with rewards and incited to pillage the enemy's lands. The enemy's rivals might also be approached with a message: "I am the bridge that links you. If I fall, this king will be your undoing. Let us unite to halt his advance." Further, messages could be sent to various states, individually or collectively, warning: "Once he's finished with me, this king will turn on each of you. Be cautious. I am your strongest ally."

- To avoid the threat posed by a close enemy, a king should regularly send gifts or offerings to a madhyama (mediator) or neutral king that would likely win their favor. Alternatively, the king could offer all his resources to the enemy, placing his entire property under their control.

[Thus ends Chapter III, "Slaying the Commander-in-Chief and Inciting a Circle of States," in Book XII, "Concerning a Powerful Enemy," of the Arthasástra of Kautilya. End of the hundred and thirty-eighth chapter from the beginning.]

CHAPTER IV. SPIES WITH WEAPONS, FIRE, AND POISON; AND DESTRUCTION OF SUPPLY, STORES AND GRANARIES.

Spies working for the conqueror, positioned as traders in the enemy's forts, farmers in the villages, or disguised as cowherds or ascetics along the enemy's borderlands, may discreetly inform a neighboring rival, a wild chieftain, a relative of the enemy, or even an imprisoned prince that the enemy's territory is vulnerable for capture. When these external forces arrive, they should be generously rewarded with wealth and honors and shown the enemy's weaknesses. Using this guidance, the spies can then target the enemy's vulnerable areas with strategic strikes.

Alternatively, a banished prince might be placed within the enemy's camp, and a spy posing as a vintner could distribute large quantities of liquor spiked with madana plant juice. On the first day, the vintner might serve regular or mildly intoxicating liquor, followed in subsequent days by liquor tainted with poison. Or, after offering pure liquor to the enemy's officers, the spy could serve them poisoned drinks while they are intoxicated.

A spy positioned as a senior officer in the enemy's army could also carry out similar strategies to weaken the troops. Spies posing as vendors of cooked meat, rice, liquor, or cakes might publicly boast of selling fresh supplies at low prices, drawing in the enemy's troops and then selling them poisoned goods under the guise of a special deal.

Women and children may receive vessels filled with poisoned liquor, milk, curd, ghee, or oil from traders, then pour these back into the traders' containers, making it seem like they intend to buy all the contents. Spies, disguised as merchants, may buy these items to be sure that enemy servants feed these contaminated supplies to their elephants and horses along with rations and grass. Spies posing as attendants could even sell poisoned grass and water directly. Others, acting as cattle traders over time, might leave herds of cattle, sheep, or goats in plain sight to distract the enemy from an impending attack. Disguised as cowherds, they may release aggressive animals like horses, mules, camels, or buffaloes whose eyes have been smeared with musk-rat blood, making them agitated and dangerous. Spies acting as hunters might release wild beasts from traps, while those pretending to be snake charmers could unleash venomous snakes; elephant keepers might set elephants loose near the enemy's camp, and spies skilled with fire could set the camp ablaze. Hidden agents might ambush enemy leaders from behind or set fires in key residences.

Traitors, enemy sympathizers, or wild tribes can be engaged to disrupt the enemy's rear or block reinforcements. Spies concealed in forests could infiltrate the border areas of the enemy's territory to wreak havoc or target their supplies and other essentials on narrow paths that can only be traversed single-file.

Following a prearranged plan, spies might, during a night raid, enter the enemy's capital and blow trumpets while loudly declaring, "We've taken the capital; the country has been conquered." Amid this chaos, they could infiltrate the palace and assassinate the king. As the king flees from one point to another, hidden Mlechchhas, wild tribes, or army chiefs lying in ambush or concealed by a post or fence might strike him down. Disguised as hunters, spies might eliminate the king while he directs his attack or during the frenzy of a planned ambush.

Taking advantage of strategic terrain, spies could kill the enemy as he marches along a single-file path, on a mountain, near a tree trunk, or under the branches of a banyan tree. Alternatively, they might unleash a torrent by breaking a dam on a river, lake, or pond, sweeping the enemy away with the force of the water. In a fort, forest, valley, or desert, the enemy might be annihilated with an explosive device or a poisonous snake. Fire is most effective against an enemy under a thicket; smoke, when he is stranded in a desert; poison, if he is in a comfortable location; crocodiles or other fierce beasts, if he is in water. Or, he might be attacked while escaping from a burning residence.

- By using methods described in the chapter, "Enticement of the Enemy by Secret Means," or through other strategies, the enemy should be captured either in areas where he is confined or in those from which he is trying to escape.

[Thus ends Chapter IV, "Spies with Weapons, Fire and Poison; and Destruction of Supply, Stores and Granaries," in Book XII, "Concerning a Powerful Enemy," of the Arthasástra of Kautilya. End of the hundred and thirty-ninth chapter from the beginning.]

CHAPTER V. CAPTURE OF THE ENEMY BY MEANS OF SECRET CONTRIVANCES OR BY MEANS OF THE ARMY; AND COMPLETE VICTORY.

Plans to eliminate the enemy may be set up in places of worship or pilgrimage that he regularly visits under religious devotion.

A wall or stone held by a mechanical device can be loosened to fall on the enemy's head when he enters a temple. Stones and weapons can be dropped from the upper stories above him, or a door panel may be released to crash down. A large rod positioned above or partially attached to a wall can be made to fall on him. Hidden weapons inside the statue of a deity might be triggered to strike him, or the floor where he usually stands, sits, or walks can be treated with poison mixed with cow dung or pure water. Poison could also be administered under the pretense of giving him flowers, incense, or perfumed smoke. Another option is to remove the supports of a cot or seat to make him fall into a pit lined with pointed spears.

If he is desperate to escape imprisonment in his country, he may be deceived and led into the hands of a nearby wild tribe or enemy lying in wait. Similarly, if he is eager to flee from his fortress, he could be misled into entering an enemy territory that is about to fall into the conqueror's hands. The enemy's people should also be held under the protection of the conqueror's family—sons or brothers—in fortresses located in mountains, forests, or river islands separated from the enemy's country by wild lands.

Measures to hinder the enemy's movements are covered in the section, "The Conduct of a Conquered King." Grasslands and firewood areas should be set ablaze up to a yojana (about 5.25 miles); water sources should be polluted and diverted; external fort structures like mounds, wells, pits, and thorn barriers should be removed. The mouth of the enemy's underground tunnel can be widened, allowing removal of their supplies and leaders—or even the enemy himself. If the tunnel has been created by the enemy for escape, the ditch outside the fort may be used to flood it. Empty pots or bronze vessels may be placed in suspicious spots along the parapet or around wells outside the fort to detect air movement from the tunnel. Once the tunnel's direction is identified, a counter-tunnel can be dug, or the discovered tunnel can be filled with smoke or water to incapacitate those inside.

Once the enemy has arranged for his fort's defense under a trusted family member, he may flee to a location where he could meet allies, relatives, or friendly wild tribes. He might go to the lands of his enemy's unreliable allies with substantial resources, hoping to split the enemy from these allies, or he may target the enemy's rear guard, territory, or disrupt the enemy's supply lines. He could head to an area where he can attack by using trees or obstacles or move to a region from which he can organize reinforcements for his own army, or he might aim for a place where peace can be negotiated on favorable terms.

The conqueror's allies might then approach this fleeing enemy with a proposal, saying: "This enemy of yours has come into our reach. Under the guise of a trade exchange or as a gift, send gold and a strong force; we will either hand him over to you, bound and chained, or expel him from here." If he accepts this offer, any gold or forces he sends could then be taken over by the conqueror.

The boundary officer of the enemy's country, having gained entry to the enemy's stronghold, may lead a portion of his force to eliminate the enemy in good faith, claiming he is moving in to subdue a local disturbance. He may also divert the enemy to an opposing force, or surround the enemy at a favorable spot and kill him under the guise of defending his own people.

A feigned ally could alert an external party, saying: "The grain, oil, jaggery, and salt supplies in the enemy's fort are nearly depleted; fresh supplies are expected at a specific location and time. Move swiftly to capture it." Traitors, enemies, wild tribes, or other appointed agents may then send in a shipment of poisoned grain, oil, jaggery, or salt to the fort. This tactic exemplifies the capture of all kinds of enemy supplies.

The fleeing enemy, having agreed to a truce with the conqueror, might begin paying the promised gold but only partially, delaying the rest in installments. He may then use this delay to create an impression of weakened defenses and then strike back with fire, poison, or direct attack. Alternatively, he could build trust with the conqueror's officials responsible for collecting tribute, using this opportunity to undermine the conqueror's resources or planning.

If his resources are entirely depleted, he may abandon his fort and flee, either escaping through an existing tunnel, a newly created hole, or by breaking through the parapet. Alternatively, he might challenge the conqueror at night, planning to confront the attack; if this fails, he can escape through a side path. He could disguise himself as a wandering ascetic with a small retinue, or he might be carried off by spies, pretending to be a corpse. Disguised as a grieving woman, he could follow another corpse, as if it were her husband's funeral procession, to the cremation grounds.

During a public event such as a ceremony honoring the gods, the ancestors, or during a local festival, he may use poisoned rice and water to harm the enemy. By collaborating with enemy traitors, he might also ambush his foe with a hidden army. If surrounded in his fort, he could consume sacramental food, set up an altar, and conceal himself in a hidden compartment within an idol. He might also hide in a concealed chamber within a wall or in a carved-out space in an underground idol. After the enemy's guard is down, he could emerge through a tunnel, enter the palace, and attack his enemy while he sleeps. Another strategy might involve loosening the fastenings of a machine to let it fall on the enemy. If the enemy rests in a chamber coated with poisonous or flammable materials, he might ignite it to trap his foe within.

Hidden spies, concealed in an underground chamber, a tunnel, or inside a wall, could ambush the enemy when he is leisurely enjoying a park or another place of relaxation. Other concealed spies might poison him, or women in hiding could throw a snake, poison, fire, or poisonous smoke over him while he sleeps in a confined area. Spies with access to the enemy's harem could seize any opportunities to harm the enemy and then disappear without detection. In these situations, they should use specific signs to indicate their intentions to members of their secret society.

- By using trumpet signals, he could gather the sentinels at the gate, along with older men and other spies placed there by others, allowing him to carry out the remainder of his plans seamlessly.

Book 13

CHAPTER I. SOWING THE SEEDS OF DISSENSION.

When a conqueror seeks to overtake a rival's village, he should actively uplift his own troops' confidence while strategically intimidating the enemy's people. This can be achieved by publicly showcasing his "omniscient" knowledge of events and a seemingly direct connection to divine forces, both of which can be used to instill fear and uncertainty in the enemy.

To showcase his omniscience, he might carry out carefully staged actions that create the impression of uncanny insight into people's private matters. For example, he could publicly dismiss high-ranking officials, revealing that he already knows personal details about their hidden lives, or expose traitors based on information gathered by spies discreetly planted to monitor them. By subtly pointing out the weak spots in any proposals given to him, he demonstrates an uncanny ability to assess the faults in suggestions, which fuels the image of his infallible judgment. Additionally, he might claim insight into far-reaching foreign affairs, attributing this knowledge to his ability to interpret signs and omens, which he could explain as a talent that allows him to foresee even distant matters—such as when a carrier pigeon arrives with a message and he can predict its contents.

To project the image of a divine connection, the conqueror might use concealed spies who stage supernatural appearances, claiming to be gods and performing feats that appear otherworldly. He could, for instance, hold "conversations" with spies dressed as deities in settings designed to look mystical, such as having spies emerge from tunnels to stand in the flames of a sacred altar or within the body of a hollow idol. These spies would pretend to be gods of fire, water, or serpents, as if appearing by divine will to bless or communicate with him. He might also stage scenes by water with spies disguised as spirits of the river or snake-gods who "rise" from the water. Further adding to the spectacle, he might instruct people to place oil and sea foam on water, lighting it at a distance to create what looks like spontaneous fire breaking out across the surface. While on a raft in the water, secretly tethered to a rock, he could put on a "divine performance" for his audience. He might even employ skilled performers who, using underwater devices created from the organs of aquatic animals, would appear to move with ease under the water while speaking in the guise of godly messengers.

Astrologers, soothsayers, and omen-readers, along with various types of spies and informers, should spread tales of the king's powers widely throughout his own land, emphasizing how gods and spirits regularly visit him and how divine beings have personally delivered valuable weapons or treasures to him. The conqueror's agents should ensure that rumors reach foreign territories as well, asserting that he has received supernatural assistance that will guide him to victory. Astrologers could also interpret signs of victory for the king, such as his ability to explain the language of animals or foresee the outcomes of dreams, contrasting this by claiming the opposite for his enemy, painting the rival as bereft of divine favor. His agents could go further by creating ominous signs in the skies of the enemy's territory, such as arranging for flaming firebrands to fall accompanied by the sound of drums on the enemy ruler's birthday, marking it as an inauspicious omen for the enemy.

Through these calculated displays and manipulations, the conqueror carefully builds his reputation, using public perception and spectacle to weaken the morale of the enemy's people, thereby advancing his conquest with psychological as well as military strategy.

The conqueror's main envoys, while pretending to be allies of the enemy, should speak highly of the conqueror's gracious treatment of guests, the formidable strength of his army, and the looming likelihood of the enemy's defeat. They should also communicate that under the conqueror's rule, both ministers and soldiers alike enjoy security and well-being, and that he treats his followers with a genuine, almost parental care in both prosperous and difficult times.

Through these and similar methods, they should gradually sway the enemy's people as previously described and as will be further detailed. They should describe the enemy ruler in unflattering terms, likening him to an "ordinary donkey" in how he treats skilled individuals, and to a "broken branch of lakucha" (Artocarpus Lacucha) in his treatment of his officers. To the frustrated and unappreciated, they should describe the enemy king as nothing more than a crab washed up on the shore. For those treated with disdain, he should be likened to a "storm of lightning," inciting only fear and chaos. To those disappointed by his promises, he should be compared to "a reed, a barren tree, an iron ball, or false clouds." To those loyal despite receiving little reward, he could be described as "the ornaments of an unattractive woman," adding no benefit to the wearer. To those previously favored but now disillusioned, the conqueror's agents should portray the enemy king as dangerous and deceptive—like "the skin of a tiger" or "a trap of death." To those who've sacrificed much on his behalf, they could liken loyalty to the enemy to "chewing on the wood of pílu" (Careya-Arborea), or the fruitless act of "churning a camel's or donkey's milk for butter."

Once the enemy's people are persuaded, the envoys may guide them to seek refuge with the conqueror in exchange for wealth and honor. For those in need of provisions, they should supply them generously with food and money, while those who prefer other support might be given jewelry for their families.

During times of famine or when thieves and wild tribes are oppressing the enemy's lands, the conqueror's spies should sow seeds of discontent, suggesting, "Let's appeal to the king for relief, but if he doesn't respond, we can seek a better place to live."

- When the enemy's people respond to these ideas, they should receive financial support, food, and any necessary aid. In this way, discord among the enemy's people can be effectively fostered.

[Thus ends Chapter I, "Sowing the Seeds of Dissension," in Book XIII, "Strategic Means to Capture a Fortress" of the Arthasástra, of Kautilya. End of the hundred and forty-first chapter from the beginning.]

CHAPTER II. ENTICEMENT OF KINGS BY SECRET CONTRIVANCES.

An ascetic, either with a shaved head or braided hair, dwelling in a cave on a mountain, may pretend to be four hundred years old. This ascetic, accompanied by a group of followers with braided hair, could set up camp near the capital of the enemy. The disciples would then present offerings of roots and fruits to the king and his ministers, inviting them to visit the revered ascetic. When the king arrives, the ascetic may recount stories of ancient kings and the history of their lands. He might say, "Every hundred years, I enter the fire and emerge reborn as a youthful being. Now, in your presence, I am about to undergo this transformation for the fourth time. It would be a great honor to have you present during this sacred event. Please, request three boons." If the king agrees, the ascetic could ask him to remain at the site with his family for seven nights to witness the ritual. Once there, the king could be captured.

Another approach involves an ascetic, either bald or with braided hair, claiming to know the secrets hidden deep within the earth. He could plant a bamboo stick wrapped in cloth stained with blood and dusted with gold, or a hollow golden tube where a snake can coil, inside an ant hill. One of his followers might then tell the king, "This holy man can locate blooming treasures buried in the earth." When the king inquires, the ascetic could confirm this skill by pulling out the bamboo stick. Alternatively, he might place more gold in the ant hill and tell the king, "A snake guards this treasure, and it can only be retrieved after a sacred ritual." Should the king agree, he could be asked to stay at the spot for seven nights, as before.

At night in a secluded area, an ascetic feigning the power to locate hidden treasures might be seated with his body seemingly ignited by magical fire. His followers could then bring the king to witness this remarkable sight, telling him that the ascetic is truly capable of uncovering such treasures. During any task requested by the king, the ascetic could then urge the king to stay for seven nights, just as before.

A skilled ascetic might deceive a king through knowledge of a magical science known as jambhaka, convincing him to stay as outlined earlier.

An ascetic may also claim to have earned the favor of the powerful deity who protects the land. He could mesmerize the king's chief ministers through amazing feats, gradually winning the king's trust.

Any individual disguised as an ascetic, living underwater or hidden within an idol reached through a secret tunnel or chamber, could be presented by his disciples as Varuna, the god of water, or as the king of snakes, and shown to the king. When going forth to fulfill the king's desires, he could again invite the king to remain for seven nights, as before.

An accomplished ascetic, halting in the vicinity of the capital city, may invite the king to witness the person (of his enemy) when he comes to witness the invocation of his enemy's life in the image to be destroyed, he may be murdered in an unguarded place.

Spies, under the, guise of merchants come to sell horses, may invite the king to examine and purchase any of the animals. While attentively examining the horses, he may be murdered in the tumult or trampled down by horses.

At night, in an altar near the enemy's capital, fiery spies could gather, blowing flames from tubes or hollow reeds filled with fire from pots. They would then shout loudly, "We are here to devour the flesh of the king or his ministers; let the gods be worshipped." Disguised as soothsayers and astrologers, other spies might spread these unsettling rumors among the people.

Spies disguised as Nagas, or snake gods, with bodies smeared in blazing oil (tejánataila), could stand in the center of a sacred pool or lake at night, sharpening iron swords or spikes, shouting threats as before. Other spies, wearing cloaks made of bear skins, might create smoky effects from their mouths, acting like demons. They could circle the city three times from right to left, then raise frightening cries in places echoing with the sounds of jackals and other wild animals. Alternatively, spies could ignite an altar or a deity's statue, coated with mica and burning oil, and again cry out as before. Other agents would then spread word of these events throughout the city.

The spies could also make blood appear to flow dramatically from revered statues of gods. Witnesses would spread this eerie news, challenging anyone brave enough to come and see the divine blood. If anyone accepted the challenge, hidden agents would ambush them, beating them to death with rods to make it appear they had been killed by supernatural forces. The spies, along with others, would then report this terrifying incident to the king. Disguised as soothsayers and astrologers, the spies might advise the king to perform auspicious and cleansing rituals to protect himself and his people from the evil consequences. When the king agrees, he might be instructed to conduct special sacrifices and ceremonies using specific mantras each night for seven days. During this time, they would plan to eliminate him as previously arranged.

To set an example and sow further confusion among other rulers, the conqueror could publicly conduct similar rites to avert evil, encouraging others to follow suit.

To ward off the negative effects of unnatural events, the conqueror may also gather funds from his subjects under this pretense.

If the enemy is particularly fond of elephants, spies might lure him with a sighting of a magnificent elephant, supposedly cared for by the officer in charge of the elephant forests. When the enemy shows interest in capturing this creature, he could be led to a remote and deserted part of the forest, where he would either be killed or captured. This demonstrates the dangers that can befall rulers who are overly eager for hunting excursions.

If the enemy has a weakness for wealth or beautiful women, spies could use this against him by presenting him with wealthy and attractive widows, seemingly seeking his help to reclaim a fortune entrusted to a relative. Then, under the guise of a private meeting arranged at night, concealed spies could kill him using weapons or poison.

If the enemy frequently visits ascetics, sacred shrines, religious pillars (stúpa), or statues of deities, spies hiding in underground chambers, secret tunnels, or within walls could take advantage of these private moments to ambush and eliminate him.

- At any location where the king personally goes to view special displays or events, or whenever he engages in activities like playing games or swimming, spies might prepare to strike.
- Similarly, they can take advantage when the king, in moments of distraction, lets out careless words or when he's preoccupied with sacrificial ceremonies, birth events, times of mourning or illness in the palace, or during moments of intimacy, grief, or fright.
- Any gatherings or celebrations held by the king's own people, where he may attend and remain unguarded, present further opportunities, as do cloudy or stormy days, or when he is amidst large, tumultuous crowds.
- Spies may also target him when he attends Brahman assemblies, goes to inspect the scene of a fire, finds himself in a secluded place, or even while he's dressing, putting on jewelry or floral garlands, resting in bed, or sitting.
- Whether during meals or drinks, or other private moments, spies, accompanied by hidden accomplices stationed there ahead of time, may wait for the signal from trumpets to carry out their mission.
- They can then discreetly leave the scene as inconspicuously as they arrived, blending into the spectators, thereby ensuring that unsuspecting kings and individuals are lured out and taken by surprise.

[Thus ends Chapter II, "Enticement of Kings by Secret Contrivances," in Book XIII, "Strategic means to Capture a Fortress," of the Arthasástra of Kautilya. End of the hundred and forty-second chapter from the beginning.]

CHAPTER III. THE WORK OF SPIES IN A SIEGE.

The conqueror might dismiss a trusted chief from a local corporation, allowing the chief to defect to the enemy as a friendly agent and offer resources like recruits and supplies gathered from the conqueror's own territory. Accompanied by a team of spies, this chief might win the enemy's favor by targeting a rebellious village, a regiment, or an ally of the conqueror, even presenting the enemy with elephants, horses, or disloyal members of the conqueror's forces or those of his allies. Alternatively, a close officer from the conqueror's ranks might request help from a section of the enemy's territory, a guild (sreni), or wild tribes. Once he gains their trust, he can steer them toward the conqueror, where they can be swiftly subdued during a staged event involving elephants or wild tribes.

This strategy illustrates the dual role that ministers and chiefs of wild tribes can play on behalf of the conqueror.

After securing peace with the enemy, the conqueror may let go of his trusted ministers, who then approach the enemy with a plea to restore their loyalty to the conqueror. If the enemy sends an envoy on their behalf, the conqueror can scold this messenger, saying, "Your leader seeks to divide me and my ministers; you should not return here." One of these dismissed ministers, accompanied by spies, traitors, unruly allies, or wild tribes without allegiance, may then offer to serve the enemy, eventually persuading him to dispose of certain leaders like the boundary guard, local chiefs, or the enemy's army commander by claiming, "These individuals are allied with your adversary." Thus, by the enemy's command, these individuals may be eliminated.

The conqueror could also propose to the enemy: "A nearby leader with a formidable army poses a threat to us both; let's join forces to defeat him. You may seize his treasury or lands." If the enemy accepts, he could be ambushed in the chaos of battle or by the conqueror's allies during the clash. Alternatively, the conqueror might extend an invitation to the enemy to attend a staged ceremony for granting new territory, naming an heir, or performing rites. At this gathering, the conqueror could capture or eliminate the enemy. If the enemy resists such events, agents may still attempt to eliminate him through covert methods or by employing the enemy's own foes.

Should the enemy insist on moving alone with his troops, the conqueror may trap him between two forces and destroy him. If the enemy decides to independently capture an unguarded enemy's territory, the conqueror can engage one of his foes or another well-prepared agent to ambush him. Should the enemy seek out his subjugated rival to raise forces, the conqueror could seize his capital in his absence. Alternatively, the conqueror might prompt the enemy to annex the territory of an ally or friend of the conqueror, where the conqueror's ally would act against the enemy, ultimately capturing him.

These strategies and maneuvers, subtle or overt, all ultimately work to the conqueror's advantage.

If the enemy shows interest in capturing the territory of the conqueror's ally, the conqueror might appear cooperative and even lend his army to aid the enemy's pursuit. Behind the scenes, however, he could form a secret alliance with his friend, feigning vulnerability and allowing himself to be attacked by the enemy, now paired with the overlooked ally. Positioned between two forces, the enemy could be cornered, either captured alive or killed, with his lands then divided between the conqueror and his ally.

If the enemy, supported by his own allies, takes refuge in a highly fortified position, nearby foes could be enlisted to devastate his territory. Should the enemy attempt to defend his lands with his forces, those forces might be neutralized in battle. When separating the enemy from his ally is impossible, both may be approached openly, with each offered the chance to make a deal with the conqueror to seize the other's territory. In this case, each would send representatives who serve both sides, relaying the message, "The conqueror, backed by my forces, plans to seize your lands." Consequently, one of the allies, provoked by anger and suspicion, would likely turn on the other.

The conqueror might discharge his own officers responsible for his forests, outlying territories, and army on grounds of alleged conspiracy with the enemy. Once these officers join the enemy's ranks, they could undermine him in moments of war, siege, or other crises. They could also create rifts between the enemy and his supporters, providing coached witnesses to back up claims of discord.

Spies, disguised as hunters, could station themselves near the enemy's fortress gate, selling meat and gradually forming friendships with the guards. By repeatedly alerting the enemy of nearby robberies, they could gain credibility, ultimately convincing him to split his forces and station troops in different parts of his land. During a village raid, they might warn of an imminent threat, suggesting that the robbers are dangerously close and require a substantial force to fend them off. The supplied army could then be handed over to the raiding commander, and later that night, some of the commander's forces could return with the spies to the fortress gate, loudly proclaiming that the robbers have been defeated and the army has triumphed. When the guards, under the enemy's orders or in confidence, open the gate, the returning army could launch a surprise attack, seizing control of the fortress.

Artists, carpenters, heretics, actors, merchants, and various other spies from the conqueror's forces could blend seamlessly into the enemy's fortified city. These agents might live under the guise of simple villagers or craftsmen, quietly preparing to act. Spies disguised as farmers can help covertly supply hidden weapons into the fortress, transporting them under layers of firewood, grass, or grains loaded into carts. Additionally, they may conceal arms and armor within items that appear harmless, such as religious images or flags of gods, allowing them to position these tools strategically within the fort without raising suspicion.

Once these resources are inside, spies posing as holy priests may alert the enemy by blowing conch shells and beating drums, proclaiming that a fierce army, intent on destruction and fully equipped, is closing in on the city. The sudden panic and confusion within the fort may create the ideal opportunity for these disguised spies to seize control of the fortress gate, along with the towers and other strategic points, preparing the way for the conqueror's forces to enter. Alternatively, amidst the uproar, the agents could disperse the enemy's guards and army, hastening the city's fall.

Further, under a pretense of peace or friendly relations with the enemy, the conqueror can have his agents smuggle both troops and weapons into the enemy's stronghold. Spies may arrive disguised as traders in caravans, processions for a bride, merchants selling horses, traveling peddlers, buyers and sellers of grains, or even wandering ascetics. These disguised troops and weapons would be strategically positioned to secure the conqueror's victory. These are the core agents assigned with the critical task of targeting the life of the opposing ruler.

The same undercover agents, along with those previously described in "Elimination of Threats," may use local thieves to destroy the enemy's cattle herds or merchandise in wilderness-adjacent areas. In addition, spies may lace the food and drink prepared for the enemy's cowherds with the intoxicating juice of the madana plant. Disguised as herders, merchants, or even opportunistic thieves, these agents could strike when the cowherds, weakened and inebriated, are least able to protect their flocks, allowing them to carry off large numbers of cattle.

Moreover, spies disguised as ascetics with shaved heads or braided hair may pretend to be followers of the deity Sankarshana. They might offer cowherds a sacrificial beverage secretly mixed with madana juice, leading to intoxication, which would enable the spies to take the cattle while the cowherds are incapacitated.

An agent posing as a vintner could exploit religious processions, funeral rites, festivals, and other public gatherings to sell liquor to the cowherds, lacing it with madana juice. Once the cowherds succumb to intoxication, other spies lying in wait could take advantage, overpowering the guards and herders to seize the cattle. Through careful preparation and deception, each of these covert operations serves the conqueror's objective of destabilizing and weakening the enemy from within.

- Agents sent into the enemy's territories under the guise of bandits, with the pretense of raiding villages and seizing valuables, yet who abandon this plundering to focus on covertly undermining or eliminating key enemy forces, are classified as spies disguised as thieves. These operatives pose as marauders but are in fact strategically directed by the conqueror to dismantle the enemy's resources and security from within. Their mission is dual-purpose, utilizing the appearance of disorder and theft to mask deliberate actions aimed at destabilizing and weakening the enemy's defenses and morale.

[Thus ends Chapter III, "The Work of Spies in a Siege," in Book XIII, "The Strategic Means to Capture a Fortress," of the Arthasástra of Kautilya. End of the hundred and forty-third chapter from the beginning.]

CHAPTER IV. THE OPERATION OF A SIEGE.

Before laying siege, it's essential to weaken the enemy's resources and morale. Any newly conquered land should be stabilized to the point where its inhabitants feel secure enough to rest without fear. If there is unrest, it can be quelled by granting rewards and reducing taxes—unless the conqueror intends to abandon it. The conqueror should also plan to conduct battles in distant parts of the enemy's territory, away from densely populated areas, as Kautilya advises that a true kingdom or country is defined by its population. If the people resist conquest, then the conqueror can weaken their resolve by targeting their supplies, destroying their crops, and cutting off their trade.

- By disrupting trade, demolishing agricultural outputs and standing crops, forcing the people to flee, and eliminating their leaders through covert actions, the land will gradually be emptied of its population.

When the conqueror sees his advantage—knowing that his army is well-supplied with staple grains, raw materials, equipment, weapons, clothing, laborers, ropes, and similar essentials, and that the season favors his side while his enemy is hampered by unfavorable weather, disease, famine, and dwindling resources—he can consider starting the siege. This is especially favorable if the enemy's forces and any allied troops are weakened and demoralized.

First, he should ensure the security of his camp, transport units, supplies, and communication routes, surrounding his camp with a trench and building a rampart. Then, to weaken the enemy's defenses, he might pollute the water in the ditches around the fort, drain the water if the ditches are full, or fill empty ditches with water to disrupt the enemy's routine. With tunnels and iron rods, he could attack the ramparts and parapets. If the trench is too deep to cross, he might fill it with earth; if it's well-defended, he could use machines to destroy it. His cavalry could attempt to break through the gate and engage the enemy inside. Periodically, amidst the chaos, he could extend an offer to negotiate terms, using one or more strategic approaches to weaken their resolve.

If birds—like vultures, crows, naptris, bhásas, parrots, máinas, or pigeons—are nesting in the fort walls, he might capture these birds, attach combustible powders to their tails, and release them toward the fort to spread fire. When his camp is set at a distance with elevated posts for archers and their flags in view, the enemy fort may be ignited from afar. Spies, disguised as fort watchmen, can secure inflammable powders to the tails of mongooses, monkeys, cats, or dogs and let these animals wander over thatched roofs to ignite them. A small fire hidden within a dried fish may also be carried by a monkey, a crow, or any other bird, delivering fire onto the thatched roofs within the fort.

Small incendiary balls can be made by mixing ingredients like sarala (Pinus Longifolia), devadáru (deodar), pútitrina (stinking grass), guggulu (Bdellium), sriveshtaka (turpentine), the juice of sarja (Vatica Robusta), and láksha (lac) combined with the dung of animals such as an ass, camel, sheep, and goat. These balls are highly inflammable and designed to sustain a flame for long durations.

An alternative incendiary powder can be prepared by blending the powder of priyala (Chironjia Sapida), the charcoal of avalguja (Serratula anthelmintica), madhúchchhishta (wax), and the dung of a horse, ass, camel, and cow. This powder is effective when hurled against the enemy as it is capable of igniting upon impact.

Another mixture involves the powdered form of all common metals, rendered to a fiery red hue, or a blend of powdered kumbhí (Gmelina arborea), sísa (lead), and trapu (zinc) with charcoal from the flowers of páribhadraka (deodar) and palása (Butea Frondosa), mixed with oil, wax, and turpentine. This combination produces another potent incendiary powder.

To create a fire-arrow, a stick coated with visvásagháti and the above mixture can be wrapped with a bark that includes hemp, zinc, and lead. These arrows are highly effective for use against enemy forces.

However, if a fort can be taken by other methods, setting it on fire should be avoided. Fire is unpredictable and dangerous, potentially incurring the wrath of the gods and destroying valuable resources, including grains, cattle, gold, and raw materials. Capturing a fort where everything has been ruined by fire also brings additional losses in terms of upkeep and repairs, making a less destructive method of conquest preferable.

When the conqueror assesses that he is sufficiently stocked with resources, supplies, and skilled workers, while his enemy is weakened, suffering from incompetent or corrupt officers, unprepared with incomplete forts, low on supplies, and isolated or even allied with untrustworthy friends, then he should recognize this as the perfect opportunity to launch a siege and storm the fort with full force.

When fire, whether accidental or set deliberately, erupts; when the enemy's people are occupied with sacrificial rituals, watching performances, involved in a brawl sparked by drunkenness, or when the troops are exhausted from prolonged battles and have suffered significant losses over repeated engagements; when the enemy's people, weary and sleep-deprived, have fallen into a deep slumber; or when there is the cover of cloudy weather, floods, thick fog, or snow — these moments are ideal for launching a full assault.

Alternatively, the conqueror might abandon his camp to hide in a nearby forest, striking at the enemy when they come out in pursuit. Another tactic involves a king pretending to be the enemy's closest friend or ally, deepening their bond and sending a messenger to convey messages like, "Here's your weak point; these are your internal enemies; this is the weakness of the besieging forces; and this person (who appears to have abandoned the conqueror to join you) is now your ally." When this supposed ally returns from the enemy with a second messenger, the conqueror can capture and publicly reveal the "traitor's" actions, banish him, and momentarily withdraw from siege activities. The supposed ally may then suggest to the besieged enemy, "Come out to join me, or let's unite to strike at the besieger." When the enemy is lured out, they can be trapped between two forces — the conqueror's and the ally's — and either killed or captured. The conqueror may then seize the enemy's territory and raze the capital to the ground, drawing out the elite of the enemy's forces to destroy them.

This approach explains the conqueror's handling of a subjugated enemy or a wild chief.

Either a conquered foe or a wild tribal chief working with the conqueror may deceive the besieged by saying, "The conqueror seems to consider retreating from the siege, fearing the spread of disease, vulnerability to a rear attack, or potential rebellion within his ranks." Once the besieged enemy believes this, the conqueror may set fire to his camp as a ruse and pull back. Then, when the enemy comes out, they can be trapped as before.

Alternatively, the conqueror may gather merchandise laced with poison and trick the enemy by sending this tainted merchandise to them. Another approach is to have a supposed ally of the enemy send a message saying, "Come out to attack the conqueror, who has already been struck by me." When the enemy complies and leaves their stronghold, they can be surrounded as before.

Spies disguised as friends or relatives, equipped with appropriate passes and orders, may infiltrate the enemy's fort and assist in its capture. Or, a feigned ally of the enemy could relay to the besieged: "I plan to strike the besieging camp at this specific time and place; when that happens, you should join in the attack with me." Should the enemy decide to attack, or if they come out upon hearing a chaotic uproar from the supposedly threatened besieging army, they may be defeated as before.

The conqueror may also persuade a friendly ally or a wild chief in alliance with the enemy to seize the enemy's land while they're under siege. If such an ally attempts to take the enemy's territory, the conqueror can deploy spies among the enemy's population or recruit leaders from the enemy's defectors to assassinate this ally, or the conqueror himself may secretly administer poison. A second fake friend may then inform the enemy that the murdered ally was acting treacherously, trying to seize the territory of his so-called friend in a time of distress. After building greater trust with the enemy, this feigned friend can sow seeds of discord between the enemy and their officers, possibly leading to their execution. By inciting unrest among the enemy's people, this spy can suppress the uprising without the enemy's knowledge. Then, after gathering a portion of his army, reinforced by fierce wild tribes, the feigned ally can enter the enemy's fort, only to let the conqueror's forces take control.

Lastly, traitors, enemies, wild tribes, or defectors from the enemy's ranks may claim to have been reconciled, honored, and rewarded, then return to the enemy's side and facilitate the fort's capture by the conqueror.

Once he has captured the fort or returned to his camp after its capture, the conqueror should show mercy to the defeated enemy's troops who surrender, whether they lie prostrate in the field, stand with their backs turned, have their hair disheveled, have thrown down their weapons, or are visibly distressed and fearful. After ensuring that the captured fort is secured, with his men guarding it both inside and out and clearing it of any remaining enemy loyalists, he can make his victorious entry.

With the territory of the immediate enemy subdued, the conqueror should next set his sights on that of the madhyama king. Upon securing this, he can then focus on the neutral king's lands, completing the first method of world conquest. If the madhyama and neutral kings are absent, he should instead earn the loyalty and trust of the former enemy's subjects through his own virtues, then turn his attention to conquering other distant enemies. This is the second path to victory. In the absence of a Circle of States to challenge, he may defeat either a friend or an enemy by positioning his forces strategically between his ally and adversary, gaining an advantage through their placement. This is the third approach.

Alternatively, he could start by defeating an almost unconquerable neighboring enemy, thus doubling his own power. With this strength, he can then take on a second enemy, tripling his power upon victory, before setting his sights on a third. This constitutes the fourth way to achieve total conquest.

Once he has conquered the land and its people, each with their own unique castes and ways of religious life, the conqueror should rule and enjoy his kingdom, governing in accordance with the noble responsibilities prescribed for kings.

- The five methods for capturing a fort are as follows: creating intrigue, employing spies, winning over the loyalty of the enemy's people, conducting a siege, and launching a direct assault.

[Thus ends Chapter IV, "The Operation of a Siege and Storming a Fort," in Book XIII, "Strategic Means to Capture a Fortress," of the Arthasástra of Kautilya. End of the hundred and forty-fourth chapter from the beginning.]

CHAPTER V. RESTORATION OF PEACE IN A CONQUERED COUNTRY.

The conqueror's military campaign may target either vast wilderness areas or single villages and small settlements. The territory he gains can be classified into three types: newly acquired land, territory reclaimed from usurpers, and inherited land.

For newly acquired territories, he should outshine the enemy by displaying his own virtues and amplifying them to overshadow any merits of the enemy. This includes adhering to his own duties rigorously, staying focused on his responsibilities, providing rewards, reducing taxes, offering gifts, and bestowing honors. The conqueror should align himself with the local leaders and influential figures. He should also fulfill any promises made to defectors from the enemy's side and continue rewarding their loyalty each time they support him.

Failure to keep promises weakens trust with both the conqueror's own people and the enemy's. Acting against the people's wishes or traditions will also damage reliability.

To build rapport, he should adopt the local customs, language, dress, and social norms. Participating in national, religious, and local festivals shows solidarity. His spies should highlight for local leaders, village heads, castes, and guilds how the enemy was punished and, by contrast, how much respect and support the conqueror offers them, aligning his prosperity with theirs. By providing gifts, tax relief, and security, he can win over the people. The conqueror should openly honor religious practices and support scholars, speakers, charitable, and courageous individuals with gifts of land, financial aid, and tax relief.

He should release prisoners and support those who are poor, helpless, or ill. To encourage compassion, animal slaughter could be restricted for two weeks during the monsoon festival (Chaturmasya), four nights around the full moon, and on his birthday or on the national day. Additionally, the killing of young animals and females should be prohibited, as should castration.

Practices or customs that threaten his revenue, military strength, or moral principles should be reformed. Known thieves and certain nomadic groups should frequently change locations, keeping them from consolidating power or influence. Loyal officers in charge of forts, rural areas, and the army, along with ministers and priests who have been caught conspiring with the enemy, should be required to live on the borders of the enemy's territory, thus reducing any internal threat.

Potentially harmful individuals who understand their own fortunes are tied to the conqueror's success should be pacified through private reprimands, while defectors captured with the enemy should be relocated to distant areas. Relatives of the enemy who pose a threat and take refuge in nearby wilderness or border regions should be granted less productive lands or a fourth of a fertile area, in exchange for taxes and soldiers. This arrangement may provoke public discontent, leading to their downfall.

Anyone who disrupts public peace or loses favor with the people should be moved to a precarious area where any actions against the conqueror may ultimately endanger them.

After reclaiming a lost territory, the conqueror should conceal the flaws that led to its loss and amplify the virtues that allowed its recovery.

For an inherited territory, he should mask the weaknesses of his predecessor and highlight his own strengths and virtues.

- He should establish any righteous practices observed in other territories but not yet followed in his own, and he should prevent the adoption of any customs, even if common elsewhere, that are considered unrighteous.

Book 14

CHAPTER I. MEANS TO INJURE AN ENEMY.

To protect the structure of the four castes, the methods discussed in the secret sciences should be used against those who act wickedly. Using individuals of the Mlechchha class skilled in various disguises that fit different regions, trades, or professions—or who can appear as hump-backed, dwarfed, short-statured, mute, deaf, mentally unsound, or blind—poisons such as kálakúta and others should be discreetly applied in the food and other pleasures of the wicked. Spies embedded in the same household or in close proximity may utilize weapons during royal events, sports, musical gatherings, or other festivities. Spies disguised as night wanderers or fire-keepers can set fire to the properties of wrongdoers.

The powder made from specific creatures—like the chitra, bheka (frog), kaundinyaka, krikana (a type of partridge), panchakushtha, and satapadi (centipede)—or from others, such as uchchitinga (crab), kambali, krikalása (lizard), with satakanda (a plant bark), or creatures like grihagaulika (house lizard), andháhika (blind snake), krakanthaka (another partridge), pútikíta (a noxious insect), and gomárika, mixed with the juices of bhallátaka (Semecarpus Anacardium) and valgaka, can produce smoke that causes immediate death when burned.

- If any of these creatures are heated with a black snake and priyangu (panic seed) and then powdered, the mixture, once set aflame, causes instant fatality.

The powder made from the roots of dhámárgava (likely lufta foetida) and yátudhána, when mixed with powder from the flower of bhallátaka (Semecarpus Anacardium), induces death within half a month when administered. The root of vyághata (Cassia fistula), ground with bhallátaka flowers and the essence from an insect (kíta), leads to death within a month. Doses differ by creature: a kalá (1/16 of a tola) for humans, twice that amount for mules and horses, and four times for elephants and camels.

When burned, the smoke from satakardama, uchchitinga (crab), karavira (nerium odorum), katutumbi (a type of bitter gourd), and fish mixed with the chaff from madana and kodrava grains (paspalam scrobiculatum), or with the chaff of hastikarna seeds (castor oil tree) and palása (butea frondosa), kills all life within the reach of the wind.

The smoke from burning pútikita (a stinking insect), fish, katutumbi, satakardama bark, and indragopa (cochineal insect), or a mix of pútikita, kshudrárála resin (shorea robusta), and hemavidári, when combined with goat hoof and horn powder, causes blindness.

Smoke from pútikaranja (guilandina bonducella) leaves, yellow arsenic, realgar, gunja seeds (abrus precatorius), red cotton seed chaff, ásphota (Careya arborea), khácha (possibly salt), along with cow dung and urine, also results in blindness.

Blindness can similarly result from smoke produced by burning snake skin, cow and horse dung, and the head of a blind snake.

To create instant lethality wherever wind carries it, one can burn a mixture of dung and urine from pigeons, frogs, carnivores, elephants, humans, and boars, plus chaff and barley powder combined with kásísa (green sulfate of iron), rice, cotton seeds, kutaja (nerium antidysentericum), and kosátaki (lufta pentandra). Add cow's urine, bhándi root (hydrocotyle asiatica), nimba (neem), sigru (moringa), phanirjaka (tulsi variant), kshíbapíluka (ripe Coreya arborea), and bhánga (a common intoxicant), along with snake and fish skin, elephant nail and tusk powder, chaff from madana and kodravá seeds, or chaff from hastikarna seeds and palása.

For assaults, a combatant may safeguard their eyes with ointment and medicinal water before burning roots like káli (Tragia involucrata), kushtha (costus), nada (a reed), satávari (asparagus racemosus), or a powder of snake skin, peacock tail, krikana (a kind of partridge), and panchakushtha. This mixture, along with previously specified or moist or dry chaff, produces smoke that blinds all exposed animals.

An ointment created by combining the secretions of the sáriká (myna), kapota (pigeon), baka (crane), and baláka (a type of small crane) with the milk of kákshiva (possibly moringa), píluka (a type of Careya arborea), and snuhi (Euphorbia plant) can induce blindness and also poison water sources.

A blend of yavaka (a type of barley), sála root (Achyranthes triandria), fruit of madana (possibly the datura plant), leaves of játí (possibly nutmeg), and human urine, mixed with powdered plaksha root (fig tree) and vidári (liquorice), along with extracts from decoctions of musta (a poisonous plant), udumbara (cluster fig), and kodrava (paspalam scrobiculatum), or with a decoction made from hastikarna (castor oil plant) and palása (Butea frondosa) is known as "madana juice" (madanayoga).

Similarly, a combination of powders made from sringi (atis betula), gaumevriksha, kantakára (solanum xanthocarpum), mayúrapadi, gunja seeds (abrus precatorius), lánguli (possibly Jussiaea repens), vishamúlika, and ingudi (possibly heart-pea), with additional powders from karavira (oleander), akshipiluka (Careya arborea), arka plant, and mrigamáríni, blended with a decoction of madana and kodrava or alternatively with hastikarna and palása, is also termed a "madana mixture" (madanayoga).

Together, these mixtures, when applied, poison grass and water sources.

Smoke produced by burning a blend of krikana (a partridge), krikalása (lizard), grihagaulika (a house lizard), and andháhika (a blind snake) severely damages eyesight and can cause madness.

The smoke from krikalása and grihagaulika alone may induce leprosy.

Adding chitrabheka (a colorful frog) entrails and madhu (possibly Celtis orientalis) to this mixture, when burned, produces smoke that leads to gonorrhea.

The same mixture, when moistened with human blood, can induce consumption.

A combination of dúshívisha, madana (possibly datura), and kodrava (paspalam scrobiculatum) destroys the tongue when applied.

A mix containing the powder of mátriváhaka, jalúka (leech), peacock tail feathers, frog eyes, and píluká (Careya arborea) brings about vishúchika disease.

Finally, a concoction of panchakushtha, kaundinyaka, rájavriksha (Cassia fistula), madhupushpa (bassia latifolia), and madhu (honey) is known to cause fever.

A mixture made from the powdered knot of the tongue of the bhája (?) and nakula (mongoose) blended into a paste with the milk of a she-donkey induces both deafness and muteness.

The doses required to bring about desired deformities in humans or animals within a fortnight or a month follow the prescribed quantities mentioned earlier.

The potency of these mixtures is enhanced considerably: in the case of drugs, by preparing them as a decoction; for animals, by creating them as powders; or, universally, by using the decoction method.

An arrow tipped with a mixture prepared from powdered sálmali (Bombax heptaphyllum) and vidári (liquorice), combined with múlavatsanábha (a type of poison) powder and smeared with musk-rat blood, can induce biting behavior in the victim. This individual bites others, causing a chain reaction where those bitten continue to bite others.

A preparation from the flowers of bhallátaka (Semecarpus anacardium), yátudhána (?), dhámárgava (Achyranthes aspera), and bána (sal tree), mixed with powdered elá (large cardamom), kákshi (red aluminous earth), guggulu (bdellium), and háláhala (a potent poison), along with goat and human blood, induces a violent madness, driving those affected to bite others.

If a half dharana (unit of weight) of this concoction, mixed with flour and oil-cakes, is cast into a reservoir a hundred bows long, it taints the entire body of water. Fish that ingest or even touch this mixture become poisonous; anyone who drinks or touches the water is also poisoned.

A condemned individual who pulls from the earth an alligator or iguana (godhá) with three or five handfuls of both red and white mustard seeds will die upon merely seeing it.

During rituals on days ruled by the stars krittiká or bharaní, if a black cobra, frothing at the mouth from a lightning shock or captured using sticks from a tree struck by lightning, is offered into a fire while performing fearful rites, that fire will continue to burn unquenchably.

- An offering of honey should be made in a fire fetched from the blacksmith's house; of wine in a fire brought from the vintner's house; and of clarified butter in the fire of a sacrificer.
- An offering of a garland should be made in the fire kept by a sacrificer with one wife; of mustard seeds in the fire maintained by an adulterous woman; of curds in the fire kept during a child's birth; and of rice-grain in the fire of a sacrificer.
- An offering of flesh should be made in the fire kept by a chandala; of human flesh in the fire burning in cremation grounds. Additionally, an offering of the serum from goat and human flesh shall be made with a sacrificial ladle in a fire that combines all the above fires.
- Repeating sacred chants to the fire, an offering of wooden pieces from the rájavriksha (cassia fistula) tree should be made into this same fire. This fire will burn unquenchably, creating illusions and confusion for the enemy.

Greetings to Aditi, greetings to Anumati, greetings to Sarasvati, and greetings to the Sun; an offering to Agni, an offering to Soma, an offering to the Earth, and an offering to the Atmosphere.

[Thus ends Chapter I, "Means to Injure an Enemy," in Book XIV, "Secret Means," of the Arthasástra of Kautilya. End of the hundred and forty-sixth chapter from the beginning.]

CHAPTER II. WONDERFUL AND DELUSIVE CONTRIVANCES.

A dose of powder made from sirisha (mimosa tree), udumbara (glomerous fig-tree), and sami (acacia suma), when mixed with clarified butter, allows a person to sustain fasting for up to half a month. Similarly, a froth concocted from the roots of kaseruka (a type of water-creeper), utpala (costus plant), and sugar cane, combined with bisa (water lily), durva grass, milk, and clarified butter, enables fasting for a month.

A blend of powders from masha (mung beans), yava (barley), kuluttha (horse gram), and the roots of darbha (sacred grass), mixed with milk and clarified butter, also sustains fasting. Milk derived from valli (a kind of vine) and clarified butter made from it, mixed equally with paste from sala (shorea robusta) and prisniparni (hedysarum lagopodioides) roots and consumed with milk, allows one to endure fasting for up to a month. Another option includes drinking a mixture of milk, clarified butter, and a spirit made from the same ingredients to facilitate a month-long fast.

Oil derived from mustard seeds soaked for seven nights in the urine of a white goat will, after being stored in a large bitter gourd for a month and a half, change the color of both bipedal and quadrupedal creatures when applied externally. Oil from white mustard seeds mixed with barley contained in the dung of a white donkey, which has been fed exclusively on butter, milk, and barley for over a week, also induces a color change.

An oil made from mustard seeds previously steeped in the urine and liquid dung of either a white goat or a white donkey results in a white color similar to the fiber of the arka plant or the down feathers of a white bird when applied. A blend of dung from a white rooster and an ajagara (boa constrictor) produces a white coloring effect.

A mixture created from white mustard seeds that have been kept for seven nights in white goat urine, combined with buttermilk, arka plant milk, salt, and grains (dhanya), will, if applied for a period of two weeks, turn the skin white. Finally, a paste made from white mustard seeds kept in a large bitter gourd along with clarified butter from valli creeper milk for half a month will turn hair white.

- A mixture made from bitter gourd, a pungent-smelling insect (putikita), and a white house lizard, when ground into a paste and applied to hair, will turn the hair as white as a conch shell.

If any part of a person's body is rubbed with a paste made from tinduka (glutinosa) and arishta (soap-berry), along with cow dung, and then coated with the juice of bhallataka (marking nut or semecarpus anacardium), that area will develop leprosy within a month.

The application of a paste made from gunja seeds that have been stored for seven nights in the mouth of a white cobra or a house lizard will also cause leprosy. Similarly, external application of the liquid from parrot and cuckoo eggs results in leprosy.

To treat leprosy, one may use a paste or decoction from priyala (possibly chironjia sapida or vitis vinifera). Eating a mixture of powders made from the roots of kukkuta (marsilia dentata), kosataki (duffa pentandra), and satavari (asparagus racemosus) for a month will lighten the skin to white.

Bathing in a decoction of vata (banyan tree) and rubbing the body with a paste from sahachara (yellow barleria) will darken the skin. A mixture of sulphur arsenic and red arsenic, when combined with oil from sakuna (a type of bird) and kanka (vulture), will also cause darkening.

Powder from the khadyota (fire-fly) mixed with mustard oil will make the mixture glow at night. The powder of khadyota (fire-fly) and gandupada (earthworm), or the powder of ocean-dwelling creatures combined with bhringa (malabathrum), kapala (a pot-herb), khadira (mimosa catechu), and karnikara (pentapetes acerifolia), mixed with the oils from sakuna and kanka, becomes tejanachurna (an ignition powder).

Rubbing the body with a powder made from the charcoal of paribhadraka (erythrina indica) bark mixed with frog serum can protect the skin from being harmed by fire. A body coated with a paste from the bark of paribhadraka and sesame seeds will burn when exposed to fire without causing harm to the individual.

A ball made from the powdered charcoal of the bark of pilu (careya arborea) can be held in one's hand while being burned without causing harm.

When a person's body is coated with the serum from frog flesh, it can be exposed to fire without injury. If this serum is combined with oils extracted from the fruits of kusa (ficus religiosa) and amra (mango tree), and if a powder made from an ocean frog (samudra manduki), phenaka (sea foam), and sarjarasa (the resin of vatica robusta) is sprinkled over the body, it will burn with fire but remain unharmed.

Applying sesame oil mixed with equal parts serum from frog flesh, crab, and similar animals to the body enables it to withstand fire. Additionally, if the body is coated in the serum of frog flesh alone, it remains protected from burns.

If the body is rubbed with a mixture containing the powder of bamboo roots and saivala (an aquatic plant) and then coated with frog serum, it will be safe from fire damage.

For someone who applies oil derived from a paste made from the roots of paribhadraka (erythrina indica), pratibala (?), vanjula (a type of rattan or tree), vajra (either andropogon muricatum or euphorbia), and kadali (banana) mixed with frog serum onto their legs, they can walk over fire without harm.

- Oil can be made from a paste using the roots of pratibala, vanjula, and paribhadraka, plants that grow near water, and blending it with serum from frog flesh.
- When this special oil is applied to one's legs, it allows the person to walk across a white-hot bed of fire as effortlessly as if strolling over soft petals.

If large birds like the hamsa (goose), krauncha (heron), and mayura (peacock) are released at night with a burning reed attached to their tails, they create the appearance of a firebrand descending from the sky. Ashes left from a lightning strike can extinguish fire. Placing kidney beans (masha) soaked in menstrual fluid, along with the roots of vajra (a type of grass) and kadali (banana), both soaked in frog serum, in a fireplace prevents grains from being cooked. Cleaning the fireplace will restore its function.

Holding a small ball of pilu (careya arborea) or a knot of the root of suvarchala (linseed tree) filled with fire inside and wrapped with thread and cotton enables a person to exhale smoke and fire. Pouring oil made from kusa (ficus religiosa) and amra (mango) onto fire keeps it burning even during a storm. Sea-foam soaked in oil will burn steadily when floating on water.

A fire started by churning a monkey's bone with a bamboo stick that has both white and black coloring (kalmasavenu) will continue to burn in water instead of being extinguished. If a fire is started by churning the left rib bone of a person who died by weapon or execution using a similarly colored bamboo stick, or by rubbing together bones of two different people, it will prevent any other fire from burning in that place when circled three times counterclockwise.

- A paste made from animals such as the chuchundari (musk-rat), khanjarita (likely a small mammal), and kharakita (unidentified animal) mixed with horse urine, when applied to shackles binding someone's legs, will cause the chains to break apart.

When the ayaskanta (sun-stone) or other similar stones are wetted with the serum from the flesh of animals like kulinda, dardura, and kharakita, they will shatter. A paste made from the powdered rib bones of animals such as naraka, a donkey, kanka (a type of vulture), and bhasa (another bird), combined with water-lily juice, can be applied to the legs of humans and animals during travel.

For long journeys, a person can wear shoes made from camel skin, coated with serum from the flesh of an owl and a vulture, and covered with banyan leaves; this preparation allows a person to walk up to fifty yojanas without tiring. When these shoes are smeared with the marrow, pith, or essence of the birds syena, kanka, kaka, gridhra, hamsa, krauncha, and vichiralla, the traveler can journey up to a hundred yojanas without fatigue.

The fat or serum from roasting a pregnant camel alongside saptaparna (Indian devil tree), or from roasting deceased children in cremation grounds, can also be applied to facilitate a journey of a hundred yojanas.

By displaying such remarkable and awe-inspiring techniques, terror can be instilled in the enemy, utilizing these wonders to evoke fear.

- While anger and terror are common responses, creating terror through such extraordinary means is considered an effective strategy for securing peace.

[Thus ends Chapter II, "Wonderful and Delusive Contrivances," in Book XIV, "Secret Means," of the Arthasástra of Kautilya. End of the hundred and forty-seventh chapter from the beginning.]

CHAPTER III. THE APPLICATION OF MEDICINES AND MANTRAS.

By removing the right and left eye-balls of animals such as a cat, camel, wolf, boar, porcupine, váguli, naptri, crow, and owl—or even from just one, two, three, or multiple animals that are active at night— one can create two types of powder from them. When someone applies the powder from the left eye of one of these animals to their own right eye, and the powder from the right eye to their own left eye, they can see clearly even in the darkest of nights.

- One effective choice is the eye of a boar, or that of a khadyota (fire-fly), a crow, or a mina bird. Applying any of these to one's eyes enables clear vision at night.

After fasting for three nights, on the day marked by the star Pushya, one should obtain the skull of a man who has been executed or killed in combat. This skull should be filled with soil and barley seeds, which are then to be watered with goat and sheep milk. Wearing a garland made from the sprouts of this barley will render the wearer invisible to others.

Similarly, after fasting for three nights, one should remove both the right and left eyes of a dog, cat, owl, and váguli (if available) on the day of Pushya. These should be ground into two types of powder and used as an ointment for one's eyes, allowing the wearer to become unseen.

On another occasion of fasting for three nights, a round-headed pin (saláká) should be crafted from a branch of the purushagháti (punnága tree) on the day of Pushya. This pin, alongside the ointment prepared in the skull of any nocturnal animal, should be inserted into the reproductive organ of a deceased woman, then burned. The extracted ointment, when applied to one's eyes, allows one to walk undetected.

If one encounters the burnt or partially burnt corpse of a Bráhman who kept sacrificial fire, fasting for three nights there and then gathering ashes in a sack made from the clothes of a naturally deceased person on the Pushya star day can be an effective way to achieve invisibility. Wearing this sack on the back renders one unseen.

The dried skin of a snake, packed with the powdered bones and marrow or fat of a cow sacrificed for a Bráhman's funeral rites, when placed on the back of cattle, will render them invisible.

The slough of a prachaláka (a type of bird) filled with the ashes of a snake-bite victim's corpse will make wild animals invisible.

A snake's skin filled with the powdered bone from the knee-joint, combined with that of the tail and the excrement of an owl and a váguli, can make birds invisible.

These are the eight specific methods known to achieve invisibility.

- I bow to Bali, son of Virochana; to Sambara, master of a hundred magical arts; to Bhandírapáka, Naraka, Nikumbha, and Kumbha.
- I bow to Devala and Nárada; I bow to Sávarnigálava. With their permission, I bring upon thee a profound sleep.
- As the boa-constrictor known as *ajagara* drifts into a deep slumber, so may the guards of this village, restless and vigilant, fall into a deep, unbreakable sleep.
- With thousands of guard dogs, hundreds of watchful geese, and donkeys all lulled into a deep, tranquil sleep, I shall step quietly into this place, and may the dogs remain calm and silent.
- Bowing to Manu and securing the roguish dogs, I also bow to the gods in the heavens and to the Bráhmans among men;
- To those skilled in Vedic wisdom, those who have reached the heights of Kailása through penance, and to all sages and prophets, I bring deep slumber to thee.

The fan of Chamari waves, and may all obstacles withdraw. I offer my respects to Manu, to you, O Aliti and Paliti.

The usage of the above mantra is as follows:—

After fasting for three nights, on the fourteenth day of the dark half of the month, specifically on the day marked by the star Pushya, one should obtain vilikhávalekhana (possibly fingernails) from a low-caste woman (svapáki). Keeping them in a small basket, one should bury them alone in a cremation ground. On the next fourteenth day, they are to be unearthed and ground into a paste with kumári (possibly aloe). Small pills are then formed from the paste. When any of these pills is placed in a location while chanting the above mantra, all living creatures in that area will fall into a deep sleep.

Following a similar ritual, three white and three black dart-like hairs (salyaka) of a porcupine should be buried separately in a cremation ground. When these are retrieved on the next fourteenth day, and scattered along with ashes from a burnt corpse while chanting the above mantra, all living creatures in that area will fall into deep sleep.

- Oblation to thee, O Amile, Kimile, Vayujáre, Prayoge, Phake, Kavayusve, Vihále, and Dantakatake, oblation to thee.
- May the vigilant dogs guarding the village fall into a deep, restful slumber; these three white dart-like hairs of the porcupine are the creation of Bráhma.

All prophets have fallen into deep slumber. I cast sleep over the entire village up to its borders until the sun rises. Oblation!

- May the dogs that vigilantly guard the village fall into a deep, peaceful slumber; these three white, dart-like hairs from the porcupine are creations of Bráhma.
- All enlightened sages have fallen into profound sleep. I cast sleep over the entire village, reaching every corner and boundary, until the sun rises. Oblation!

To apply the mantra above:

After fasting for seven nights, a person should obtain three white, dart-like hairs from a porcupine. On the fourteenth day of the dark half of the month, they must make 108 oblations into a sacred fire using sacrificial wood from khadira (mimosa catechu) and similar trees, adding honey and clarified butter while chanting the mantra. Then, chanting the mantra again, they should bury one of the hairs at the entrance of a village or any house within it. This will cause all animal life inside to fall into a deep sleep.

- I offer my respects to Bali, son of Vairochana; to S'atamáya, S'ambara, Nikumbha, Naraka, Kumbha, Tantukachchha, and the mighty demon.
- I honor Armálava, Pramíla, Mandolúka, Ghatodbala, Krishna with his followers, and the renowned woman, Paulomi.
- Reciting the sacred mantras, I retrieve the essence or bone of

the corpse (savasárika) that fulfills my desired intentions—may the S'alaka demons be triumphant; I bow to them with offerings. May the vigilant dogs guarding the village enter a deep and peaceful sleep.

- May all enlightened ones (siddhárthāh) rest in contentment regarding our goal from dusk to dawn, until my aim is achieved. Oblation!

The method of applying the above mantra is as follows:

After fasting for four nights, on the fourteenth day of the dark half of the month, perform an animal sacrifice (bali) in the cremation grounds. While chanting the above mantra, gather the essence (savasárika) of a corpse and place it in a basket made from leaves (pattrapauttalikā). When this basket is pierced in its center with a dart-like hair of a porcupine and buried while reciting the mantra, all animal life in that area will fall into a deep slumber.

- I seek protection from the god of fire and all goddesses in the ten directions; may all obstacles be removed, and may everything come under my control. Oblation.

The application of the above mantra is as follows:--

Having fasted for three nights and having on the day of the star of Pushya prepared twenty-one pieces of sugar-candy, one should make oblation into the fire with honey and clarified butter; and having worshipped the pieces of sugar-candy with scents and garlands of flowers, one should bury them. When, having on the next day of the star of Pushya unearthed the pieces of sugar-candy, and chanting the above mantra, one strikes the door-panel of a house with one piece and throws four pieces in the interior, the door will open itself.

Having fasted for four nights, one should on the fourteenth day of the dark half of the month get a figure of a bull prepared from the bone of a man, and worship it, repeating the above mantra. Then a cart drawn by two bulls will be brought before the worshipper who can (mount it and) drive in the sky and tell all that is connected with the sun and other planets of the sky.

O, Chandáli Kumbhi, Tumba Katuka, and Sárigha, thou art possessed of the bhaga of a woman, oblation to thee.

When this mantra is repeated, the door will open and the inmates fall into sleep.

Having fasted for three nights, one should on the day of the star of Pushya fill with soil the skull of a man killed with weapons or put to the gallows, and, planting in it valli (vallari ?) plants, should irrigate them with water. Having taken up the grown-up plants on the next day of the star of Pushya (i.e., after 27 days), one should manufacture a rope from them. When this rope is cut into two pieces before a drawn bow or any other shooting machine, the string of those machines will be suddenly cut into two pieces.

When the slough of a water-snake (udakáhi) is filled with the breathed-out dirt (uchchhvásamrittika?) of a man or woman (and is held before the face and nose of any person), it causes those organs to swell.

When the sack-like skin of the abdomen of a dog or a boar is filled with the breathed-out dirt (uchchhvásamrittika) of a man or woman and is bound (to the body of a man) with the ligaments of a monkey, it causes the man's body to grow in width and length (ánáha),

When a figure of an enemy carved from the rájavriksha (cassia fistula) tree is coated with the bile of a brown cow that was sacrificed on the fourteenth day of the dark half of the month, it induces blindness in the enemy.

After fasting for four nights and performing an animal sacrifice (bali) on the fourteenth day of the dark half of the month, create several bolt-like pieces from the bone of a man who was executed on the gallows. If one of these pieces is placed in the feces or urine of an enemy, it will cause the enemy's body to swell (ánáha). If the piece is buried beneath the enemy's feet or seat, it will cause him to suffer a wasting illness, leading to death. If it is buried in the enemy's shop, fields, or house, it will cause him financial ruin and a loss of livelihood.

This method of smearing and burying also applies to bolt-like pieces (kílaka) crafted from the vidyuddanda tree.

- If the nail of the little finger, along with nimba (neem), káma (bdellium), madhu (celtis orientalis), a monkey's hair, and a human bone,
- Is wrapped in a garment of the deceased and buried in a person's house or trodden underfoot by them, that individual and their family—including spouse, children, and wealth—will not survive beyond three fortnights.
- Similarly, if the little finger nail, along with nimba, káma, madhu, and the bone of a person who died of natural causes, is buried under a person's feet or close to their residence,
- Or near the camp of an army, village, or city, the affected person (or community) along with their spouse, children, and possessions will not endure beyond three fortnights
- Collecting the hairs of a sheep, monkey, cat, and mongoose, as well as the hair of Bráhmans, those of low caste (svapáka), and of a crow and owl, can bring about specific outcomes.
- When the collected hairs of a sheep, monkey, cat, mongoose, Bráhmans, those of low caste (svapáka), and of a crow and owl are ground into a paste with feces, its application causes instantaneous death.

If a garland taken from a deceased person, the ashes from a burnt corpse, the hair of a mongoose, and the skins of a scorpion, bee, and snake are buried under a person's feet, that person will lose all human appearance As long as these items remain in place, the effect continues.

After fasting for three nights and, on the day of the star of Pushya, planting gunja seeds in the soil-filled skull of a man who was executed or killed by weapons, one should water them. On the next new or full moon day under the star of Pushya, the grown plants can be removed and used to create circular pedestals (mandaliká). Any food or water vessels placed on these pedestals will remain undiminished in quantity.

During a grand night procession, cut off the nipples from a deceased cow's udder and burn them in a torch flame. The ashes should be mixed with bull urine to coat a fresh vessel. When this vessel is carried around the village in a counterclockwise direction and then set down, it will attract all the butter produced by the cows in the village to itself.

On the fourteenth day of the dark half of the month aligned with the star of Pushya, insert an iron seal into the reproductive organ of a dog, and retrieve it once it falls out on its own. When this seal is held and the magician calls for a collection of fruits, they will arrive of their own accord.

• By using mantras, specific substances, and other magical practices, one can safeguard their own people and bring harm to the enemy.

[Thus ends Chapter III, "The Application of Medicine and Mantras," in Book XIV, "Secret Means," of the Arthasástra of Kautilya. End of the hundred and forty-eighth chapter from the beginning.]

CHAPTER IV. REMEDIES AGAINST THE INJURIES OF ONE'S OWN ARMY.

To counteract the effects of poisons and toxic compounds used by enemies against one's own army or people:

When items intended for the king's use, including parts of the body of his consorts, as well as military equipment, are cleansed in warm water made from a decoction containing sleshmátaki (sebesten or cordia myk), kapi (emblica officinalis), madanti, danta (ivory), satha (Citron tree), gojigi (gojihva or elephantophus scaber), visha (aconitum ferox), pátali (bignonia suaveolens), bala (lida cardifolia and rombifolia), syonáka (bignonia indica), punarnava, sveta (andropogon aciculatum), and tagara (tabernæmontana coronaria), mixed with sandalwood (chandana) and the blood of a jackal (salávriki), it neutralizes the harmful effects of poison.

A compound made from the bile of prishata (red-spotted deer), nakula (mongoose), nílakantha (peacock), and godhá (alligator), mixed with charcoal powder (mashíráji) and the young shoots (agra) of sinduvára (vitex trifolia), tagara (tabernæmontana coronaria), varuna (teriandium indicum), tandulíyaka (amaranthus polygamus), and sataparva (convolvulus repens), along with pindítaka (vangueria spinosa), can counteract the effects of a madana poison mixture.

Decoctions made from the roots of srigála (bignonia indica), vinna, madana, sinduvára (vitex trifolia), tagara (tabernæmontana coronaria), and valli (a type of creeper) can be taken individually or together with milk to neutralize madana poison.

The pungent oil extracted from kaidarya (vangueria spinosa) acts as an antidote to madness.

A blend made from priyangu (panic seed) and naktamála (galedupa arborea) alleviates leprosy when applied nasally.

For consumption (a wasting disease), a preparation from kushtha (costus) and lodhra (symplocus) is beneficial.

A combination of katuphala (glelina arborea), dravanti (anthericum tuberosum), and vilanga (a type of seed) can relieve headache and other head-related ailments when applied through the nose.

The application of a mixture made from priyangu (panic seed), manjishtha (rubia manjit), tagara (tabernæmontana coronaria), lákshárasa (lac essence), madhuka, haridrá (turmeric), and kshaudra (honey) revives individuals who have lost consciousness due to incidents like being struck with a rope, falling into water, ingesting poison, being whipped, or taking a fall.

The recommended dose is approximately one aksha for humans, double for cows and horses, and quadruple for elephants and camels.

A spherical amulet (mani) prepared from this mixture and embedded with a core of gold (rukma) serves as an antidote for any poison.

An amulet made from the wood of asvattha (sacred fig tree) entwined with medicinal plants such as jívantí, sveta (andropogan aciculatum), mushkaka flowers, and vanadáka (epidendrum tesseloides) also neutralizes any form of poison.

- The sound of trumpets coated with the above mixture neutralizes poison, while anyone who gazes upon a flag or banner smeared with this mixture will be protected from poison.
- Once a king has employed these remedies to ensure his and his army's safety, he may proceed to use toxic smokes and other preparations to contaminate the enemy's water supply.

Book 15

CHAPTER I. PARAGRAPHICAL DIVISIONS OF THIS TREATISE.

The term artha, or wealth, refers to the foundation of human livelihood; the earth that sustains human life is also termed artha, or wealth. The science that explores the methods to acquire and sustain this earth is the Arthasástra, the Science of Polity.

This science is divided into thirty-two sections: the book (adhikarana), contents (vidhána), reference to similar cases (yoga), the meaning of a term (padártha), the purpose behind reasoning (hetvartha), summary (uddesa), detailed explanation (nirdesa), instruction (upadesa), quotation (apadesa), application (atidesa), place of reference (pradesa), analogy (upamána), implication (arthápatti), doubt (samsaya), reference to similar practice (presanga), contradiction (viparyaya), ellipsis (vakyasesha), approval (anumata), explanation (vyákhayána), etymology (nirvachana), example (nidarsana), exception (apavarga), special terms by the author (svasanjá), preliminary view (púrva paksha), counterview (uttrapaksha), conclusion (ekánta), future reference (anágatávekshana), previous reference (atikrantávekshana), command (niyoga), alternative (vikalpa), compilation (samuchchaya), and deduction (úhya).

A book is the portion of a work in which a particular subject or topic is addressed. For example, the Arthasástra is presented as a condensed guide of all Arthasástras, serving as a manual for kings in acquiring and sustaining the earth, as written by the teachers of old.

The contents of a book provide a concise outline of its topics, such as: "The purpose of learning; association with elders; control over the senses; selection of ministers, and similar topics."

Suggestion of similar facts is achieved by using phrases like "These and the like" to point out comparable instances; for example, "The world comprising the four castes and the four religious divisions, and the like."

The meaning of a word refers to its intended sense; for instance, in the term múlahara: "One who squanders wealth inherited from father and grandfather is known as a múlahara, or prodigal."

The purport of reason conveys the purpose behind an assertion; for example: "Charity and the enjoyment of life rely on the possession of wealth."

Mentioning a fact in brief expresses an idea in a single word or phrase; for instance: "Control over the senses is foundational to success in learning and discipline."

Detailing a fact provides an expanded explanation; for example: "The restraint of the senses refers to harmonious perception through hearing, touch, sight, taste, and smell via the ears, skin, eyes, tongue, and nose."

Guidance is conveyed through statements like, "Thus, one should live," as in: "One should live without violating the principles of righteousness and economy."

Quotation uses phrases like "he says thus" to reference other teachings; for example: "The school of Manu suggests that a king's council should have twelve ministers; Brihaspati's school advises sixteen; Usanas' school recommends twenty; Kautilya holds that the council size should suit the kingdom's needs."

Application refers to extending a discussed rule to another matter; for instance: "What applies to an unpaid debt also applies to the failure to fulfill a promised gift."

Place of reference is a method of establishing a fact or principle based on a point to be covered in greater detail later. This approach creates a preparatory context for ideas that will soon follow, offering readers a way to anticipate future discussions. For example: "Utilizing strategic methods like conciliation, bribery, dissension, and coercion, as we'll explain fully in our section on calamities." This points forward, promising further elaboration and depth regarding these tactics.

Simile is used to clarify an unseen or abstract situation by drawing a parallel with a familiar, visible circumstance. It's a way of illuminating complexities by highlighting similar, known instances. For example: "Just as a father provides guidance and security for his son, so should the ruler protect subjects who have outgrown exemptions from taxes." This analogy encourages readers to understand leadership as an extension of familial care, lending insight into the protective duties expected of a ruler.

Implication occurs when facts lead logically to an unstated, inferred truth. It's a way of suggesting principles or rules indirectly by presenting context and letting readers recognize what logically follows. For example: "A knowledgeable person, well-experienced in worldly matters, should gain the favor of a worthy and ethical king through friends and trusted advisors, implying that it is unwise and even dangerous to seek favor through those who oppose the king." Here, the underlying idea is the strategic importance of approaching a leader via trusted channels rather than through adversaries.

Doubt presents a situation where reasoning could apply to multiple options, creating an intentional ambiguity that reflects the complex nature of certain choices. It highlights scenarios where decision-making isn't straightforward but rather subject to thoughtful consideration. For example: "When deciding on a military campaign, which is more strategically sound: should a conqueror focus on an adversary whose subjects are impoverished and inclined to defect, or one whose subjects feel oppressed and resentful?" This showcases situations requiring critical evaluation without clear, singular answers.

Reference to similar procedure applies a previously discussed method or action to new and different circumstances, allowing a familiar process to serve as a guide for consistency. It extends established procedures to similar scenarios for simplicity and coherence. For example: "In cultivating lands newly allotted for agricultural use, he should follow the methods and processes already established, as before." This maintains continuity, applying proven approaches in new areas for dependable results.

Contrariety is inferred by taking the opposite meaning from a positive statement, providing insight by suggesting an alternative outcome. It's a way of deducing what could happen under contrasting conditions. For example: "When a king shows displeasure with the messenger, it implies that his response will contrast sharply with the respectful reception given to a valued emissary." This gives context by revealing likely behavior based on emotional signals.

Ellipsis omits a portion of a sentence that's implied, completing the sense in the reader's mind. This form creates a space for interpretation while conveying a complete idea. For example: "Once stripped of his feathers, he will lose his power to move." Here, "like a bird" is implied but omitted, enhancing the image by assuming familiarity with the analogy.

Acceptance acknowledges another's perspective or teaching without challenge, representing open acknowledgment of varied viewpoints. It's a way of presenting ideas within a neutral context. For instance: "The structure of an army formation, with wings, front, and reserve, is an arrangement as recommended by the school of Usanas." This citation honors a viewpoint without necessarily aligning with it, leaving space for differing interpretations.

Detailed description, known as explanation, refers to an expanded discussion of a topic, clarifying its nature and implications. It deepens understanding by breaking down complex ideas. For instance: "In assemblies of kings or confederacies marked by the characteristics of such gatherings, quarrels frequently arise due to gambling, leading to the potential downfall of individuals involved in these disputes. This is why gambling stands as the most dangerous vice, as it deprives the king of his capacity for effective leadership and action." This explanation sheds light on gambling's destabilizing effect on governance.

Derivation involves breaking down a word to reveal its core meaning or purpose, often pointing to the word's etymological or functional essence. For example: "That which diverts (vyasyati) a king from his successful path is termed propensity (vyasana)." This offers a linguistic insight that clarifies the underlying purpose or consequence of the word.

Illustration provides a concrete example to support a concept, helping readers to visualize or understand the principle being discussed. For example: "In a battle against a far superior force, an inferior army is much like a lone foot soldier facing an elephant—it's likely to be overwhelmed." This illustration reinforces the concept of power imbalance.

Exception is applied to limit or clarify a general statement by introducing specific conditions under which the rule doesn't apply. It removes potential misconceptions. For example: "A king may allow his enemy's forces to camp near his borders unless there's a reason to suspect internal dissent or disloyalty." This clarifies that, while proximity can be tolerated, signs of internal unrest could make such proximity risky.

Technical terms, unique to an author's framework, are words or phrases used in a particular, specialized way that may not be common in broader discourse. They are essential for understanding the author's intent. For example: "The term 'first member' refers to the territory closest to the conqueror's, followed by 'second member' for the next in line, and so forth." This terminology specifically organizes the geopolitical landscape for the author's analysis.

Prima facie view is the initial stance or argument introduced for scrutiny, serving as a hypothesis to test or refute. For example: "Between the king's distress and his minister's, the minister's distress is viewed as the greater harm." This opens a line of reasoning that can be evaluated in subsequent discussion.

Rejoinder is a settled opinion that follows a prima facie view, clarifying the author's stance on the issue. For example: "The king's distress is ultimately more consequential, as the kingdom's stability pivots on his leadership." This counters the previous view with a final conclusion emphasizing the king's central role.

Conclusion or established fact refers to a universal or broadly applicable statement that forms a foundational principle. For example: "A king must always be prepared for diligent and vigorous action." This reflects a general truth about the nature of kingship.

Reference to a subsequent portion signals where a concept will be expanded upon later, helping the reader anticipate a more comprehensive discussion. For example: "The topic of balance and weights will be discussed in full in the upcoming chapter, 'The

Superintendent of Weights and Measures.'" This directs readers forward for further elaboration.

Reference to a previous portion points back to an earlier discussion, reminding the reader of groundwork already covered. For example: "As previously discussed, a minister's qualifications have already been outlined."

Command indicates a directive that leaves no room for deviation. It mandates specific behavior or choices. For example: "Thus, he should be taught the principles of righteousness and wealth, and never unrighteousness or unproductive paths."

Alternative provides options, showing the existence of more than one possible route. For example: "Or daughters may be born from an approved (dharmaviváha) marriage."

Compounding together brings together elements from different origins or paths to form a cohesive idea. For instance: "A child born to a man and his wife is considered agnatic both to the father and the father's kin."

Finally, determinable fact highlights areas requiring careful assessment before reaching a judgment, especially in cases where various factors influence the outcome. For example: "Gifts' validity or invalidity shall be evaluated by experts to ensure fairness, safeguarding the interests of both giver and recipient." This underscores the need for expertise and careful judgment.

- Thus, this Sástra, adhering to these structured divisions, is composed to serve as a comprehensive guide for acquiring and safeguarding success in both this world and the world beyond.
- In the context provided by this Sástra, one can initiate and sustain actions rooted in righteousness, economic prudence, and aesthetic value while effectively curtailing actions that are unrighteous, wasteful, and unappealing.
- This Sástra was created by him who, motivated by an aversion

to injustice and misrule, swiftly reclaimed the sacred scriptures, the science of warfare, and the realm itself, which had fallen under the control of the Nanda king. Through his efforts, order, wisdom, and prosperity were restored, and this work stands as a testament to that enduring vision of governance.

The Commentaries of Julius Caesar

Julius Caesar

Chapter I.

Introduction.

It could be said that Cæsar's Commentaries mark the beginning of modern history. Although written nearly two thousand years ago, Cæsar documented events as he experienced them, recounting his own actions and the events he observed firsthand. He wrote about regions that are familiar to us today—such as Britain, which he invaded twice—and about peoples close enough to be recognizable as our neighbors and predecessors. His accounts bring us actual history, not fictionalized tales. The straightforward style of his narrative is perhaps its greatest strength; it convinces us that the events he describes truly took place, almost exactly as he recorded them. Cæsar describes large-scale movements across Europe that shaped the current political landscape of nations. While readers may find fascination in the great exploits of Greek heroes or the powerful words of Greek orators, it is challenging to find any direct and reliable connection between the fortunes of ancient Athens, Sparta, or Macedonia and our own time. The same can be said of the earlier history of Rome, prior to Cæsar's era.

The Punic Wars, the Social War, the lives of the Scipios and the Gracchi, or even the power struggle between Marius and Sulla, do not resonate as personally as the Gallic Wars or the Roman invasion of Britain. Through these latter events, Roman civilization was first extended westward, setting the stage for the "Bellum Civile" (Civil War), which initiated a long line of emperors, whose legacy extends almost to our own time. These events lay the groundwork for the development of nearly every European nation we know today. Admittedly, if all facts were available to us, we might trace every current political and social structure back to the earliest days of humanity. But our interest often wanes when facts become uncertain and history seems entangled with legend. While Herodotus captivates with his myths, the enjoyment we derive from his writings rarely comes from a desire to trace a direct line from his time to ours. There is a vast difference between the mythical wonders of Herodotus and the documented realities of Cæsar.

With Cæsar, there is a level of clarity that we associate with modern history. From the start, it's essential to remember that Cæsar wrote only about events he personally experienced or directed. His two surviving works, his Commentaries, are all that remain of his writings. We are told that he produced other works as well, including a poem, but these two Commentaries are the only complete texts that have come down to us. The first, consisting of seven books, describes the events of his initial seven campaigns in Gaul over seven consecutive years, where he subdued the tribes living between the Rhine, the Rhone, the Mediterranean, the Pyrenees, and the English Channel. The second Commentary recounts the details of the civil war in which he clashed with Pompey—his former partner in power, along with Crassus, in the first triumvirate—and established the empire that would later pass to Augustus after a second, short-lived triumvirate between Augustus, Lepidus, and Antony.

This little book aims to describe Cæsar's Commentaries for those who do not read Latin, rather than to provide a full history of Rome. Still, it may be helpful to begin with a brief look at the life and character of Cæsar himself. Most of us recognize the name Julius Cæsar. As children, we learned he was the first of the twelve Roman emperors whose names we memorized in school. We were taught that when Cæsar came to power, the old republican system—where two consuls, elected annually, governed Rome—came to an end. First, there were the seven kings of Rome, whose names we also know, then the consuls, and finally, the twelve Cæsars, beginning with the renowned Julius. This much we all remember about him, and we're also familiar with the fact that he was assassinated by conspirators in the Capitol just as he was about to take on the role of emperor—a detail that, ironically, seems to contradict his claim as the first of the Cæsars.

We also know Cæsar as a brilliant general, conqueror, and writer who recorded his deeds in his famous "veni, vidi, vici" style, famously proclaiming, "I came, I saw, I conquered." We're aware that he commanded a powerful Roman army and used this force to establish his own rule in Rome. He did so by leading part of his army across the Rubicon, a small river that marked the boundary of his provincial authority. By crossing it, he entered Roman territory in a manner forbidden to generals serving the Republic, setting the stage for his rise to power. This is the basic story most of us learned.

In this brief introduction to the life of the great commander and historian, there is no need to question or alter these early lessons, as has so often been attempted in recent years. Those lessons were generally correct. Here, I'll simply add a few details that, while once learned by schoolchildren, may have faded from memory over time.

Dean Merivale, in one of the first chapters of his well-regarded history of the Romans under the Empire, declares that Caius Julius Cæsar is the greatest name in history. He makes this statement without holding back, and without suggesting that it is only his own opinion. We often find such claims made by authors in favor of their heroes, and usually, we are inclined to challenge them. Yet, even though this claim is huge, it is difficult to deny. Dr. Merivale doesn't claim that Cæsar was the greatest person who ever lived. When people measure greatness, they do so by different standards. One might think a poet is the greatest, another might choose a religious leader, a third might select a thinker who unlocked nature's mysteries, and another still might see a powerful ruler as the greatest. But the names of some of these people cannot be called great purely from a historical perspective. Homer, Luther, Galileo, and Charles V. are all famous names, as are Shakespeare, Knox, Queen Elizabeth, and Newton. However, the two rulers in this list would probably be the least admired overall. But no one can argue that the poets, religious leaders, and scientists are necessarily greater in history than these rulers. Dean Merivale means that of all the people whose actions we know, Julius Cæsar did the most to change the world, and we agree that he is right.

Those we might compare to Cæsar are Alexander, Charlemagne, Cromwell, Napoleon, and Washington. For the first two, when we make comparisons to them, we do so knowing we have only partial records of what they achieved. In Alexander's time, history was still somewhat obscure, and by the era of Charlemagne, it had once again become vague. What Cromwell achieved was limited to Britain, and though he was immensely important for the British Isles, he does not appear as significant to the world at large as someone who influenced all of Europe, both in the present and the future. If Cæsar has any true rival for this title, it is Napoleon. As a soldier, Napoleon was just as remarkable, and he operated across just as wide an area. But there is an old saying that no one's fortune is truly secure until the end, and Cæsar's dramatic death on the steps of the Capitol feels more aligned with our sense of greatness than Napoleon's passing on St. Helena. Furthermore, there seem to be fewer flaws in the personal character of the Roman "Imperator" and Dictator than in the character of the French Emperor. Technically, Julius Cæsar was never really an emperor as we understand the term; his successor Augustus was the one who truly became emperor.

As for Washington, we might agree that he was perhaps the greatest of all in terms of moral qualities. He risked everything for his country, even the disgraceful death of a rebel, had he not succeeded in a venture that seemed very unlikely to succeed. He succeeded in all he set out to do. His name is the crowning one among those who created the United States, and all its people celebrate him for that. His achievements were driven by love of country, without any trace of personal ambition. But it cannot be said that his achievements were as momentous as those of Cæsar, nor that he was as powerful in carrying them out. Washington risked everything with as noble a purpose as any person could, and he succeeded, yet the deeds he accomplished are small in comparison to those of his less honorable rival for fame.

Mommsen, the German historian, describes Cæsar as a man too vast for the reach of his intelligence and ability to portray. "The historian," Mommsen writes, speaking of Cæsar, "when once in a thousand years he encounters perfection, can only be silent about it." Napoleon, too, in his biography of Cæsar, portrays him as perfect. But Napoleon's portrayal is, in reality, a way of claiming godlike perfection for his own uncle, the second Cæsar. And the perfection Napoleon describes is different from what Mommsen suggests. Mommsen wants to convey that Cæsar was flawless in his human capabilities and intelligence, while Napoleon credits him with moral perfection. "We may be sure," says the Emperor, "based on the above facts, that during his first consulship, Cæsar was driven by only one motive—the public good." However, we cannot completely accept the facts as the French Emperor presents them, nor can we fully share his confidence. Yet, most readers would likely agree that no name in history is as great as that of Julius Cæsar, and this volume will offer some account of his writings in the following sections.

He was born exactly one hundred years before the birth of Christ, into an old and noble Roman family, known for the name Julius rather than Cæsar. The origin of the name "Cæsar" is uncertain and surrounded by stories and myths. Some say it came from the thick hair of an early member of the Julian family, while others claim it's from a child of the family being, like Macduff, "ripped from his mother's womb"—with Latin words conveniently supporting these ideas. Another story says that a member of the family once kept an elephant, and that "Cæsar" sounds like the word for elephant in some Eastern language. Yet another legend, which fit well with Cæsar's Gallic campaigns, claimed that in the Gallic language of the time, "Cæsar" sounded like a phrase meaning, "Send him back." Supposedly, when Cæsar's horse once bolted and carried him over to the enemy, a Gaul who recognized him shouted "Cæsar, Cæsar!" Hearing this, the other Gauls mistook it for an order to let him go, so he safely returned. The German historian who recounts this tale dismisses it with great skepticism. Whatever the true origin, the name "Cæsar" gained huge importance due to Caius Julius Cæsar's achievements and writings. It eventually came to signify, in multiple languages, a ruler with absolute power. And although the Russian title "Czar" is said to be unrelated to the Roman word, the association is so strong that people will likely always connect the Russian Emperor's title with the Roman legacy.

Cæsar was related by marriage to Marius, the influential general who, through a mix of brutal victories and near-disastrous failures, battled Sulla for the top position in the republic. In these power struggles, Sulla represented the aristocratic and patrician faction—the side we might today call "Conservative." Marius, on the other hand, came from humble origins. He had started as a common soldier, earned his way up the ranks, and eventually became a favorite of the army and the people. If the term "Liberal" had existed back then, he might have identified with it. Like other political leaders after him, Marius's so-called "liberal" stance led him to personal power. He served as Consul seven times, securing his final election through horrific violence against his opponents in the city. He died during this last consulship.

Although young Cæsar was born into the patrician class, he succeeded Marius in leading the popular party. From a very young age—even in his teenage years—he seemed to have set his sights on the power he could achieve by skillfully navigating the political landscape.

Cæsar was highly cautious and showed an impressive level of confidence and patience. Most readers probably know the story of how the Roman Republic fell and turned into the Roman Empire after a series of civil wars that began with Marius and ended with "young Octavius," better known as Augustus Cæsar. Julius Cæsar was Marius's nephew by marriage, and Augustus was Julius's great-nephew and chosen heir. The power Marius gained almost by accident—and which Julius Cæsar pursued strategically throughout his life—was finally secured by Augustus through brutal acts of conscription and killings. These events, while perhaps fewer in number, were no less horrific than those of the French Revolution. This power, which Augustus received and held, was then passed down to the emperors after him.

When we look back at history, we often find that despotic power tends to arise from popular uprisings against authority. This happened with Cromwell, twice in modern France, and certainly in the rise of the Roman Empire. Establishing this empire relied on Cæsar's intellect, skill, and courage, regardless of whether we see this as good or bad. And when we compare the lives of Marius, Cæsar, and Augustus, who each worked toward the same end—the destruction of the oligarchy disguised as a Republic—we see that Cæsar was the only one with any true humanity. Marius, as an old man, and Augustus, as a young man, committed atrocities so horrific that they still shock readers today, even considering that these acts occurred before the influence of Christianity. Marius, along with his rival Sulla, drowned his enemies in blood. Meanwhile, Octavius—who later became the godlike Augustus—secured his position by executing close friends to appease his allies, Lepidus and Antony, in the second triumvirate. Cæsar, by comparison, is remembered for his mercy. Yet, as one reads his accounts, the sheer scale of the cities he razed and communities he destroyed can be overwhelming. He could recount the slaughter of women and children in just one line without any hint of emotion. Nevertheless, Cæsar didn't relish bloodshed. He saw it as a means to an end—an action taken without hesitation when it served his purpose. But he was not drawn to violence for its own sake. He was a calculated, cautious thinker, and could carry out orders with calm resolve when he deemed them necessary.

Cæsar also seemed to be motivated by a sense of duty and love for Rome, much like his contemporaries Pompey and Cicero. However, it's hard to say the same for those before and after him, like Marius, Sulla, Antony, and Augustus, whose actions seemed driven solely by power, greed, vengeance, personal ambition, and a belief in their own fates pushing them toward greatness. These desires existed in Cæsar as well, as they do in today's leaders, but he also carried a noble vision—to stay true to Rome's greatness and to claim power with the hope of ensuring its empire was governed wisely. Augustus, to be fair, ruled well. And while Cæsar had little time to govern after his conquests, Augustus's intelligence can be credited with recognizing that maintaining the well-being of Rome's citizens was key to his own security.

In his early years, Cæsar rose to a high position, even though his rise was fraught with dangers. People around him were amazed that Sulla hadn't killed him when he was still young—when he could have been "crushed in the shell," so to speak. But Sulla spared him, and Cæsar advanced steadily. We learn that he was appointed priest of Jupiter at seventeen, and at that time, he was already married. He began training himself as a public speaker early on, and amid constant threats, he took up the popular cause in Rome. He served Rome in the East—likely in Bithynia—avoiding the dangers he might have faced if he had stayed in the city. He was made Quaestor and later Ædile, with the backing of the Marian party, which supported him as a rising leader they saw as their future head. Cæsar attacked and was also attacked in turn, becoming known for his "tireless harassment of the aristocracy," who tried, but failed, to crush him. Though he was young and embraced all the pleasures of youth—Sulla once even called him a "trifler"—he made sure to learn everything he needed as the head of a powerful party and as the leader of great armies. At thirty-seven, he was appointed Pontifex Maximus, the head of the Roman priesthood, which was the most honored role in the city. He achieved this despite opposition from the entire aristocracy and the candidacy of Catulus, who was the most admired and virtuous member of their party. The following year, he became Prætor, though he faced fierce opposition from those who feared him. After completing his twelve-month term, he took up the governorship of Spain, the province granted to him as Proprætor according to

Republican tradition, defying a Senate decree that ordered him to stay in Rome. It was in Spain that he achieved his first major military success, winning the loyalty of his soldiers, and returning to Rome eligible for the honor of a triumph.

But there was still one more step in his political career that he had to achieve before he could reach the position he likely already envisioned for himself. To command many legions, he needed to become Consul. And in order to officially apply for this position, he had to give up his triumph. Triumphs were only possible for those acting as Generals for the Republic's armies, and as an Imperator, or General, he couldn't enter the city. Cæsar gave up the Triumph, sought the consulship in the usual way, and by doing so, allowed the people to believe he valued their service over his own personal honors. At forty-one, he became Consul. During his struggle for this office, the famous triumvirate was formed—an alliance so well-known to later generations, though it was likely less talked about among Romans at the time. Pompey, who had once been under Sulla's guidance and had been the hope of the patricians to whom he belonged, had returned to Rome after achieving several victories as Proconsul in the East. He had celebrated his triumph and thought he could retire on his honors, disbanding his army and assuming he could live quietly. However, the political environment was too chaotic for such a simple course of action, and Pompey, though he wished to step away from power, found it difficult to be sidelined by his own party. He may have thought that he could lead Rome using his influence alone, without needing the support of his legions. Seeing this, Cæsar approached him with an offer, and together with Crassus, whose wealth made him valuable, they formed the first triumvirate. Their agreement allowed them to control Rome and its provinces together. However, though it was a shared plan, Cæsar no doubt secretly aimed to take ultimate power for himself. In the years that followed, as Cæsar fought in Gaul, Pompey stayed in Rome. He was not, in truth, Cæsar's ally—their superficial friendship had ended with the death of Julia, Cæsar's daughter, who was Pompey's wife, despite him being five years older than Cæsar—but rather, he remained in cautious rivalry with the ambitious man who was training his armies abroad to eventually seize power at home. Later, after Cæsar crossed the Rubicon, as we will discuss, their rivalry became open hostility. It was, perhaps, only natural that they should become enemies. In his middle years, Pompey, as we have noted, had married Cæsar's daughter, and Cæsar's second wife was a Pompeia. But when they were younger, and each man was more committed to the politics of his own faction, Pompey had married Sulla's daughter-in-law, while Cæsar married the daughter of Cinna, who had almost joined Marius in leading the popular faction. Given these connections in their early lives, it is not surprising that Pompey and Cæsar would become adversaries, and that their joining forces with a third member in a triumvirate was a shallow compromise, designed only to buy them time.

Now, as Consul, Cæsar openly mocked the Senate and the aristocratic partner assigned to him, Bibulus, who will appear again in his account of the civil war. Throughout his year in office, he seemed to govern almost solely, wielding immense power. The Senate was compelled to follow his lead, and during this period, Pompey stood by him as an ally. We know that once prætors and consuls completed their terms within the city, they were granted authority over the Republic's major provinces, where they governed as proprætors and proconsuls. After serving as Prætor, Cæsar spent a year in southern Spain, the province allotted to him, returning victorious—though he chose not to claim his Triumph. Following his consulship, he was assigned the joint provinces of Cisalpine Gaul and Illyricum, not for the typical one-year term but for five years; Transalpine Gaul was also added to his command. This appointment gave him control over Northern Italy, Illyria to the east, and across the Alps to the west, over the Roman-established province in southern France. The Transalpine Gaul province, bordered to the north by Lake Geneva and the Swiss mountains, stretched south to the Mediterranean and westward halfway across the neck of land connecting Spain to continental Europe. This region was already under Roman control, and it was now Cæsar's responsibility to protect it and defend Rome itself from the fierce Gauls. To achieve this, he gathered his legions in the area we now recognize as northern Italy.

It seems there was no original intent for Cæsar to conquer all of Gaul. Up until then, Rome had viewed the Gauls with fear, having suffered from their incursions in the past. In earlier times, the Gauls had even invaded Rome, leaving only when they were paid a ransom. They had spread through Northern Italy, which became known as Cisalpine Gaul once conquered by Rome. Over the century before Cæsar's campaigns, Rome gradually extended its influence across southern France, with Marseilles, or Massilia—a colony of Greek merchants allied with Rome—serving as the focal point. Readers of history know well where alliances with Rome typically led. The Greek colony became a Roman town, and the province expanded around it. As the governor of Transalpine Gaul, it was Cæsar's duty to protect the region from marauding Gauls. His first Commentary recounts how he took on this responsibility.

During the fourth year of his term, while Pompey and Crassus, his partners in the triumvirate, were consuls, his command over these three provinces was extended for an additional five years. However, he would not complete the full ten years in this arena. Julia, his daughter, had passed away, creating a rift between him and his powerful ally, Pompey. The Senate demanded his recall, and Pompey, though hesitant, agreed. At the Senate's order, Cæsar released part of his army, which was sent back to Italy and soon came under Pompey's control. At that point, Cæsar decided that the Italian side of the Alps was the better place to be. The territory known as Cisalpine Gaul, just across the Rubicon, needed his attention, making it a strategic base. His second Commentary, De Bello Civili, in three books, covers the events and experiences of the civil war and documents his actions and outcomes in the years 49 and 48 B.C. His career as a general continues in three more Commentaries written by others, which, while significant, fall outside the main scope of this account and will be briefly noted. This period was followed by one final year of supreme power, marked by triumphs, achievements, and notable, if short-lived, governance. Then came his end, famously and frequently recounted, when he was struck down by allies and adversaries alike at the base of Pompey's statue in the Capitol.

It's important to add a few words about the nature of Cæsar's writings, as the purpose here is to give some insight into them for readers who may not have the chance to read the works themselves. This volume is not meant to tell the full story of Cæsar's life, as that would be to cover the history of the world as it was in his time. The term that Cæsar chose for his work—"Commentary"—has become so associated with him that anyone using it now might seem to be referring directly to Cæsar himself. In Cæsar's sense, "Commentary" essentially means a memoir. Without Cæsar's use of the term, the word "Commentary" would typically mean an addition from a critic rather than an original work by an author. Cæsar's Commentaries are personal memoirs, written by him about his campaigns, where he refers to himself in the third person, telling his story as though a scribe or secretary traveling with him were recording it. Given this, we naturally wonder if perhaps a scribe or secretary may indeed have written these accounts. There is a compelling reason to consider this: the sheer amount of work Cæsar undertook—not only in his military campaigns but also in his political life—would have been overwhelming without adding the effort required to write detailed memoirs. He was probably the most burdened man of his time, as the idea of "division of labor" was far less practiced in large matters then than it is now.

Cæsar was far more than a general. He was also an engineer, an astronomer, an orator, a poet, and a high priest. In that last role, though a non-believer in the gods of Olympus, he still had to understand the intricacies of the Roman religious system. Politically, he was constantly engaged with opposition—yet without any relief from the intense workload it brought. We've had our own examples of busy statesmen who were also writers: two prime ministers translated Homer, another wrote novels, and yet another made a name as a historian, dramatist, and biographer. But none of these men led armies while managing Parliament, nor did they face the unending demand of Cæsar's political life, where opposition rarely allowed time for rest or reflection. From the beginning of the Gallic War until his death, Cæsar was in active combat every year but one, and his successes were achieved only through his personal leadership. In the pages that follow, the reader will see that with one notable exception—the siege of Marseilles—no major achievement happened in his absence. Cæsar had to build his army himself, as well as command it. Each legion had to be raised by him, drawn together by the strength of his name and his leadership.

The extraordinary rewards necessary to inspire his soldiers to remarkable bravery and effort were handed out as if from his own resources. He was responsible for every aspect of his soldiers' tasks, and at the same time, he had to navigate the political dangers back in Rome. This required not only managing his rivals but, even more challenging, keeping his allies under control to prevent political disaster. With so many demands, could Cæsar actually have written his own Commentaries? It's likely that he gathered a great deal of material, with the help of his secretaries, which was known as the Ephemerides of Cæsar—notes or records kept daily. Could it be that the Commentaries bearing his name were crafted from these notes by a skilled and knowledgeable secretary?

These notes have stirred up considerable debate among editors and scholars. One German scholar, passionately asserting that Cæsar never wrote any Ephemerides, grudgingly concedes that someone must have recorded certain details—like distances traveled, elevations of mountains, the sizes of rivers, and the counts of prisoners and slaves. "Not even I," he says, "not even I believe that Cæsar could have kept all these figures in his head." He then goes on to argue that any scribe could have taken down such notes, and that it seems improbable Cæsar would have had time to make meticulous records while actively engaged in the field. Although the critic's indignation is somewhat amusing, his logic is sound. It's likely that these notes were compiled by Cæsar's secretaries under his close supervision; yet there is ample evidence that the Commentaries themselves are Cæsar's own writing.

The Commentaries seem to have been known to the educated Romans of the time almost immediately. Cicero, who was perhaps the most learned and certainly the most discerning critic of his day, discusses them without any question as to their authorship. It was clearly recognized that Cæsar wrote the first seven books of the Gallic War himself, whereas the eighth book was completed by another. This point alone appears to settle the matter. Moreover, there is internal evidence within the works themselves. Although Cæsar carefully maintains a third-person narrative throughout, he slips into the first person three or four times, momentarily forgetting himself. No ghostwriter, tasked with writing for Cæsar, would likely have done this. There are also personal touches in the way he tells certain details— such as his references to "young" Crassus and "young" Brutus—small nuances that a scribe would not have likely included. He also subtly conveys his pride when receiving a legion from Pompey as a token of friendship, followed by his intense dismay when the Senate requisitions that legion and another one, which Pompey then turns against him. These elements lend authenticity to the Commentaries, but they are hardly necessary; the confidence of Cæsar's contemporaries alone is convincing enough.

It appears the Commentaries were written in parallel with the campaigns, with each book likely published soon after completion. If this were not the case, it would be hard to explain why Cæsar began his Civil War commentary before completing the account of the Gallic War. The pressing demands of the civil conflict likely prevented him from finishing the last two books of the Gallic War, so he entrusted this task to his friend Hirtius, who summarized those two years in a single book. Additionally, Cæsar's descriptions of individuals who were once his allies but later turned adversaries suggest that his first Commentary was already completed and published before he started on the next one. For example, Labienus, once Cæsar's most trusted lieutenant during the Gallic campaigns, defected to Pompey's side during the civil conflict. If Labienus had joined Pompey while the first Commentary was still in progress, Cæsar almost certainly would have referred to his betrayal within that work.

The style Cæsar employed was quickly acknowledged by the foremost literary critic of his time as perfectly suited to its purpose. It's clear that Cæsar wasn't aiming for literary acclaim but was focused on delivering a vivid, concise, and understandable account of his actions. He sought a style that would capture the reader's attention through clear and effective narration. Cicero, the great critic, commented on the Commentaries, saying, "Valde quidam, inquam, probandos; nudi enim sunt, recti, et venusti, omni ornatu orationis, tanquam veste, detracto." This passage is simple to grasp in Latin, though not easily translated into English. It means something like, "I consider them very commendable; they are plain, direct, and graceful, with all the decorative flourishes of rhetoric stripped away, like a garment removed." This remark was made by Cicero while Cæsar was still alive, as indicated by the context. Cicero's praise isn't to imply that Cæsar's writings are rough or lacking elegance; the word venusti (graceful) makes this clear. In another instance, Cicero notes that Cæsar spoke with a refinement and precision of language that surpassed nearly all other speakers of his day. Given that Roman orations were often carefully composed in writing, it stands to reason that Cæsar's written style would reflect his spoken elegance.

Montaigne, for his part, held Cæsar in great admiration, saying, "I read this author with a respect that surpasses what I'd normally grant human writings, sometimes contemplating him in his own person, through his astonishing deeds, and sometimes admiring the pure, inimitable polish of his language and style, by which he outshines all other historians, as Cicero acknowledges, and perhaps even rivals Cicero himself." Montaigne, however, stretches Cicero's words a bit too far; Cicero never went so far as to claim that Cæsar surpassed him. But Montaigne's fondness for Cæsar is evident, and he often speaks of him with great enthusiasm and reverence.

For us, who tend to clarify our ideas by using many words and rarely prioritize brevity in writing, Cæsar's tightly condensed style can initially be challenging to grasp. Reading his work demands a slow, deliberate approach until one becomes accustomed to his way of packing meaning into brief phrases. After this, though, speed reading is still not advisable. Often, he conveys what would, in English, require three or four sentences, through a single phrase with two or three adjectives or, more likely, participles. Capturing Cæsar's full meaning in English often requires three times the number of words he used. This characteristic isn't unique to Cæsar but extends to many, if not most, Latin authors—owing to the Roman penchant for conciseness, while ours leans toward expansion. However, with Cæsar, though every word is weighty, sentences themselves are often long, which soon makes it clear to the reader that skipping is impossible and rapid reading is counterproductive.

What will likely stand out most to the typical English reader in Cæsar's narrative is the sheer cruelty of the Romans—a cruelty that Cæsar himself exhibits to a shocking degree, without any sign of regret. Despite this, he gained and retained a reputation for clemency that has lasted even to this day. Assessing Cæsar's character solely on his own actions, without considering those of his contemporaries, it's hard to avoid the conclusion that he was exceedingly ruthless. He never killed for the pleasure of it, but he also didn't spare anyone out of compassion. Everything he did was calculated for political purposes; when his strategies required it, he could order widespread killing without hesitation, and seemingly without remorse, regardless of the victims' numbers, gender, age, innocence, or defenselessness. Our only explanation for this is that he was Roman, and that Romans as a whole were indifferent to human life. In their culture, suicide was a common response to unavoidable misfortune, and it followed naturally that people who could easily dismiss their own lives would also be untroubled by ending the lives of others.

Nearly all the figures mentioned in these pages met violent deaths. Cæsar and Pompey, the two most prominent, were murdered. Dumnorix, the Æduan leader, was killed on Cæsar's orders. Vercingetorix, the courageous Gallic chieftain, was kept alive only to be executed as part of Cæsar's Triumph. Ariovistus, the German, managed to escape from Cæsar, but he soon met his end, reportedly at Roman hands. The fate of the fugitive Ambiorix remains unknown, but his fellow king, Cativolcus, poisoned himself with yew-tree sap. Crassus, who had joined with Cæsar and Pompey in the first triumvirate, was killed by the Parthians. Young Crassus, an officer serving Cæsar in Gaul, chose to be slain by his own soldiers to avoid capture by the Parthians; his head was cut off and sent to his father. Labienus perished at the Battle of Munda during the final civil war in Spain. Quintus Cicero, one of Cæsar's officers, his brother the orator, and his nephew all perished in the purges of the second triumvirate.

Other fates were equally grim: Titurius and Cotta, with their army, were slaughtered by Ambiorix. Afranius was killed by Cæsar's troops after the last battle in Africa. Petreius died in a brutal contest with King Juba. While Varro lived to an old age and wrote many books, Domitius, who defended Marseilles for Pompey, was killed in the aftermath of Pharsalia. Trebonius, who led the assault on Marseilles by land, was later killed by Cicero's son-in-law at Smyrna. Decimus Brutus, who attacked Marseilles by sea, was beheaded by Camillus, who sent it to Antony as a gift. Curio, leading forces on Cæsar's behalf in Africa, charged into enemy swords and was cut down. King Juba, who defeated Curio, had a slave kill him when he failed to take his own life. Attius Varus, who had held the province of Africa for Pompey, fell later at Munda.

Marc Antony, Cæsar's leading general during the Pharsalian campaign, committed suicide. Cassius Longinus, another of Cæsar's officers, drowned. Scipio, Pompey's ally at Pharsalia, ended his own life in Africa. Bibulus, his chief admiral, wasted away and died. Young Ptolemy, to whom Pompey fled, drowned in the Nile. His sister, Cleopatra's, tragic end is well known. Pharnaces, who opposed Cæsar in Asia, was killed in battle. Cato died by his own hand in Utica. Pompey's eldest son, Cnæus, was captured and killed in Spain. Sextus, the younger son, was killed years later by a soldier under Antony. Both Brutus and Cassius, the prominent conspirators, committed suicide.

In all these events, scarcely three individuals met their end in fair battle, if even that many. The vast majority died through murder, suicide, or assassination.

The above list is filled with notable figures—primarily warriors, men who knowingly and willingly faced danger to achieve specific goals. The bloody roll call is so extensive, so close to encompassing everyone mentioned, that it almost gives the reader a dark, uneasy sense of humor. But when we turn to the outright slaughter of entire towns, to the calculated destruction of lands so that men and women would be left to starve, to the cold abandonment of the elderly, the young, and the vulnerable so they might die alone on the hillsides, to the brutal mutilation of masses of men, to cities being set aflame in passing, and to thousands drowned as casually as if one were discussing the extermination of pests—the dark humor evaporates, and only a deep sickness in the heart remains. It is then we recall how the coming of Christ changed everything and recognize that, even though terrible acts have been committed since, people today are no longer as they were in Cæsar's time.

Chapter II.

FIRST BOOK OF THE WAR IN GAUL.— CÆSAR DRIVES FIRST THE SWISS AND THEN THE GERMANS OUT OF GAUL.— B.C. 58.

In the previous chapter, it was noted that Cæsar didn't appear to have any specific mandate to conquer Gaul when he first took charge of his three provinces. The people of Rome still harbored a fear of the Gauls, and his responsibility was to ensure that they did not cross the Alps into Roman territory. He was also tasked with defending against invasions and preventing rebellion in that part of Gaul already established as a Roman province, though the local sympathies leaned more toward their former allies than their new rulers. History shows us that once a powerful empire begins to protect what it already possesses, it often extends its hold over more, until it controls everything in reach. This is how the British Empire expanded in India. It's how Spain established dominion over America. It's how the United States continues to expand its influence. And it's how Prussia, as we recall, recently took Nassau, Hanover, Holstein, and Hesse, all under the pretext of self-preservation. It's the same as when the wolf claimed the whole river, claiming it couldn't tolerate the nearby lamb. The compassionate reader of history may curse the ruthless, all-consuming, greedy wolf. But the reflective reader understands that, in this way—and no other—civilization reaches distant lands. The wolf, however ravenous, brings energy and knowledge along with him.

We don't have any clear insight into what Cæsar's ambitions were regarding Gaul when he was first assigned to govern the provinces. However, we might guess—and, indeed, we feel certain—that he had a plan in mind that was far more significant to him than merely adding new territory to the Republic, no matter how vast Gaul might be.

Cæsar had seen enough of Roman politics to understand that true power in Rome lay in the control of legions. Both Marius and Sulla had asserted themselves in Rome with armies they had raised as esteemed generals of the Republic. Pompey, too, had led a successful army in the East, and there had been an expectation that he would use his forces similarly. Yet Pompey, whether out of nobility, indecision, or poor judgment—depending on one's perspective—chose to disband his legions when he returned to Italy. As a result, he was left, at the very time Cæsar was planning his future course, to seek influence within Rome through an alliance with Cæsar, his natural adversary, and Crassus. Seeing this, understanding the paths to power taken by Marius and Sulla, and witnessing Pompey's diminished influence, Cæsar surely resolved that, regardless of the wars he would fight, he would keep a loyal and trained army at his command. So, when he first encountered a reason for conflict, he was already prepared. Not long into his term as proconsul, a wayward lamb came to drink from his stream.

As he describes his conquest of one tribe after another across the land he calls Gallia, Cæsar shares almost nothing personal about himself. He keeps silent on his political ambitions, his vision for Rome, and even his activities in Italy during those winter months he spent on the Roman side of the Alps, while his army wintered under the command of his lieutenants. He writes solely about the campaigns, and although he occasionally mentions the dignity of the Republic, he rarely pauses in his account to reveal the motivations that drive him. In these seven commentaries on his seven years of warfare in Gaul, only once does he refer to a personal motive. After defeating a fourth of the migrating Swiss—the first military victory he won in Gaul—he notes that he had avenged both an offense to the Republic and a personal injury. The tribe he defeated had once killed the grandfather of his father-in-law in a previous conflict.

It's also worth noting that he generally avoids speaking in the first person. When he does, it's in minor passages where the personal tone feels unintentional and insignificant. Instead of saying "I" or "me," he refers to himself simply as "Cæsar," as if the writer of the Commentary is somehow separate from the Cæsar he writes about. He sometimes speaks highly of his own actions, but in doing so, he uses a tone devoid of both humility and pride. Even when he praises his own achievements, there's no sense of boasting—he recounts his accomplishments in the same straightforward way he talks about the deeds of his generals and soldiers. He mentions without hesitation that, at the close of certain campaigns, Rome declared "supplications"— public festivals and ceremonies of thanksgiving for his victories— lasting fifteen or twenty days upon hearing news of his triumphs.

When it comes to the challenges he faced in Rome, the political obstacles that arose in his absence, he leaves us in the dark. Yet these struggles must have weighed heavily on him. Other sources tell us that his actions in Gaul were hotly criticized in Rome, where he was accused of brutal aggression against states believed to be friendly to the Republic. At one point, it was even suggested that he should be handed over to his enemies as punishment for his alleged treachery. Had the Senate decided to act on such a proposal, it's unlikely they could have enforced it. It was far easier to grant him a "supplication" lasting twenty days than it would have been to halt his momentum once his legions had come to know him.

Cæsar rarely discusses his strategic struggles in detail; however, occasionally, he lets us glimpse the challenges he faced—like when his ships were battered on the British coast, or when he had crushed the Gauls so severely that they united against him under Vercingetorix. Yet, his approach is to simply state his intentions, describe his actions, and report the final outcome—all with the fewest words possible. If a reader were to examine both Cæsar's seven books on the Gallic War and the first four volumes of Mr. Kinglake's 'Invasion of the Crimea,' they would find two excellent examples of precise word usage: Cæsar's narrative is remarkably concise, while Kinglake's is almost exhaustively detailed. And yet, each narrative is equally clear, both skillfully arranged to make the reader appreciate the mastery behind the storytelling.

Cæsar is generous with praise—whether for his lieutenants, his soldiers, or occasionally even his enemies. His enthusiasm shines through, though often in just a single word or a carefully placed epithet within a sentence designed for an entirely different purpose. He's sparing with blame; so much so that it seems he viewed some flaws, even those involving trustworthiness or bravery—or wisdom—as natural human weaknesses, and thus excusable because of that necessity. He describes the complete destruction of a legion due to the failings or possible cowardice of one of his lieutenants without uttering a single harsh word against the man's name. He also recounts how a favored tribe repeatedly broke their word to him without showing anger, simply explaining how he accepted them back as allies—not out of forgiveness, but because it served his purposes. But he can also tell us, without a hint of hesitation, how he wiped out a city with all its women and children so that other cities might learn what would happen if they resisted, refusing to bow down and become subjects under the divine hero in whose hands Providence had placed their fate and wealth.

It seems Cæsar always had confidence in himself. His words are so plain, and his awareness of his own dignity so clear, that he never has to insist he has never been defeated. His very simplicity implies that no campaign he undertakes could ever end in failure. His writing suggests that victory is so assured for him that to question its likelihood would be pointless. He feared no one, and because of this, he commanded the fear of others. He could confront his legions when they refused his call to arms and bring them to obedience with just a word. Lucan, who understood Cæsar's character well, wrote that "he deserved to be feared, for he feared nothing"; "meruitque timeri Nil metuens." He writes of himself as one might expect a god to write, secure that his divine purpose would surely prevail, never needing to question it. With Cæsar, there is always this godlike simplicity that makes his "Veni, vidi, vici" a natural expression of how he views his own approach to action. The same quality comes through in the many brief mentions of the punishments he administered. Cities are left desolate, almost as though by a wave of his hand, though he scarcely bothers to mention that his hand even moved. He tells of one Acco who opposed him, that "Graviore sententiâ pronunciatâ,"—as if there had been some jury to hand down this severe sentence, which in reality came only from Cæsar himself—he sentenced him "more majorum." We learn from other sources that this punishment involved stripping him, binding his neck in a cleft stick, and flogging him to death. After a half-sentence telling us how he forced the accomplices of the tortured chief to flee from their own country, he moves on into Italy with a dignity so imposing that he seems far too grand to linger on these small yet distasteful details. And we feel he truly is grand enough for such restraint.

It has already been mentioned that the great proconsular "wolf" soon learned of a "lamb" coming down to drink from his stream. The Helvetii, or Swiss as we now call them—those tribes living by Lake Leman and scattered throughout the hills and valleys to the north of the lake—had decided that their homeland was lacking. They believed they could greatly improve their lot by leaving their mountainous territory and moving into parts of Gaul, where they might prove stronger than the tribes already there and take hold of the fertile lands. In order to do so, the easiest path out of their own region led down the Rhone, where it now flows through Geneva into France. However, to follow this route, the Swiss would need to cross a portion of the Roman province. Here, indeed, was a case of the "lamb" stirring the waters with a vengeance. Upon hearing that these Swiss planned to "facero iter per Provinciam nostram"—"make their way through our Province"—Cæsar rushed over the Alps into Gaul, arriving in Geneva as quickly as he could.

He opens his first book with a geographical outline of Gaul. Though it may not be perfectly accurate, it provides us with a remarkably clear picture of what Cæsar wanted to convey. When he speaks of Gallia, he refers to the entire territory stretching from where the Rhine empties into the ocean down to the Pyrenees and eastward to the Rhone, the Swiss mountains, and the borders of the Roman province. He then divides this territory into three regions: the Belgians inhabited the northern part, above the Seine and Marne; the Aquitanians held the land south of the Garonne; and the Gauls or Celts occupied the intermediate territory. Having thus set the stage, he plunges at once into condemning the Swiss for their grievous offense in seeking to pass through "our Province."

He has only one legion stationed in Further Gaul—that is, in the Roman province located beyond the Alps from Rome. So, when Swiss ambassadors approach him, asking for permission to cross through the small patch of Roman land and pledging to cause no harm as they pass, he stalls for time. He tells them he can't provide an immediate answer and needs to consider the matter. He instructs them to return on a certain day—by which time he will have gathered more soldiers. Of course, when the day arrives, he refuses their request. The Swiss attempt to cross but quickly abandon the plan in frustration. They find an alternate route to exit their mountainous homeland through the territory of a people called the Sequani, securing permission to do so. However, Cæsar knows how dangerous the Swiss "lambs" could be to him and his "wolves" if they succeed in reaching the back of his province—that Roman territory which left behind the name "Provence" in modern France, until France insisted on unifying into a single nation. Moreover, certain allies of the Roman Republic, called the Ædui, ask him to come and halt the advance of these rough Swiss travelers. Cæsar is always willing to aid the Ædui, though they are a fickle and unreliable people—and, above all, he is eager for war. So he maneuvers to intercept the rear of the Swiss, striking when three parts of the people have crossed the river Arar (Saone) and one portion remains behind. This unfortunate group—since all these people belong to one tribe or mountainous canton—he falls upon and completely destroys. And in this instance, he congratulates himself for avenging the death of his father-in-law's grandfather, slain by this very tribe.

This tale of the Helvetii's attempted migration stands as one of the most extraordinary in history, told by Cæsar without a hint of astonishment. The entire population decided that, because their lands were cramped, their numbers growing, and their spirits high, they would venture out—taking men, women, and children—to seek new homes. We frequently read of large-scale migrations—like those of the Northmen sweeping south, or Danes and Jutes coming into Britain, or people from Scandinavia crossing the Rhine. We know that it's by this method that many lands came to be populated. But we often imagine such movements as being dominated by warriors, leaving behind homes and families, with the option of returning later. These Swiss wanderers, however, had no intention of returning. Anything they couldn't carry with them, they destroyed, even burning their homes and crops so there would be no chance of turning back.

They do make significant progress, reaching as far as Autun in France—at least three-fourths of them get that far. But it's there that they face Cæsar, who outmaneuvers them on a hill. At this time, Roman power had not fully established its fearsome reputation in the area, so the Swiss almost gain the upper hand. Cæsar acknowledges, as he does only once or twice more in his Commentaries, that the battle was long and the outcome uncertain for much of it. But eventually, the unfortunate Helvetii are routed in a bloody defeat. However, Cæsar is not content to simply see them flee; he forces them back to their original territory—back to their burned homes and ruined fields—fearing that otherwise, certain German tribes might settle there and cause problems. And so, they return—at least, those who survive the ordeal. With careful attention to detail, Cæsar records that 368,000 people embarked on the expedition, but only 110,000, or less than a third, managed to make it home. Among those who perished, countless were sacrificed to honor the shade of his father-in-law's grandfather.

Following this, the Gauls begin to realize just how formidable a man Cæsar truly is. He informs us that no sooner had he concluded the war with the Swiss than nearly every tribe in Gallia sent representatives to congratulate him. In particular, one tribe, the Ædui—whom we hear much about and never quite warm to, given that they are untrustworthy allies, loyal to Cæsar only until they sense he's in difficulty—now come to request a significant favor. Two tribes, the Ædui, whose name has left little trace in modern France, and the Arverni, who are still known in the region of Auvergne, have long been in a struggle for dominance. In response, the Arverni and their allies, the Sequani, have called upon certain German tribes from across the Rhine for support. The Ædui have been on the losing end of this conflict. One of their leaders, Divitiacus, now entreats Cæsar to intervene. Would he be willing to expel these troublesome Germans, retrieve their hostages, free them from oppressive rule, and set things right? Indeed, not only are the Ædui suffering under these Germans and their king, Ariovistus, but the situation has worsened for the Sequani as well, who had invited the Germans in the first place. In fact, Ariovistus has become an unbearable menace to the eastern part of Gaul. Would Cæsar please be so kind as to drive him out?

Cæsar consents, and we are reminded of another fable—the story of the horse who asked the man for help in a fight against a stag, only to find the man mounted on his back and never dismounting. Cæsar wasted no time in taking the reins, and, once in control, had no intention of letting go.

Cæsar then explains his reasoning for accepting this commission. The Roman Senate had often referred to the Ædui as "brothers" and "cousins," and it would be unfitting for men honored in such a way to be dominated by Germans. Moreover, if these marauding Germans weren't stopped, they might develop the habit of crossing the Rhine, eventually encroaching on the Roman Province and even posing a threat to Italy. And Ariovistus was personally so arrogant that this situation needed to be dealt with. So Cæsar sends ambassadors to Ariovistus, inviting the German leader to a meeting. Ariovistus refuses to attend. If he wanted to see Cæsar, he would come to Cæsar; if Cæsar wanted to see him, he was welcome to come to him. Such was Ariovistus's reply. Ambassadors shuttle back and forth between them, and a good deal of argument ensues, in which Ariovistus, surprisingly, presents the stronger logic. Cæsar, with his characteristic simplicity, does not hesitate to let Ariovistus's arguments be fully heard.

Ariovistus reminds Cæsar that the Romans have governed their conquered tribes in their own way without interference from him, Ariovistus, and that the Germans claim and intend to exercise the same right. He goes on to say that he is quite open to living in peace with the Romans, but asks Cæsar to bear in mind that the Germans are an undefeated people, trained to fight, and used to hardship—as Cæsar might judge by the fact that they had not slept under a roof for fourteen years. Meanwhile, other Gaulish tribes are appealing to Cæsar for help. The Treviri, whose territory corresponds to present-day Trier, are suffering attacks from the fierce, fair-haired Suevi, a people who at the time seem to have dominated what we now know as Prussia on the far side of the Rhine, driven westward by the same desire that has since characterized the region. Additionally, a people called the Harudes, coming from the Danube, are also harassing the Ædui.

Observing all of this, Cæsar realizes that unless he acts swiftly, the northern and southern German forces may join together. He gathers his supplies and advances on Ariovistus with remarkable speed.

In all his campaigns, Cæsar, much like Napoleon would later, achieved everything through swift and decisive action. He doesn't lecture us on the importance of speed in warfare or give lengthy explanations; he simply tells us again and again that he moved his army "magnis itineribus"—by very rapid marches; that he worked tirelessly day and night, and took "magno opere" measures—with much effort and utmost care—to stay ahead of the enemy. In this particular instance, Ariovistus is attempting to reach a town belonging to the Sequani, called Vesontio—known to us now as Besançon, though the name has evolved significantly. This town sat atop a hill, a natural fortress nearly encircled by a river that served as a natural moat. Cæsar notes that nothing is more advantageous in war than possessing such a naturally strong position. So he rushes forward, outpaces Ariovistus, and occupies the town.

At this point, the reader begins to sense that Cæsar is destined for almost supernatural success. We know this in advance, and expect nothing worse for him than narrow escapes. But, at that time, the Romans themselves didn't share the same confidence in him. While stationed at Vesontio, Cæsar receives news that his soldiers are terrified of the Germans. And understandably so. Though Roman soldiers had become hardened by the art of war and trained through conquests in the East, the Punic wars, and battles with surrounding nations, they were still, even up to this point, quite fearful of the Gauls. Ever since the days of Brennus, the invasion of the Gauls into Italy had struck terror into Roman hearts. The Germans, however, were even more frightening than the Gauls. Ariovistus's claim that his men had not slept under a roof for fourteen years was not merely boastful or empty; it reflected their raw, untamed nature. These Germans were a terrifying, rough, yellow-haired people whose fierce gaze was unsettling to Italians.

The soldiers were so overwhelmed with fear that they were "sometimes unable to hold back even their tears"—"neque interdum lacrimas tenere poterant." When we consider what these men later became under Cæsar's command, their initial tearful dread of the Germans seems almost humorous. And it reminds us that Italians, then as now, were generally more open with their emotions, in contrast with the reserved demeanor expected in northern countries. It's hard to imagine soldiers crying out of sheer fear. Cæsar's centurions inform him that the anxiety is so intense that the troops might outright refuse to take up arms when ordered to fight. Cæsar then addresses his officers in a speech full of bravado, full of scorn, and likely embellished with a good deal of untruth, though he uses truth whenever it serves him. Cæsar was renowned for his gift of persuasion. His words could flow "sweeter than honey" or cut "sharper than steel," just as Nestor's did. In any case, if others wouldn't follow him, he could count on his tenth legion to stand with him. He would go forth with that one legion of loyal soldiers if need be.

Though he had been commanding his forces for only a short time, Cæsar already had his elite troops, his guards, his beloved tenth legion. He knew well how to harness their strength and valor to inspire similar qualities in others.

Then Ariovistus sends ambassadors, stating that he is now willing to meet with Cæsar. He proposes a meeting on a certain plain, with each bringing only his cavalry guard, pointing out that foot-soldiers could be risky—aware, of course, that Cæsar's foot-soldiers would be Roman, while his own cavalry were Gauls. Cæsar agrees, but cleverly has men from his tenth legion mount the horses of his less-trusted allies. The accounts of these meetings, and the arguments given on each side, are quite fascinating. While we must remember that Cæsar is narrating both sides of the story, it feels as though he aims to tell it fairly. Ariovistus has little response to Cæsar's demands but speaks at length about his own accomplishments. The meeting is broken up, however, when the Germans launch an attack on Cæsar's mounted guard, and Cæsar withdraws—not before he has, however, expressed to Ariovistus Rome's grand principle of protecting her allies.

Ariovistus then suggests another meeting, but Cæsar declines to attend personally, instead sending some ambassadors. Immediately, Ariovistus captures these ambassadors and throws them into chains, leaving no option now but battle.

Due to space, the details of all these battles can't be fully covered here, and nothing particularly unique about this battle demands special focus. Cæsar describes the German tactic where their cavalry and infantry fight together, with the footmen advancing out from the midst of the horsemen and then retreating for cover. Cæsar's own men fight well, and the Germans, despite their fierce looks, are eventually driven in a complete rout back toward the Rhine. Ariovistus manages to escape over the river, saving himself, but has to abandon his two daughters and his two wives. Both wives and one of his daughters are killed, while the other daughter is captured. Cæsar had sent a dear friend as one of the ambassadors to the German leader, and, as we recall, he and his fellow envoy were immediately put in chains. During the German flight, this ambassador is recovered.

Cæsar tells us that this event brought him as much joy as the victory itself—seeing "one of the most honest men of the Province of Gaul," his close friend and guest, freed from enemy hands and safely returned. Fortune did not lessen this joy by inflicting any harm upon the man. Thrice, as the ambassador himself reported, it was decided by lot before his eyes whether he would be burned alive then or be held for a later date. Cæsar's telling of the story makes us appreciate his genuine enthusiasm, and we're glad to hear that the fellow envoy was also rescued.

When the yellow-haired Suevi hear of all this, they immediately halt their advance along the lower Rhine and hurry back to their own lands, suffering some misfortunes on the way. Such is Cæsar's growing reputation that tribes, almost in alliance with him, even dare to challenge the Suevi. Then, in his "Veni, vidi, vici" manner, he informs us that, having wrapped up two wars in a single summer, he can put his troops into winter quarters even earlier than required, allowing him to return to his other Gaul across the Alps—"ad conventus agendos"—to hold some form of session or council for governing his province, and especially to raise more soldiers.

Chapter III.

SECOND BOOK OF THE WAR IN GAUL.—
CÆSAR SUBDUES THE BELGIAN
TRIBES.—B.C. 57.

The man had now firmly seated himself on the horse's back, but the horse still faced a number of troublesome enemies, against whom the man could be very useful, so the horse was in no hurry to unseat his rider. Could Cæsar kindly go and subdue the Belgian tribes? Cæsar, naturally, finds reasons to comply. The Belgians are conspiring against him, believing that now, with all Gaul "pacified"—as Cæsar describes it—the Roman conqueror will surely turn his sights on them, and so they had best prepare. Cæsar proposes that they would understandably see it as a major grievance for a Roman army to spend the winter so close by. Thus, by this rationale, these Belgian lambs have greatly disturbed the waters, and the wolf must respond. He gathers two more legions, and, as soon as the earth provides enough food for his increased numbers of men and horses, he rushes off to confront these Belgian tribes in Northern Gaul.

One tribe, the Remi, immediately reaches out, insisting that they are not rebellious lambs like the others; they have never disturbed the waters. According to the Remi, all the other Belgians—and some Germans with them—are conspiring together. Even the Suessiones, their closest neighbors, brothers, and cousins, are guilty; but they, the Remi, have steadfastly refused even to approach the stream, acknowledging that it rightfully belongs to the benevolent wolf. Would the wolf kindly take them and all they possess under his protection, allowing them to be the humblest of his friends? We come to detest the Remi as we do the Ædui; but their cleverness spares them from much of the starvation, slaughter, and ruin that the other tribes endure. Among most of these Belgian tribes, we recognize the familiar names of present-day regions. The old land of the Remi is now Rheims, the Suessiones now Soissons. Beauvais is where the Bellovaci lived, Amiens is the former land of the Ambiani, Arras that of the Atrebates, and Treves of the Treviri, as previously noted. The Silva Arduenna, of course, is today's Ardennes Forest.

The campaign starts with an attack by the other Belgians on the Remi, those disloyal traitors who have sided with the Romans. There's a town of theirs called Bibrax, now a small place known as Bievre, where the Remi are besieged by their fellow Belgians. When Bibrax is close to falling—and we can imagine the dire fate that awaited the townspeople—the Remi send word to Cæsar, who is only eight miles away. They inform him that they can't hold out any longer unless he sends help. Waiting for the right moment, Cæsar promptly sends assistance, and the Belgian besiegers fall into utter confusion. They agree to retreat to their respective territories, planning to defend any tribe that Cæsar might next choose to attack. "Thus," Cæsar says, as he concludes this minor episode, "without any risk to us, our soldiers killed as many of them as daylight allowed." Only when the sun set did the killing stop, just as Cæsar had ordered.

There is no real evidence that these Belgians had any intention of attacking the Roman province or even any Roman ally, other than Cæsar's statement that they had all conspired. But regardless of any actual wrongdoing or lack thereof on their part, Cæsar is set on carrying forward his campaign until he completely subdues them. The very next day, he advances on the Suessiones and reaches Noviodunum—now known as Noyons. When the inhabitants witness the power of his war engines, they abandon any thought of resistance and ask for terms. The Bellovaci soon follow suit. Thanks to the recommendations of his allies, the Remi, Cæsar spares one city, and to please the Ædui, he spares the other as well. Yet, he still takes their weapons and demands hostages. From the Bellovaci, known as a strong and influential people, he demands no less than 600 hostages. Through all these campaigns, we can only wonder how Cæsar managed and housed so many hostages. However, it was clearly understood that any town, state, or tribe providing these hostages would face their deaths if they opposed the great conqueror in any way.

Next come the Ambiani, whose forebears of our modern Amiens surrender almost immediately. Then he encounters the Nervii, who live much farther north, near present-day Lille and a considerable part of Flanders. Cæsar had heard astonishing stories about this tribe. Unlike modern-day Belgians, they allowed no traders among them, abstained from wine, and avoided all luxuries, fearing such indulgences might weaken their warrior spirit. Unlike other tribes, they send no ambassadors to Cæsar and resolve to defend their land if possible. They rely solely on infantry in battle and lack any cavalry. To guard against the cavalry of other nations, however, they construct thick artificial hedges, nearly as impenetrable as walls.

When Cæsar faces the Nervii, he commands eight legions, and he explains how he advanced on them in "his usual manner." The Nervii had apparently received incorrect information on this approach, which led them into serious difficulties. Cæsar begins by sending his cavalry ahead, followed by six legions—all foot soldiers. After these, he moves the baggage, supplies, and all equipment required for sieges. Finally, he brings up the rear with the two most recently enrolled legions. It is worth noting here that a legion in Cæsar's day, theoretically, consisted of six thousand heavily armed infantrymen. Each legion was divided into ten cohorts, and each cohort into six centuries or groups of about six hundred men. As with modern regiments, the actual numbers likely varied. Thus, eight full legions would represent an army of approximately 48,000 infantry. Cæsar, however, does not specify the exact count of his forces here or elsewhere.

By his own account, Cæsar found himself forced into battle almost before he realized what was happening. He claims that he had to manage everything himself, all at once—raising the battle standard, giving the signal with the trumpet, recalling the soldiers from their work, summoning back those who had gone a distance for materials to build a rampart, arranging the army, giving the soldiers a short address, and finally giving the battle cry. As for his speech to them, he kept it simple, telling them only to remember their past valor. The enemy was so near and eager for battle that the Romans could barely put on their helmets and pull their shields from their covers. The confusion was so intense that soldiers couldn't reach their own ranks but had to fight wherever they stood, under whatever flag was nearest. With so many challenges—especially the thick, artificial hedges blocking their view—it was impossible for them to fight in any organized fashion, leading to moments of shifting fortune. One is left with the impression that, in this case, Cæsar was caught off guard. At times and in certain places, the Nervii seemed to be gaining the upper hand.

The ninth and tenth legions chased one tribe into a river, where they had to fight them again and drive them out. The eleventh and eighth legions, having already put another tribe to flight, were attacked at the river's edge. The twelfth and seventh legions faced similar difficulties when Boduognatus, the Nervian leader, broke into the very heart of the Roman camp. The confusion was so severe that even the Treviri—considered the bravest cavalrymen in Gaul and fighting on Cæsar's side as allies—fled back home, claiming the Romans had been defeated. However, Cæsar managed to save his army through his own daring. Seeing the dire situation—"rem esse in angusto," as he describes it, meaning the battle was in a tight spot—he grabbed a shield from a common soldier, as he had come without one, and charged into the fray. When the soldiers saw him in the midst of the fight, and realized he was watching their every move, they rallied with renewed strength, and the Nervii's advance was finally stopped.

Readers might wonder how much of this is strictly true. It reads as though it were. We might not fully understand today how one brave man, especially at such a moment, could have such a profound effect, or how Cæsar, in such a large army, could know his soldiers personally enough to call the centurions by name. Yet, the account feels genuine, as though Cæsar, too proud to boast, would not be hindered by any modern restraint from stating the truth of his actions. It's as if the goddess Minerva were recounting a moment when she descended among the Trojans.

The Nervii continued to fight but, inevitably, they were driven back in defeat. According to Cæsar, the tribe was nearly annihilated—so thoroughly that barely a trace of their name remained. We are told that out of six hundred senators, only three survived, and from sixty thousand warriors, barely five hundred were left. Then, Cæsar extended his mercy to the few who remained. He allowed them to return to their homes and even forbade neighboring tribes from disturbing them. There's little doubt that Cæsar came close to defeat in this encounter, and we might guess that the experience taught him a valuable lesson for future campaigns.

But there still remained the Aduatuci to deal with before the summer ended—a group that had aided the Nervii, who had a town of their own and were located in what is now roughly the Namur region. At first, they put up a little resistance around their town's walls. However, when they saw the frightening siege engines Cæsar had—devices designed to reach them over their very walls—they became alarmed. They watched him construct a massive turret at a distance, laughing at its size, but as he moved it closer, looming above them, threatening them with stones and arrows, they realized they had no defense against such height. In awe, they sent out envoys to plead for mercy. Surely, they reasoned, Cæsar and his Romans must wield powers beyond human. They promised to surrender everything if Cæsar would only be merciful enough to let them keep their arms, explaining that they were constantly at war with neighboring tribes and that without weapons they would be defenseless.

Cæsar responded. As for deserving mercy, they had no claims. How could any tribe merit mercy when it stood against him in war? Yet, as was his usual practice, he would grant them some terms of grace if they surrendered before his battering ram touched their walls. But the idea of keeping their arms was clearly absurd to him. Naturally, they would need to surrender all their weapons. Just as he had done for the Nervii, he would instruct their neighbors not to harm them. They agreed and threw their weapons into the outer ditch of the town—but not quite all. They cunningly kept back a third, hiding these weapons for a later opportunity. When Cæsar entered the town, those who still had arms, along with others without, attempted to flee. A battle ensued; thousands of Aduatuci were killed, while the rest were driven back and subsequently sold into slavery. We can't help but wonder who purchased these captives and what price each man fetched on that day in the Aduatuci's city.

Then, word came to Cæsar through his young lieutenant, Crassus, the son of his fellow triumvir, that the Belgian states, from the Scheldt to the Bay of Biscay, had been brought under the Roman yoke. Even the Germans sent ambassadors to him, so convinced were they that fighting him was useless—such a deep impression this last campaign had left on the minds of the barbarian tribes. But Cæsar was in a hurry; he had no time for ambassadors now, wishing to get into Italy. They were told they would have to return to him next summer.

Upon hearing of these achievements, Rome decreed a public thanksgiving, lasting fifteen days, in honor of Cæsar's glorious accomplishments.

Chapter IV.
THIRD BOOK OF THE WAR IN GAUL.— CÆSAR SUBDUES THE WESTERN TRIBES OF GAUL.—B.C. 56.

In the opening of the third book, we see that Cæsar was concerned not just with conquering lands but also with securing the benefits that conquest could bring. After his last campaign, when he traveled into Italy, he sent one of his lieutenants, Galba—whose descendant would later become an emperor after Nero—along with the Twelfth Legion, to spend the winter in the upper Rhone Valley. The aim was to open up an easier trade route over the Alps for merchants coming in and out of Northern Italy. This route appears to have been through the Great St. Bernard Pass, and Galba stationed his forces at Martigny, a location many people know today. However, he soon faced a violent attack from the local inhabitants of the valley, who likely didn't appreciate being told how much toll they should charge the passing traders. In the struggle, Galba and his legion were nearly overrun. Yet, when the Romans found themselves nearly out of weapons and provisions, they decided to fight their way out. They did so with such success that they reportedly killed more than ten thousand enemies, while the remaining twenty thousand Swiss warriors fled. Even so, Galba thought it best to leave the area, which proved difficult to sustain during the winter, and he retreated down the valley toward the lake and into the Roman province, setting up winter quarters among the Allobroges, a people south of present-day Lyon. While we don't know if the Allobroges were pleased with his presence, they were considered loyal at that time, though they had caused trouble in the past. Their position made loyalty to Rome almost a necessity. Whether Cæsar's commanders compensated the locals fairly for their food and supplies or simply took what they needed remains unclear. It was Cæsar's practice, however, to have the lands his army occupied support them.

When we think about the number of troops Cæsar took into unfamiliar lands and the boldness he showed in doing so, it's striking how little he says about the difficulties he must have faced. His armies likely needed supplies for as many soldiers as the British and French forces combined in the Crimean War, and unlike them, he couldn't rely on ships to carry everything. We know the road from Balaclava to the heights over Sebastopol was terrible, though short. Cæsar's route, stretching from the base of the Alps in the Roman province to the lands he sought to conquer, would have been no easier and many times longer—almost a hundred miles for each mile that caused so much hardship in the Crimea. However, Cæsar traveled lightly, with few supplies beyond weapons and essential tools, which he likely crafted along the way. His soldiers were given a daily ration of grain and some pay. Before Cæsar's time, legionaries received 100 asses a month—an as being worth less than a penny—but Cæsar doubled it. We can imagine that paying his men was not his main worry, though finding daily grain and forage for so many soldiers and horses must have been a constant challenge. He mentions these difficulties at times, but not with the frustration we associate with the struggles over coffee and supplies in the Crimea. Sometimes he waited for forage to grow, and there were necessary discussions on provisioning, yet he barely speaks of overwhelming obstacles and says nothing at all about rough roads. One advantage Cæsar had over Lord Raglan was that he was his own reporter. His soldiers certainly didn't get coffee, and if their grain wasn't well-prepared, Cæsar had no reporters at hand to broadcast their complaints to the world.

When Galba's affair was settled, and Cæsar, by his own account, believed that all of Gaul was "pacified," or at least brought under control—having subdued the Belgians, driven off the Germans, and slaughtered the Swiss in the Rhone valley—he thought he might take a brief trip into his other province, Illyricum, to see what it was like. Just then, however, he learned of yet another uprising in Gaul! Young Crassus, needing to find winter provisions for the seventh legion he was ordered to lead into Aquitania, had sent his men out to neighboring regions to gather grain. Being a well-trained young general, Crassus had already taken hostages, as was proper, before allowing his soldiers to roam among unknown and potentially hostile barbarians. But despite this precaution, the Veneti—a seafaring people from ancient Brittany, in the same area where we now find the Druid monuments of Carnac and Locmariaker—decided to detain two of his officers, who would later be referred to as ambassadors, though initially Cæsar called them prefects and tribunes. The name of this tribe lives on in the capital of Morbihan, Vannes. These Veneti, who were powerful at sea, saw no reason why they should have to give up their grain to Crassus. When Cæsar heard that his officers, his sacred ambassadors, had been detained, he was filled with both outrage and indignation, and rushed back, probably with only a glimpse of Illyricum.

Cæsar's fury over the detained ambassadors—a sentiment that extended to the Gauls themselves, who soon realized the severity of what they'd done by imprisoning these "legates," a term held sacred and inviolable by all nations—was intense. This anger, he felt, made his resolve even more necessary. It reminds us of the Spanish conquistadors, who issued proclamations (in Spanish) to native people in Venezuela and New Granada, ordering them to obey a faraway king authorized by an even more distant pope, who claimed the authority of an even more distant God. The pain in history often lies in the injustice of the wolf preying on the lamb, yet the belief remains that only through such conquest could the lamb rise above a simple, subjugated life. And Cæsar was serious about his mission.

Cæsar gives a translated summary of his reasoning for this campaign in section ten of the book: "There were challenges in this war, which I have already described"—referring to the Veneti's strong naval power. "Still, there were many reasons urging Cæsar toward this campaign: the wrongs done to those Roman knights who had been detained, the rebellion stirred after a surrender had supposedly been agreed upon" (though there's no indication in the text of any formal surrender, only that Crassus had taken hostages); "the breach of alliance after hostages were given; the conspiracy among so many tribes; and, most importantly, that if this part of the region were left unchecked, others might feel emboldened to do the same." Furthermore, since the Gauls were naturally inclined to revolt and were quick to be stirred into war, and since all men, he noted, are drawn to freedom and hate subjugation, he decided it would be wise to station his army more widely rather than risk a mass conspiracy in Gaul.

Treating Gaul as if it were a grand chessboard, he made plans to secure every area: he would keep the Treviri subdued in their territory (as readers may recall, Treves is far from Brittany). The Belgians needed to be watched, in case they rose up to assist others. The Germans had to be prevented from crossing the Rhine. Cæsar's most trusted general during the Gallic wars, Labienus, was given this responsibility. Crassus was to return to Aquitania and keep the south stable. Titurius Sabinus, who would later meet a tragic end, was sent with three legions, totaling about eighteen thousand men, to the neighboring tribes in Northern Brittany and Normandy. And young Decimus Brutus—whom Cæsar mentions with a fondness reflected in his choice of the word "young," though this Brutus would later play a part in Cæsar's assassination—was given command of the fleet, tasked with defeating these rebellious maritime tribes. Cæsar himself took command of his legions on-site.

All of this was conveyed by Cæsar in fewer words than have been used here to retell it. The reader feels the force of an extraordinary leader whose vision seemed limitless, making any ordinary enemy likely to think, "Surely this is no man, but a god."

Cæsar recounts the powerful effect his presence on the shore had during the battle at sea, even though young Brutus was leading the combat. Describing the action, he states, "What remained of the conflict depended on valor, in which our men were far superior; and this was especially true because the engagement took place so openly within sight of Cæsar and the whole army that no brave act could go unnoticed." The entire hillside and high ground overlooking the sea were crowded with his troops, who were able to watch the battle unfold below, allowing them to witness firsthand the bravery of their comrades.

Of course, Cæsar triumphs over the Veneti and the other seafaring tribes, defeating them even on their own waters. In the end, the Veneti surrender themselves, along with all their possessions, to Cæsar. Wanting to make an example of them and to ensure that the rights of ambassadors would be respected by other "barbarian" tribes in the future, he decided that a particularly harsh punishment was necessary. "Gravius vindicandum statuit," he says—"he resolved that the offense should be punished with exceptional severity." He thus orders the execution of the entire senate and sells the remaining men of the tribe into slavery. The striking brevity and unapologetic forcefulness of this sentence, both in the way he delivered it and in how he recounts it, is as shocking as it is fascinating to read from such a distance in time. "Itaque, omni senatu necato, reliquos sub coronâ vendidit"— "Therefore, having slaughtered the entire senate, he sold the rest of the men with chaplets on their heads," following the Roman custom of marking captives meant for sale with these garlands. We can almost picture him, with a commanding gesture, moving on from the scene. Surely, he appears not merely as a conqueror but as a figure larger than life, almost divine.

His generals were just as successful in their own campaigns. One Gallic leader, Viridovix, based in what is now the Normandy region— perhaps near Avranches or St. Lo—was lured into a trap and defeated along with his army. Meanwhile, in Aquitania, Crassus faced resistance but ultimately forced the region into submission, with the inhabitants relinquishing their arms.

At this point, Cæsar considers that two tribes—the Morini and the Menapii—have yet to submit to him. The Morini lived in the region now known as Boulogne and Calais, while the Menapii were farther away, scattered across the Low Countries, up near the mouths of the Scheldt and the Rhine. These tribes were a challenging group to subdue; they had no permanent towns or structures that could be easily destroyed. Instead, they roamed through dense forests and marshlands, taking refuge in them whenever they faced defeat. By now, summer was almost over, and the journey from Vannes in Brittany to regions as far north as Breda or even Antwerp was no small feat, especially given the vast wilderness of the land and the size of Cæsar's army. Yet he had a few weeks left before winter and was motivated to finally claim that all of Gaul was "pacified." For the moment, though, there was this stubborn northern corner that still defied him: "Omni Galliâ pacatâ, Morini Menapiique supererant"—"all Gaul having been pacified, the Morini and Menapii remained." He also likely started to contemplate that, from the Morini's territory, he could launch the shortest journey to the mysterious land beyond—the island of Britannia.

Seeing an opportunity, Cæsar launches an assault on these evasive tribes. When they retreat into the woods, he orders his men to cut down the forests. Despite felling large stretches of woodland, however, the tribes only retreat further into denser and deeper woods. Bad weather sets in, and his soldiers, accustomed to the warmer climate of Italy, struggle to endure the harsh conditions in their simple tents made of animal hides. Picture these Italian soldiers, unprotected by solid walls or roofs, battling through the raw, damp winters of undrained Flanders, ordered to chop down seemingly endless forests. If a contemporary report like the Times had been available then, instead of Cæsar's Commentaries, we might have heard a lot more about their suffering. Instead, Cæsar simply notes that he was forced to abandon the campaign for that year.

Before leaving, though, he makes sure to leave a lasting mark on the land. He sets fire to all the villages, devastates the fields, and finally withdraws his army to a more hospitable area south of the Seine. There, he places his troops in winter quarters, though probably to the considerable discomfort of the local population who would have to host his soldiers for the season.

Chapter V.

FOURTH BOOK OF THE WAR IN GAUL.—
CÆSAR CROSSES THE RHINE,
SLAUGHTERS THE GERMANS, AND GOES
INTO BRITAIN.—B.C. 55.

In the following year, certain German tribes, including the Usipetes, crossed over the Rhine into Gaul, near where it meets the sea, as Cæsar tells us. He also notes that when he forced these Germans back across the river, it was close to the confluence of the Meuse and the Rhine. Considering the limited information available to Cæsar, it's impressive how accurate his geographical knowledge was regarding the Rhine's flow to the sea and the junction of the Rhine and the Meuse through the Waal. The spot he describes, where the Germans were driven into the river, seems to be close to modern-day Bommel in the Netherlands, where the Waal and Meuse rivers converge at the head of Bommel Island, where Fort St. André now stands or once stood.

The Suevi, those remarkable people of whom he writes, have customs that stand out starkly even by today's standards. Among these Suevi, the men alternate each year between fighting and farming, though they seem to value their cattle more than their crops. They practice a form of communal land ownership, with no private property for their fields. From a young age, Suevi men follow their own will, each living as he pleases. They are tall, strong men, accustomed to a harsh climate, wearing only minimal coverings made of animal skins, even in the cold. They regularly bathe in rivers throughout the year, and they only trade with others to sell the spoils of war. Unconcerned with luxury, they care little for their horses and, when they do ride, prefer to do so without saddles, feeling contempt for men who rely on such "delicate" additions. Wine is foreign to them, and they maintain a strict distance from neighboring tribes, unwilling to live near anyone.

It is these fierce Suevi who have driven other German tribes over the Rhine and into Gaul. Cæsar, upon hearing this, grows deeply concerned. He is keenly aware of his Gaulish allies' weaknesses—how easily they become unsettled, their fondness for rumors, and their tendency toward restlessness. These Germanic tribes have now begun to settle in the lands of the Menapii, the very tribe with whom Cæsar had left some unfinished business in the previous year. With Germans encroaching on Gallic territory, Cæsar realizes that if he allows these newcomers to become comfortable on the Roman side of the river, they could pose serious trouble. Without delay, he sets out to aid the Menapii and put a stop to the German advance.

Naturally, the Germans send ambassadors to negotiate. They explain that they have been forced out of their own lands by their own kin, the Suevi, who, they admit, are stronger than they are. They declare that, in matters of combat, only the Suevi are superior to them—not even the immortal gods could withstand the Suevi. But they insist they are also Germans and are certainly not afraid of the Romans. Yet, in the proposal they present, they show a hint of caution. They ask if Cæsar would permit them to stay where they are or perhaps assign them a different region on the Roman side of the Rhine.

Cæsar responds with an offer of his own: they are welcome to settle among the Ubii, another German tribe living along the Rhine, possibly around where Cologne now stands, or slightly farther north. Some of the Ubii appear to have already been pushed across the Rhine by the Suevi and have managed to secure a place in the region where Charlemagne would later establish his famous chapel, now known as Aix-la-Chapelle. Here, though they are Germans, they have survived because they successfully defended their ground. The Ubii, too, face trouble with the Suevi, so if these newcomers are willing to go and join the Ubii, Cæsar will see to it that things are arranged fairly for all parties.

The German tribes hesitate but ultimately decide not to relocate, and eventually, they launch an attack on Cæsar's cavalry, achieving some success. In this encounter, there is treachery on both sides—first by the Germans, then by Cæsar—a double deception that later sparked intense criticism against Cæsar in Rome. Because of the deceitful actions in this engagement, some of Cæsar's enemies in the Senate proposed that he should be handed over to the Germans by the Republic itself. But, had such a decree been passed, carrying it out would have been nearly impossible—Cæsar's hold on the army and his influence were far too great.

As expected, the Germans are defeated, and they are driven back toward the river, fleeing into the low, marshy land where the Rhine, Meuse, and Waal intertwine, creating a landscape that was as confusing for armies as for travelers. This may have taken place here in the vast river delta or, perhaps, much farther upstream near Coblentz. The reader may recall the potential location mentioned at the start of this chapter. Cæsar describes the aftermath as if nearly all of the Germans—men, women, and children—were swept away. They had brought their families with them, and when the tide turned against them, the whole group, desperate to escape, fled en masse toward the river. Pursued closely by the Romans, they threw themselves over the banks. Overwhelmed by fear, exhaustion, and the strong currents, they perished in large numbers. The estimated count was 180,000 Germans who were destroyed, while the Roman army emerged from the conflict unharmed to the last man.

Cæsar then decided to cross the Rhine. While it's clear he didn't intend to permanently expand the Republic's control into what he termed Germany, he felt it necessary to show the Germans his strength. The cavalry of the intruding Usipetes had been on the other side of the river foraging, and Cæsar seized the opportunity to demand that the Sigambri, a tribe with whom the cavalry had taken refuge, surrender these horsemen to him. However, the Sigambri refused to comply. The Germans appeared to accept that Cæsar controlled Gaul and could manage it as he wished, but they fiercely opposed his interference beyond the Rhine. Yet, Cæsar, as he often did, managed to maintain allies even among potential foes. Just as he had the support of the Ædui in central Gaul and the Remi in the north, he had the Ubii as his German friends. This tribe, which likely occupied areas on both sides of the Rhine at that time, encouraged him to cross the river and demonstrate his power to intimidate their neighboring rivals. Cæsar agreed to their request. However, crossing the river in boats wouldn't suit either his sense of security or his sense of pride, so he decided that he would build a bridge.

Is there a student in England, or one who has attended any school where Cæsar's writings are taught, who doesn't recall the famous phrase "Tigna bina sesquipedalia"? With these words, Cæsar begins his vivid account of constructing the bridge. Considering the Rhine's width, swift current, and the limited availability of tools and building materials in such a wild and remote region, the construction of this bridge astonishes us. It reveals the brilliance of Cæsar's planning and his remarkable ability to execute ambitious projects. He drove paired piles into the riverbed, positioning them to counter the flow of the river, with each pair slanting against the current. In our time, we might accomplish this as well, but we would rely on coffer-dams, steam-pumps, mechanical rammers, and a team of engineers. Cæsar explains that he designed the supports in such a way that the current's force only served to further stabilize them. In an astounding ten days, the bridge was complete, and the entire army, including the cavalry, was led across.

Cæsar doesn't delve into the hardships involved or mention if any soldiers were lost during the process. This simplicity in his writing is a striking feature of his Commentaries. We're familiar with the construction challenges faced by modern armies, as well as projects that today's armies would find nearly impossible. We can think of the infamous road up from Balaclava, or the railway that was sent from England during another campaign. With all the advantages of modern technology, such feats require an immense amount of time and resources. Yet, for Cæsar, the obstacles seem minimal, barely worthy of mention. He simply built his bridge, crossed with his entire army in ten days, and said nothing of the inevitable difficulties, harsh conditions, or potential casualties involved.

Once the bridge was completed, German ambassadors arrived without delay. From the moment construction began, the Sigambri fled and concealed themselves in the woods. Cæsar responded by burning their villages, destroying their crops, and advancing into Ubii territory. Once there, he reassured the Ubii, solidifying their alliance. News of his approach soon reached the formidable Suevi, who immediately began preparations for large-scale combat. However, Cæsar, noting that he hadn't crossed the Rhine to wage war against the Suevi specifically, decided that he had already achieved enough in terms of demonstrating the might of Rome and intimidating the Germans. After spending eighteen days across the river, he led his troops back and dismantled the bridge, erasing this remarkable feat as efficiently as he had created it.

Then follows a section that stirs mixed feelings in a Briton's heart—feelings of embarrassment over our remote ancestors' supposed insignificance and irritation at what seems like Cæsar's clear misunderstanding of our ancient character. After returning across the Rhine, he found only a few weeks of the fighting season remaining. What better way to spend this leftover time, Cæsar thinks, than to cross the sea and conquer Britannia? This first record of an invasion of our island is mentioned almost as an afterthought, as if Cæsar intended it merely to make productive use of the remaining days of summer. Though the island seems distant and mysterious, Cæsar claims that British warriors had been aiding the Gauls throughout his campaigns. This sense of interference from across the water sparks his interest in a reconnaissance mission.

Before embarking with his army, he sends over a reliable messenger to scope out the coasts and harbors of Britain. This envoy, however, doesn't muster the courage to actually land. He returns to Cæsar with a limited report—essentially a brief summary of what he glimpsed from the safety of his ship. Meanwhile, Cæsar, ever efficient in his planning, assembles a substantial fleet in the region of Boulogne and Calais, mobilizing it for his daring voyage across the Channel. Word of his intended invasion has evidently spread, as he receives messages from Britain—at least according to his account—pledging submission to the Roman Republic. Whether we take this account at face value or not is another question, but it's clear that Cæsar at least implies a slight acknowledgment of Britain's willingness to submit, a hint of respect for the land that even the people of Boulogne and Calais didn't quite receive.

As Cæsar recounts, these Gallic people—known as the Morini—approach him asking for pardon for their past resistance. They come with offers of hostages and excuses, claiming they were misguided by poor counsel. Cæsar graciously extends them some measure of clemency. He admits that he was inclined to accept their submission and move forward, not wishing to let these minor affairs in Gaul interfere with his new purpose. "Nor did he consider that such trifling affairs as these should stand in the way of his expedition to Britain," he explains. One hopes the Boulogne and Calais people still remember and appreciate Cæsar's choice of words—dismissing them as "trifling matters" when his sights were set on Britain.

With ample hostages taken to secure peace on the mainland, Cæsar turns his focus to preparing for the crossing. He organizes his fleet, and they set out around the third watch, roughly around midnight. As often happens on this particular crossing even in modern times, the cavalry detachment faced delays, no doubt made worse by the fact that they were leading horses along with them. Cæsar himself, however, crosses successfully and arrives near the British coast around the fourth hour—roughly eight or nine in the morning. Approaching the white cliffs of Kent, he sees Britons lined up along the heights, braced for his arrival and ready for resistance.

He anchors offshore and waits for his full fleet to assemble, holding his position until around two in the afternoon. The cavalry unit is delayed further and doesn't manage to cross until four days later. Once his forces are in place and he has surveyed the coast, Cæsar gives the command to land. Seizing the right moment and finding an appropriate stretch of shore, he orders his vessels toward the beach and initiates the landing, a historic moment marking the beginning of Rome's encounters with the people of Britain.

Cæsar admits he faced significant challenges in landing his troops on British shores. Knowing the difficulties we face today in making a similar crossing to the Kent coast, even with modern technology, one can appreciate Cæsar's struggle. His large ships, loaded with heavily armed Roman soldiers, could not come in close to shore because of the shallow water. This forced the soldiers to jump overboard, fully equipped, and wade through the waves to reach land—all while battling not only the rough seas but also the fierce Britons waiting to confront them. The British fighters, unencumbered by heavy armor and far more agile, knew the shallows well. They maneuvered easily, attacking from the shore and darting into the surf to hinder the Roman troops. Cæsar observes that his men, unsteady in the water, were less surefooted and less effective in combat than they typically were on dry land—something he explains without surprise.

Cæsar had two types of ships at his disposal: "naves longæ," or long ships, designed for carrying soldiers, and "naves onerariæ," larger ships meant to transport supplies. The long ships were more maneuverable and versatile than the transports, though they were not the dedicated war vessels Romans typically used in naval battles. To gain an advantage, Cæsar brought his long ships broadside to the shore, allowing his men to launch stones and arrows at the Britons, unsettling the defenders and buying time for his troops to make their way onto land.

In a moment of intense bravery, the eagle-bearer of the tenth legion jumped into the sea, shouting to his comrades that he would fulfill his duty and challenging them to follow if they did not wish to see their standard—their sacred eagle—fall into enemy hands. "Jump down, my fellow soldiers," he called, "unless you wish to betray your eagle to the enemy. I, for one, will do my duty to the Republic and to our General!" Inspired by his courage, the rest of the soldiers plunged into the water, leaving the safety of their ships. A fierce battle ensued, with the Britons doing their best to drive the Romans back into the sea. Cæsar describes the clash as sharp and intense—"Pugnatum est ab utrisque acriter," he says, which roughly means "Both sides fought fiercely." Yet, despite the resistance, the Romans pushed forward, and the Britons eventually retreated.

The only thing missing from Cæsar's customary fortune, he notes, was a strong cavalry force to pursue the fleeing Britons and fully secure the island. Considering his short stay, though, this complaint seems a bit exaggerated; Cæsar wasn't planning to remain in Britain for long. Still, he could claim victory: the Britons offered a general surrender and handed over hostages. However, a sudden storm disrupted his plans, damaging his fleet and leaving him unsure if he could even make it back to Gaul. He was further confounded by unusually high tides, which he had not anticipated. Since he had only prepared for a brief incursion rather than a prolonged campaign, he lacked sufficient food supplies and urgently needed to return to the mainland. Observing his difficulties, the Britons regained their courage, believing they could perhaps overpower him. They launched an attack, putting the seventh legion at risk, which had ventured out to forage. Cæsar managed to rescue them, but his damaged fleet was still a major concern.

Realizing the necessity of repairs, Cæsar decided to dismantle some of the most severely damaged ships to use their parts to fix the others. It's astonishing to think of the speed and efficiency with which he managed this, especially given that they had no access to the sort of facilities—dry docks, tools, or even stable work environments— that we rely on for similar repairs today. Despite these challenges, he succeeded in getting his ships seaworthy again. During this time, he also faced another assault from the Britons but was able to repel them, inflicting damage and destroying their resources to quell resistance. Once again, British leaders approached Cæsar to sue for peace, and this time, he demanded twice as many hostages as before. Due to the lateness of the season and the damage to his ships, he arranged for these hostages to be sent to him later in Gaul rather than taking them with him.

With his fleet now repaired, Cæsar prepared for the return journey. Amazingly, only two of his transports went missing, drifting down the coast with about three hundred men aboard. These soldiers soon found themselves threatened by the Morini, who demanded their surrender. But Cæsar quickly dispatched reinforcements, rescuing them from a dangerous predicament. Following this minor skirmish, he continued with his signature tactics—burning villages, destroying fields, and leaving a desolate landscape behind to deter any further defiance.

One can only wonder what might have changed in the world's history if the Britons had seized this opportunity to destroy Cæsar's fleet and end his incursion, leaving not a single Roman ship to carry word back to Gaul. But instead, Cæsar was able to report his "victory" to Rome, securing his desired outcome: a formal public thanksgiving, decreed to last a full twenty days, in recognition of his conquests and achievements.

Chapter VI.
FIFTH BOOK OF THE WAR IN GAUL.—
CÆSAR'S SECOND INVASION OF

BRITAIN.—THE GAULS RISE AGAINST HIM.—B.C. 54.

Upon his return from Britain, Cæsar, as was his custom, crossed over the Alps to oversee his other provinces and manage affairs in Italy. Yet he was resolved to undertake another expedition to the island. He could not yet claim to have truly "conquered" it, so he left detailed orders with his generals for constructing new ships and repairing the damaged ones. He sent requests to Spain for various supplies and materials to fully equip his fleet. Remarkably, there's never any mention of financial obstacles. Though he received substantial funds from Rome to support his legions, Cæsar made no hesitation in letting the spoils of war fund further military endeavors whenever possible. In fact, Cæsar had started his campaigns heavily in debt; he had borrowed an immense sum—over 830 talents, or about £200,000—from Crassus, Rome's wealthiest man at the time, just to take on his Spanish province. When the wars concluded, however, Cæsar returned to Rome with immense wealth, having collected a considerable fortune. Like Clive in India centuries later, who came across hoards of treasure among the locals, Cæsar likely took his share from the barbarians he defeated—though unlike Clive, Cæsar probably took all he found.

Once he'd secured his ship orders, Cæsar turned his attention to a brief matter in Illyricum, where he managed to raise additional tribute. He notes this winter activity in no more than a dozen lines, showing his preference for brevity when recording the less remarkable episodes. With his affairs quickly handled, he made haste to rejoin his army and fleet. By the time he returned, his instructions had been followed to such precision that he found a fleet of the newly-designed ships awaiting him—these were lighter, faster vessels, each fitted with just one bank of oars. He counted six hundred of these ships and an additional twenty-eight of the larger kind. Cæsar acknowledged the efforts of his soldiers, commending their hard work and efficiency. He promptly ordered his fleet to sail for the Portus Itius, which historians believe lay somewhere between modern Boulogne and Calais, likely near Wissant.

With his second British expedition nearly prepared, Cæsar quickly diverted his attention to a separate matter brewing in the land of the Treveri. Two rival chieftains were locked in a dispute, and Cæsar thought it best to intervene before their quarrel destabilized the region. With four legions and eight hundred cavalry—totaling around 25,000 men—he marched into the Treveri lands. In typical fashion, he resolved their conflict swiftly, in a manner not unlike the clever monkey settling the dispute over the oyster. Satisfied with his intervention, Cæsar wrapped up the affair almost as quickly as he'd begun it, returning to his fleet at the Portus Itius in little more than a page and a half of his account.

Cæsar decides to take five of his legions to Britain along with two thousand mounted Gaulish allies. In total, he has gathered around four thousand horsemen from various parts of Gaul, many of them chieftains and nobles. These allies serve a dual purpose: they will provide additional military support, but their presence also helps ensure that the tribes in Gaul remain loyal while he is absent, as their chieftains are effectively held as hostages. Cæsar divides this cavalry force, taking half with him to Britain and leaving the other half behind with three of his legions under Labienus, stationed in the Boulogne area. This contingent would serve as a base, maintaining provisions and guarding against any disturbances in his absence.

However, a complication arises with Dumnorix, a prominent Æduan chieftain, who was supposed to be one of Cæsar's staunchest allies. Instead, Dumnorix tries to flee with all the Æduan horsemen, apparently unwilling to join the campaign. Cæsar, resolute in his discipline, orders a pursuit, resulting in Dumnorix's capture and death. With this matter resolved, Cæsar is ready for departure. He sets sail with a fleet of over 800 ships at sunset, benefiting from a favorable south-west wind. By noon the next day, he reaches the coast of Britain, but the cliffs are deserted, with no Britons in sight. He suspects that the sheer number of his ships has intimidated the locals into hiding. Wasting no time, he establishes a secure camp near the shore.

That very night, Cæsar advances roughly twelve miles inland—about eleven Roman miles, as their measurements were slightly shorter than ours today. There, he encounters the Britons, who have gathered their forces for resistance. A skirmish ensues, after which Cæsar returns to fortify his camp on the coast. Shortly thereafter, a fierce storm hits, wreaking havoc on his fleet despite his efforts to secure them in a sheltered spot. The tempest tears the ships from their anchors, tossing them onto the shore and smashing them against one another. The damage is extensive, forcing Cæsar to send a message to Labienus, instructing him to construct additional ships to replace the wrecked ones.

Determined to salvage what's left, Cæsar orders his men to haul the damaged ships onto land, closer to the camp. This task is grueling, requiring around ten days of continuous labor, day and night. His soldiers endure incredible strain to complete the task, but with the fleet finally secured, Cæsar advances once more into the heart of Britain to confront the assembled tribes.

At this point, the Britons, who had often been at odds with one another, have united under a single leader: Cassivellaunus, a powerful chieftain from across the Thames, likely in what we now know as Middlesex or Hertfordshire. The internal conflicts of Britain have been set aside temporarily, as the tribes rally together to resist the Roman invasion under Cassivellaunus's command.

Cæsar's description of the island and its people is fascinating. He notes that the interior is inhabited by "aborigines" or native Britons, while the coastal areas are dominated by immigrants from Belgium, who have retained the names of their continental tribes. The population is dense, with houses that are numerous and closely grouped, much like those in Gaul. The Britons possess an abundance of cattle and use currency, either in the form of copper coins or iron rings, which are quite heavy. Tin, he observes, is plentiful in the center of the island, while iron is only found near the coast and in limited quantities. Brass is an imported metal. Their timber is similar to that in Gaul, except that Britain lacks beech and fir trees.

Interestingly, he notes cultural practices that strike him as peculiar. The Britons keep hares, chickens, and geese not for food but as pets, believing it wrong to eat them. The climate is milder than in Gaul, and Cæsar provides a rough description of the island's shape, which he describes as a triangle. He estimates the southern side (the Kentish coast) to be 500 miles long, overshooting the real distance by about 150 miles. His geographical knowledge becomes a bit less precise when describing the western side, which he suggests is oriented toward Spain and where Ireland lies. He speculates that Ireland is roughly half the size of Britain and situated about the same distance from Britain as Britain is from Gaul. He also mentions an island named Mona (likely the Isle of Man) and suggests the existence of other islands where, he claims, thirty days of continuous darkness occur at midwinter—a notion that veers into myth.

Moving on to describe the British people, he praises the men of Kent as the most "civilised" among the Britons, stating they are nearly as advanced as the Gauls. Those further inland, however, lead simpler lives, subsisting on milk and meat rather than corn, and they wear garments made of animal skins. They stain their skin with woad, which gives them a blue tint, and sport long hair, though they shave everything but the head and upper lip. A rather shocking detail is that it's customary for groups of ten or twelve men to share wives. Cæsar's observations, colored by Roman attitudes, provide an intriguing glimpse into what he perceived as both the peculiarities and barbarism of the Britons.

In his detailed account, Cæsar provides a fascinating and even somewhat admiring description of the impressive skill and agility with which the ancient Britons maneuvered their war chariots in battle.

"This," he explains, "is the nature of their chariot-fighting." He tells us that they begin by speeding across the battlefield "per omnes partes"—in all directions—causing confusion in their enemies' ranks through the sheer terror induced by the powerful sight of their horses and the thunderous clatter of the chariot wheels. As they race forward, they skillfully hurl darts, disrupting and disordering the enemy ranks by both the weapons and the intensity of their approach. Once they have created an opening, these Britons leap from the chariots, abandoning their initial positions, and join the fight on foot, facing their enemies as infantry soldiers.

The charioteers, meanwhile, maintain a clever strategy: they drive just far enough away from the active battle to stay clear of immediate danger but remain close enough to provide rapid support when needed. The chariots are positioned in such a way that, if their comrades on foot are overwhelmed, they can quickly and efficiently rejoin the fray to either support a retreat or bolster an offensive. In this way, the Britons ingeniously combine "the speed of cavalry" with "the endurance and stability of infantry." Their continual practice has made them extremely adept at managing this dual approach, so much so that they can keep their highly energized horses steady even on rugged, sloped, or otherwise treacherous terrain. The Britons' skill extends to remarkable feats, such as maneuvering the horses at a full gallop, running along the chariot pole, balancing on the yoke that binds the horses, and then, as swiftly as they departed, leaping back into the chariot—all while in motion. "All of which is very wonderful," Cæsar remarks, highlighting his genuine amazement at their skill and technique.

Naturally, there is a considerable amount of fighting throughout this campaign. As Cæsar's legions make headway, the Britons, gradually becoming familiar with the Romans' strategies, adapt their tactics, avoiding large-scale confrontations in favor of smaller, guerrilla-style skirmishes. This shift to more evasive and sporadic attacks slows Cæsar's progress, yet he presses onward, making his way deeper into the heart of Britain and reaching the banks of the Thames. Here he encounters yet another significant challenge: crossing the river. The passage is treacherous, and Cæsar can only ford the river at one particular spot—and even then, with great difficulty. While he doesn't specify the exact location, historians later speculated that this ford might have been near what we now call Sunbury. The crossing was perilous, with the Roman soldiers nearly submerged, their heads barely above the water, but even in these conditions, their advance was so fierce that the Britons, seeing the determination of the Romans, abandoned their defensive positions on the opposite bank and fled.

Once across, Cæsar soon compels the Britons to yield, leading to a series of unconditional surrenders, hostages taken in his favor, and promises of tribute to Rome. Cassivellaunus, the British leader, recognizing that his position is becoming increasingly precarious, seeks refuge in what he considers a fortified settlement, believed to have been located near the modern site of St. Albans. Cæsar, however, points out that the British concept of a town, or "oppidum," is somewhat rudimentary by Roman standards, consisting simply of an area where they have surrounded dense woods with a ditch and a rampart. Despite this fortification, Cæsar's legions force their way into the stronghold, driving out the Britons and effectively dismantling their defensive position.

With their defenses breached, the Britons have little choice but to surrender once again. Cæsar secures further hostages and reaffirms the demand for tribute. He leaves behind strict orders as he departs, speaking with the authority of one who expects immediate and absolute compliance. Cassivellaunus, the British leader, is now required to relinquish his authority in favor of Mandubratius, whom Cæsar installs as the new ruler of the Trinobantes—the tribe inhabiting what we know today as Middlesex and Hertfordshire. He specifies the annual tribute that the Britons are to send to Rome as a token of their subjugation and, notably, orders that Cassivellaunus must not interfere with Mandubratius's rule.

Once these arrangements are in place, Cæsar prepares to leave Britain. His fleet is insufficient to carry the entire army in one crossing, so he divides his forces, sending half of his soldiers across the Channel and instructing the ships to return for the remaining troops. He observes, almost with a sense of pious gratitude, that although he lost many ships when they were empty, during the return voyage—when they were filled with soldiers—hardly any were damaged.

Cæsar's second expedition to Britain marked the end of his attempts to conquer the island. Though he could claim certain accomplishments—landing twice on British shores, establishing some measure of dominance, and returning his army safely—he was far from subduing Britain as he had done with Gaul. His achievements were by no means the complete victory that Cicero's brother had reported back home with the word "confecta"—implying that Britain was "finished." Indeed, Cæsar's incursions into Britain felt more like probes into an uncharted land than decisive campaigns for conquest. The insurmountable natural barrier posed by the English Channel was an unyielding ally to the Britons, one that made it difficult for the Romans to establish a true foothold. Both landings had been challenging, and Cæsar found his army's very survival often hanging in the balance. In each attempt, the struggle against the channel's treacherous waters was nearly as daunting as the battles against the Britons themselves.

One might conclude that Cæsar's primary motive for invading Britain was to demonstrate his reach rather than to permanently extend Roman control across the channel. His objective may have been more psychological and strategic—showing the Gauls that no land, not even distant islands, was safe from Rome's influence, thus reinforcing his authority. Since Britons had supported the Gauls against him in previous battles, it was crucial for Cæsar to discourage them and anyone else who might think of assisting Rome's enemies. Whether his orders to the British chiefs after his departure were actually obeyed is uncertain. It seems unlikely, however, that the tribute he demanded would be delivered with consistency or enthusiasm. Ultimately, Cæsar returned to Gaul without achieving full subjugation, marking his invasions as symbolic more than substantive.

Upon his return to Gaul in the late summer, Cæsar encountered a significant problem: a severe shortage of provisions due to an unyielding drought that had left the crops in poor condition. To feed his army, he was forced to split his forces and disperse them across various tribes, stationing each legion in a different area. He assigned one legion and a half under his generals L. Titurius Sabinus and L. Aurunculeius Cotta to the Eburones, a tribe living near the Meuse in what is now the region of Liège and Namur. The Eburones were known for their strong resistance to Roman control, and placing his men among such a tenacious people was a calculated risk. Cæsar hoped that dispersing his legions this way would alleviate the strain of food scarcity, though he understood the dangers of dividing his forces in such a contentious land. Taking care to position most of his legions within a hundred miles of each other for mutual support, he stationed one particularly isolated legion in a more subdued region—the territory of the Essui, near modern-day Alençon. But despite this attempt at prudence, the decision to spread his army would soon lead to one of the greatest disasters Cæsar would face in his entire career.

Throughout Cæsar's campaigns in Gaul, the spirit of the Gauls to reclaim their autonomy never wavered. Their longing for freedom from Roman subjugation simmered just beneath the surface, with each tribe harboring a deep resentment toward the occupying force. To the Gauls, Cæsar was nothing short of a monstrous curse—a figure of incomprehensible power whose presence was as inescapable as it was destructive. Though some tribes aligned with him temporarily, he had no true allies among the Gauls. Even the Ædui, who had enjoyed a privileged alliance with Rome, chafed under his authority. Dumnorix, the Æduan chieftain who defected with his horsemen during Cæsar's second invasion of Britain, had resisted fiercely before his death, protesting his right to freedom as a member of a free state. His resistance was a tragic illustration of the Gauls' struggle against Rome's harsh demands. To Cæsar, who wielded authority with "godlike simplicity," this opposition was little more than an inconvenience. He expressed no remorse for the countless lives lost or villages burned under his command, viewing these acts as mere steps in a grand design. His power was exercised with the impassive detachment of a deity who believed such matters inconsequential—a means to an end. If brutality was required to maintain order, he considered it justifiable, his actions calculated for their effect on both the Gauls and his Italian supporters. The display of might was intended to reinforce the invincible image of Rome, making it clear that resistance to Cæsar was futile.

Yet, as the reader witnesses the unyielding spirit of the tribes crushed under Roman might, the narrative evokes a profound empathy for the Gauls. Figures like Dumnorix, asserting his freedom to the last breath, resonate as symbols of defiance. Even tribes like the Carnutes, who were nominally under Cæsar's control, refused to fully submit. When Cæsar installed his own puppet king, Tasgetius, among the Carnutes, they promptly revolted during his absence in Britain and killed Tasgetius, rejecting his rule as an affront to their sovereignty. Now, the Eburones—strongly independent and led by their two kings, Ambiorix and Cativolcus—recognized an opportunity in the scarcity and division of Cæsar's forces. They saw their chance to break free from the grip of Rome and dared to strike at the legion under Titurius and Cotta, igniting a revolt that would soon reveal the vulnerabilities in Cæsar's formidable empire.

Ambiorix, the crafty and cunning chieftain of the Eburones, hatches a plan that reveals his deep understanding of both diplomacy and deception. With smooth words and clever maneuvering, he convinces the Roman generals to meet with him under a flag of peace, where he begins his tale with apparent sincerity. Ambiorix professes admiration and gratitude toward Cæsar, expressing the highest regard for the Roman leader who has shown him kindness in the past. He assures them that he harbors no personal ill will against Cæsar or his soldiers. However, he explains, the situation has escalated beyond his control: an immense force of Germans has crossed the Rhine and is rushing toward the Roman camp with overwhelming numbers. There is no possibility, he says, of the Romans withstanding such a force if they remain where they are; destruction is inevitable.

Ambiorix suggests, with feigned concern, that the best course of action would be for the Romans to abandon their camp and join their allies, either the legion stationed under Quintus Cicero, the orator's brother, among the Nervii to the east, or Labienus's legion on the southern borders, near the Remi and Treviri. As a token of his supposed allegiance to Cæsar, Ambiorix offers to personally guide the Romans safely through Eburone territory, allowing them to escape while they still have the chance. It is an offer he presents as one of goodwill, a gesture of reverence for Cæsar himself. Ambiorix even pleads with Titurius and Cotta to take his advice, pressing them to make a swift decision.

Faced with this proposal, the two generals are divided. Titurius, convinced by Ambiorix's seemingly heartfelt warning, is in favor of taking the advice and evacuating the camp. But Cotta, along with several tribunes and experienced centurions, remains skeptical. He argues that it is foolish to place trust in the words of an enemy and warns against acting without orders from Cæsar. Cotta points out the risk of basing their strategy on the suggestions of a potential adversary and urges that they stand their ground and await further instructions. However, Titurius, undeterred by the caution of his colleague, insists upon immediate action. After heated debate, and likely weary from Titurius's persistence, Cotta reluctantly agrees.

At the break of dawn, the Roman forces, carrying all their baggage and supplies, set out from the camp with an air of misguided confidence, as though they were marching through friendly lands. They assume, in their naïveté, that Ambiorix's offer of safe passage was sincere. Yet no sooner do they leave the relative safety of their encampment than Ambiorix's true intentions reveal themselves. The Eburones had, as expected, prepared a deadly ambush. With the Romans caught off guard, an assault is launched on both their rear and front, throwing the legion into a state of complete disarray and panic.

The battle unfolds in a series of tragic events. Outmaneuvered and overwhelmed, the Roman soldiers are struck down, their formation shattered by the surprise attack. Titurius, in a desperate bid for peace, steps forward to plead for mercy. He is met with a demand to lay down his arms—a request that, to a Roman, represents the ultimate dishonor. Nevertheless, Titurius, consumed by a flicker of hope, complies, casting aside his weapons. But Ambiorix's apparent mercy is merely a ploy. As Titurius stands weaponless and vulnerable, Ambiorix distracts him with a speech, drawing out the moments until, finally, the Roman general is surrounded and mercilessly slain. Cotta, unwilling to surrender, dies fighting, refusing to abandon his men or his honor in the face of overwhelming odds. More than half the soldiers fall in battle; the remainder, horrified and desperate, retreat to the camp under the cover of night.

The survivors, once within the camp's confines, realize the gravity of their predicament. With no hope of rescue and burdened by the shame of their defeat, they decide to end their own lives rather than face the dishonor of capture. In the end, only a handful of soldiers manage to slip away, escaping through the chaos and eventually bringing word of the disaster to the camp of Labienus.

Despite the usual sympathy that the reader might feel toward the Gauls' fight for freedom, the fate of the Roman legion stirs a particular sense of tragedy. One can't help but feel that the ambush was an unnecessary cruelty, and that Titurius, though tragically flawed, should not have led so many men to their deaths. The story is especially poignant when we hear of the gallant eagle-bearer, Petrosidius, who, in the throes of battle, hurls the eagle standard over the camp's fortifications to protect it from capture, and then dies defending it. It is a moment of Roman honor in the midst of a doomed struggle, making us wish, if only for a moment, that Ambiorix's treachery had not met with such success.

However, there is a sense of ominous certainty as well. Knowing Cæsar's relentless determination and his unwavering sense of retribution, one can be sure that Ambiorix's betrayal will not go unpunished for long.

Having achieved such a devastating blow against the Romans, Ambiorix and the Eburones press on, seizing the moment when Cæsar's forces are still scattered and the Romans are grappling with their recent disgrace. It's clear to the Gauls that if they are to prevail against Roman domination, now is the time. Ambiorix, emboldened by his success, leads his forces toward the camp of Quintus Cicero, who is stationed with his legion among the Nervii. The Nervii, fierce opponents of Rome, are eager to join the fight, and together with the Eburones, they lay siege to Cicero's encampment.

The assault is brutal. The Romans, outnumbered and caught off guard, find themselves struggling to hold their defenses. The barbarians unleash red-hot balls of clay and fiery arrows into the camp, igniting fires and creating chaos. Cicero's situation grows more desperate with each passing day. Several attempts to send messengers to Cæsar for reinforcements end in tragedy, as the couriers are intercepted and slain before they can reach him. Hope dwindles among the Romans, who begin to despair of any escape. They know, with a kind of fatalistic certainty, that without Cæsar, their defenses may not hold. The might, the renown, and the very essence of Roman invincibility seem to reside solely in their general. Cicero, though both a courageous and prudent leader, is aware that he and his men are in dire straits. Eventually, he manages to send a Gaulish slave, who cleverly conceals a message in a hollowed-out dart, hoping it will find its way to Cæsar.

In the midst of this tense standoff, Cæsar offers a brief but memorable episode featuring two Roman centurions, Pulfius and

Varenus, who are constantly arguing about who is the braver man. When Pulfius, in a fit of bravado, charges out alone against the enemy, Varenus, not to be outdone, follows him into the fray. Pulfius soon finds himself in danger, and Varenus rushes to his rescue, fighting off the attackers. Just as Varenus begins to extricate Pulfius, he too is surrounded by enemies, only to have Pulfius come to his aid in turn. Against all odds, both centurions manage to return to camp, unharmed. It's a rare moment of levity amid the grim reality of war, and it leaves the question of their rivalry unresolved — to this day, no one can say who was truly the better man.

Meanwhile, Cæsar, upon receiving the concealed message, wastes no time. He prepares a relief force and sends word back to Cicero, attaching a reassuring letter to another dart. Though the dart barely reaches Cicero before Cæsar himself arrives, the distant smoke and fires that mark the advancing legions' line of march give the beleaguered Romans the first glimmer of hope. Soon after, Cæsar's forces engage the Gauls. The fighting is fierce, but Cæsar, as always, prevails, rescuing Cicero and his legion from what had seemed an inevitable defeat.

Labienus, stationed on the borders of the Treviri, also faces his own challenges. The Treviri, another tribe with a deep-seated enmity toward Rome, prepare to launch an assault on his position. However, word of Cæsar's victory over the Eburones and Nervii spreads swiftly, instilling fear in the Treviri, who decide to abandon their plans rather than risk a battle against a freshly reinforced Roman force.

Yet, despite these successes, Cæsar is no longer under the illusion that Gaul is pacified. He realizes that, although he has repeatedly claimed to have subdued the region, Gaul as a whole is still seething with resistance, prepared to rise against Roman rule whenever the opportunity arises. It is during this winter that Cæsar comes to an important understanding: the Gauls have no desire to submit quietly to his authority. His presence is unwelcome, and his work in Gaul is far from over. The opposition against him has grown not only in strength but in unity, and the resistance is now so widespread that he decides to remain in Gaul for the winter, foregoing his usual return to Italy.

In the meantime, Labienus takes action against Indutiomarus, the chief of the Treviri, killing him in an effort to quell the unrest in that area. However, even with this victory, Cæsar can only report that Gaul is now "a little quieter" — a small step toward submission, but still far from the subjugation he seeks. The land remains turbulent, with Roman control tenuous at best. These events underscore for Cæsar the monumental challenge he faces in taming the Gaulish spirit.

Notably, it is during this turbulent winter that Cæsar's authority as proconsul is extended for another five years, granting him additional time to realize his ambitions in Gaul and beyond. Though he has achieved much, Cæsar knows that his work is not yet complete. His empire-building efforts will demand even greater resolve, cunning, and strength in the campaigns to come.

Chapter VII.

SIXTH BOOK OF THE WAR IN GAUL.— CÆSAR PURSUES AMBIORIX.—THE MANNERS OF THE GAULS AND OF THE GERMANS ARE CONTRASTED.—B.C. 53.

Cæsar wastes no time in launching the next campaign, even before winter has released its grip. The previous campaign had extended far beyond the usual season, with the cold creeping in while battles still raged across Gaul. The situation had grown increasingly dire: the Gauls were learning the power of unity, and their resistance was more determined than ever. Cæsar had already suffered severe losses—an entire Roman force of likely ten thousand men had been wiped out along with its generals, Titurius Sabinus and Aurunculeius Cotta.

Another legion, led by Quintus Cicero, was only saved from the same fate by Cæsar's timely intervention. Labienus's troops had also been engaged in fierce conflict. It seemed as though all of Gaul was preparing for war, and although Cæsar had managed to claim at the end of the last campaign that the region was a little quieter, he understood full well that his work was far from over.

At the start of the new campaign, Cæsar had formidable resources: eight legions, comprising 48,000 soldiers, all recruited from the Italian side of the Alps. Alongside these were substantial contingents of Gaulish cavalry and light infantry, supplementing the core of his army. Yet he had also experienced losses. An entire legion and a half had been obliterated, and further gaps had been made during his campaigns in Britain and in the battles with the Nervii under Cicero. But Cæsar intended to demonstrate to the Gauls that Rome's power would not falter—even after such setbacks. In fact, he would show them that Rome's strength could grow even greater in response to opposition. He would astonish them with a display of Rome's might, aiming to instill a lasting impression on Gaul's people that Rome could rebound swiftly and with even greater force after any defeat. To this end, he not only raised new troops but also borrowed a legion from Pompey, stationed outside Rome's walls.

Cæsar tells us that Pompey lent the legion out of "Friendship and for the Republic." Though Pompey and Cæsar were partners in the Triumvirate, Pompey likely felt he had no real choice. Replenished and reinforced, Cæsar reestablished the annihilated legion, filled the ranks of the others, and, with two new legions, now commanded an army probably numbering as many as 80,000 men.

His first strike was directed at the Nervii—an old and persistent foe, who had come close to defeating Cicero's forces before Christmas and were now conspiring again with various Germanic and Belgic tribes. The reader may remember that, in a previous book, Cæsar claimed to have nearly wiped out the Nervii, leaving hardly a trace of them. But evidently, enough of them survived to threaten the Romans once more. After quelling this latest resistance, Cæsar moved toward Paris, known in his writings as Lutetia Parisiorum—a city that now appears for the first time in recorded history. With the support of his allies, the Ædui and the Remi, he negotiated a peace with the tribes of the central region, including the Senones and the Carnutes.

With this accomplished, Cæsar focused his full attention on Ambiorix. The memory of his lost legion, his fallen generals, and the heavy blow Ambiorix had dealt to Roman pride drove him to a personal vendetta against the chieftain. According to legend, Cæsar vowed not to cut his hair or shave until he had avenged their deaths. However, he knew that before he could punish Ambiorix directly, he would need to deal with his allies. One of these was the Menapii, a tribe that had eluded Cæsar's control in previous campaigns. The Menapii lived along the southern banks of the Meuse near the sea and had yet to send any emissaries to Cæsar to plead for peace. He responded by devastating their villages, seizing their cattle, enslaving their people, and taking hostages, compelling them to forswear any alliance with Ambiorix.

Meanwhile, Labienus, Cæsar's trusted lieutenant, achieved a decisive victory over the powerful Treviri, a prominent tribe in the northeastern region. By skillfully luring the Treviri into a confrontation just before they were to receive reinforcements from the Germans, Labienus effectively crushed their hopes of mounting a successful resistance. The ancient adage, Quem Deus vult perdere prius dementat—"Whom the gods wish to destroy, they first make mad"—seems almost tailor-made for the unfortunate Gauls and Germans, who repeatedly fall into Roman traps. Cæsar provides a memorable recounting of Labienus's speech to his troops, urging them to take advantage of the moment. "Now," Labienus said, "you have your opportunity. You have your enemy thoroughly at a disadvantage. Show now the valour that you have displayed so often before the Imperator, Cæsar. Imagine that he is here, watching you." The respect and reverence with which Labienus invokes Cæsar's name speaks volumes about how Cæsar was regarded by his officers and men. Indeed, Cæsar describes this moment as though it were perfectly natural that Labienus and the soldiers should view him with almost divine reverence.

Through his relentless tactics and remarkable tenacity, Cæsar was determined not only to reclaim any ground lost to the rebellious Gauls but to ensure that Rome's dominance would be unshakable.

After this battle, in which the Treviri are, predictably, thoroughly defeated and slaughtered, Cæsar decides to construct a second bridge over the Rhine, a little upstream from the location where he had previously crossed. He explains that he undertakes this for two main reasons: first, because the Germans had sent aid to the Nervii, and second, because he wants to prevent his formidable enemy, Ambiorix, from finding refuge among the Suevi on the German side of the Rhine. This bridge-building feat also gives him an occasion to share some insights on the distinct customs of Gaul and Germany.

Cæsar observes that, among the Gauls, there are always two factions within each tribe, village, and even family, ensuring that one group can always check the other, preventing either from gaining absolute power. He provides this explanation here to clarify his original choice to ally with the Ædui and intervene against the Germans—especially in driving Ariovistus back across the Rhine. In eastern Gaul, a longstanding rivalry existed between two powerful tribes, the Ædui and the Sequani, each vying for dominance. The Sequani, seeking an advantage, had invited the Germans to assist them, leaving the Ædui in a dire situation. Desperate, the Ædui had appealed to Rome, citing their previous alliance with the Republic. Divitiacus, the high-ranking magistrate of the Ædui and brother of Dumnorix (whom Cæsar later had executed for his defection with the Æduan cavalry before Cæsar's second British invasion), had spent time in Rome and enjoyed influential friendships there, including that of Cicero.

Initially, there had been some debate in Rome about whether to support the Ædui, but Cæsar ultimately decided in their favor, thus setting the course for the confrontations that ensued. As we know, he succeeded in expelling Ariovistus back into Germany, and Ariovistus's family—his wives and daughters—were lost in the process. Thus, Cæsar explains, the Ædui were recognized as the preeminent allies of Rome among the Gauls, while the Remi, who had quickly joined Cæsar's cause when the Belgians rose against him, were given the status of Rome's second most honored allies.

Cæsar delves deeper into the social structure of the Gauls, highlighting that two classes of men are held in particular esteem: the Druids and the knights. This implies that for the Gaulish elite, there are essentially two noble professions—priesthood and the military. Meanwhile, the ordinary populace, he says, lives in a condition barely better than servitude. When burdened by debt, high taxes, or fear of powerful foes, common people often surrender their freedom, willingly entering a form of servitude to gain protection. Among the Gauls, the Druids wield the greatest influence, possessing supreme authority not only in religious matters but in civil life as well. They enforce this power through the dreaded sentence of excommunication, rendering any man who disobeys them an outcast, deprived of all civil rights.

The Druids are led by a single chief Druid who, upon death, is succeeded through a general election among the other Druids—unless one member is so clearly preeminent that no election is necessary. Their most sacred site is in the territory of the Carnutes, located at the heart of Gaul, and their spiritual and disciplinary teachings originate in Britain. Whenever faced with complex issues, they make pilgrimages to Britain to consult with their British counterparts. The Druids are exempt from military service and from paying taxes, a privilege that makes their role highly desirable among the Gauls. However, the path to becoming a Druid is arduous; training can last twenty years, as everything must be committed to memory. All

Druidic knowledge is passed down orally, for their laws and doctrines are never to be written. Their core belief is in the transmigration of souls, so that people are taught that death is merely a transition rather than an end, removing much of the fear associated with it. Beyond this, they are esteemed for their knowledge of astronomy, geography, natural science, and, naturally, theology.

Through these explanations, Cæsar offers a fascinating window into Gaulish life, illustrating not only the complex social structure but also the impressive and revered position held by the Druids. Their influence, coupled with the loyalty of the knights and the submission of the general populace, shaped a society that, while diverse in customs, was unified by powerful, controlling forces.

The knights, or nobles of Gaul, according to Cæsar, had no calling or pursuit other than that of war. Before the so-called "benefits" of Roman order and control, they found themselves in a rather unpleasant predicament of perpetual warfare with each other, year upon year, driven by necessity to fight among their own. Of all peoples, Cæsar observes, the Gauls are steeped most deeply in superstition. So fervent is their belief that, in times of great peril or crisis, they frequently resort to human sacrifices, with the Druids, their spiritual leaders, officiating as the grim mediators between man and their fierce gods. These sacrifices are conducted by fire, where victims are burned alive to appease the deities. They have a particular preference for burning criminals—thieves and murderers—believing that the gods take special delight in such tainted offerings. However, when such morally compromised individuals are not available, they will even sacrifice the innocent.

In terms of their gods, Cæsar tells us that the Gauls chiefly worship Mercury, whom they revere as the most clever and versatile of all gods. Beyond Mercury, they also honor Apollo, Mars, Jove, and Minerva, assigning them the familiar attributes recognized by other nations. While Cæsar uses the Roman names for these deities, he doesn't imply that the Gauls themselves used these terms. Rather, they had their own names and mythologies, adapted from their native beliefs. How precisely the Roman gods merged with Druidic practices is left unexplained; Cæsar himself expresses no particular surprise at this amalgamation. Among the Gauls, trophies captured in war are consecrated to Mars, and some states even maintain vast reserves of these sacred spoils. Few Gauls would dare to appropriate these sacred items for their own use, but if anyone commits this sacrilege, they face a terrible punishment—death by torture.

In family life, the Gauls hold fathers in the highest veneration. Sons do not dare to approach or even stand publicly in the presence of their fathers until they are mature enough to bear arms, a rule that underscores the respect accorded to paternal authority. Marital property arrangements are also unique: a husband's fortune must be made to equal his wife's dowry, and afterward, their wealth is held in common. This system of shared assets would likely appeal to many British wives today, Cæsar notes approvingly. However, the next custom he describes would be met with quite a different reception. Among the Gauls, husbands have the power of life and death over their wives and children. When a man of importance dies and there is suspicion of foul play, his wives are questioned under torture. Should any incriminating confession be extracted, the guilty party is put to death by torture. This practice reveals that polygamy was not uncommon among the Gauls.

The Gauls are also known for their grand funeral rites. Objects and creatures that were cherished by the deceased are committed to flames as part of the ceremony. In Cæsar's time, this included animals, but in earlier days, it extended even to slaves and other close dependants who had been especially beloved by the departed. In matters of governance, Cæsar notes that the best-organized Gaulish states are scrupulously careful about public discussions of state affairs. It is forbidden to spread rumors or debate matters of public importance outside of the formal council. Instead, any news or intelligence must be relayed directly to a magistrate, ensuring that discussions on critical matters are limited to official gatherings. Thus, Cæsar provides a fascinating insight into Gaulish society, highlighting both their superstitious devotion and their structured approach to public order.

Turning his attention to the Germans, Cæsar explains that they diverge significantly from the Gauls in customs and beliefs. They do not have Druids, nor do they care much for sacrifices or ritualistic practices. Instead, their worship is directed solely toward the natural elements that they can observe and derive benefit from—principally the sun, fire, and the moon. The Germans live with a single focus on hunting and warfare, caring little for agriculture or cultivation of the land. Their diet consists mainly of milk, cheese, and meat, and they treat land communally, moving on after a year rather than establishing permanent homesteads. This way of life is deliberately maintained to discourage any attachment to the land that might detract from their warlike spirit. They avoid fixed settlements to prevent the emergence of social divisions, where the wealthy might gain dominance over the poor, and to forestall a dependence on comfort that could erode their resilience to cold and heat. By resisting these trappings of civilization, they aim to stave off the allure of wealth, so that no one individual can aspire to be higher or more powerful than another.

In this account, Cæsar presents the Germans as a society with an almost modern-sounding grasp of political philosophy, favoring equality, communal property, and a rugged lifestyle that keeps them ready for war and free from the corrupting influence of wealth and social hierarchy. Through these contrasts, Cæsar paints a portrait of two cultures—one marked by its spiritual and familial rituals, the other by its stern simplicity and communal ethos—each with unique customs that defined their societies.

The Germans, as Cæsar observes, take great pride in having no close neighbors. For them, an ideal arrangement is to have a broad, empty buffer zone surrounding their territory, enhancing both their security and their independence. Each tribe, therefore, cultivates this wide margin of separation, holding it as a matter of honor and protection. In times of war, the chieftains wield absolute authority over life and death, a reflection of the Germans' rigorous approach to leadership in battle. In times of peace, however, they have no appointed magistrates or formal legal systems. Justice is instead a matter for the chiefs, who strive to mediate and resolve disputes as best they can within each canton. Interestingly, among the Germans, theft within one's own tribe is punishable, but theft from a neighboring state is considered honorable. In fact, they organize expeditions specifically for this purpose, allowing individuals to join voluntarily. However, should anyone join and then back out, serious consequences await. Despite this penchant for thieving expeditions, they are notably hospitable to foreign travelers passing through.

Cæsar reflects on the evolving power dynamics between the Gauls and the Germans, noting that there was once a time when the Gauls were the stronger people, capable of invading and conquering German lands. In fact, even in his own time, some Gaulish tribes were still living across the Rhine, having adopted German customs and lifestyle. However, Cæsar suggests that the Gauls' proximity to the Roman Province has softened them, introducing them to luxuries that have made them less capable in battle. Thus, as Roman civilization advanced and introduced refinement, the Gauls have gradually lost some of the fierce resilience they once possessed. In contemplating these accounts of the customs and beliefs of various tribes, one gains insight into what was considered beneficial or harmful by different European peoples long before the rise of Christianity.

Cæsar goes on to describe the Hercynian Forest, an immense, dense woodland stretching from what is now northern Switzerland across the Danube. This vast forest was formidable in its size: it would take nine days for a traveler to cross it in width, while its length was seemingly endless, requiring sixty days to reach the farthest point. This Hercynian expanse, likely including the Black Forest region, was home to several strange and fascinating animals. Among them were bisons with a single horn and elks that resembled large stags but lacked joints in their legs, meaning they could neither lie down nor get back up if they fell. These elks, Cæsar tells us, sleep leaning against trees, though they sometimes topple when a tree breaks, leaving them helpless. Another extraordinary creature in the forest is the "urus," a fearsome beast nearly the size of an elephant, which is aggressive toward both humans and animals. Killing a urus is a significant feat for any German, and its horns are prized, often mounted in silver to be used as drinking vessels.

Though Cæsar ventures into the German lands briefly, he does not linger long. He crosses back over the Rhine, partially dismantles the bridge, and resumes his pursuit of Ambiorix, the elusive chieftain who has continually evaded him. Cæsar's lieutenant, Basilus, nearly captures Ambiorix, but the crafty king escapes once again, leading Cæsar to reflect philosophically on the capriciousness of fortune. Ambiorix, as we may remember, shared his kingship over the Eburones with an elder named Cativolcus. However, Cativolcus, worn down by the relentless pressure on his people, curses Ambiorix for bringing these misfortunes upon their nation and ultimately takes his own life by poisoning himself with yew-juice.

The Belgic tribes—comprising both Gaulish and Germanic peoples—were now under intense pressure. Many had assisted, or might have assisted, Ambiorix and the Eburones, or, if left unchecked, could potentially aid them in the future. To deal with this widespread unrest, Cæsar decides to split his forces, yet he remains committed to tracking down Ambiorix himself, pushing deep into the damp, challenging landscapes near the mouths of the Scheldt and Meuse rivers. Here, Cæsar faces a difficult dilemma: he is driven by an unyielding determination to annihilate the entire tribe that dared to strike down his army—a crime, in his eyes, so grave that it demands nothing less than their total eradication. Yet he is also wary of the toll that such a campaign in these inhospitable regions might take on his own troops. He resolves this by inviting neighboring Gaulish tribes to assist in his mission, thus ensuring that Gauls, rather than his Roman legionaries, would suffer the brunt of hardship in this hostile terrain.

Cæsar's objective, however, is crystal clear and unbending: the Eburones must be obliterated, so that their very name will be erased from history. "Pro tali facinore, stirps ac nomen civitatis tollatur" — "For such a crime, the very lineage and name of their state must be wiped out."

In dividing his forces, Cæsar had stationed Quintus Cicero, with a single legion and a considerable amount of the army's heavier baggage and spoils, in a fortress strategically located precisely where the previous tragedy had occurred—the place from which the unfortunate Titurius Sabinus had been drawn out and killed due to the deceit of Ambiorix. Cæsar had made it known that the wealth of the Eburones was fair game for any who could claim it, hoping to encourage the complete decimation of that rebellious tribe by turning them into prey for other tribes. Learning of this opportunity for plunder, a group of Germans, known as the Sigambri, crossed the Rhine to gather the spoils left by the Eburones.

However, their focus soon shifted when they were tipped off about a potentially much richer target: the fortress of Quintus Cicero, where Cæsar's stores and wealth lay heavily guarded. Encouraged by this suggestion, the Germans seized the moment, launching an attack on Cicero's camp just as much of his force was away, searching for provisions. For the Romans, this position in the heart of the Eburones' territory once again proved nearly disastrous, with Cicero's legion narrowly escaping annihilation. Yet, while the Germans gained some success in the initial assault, they lacked the skill and experience to press their advantage fully. Satisfied with the spoils they had gathered, they chose to retreat and crossed back over the Rhine, leaving Cicero's force battered but alive.

As before, Cæsar arrives on the scene with divine-like timing, but Ambiorix, that relentlessly elusive leader, still manages to evade capture. Cæsar expresses bitter frustration that the Sigambri, rather than helping to harm Ambiorix as intended, had instead indirectly aided him, allowing the Eburones to slip through Cæsar's grasp once again.

Determined to capture Ambiorix, Cæsar spares no effort, offering substantial rewards to any who can help bring him in. He even persuades his soldiers to endure unimaginable hardships in their relentless search. Despite this, Ambiorix, accompanied by a small band of trusted companions, always manages to stay just a few steps ahead, eluding Cæsar with daring and skill at every turn. Nevertheless, Cæsar exacts his revenge in other ways. He methodically burns every village of the Eburones, laying waste to their land so thoroughly that even after his army withdraws, no one will be able to live there. Only when he has accomplished this complete devastation does he likely feel content enough to end his vow and shave, having finally satisfied his need for retribution.

Ambiorix continues to be spotted here and there, appearing briefly before slipping away again. In the meantime, Cæsar moves southward as winter approaches, settling in Rheims—then known as Durocortorum. Briefly, almost as an afterthought, he mentions his treatment of Acco, a leader among the Carnutes and Senones who had incited a conspiracy within central Gaul. With typical severity, Cæsar has Acco tortured to death and ruthlessly punishes others involved in the plot, exiling or outlawing those who managed to escape his grasp. Having quelled this rebellion and secured his legions in their winter quarters, Cæsar once again turns back to Italy to hold court, tending to his personal and political matters amid the complex affairs of the Republic.

So, with his vengeance taken against the Eburones and his dominion in Gaul once more firmly established, Cæsar concludes another campaign season, retreating momentarily from the constant demands of war to focus on the wider ambitions of his burgeoning empire.

Chapter VIII.

SEVENTH BOOK OF THE WAR IN GAUL.— THE REVOLT OF VERCINGETORIX.—B.C. 52.

In the opening of his account of this seventh campaign, Cæsar makes one of the rare references to events in Rome that appears in these Commentaries. Clodius, the notorious political agitator, had been assassinated, an incident that had caused great upheaval in the city. By this time, Crassus had also perished in his ill-fated campaign in the East, meeting his end at the hands of the Parthians. In the aftermath of Clodius's death, Pompey had been appointed sole Consul, effectively granting him dictatorial powers. Yet Cæsar only briefly mentions Clodius's murder, quickly pivoting back to events in Gaul. He notes that the Gaulish tribes, aware of the volatile state of affairs in Rome and sensing the gravity of Cæsar's involvement there, believed that he would be unable to leave Italy. They saw an opportunity to rise against Roman rule, hoping to cast off the Roman yoke while they assumed Cæsar's attention was entirely on the troubles in his homeland.

Indeed, the events in Rome must have weighed heavily on Cæsar. He likely saw in these developments the looming clash for supremacy within the Republic. Clodius, a political figure with whom Cæsar had maintained an uneasy but strategic alliance, was now gone. Crassus, once a wealthy and influential member of the Triumvirate, was also gone, leaving only Pompey to share power with Cæsar. Pompey, who just a year prior had sent a legion to aid Cæsar "for the sake of the Republic—and of friendship," was now firmly positioned in Rome with unprecedented authority. By now, Cæsar undoubtedly foresaw the inevitable showdown between himself and Pompey. The Republic was already shedding its traditional forms, and both Cæsar and Pompey must have realized that a new power structure would soon emerge. It was clear that the strength required to seize control of such a force would need to be formidable, and Cæsar knew that time was not yet ripe. Having dedicated six years to subduing Gaul, he would not forfeit the prestige, strength, and resources that such a conquest offered him. Though Rome's affairs were urgent, his most prudent course was still to return to Gaul and complete his campaign. News reached him that the tribes of Gaul were conspiring, assuming that the emergency in Rome would prevent Cæsar from leaving Italy to suppress them.

In this final book of the Commentaries, Cæsar recounts the extraordinary story of Vercingetorix, the brave leader from the Arverni (a region known today as Auvergne), whose father, Celtillus, had once sought to be the supreme leader of Gaul but was executed by his own people for his ambition. Vercingetorix stands out as the foremost hero of the Gaulish resistance, though we hear of him for the first time in this seventh campaign. The conspiracy against Rome began with the Carnutes, whose chief city, Genabum (modern-day Orleans), was the starting point of the revolt. Vercingetorix attempted to rally his own people, but they expelled him from their town of Gergovia, fearing the wrath of Rome. However, he continued to gather support, attracting followers from all over the region, including from as far north as Paris and from the western shores by the Atlantic.

Assuming command, Vercingetorix implemented harsh laws to maintain discipline. For severe offenses, he would burn the offender alive after subjecting them to excruciating tortures. For minor infractions, he would cut off a man's ears, gouge out one of his eyes, and send him back home as a stark, visible warning to others. With these ruthless methods, he managed to rally a significant force, threatening extreme punishment to any who resisted his call to arms and meting out punishment to those who wavered in their loyalty or showed even a hint of cowardice. Hearing of these escalating threats, Cæsar—still in Italy—realized that he could not delay any longer. He settled his affairs with Pompey as best as he could under the circumstances, then rushed back into Gaul.

Cæsar recounts the difficulties he faced just in reaching his forces, underscoring the urgency of protecting even the Roman Province itself from possible invasion. In the depth of winter, he forced his way through the Cevennes, a mountain range considered impassable at that time of year due to the heavy snows. His daring passage over these snow-clad peaks astonished even his allies and inspired fear among his enemies. Forced into early battle due to the tenuous loyalty of certain tribes (such as the Ædui, who could easily be swayed to join the revolt if not convinced of Roman strength), Cæsar had to balance the risks of a winter campaign with the very real threat of a Gaulish uprising.

Cæsar acknowledges the difficulty of his decision, recognizing that he would have preferred to wait for spring. But seeing that hesitation would allow the tribes to rally further support, he resolved to act at once. Thus began his seventh and most decisive campaign, in which he would face not only the bravery and skill of a single Gaulish hero but a widespread and deeply rooted Gaulish insurrection determined to restore their independence.

With remarkable swiftness, Cæsar maneuvers his forces across central Gaul, capturing three towns in quick succession, beginning with Genabum (modern-day Orleans), thus securing essential provisions for his army. This development unsettles Vercingetorix deeply. He realizes that, with the Romans gaining access to the very food and supplies of Gaul, his forces face a critical threat. Vercingetorix, therefore, proposes a drastic strategy to his followers: they must destroy their own towns and resources, leaving Cæsar with no way to sustain his army off the land. He addresses his people, urging them to endure the destruction of their homes and possessions, arguing that it would be far more devastating to suffer the capture of their wives and children as slaves under Roman rule. Convinced by his words, they act upon his order and burn twenty cities within a single tribe's territory, reducing them all to ashes. Neighboring states follow suit, embracing this scorched-earth tactic as their last defense.

However, one city stands out: Avaricum, known today as Bourges. Its beauty and strategic value as the pride of the surrounding region make it difficult for the Gauls to consider destroying it. They insist that Avaricum's strong natural defenses would make it a valuable asset rather than a risk. Vercingetorix initially insists that Avaricum should be burned just like the others, but eventually, he yields to his people's pleas, allowing the city to remain standing—for now.

Cæsar, determined to capture Avaricum, soon finds that his task will be challenging. The Gauls have systematically removed all sources of food and livestock from the area, leaving his army with no easy means of sustenance. Even the Ædui, who were supposed to be Cæsar's allies, do little to support him, and their neighbors, the Boii, a smaller and less capable tribe, are equally unhelpful. For days, Cæsar's soldiers endure grueling hunger, with the army at times entirely without food. Yet, Cæsar notes with pride that despite the suffering, his soldiers maintain their discipline and morale. "No word of complaint is heard unworthy of the majesty and former victories of the Roman people," he writes, underscoring their unwavering resolve. When Cæsar offers to lift the siege, seeing the difficulties they face, his men adamantly refuse. They declare their readiness to endure any hardship rather than abandon a siege once begun. They remind Cæsar of their unbroken record of success under his leadership and insist on finishing what they've started, to avenge the Roman citizens killed by the Gauls at Genabum. Cæsar describes this in a way that convinces the reader of the soldiers' loyalty and commitment. By now, Cæsar's legionaries have grown into seasoned warriors who no longer flinch in the face of adversity.

Meanwhile, Vercingetorix faces dissent among his own people. As the Romans close in on Avaricum, doubts and suspicions start to plague the Gauls. Fearing betrayal, they accuse Vercingetorix of conspiring to hand them over to Cæsar. The situation grows tense until Vercingetorix gathers his followers and delivers a speech to reassure them. To back up his words, he brings forth Roman prisoners and presents them as proof of the Romans' struggling condition. Vercingetorix insists that these men are Roman soldiers, claiming that their presence shows the dire state of Cæsar's army. This demonstration temporarily quells the unrest among his forces.

In response, Cæsar defends his legionaries against Vercingetorix's claims, asserting that the prisoners paraded before the Gauls were merely slaves, not soldiers. As the siege continues, the contrast between the two leaders becomes more pronounced—Vercingetorix relies on persuasion and unity among the Gauls, while Cæsar depends on the discipline, loyalty, and resilience of his legionaries, determined to see through the siege of Avaricum despite the mounting difficulties.

While Vercingetorix holds his position in a camp some distance from Avaricum, Cæsar is resolute in his determination to capture the city. The account of the siege is vivid and sharply drawn, capturing the intensity of the struggle on both sides. Cæsar describes the city's walls and how skillfully the Gauls defended against his troops. They proved adept in mining and countermining, constantly countering the Romans' advances with a relentless energy that included flinging hot pitch and boiling grease upon the invading soldiers. As each Gaul fell in the defense, another took his place, stepping forward undeterred to continue the fight. When a plan emerged among the defenders to abandon the city at night and escape to the safety of Vercingetorix's camp, their own women, in fear of Roman retribution, begged them to stay. Ultimately, however, the Gauls could not hold out, and the city fell to Cæsar's forces.

The fate of Avaricum's people is chilling. Cæsar recounts with cool detachment the massacre that followed, sparing neither the elderly, the women, nor the children. Of the forty thousand Gauls within Avaricum's walls, Cæsar states that only around eight hundred managed to reach Vercingetorix, who awaited them outside. While the exact number might be debated, there is no doubt that the Romans left almost no survivors, slaughtering the entire population with ruthless efficiency. Cæsar rationalizes the carnage as retaliation for the earlier murder of Roman traders in Genabum—traders, who, it should be noted, were primarily usurers exploiting the local population. According to Cæsar, this incident alone justified the massacre of Avaricum's innocents. One might concede that Gaul, if it were to be conquered, required decisive action of this kind; but it is difficult not to recoil from Cæsar's calm acceptance of such a brutal method.

Remarkably, Vercingetorix does not falter after this staggering loss. Displaying resilience, he reminds his followers that had they listened to his initial advice, Avaricum would have been burned by their own hands, sparing them the bloodshed that followed its defense. He maintains that, despite this setback, Gaul's many tribes are now prepared to rally to their cause. Vercingetorix then sets about fortifying his camp in a style influenced by the Roman methods he has observed, signaling a new determination and a tactical shift in the conflict. Until now, the Gauls had relied either on the defenses of walled cities or on the natural cover of forests and hills when they fought in open terrain.

Meanwhile, Cæsar faces yet another problem with his allies, the Ædui, whose internal divisions threaten to disrupt his campaign. A dispute has arisen over who should serve as their chief magistrate: an elderly contender or a younger rival. The Ædui appeal to Cæsar to settle the matter, despite the fact that he is fully occupied with the war effort. Recognizing the necessity of maintaining order among his allies, Cæsar goes to one of their towns in person to make a decision. He appoints the younger man as magistrate but seizes the opportunity to request reinforcements from the Ædui, asking for ten thousand infantry and all their cavalry to assist him against Vercingetorix. Bound to comply, the Ædui send their forces—but the arrangement is far from amicable.

As it turns out, the dismissed elder magistrate conspires with the Æduan general, leading their army to side not with Cæsar but with

Vercingetorix instead. Treachery and deceit abound among the Ædui, and their schemes inevitably reach Cæsar's ears. Time and again, they deceive him, working covertly to undermine his efforts, yet Cæsar continually chooses to overlook their betrayals, or at least he pretends to. It is part of his calculated approach to demonstrate to the Gauls the benefits of Roman friendship and the generosity of his own character. One might wish that he had directed his wrath toward the disloyal Ædui instead of the defenseless citizens of Avaricum, but then, if he had acted differently, he would not have been the Cæsar history knows—the Cæsar whose combination of ruthlessness, clemency, and political acumen kept him advancing inexorably toward his objectives.

While dealing with the fickle loyalties of his supposed allies, Cæsar also faces the mounting threat posed by his enemies. After the brutal loss at Avaricum (modern Bourges), Vercingetorix retreats with his followers to the heart of his homeland in Auvergne, where he strategically positions his forces on the hill of Gergovia. This hill, topped with a flat surface, is a natural stronghold, well-known to those who have visited Clermont, as it dominates the landscape. There, Vercingetorix sets up three camps, securing the approach with a river between him and Cæsar. Confident in his advantage, Vercingetorix anticipates that this river, difficult to ford, will keep the Romans at bay.

Cæsar, however, is undeterred. He builds a bridge and positions his legions before Gergovia, determined to seize the town. Though we cannot delve deeply into each maneuver, this siege of Gergovia stands out as one of Cæsar's most dramatic encounters. Against all odds, he captures the three Gaulish camps. The women of Gergovia, fearing the worst, lean over the walls, pleading for mercy from the Romans, begging not to suffer the fate of the women of Avaricum. Driven by courage or desperation, some Roman soldiers even climb into the town, as if victory is within reach. Readers, familiar with Cæsar's unbroken string of successes, expect him to prevail as he usually does. Yet, this time, Cæsar faces a surprising defeat and is forced to withdraw. Vercingetorix emerges victorious, masterfully defending Gergovia.

Cæsar explains the setback with a rationale that resonates with readers inclined to trust his account, even when disliking his methods. He attributes the loss to the over-eager bravery of his soldiers rather than any strategic misstep on his part. It's plausible, given Cæsar's track record and the unwavering confidence he inspires in his men. Nevertheless, after suffering a loss of 700 men and 46 officers, he retreats, crossing the Allier River back into the territory of his unreliable Æduan allies. Here, Cæsar narrowly avoids disaster, as his position grows increasingly precarious. Had Vercingetorix capitalized on his victory and blocked Cæsar's retreat over the Allier, the Roman general might have faced total defeat. But, as Cæsar suggests, the Gauls lack the tactical awareness and experience the Romans possess.

The Ædui, predictably, betray him once more. His stores, treasure, and essential supplies, safeguarded at Noviodunum (modern Nevers), are seized by these disloyal allies. The Ædui destroy what they can't carry off, leaving Cæsar's army at risk of starvation. The land around him is stripped bare, and with no bridges or fords available, the Loire River stands as an additional barrier between his troops and the food they desperately need. Still, Cæsar's resourcefulness prevails: he identifies a shallow stretch and orders his men to cross with water nearly up to their shoulders. Despite the risks, they manage the ford and secure much-needed provisions.

Meanwhile, Cæsar's lieutenant Labienus, stationed with four legions near modern Paris, is also feeling the strain. Hearing of Cæsar's defeat at Gergovia, Labienus recognizes the urgency of rejoining his commander. He fights his own battle, securing a hard-won victory, which Cæsar recounts with as much fervor as if he himself had led the charge. With this victory achieved, Labienus brings his troops south to reunite with Cæsar.

But the Gauls are far from conceding. They assemble a grand council at Bibracte, the Ædui's principal city (modern Autun), to further their resolve in ousting the Romans. The Ædui, confident of their stature as Cæsar's longest-standing allies in Gaul, insist on leading the fight against Rome, believing themselves entitled to command. However, the assembled tribes instead elect Vercingetorix as their leader, recognizing his skill and commitment to their cause. The Æduan leaders, disappointed at being overlooked, nurse their grievances.

Undeterred, Vercingetorix takes advantage of Cæsar's apparent retreat southward to the Roman Province. Declaring that Cæsar's forces are retreating, he rallies his troops to launch an offensive. Although Cæsar may indeed be falling back to regroup, he soon turns to meet the Gauls head-on, dealing them a heavy defeat and killing around three thousand in the ensuing skirmish. Once again, Vercingetorix is forced to retreat, this time barricading himself within the fortified town of Alesia. With his enemy entrenched, Cæsar prepares for yet another intense siege, signaling that the struggle for Gaul is far from over.

The siege of Alesia marks the final, brutal episode of Cæsar's Commentary on the Gallic War, and it stands out as perhaps the most harrowing of all. Here, civilization advances, but in the most ruthless manner imaginable. Besieged in the town with his entire army, Vercingetorix finds himself trapped as Cæsar constructs extensive fortifications, ditches, ramparts, and lines surrounding the town, cutting off every possible route of escape. Yet, before the Roman works are fully completed, Vercingetorix sends out a group of his horsemen, desperate for reinforcements. Their mission is to rally Gaul's tribes, urging them to bring all available fighting men to lift the siege and drive away the Romans.

The urgency is clear: Vercingetorix warns them that he has only thirty days' worth of provisions for the town. Though they may find ways to stretch the food supply slightly, beyond that, if no help arrives, he and the eighty thousand souls with him will be doomed. Cæsar's account portrays Vercingetorix's plea as heartfelt and desperate, aware that their fate lies entirely with the resolve and speed of their Gaulish kin. These horsemen successfully escape, while the chief and his people inside prepare to wait out the harrowing days ahead.

The challenges in uniting Gaul for a concerted effort seem daunting, especially given the distance and fragmented loyalties of the tribes. Yet Cæsar, with characteristic matter-of-factness, tells us that nearly all Gaul responds, each tribe sending the number of men requested, with the only exception being the Bellovaci, the people of Beauvais. They declare that they prefer to wage war independently, but in a show of solidarity still lend two thousand men for the cause. Even Cæsar's Gaulish allies, including Commius—whom he had raised to kingship over the Atrebates and who had aided him in Britain—join this national uprising, motivated by a fervent desire to free Gaul from Roman domination. So deep runs this yearning for liberty that memories of Cæsar's friendship and past favors prove no deterrent. An immense force of eight thousand cavalry and two hundred and forty thousand foot soldiers assembles in the lands of the Ædui, ready to march on Alesia and liberate Vercingetorix.

Inside Alesia, however, hope is fading fast. The days of waiting drag beyond the promised thirty, with no word reaching them of any coming relief. As food supplies dwindle, desperation rises among the trapped men and women. Some argue for unconditional surrender, while others propose a daring escape attempt, cutting their way through the Roman lines. In this grim moment, one figure, Critognatus, takes the floor to offer his own horrifying solution, and Cæsar chooses to recount his speech in vivid detail.

Critognatus disregards those speaking of surrender, finding their proposal so disgraceful that he barely acknowledges it. As for those advocating a suicidal breakout, he argues that enduring suffering is nobler than seeking a quick end. "Many a man can die," he insists, "but only the bravest can suffer and survive." Rather than rushing to die, he urges them to hold out a little longer and trust in the loyalty of the Gaulish tribes.

Then he makes a shocking suggestion: let those who can fight survive by consuming those who cannot—the weak and the sick. By rationing in this way, he argues, the defenders can hold out until the promised relief arrives. It's a proposition so dreadful that even the leaders of Alesia, though desperate, cannot bring themselves to adopt it fully. Yet they implement an equally tragic measure: all the women, the elderly, and the infirm are forced to leave the town, a last attempt to stretch their meager rations. If this act of brutal self-preservation proves insufficient, they are ready to resort to even more unimaginable actions.

Alesia itself belongs not to Vercingetorix's tribe but to the Mandubii, who are now the most pitiful of victims in this grim episode. Pushed out of the gates with their children, these helpless civilians find themselves caught between the Romans and their own people, no longer welcome inside the besieged town, yet facing certain death or enslavement if they try to pass the Roman fortifications.

Memory updated

But where would they go? Cæsar has told us that there was a strip of ground between his lines and the city wall—an enclosed space from which there was no escape except into Cæsar's camp or back to the besieged town. The weak ones—elderly men, women, and children—stand here and beg Cæsar to let them enter his camp so they could make their way into the open country. There they stood, pleading for mercy, on that narrow strip of land between the two armies. Their own people, without enough food, had driven them from their homes. Would Cæsar show mercy? With a wave of his hand, Cæsar showed he would not. He tells us his decision in just eight words: "At Cæsar, depositis in vallo custodiis, recipi prohibebat." "But Cæsar, placing guards along the wall, forbade that they should be allowed in." We hear no more about them, but we know that they perished.

The gathered forces of Gaul do finally arrive to try to rescue Vercingetorix—and they arrive just in time; but was their arrival enough to change anything? They attack Cæsar in his camp, and a huge battle takes place, watched closely by those inside Alesia. Cæsar, however, is very careful to ensure that the people now trapped in the town don't manage to join up with the Gauls who were scattered around him in the countryside. We read how, during the battle, Cæsar himself appears, recognized by the color of his cloak. As we read his account of the fighting, we again feel that the Gauls nearly win, and that they should win. But in the end, they are pushed back in a chaotic retreat—all the gathered forces of all the tribes. The Romans kill many, and if the task of killing were not so difficult, they might have killed everyone. However, a huge crowd does manage to escape, scattering back into their tribes.

The next day, Vercingetorix surrenders himself and the city to Cæsar. During the battle, he and his men, shut up inside the walls, had only watched the fighting. Cæsar sits in his lines before his camp; and there, the chieftains, led by Vercingetorix, are brought to him. Plutarch tells us a story about the chieftain riding up in front of Cæsar to surrender himself, wearing gilded armor, on a grand horse, circling and prancing. It's hard to imagine any horse from inside Alesia being fit for such a display after the siege. The horses from Vercingetorix's stables had probably been eaten many days before. Then, once more, Cæsar forgives the Ædui; but Vercingetorix is taken as a prisoner to Rome, where he is kept for six years. He is then displayed in Cæsar's Triumph, and after these six years, he is killed as a sacrifice to add to Cæsar's glory, so honor can be brought to Cæsar! Cæsar places his army in winter quarters and decides to stay in Gaul through the winter. When the news of these events reaches Rome, a "thanksgiving" of twenty days is declared in his honor.

This is the end of Cæsar's Commentary on the "Gallic War." The conflict continued for two more years, and an account of Cæsar's actions during these years—51 and 50 B.C.—was written in Cæsar's style by Aulus Hirtius. Hirtius makes no claim that this was Cæsar's own work, as he includes a brief introduction where he apologizes for daring to continue what Cæsar had started. The most notable event in these two campaigns is the capture of Uxellodunum, a town in southwestern France, though its exact location is unknown today. Cæsar took the town by cutting off the water supply, and then he horrifically mutilated the inhabitants who had dared to defend their homes. "Cæsar," says the historian, "knowing well that his clemency was acknowledged by all, and feeling secure that no punishment he inflicted would be blamed on cruelty, realized that he could never know where his plans might lead if such rebellions continued. He decided that other Gauls should be deterred by the fear of punishment." So he cut off the hands of all those who had fought at Uxellodunum and turned the helpless victims loose in the world. His defender then adds that Cæsar spared their lives so that the punishment of these rebels—who had only fought for their freedom—would serve as an example to all! This was perhaps the height of Cæsar's cruelty, justified, as we see, by the reputation he had built for mercy!

Soon after this, Gaul was truly conquered, and we begin to hear the first hints of the coming civil war. At Rome, attempts were made to ruin Cæsar in his absence. One of the consuls in 51 B.C. tried to cut short his term as proconsul and prevent him from running for the consulship in his absence. He was also ordered to return two of his legions. Cæsar complied, though he hadn't yet decided to cross the Rubicon. The official demand was for one legion from Cæsar and one from Pompey, but as the reader may recall, Cæsar had with him a legion borrowed from Pompey—meaning, in effect, Cæsar was required to give up two legions. And he surrendered them, not yet fully prepared to make his decisive move.

Chapter IX.

FIRST BOOK OF THE CIVIL WAR.—CÆSAR

CROSSES THE RUBICON.—FOLLOWS POMPEY TO BRUNDUSIUM.—AND CONQUERS AFRANIUS IN SPAIN.—B.C. 49.

Cæsar now begins his account of the civil war in which he and Pompey struggled for control over Rome and the Republic. In his first Commentary, he recorded his campaigns in Gaul—campaigns where he subdued tribes that, even if not exactly hostile, were at least foreign. Through his success, he carried forward the strength, traditions, and mission of the Roman Republic. Romans aimed to rule the known world, and to them, only those lands that had become Roman were truly "known." Any expansion of this world could happen only by adding so-called barbarian tribes to the number of Roman subjects. By conquering Gaul, fighting the Germans, and even crossing into Britain, Cæsar was doing what all loyal Romans hoped to see done, matching in the West the great accomplishments of Pompey for the Republic in the East. But in this second Commentary, he has to address a topic less pleasant for Roman readers: he describes the victories he won with Roman legions over other equally Roman legions, which led him to dismantle the Republic's freedom.

In fairness to Cæsar, liberty in Rome had already decayed before his time. Power had led to wealth, and wealth to corruption. Roman tribes were bought and sold during elections, while a few powerful oligarchs, from either faction, shared the top roles of trust, honor, and authority—always reaching for public wealth. An honest man with clean hands, principles, and love of country had little place in public office. In these times, Cato seemed almost laughable, and even Cicero, though he tried to adapt to changing circumstances, was too honest for the era. Laws were twisted from their purpose, and even the Tribunes, meant to protect the people, had become tyrants. Perhaps a master was needed—and Cæsar thought so, at least. Undoubtedly, he recognized this need throughout his years of fighting in Gaul and resolved to be no less than First in the new order. So he crossed the Rubicon.

Readers may find this second Commentary less captivating than the first. It has fewer elements of adventure, less of the new and unfamiliar, and lacks the healthy, exuberant sense that Cæsar felt while fighting in Gaul—that, by crushing the Gauls, he was achieving something unquestionably good. To us today, his actions in Gaul seem cruel, but to him and the Romans, they were no stain on his character. How other Roman conquerors treated the defeated can be judged by the fact that Cæsar was considered merciful for his restraint in Gaul. He writes as if free from any guilt, as he describes the punishments he felt policy required. Yet, in recounting the civil wars, there is no such tone of complete self-satisfaction, and he is, in fact, much less cruel.

He could witness or order the deaths of countless Gauls—men, women, or children—without hesitation, whether they were burned, drowned, starved, mutilated, or tortured. He gave such commands without more regret than one might have ordering the removal of a litter of unwanted puppies. But he could not bring himself to kill Roman soldiers, even in fair combat, with any sense of ease. Either he was more compassionate or he had a deeper patriotism than many who have fought in civil wars since. In the Wars of the Roses or Cromwell's battles, we see no such restraint. American generals did not show it either. But Cæsar seems to have valued a single Roman legionary above an entire tribe of Gauls.

Cæsar, however, crossed the Rubicon. We've all heard of this famous crossing, yet Cæsar himself says nothing about it. The Rubicon was a small river, now almost unknown, flowing into the Adriatic between Ravenna and Ariminum—modern-day Rimini—and marking the boundary between Cisalpine Gaul and territory directly under the authority of Rome's magistrates. North of the Rubicon, Cæsar was effectively within his own province, where he held complete command. But according to the law, he was strictly forbidden from even entering Rome's territory while in command of a Roman province. Thus, by crossing the Rubicon, Cæsar directly broke the law and challenged the authority of the city's governing officials.

However, it doesn't appear that this specific act was viewed as especially significant at the time, nor was the crossing itself seen as an unmistakable sign of Cæsar's intentions or as an irrevocable action. Many stories describe Cæsar hesitating at the river's edge, debating whether he should take a step that would plunge the world into civil war. These tales recount how a mysterious spirit appeared to him, leading him across the river to the sounds of martial music, and how Cæsar, declaring "the die is cast," crossed over the fateful stream. But all this was myth, later invented by Romans who wanted to add drama to Cæsar's life. In reality, Cæsar's intention was likely well known when he brought one of his legions down to that part of his province, but offers to negotiate were still made by Pompey and his allies after Cæsar had entered the Roman side of the river.

When the civil war began, Cæsar still had two and a half years remaining in his assigned period of governance over the three provinces; but his victories and increasing power had been carefully monitored with great concern from Rome, and the Senate had attempted to order his recall. By now, Pompey was no longer Cæsar's ally, nor did Cæsar expect Pompey's friendship. Pompey, who had recently made a series of strategic mistakes and must have felt their weight, was now free from any alliance with Cæsar due to the deaths of Crassus, their fellow triumvir, and Julia, Cæsar's daughter, along with the changing political climate in Rome. This alliance had been a calculated arrangement created by Cæsar, mainly to curb the influence of his rival. Pompey's earlier successes had always made him seem almost godlike to the Romans.

While still a young man, Pompey had led armies and won decisive victories. Women adored him, soldiers idolized him, and even Sulla had given him the title of "the Great," raising his hat in respect. Pompey had been granted the honor of a Triumph while still a youth, celebrated a second Triumph before reaching middle age, and went on to earn a third Triumph—each one symbolizing a conquest in a different quarter of the world. In all his undertakings, he had known nothing but success and widespread admiration. He had driven pirates out of Mediterranean harbors, securing Rome's food supply by ensuring a steady flow of grain. He returned victorious with his legions from the East, then dared to disband his forces in order to live again as an ordinary citizen. Later, when the city faced internal disorder, he was appointed sole consul to restore stability.

Today, we better understand Pompey's character than we do the special position his consistent success had won him in the minds of both Rome's aristocracy and its people. Even after Cæsar's successful campaigns in Gaul, Pompey retained a certain aura of divine power that inspired trust among Romans. Pompey was proud, controlled, and self-possessed, permitting no equal, yet enforcing his status with a calm restraint. He was grand, handsome, and generous when necessary; ruthless when required; cunning, heartless, intensely loyal to Rome, and fiercely brave.

However, Pompey possessed one fatal flaw: when the time came for the final conflict, he was uncertain about his own intentions. He hadn't formed a clear vision of his future. The challenges he faced were immense, and he was left undecided when certainty was crucial. In contrast, Cæsar fully understood the situation and harbored no doubts. The story of Cæsar standing on the bridge over the Rubicon, torn between obedience and rebellion, may be captivating, but in truth, there was no hesitation and no inner conflict. Cæsar knew precisely what he intended and exactly what he wanted.

Cæsar begins his second account with a focus on the wrongs he feels have been done to him. He describes how his own supporters are silenced both in the Senate and throughout the city, while his enemies—Scipio, Cato, and Lentulus the consul—dominate the discussions, leaving no one able to speak on his behalf. "Pompey himself," he claims, "urged on by Cæsar's opponents and unwilling to share his honor with anyone else, has completely broken off their friendship and returned to the company of the very enemies he had made for Cæsar during their alliance." Additionally, Pompey, troubled by the "scandal" surrounding the two legions he had kept from going to Asia and Syria, is eager to see the matter resolved by force. Those two legions weigh heavily on Cæsar's mind. One of these legions, as we recall, had been lent by Pompey "for the sake of friendship—and the Republic." At the start of the power struggle between them, the Senate had sought to reduce both leaders' forces by demanding one legion from each. Pompey had then asked Cæsar to return the one he had lent in good faith, and Cæsar, too proud to refuse, sent it along with another legion as ordered. These legions were supposedly meant for service in the East, but now they were under the control of Pompey, once his friend and now his foe. It's little wonder that Cæsar speaks with anger about the "scandal" of these two legions. His frustration about them comes up repeatedly.

In January, Cæsar was in Ravenna, just north of the Rubicon, still within his province. Messages were exchanged between him and the Senate, where he made his demands, and the Senate made theirs. They insisted that he must lay down his arms or else be deemed an enemy of the Republic. The city of Rome was in turmoil. While this account is Cæsar's, it seems clear that Rome truly was in an uproar. "Soldiers are recruited all over Italy; weapons are gathered, taxes are imposed on the municipalities, and funds are taken from sacred shrines; all divine and human laws are disregarded." Cæsar then gathers his soldiers and tells them of his grievances and Pompey's crimes. He reminds them of their shared victories and of how, under his leadership, they have "pacified" all of Gaul and Germany. He calls on them to defend the leader who made these achievements possible. He has only one legion with him, but that legion pledges its loyalty—to him and to the tribunes of the people, some of whom have joined him in Ravenna from Rome in support of his cause. We can sense Cæsar's aim in mentioning the tribunes: it's a move to suggest that there remains some connection between himself and the governing authorities. With his soldiers' support assured, Cæsar heads to Ariminum, and in doing so, he crosses the Rubicon.

More messages follow, and Cæsar says he feels deeply saddened by being forced to wait in such suspense. Yet, for the good of the Republic, he is prepared to endure everything—"omnia pati reipublicæ causâ." All he asks is that Pompey go to his province, the legions stationed around Rome be disbanded, the old forms of free government be restored, and that panic be put to rest. If all that is done, then any remaining issues can be settled in a short conversation. In response, the consuls and Pompey reply that if Cæsar returns to Gaul and disbands his army, then Pompey will go to Spain. However, Pompey and the consuls refuse to budge with their troops until Cæsar provides assurances that he will leave first. Essentially, each side insists that the other move first. These messages, of course, lead nowhere.

Bitterly denouncing the injustice he faces, Cæsar sends part of his small force deeper into Roman territory. Marc Antony leads five cohorts to Arezzo, while Cæsar stations a cohort in three other towns. The real wonder is that Pompey didn't attack him and push him back. We can assume that Pompey's troops weren't particularly trustworthy when it came to opposing Cæsar, likely because these soldiers had served under him before. Cæsar misses his two legions, and it's likely those two legions miss him as well. Regardless, the consuls and Pompey, along with their forces and many senators, retreat southward to Brundusium—Brindisi—planning to depart Italy from the same port we all now use to travel eastward. During this retreat, the first blood of the civil war is spilled at Corfinium, a town that would now be found in the Abruzzi, if it still stood. Cæsar achieves a small victory there and captures the town. He spares the captured Pompeian officers, even allowing them to take money which, he believes, they had seized from the public treasury.

As he moves south, Pompey's soldiers—many of whom had once served Cæsar—rejoin him along the way. Pompey and the consuls keep retreating, and Cæsar keeps pursuing them, despite Pompey's previous boast that he only had to stamp his foot on Italian soil and legions would rise up ready to obey him. Pompey is fully aware, however, that beyond Italy, in Rome's provinces like Macedonia, Achaia, Asia, Cilicia, Sicily, Sardinia, Africa, Mauritania, and the two Spains, there are legions that remain loyal to Rome and are yet untouched by Cæsar. Perhaps it would be wiser for Pompey to stamp his foot somewhere outside of Italy. He sends the consuls and attending senators along with part of his army across the sea to Dyrrachium in Illyria, and he follows with the rest as Cæsar closes in. Cæsar tries to intercept Pompey's fleet but fails. And so, Pompey leaves Italy and Rome—never to see the imperial city or its beautiful lands again.

Cæsar explains his decision not to follow Pompey immediately to finish the fight. Pompey has ships, and he does not, and Cæsar knows that Rome's power lies in her provinces. Moreover, Rome could be starved by Pompey if Cæsar doesn't ensure that the grain-producing lands, which serve as Rome's granaries, are kept accessible for the city's needs. He must secure Gaul, Sardinia, Sicily, and even Africa if he can. He also needs to win over the two Spains, especially the northern region, which currently leans toward Pompey. He sends one lieutenant to Sardinia with a legion, another to Sicily with three legions—and from there, on to Africa. These regions were controlled by Pompey's supporters, but Cæsar quickly gains the upper hand. Cato, known for his uprightness, had been assigned to govern Sicily, but without an army, he finds himself defenseless. Bitterly complaining that he has been abandoned and betrayed by the head of his faction, Cato flees, leaving the province to Cæsar's officers. Cæsar then resolves to take the war to Spain himself.

However, before heading to Spain, Cæsar found it necessary to stop in Rome. His account of what he did there, though, may not be entirely candid. We believe him when he explains that, gathering what senators he could—since Pompey had already taken those he could persuade to join him—he proposed to this diminished Senate the idea of sending ambassadors to negotiate with Pompey. The Senate accepted the idea, but no one was willing to take on such a dangerous task, especially after Pompey had already declared that those who stayed in Rome were his enemies. It's likely true, as Cæsar claims, that he found a particular tribune in Rome who opposed all his actions, though we doubt the resistance was very strong. Still, his real motive in coming to Rome was to seize the Republic's treasury—the sacred funds, the sanctius ærarium, stored in the Temple of Saturn for the state's direst emergencies. It's not surprising he would take this treasure, but it is surprising that he tries to claim he did not. He insists he was so obstructed by this pesky tribune that he couldn't complete the plans he came for. Yet, it's clear he did take the money, and there's little doubt he came to Rome specifically to secure it.

En route to Spain, Cæsar stops in Marseilles, known in ancient times as Massilia. Like today, it was then a major Mediterranean port, full of thriving commerce. Although located in the province of Further Gaul, Massilia was actually a Greek colony and quite prosperous. Now, however, Cæsar needs control of the city. When the local magistrates are called upon for their support, they give a very diplomatic reply: they assure him that they hold both him and Pompey in high regard, that they are troubled by this dispute between two such worthy men, and that they prefer to keep to their own affairs. Cæsar takes this decision as an affront and uses it to justify a siege. He lays siege to the city by both land and sea, appoints officers to continue the blockade, and proceeds to Spain.

At that time, all of Spain was under the command of three generals loyal to Pompey. However, judging by his earlier comments, Cæsar seems less concerned about resistance in the south. Afranius commands in the north and east, holding key passes in the Pyrenees. Petreius, stationed in Lusitania in the southwest, quickly marches north to support Afranius as soon as Cæsar approaches. The two armies soon face off near Ilerda (modern-day Lérida), by the small river Sicoris (now the Segre), which flows into the Ebro. The proximity of the mountains, the swift rivers, and the rugged terrain all shape the course of the campaign. Cæsar gives an extremely detailed account of this campaign, making it thrilling by the clarity and intensity of his narrative. Afranius and Petreius occupy Ilerda, well-stocked with provisions, while Cæsar's army suffers from shortages. The crops and grass are not yet grown, and last year's harvest is nearly gone. The situation becomes so dire that reports reach Rome suggesting Afranius has already defeated Cæsar, leading many still undecided in Rome to choose Pompey's side.

Despite these difficulties, Cæsar eventually forces Afranius and Petreius to abandon Ilerda. Using techniques he learned in Britain, he ferries his men across a river on coracles, diverts another river, fords a third by breaking up its flow with his horses, and even builds a bridge over a fourth. Realizing they can no longer hold their ground, Afranius and Petreius try to escape south across the Ebro and seek refuge among the more primitive tribes there, hoping to reach the Celtiberians farther south in what would later be called Castile. Cæsar notes that while these tribes know Pompey's name, his own reputation has not yet spread to these distant peoples. But Afranius cannot cross the Ebro without Cæsar's consent, and Cæsar has no intention of giving it. He cuts off their path, using that severe tactic of deprivation that he himself had endured. Now he drives the Pompeians across the land, keeping them north of the Ebro and denying them access to water, until they are ultimately forced to surrender.

In the final days of this conflict, the soldiers under Afranius—known as the Afranians, who are, after all, Roman legionaries just like those under Cæsar—start to fraternize with the troops in Cæsar's camp. Soon enough, there's a sort of informal communication happening between the two armies. Eventually, the soldiers serving Afranius come to a decision: they resolve to surrender to Cæsar, but they insist on a condition—that their own generals be kept safe. Afranius is agreeable to the idea; however, his fellow commander,

Petreius, is staunchly opposed. With a heart firmly loyal to Roman pride, Petreius is horrified at the thought of surrender. As we'll see later, Petreius meets a rather unusual fate in his own right. For now, he crushes the brewing plot with vigorous resolve and even forces an oath against surrender from his men and from Afranius himself. He issues a strict order that any of Cæsar's soldiers found mingling in their camp are to be killed. As Cæsar recounts, Petreius effectively "restores the affair to the old form of war." But ultimately, even Petreius's fervor cannot alter their dire situation. The lack of water becomes so desperate for the Afranians that their generals have no choice but to capitulate and formally surrender their arms.

Cæsar's account of these moments demonstrates his remarkable skill with concise language, and the flexibility of Latin itself. In describing the Afranians' distress, he uses just five Latin words: Premebantur Afraniani pabulatione, aquabantur ægre. This translates roughly to, "The soldiers of Afranius were much distressed in the matter of forage, and could obtain water only with great difficulty." Translating Cæsar's five words into English requires about twenty words to capture the same sense accurately, and likely more than twenty in any English historical retelling.

Upon winning, Cæsar displays extraordinary generosity toward his fellow Romans. Had his defeated foes been Gauls, he would have likely sold them into slavery, executed their leaders, cut off their hands, or driven them down to the river, letting them die in the waters. But here, his enemies are Roman soldiers. Cæsar's only condition is that Afranius's army be disbanded and its leaders free to go wherever they choose. He delivers a speech in which he explains how unfairly they have treated him, yet assures them he will not harm anyone. He tells them that he has borne these wrongs and will continue to bear them with patience. His only requirement is that the generals leave the Province and that the army they commanded disband immediately. Cæsar even assures the soldiers that he won't keep anyone who doesn't wish to stay with him, and he promises to pay those who haven't yet received compensation from Afranius, using his own funds. Those who own homes and lands in Spain are free to remain; those who have nothing, he will first feed and then escort—if not back to Italy itself, then at least to the edge of Italian territory. As for any belongings taken from them by his own soldiers during the battle, he promises that those items will be returned, and he will personally make up any losses. Keeping his word, Cæsar leads those unwilling to stay under his command to the banks of the Var River, which marks the boundary between Italy and the Province, releasing them there. Surely, they left filled with gratitude toward their merciful conqueror. This was mercy indeed—or, perhaps, the most strategic foresight imaginable! Cæsar had completed his entire campaign in Spain within just forty days.

Meanwhile, Decimus Brutus—whom Cæsar had appointed over the ships prepared against the Veneti in western Gaul, and who would later become one of his assassins in the Senate—secures a naval victory against the much larger fleet of the Massilians. The Massilians had prepared seventeen large ships—referred to by Cæsar as naves longæ—but Brutus either captures or destroys nine of them. In his next account, Cæsar will continue describing the siege of Marseilles, detailing the events both at sea and on land after this decisive battle.

Chapter X.

SECOND BOOK OF THE CIVIL WAR.—THE TAKING OF MARSEILLES.—VARRO IN THE SOUTH OF SPAIN.—THE FATE OF CURIO BEFORE UTICA.—B.C. 49.

In his account of the Gallic war, Cæsar structured each book to tell the story of a full year's campaign. When describing the civil war, however, he uses the first two books to recount just one year. The second book narrates three major events from that year's campaign: the siege and capture of Marseilles, the submission of southern Spain—which, though it surrendered quite easily, is described as being subjugated—and the defeat of a Roman army in Africa by a barbarian king. This section is perhaps the least compelling of Cæsar's writings, as it shares little of Cæsar's personal actions, instead focusing on the deeds of his lieutenants both on land and at sea.

Cæsar begins by recounting the immense efforts made by both the besieging forces and the defenders at Marseilles, which was being held for Pompey by Domitius. To strengthen their naval defense, Pompey sent a fleet under Nasidius. Brutus the Younger, who, as we recall, was leading Cæsar's forces in the harbor, had already won a victory over the Massilians even before Nasidius arrived; meanwhile, Trebonius was conducting the siege from the land side for Cæsar. Interestingly, Decimus Brutus, one of the commanders here, would later become one of the conspirators who ultimately turned against and killed Cæsar, along with Trebonius, who would also join that plot.

The sensible Greeks of the city had explained to Cæsar, when he initially asked for their support, that they genuinely cared for both Pompey and Cæsar equally. However, they had felt compelled to take Pompey's side because Domitius, Pompey's general, was the first to enter their city. Now, out of necessity, they found themselves fighting as Pompeians, not only to defend their wealth but also to protect their homes. So, by circumstance, they became staunch defenders of the Republic against the autocracy, as it was during the siege of Marseilles that Cæsar was appointed Dictator—a decree passed in Rome, where such decisions were easily made in the absence of Pompey, the consuls, and most senators who sided with him.

Now fully committed to their chosen side, the people of Marseilles fought with everything they had. We learn that Cæsar's troops, from their elevated camp positioned by Trebonius, could look directly down into the city and see "how all the youth left in the city, along with the elders, their children, wives, and the guards, either stretched their hands to the heavens from the city walls or entered the temples of the immortal gods and cast themselves down before the statues, praying for divine assistance in winning this battle." None of them, Cæsar tells us, doubted that the outcome would determine all they held dear—their liberty, property, and lives. It's clear that the Massilians knew well of the fates of Avaricum, Alesia, and Uxellodunum. "When the battle began," Cæsar writes, "the Massilians showed no lack of courage. Remembering the recent speeches made to them by their own people, they fought as if this battle was their one hope of survival. For those who fell in combat, it was only an early end to what the rest would face if the city were captured."

As he wrote this, Cæsar must have recalled the harsh actions he had taken in Gaul, where his policies sometimes demanded severe measures. Here, however, he skillfully emphasizes his own mercy, as he is about to describe his lenient treatment of Marseilles. He knew that depopulating a wealthy city would be unwise, as the trade it generated benefited both Rome and the Province. Thus, Cæsar carefully highlights how little mercy the besieged expected from him, making his ultimate decision seem all the more generous. Reading his words, we sense that each line has been thoughtfully crafted, even though Cæsar must have had little time for such careful composition given his constant state of action and the many demands on his attention.

Nasidius, whom we may call Pompey's admiral, proved to be of no help at all. The Massilians, emboldened by his arrival, launch a bold attack on the ship carrying young Brutus's flag; but Brutus is too swift and skillful for them. The desperate Massilians end up crashing two of their largest ships into each other as they try to trap Brutus's flagship between them. In the end, the Massilian fleet is completely scattered. Five ships are sunk, four are captured, and one manages to escape with Nasidius, who flees without even attempting to fight. According to Cæsar, Pompey may have sent Nasidius merely to give an appearance of help, not to truly engage in the battle. One lone ship makes it back to the harbor with the grim news, and the Massilians—though briefly disheartened—resolve to continue defending their walls.

The town of Marseilles was well prepared for a defense, the people being resourceful, well-trained, and equipped with necessary materials. They had strong twelve-foot poles with iron tips that could be hurled from their wall-mounted engines with such force that they pierced through four layers of the wicker screens and stationary shields that Cæsar's forces had set up for their protection, thinking nothing could penetrate them. This part of the description inevitably brings to mind modern artillery, with our cannons, armor plating, granite forts, and earthen defenses. These dreadful missiles, launched from the "balistae," were hard on Cæsar's troops, so they came up with the idea to build an enormous tower, constructed so high that it could not be reached by enemy weapons and reinforced so that nothing flammable was exposed. They built this tower one level at a time, each level reinforced against fire and the enemy's projectiles.

As we read about this careful engineering feat, it's easy to think Cæsar himself might have been trained as an engineer, especially given his attention to detail. Yet, in truth, Cæsar was not even at this siege himself and didn't oversee the tower's construction. He must have received a written description of this effort from his officer on site—just as he likely did earlier when constructing the famous bridge over the Rhine. Once the tower was completed, his forces created a covered passage or "muscle," as Cæsar calls it. This structure extended from the massive tower to a strategic point in the town's walls. The muscle's sloped roof was so solid that nothing hurled at it could penetrate or set it aflame. The Massilians tried to stop it with flaming tubs of pitch and large stones, but these simply slid off and were cleared away with poles and prongs. Cæsar's troops, from the height of their impressive tower, gained a deadly advantage, making it nearly impossible for the Massilians to defend their walls, and a breach was nearly made.

At last, the Massilians had nothing left to give. The very gods seemed against them. So, in the humble garb of supplicants, they went to meet the conquerors, offering to surrender the city to Cæsar. They requested Trebonius to wait for Cæsar himself to arrive. Trebonius understood well enough that if his soldiers broke through into the city before Cæsar's arrival, there would be dire consequences. A slight delay would do no harm. No action would be taken until Cæsar came. Fortunately, Cæsar had previously ordered that the city be spared, and a truce was arranged until he arrived to accept the surrender. Trebonius struggled to keep his soldiers from plundering the town, but he managed to hold them back. The two sides, attackers and defenders alike, waited together for Cæsar's arrival.

But these Massilians were clever and cunning. The Cæsarean soldiers, having agreed to wait for Cæsar's arrival, let their guard down and passed the time in idle amusement. Seeing this, and with a strong wind to aid them, the Massilians suddenly rushed out and managed to set fire to the tower, the covered passage, the rampart, the sheds, and all of Cæsar's siege equipment. Though the tower was made of brick, it burned easily in the fierce wind. Trebonius, however, set to work again and rebuilt everything. Since no more wood was available near the camp, he created a new kind of rampart—one built from bricks, something unheard of before. The Cæsarean soldiers likely had to make these bricks themselves, and we can imagine their growing resentment toward the Massilians. Still, they worked with such diligence and determination that the Massilians soon saw their recent victory was useless. They had nothing left. Neither trickery nor courage would save them now, and once again, they surrendered— this time, intending no further deceit. "Sese dedere sine fraude constituunt," Cæsar writes, which means, "They resolved to surrender themselves without treachery."

Domitius, the general for Pompey, managed to escape on a ship. He set out with three ships, but only the one he was on managed to avoid capture by "young" Brutus. Surely now Marseilles would face harsh punishment, similar to what befell the Gaulish cities. But Cæsar had other plans. He took their public treasury and ships, and reminded them that he spared them more for the city's reputation and ancient standing than for any loyalty shown to him. He left two legions stationed there and departed for Rome.

At Avaricum, where the Gauls had fought to protect their freedom, he had ordered the destruction of everyone. At Alesia, he had condemned every inhabitant when they had merely requested permission to pass through his camp. At Uxellodunum, he had cut off the hands and gouged out the eyes of Gauls who had dared to fight for their homeland. But these Gauls were barbarians, whom Cæsar believed needed to be pacified. The Massilians, on the other hand, were Greeks—a cultured and civilised people who might still serve a useful purpose.

Before turning his attention to Marseilles, Cæsar still had some business to finish in Spain. As mentioned in the previous chapter, he had already forced Afranius and Petreius to surrender their arms and disband their legions. Among those aligned with these generals was a third Pompeian leader named Varro—a respected figure, though not necessarily a skilled military strategist. Cæsar describes how Varro, trying to navigate the political currents of Rome, initially wavered between supporting Pompey and Cæsar. However, once Varro heard that Afranius was successful around Lerida, he ultimately chose to support Pompey—a decision that did not work in his favor.

Varro, stationed further south in Spain, in the region known then as Bætica (present-day Andalusia), found that Cæsar's cause was significantly more popular in that part of the country than Pompey's. Consequently, Cæsar encountered minimal resistance. The legions under Varro's command soon deserted him, and Varro, seeing little chance for victory, quickly surrendered. Although Cæsar does not delve into the specifics of how he handled Varro, history records that he extended his usual courtesy and respect toward this fellow Roman. Varro was a highly learned man, a friend of Cicero, and a prolific author, credited with writing 490 volumes. He was considered a true scholar—a source of pride for Rome due to his literary contributions, if not his military prowess. Remarkably, Varro lived to the age of eighty-eight, a rare feat for a Roman involved in political affairs during these tumultuous times.

Cæsar swiftly restored order in southern Spain, returning the money and valuables Varro had seized from the towns and expressing his gratitude to the local people for their support. With matters in Spain settled, he then crossed over the Pyrenees and proceeded to Marseilles, where he again restored stability to the region.

In the meantime, however, matters were far from calm in Africa. At this time, "Africa" referred to a small province under the Republic's control, lying to the east of Numidia, where the ancient city of Carthage had once stood. This province included the promontory that extends toward Sicily, with Utica serving as its Roman administrative center. Earlier, when Cæsar had decided to secure certain provinces of the Republic before pursuing Pompey across the Adriatic, he had sent a lieutenant to Sicily with three legions, instructing him to advance to Africa as soon as things were settled on the island in favor of Cæsar's cause. In Sicily, there was little resistance, as Cato, the upstanding man to whom Pompey had entrusted the island's governance, chose to depart when Cæsar's legions arrived. He left with a strong sense of grievance, bitterly criticizing Pompey's management.

Afterwards, Cæsar's lieutenant sailed to Africa with two legions, tasked with driving out one Attius Varus. According to Cæsar, Varus had taken control of the province without proper authority and was holding it for Pompey, blocking the rightful governor from even setting foot on its shores. This lieutenant was a favorite of Cæsar's, a young man named Curio. Curio had been elected tribune of the people around the time the Senate was attempting to recall Cæsar from his command in Gaul. At that critical moment, Curio, as tribune, had come to Cæsar's aid, and Cæsar, in turn, held a deep affection for him.

Curio belonged to a class of men who, despite noble birth, had thrown themselves into popular causes, much like Catiline and Clodius had done. He was unpredictable, turbulent, unprincipled, prone to vices, reckless with money, indulgent in pleasure, greedy, yet also well-educated, brave, and smart. Cæsar himself had been somewhat like this in his youth and could overlook such flaws in a man who, along with these traits, possessed the even greater virtue of loyalty to Cæsar. Cæsar trusted Curio completely and expected significant accomplishments from him.

Curio, with a sizable fleet and his two legions, landed in Africa, preparing to capture the province on Cæsar's behalf. He gained some initial success and was even hailed as "Imperator" by his troops—a title reserved for a general after a victorious battle. However, Cæsar's account suggests that Curio's officers and soldiers had little confidence in him, uncertain whether to continue following him, take over the ships and return to Sicily, or perhaps switch sides to Attius Varus, who had previously commanded them in Italy before they defected from Pompey to Cæsar. A war council was held, full of uncertainty and debate. Their concern lay not only with Varus, their Roman opponent, but also with Juba, the Numidian king, who would surely join Varus and fight against Curio. Juba was a declared ally of Pompey and an equally declared enemy of Cæsar, harboring a particular grudge against Curio. If Juba arrived personally with his full forces, Curio would find himself in dire straits, especially if caught away from his camp. Driven by the council's hesitation, Curio, wanting to secure his soldiers' support for a battle, addressed his legionaries with a rousing speech. And, of course, we must remember that this speech, as recorded by Cæsar, was likely crafted by Cæsar himself.

The speech begins with Curio speaking in the third person, referring to himself indirectly as he reminds the soldiers of how helpful they were to Cæsar at Corfinium, the town where they had switched allegiance from Pompey to Cæsar. Then, Curio shifts into the first person, putting direct words in his own mouth. "For it was you and your actions," he says, "that set an example for every town; and it's no surprise that Cæsar thinks kindly of you, while the Pompeians bear you no love. For Pompey, though he hadn't yet lost a single battle, fled from Italy simply because of what you accomplished. And now, Cæsar—who holds me in highest regard and who relies on Sicily and Africa to secure Rome and Italy—has entrusted these territories to your honor. Some suggest that you desert me—what could be more satisfying to such people than trapping me and staining your reputation with betrayal? But tell me, haven't you heard about what Cæsar achieved in Spain? Two armies defeated, two generals subdued, and two provinces taken—all in the span of just forty days from the moment Cæsar first set eyes on his enemy. How can those who couldn't resist him before even losing, hope to stand against him now in defeat? And you—who followed Cæsar even when his victory was uncertain—would you now switch sides, aligning with the defeated just as you're about to reap the rewards of your loyalty?

"But perhaps you love Cæsar yet still distrust me. I won't boast about my own services to you—they may be less than I hoped to achieve or than you expected of me." Though he claims not to speak of himself, Curio does indeed take a moment to address his own efforts. "But why should I skip over my own accomplishments, the progress we've made so far, or the good fortune I've had in battle? Does it not matter to you that I brought our entire army here safely, losing not a single ship? That, upon my arrival, I scattered the enemy's fleet at my first strike? That, within two days, I had won twice with our cavalry; that I seized two hundred transport ships from the enemy's harbor; that I weakened them to the point that neither by land nor sea could they gather enough food to sustain themselves? Do you really wish to turn your backs on such fortune, such leadership, to align yourselves instead with the disgrace of Corfinium, the flight from Italy"—referring to Pompey's escape to Dyrrachium—"the surrender of Spain, and all the misfortunes of this African campaign?

"I have wanted nothing more than to be known as Cæsar's soldier, and you yourselves have called me your commander. But if you regret calling me so, I gladly return the title to you. Restore to me my name if you feel it was in mockery that you ever honored me with that title."

This account is filled with energy, and Cæsar's rhetorical description of Curio's speech to his troops is fascinating in itself, as it reflects how Roman commanders were expected to inspire and interact with their soldiers. It also gives insight into the unique challenges of civil war, where loyalty to either side could waver, as soldiers faced the prospect of fighting for one Roman leader they respected against another. Both sides of the conflict were led by Roman Imperators whom the soldiers had come to admire. Curio, we know, was a man capable of persuasive words in moments like these. However, it's unlikely he actually spoke the precise words that Cæsar attributes to him. Cæsar was eager to offer a tribute to his gallant young friend, who had given his life for Cæsar's cause, memorializing him for all time with a speech crafted to glorify his legacy.

Yet, before his ultimate fall, the young commander experiences a brief period of success, one that, had he truly spoken Cæsar's words, would have seemed to justify his confidence. Curio launches a bold attack on the army of his fellow Roman, Varus, and achieves a victory, pushing Varus and his men back to the town of Utica. Curio then resolves to lay siege to the town, and Cæsar hints that the outcome could have been in his favor, due to the sympathies of some townspeople for Cæsar's cause—if not for the advancing threat of the dreaded Juba, king of Numidia. News reaches Curio that Juba has swiftly resolved another matter and is now free to confront the Roman forces in Africa. Varus, too, hears the rumor inside the town. Craftily, Juba sends ahead only a small contingent under his lieutenant, Sabura, giving Curio the false impression that the approaching force is limited. Confident, Curio believes he can handle Sabura and his band of Numidian cavalry with ease.

From this moment, however, we sense that Curio is doomed. Cæsar, in a few poignant lines, offers his apology for his friend's ill-fated decision: "Youth itself was to blame, as well as his high spirits; his earlier successes and trust in his fortune also misled him." There is no trace of reproach in Cæsar's words. Curio makes another speech, rallying his men with, "Hasten to your reward, hasten to your glory!" And hasten they do—but not as Curio had hoped. His troops advance with such speed that the front lines are far ahead of the rest, scattered along the road. When they reach Sabura's force, they find themselves hopelessly outmatched and are swiftly defeated by Juba's soldiers.

As the battle takes its toll, one of Curio's officers urges him to retreat back to camp. But Cæsar records Curio's tragic response, his last words, declaring he would never face Cæsar again after losing the army that had been entrusted to him. These words, reported to Cæsar by that officer, likely bear some truth. "So, fighting, he was slain," Cæsar concludes, and with this, the life of the man Cæsar loved comes to an end.

What happened next was deeply tragic for a Roman army. Many soldiers rushed down to the ships by the sea, hoping to escape, but the scene was one of utter panic and confusion. Things were so chaotic that only a few managed to reach Sicily safely. The others tried to surrender to Varus, and if they had succeeded, their situation might not have been so terrible. A Roman surrendering to another Roman, after all, would likely face little worse than a forced change of allegiance. But Juba, the Numidian king, arrived and claimed the defeated soldiers as his prize, and Varus did not dare to stand against this powerful ally.

Juba ordered most of the captives to be killed but spared a few whom he thought could serve his purposes and add to his renown. In doing so, Juba behaved no worse than Cæsar had often acted in Gaul; yet Cæsar always wrote as though not only Romans but the entire world should view a Roman as something more than an ordinary human. By demanding such respect and making these assertions of superiority, the Romans were often indeed viewed that way. We are then told that the barbarian king of Numidia rode into Utica in triumph, with captured Roman senators trailing behind him—a symbol of his victory. Cæsar makes sure to record the names of two particular senators in this humiliating procession, marking them for posterity. Wherever possible, we'll let them rest in peace.

As for King Juba and his eventual fate, we will hear of him again.

Chapter XI.

THIRD BOOK OF THE CIVIL WAR.— CÆSAR FOLLOWS POMPEY INTO ILLYRIA.—THE LINES OF PETRA AND THE BATTLE OF PHARSALIA.—B.C. 48.

Cæsar begins the final book of his last Commentary by stating that this was the year in which he, Cæsar, had the legal authority to appoint a consul. He selects Publius Servilius to serve alongside him. This means that, since Cæsar had been made Dictator and Pompey had taken the previous year's consuls with him to Illyria, Cæsar was now the sole magistrate with the power to elect a consul. Although he certainly chose the man himself, the election was conducted in a way that maintained the appearance of following the Republic's established procedures. He stayed in Rome as Dictator for only eleven days, during which time he passed several laws aimed at reducing the instability caused by the breakdown of usual governance. Then he departed for Brindisi, following Pompey's path.

Cæsar had twelve legions with him, but lacked sufficient ships to transport them, and he admits that his soldiers were suffering from poor health after enduring a harsh autumn in southern Italy—a climate much tougher than the healthy air of Gaul and northern Spain, to which they were accustomed. He tells us that Pompey had had an entire year to prepare his forces, a year without active warfare, during which he gathered soldiers, ships, and funding, as well as support from many places—Asia, the Cyclades, Corcyra, Athens, Bithynia, Cilicia, Phœnicia, Egypt, and the free states of Achaia. Pompey had nine Roman legions and was awaiting two more with his father-in-law, Scipio, coming from Syria. He had assembled three thousand archers from Crete, Sparta, and Pontus, as well as twelve hundred slingers and seven thousand cavalry from Galatia, Cappadocia, and Thrace. A bold prince from Macedonia had brought him two hundred mounted men, and five hundred Galatian and German cavalry—who had been stationed in Egypt to secure Ptolemy's loyalty—were sent to Pompey by his son Cnæus, who had also brought along eight hundred armed members of their own retainers.

Antiochus of Commagena contributed two hundred mounted archers as mercenaries, with a promise of significant pay. Warriors from the regions of Dardania (from the lands of ancient Troy), the Bessi (from the banks of the Hebrus), Thessaly, and Macedonia had all flocked to Pompey's side. We sense that Cæsar lists these forces with a degree of anticipation, savoring the impressive strength of Pompey's assembled forces even as he prepares us for the outcome— Cæsar will soon reveal how he, with his smaller force of Roman legionaries, would scatter these armies to the winds after successfully landing on the shores of Illyria.

Pompey has also gathered an impressive stock of grain— "frumenti vim maximam," as Cæsar phrases it. If literally translated, it would be "a great power of corn," like an expression from an old Irish tale. Pompey's forces have filled the seas with ships to block Cæsar's exit from Italy. Eight vice-admirals command these fleets, each named by Cæsar, while the overall commander is Bibulus, who was once Cæsar's co-consul before the Gallic campaigns. Bibulus had been so overwhelmed by Cæsar's influence during that time that he secluded himself in his house, leaving Cæsar to act as if he were sole consul.

Now, Bibulus is bent on revenge, but Cæsar seems to imply that Bibulus's efforts to retaliate will be just as ineffective as before.

With his legions at Brindisi, Cæsar makes a speech to his troops, displaying an audacity that surpasses most of his actions. He tells them that since they've nearly completed all his "business" for him—the last task being to bring down the Republic itself, with Pompey, his legions, and all the forces loyal to the Republic, not to mention King Ptolemy in Egypt, King Pharnaces in Asia, and King Juba in Numidia—they should leave behind their belongings from previous wars. Doing so will allow them to pack more tightly in the boats he intends to use to get them across to Illyria. There's no promise of recovering their possessions later; Cæsar simply expects his soldiers to rely on his goodwill for their future gains. They respond with one unified cheer, showing their readiness to follow him without hesitation. With seven legions, he makes the crossing, skirting those dreaded "rocks of evil fame," the Acroceraunia, known to us from Horace, and manages to avoid Bibulus, who, it seems, has retreated to his ship as he once withdrew into his house.

Cæsar appears to have taken on this dangerous voyage fully aware that a run-in with Bibulus could spell disaster. Indeed, with a bit of vigilance and effort, Bibulus could have turned the situation in his favor. Yet Cæsar still tries his luck, relying on "Fortune," and succeeds, landing at a site he calls Palæste on the Epirus coast, considerably south of Dyrrachium in Illyria, where Pompey had landed the year before. There, Pompey has stored the vast provisions Cæsar mentions.

Finally, Bibulus decides to take action and attacks the ships Cæsar sends back to bring the rest of his army. Coming across thirty empty vessels, Bibulus vents his frustration by burning them all, as well as killing their sailors and captains, supposedly to discourage others from making the trip. Cæsar tells us this, adding that Bibulus acts "with all the wrath caused by his own negligence and regret." It's not hard to feel a sense of grim satisfaction when we learn that, although Bibulus continues to roam the seas, seemingly tireless, he achieves little and eventually dies—possibly of sheer frustration.

Bibulus does manage to capture another ship later, but this time it's not a military vessel. Instead, it carries the non-combatant followers of Cæsar's camp—families, servants, and others traveling for personal reasons. Bibulus, showing no mercy, slaughters everyone on board, down to the youngest child. However, we should remember that this account is from Cæsar's perspective, and he was not known to speak kindly of Bibulus.

Mark Antony remains at Brindisi, commanding the legions that Cæsar couldn't transport on his initial trip due to limited ship capacity. Cæsar presses Antony urgently to make the crossing. Meanwhile, negotiations for peace begin, though Cæsar appears to use them primarily to buy time until Antony and the remaining legions can arrive. We learn that by now, Cæsar and Pompey's camps are positioned very close, separated only by the river Apsus, as Cæsar has advanced northward toward Pompey's stronghold. Soldiers from both sides talk across the river, agreeing not to throw any weapons as they converse.

Cæsar seizes this opportunity and sends Vatinius to the riverbank to discuss peace. Vatinius shouts across, questioning whether "citizens should be allowed to send ambassadors to fellow citizens to discuss peace," adding that even deserters and brigands had been permitted to negotiate, especially when the aim was to prevent citizens from fighting one another. This logic seems compelling, and a date for further talks is set. Labienus, who had once been loyal to Cæsar but has since joined Pompey's side, arrives at the river to negotiate on one side, while Vatinius stands on the opposite bank.

But then, according to Cæsar's account, Cæsar's own soldiers suddenly hurl their weapons at Labienus, likely unable to tolerate the sight or sound of a man they now consider a traitor. Labienus manages to escape, shielded by his men, but leaves seething with anger. "From now on," he declares, "let us speak no more of peace. There will be no peace until Cæsar's head is brought to us." Despite this turn, these riverside talks likely serve Cæsar's purpose by stalling for time.

Eager to get his troops across from Italy, Cæsar grows frustrated with Antony for the delays. A famous story—one Cæsar doesn't tell himself—circulates that Cæsar, in his impatience, attempted to cross the sea back to Brindisi himself. Boarding a small boat in the midst of a storm, he reportedly encouraged the fearful boatmaster by declaring, "You carry Cæsar and his fortunes." They attempted the crossing but were ultimately forced back by the fierce winds.

At last, a southwest wind rises, giving Antony the chance to set sail with his fleet, despite Pompey's warships still patrolling the waters and guarding the Illyrian coast. But fortune is on Antony's side, and the second half of Cæsar's army catches favorable winds and is carried northward toward the shore, right in view of Pompey and his soldiers stationed at Dyrrachium. However, two ships fall behind and are captured by Otacilius, a Pompeian officer. One ship is filled with recruits, the other with seasoned veterans. Both groups are asked to surrender, and Otacilius swears not to harm them if they comply.

Cæsar then remarks on the importance of presence of mind in securing safety. The recruits, trusting Otacilius's oath, surrender, only to be killed when he goes back on his word, ignoring his promise. But the veterans are not so easily deceived. They refuse to surrender, well aware of how little they can trust Otacilius. Instead, they run their ship ashore in the night, fighting fiercely and ultimately making it safely to Antony. Cæsar wryly notes that the recruits might have done the same had they not been weakened by seasickness, but even the storm and the ship's foul conditions couldn't shake the courage of the old soldiers, who endured it all without faltering.

Then, we hear of Metellus Scipio, who, on his journey from Syria to join Pompey in Macedonia, nearly robs the temple of Diana at Ephesus. Scipio gathers a group of senators to act as witnesses to ensure that he fairly counts the money as he removes it from the temple. But just as he's about to complete this profitable task, letters from Pompey arrive, urging him onward. Scipio decides not to delay his journey further, even though he misses the chance to complete the theft. He hurries to meet Pompey, eager to share in the command in the coming decisive battle.

Meanwhile, Cæsar sends his lieutenants into Thessaly, Aetolia, and Macedonia to secure allies, capture cities, and gather supplies. Although this territory is thought to be loyal to Pompey, many have heard of Cæsar's successes, and the Greeks are keen to align themselves with the strongest Roman of the moment. They must decide whom to support based on who is likely to win, and the decision is not easy. Soon, we'll see Cæsar's way of clarifying matters for the citizens of Gomphi, who waver in their support.

In the meantime, Cæsar unites his forces with those Antony has brought from Italy. Now, he is determined to force Pompey into a decisive confrontation.

We can divide the rest of this final book of Cæsar's second Commentary into two main episodes. The first is the account of what happened within the lines at Petra, where Pompey emerged victorious. However, despite the scale of his success, this victory has received little recognition in history. The second episode, which the whole world knows, is the battle of Pharsalia, where Cæsar emerged triumphant and assumed ultimate control. Ironically, the events at Petra should have made Pharsalia unnecessary, as Pompey's complete success there could have halted further conflict. Yet two factors worked against this outcome: the fact that the Commentary was written by Cæsar rather than Pompey, and that, unfortunately for Pompey, the battle of Pharsalia came after Petra.

Cæsar's description of the movements and strategies employed by both armies at Petra is complex and difficult to untangle. Even if it were simpler, our purpose here wouldn't allow us to present the full narrative in detail. By now, Cæsar had successfully combined his own legions, which he brought over from Italy, with those that had arrived later with Antony, and was eager to force a battle. His soldiers, although fewer than Pompey's in number, were battle-hardened and experienced in the arts of war. Pompey's soldiers, on the other hand, were mostly new to fighting; yet they were steadily learning, and each week they spent in preparation worked in Pompey's favor.

Hoping to compel a confrontation, Cæsar managed to position his forces between Dyrrachium, where Pompey kept his military supplies and stores, and Pompey's army itself, effectively cutting Pompey off from his base by land. Yet the sea remained open to Pompey. His fleet was well-established along the coast, whereas Cæsar's forces had not a single ship capable of challenging Pompey's naval forces.

North of Dyrrachium lay a rugged, rocky promontory, known as Petra, which had direct access to the sea. Here, Pompey positioned his army, taking advantage of a broad strip of pastureland at the base of the rock. He fortified this position with impressive Roman defenses— a continuous trench, bank, and wall stretching across fifteen Roman miles, or just over thirteen English miles, from sea to sea. His fortifications included twenty-four towers and numerous earthworks, creating a line so secure it seemed nearly impregnable. Within this perimeter, Pompey secured ample grazing land for his horses, while the open sea allowed him access to supplies and reinforcements. From the vast stores he had amassed at Dyrrachium, all along the coasts of Greece, Asia, and Egypt, Pompey could freely draw provisions. His only limitations were adequate grass for his horses and access to fresh water. In contrast, Cæsar faced extreme shortages of nearly everything but grass and water, as he was backed against the harsh, mountainous lands of Illyria. The local inhabitants, who typically relied on imported corn to survive, were already struggling due to Pompey's strategic foresight in emptying the storehouses and leaving nearby towns desolate.

Yet, undeterred, Cæsar resolved to confine his opponent. He began constructing lines around Pompey's position, effectively trapping him at Petra. Small garrisons and towers were set up on hills surrounding Pompey's encampment, gradually connecting these posts with continuous fortifications from one sea to the other. This strategy was aimed at blocking Pompey's horsemen from venturing out for forage and weakening the horses trapped within. Furthermore, Cæsar believed that news of Pompey being besieged would diminish Pompey's reputation—his auctoritas—in the eyes of foreign nations and make it seem that Pompey dared not engage Cæsar in direct combat.

In modern retellings of history, Cæsar is often depicted as an unstoppable force, with Pompey almost overshadowed. But in passages like these, we see that this was far from the case. Up to this point, Pompey was the more accomplished man; he had achieved great deeds and commanded immense respect. On his side were Rome's wealthiest and most respectable citizens. Pompey was, in essence, the leader of the Conservative faction, confident that he simply had to hold his position until Cæsar's rebellion exhausted itself. To Pompey, Cæsar and his followers were like the fringe revolutionary forces of France before they proved their strength, or the Reform Bill and Catholic Emancipation to figures like George IV and Lord Eldon—an unwanted upheaval that might still be quashed.

Pompey's confidence is evident in a boast he reportedly made to his men, which Cæsar recounts: Pompey would consider himself a failed general if Cæsar's legions could escape the precarious position they had recklessly created for themselves without "very great loss"—maximo detrimento—a loss so significant it would approach ruin. And Pompey's assessment was nearly correct.

There was a lot of fighting over the grassy areas and the good spots to take cover. Most of this fighting happened right between the two opposing lines. Cæsar faced a disadvantage because his fortifications, being much longer, required a larger number of men to build, extend, and maintain them. On the other hand, Pompey, with the inner line, needed fewer men for his works, so he had more soldiers free to fight. Although Cæsar's men, being experienced, had the upper hand in actual combat, Pompey's inexperienced soldiers were gaining the practice they needed. Even so, Pompey was struggling a lot. They couldn't find water on the rocky ground, and whenever he tried to dig wells, Cæsar would divert the water sources, leaving Pompey's wells dry. Cæsar says he even blocked off streams to create small lakes, preventing the water from flowing underground to where Pompey's men could reach it. However, it seems that any reservoirs like this would eventually overflow and become useless.

Meanwhile, Cæsar's soldiers had no bread except what they made from a wild cabbage called "chara" that grew there. They mixed it with milk, eating it without complaint, even though it didn't taste very good. To show Pompey's men the kind of food seasoned soldiers could make do with, they tossed loaves made from this mix across the lines, since they were close enough to talk and taunt each other. Pompey's men mocked Cæsar's troops for their lack of food, but Cæsar's forces had plenty of water and meat, and they assured him they would rather eat tree bark than let Pompey escape.

Cæsar always had one big concern: that Pompey might land troops behind him and attack from the rear. To prevent this, Cæsar built another trench and bank running from the shore at a right angle to his main line, intending to connect this new line to his main fortifications along the coast between his two positions. But then, just as he was working on these defenses, disaster struck, nearly leading to his defeat. While his men were digging trenches and building towers, the fighting was so intense that, according to Cæsar, there were six battles in a single day. Pompey lost two thousand soldiers, while Cæsar lost only twenty. However, every Cæsarean soldier defending a certain tower was wounded, and four officers lost their eyesight. Cæsar estimated that thirty thousand arrows were shot at the men guarding that tower and mentions an officer named Scæva who had two hundred and thirty arrow holes in his shield. It must have been a large shield, and counting all the holes would have taken a lot of time. Cæsar was so impressed that he rewarded Scæva with a large sum of money—over £500—and promoted him six ranks up to become the first centurion, or Primipilus, of the legion. We know of no other instance of such rapid promotion in a true account, though there is a story in verse about a brave sailor who was made first-lieutenant on the spot, but that sailor was actually a woman.

Two perfidious Gauls to whom Cæsar had Cæsar had some Gallic soldiers who had once been loyal to him but whom he had to discipline for some serious thefts they committed. Though he didn't have time to punish them, they went over to Pompey and revealed all of Cæsar's plans—details about his ditches, forts, and walls, whether they were completed or still under construction. Before this, Cæsar assures us that none of his men had defected to the enemy, even though many of the enemy's soldiers had joined him. But these untrustworthy Gauls caused a lot of damage. Hearing from them how far Cæsar was from finishing his defenses along the seashore, Pompey gathered a large fleet of boats and managed to land a large force during the night between Cæsar's two lines, splitting his army and hitting him at his weakest point.

Cæsar admits that his troops panicked and that many were killed. It seems that the sheer size of his own defenses led to his downfall, as the different sections were separated, leaving each group unable to help the others. This event ended in the complete defeat of Cæsar's forces. Cæsar himself had to flee, and if Pompey had pursued him, it might have been the end for Cæsar. He confesses that he lost 960 legionaries, 32 officers, and 32 standards in the two battles fought that day.

Then, Cæsar recounts a story about Labienus, who had been his most trusted lieutenant during the Gallic wars but had now joined Pompey, unwilling to fight against the Republic. Labienus requested the prisoners from Pompey and had them all killed, mocking them and asking if seasoned soldiers like them were used to running away. Cæsar was very angry with Labienus, but Labienus might have argued that executing prisoners was something he learned in Gaul. As for those mocking words, Cæsar couldn't have heard them himself, and it's understandable that he would want to speak harshly of Labienus.

Pompey was immediately declared "Imperator," and he accepted the title, even though his victory had sadly been over fellow Romans. "The effect of this victory on the spirits and confidence of Pompey's followers was so great that they no longer thought about continuing the war, only about the success they had just achieved." Then, Cæsar criticizes the Pompeians, defending himself in the same words. "They didn't consider that it was the small number of our soldiers that led to their victory, or that the uneven ground and narrow passages played a part, or that our men were thrown into confusion by being trapped between two sets of defenses. Nor did they remember that our forces were split in two, so one part couldn't assist the other. They also overlooked how our soldiers, constrained as they were, couldn't fight a fair battle and that their own crowding in the narrow gorges caused more trouble than the enemy did. They forgot the usual risks of war— that small issues, like a baseless fear, a sudden panic, or a superstition, can lead to disaster. They ignored how easily a general's error or an officer's misjudgment can harm an army. Instead, they spread the news of their victory across the world, sending letters and stories as if their success was purely from their own bravery, and they believed there could be no setback for them after this." This was the event at Petra, which nearly reversed Cæsar and Pompey's places in history.

Cæsar now admits that he must change his entire campaign strategy. He addresses his troops, explaining that this defeat, like the one at Gergovia, might still bring success in the future. The victory at Alesia had come after the setback at Gergovia because it encouraged the Gauls to fight, and the losses at Petra might lead to similar fortune—since surely now Pompey's army would no longer shy away from battle. He punishes and demotes a few officers. His remarks about his army after their defeat are very moving. "Such sorrow fell over the whole army from this loss, and such a strong drive to redeem their honor, that no one now wanted the role of tribune or centurion in his legion. All, as a form of self-imposed punishment, took on more work, and every man was eager for battle. Some of the higher-ranking soldiers were so inspired by Cæsar's words that they believed they should stay and fight right where they were." But Cæsar, being a wise general, did not do that. He marched southeast, and while retreating, managed to outmaneuver Pompey, who only half-heartedly pursued him. Soon, Pompey abandoned the chase. His father-in-law, Scipio, had brought a large army from the east and was now in Thessaly. As we read this, we can't help but recall how recently it was that Cæsar had been Pompey's father-in-law and friend, as Pompey, deeply devoted, clung to Julia, his young wife. Now, Pompey moved east to unite his forces with Scipio's army, while Cæsar, taking a more southern path into Thessaly, joined up with troops under his lieutenant, Calvinus, who had been keeping an eye on Scipio and barely avoided capture by Pompey before reaching Cæsar. But wherever fortune or chance could play a role, the gods always favored Cæsar.

Then Cæsar recounts how he dealt with two towns in Thessaly, Gomphi and Metropolis. The situation for Gomphi was unfortunate; Cæsar arrived there first. By now, the news of Pompey's victory at Petra had spread widely, and the people of Gomphi—who, in fairness, would have supported either Cæsar or Pompey depending on who appeared stronger, as they only wished to secure their town's safety—believed that Cæsar was struggling. Seeing him as a losing force, they decided to shut their gates against him and quickly sent messengers to Pompey, hoping he would come to their aid. They believed they could hold out for a short time, confident that Pompey would arrive soon to help defend them.

However, Pompey did not arrive in time, and the Gomphians' ability to withstand Cæsar's forces proved brief. At around three in the afternoon, Cæsar began his siege on the town. By sunset, the walls had fallen, and Cæsar's soldiers poured into Gomphi, plundering it as a punishment for resisting him. News of Gomphi's fate reached the nearby town of Metropolis just as they were preparing to bar their own gates. Realizing what Cæsar's wrath might mean, they quickly changed their minds and opened their gates to him. Cæsar, in turn, rewarded Metropolis with his protection, allowing the townspeople to remain safe. Word of these contrasting fates spread throughout Thessaly, and the towns learned the benefits of staying in Cæsar's good graces.

Meanwhile, Pompey, after merging his forces with those of his father-in-law Scipio, shared his honors and command with him. This gesture hinted at Pompey's difficult position; he was known to be a proud leader who would never share his status unless compelled. Commanding with Scipio by his side and a Senate of Roman officials in his camp was no easy task for Pompey. Although having the Senate with him might have been a mark of his authority, these senators, unused to strict military discipline, were likely more challenging to control than seasoned soldiers. They even accused Pompey of keeping them in Thessaly simply to exercise power over them. Yet, despite these internal disputes, they were all confident that Cæsar's downfall was near. In Pompey's camp, the senators and officers eagerly discussed the rewards they would claim in Rome once their old order was restored by Pompey's victory.

As the anticipated battle drew near, Labienus, Cæsar's former trusted lieutenant, reappeared and delivered a speech that Cæsar retells, clearly intending for readers to measure its words against the battle's outcome. Labienus, who had once served Cæsar faithfully in Gaul and Germany as his second-in-command, now spoke to Pompey with scorn for Cæsar's current army. "Do not think, O Pompey, that this is the same army that conquered Gaul and Germany," he declared, emphasizing his personal experience in those campaigns. "I was there for every battle and know what I speak of. Only a small part of that original army remains. Many have died in countless battles. Disease took many in Italy during the autumn, others have returned home, and many were left behind on the far shore." Labienus went on to remind Pompey of news they'd received from their friends who had remained behind in Italy, mentioning that "these cohorts of Cæsar's were pieced together just recently at Brindisi." He implied that Cæsar's current army had been hastily assembled, filled with recruits from both Gauls, but that its real strength had been lost in previous battles, particularly during the fierce confrontations at Dyrrachium within the defenses of Petra.

As if to seal their confidence, Labienus swore that he would not rest under a tent again until he had claimed victory over Cæsar, and Pompey, along with all the officers around them, joined in the oath, each pledging to share in the imminent triumph. They all departed filled with certainty about their upcoming victory. There was, no doubt, a strong sense of overconfidence. As for the words attributed to Labienus, we can clearly sense Cæsar's resentment toward him and might question whether Labienus truly spoke them. Nonetheless, Cæsar uses this account to emphasize the opposition's bold yet ultimately misplaced confidence before the decisive clash.

Finally, the location of the decisive battle was chosen—near the town of Pharsalus, along the Enipeus River in Thessaly. This battle would later become legendary, known as the Battle of Pharsalia, with "Pharsalia" widely considered the name of the plain where it occurred. However, neither "Pharsalia" nor "Enipeus" are mentioned in Cæsar's Commentaries, and the exact spot of the battle remains somewhat uncertain. The battlefield now lies within Turkish territory, near the mountains that form the border between modern Greece and Turkey, a difficult area for historical researchers to access. Cæsar had been maneuvering his forces close to Pompey's, pressing him until Pompey found himself forced to engage in battle. Labienus had already delivered his boasts and made his oath, and so, at last, the date and place were set. Cæsar, for his part, was fully prepared. At this point, Cæsar was fifty-two years old, and Pompey was fifty-seven.

Cæsar reports that Pompey commanded 110 cohorts, or eleven legions. If these legions were at full strength, Pompey's forces would have numbered 66,000 legionaries. However, Cæsar states that Pompey's army was closer to 45,000 men, meaning about two-thirds of their potential capacity. He doesn't miss the chance to remind us that among these eleven legions were the two he had once turned over to the Senate by their demand. Pompey stationed himself with these very two legions on the left flank, away from the river, alongside all his auxiliary troops—slingers, archers, and cavalry, who were not counted among the legionaries. In the center, he placed Scipio, who had brought legions from Syria, according to Cæsar's account. Additional sources indicate that Lentulus commanded Pompey's right wing by the river, while Domitius, remembered for his attempt to defend Marseilles against young Brutus and Trebonius, commanded the left.

Cæsar's army consisted of 80 cohorts, or eight legions, which, at full strength, should have numbered around 48,000 men. However, as Cæsar notes, he led only 22,000 legionaries into battle, meaning his forces were short by more than half. Following his usual formation, he placed his elite tenth legion on the right, farthest from the river. His ninth legion, severely weakened by earlier battles at Petra, was joined with the eleventh and positioned on the left wing near the river. Antony commanded the left wing, Domitius Calvinus (whom Cæsar refers to by both names at different times) took charge of the center, and Sulla led the right. Cæsar positioned himself on the right flank with his tenth legion, directly across from Pompey.

From what can be gathered, the battlefield itself offered neither side much advantage in terms of terrain. Thus, with both armies set, the historic confrontation began.

The account Cæsar provides of the actual battle is relatively straightforward and perhaps lacks the drama we might expect. As was customary, he made a speech to his troops beforehand. But if Cæsar truly spoke the words he records, it was one of the most misleading speeches ever given. He began by reminding his soldiers that they themselves had seen his efforts to secure peace. He then referenced past treaties he'd supposedly pursued in good faith, though these had often been little more than strategic delays he used to outmaneuver Pompey. He claimed he had no desire to waste the lives of his soldiers or to harm the Republic by destroying either army—whether it be Pompey's or his own. Both armies were Roman, and he professed that he wished to spare all that belonged to the Republic. It's worth acknowledging that Cæsar was indeed cautious with Roman lives when he could be, yet he was also quick to sacrifice them without hesitation if it served his purpose. He was exceptionally strategic, but tender-hearted? That quality was foreign to him—and perhaps to any Roman of his time.

Then there's a story about one soldier, Crastinus, who vowed to Cæsar that, dead or alive, he would bring him honor in the battle. True to his word, Crastinus hurled the first spear at the enemy and fulfilled his promise—but only in death, as he was killed in his effort to please Cæsar.

Pompey's strategy was conservative; he ordered his first line to hold their position and await Cæsar's charge. Cæsar points out this as a flaw in Pompey's approach, as the surge of adrenaline and momentum often give soldiers a distinct edge in the initial rush of battle. Following their orders, Cæsar's soldiers advanced across the open ground, but, being disciplined veterans, they paused to catch their breath before unleashing their spears. They then hurled their javelins, drew their swords, and closed in on Pompey's forces for hand-to-hand combat.

Pompey's main strategy, however, relied less on his legionaries and more on his substantial cavalry and auxiliary troops. He outnumbered Cæsar overall and believed he could overwhelm him with a formidable array of horsemen, archers, and slingers. Pompey counted on this maneuver to crush Cæsar's forces from the flank, effectively winning the battle without exhausting his legionaries. Yet Cæsar had anticipated this move. Arranged in his usual formation of three lines, he had a surprise fourth line—a select group of soldiers positioned just behind and to the right of his third rank. This special reserve force was tasked specifically with countering Pompey's cavalry when they inevitably attacked the right flank.

As expected, Pompey's cavalry, along with the archers and slingers, moved to encircle Cæsar's right side. At first, Cæsar's own limited cavalry began to fall back before the onslaught. Pompey's horsemen and archers moved in what seemed like an unstoppable wave, sweeping around the flank with the apparent goal of shattering Cæsar's forces. But Cæsar's fourth line was ready. At his command, this reserve line surged forward with fierce speed, charging directly into Pompey's cavalry. According to Cæsar, his soldiers advanced with such force that Pompey's cavalry had no choice but to retreat. They were not just forced back but were quickly driven into full-scale panic, fleeing to the safety of the nearby high ground. This retreat left Pompey's archers and slingers completely vulnerable. With no one to defend them, they were left isolated and were swiftly cut down in large numbers.

This was the undoing of Pompey's grand cavalry assault, which he had hoped would decide the battle without requiring much effort from his legionaries. Instead, it turned into a decisive and devastating failure, with his auxiliary forces overrun and his carefully planned strategy collapsing around him.

Cæsar acknowledges that Pompey's legionaries The soldiers of Cæsar drew their swords with courage and joined the battle with great determination. But immediately after beginning his account of this fight, Cæsar shifts to describing the collapse of Pompey's cavalry and the massacre of the vulnerable auxiliary slingers. In his next breath, he gives the impression that the battle's outcome was already decided. Although Pompey's forces far outnumbered Cæsar's, we learn that Cæsar's third line ultimately pushed against Pompey's legionaries when they were already exhausted—"defessi," as Cæsar puts it. The small, elite group of soldiers who had brilliantly routed Pompey's cavalry on the flank now used their momentum to turn the tide, breaking through the lines of Pompey's main legions and securing the victory.

According to Cæsar, the outcome was swift and decisive, with no doubt left about who had won. Pompey, realizing the battle was lost, retreated to his camp, hoping to make a last stand there. But resistance was futile, and Pompey was forced to flee altogether. Mounting a horse with a few loyal companions, he did not stop until he reached the coast. There, he boarded a supply ship, lamenting bitterly that those same men he had relied on for victory had now betrayed him.

Cæsar paints a vivid picture of what his men found upon entering Pompey's camp—a place prepared for victory with every luxury. Hungry, disciplined, and hardened by their hardships, Cæsar's soldiers entered a scene that was more fit for celebration than for a war camp. Lavish couches were set out, silver dishes were arranged, tables were laden with food, and the tents of the Senate's elite were adorned with fresh ivy. These senators, so certain of victory, had either perished in the chaotic retreat or fled to the barren, desolate mountains, abandoning their once-grand camp to Cæsar's men.

The day after the battle, Cæsar continued his pursuit of the fleeing forces, ultimately forcing a large group of them to surrender. He cornered these fugitives on a hilltop, cutting them off from water. With no choice left, they surrendered unconditionally. In a dramatic moment, these former elite warriors of the Roman Republic, the finest representatives of its military strength, lay prostrate on the ground, hands outstretched, begging Cæsar for mercy. Only the day before, they had sworn not to rest until they had conquered. Now, weeping, they implored Cæsar for their lives. Cæsar, giving a brief speech on his famed clemency, granted them mercy, sparing their lives. He handed them over to his soldiers, ordering that they be neither harmed nor looted.

Cæsar claims he lost only 200 soldiers in this decisive battle, including 30 officers—brave men like the gallant Crastinus, who had vowed to honor Cæsar even if it cost him his life. In contrast, Pompey's losses were staggering: 15,000 of his men had been killed, and 24,000 had surrendered. Cæsar's forces captured 180 standards and 9 eagles, a testament to the scale of his victory. These numbers may seem almost unbelievable, whether for the conqueror's minimal losses or the scale of the vanquished, yet Cæsar's account has been widely accepted as accurate, and it stands as the official record of that day.

Thus, the Battle of Pharsalia was won, marking a turning point that signaled the collapse of the Roman Republic as it had been known.

Yet Cæsar by no means believed his task was complete—far from it. His immediate duty now was to pursue Pompey, for if Pompey managed to escape, he could quickly gather a new army from the Republic's distant provinces and loyal allies. Cæsar's focus, as he says, was to chase Pompey "to the neglecting of all other things." Meanwhile, Pompey, seemingly overwhelmed by the disaster of his defeat, fled across the Aegean Sea with a small group of followers. Along the way, he collected his young wife, who was waiting on an island, and together they made their way toward Egypt.

The story of Pompey's tragic death is well-known. In need of refuge and assistance, Pompey appealed to the young King Ptolemy of Egypt, relying on the past friendship between himself and the boy's father. But Ptolemy, controlled by a treacherous group of advisors—eunuchs, mercenaries, and ruthless soldiers—had no real power over the decision. These men, considering Pompey a threat, concluded that it would be better to eliminate him than to offer help. A royal satrap named Achillas and a Roman soldier, Septimius, acting as messengers from Ptolemy, rowed out to Pompey's ship and coaxed him into their small boat. Then, in full view of his wife, Pompey was assassinated, and his head was severed and taken away as evidence of the deed. This was the end of Pompey, who had once been blessed with boundless fortune—until Cæsar appeared on the scene.

The Roman poet Lucan, who wrote an epic centered on the battle of Pharsalia, remarked that Cæsar could tolerate no superior, and Pompey no equal. Perhaps Lucan sought to cast Pompey in a more noble light by comparison. Yet when we look closely at both men, it becomes evident that Cæsar was just as determined as Pompey to dominate the political landscape, though he proved far more adept at removing any who might share the power he so intensely desired. When Pompey held the position of power in the triumvirate, he admitted his younger ally, Cæsar, to what he must have regarded as an equal share. By contrast, Cæsar, also part of the triumvirate, merely used his elder Pompey as a stepping stone. At Thessaly, Pompey was even forced to share the authority of his position with his father-in-law Scipio. But Cæsar never allowed another to carry any portion of his authority or to share in the mantle of his command.

When comparing Pompey's character to that of his formidable rival, one could argue that Pompey, in his battles both on the field and in the political arena, was motivated by a profound love for the Republic and for Rome as the grandest institution the world had ever known. He was guided by a sense of patriotism that Cæsar, perhaps due to his singular ambition, could not fully grasp. Pompey wanted to lead, but he wished to lead the Republic, preserving its traditions and structure. In contrast, Cæsar held little regard for the institutions of the past; he lacked reverence for Rome's established order. He was without that attachment to tradition, that loyalty to the footsteps of predecessors, which makes many of us cling to our beliefs, even when they are proven flawed. Instead, Cæsar sought to create something entirely new from the ashes of the Republic—an order that, shaped by his ambition and genius, might rise as something better and more enduring than the Republic had been.

The final seven chapters of the third book in Cæsar's Commentary mark the beginning of his account of the Alexandrine war—a record he did not continue beyond these chapters. The fact that Cæsar managed to write any Commentary at all during the intense demands of military campaigns, coupled with the urgent needs of his political situation, stands as one of the most astonishing feats of human capability. Now, he recounts how, after a brief pause in Asia, he set out in pursuit of Pompey, first to Cyprus and then to Egypt, accompanied by a mere 3,200 men. "The rest," he explains, "worn out by wounds, battles, exhaustion, and the vastness of the journey, could not follow him." Nonetheless, he commanded that fresh legions be formed from the scattered remnants of Pompey's defeated army, and, with remarkable confidence in the loyalty of his distant allies, continued on his way to Egypt.

Cæsar notes that he was delayed in Alexandria due to the Etesian winds, yet we also know that Cleopatra sought him out in Alexandria, appealing to him for aid in her struggle to secure the throne of Egypt. Knowing what ultimately transpired between them, it seems fair to question how much of the delay was genuinely caused by the winds. Had Cleopatra been an unremarkable, swarthy Nubian, as some have claimed, one might suspect that Cæsar would have left Alexandria, defying even the strongest winds. But for Cæsar, every wind seemed to fill his sails in the direction he desired.

Once in Alexandria, Cæsar gained control over Cleopatra's brother, Ptolemy, who, according to their father's will, was supposed to rule Egypt jointly with Cleopatra. This arrangement provoked an uproar among the Alexandrians, who revolted against Cæsar in great numbers. In response, Cæsar executed Photinus, one of King Ptolemy's key advisors, saw his own ambassador assassinated, and set the Egyptian royal fleet ablaze—an act which, unfortunately, also led to the destruction of a large portion of Egypt's royal library. "These events marked the beginning of the Alexandrine war," he writes, closing the last chapter of his final Commentary with these words.

Chapter XII.
CONCLUSION.

Having completed these ten concise chapters summarizing the ten books of Cæsar's Commentaries, the author of this brief volume now brings his work to a close. Since he wishes to avoid any impression that he intended to write a history, he would not add further remarks, except that three additional Commentaries about Cæsar's later wars were appended to his original works by other authors. There exists a Commentary on the Alexandrine war, likely penned by Hirtius, who wrote the final book of the Gallic war, along with Commentaries on the African and Spanish wars, which critics believe were written by Oppius, a trusted friend of Cæsar. The Alexandrine war stands as a distinct conflict, one into which Cæsar was drawn by his unparalleled boldness in pursuing Pompey into Egypt, and possibly by the allure of Cleopatra herself. This Egyptian campaign subsequently led to an additional war in Asia Minor, detailed within the same Commentary. The African and Spanish wars, aimed at quelling the lingering sparks of Pompeian resistance, were effectively extensions of the civil war, and their accounts could have easily served as further chapters of Cæsar's "De Bello Civili."

When Cæsar landed in Alexandria in pursuit of Pompey, he was greeted with the unsettling tribute of his rival's severed head—a gift offered to him by the Egyptians upon his arrival. Alexandria at this time was nearly as populous and wealthy as Rome, and throughout its thriving lands, a force of Roman soldiers remained to support and oversee the rule of the Ptolemies. Despite arriving with barely half of a full legion, Cæsar entered Alexandria as if Egypt's obedience to him as Roman consul was a foregone conclusion. Almost immediately, he demanded a vast sum of money, claiming it as repayment for services he had rendered to an earlier Ptolemy. He took young King Ptolemy into custody and, in turn, was captivated by Cleopatra, Ptolemy's sister and co-heir to the throne.

In all of Cæsar's career, his actions in Egypt were perhaps his most daring. The Alexandrians—or rather, the Roman soldiers stationed there under the influence of the young king's satraps—rose against him, forcing Cæsar to fortify his position within the city. Still, he managed to burn the entire Egyptian fleet, and, as he previously recounted in his Commentary, much of the royal library was lost in the flames. Eventually, Cæsar released Ptolemy, thinking that the king's return might ease tensions with the Alexandrians. When the young king left, he shed tears, professing that he valued Cæsar's company even above his own kingdom. Yet, the cunning boy quickly turned against Cæsar as soon as he was free.

Cæsar found himself in grave danger, and it becomes nearly impossible to call his actions in Alexandria anything but recklessly audacious—until we recall that Cæsar was, indeed, Cæsar. He had walked into Alexandria, nearly alone, with the casual assumption of his own invincibility. Driven first by the desire for immediate funds, and perhaps swayed by Cleopatra's charm, Cæsar came perilously close to losing everything in Egypt.

In Cæsar's time of need, a barbarian ally named Mithridates of Pergamus—a supposed son of the legendary Mithridates of Pontus—comes to his aid, bringing with him a much-needed army. Mithridates's arrival changes everything; with his support, Cæsar finally has the resources to mount a counterattack. A decisive battle unfolds along the Nile, one that Cæsar could not have fought alone, and the Egyptian forces are thoroughly defeated. In the aftermath, young King Ptolemy is drowned, Cleopatra is restored to her throne under Cæsar's protection, and Egypt falls under his influence.

Cæsar quickly shifts his focus to Asia, where a troublesome local ruler has dared to defeat a Roman general. This new adversary is Pharnaces, the legitimate son of Mithridates of Pontus. Cæsar, renowned for his relentless pursuit of enemies, wastes no time in dealing with Pharnaces. He confronts him at Zela, utterly decimates his forces, and reportedly inscribes the bold words "Veni, vidi, vici"

("I came, I saw, I conquered") upon his banners. By this point, Cæsar had already been declared Dictator of Rome for a year, had enjoyed the luxury of Alexandria alongside Cleopatra, and was beginning to consolidate power in a manner that foreshadowed true monarchy.

These campaigns, all occurring in 47 B.C., are chronicled in the Commentary "De Bello Alexandrino." Yet, while Cæsar's influence spreads abroad, things are far from settled in Italy. Although his allies in Rome have appointed him Dictator, his soldiers are growing restless, mutinying against their commanders and even challenging Cæsar's own authority. Meanwhile, the Republican forces are regrouping across the Mediterranean in the province of Africa, where poor Curio had previously suffered defeat at the hands of King Juba—a defeat marked by the humiliating presence of Roman senators in Juba's retinue and the complete destruction of Cæsar's forces.

This African province, lying just across from Sicily, was enriched by the Roman culture that radiated from the Republic's closest territories. Now, it has become the stronghold of the Republican faction—the last Roman territory where Cæsar has yet to secure a victory. Although Pompey is gone, his cause lives on, with both of his sons rallying here. Joining them is Scipio, Pompey's father-in-law, whom Pompey had elevated to share command at Pharsalus; Labienus, once Cæsar's trusted lieutenant, now a fierce Pompeian; Afranius, whom Cæsar had spared in Spain; and Petreius, along with King Juba himself, each harboring personal scores to settle with Cæsar.

There is also Varus, who defended the province against Curio, and, most notably, Cato—a towering figure, famed for his uncompromising virtue and his unyielding resistance to Cæsar's rise. Cato, though respected, is seen by many as rigid to a fault; his unbending principles often leave him isolated, and he is remembered as much for his fondness for wine as for his tragic end in Utica, where he chose death over submission to Cæsar.

This gathering of Pompey's former allies and loyalists represents a formidable challenge, a final bastion of Republican resistance against the ambitions of Cæsar.

In Utica, the remnants of Pompey's loyalists gather, making the city their temporary Rome. They establish a Senate, seeking to emulate the governance of the Republic, and place Scipio, a man unworthy of his famous name and inept as a general, as their commander-in-chief. Cato, unwavering in his belief in law and order, insists that rank and precedent demand Scipio's appointment, as he once served as consul and had held joint command with Pompey. The same rigid adherence to rank had previously granted Scipio command, and Bibulus the Republican fleet, purely due to their consular status, regardless of actual skill.

Cæsar, in contrast, rarely promotes based on titles alone. His flaw, if any, is trusting people based on personal affection—what we might call favoritism—as seen when he entrusted Curio with a mission in Africa, a decision that led to disaster and, ultimately, the present troubles. Yet, despite questionable leadership, the Pompeians muster a massive force, with ten Roman legions backed by the entire army of King Juba. Their numbers reportedly match those of Pompey's forces at Pharsalus. But with their ranks come internal strife: disputes over command, disagreements on tactics, resentment toward their reliance on the barbarian Juba, and an underlying sense that this effort is futile.

Meanwhile, Cæsar, undaunted, pacifies a mutiny among his veteran soldiers in Italy with a few decisive words. Facing them without fear, he listens as they demand to be discharged, and he grants it without hesitation. When they demand their promised rewards, he tells them they'll receive their dues—after he has earned the funds in battle with fresh troops. He then addresses them as "citizens" rather than "soldiers"—"Quirites"—a term they cannot tolerate, as it implies they are no longer his battle-hardened legionaries. The effect is immediate; his veterans rally to him, the legions are re-formed, and Cæsar sails for Africa, initially with little more than three thousand men. In the first engagement, he nearly faces disaster, but his fortune holds.

After a few months of relentless campaigning, the inevitable outcome takes shape. In a climactic battle at Thapsus, fought a year and five months after Pharsalia, the Republican forces face total defeat. The battle marks the final end of the Republic's military resistance. On this occasion, the ferocity of Cæsar's veterans knows no bounds; neither orders nor pleas can stem the bloodshed, as his soldiers, driven by their own intensity, continue to cut down the enemy without restraint.

Separate stories recount the tragic fates of each of the defeated leaders. Cato's story is perhaps the most famous. Realizing he must surrender Utica to Cæsar, Cato calmly arranges his affairs, entrusting his children to Lucius Cæsar, his quæstor. Without betraying his intentions, he retires to his room with his sword and, with quiet resolve, takes his own life. Scipio also ends his life, while Afranius is killed by Cæsar's soldiers. Labienus, Pompey's two sons, and Varus manage to flee to Spain.

Then comes the dramatic tale of King Juba and Petreius. Juba, anticipating defeat, gathers his wives, children, wealth, and treasures into the town of Zama, where he constructs a grand funeral pyre. His plan, if conquered, is to perish in the flames with his family, followers, and riches. However, upon returning to Zama after his defeat, he finds that his wives, children, and subjects, unwilling to share his grim fate, have barred him from entering the town. With no other recourse, he seeks out Petreius, an old Roman ally who once refused to let Afranius surrender to Cæsar at Lerida. The two sit down for a final meal together, and afterward, Juba proposes a duel, allowing one of them to die with honor. They fight, and Juba, being the stronger, swiftly kills Petreius. Then, attempting to take his own life, he fails and ultimately orders a servant to finish the task. Thus, with the Battle of Thapsus in 47 B.C., Numidia becomes a Roman province, and Africa is brought under Cæsar's control. The Republic, in a symbolic sense, dies with Cato at Utica.

The Spanish war, which serves as the subject of the last of the Commentaries, is more an effort to extinguish the final embers of resistance. After his success in Africa, Cæsar returns to Rome, where he is detained by "muneribus dandis"—the distribution of rewards—as he fulfills promises to the veterans who had rejoined him in Italy. Meanwhile, Pompey's sons, Cnæus and Sextus, gather a substantial force in Spain to revive their father's cause. The war culminates in the bloody Battle of Munda, where over 30,000 lives are lost. This is the end of the conflict; Labienus and Varus are slain, and the historian notes that they are given a proper funeral. One of the rebel leaders, Scapula, makes a defiant end—he eats a final meal, is anointed, and dies on a funeral pyre. Cnæus, Pompey's elder son, escapes the battle wounded but is later discovered hiding in a cave and killed. Sextus, the younger son, escapes and remains a rebel leader for several years, until eventually he too is killed by one of Antony's officers.

The final Commentary ends abruptly, cutting off in the middle of a speech in which Cæsar chastises the citizens of Hipsala (modern-day Seville), reminding them of his benevolence and their disloyalty. After the Battle of Munda, Cæsar returns to Rome, where he enjoys a single year of grand authority and splendor. He is appointed Consul for ten years, Dictator for life, and, finally, is even called "King." His achievements in this final year are significant: he passes numerous laws and, perhaps most enduringly, reforms the calendar, establishing the Julian system that orders months and days into a properly divided year.

However, as there is no Commentary on this last year of Cæsar's life, we will not delve further into it here. His assassination—struck down by Brutus, Cassius, and the other conspirators at the base of Pompey's statue—is familiar to all. Cæsar fell with grace, gathering his garments around him, even in death displaying the dignity and resolve that defined his life.

"Then burst his mighty heart; And in his mantle muffling up his face, Even at the base of Pompey's statua, Which all the while ran blood, Great Cæsar fell."

In the end, it was perhaps a stroke of fortune that he died before the unchecked power of the State could corrupt his legacy. His career, unparalleled in success, closed at a moment that spared his name from the consequences of absolute rule.

THE END.

Thank You for Reading

Dear Reader,

We hope this timeless classic has sparked your imagination and enriched your literary journey. Now that you've turned the final page, we want to share a vision for the future of reading—one where every classic you've ever wanted to explore is at your fingertips, in a format that best suits your life.

We'd like to invite you to gain immediate, unlimited digital & audiobook access to hundreds of the most treasured literary classics ever written—along with the option to secure deluxe paperback, hardcover & box set editions at printing cost. Together, we can spark a new global literary renaissance alongside our small, independent publishing house called "The Library of Alexandria."

Thousands of years ago, the Library of Alexandria stood as a beacon of knowledge—until it was lost to history. We aim to reignite that spirit of preservation and discovery right now, in the modern age—only this time, it's accessible to all, in every language and every format.

Picture a world where every timeless classic, novel, poem, or philosophical treatise is not only available to read but also updated for today's readers—modernized, translated into any language or dialect, and ready to enjoy in any format you choose, whether that is in an eBook, audiobook, paperback, or deluxe hardcover & box set version a printing cost.

By joining our movement to rebuild the modern Library of Alexandria, you become part of an unprecedented mission to offer:

- **Unlimited Audiobook & eBook Access to the Greatest Classics of All Time**

  Instantly explore thousands of legendary works, from Plato and Shakespeare to Jane Austen and Leo Tolstoy. All are instantly ready to read or listen to, giving you a complete literary universe at your fingertips.

- **Paperback & Deluxe Editions at Printing Costs:**

  Purchase any title in a paperback, deluxe hardbound, or deluxe boxset edition at printing costs, shipped right to your doorstep. Curate your personal library of Alexandria with editions worthy of display—crafted to last, designed to captivate, and delivered straight to your door.

- **Modern translations for Contemporary Readers in all languages and dialects**

  Discover a vast selection of classics reimagined in clear, current language—no more struggling with outdated phrases or obscure references. Next to the original versions, we aim to offer translations in as many languages and dialects as possible.

  As we continue our translation efforts and add new languages, readers everywhere can connect with these works as if they were written today. By bridging linguistic divides, you're contributing to ensuring that these timeless stories become more meaningful, accessible, and inspiring for people across the globe.

- **Your Personal Library of Alexandria:**

  Over the months and years, you'll curate a unique physical archive of classics—each volume a testament to your taste, curiosity, and love of knowledge. It's not just about owning books—it's about curating a cultural legacy you'll cherish and pass down for generations to come.

- **Join a Global Literary Renaissance:**

  Your support fuels an ongoing mission: allowing us to reinvest in offering deluxe print editions (including special boxsets) at their true cost, broaden the range of available formats and translations, and extend the reach of these works to new audiences worldwide. By joining today, you're not just preserving a legacy of masterpieces; you set in motion a powerful wave of literary accessibility.

  We are more than a publisher—we're a movement, and we can't do it alone. Your support lets us scale our mission, preserving and reimagining history's greatest works for tomorrow's readers.

Become a Torchbearer of knowledge.

Thank you for picking up this book and allowing us into your literary journey. As you turn the pages, know that you're part of something larger: a global effort to keep these stories alive, share their wisdom across borders and generations, and spark a true cultural revival for the modern era.

If this resonates with you—please consider taking the next step by visiting:

www.libraryofalexandria.com

With gratitude and a shared love of knowledge,

The Modern Library of Alexandria Team

Visit:

www.libraryofalexandria.com

Or scan the code below:

www.ingramcontent.com/pod-product-compliance
Lightning Source LLC
Chambersburg PA
CBHW010708060726
47498CB00018B/2859